Inspirational Romance Reader No. 1

A Collection of Four Complete, Unabridged
Inspirational Romances
in One Volume

• Contemporary Collection No. 1 •

Restore the Joy
Sara Mitchell

Heartstrings
Irene B. Brand

A Matter of Choice
Susannah Hayden

Passage of the Heart
Kjersti Hoff Baez

A Barbour Book

Restore the Joy

Sara Mitchell

Introduction

Death was lurking in the room. Lying in a huge tester bed, a man breathed in labored gasps, his complexion beneath the full black beard and mustache waxen, the flesh clammy. His eyes opened and fixed upon a weeping woman sitting beside him.

"Do you understand?" he repeated hoarsely, with great effort. "Do you understand why I had to do it this way?"

The woman fingered the lace of her cashmere breakfast jacket, then reached and laid her trembling hand over his where it lay clutching the bedclothes. "I understand, Everett," she murmured in a tearful voice. "Please try not to tire yourself now." Her voice caught, and she turned her head aside so the man would be spared the sight of her stricken face.

She was a lovely woman, with rich black hair gathered in a bun on top of her head and fashionably fuzzy ringlets framing her face. But deep unhappiness and shame had left their marks. She had had to pay a heavy price to be with this man, and she knew that, as he prepared himself to meet his Maker, he was trying to atone for both their sins.

"You . . . and Harold . . . will be . . . comfortable," he was gasping out now, his breathing even more labored. "Won't have to worry about yourself . . . or our son."

"Thank you," the woman whispered humbly. He might have built her this mansion and showered her with material possessions, but she had always known of his feelings of guilt.

"Must do what's fair, what's right." For a minute he rested, gathering the strength to finish. "I can't rest in peace . . . through eternity . . . with the VanCleef name tarnished. This—this will help restore honor . . . to rightful . . . heirs."

His chest rose heavily and fell, and his eyes closed so he did not see the fresh pain washing into the woman's face. Suddenly he roused and with surprising strength gripped her hand. "But I did love you, Gwinette. . . ." His parched lips parted in a smile and the unfocused eyes assumed a satisfied, faraway cast. "Got you the window like I promised, didn't I?"

"Yes, Everett, you got me my beautiful Tiffany window. And I love you for it." Tears crowded her throat and she stopped, her heart breaking.

"Only one other window like that. . . ." His eyes dimmed now, and the strength went out of his grip. "It's still there, I imagine . . . I wonder . . . if she ever forgave me. . . ." The words died away, and his hand slipped from her fingers to the heavy silk counterpane.

He died an hour later, and the sober attending physician laid the covers over his head and put a comforting hand on the woman's shoulder. She waited until the doctor left the room, then walked slowly around the bed to pick up a document lying on a table. Carefully and quietly, she found the safety deposit box Everett had kept hidden in the secret place at the back of the closet.

It would be so easy to destroy the document, to tell the lawyer Everett had changed his mind and dictated a new one to her. But she couldn't. She had given herself to Everett, thereby blighting her reputation and his, so she could not destroy his feeble effort to redeem himself.

She had this house—with the window she had coveted from the moment she saw its twin at his home in New York—and she had their son. Everett had been as faithful to her as he knew how to be. In the end, though, it hadn't been enough. Man's faithfulness alone never is.

Chapter One

Dear Emily,
Just thought we'd drop a line and let you know
we've made it as far as Virginia.   Beautiful
scenery—it's great having all this freedom to go and
come as we please. Keep the home fires burning.
                                    Love, Mom and Dad.

What home fires? Emily Carson thought with resigned humor as she read the
postcard from her parents. The little square frame house she had lived in all her
life had been sold three months before. In its place, Dad had purchased a mono-
lith motor home, complete with every luxurious appointment known to man.
He and Mom had kissed Emily good-bye, asked her to maintain contact with her
younger brother Jimmy-Joe, and taken off for parts unknown.

Emily dropped the postcard in the round straw basket she had purchased to
hold the sporadic remembrances from her mother. Let's see—today's note
made three, so that was about one a month. She sighed.

It was a hot, lazy day in early June. School had just been released, with
shouts of freedom from the students and gasps of relief from the teachers.
Emily Carson was a teacher, only she had not gasped in relief. She missed her
kids already because for the past five years it was from them—and them
alone—that she drew meaning and purpose for her life.

A plain, quiet girl with straight nut brown hair and solemn brown eyes, Emily
had learned early in life to combat her poor self-image and lack of popularity
by working as hard and as long as she could. Gainfully employed since the age
of fifteen, she had opened her own bank account when she started college. Now
at twenty-six, she had—thanks to her parents' radical lifestyle transformation—
her own apartment, a compact car, and an overwhelming sense of loneliness.

The loneliness was harder to ward off in the summer months, so Emily had
taken to driving around the south Georgia countryside since school let out the
previous week. She never drove with a destination in mind; if a road looked
inviting, she simply turned and followed it. Narrow country lanes of packed
clay or sand crisscrossed paved county roads, which intersected the larger state
highways she invariably left to follow those other winding, bumpy lanes and
roads. Eventually she would happen onto a signpost, and when she was ready,
she'd wander back toward Sylvan, the sleepy, slow-moving town where she had
lived all her life.

Today her beat-up Toyota headed east, where forests of pine, fields of corn, soybeans, and tobacco, tumble-down shacks, and one-corner communities all blurred together as the miles ticked away on the odometer of the car. She would have missed the house outside Timmons altogether if it hadn't been for rays of sunlight striking off one of its windows directly onto Emily's windshield. Wincing, Emily glanced over to the right to see what had caused the sudden glare and caught her breath. The car swerved as she jammed the brakes. then backed up with careless haste and stopped dead in the middle of the ancient dirt road upon which she had been traveling.

Half hidden by towering oaks and elms, almost strangled by overgrown azaleas, rhododendrons, and a healthy crop of weeds, a house straight out of nineteenth century Victorian America resided in faded splendor right there before Emily's incredulous eyes. In that first astonishing moment of discovery, all she saw was that the two story structure was constructed—incredibly for south Georgia—entirely of brick. Then, as her delighted eyes moved over the gables and steeply pitched slate roof and the wooden gingerbread porches, her gaze fell at last on the huge bay window. In spite of the accumulation of dust and dirt and years of neglect, the sunbeams had found this diamond in the rough and offered it to her—plain old Emily Carson.

She had never seen a window quite like this one. She had never seen a *house* quite like this one. With careful but eager movements, she stepped across a ditch and picked her way through beggar's lice and tall scratchy grasses and a multitude of other undesirable weeds to stand in front of the bay window.

The side panels were of clear beveled glass panes. Matching smaller panes created a frame for the center panel, which was of leaded glass. Emily reached trembling fingers and gently smoothed away some of the layers of grime. A shimmering, soft shade of luminous lemon-gold appeared.

Clumsy with excitement, she used the hem of her shirt to clean a larger space, and a minute later her eyes confirmed what her brain refused to believe: the front panel of leaded glass depicted an intricate floral pattern complete with leaves and branches intertwined in glorious, richly hued colors. Lips parted, breathing suspended, Emily stared at this vision of delight with the growing seed of an idea clamoring to take root.

She wanted this house. More than anything else on this earth, she wanted this house. She wanted to restore it, uncover all its dignity and charm and elegance, resurrect this huge, decaying ghost from out of the past and give meaning and purpose to her own life as well. She would live here and become something beyond plain old Emily Carson, abandoned and rootless. She *needed* this house. This house needed *her.*

An unfamiliar, tantalizing emotion bubbled up and through her. She stood a moment longer, staring at the house, hands clasped to her chest as if to keep her heart from bursting through. Then she whirled, scrambled into her car, and tore off down the dirt lane with unladylike haste.

Over the next weeks Emily Carson acquired three things. The first was an alarmingly large dog whom she dubbed Ivan the Terrible. Ivan had just passed his first birthday and was housebroken. The second was a scruffy, flea-ridden kitten. Two former students begged Emily to save the animal from its dismal, but certain, fate. Her third acquisition was the house.

Upon closer inspection of the latter, Emily learned that the room with the beautiful bay window must have been a library. Floor-to-ceiling shelves on two walls, empty now of books and coated with dust and dead insects, clued her to this snippet of information.

Upstairs, she also discovered traces of former residents—someone who must have camped out in a couple of the rooms for awhile. Emily stuffed empty beer cans and filthy litter into a sack and stomped angrily downstairs. If any wandering hoboes made a return visit, she'd toss them out on their ears. This was *her* house now.

She planned to restore it one room at a time as finances permitted. The library would be first—except for her hidden treasure of a window. That jewel she would save for last.

Where had it come from? She had seen stained glass windows before, but only in churches, and even those did not resemble the one here. And it was hers now. Hers to savor, hers to dream over and wonder about its past.

By the middle of July, Emily was sanding down the mantel over the fireplace with the belt sander a man at the Timmons hardware store had recommended. The wood, she was told, was mahogany, although the bookshelves and molding were oak. Fingers now as red and rough as the sandpaper on the tool she was using, Emily nonetheless delighted in each new discovery she made about her new home. Solid oak floors, five fireplaces including one in the kitchen, large airy rooms fringed with intricate crown molding and filled with sunlight—every day she stumbled onto a bonus she was sure had to be the last.

Buying the house may have taken almost every penny in her savings account, but it was worth it. It was doubly worth it considering the weeks of trouble and uncertainty and tedious searching and waiting before this glorious palace was hers . . . all hers.

Emily rubbed her hands hard against the small of her back, sitting on her heels to rest a minute as her mind idly mulled over the past hectic month. If it hadn't been for a nice, but nosy, old man shamelessly eavesdropping in the county courthouse that day—

From outside came the sound of a car door slamming, and Emily twisted her head. What on earth? She wasn't expecting the electrician until tomorrow. He had checked and repaired the existing wiring already, but Emily wanted some new outlets, and he had promised to drop by in the morning.

"Anybody home?" a man's voice called out a moment later, and Emily stood up with a sigh. She might have known it! This was probably one of those disgusting vagrants who made free with other people's property. Well, he had a surprise in store.

"In here," she answered grimly, rising to her full five feet six inches and preparing to intimidate with her best stern schoolteacher's demeanor. She shoved a few straggling locks of hair out of her face, then froze.

Like Emily, the man was wearing jeans, but his weren't covered with sawdust. A shaft of sunlight glinted off sandy brown hair, revealing deep chestnut highlights among the rebellious waves spilling haphazardly about his face. Although he obviously tried to control his hair by keeping it cropped about the ears and neck, the first impression was quite dramatic. To Emily, he resembled the statue of an ancient Greek.

His eyes, warm and a startling shade of green, were amused. Emily realized with a start that she was staring. "I'm sorry," she apologized, and grinned sheepishly. "I wasn't expecting anyone—especially someone who looks like you."

"Someone who looks like me?" the stranger repeated with a charming, white-toothed grin. "What does that mean, or should I ask?"

Emily laughed. "Oh, nothing special, I assure you. My first thought was that you were one of the bums who had used my home for a pit stop sometime in the past." She tilted her head to one side and studied him. "But somehow I don't think you're a bum . . . and you're definitely an improvement over the plumber. He was about fifty years old and that many pounds overweight. The termite man was just the opposite—in his twenties and skinny as a maple sapling. He also chewed tobacco."

As she talked, she ticked the numbers off on her fingers, enjoying the frank appreciation of the man's response without analyzing why she felt so free to tease. "The roofing man wasn't too bad, but he had a wife and four kids. He showed me their pictures."

"Well, I'm not married, I'm thirty-three, and I don't chew tobacco. And I'm definitely not a homeless vagrant."

"You're not overweight either," Emily couldn't help adding, and they both laughed.

The stranger began prowling slowly about the room, eyeing it with entirely too much interest to suit Emily. Stroking the mantel with a proprietary hand, she watched him with the wariness of a mother dog defending her pups. He ran a finger along a section of the molding she had sanded down, then knelt suddenly to examine the tongue-in-groove hardwood floors.

"What *did* you want?" Emily prodded, his easy silence making her somehow nervous.

The man dusted his hands and turned back to her. For a minute he studied her in silence, then remarked casually, "I understand you've bought this old place. Is that correct?"

"Yes." Emily stared back, her own gaze speculative. "How did you find out—and why do you want to know?"

"I asked in Timmons. Apparently you've generated more business—and gossip—than they've enjoyed in a decade or more."

He sounded half-amused, half-bemused, and in some confusion Emily turned and picked up the belt sander from the mantelpiece. "Everyone has been . . . mostly helpful. Look, I don't want to be rude but I am busy, as you can see. If you're tying to sell insurance or something, you're wasting your time. I've spent every dime I have in the world on this place, and every dime I hope to make in the future as well."

"I'm not an insurance salesman." He paused, then added, "But you do need adequate, specialized insurance on a place like this. It's financial suicide not to."

"I'm not stupid," Emily replied stiffly. "It's insured. Now if you don't mind . . . who are you and would you please hurry up and go?"

One thick sable eyebrow shot up, and a chuckle echoed deep in his throat. "Yes, ma'am!" His gaze wandered over the room again, ending with another examination of Emily. A strange expression flitted through his eyes, but his voice remained pleasantly bland. "The realtor—a Mrs. Davis, I believe—told me you were doing most of the work yourself."

Emily's chin lifted. "Yes, I am."

"You've taken on an overwhelming project, you know. Do you have any idea what you're demanding of yourself to try and do it alone?" He hesitated, then spoke as if choosing his words with more than usual care. "There are businesses devoted to this kind of work, and it seems like it would be prudent to take advantage of their expertise. As a matter of fact—"

"All they would do is take advantage of my pocketbook," Emily retorted. "Besides, I *want* to do it myself." She waved her hand with the sander in it. "I don't think I've done too badly for a rank beginner in home restoration." She flashed him a determined grin. "I realize I jumped in the deep end before I learned more than a dog paddle, but I'm not a klutz. Besides, I couldn't afford to hire someone who had to be paid to do what I'm doing for free. I told you it took every penny I had to buy the place."

Her own gaze roved fondly about the room, ending on the window—her pot of gold, the reward for the hours and days and weeks of labor. She was saving the window to do last because the anticipation of what it would look like kept her going long after her body begged for rest. "But it's worth it," she whispered almost to herself. "Oh, it's worth it."

She abruptly became aware that the stranger was watching her with a peculiar expression, his body posed in an attitude of unnatural stillness. Coloring a little, she started to change the subject, but even as she opened her mouth, he moved, walking in swift sure strides across to her window.

"What's this?"

There was sufficient excitement in his voice for Emily to become alarmed. She didn't want to share her window with anybody. It was her secret, and no one else—especially some nosy stranger—was going to poke around and discover what lay beneath the concealing layers of grime.

"It's a window," she understated.

The man tossed an impatient glance over his shoulder. "It's more than just a window, and I think you know it."

He reached into his hip pocket and withdrew a neatly folded white handkerchief. Before Emily could reach him, he had carefully cleaned off a six-inch square, revealing a deep-wine-colored rosebud. Inhaling sharply, he muttered something Emily didn't catch because she was too busy scurrying over and grabbing his arm.

"Leave it alone!" she snapped, too desperate to be polite. Her fingers dug into a forearm covered with soft, curling brown hair, but the muscles beneath were as hard and unyielding as the oak banister out in the hall.

His hand came up and very gently covered hers. "I'm not going to hurt your window." He withdrew his hand and moved away. "It is yours, I take it? According to the realtor you paid cash and closed the deal as fast as the reports came in attesting to the basic soundness of the place."

"Yes. It's mine," Emily stated flatly. "I found it and spent a week unearthing as much as I could of its history at the county courthouse. I found the real estate company who handled it, and they sold it to me. I'm going to restore it and turn it back into the thing of beauty it used to be, and no one is going to stop me."

Her impassioned speech rang into the hot stillness of the day, and she stared up into the stranger's impassive face with her own feelings shamelessly exposed.

"You feel pretty strongly about it, don't you?" he commented after a moment, his voice and green eyes suddenly softening.

"Yes," said Emily. "I do." She was amazed at how much she was letting a perfect stranger see, but she sensed on a subconscious level that he posed a threat of some kind. Perhaps if he were convinced of her dedication and determination, he would go away and leave her alone.

"About five months ago my parents up and sold the only home I've ever known," Emily explained. "They bought themselves one of those mile long motor homes and took off for the wild blue yonder. My brother joined the Air Force. He just shipped out to Germany, and I probably won't see him for three years."

Hands planted on her hips, head held high, she stared the man straight in the eye. "This house is all I have in this world that means something to me besides the dog and cat that got dumped on me a month ago. I need it—and it needs me. So, I don't know who you are or what you want, but if it has to do with this house, forget it. I'm not interested."

"My name is Simon Balfour, and I'm afraid I am here about the house, and I'll have to have your interest whether desired or not." His disconcerting green eyes probed hers briefly, but then, to Emily's amazement, Simon bowed his head and closed his eyes as if he were about to offer up a prayer.

For the first time Emily knew fear, and she found herself wanting to pray, too. Although she had come to an awareness of her need for God while in college, she had never felt the need to bother Him overmuch with the petty day-to-day details of her life. She had always felt the Lord had more important things on His mind than the niggling problems of Emily Carson. Right now, however, her problems loomed with the significance of the last trumpet call, and she found herself sending up a desperate plea for divine intervention in her behalf.

Simon Balfour opened his eyes and looked at her again, this time with pain— and pity. He turned abruptly away. "There's a title dispute," he declared without looking at Emily.

"Title dispute?" she echoed stupidly.

Simon turned back, his face a mask of frustration. "Yes," he confirmed harshly, then, as he watched the impact of his message register, his voice softened. "I'm sorry. If it's any consolation, I feel like I've just booted a baby bird out of its nest . . . from what you tell me of your parents."

"There can't be a dispute. It's legal. Mildred didn't say anything." She stared at him, so stunned she couldn't even take offense at what he had called her.

"Why don't we go sit outside on the steps, and I'll explain?" Simon suggested.

As they walked across the creaking, slightly sagging porch, Emily's shell-shocked gaze wandered over the wild beauty of the front yard. "Prove it," she demanded suddenly in an upsurge of sheer protectiveness. "Give me some proof of your allegation or I'll throw you off this property. My property, I might remind you."

"I don't have any proof with me right now," Simon admitted slowly, a spark of reluctant amusement lighting his face at her outrageous threat. "I came out here to meet you, introduce myself." Amusement spread as he surveyed Emily from the dust-streaked, frazzled braid unraveling down her back to the equally dust-streaked, frazzled sneakers on her feet. "Just to satisfy my curiosity, how would you go about throwing me off your property?"

Emily put two fingers to her lips and whistled with the easy expertise of a ten-year-old boy. In a minute, Ivan came bounding across the yard through the three-foot high weeds. One Sunday afternoon, Emily and her friend Barb had passed the time speculating on Ivan's ancestry. They stopped after Great Dane, German shepherd, collie, and Doberman pinscher, deciding the effort was fruitless and it was easier just to call the animal a gigantic mutt. His back came almost to Emily's waist; his face, almost shaped like that of a Great Dane, had the longer hair of a shepherd. He looked horribly ferocious and had a bark to send shivers down the spine of a sumo wrestler, but it was all show. He retained the gregarious personality of a puppy. Of course Simon Balfour didn't know that.

The man's eyes opened wide at the sight of the dog, who leaped up the steps and stopped short when he saw Simon. Ivan growled, then barked twice—his invitation to play. Emily stood with arms crossed and a smug expression on her face. She gave Simon Balfour credit, however, for although he looked uneasy, he didn't bolt.

"Nice dog," he intoned dryly, holding out his palm for Ivan to sniff.

"Sometimes," Emily murmured back provocatively. Ivan turned from licking Simon's hand to whining playfully around Emily's feet, acting about as threatening now as he actually was. When Emily's eyes met Simon's again, she smiled reluctantly. "Okay. So I couldn't throw you off the place, and my watch dog would welcome Genghis Khan if he offered to play catch first." She sat down abruptly, humor wilting as she shooed her pet away after failing to dodge his wet tongue. "Please. Don't lie to me. Tell me why you're here."

Ivan padded off with an injured air and collapsed with a loud sigh in the corner of the long porch. "I wouldn't lie to you, Emily Carson," Simon promised with quiet sincerity. "Or to anyone else, for that matter."

"How noble," Emily retorted with a touch of acerbity. "Everyone lies if it suits his purpose to do so."

"You don't have much faith in people, do you?"

Emily shrugged. "I suppose not. No one has ever given me much reason why I should."

"What about God. Can even He earn your trust?"

Emily jerked her head around, wondering if she had heard right. Was he joking, being sarcastic? He met her astonishment and wariness with a clear-eyed serenity that was either completely guileless or the product of years of polished acting. "I don't see where my views on God have anything to do with the situation here," she finally hedged. "Are you stalling or something?"

Simon gave a rueful laugh and sat up. "I was perfectly serious in my question, but yeah—I was stalling." He paused. "I've discovered I have this tremendous aversion to hurting you. And I'm afraid, after talking with you these few minutes, that what I have to tell you is going to hurt you pretty badly. I've been praying ever since I saw what this place meant to you, if you want to know."

"The title dispute. . . ." She spoke the words as if referring to a repugnant, noxious weed. "Are you trying to tell me you're claiming this as your house?"

"Not exactly." He stirred restlessly. Emily sat unmoving, her very stillness betraying a fear she didn't want to admit. "It's my great aunt, actually. She claims the house belongs to her by virtue of a will that—unfortunately—hasn't been found yet. The property was supposed to have been left in trust with the realtors you dealt with."

Emily shook her head, trying to understand. "My real estate agent never said a word. Mildred didn't know anything about the place other than referring to it as the old deCourier place like everyone else in Timmons. We searched for the deed together. She was just as excited as I was. . . ." Emily's voice faltered. "It doesn't make any sense. In fact, I don't believe you." Bewilderment hardened to accusation. "You're just trying to take my house away from me so you can tear it down and build condominiums or something."

"No, I'm not." Simon's voice and face oozed compassion and regret, and Emily's suspicion faltered. "I don't understand about your realtor, although she did mention something about her mother being her partner, but away for a three-month Mediterranean cruise. Maybe *she* would have known."

He fingered the wilting blossoms of a huge, lavender hydrangea planted by the front porch steps decades before. "All I know is what I learned from Aunt Iris, who might be seventy-six years old but has the finesse of a Sherman tank. She called my mother about a month ago ranting and raving about someone snatching her inheritance out from under her."

His gaze wandered over the wild, overgrown yard, a reflective, somewhat calculating look on his face as if he were imagining what it would look like all cleaned up. "Apparently some old codger who lives around here mentioned the sale to his sister, who is a longtime acquaintance of Aunt Iris. The woman commented on the sale in a letter to my great aunt, who promptly declared war over it. Included in her campaign was a rather heated call to my mother—Iris's niece. Mother got hold of me and persuaded me to see if could find out what was going on."

He sighed, and muttered in an undertone, "I don't know why she didn't call my brother Geoff, but I suppose due to the circumstances. . . ." He raised his voice and smiled at Emily, who did not return the gesture.

"Aunt Iris is a little less than five feet high and weighs maybe ninety-five pounds. But she's Attila the Hun and Queen Victoria all wrapped up in one package, and it's sort of hard to refuse when she gets a bee in her bonnet." In spite of herself, a smile tugged at Emily's lips. He sounded like a little boy and resembled one at the moment, the way he was toying with the flowers and avoiding her eyes, talking about this great-aunt as if she were some monstrous dictator holding a gun to his head.

"Anyway," Simon continued, "Aunt Iris swears there is a will somewhere in this house that stipulates the place has to remain in our family for a hundred years from the date of the will."

"Is that legal?"

"I've talked to my brother, who is a lawyer. If the will is found and is a proper will, then yes, it's legal."

"Why didn't your brother take care of all this then? Why did your great aunt want you to get involved?"

Simon heaved a bone-deep sigh, contemplated his jogging shoes, then faced Emily squarely. "She wanted me to find out the details so I could get rid of you before you did too much damage to the house. Aunt Iris wants it renovated as well, but she wants *me* to do it." He paused, then finished almost roughly, "You see, I'm a professional contractor, Emily, and head a company specializing in period home restoration."

Chapter Two

Emily jumped to her feet, face white beneath the streaks of dirt and perspiration. "You won't *touch* my house! No so much as pound a nail or paint a single board! Get out."

"Miss Carson—Emily—"

Panicked now, Emily ignored him. "There's no aunt, no will—you just heard about my house and want it for yourself!" Her voice rose. Ivan, hearing the unusual sound of his mistress yelling, rose and trotted over, nudging her with a damp inquisitive nose. Simon rose, too, and put his hand on Emily's arm. She knocked it away with a force that surprised both of them.

"Get him, Ivan!" she commanded the dog, her voice almost breaking now. "Attack, you stupid animal. He's trying to take away my house." Her gaze ricocheted around wildly, ending with Simon, who stood a little ways from her now, his eyes very green. The outburst died as abruptly as it had erupted, and Emily plopped back down on the top step, shoulders slumped in exhaustion and mortification. Ordinarily, she was not a demonstrative, passionate woman, one who wore her feelings on her sleeve. She had a reputation as an easygoing, absentminded, tolerant creature with a heart like warm oatmeal. She never got angry, never lost her temper, and was frankly appalled to discover she *had* a temper.

But she had also never been as unnerved as she was at this moment.

Simon came down the steps and hunkered down in front of her, balancing on the second step from the bottom with the ease of a gymnast. "I am truly sorry," he repeated quietly. "It's a mess, and we're just going to have to work together to find a way out of it."

"You and your family can work any way you please," Emily responded in a tight, cold voice. "Until you present me with an affidavit proving otherwise this is my property, my house. And I plan to keep on restoring it the way I please." She glared at Simon. "And you can tell your Attila the Hun of an aunt that just because it's your job and I haven't done it before, doesn't mean I can't restore *my* home just as well as you can."

Incredibly, Simon grinned. "So there," he finished for her, and stood up. "Well . . . I think I'll take myself off now, since you're obviously not interested in negotiation at the moment. Not," he added with a rueful sigh, "that I blame you." He started down the steps then stopped, turning back. "There's an old hymn I love . . . it reminds me that God's eye watches over us all the time—"

"His Eye is On the Sparrow?" I've been thinking about it the last few minutes, when I had to warn a sparrow that she might be kicked out of her nest."

He stared down at her a minute more, then loped off toward his car. Ivan bounded after him, leaping and running in circles and barking happily. Simon ignored the dog, but just before he climbed back inside his snappy little sports convertible, he looked across the yard at Emily one last time. She returned the look, refusing to move until he ducked into the car, started the engine, and drove away.

Emily had been working in the daytime at the house, then driving the thirty miles or so back to her apartment at night. After the confrontation with Simon Balfour, however, she determined to move in lock, stock, and barrel as fast as she could. Possession, after all, was nine-tenths of the law.

It took almost a week to transfer her belongings, during which time Emily also resigned her teaching position in Sylvan. She crammed most of her things into the dining room since she had no plans for entertaining until she finished restoring her new home. Her parents had told her she was welcome to the contents of the house they'd lived in for over thirty years. Emily never let them know how much their attitude hurt. They discarded it all—as if everything had the sentimental value of a worn-out shoe.

About like they discarded J.J. and me, Emily found herself thinking late one night. She kicked the crumpled sheet, rolled on one side and then the other, and finally fluffed her pillow so she could sit up and be miserable. And alone. Thanks to her best friend, she was acutely aware that she was a single woman, living alone.

Barb and Taylor Chakensis and their two children had helped her move, and Barb—a perpetual worrier—fretted over Emily. She made such a fuss over Emily's job situation, her isolation, and the possible re-appearance of Simon Balfour that Emily herself was becoming paranoid.

"Look," Emily had finally said, "I've applied in Timmons for a teaching position, and I should have the phone in a few more weeks. Until then, if a motorcycle gang from L.A. decide to camp out here, I'll feed 'em lunch." She ignored Barb's rolling eyes. "At least I have Ivan."

Ivan. . . . Emily sat up a little straighter in the bed, listening. He was barking again. Emily started to yell at him when her ear caught the faint sound of an idling car engine. Suddenly it revved up and gunned down the dirt road. Ivan barked three more times, and Emily finally yelled at him to hush. Honestly, did he have to bark at every car that passed?

"Give me a break, dog," Emily groaned, plumping her pillow and flopping back. "I'm finally in a position where I don't have to listen to Mom and Dad fighting about what to do with him. I don't have to listen to creaking floorboards when people walk across the floor in the apartment above mine, or hear the water running down the pipes every time they turn on a faucet. I have a home of my own now."

But for how long? The uncertainty lingered even though she hadn't heard from Simon Balfour again. Emily tried to convince herself he had been a slick con artist who had discovered she couldn't be conned, so he had given up. And yet what kind of con artist talked about old hymns and . . . and called her a sparrow?

The metaphor hurt because sparrows were nondescript, pesky birds everyone ignored.

And yet . . . Emily had taken time to run by her church, where she rifled through the pages of an old hymnbook Mrs. Jenkins, the church pianist, unearthed for her. Why *would* a slick con artist talk about God as Simon Balfour had and refer to a song about how God watches over individuals as He does an insignificant bird? It had been a rather comforting song, actually, and when Mrs. Jenkins told her she was welcome to the hymnbook since the church used newer ones now, Emily had accepted the offer with thanks.

Ivan didn't bark again, and eventually Emily slid back into sleep.

The next morning was gray and sullen. Emily donned her jeans and an old, oversize t-shirt with an arrow on the front pointing down to her stomach and the word 'BABY' printed above it. Another arrow beside it pointed upward with the word 'MOTHER' printed at its point. Barb had donated the garment after declaring she would never need it again, teasing Emily about what would happen if Emily wore it in public. Emily had laughed and said it was going to be a work shirt, and if Ivan and Samson took offense, she could shove them both outside.

She had finished stripping and sanding all the wood in the library and was going to start painting it a lovely creamy gold color. It would be nice to wallpaper, of course, but that would have to wait. One day. . . .

A light rain started when she had been painting an hour, and with a sigh Emily put the brush down to close all the windows but the two opening to the side veranda. Even if the shower turned into a downpour, the overhanging porch would keep the water from splashing inside and ruining all her work.

Sure enough, within the next hour the sky darkened and rumbles of thunder heralded a good, old-fashioned summer storm. Emily ignored the sound and fury and continued to paint in long, even strokes just like the instructions recommended. It was actually sort of soothing, and she began humming a tuneless song to the rhythm of the strokes, oblivious to the rest of the world. She was so oblivious that she didn't hear Ivan's welcoming barks over the steady beating of the rain on the roof, nor the sound of the buzzer-style doorbell that didn't work half the time anyway.

Balanced on the top step of her new ladder, reaching to paint over the crown molding that framed the walls next to the ceiling, Emily didn't hear the footsteps scraping across the floor and pausing momentarily at the entrance of the library. When Simon Balfour's voice offered in approving tones, "This is looking good," Emily was so startled she let out a small yelp, jerked around, and promptly lost her balance.

She would never know how he managed to move so quickly, but Simon caught her as she toppled, the wildly waving paintbrush missing his head by inches. His arms folded around her in a hard, bruising grip, and for just a moment he held her tightly against his chest before setting her gently on her feet.

"I'm sorry. I suppose I should have kept ringing the bell, but I was getting soaked out there and, besides, I was concerned about you." He stopped, his gaze dropping to the paint-spattered t-shirt, then lifting to search her face.

Emily was still too busy recovering her breath as well as her balance. She lifted her hand to swipe at her hair, saw that she was still clutching the brush, and laid it carefully down across the top of the can of paint. What on earth was he doing here? She straightened slowly, using the brief seconds to marshall her scattered senses. Her eyes lifted to meet Simon's, where the blankness of a stone wall had replaced the engaging air of apology and concern and interest.

That threw her all over again, and instead of demanding to know what he was doing she gaped at him, not understanding the aura of disapproval, almost censure, that hovered behind the carefully expressionless face.

"I wasn't aware of your condition," Simon said finally after a moment of uneasy silence. "It's none of my business, but I don't think it's such a good idea to be perched up on ladders, much less inhaling all these fumes without adequate ventilation."

"Just what," Emily demanded incredulously, "are you talking about? I'm as healthy as a Berkshire hog at the county fair, and you're right, it *is* none of your business. Speaking of that, what are you doing here, anyway?"

He was staring at her front again, so fixedly that Emily finally followed suit to see what was causing him to be so abominably rude. Color climbed hectically all over her cheeks; she groaned and covered her face with her hands.

"I will never tell my best friend Barb about this," she mumbled from behind her splayed fingers. "This is one of her old maternity tops she gave me to work in. I'm not pregnant. In fact, I've never—she stopped, so embarassed she wanted to leap through the open window and see if the rain would melt her . . . or maybe lightning would strike her dead. . . .

Simon was laughing. "I'm relieved you're not pregnant," he finally managed to say between chuckles. "I'm also just as pleased to hear about the other, even if that's none of my business, either. Young women like you are a rare and wonderful species nowadays, and speaking as a Christian and a man, I'd like to ask you to marry me."

Emily jerked back, then realized he was teasing her. It was a kind thing for him to do, and it worked. She found herself laughing, the awkwardness and humiliation of the moment dissolving. "If I wasn't so sure you were asking mainly in order to get your hands on my house, I just might consider accepting and teaching you a lesson," she tossed back.

Simon shook his head and preceded to wander around the library examining her work. Emily found herself feeling like one of her eighth graders taking mid-terms. Would he truly approve of what she had done? More to the point—why did she care *what* Simon Balfour thought? Because she was so uncomfortable with the direction of her thoughts, she sidelined the whole issue. "I need to go check on my cat," she blurted. "He's not too wild about thunderstorms."

With cool dignity she marched from the room as if her hair were bound in a strikingly elegant coronet and she were dressed in a suit, silk stockings, and three-inch heels.

When she hadn't reappeared in ten minutes, Simon went searching, taking note of the fact that she had moved all her furniture in. The bulk of it was crammed in haphazard fashion in a room down the front hall: boxes stacked on top of each other and tables on top of tables, chairs with their legs stuck up in the air mingling with lamps and knickknacks and other odds and ends. Simon shook his head again, smiling a little of this evidence of Emily Carson's deter-mination to stake her claim. Hey, Lord, this is a lot harder than I thought it *would* be. Why couldn't she be some hard-nosed female who could just be bought off with appropriate monetary compensation? Why a vulnerable, appealing young woman with gumption and grit and the most expressive pair of brown eyes he'd ever encountered?

"I'm storing it in here," Emily informed him from over his right shoulder.

He turned, taking note of the cat purring contentedly in her cradled arms. Not another furry animal to contend with? How many did she have, anyway? She had mentioned the two last week, but Simon was rapidly coming to realize that Emily Carson was an unpredictable creature at best. She just might produce a rabbit or two from under the staircase if he wasn't careful.

"I can see that. What are your plans—a room at a time?"

The cat was kneading its paws with the pin-like claws against her breast. Emily transferred him to her shoulder, where he draped about her neck as con-tented and limp as only felines can be. "Yes," Emily agreed almost defiantly. "One room at a time, and you saw for yourself how capable I am."

"How would you like a job working for me then? I could always use capa-ble, dedicated help." He watched her closely, wondering how someone with so expressive a face could be so wary and cynical about people.

"If that's a subtle way of re-introducing our previous discussion on a sup-posed title discrepancy, it worked." She gently dumped the cat on top of what was presumably a cushioned kitchen chair, residing at the moment on top of a coffee table. "Would you like a Coke or something to drink? And come find a chair somewhere. If we're going to fight, we might as well be comfortable."

"A Coke would be nice, and I didn't come wanting to fight you." He followed her into a small galley kitchen with ancient, grease-filmed gas appliances. A small dinette table with metal legs had been positioned under a window, with one of the mates to the chair Emily had put the cat on next to it. Simon back-tracked the few steps to the dining room and helped himself to the chair next to the cat, who stared at him with unblinking disdain.

When he returned, Emily handed him a paper cup filled with ice cubes and cola. "I haven't unpacked dishes yet," she said, sounding defensive.

Simon shrugged amiably. "This is fine." He took a long swallow, put the cup down, and leaned forward on his elbows. "Emily, I flew up to Connecticut to try and persuade Aunt Iris to drop the whole thing. She's never even seen this place and has apparently looked on it as sort of a nest egg security for her old age all these years."

"Connecticut?" Emily spluttered. "Why on earth should someone from Connecticut be interested in a house in the backwoods of south Georgia?" She searched his face. "Can you prove any of this today?"

"Yes. I brought papers and letters and identification—I left them in the car, though." He stood, glancing out the window at the pouring rain. "Do I have to go get them right now?"

"No," Emily allowed, relenting in the face of Simon's plaintive plea. "You can wait until it lets up some. But I do want to see some proof of all this."

"I understand. In the meantime, can I explain the situation and try to convince you that I'm as frustrated by it all as you are?"

"I can imagine your level of frustration," Emily responded dryly. "How much profit would you realize restoring a place like this?"

"That," stated Simon a little too evenly, "was uncalled for." Emily ducked her head, but Simon knew she sensed the temper flicking beneath the words.

"I'm sorry." She traced the faint brown stain made from a too-hot pan, her gaze wandering around the room and settling on the stain again. "This was my fault," she murmured absently, as if Simon had asked. "I was twelve. Mom yelled at me about how clumsy and stupid I was. Then—like she always did—she turned around five minutes later and apologized. Another five minutes later she breezed out the door to go—I've forgotten where she went. . . ."

Her voice remained offhand, neutral, but Simon suddenly had the uncomfortable urge to wrap her in a tender embrace. He also had a feeling the scar on Emily's soul was as permanent as the scar on the table.

"Hey."

She lifted her eyes.

"We'll work it out, okay?" Briefly, deftly, he brushed the back of her hand.

"I understand the sense of panic and desperation you must be feeling, and I really would like to avoid your losing your home. But unfortunately for us both, there's still Aunt Iris."

"Blood is thicker than water," Emily murmured, but there was no sarcasm in the observation, and she managed to give Simon enough of a smile to convince him she was merely trying to inject a lighter note.

"I don't think Aunt Iris had blood—not her own, anyway," Simon returned. The ensuing laughter was strained, but somehow after that the atmosphere lightened, and when Emily offered to make sandwiches to go with the drinks, Simon agreed easily.

"From what I can gather, my grandmother couldn't have cared less about this property—but then she married my grandfather pretty young and had no need of it anyway." He took another huge bite of his ham and cheese sandwich. "Iris never married, though, and from what Mother tells me she's always had a 'thing' about the 'family estate.' I suppose, when you grow up in the Depression years, land is about as valuable as money in your pocket. Aunt Iris felt that as long as she had property down in Georgia, she would never have to be beholden to anyone or be totally destitute."

"Where did this"—Emily waved her sandwich—"family estate come from? Who built it? Any why here in Georgia instead of Connecticut?"

Simon smiled across at her. The bruised look was fading from her eyes now, and she was almost as relaxed as her cat, who at the moment was sitting at his feet with a hopeful, expectant look on his face.

"I'm still working on that one. All my great-aunt can remember is her mother talking about a family scandal and amazement that she would even *consider* having anything to do with this property. I gather it was more or less a taboo subject for my grandmother and Aunt Iris, so little was said until their mother—my great-great grandmother—had died. Some mention of the will and the property were made in her will, and Aunt Iris must have jumped on it like a spinster would an eligible male."

"Watch it, fella. I'm a spinster schoolteacher and take exception to such remarks. Who needs men?"

"Such belligerence," Simon lifted his hands in mock surrender, relieved that she had recovered enough to tease like she had when they first met. "Does this mean I can't make you swoon with a display of all my muscles or my just-as-healthy bank account?"

Emily wrinkled her nose. "Yucch. You would doubtless impress the girls in my science classes, but it doesn't do much for me."

Simon gave in and dropped the last bite of his sandwich to the floor. It disappeared immediately. "I take it you disagree with the biblical observation that it is not good for man to be alone."

His gaze wandered over her smooth, high forehead, the huge brown eyes framed with dark lashes and several spatters of cream-colored paint, traced the line of her cheek and jaw back to her mouth, which at the moment was pressed in a tight line.

She was not used to such a frank, masculine survey. Simon found himself wondering why. She was not particularly beautiful, but there was nonetheless something incredibly appealing about her. "What put you off the male of the species?" he asked.

Emily pondered his question a moment, brow wrinkled in thought. "I never really thought about it like that," she confessed at last. "And it's not that I don't *like* men—I suppose I've just been occupied with other things."

She contemplated her supple, slender fingers. "I've had a job of some kind ever since I was fifteen. There was never any time to date much or do all the other things the kids were doing." She began twirling the end of her braid round and round her fingers. "Besides, I have a younger brother who was pretty wild. I spent a lot of time trying to keep him—and his friends—out of trouble."

Emily flung the braid over her shoulder and stood up, dumping the trash in a paper grocery sack on the floor. "My parents had no idea what to do about J.J., and they quit trying. I finally persuaded him to join the Air Force and he's in Germany now."

She turned back to Simon. "That's enough biography. What about the title dispute? What are you going to do now that your great-aunt refuses to give up her notion of a lost will?"

Simon stood up, too, dumped his trash in the bag, and came to stand in front of Emily. "I'm going to have to try and find the will," he admitted, inwardly wincing at Emily's expression. "She claims it's hidden somewhere in this house. I'd like your permission to search for it."

Chapter Three

Emily closed her eyes. She should have known what he was going to say, but she was so thrown by the whole situation her brain wasn't functioning. "I don't want you nosing around," she whispered, opening her eyes but avoiding looking at Simon. "And if I let you, and you find the will, it's like I'm signing my own death warrant."

"I know."

She hated it when he spoke like that. Why couldn't he be mean and obnoxious, a bully and a crass gold digger she could fight, someone who was easy to harden her heart against?

"But I also know I have to make the effort," Simon continued, his voice flat, expressionless. "And if I can't do it with your cooperation, I'll have to do my job without it."

Emily changed her mind. It was *very* easy to harden her heart against him. "Go ahead, then. But don't expect any help from me." She scooped Samson off the floor and stalked out the door down the long, narrow hall.

Moments later, Emily heard Simon come into the library. "Go away," she said without pausing in her strokes, her voice husky. "Go look for you stupid will."

"Can I help paint a while instead? The way you're going about it, you're going to smack the brush through the wall any minute." Emily paused in mid-stroke, stared at the section of wall she had been painting, and winced. The strokes of her brush were short and abrupt, almost vicious, and as a consequence the wall was a mess. She laid the brush down, wiped her hands on a rag, and rubbed them over her eyes and face.

"I don't want your help," she muttered tiredly. "Could you please either look for the will or leave? I don't mean to be rude, but I'm not very good company right now." Her gaze bounced off his, then returned to a dejected contemplation of the floor. "I don't know why I'm apologizing. It's your fault I'm in this predicament."

Simon studied her with assessing eyes Emily was afraid saw a lot more than she was comfortable with. His next words confirmed it. "Someday I'd like to find out why you have so little faith in yourself and in other people. I'd like to change that, starting with teaching you to have faith in me and my intentions."

He leaned and picked up the paintbrush and placed it in Emily's hand, closing her limp fingers around the handle. "So I'm leaving you right now, giving you some space. I'll come back to start hunting for the will after you've had a little time to adjust. Try not to let your burdens get you down too much, sparrow-girl."

He left, but it was a long time before Emily could concentrate on painting the library wall. She tried to undo the damage she'd inflicted, but her heart wasn't in it. Grumbling, muttering vague threats, she ended up rummaging around upstairs, looking for Simone Balfour's blasted will.

How, she asked herself furiously as she sneezed and coughed through the dust and dim corners of the upstairs rooms, was she supposed to concentrate on restoring her house when she couldn't even be sure it *was* her house? If she found the stupid document before Simon did she would burn it.

No. . . . She wouldn't, couldn't do that, even if she could get away with it. She might not be the best Christian on the face of this earth, but she did know right from wrong. Even back in high school, before she committed her life to Christ, she had been unable to cheat on tests, or lie about her whereabouts, or experiment with drugs and sex. It had been such a relief to find out the reason why, thanks to a compassionate, caring college roommate. Her body was the temple of God, and He had laid out specific rules as to its care.

Somehow, though, in the last couple of years, the Lord hadn't seemed to figure as prominently in her life. She had been so busy working, so worried trying to keep J.J. out of trouble, and the last couple of months so . . . disillusioned with life and people that her faith had more or less taken a back seat.

Wiping her hands on her paint-splattered jeans, Emily trudged down the narrow hall into her bedroom. Over in the corner was the box holding all her important documents and papers. Emily rummaged until she came up with the folder holding all the papers on the house, tugged it out, and began reading.

For almost thirty minutes she sifted through legal jargon and page after page of photostated documents and certifications and contracts. Everything looked straightforward, as it should be: On July 10, she and Mildred Davis, realtor, with a lawyer and secretary as witnesses, had signed all the papers for the property known as the deCourier estate over to Emily Elizabeth Carson.

Mildred's mother had handled the property for the past twenty years or so, but since she had been out of the country, the lawyer hadn't seen any problem with Mildred handling things. No one stepped forward protesting the change in ownership—and as Simon pointed out, virtually the whole town knew what was happening in the office of Shady Tree Realtors.

The only other names Mildred and Emily had been able to unearth in the dusty tomb of the records office at the county courthouse had been someone named VanCleef and some man whose first name was Harold (the last name had smeared to an indecipherable blot). The only other owner had been a woman name Gwinette deCourier.

Emily squinted at all the faded type. Where on earth did Simon's Great-Aunt Iris come into all this? What would happen when all the citizens of Timmons heard—as they would, Emily knew. Human emotions were fickle at best. Emily mentally vowed to gird her armor more tightly against whatever weapons Simon Balfour chose to fire at her.

A week passed. Emily worked with single-minded desperation, falling exhausted into bed at night. Her sleep remained restless, uneasy, and twice more Ivan woke her barking at passing cars. A random thought flitted through her mind that there was a lot more traffic out here in the country than she would have anticipated.

Simon returned late one afternoon, just after the whippoorwills began their haunting calls to each other from the wood surrounding the house. Ivan barked and galloped across the yard to meet him. Simon irritably ordered him to get down and go away, wondering again why anyone would want a dog the size and disposition of a bouncing kangaroo.

Emily met him at the door, looking even more like a ragpicker's child. "I wondered when you'd come back," she said, chin up and bristling with defiance.

Simon looked closer, noting the signs of exhaustion and apprehension her tired defiance couldn't hide. "I was going to give you a few more days," he replied, following her inside and into the front hall, "but every night my great-aunt calls both my parents in Florida and me at Timmon's one-and-only motel, to see if I've found anything. And . . . since you're more or less being dangled on a fraying rope over a precipice, I decided the sooner we resolve things, the better for everyone."

"That was a lovely line," Emily murmured, looking both stunned—and close to tears. "You really sounded as if you meant it." She lifted a hand to mop at the perspiration trickling down her temple, and Simon noticed her trembling fingers. He frowned down at her, then peered over her shoulder into the library. "How long have you been working without a break?" he asked quietly.

Emily shrugged. "Since Barb left this afternoon. She and her two kids brought cookies and lemonade. I don't know. What time is it, anyway?"

"It's going on eight o'clock. Have you eaten anything?"

"Lemonade and cookies."

His frown deepened to a scowl. "You stubborn little mule. You're going to kill yourself over this place if you don't take better care." If he had an ounce of sense, he'd hunt out the blasted will and get it over with. . . . "Go clean up and put on some decent clothes. I'll take you into Timmons for a meal and come back in the morning to search for the will."

She stared at him as if he'd lost his mind, and Simon didn't blame her. He couldn't believe himself, either.

"Do I have any say-so in the matter?"

Suddenly they grinned at each other, and the aura of tension evaporated.

"No," Simon promised, eyes warm and twinkling now but his stance faintly foreboding. "If you don't do as I ask, I'll take you as you are. We might be refused service in the first couple of places, but I daresay someone will eventually overlook your extreme grubbiness."

"Thanks a lot. I'll go clean up—it will probably only take fifteen minutes or so. Do you want to wait in the kitchen? I don't have chairs set up anywhere else."

"I'll wait on the front porch. Take your time, but hurry."

Simon sat on the porch steps, elbows on his knees, feeling buffeted by conflicting feelings of depression and guilt, excitement and determination. Never in his life had he found himself in such an untenable situation, and he didn't know what to do.

Bowing his head in prayer, he sent up a heartfelt petition for guidance and direction. Solomon had been granted the wisdom to handle two women who claimed the same child; surely he could come up with an approach to offer Aunt Iris and Emily Carson which would achieve a similar resolution. Unfortunately, with Emily he seemed to be losing his ability to remain neutral. He stood when he heard her footsteps crossing the porch, something very unnerving stirring deep inside as she came to stand quietly in front of him.

"I don't have any dresses unpacked," Emily gestured apologetically to her plain khaki slacks and the oversized turquoise sleeveless knit sweater. "Will this do?"

Simon studied her face, bare of any makeup, the vulnerability and openness of her nature shining out at him like a beacon. She had washed her hair and coiled it in a wet bun on top of her head. Drying wisps were already slipping out and feathering her slender neck and forehead, and they seemed to accent the slenderness of her form.

She was not beautiful—she was not really even pretty—but Simon felt a giant hand squeezing his heart. She was somehow beyond either of those trite descriptions, and all he could think of was that she was the most gallant person he had ever known. Her dark brown eyes were filled with worry and fatigue, but she had lifted her chin and was gazing at him with that tiny spark of defiance flickering away, distinguishable even in the purple shadows of early evening.

She had a rare beauty of spirit, yet such a thick veneer of disillusionment, the spirit was only allowed to shine at brief unguarded moments he was beginning to cherish. What had made her the way she was? And what *was* he going to do if and when he found the will?

Chapter Four

They ate at a steakhouse in Timmons, and Emily—with a challenging gleam in her eye—ordered the most expensive steak on the menu. She had just laughingly promised Simon she would, too, eat every bite when a medium-sized man with carefully combed hair and an intimidating scowl stopped by their table.

"Excuse me, but you're Emily Carson, aren't you?"

Emily looked up, smiling in surprise and anticipation. "Mr. Radford! How are you?" He was the principal of the junior high school in Timmons, and Emily hoped he was going to tell her about the position she had applied for. It had worried her to be without a job more than she had allowed Barb to know.

Mr. Radford ignored her question. "Miss Carson, I've been trying to get in touch with you for a week. You apparently had your phone disconnected in Slyvan and have yet to have one installed in your new place of residence." He paused and added bitingly, "It's very annoying, as I'm sure you agree."

Emily colored. "I finally had my secretary send you a letter Friday, but since I saw you here I thought I'd go on and let you know." Mr. Radford glanced at Simon, who was sitting without moving, watching Emily. "The teacher who was considering retiring changed her mind. There are thus no available openings at this time. Since you do have excellent references, we're keeping your name on file for mid-season replacements. We'd also be happy to use you as a sub."

He glanced at his watch, then over toward the entrance. "It's a shame you don't have any training in foreign languages. The high school is looking for a Spanish teacher."

"I see," Emily said very faintly. "Thank you for telling me, Mr. Radford."

"I'm sorry, Emily," Simon offered after Mr. Radford left. "That's a tough break."

"Yes. First you and your will. Now this. God must not want me around here." Her chin lifted. "But I'm staying. I'll handle it—I'll find another job." She picked up her water glass and took a swallow, put it down and toyed with the silverware until the prickling tears receded and the hot poker in her chest cooled a little.

"Emily—look at me." Emily lifted dull brown eyes. "Don't shut God out, or convince yourself He's trying to crush you in defeat. It's not true—He cares very much what happens to you."

"His eye is on the sparrow, right? I found a copy of the song— it's a nice song." She stared down at her steak. "Maybe God does watch out for sparrows—I don't know. I do know He obviously has more important things on His mind than watching out for *me*." She lifted her gaze back to Simon. "So please don't try to convince me otherwise."

"No."

He said the word softly, but with unyielding emphasis, and Emily felt a shaft of something hot and alien stirring to life deep inside her. "Exactly what do you mean by that?" she asked carefully.

"I mean you're wrong, dead wrong, and I'm going to convince you of it if it takes the rest of the summer. Or longer. I have a crew of well-trained men and women who can function on their own awhile."

He placed his palms flat on the table and leaned across, trapping Emily within the compelling depths of his determined gaze. "You, on the other hand, have no job, a house that might not be yours, and the insane notion that God has turned His back on you. If anyone ever needed to be convinced that God has His loving eye on you at all times, you do. And since I feel responsible for at least half your problems, I plan to be responsible for the solutions as well."

"I want to go home, please." If he thought for one minute she was naive enough to fall for *that* approach. . . . Abruptly, she shoved her chair back and stood. "Thanks for the meal, but I'm not hungry after all. Please enjoy yours— I'll get a taxi. See you in court, Mr. Balfour."

Shamefully glad to see signs of temper flickering across his face, Emily swiveled and marched out of the dining room. Her behavior was irrational, rude—totally out of character—and her parting shot ridiculously childish. But right now she just didn't care.

Simon caught up with her outside.

"Come on," he said, his voice short, clipped. Cupping her elbow, he added, "I'll take you home."

Emily jerked free. "I'm not a helpless old woman yet! You can take me home only because it'll be *hours* before I could rouse a taxi." Stalking across to his car, she reached for the handle, then rounded on the hovering man at her heels.

All the suppressed rage and denied fear welled up and burst free. She glared up into his shadowed face, almost shaking with emotion. "I don't need you, or your—your pity! And if you ever compare me to a sparrow again, I'll wallop you. They're disgusting little creatures nobody cares two straws about—and that song is wrong!"

His figure loomed above her, radiating temper and something even more ominous. "Maybe," he growled, "just maybe *now's* the time to do what I've wanted to do since the second time we met."

Suddenly his arms wrapped around Emily and she was held immobilized against a damp chest that smelled equal parts of after shave, sweat, and rib-eye steak. Without warning his mouth covered hers and Emily Carson, placid, easygoing schoolteacher, was kissed more thoroughly, more expertly, than she had been in her entire twenty-six years.

When Simon lifted his head at last, Emily gawked up at him, mouth tingling, ears ringing, and all round them moths and gnats fluttered in the wavering streams of yellow light from the restaurant parking lot.

"Oh," she stammered out at last, "I thought you were a . . . a gentleman . . . a *Christian* gentleman."

Simon stared at her as if he couldn't quite believe what he had heard. His gaze moved from her eyes to her mouth, and a muscle twitched in his jaw.

"Being a Christian doesn't mean I'm a eunuch, woman!" He turned away with an infuriated jerk and braced his palms flat on the hood of his little green Jensen-Healy. Head bowed, breathing heavy, he stayed thus for several moments without speaking.

Emily considered and cast aside a baker's dozen comebacks, but she was bitterly aware that nothing could erase the unbelievable naivete of her comment. Nor could she deny the fact that the kiss had somehow transformed all her anger to a far more frightening emotion.

What had possessed her to behave so? She had been kissed before, had even successfully repulsed the heated advances of one of J.J.'s drunken companions. What bewildering alchemy had Simon performed to metamorphose the plain, unexciting woman of humdrum lifestyle into a starry-eyed, pliable creature fairly throbbing with—with passion?

She didn't like Simon, she didn't trust Simon, and he was making her feel all sorts of violent emotions she never would have associated with passion and desire: anger, frustration, helplessness, fear. Yet when his mouth had covered hers, all those seething emotions had swirled into something so sweet, so wildly wonderful, so mindlessly bone dissolving that all she could do was gape at him like a bug-eyed frog and utter foolish banalities.

"What are you standing there for? Waiting for an apology—or seconds?" Simon snapped with unforgivable irritation. She had no idea what he must have read on her face, but after pinching the bridge of his nose between thumb and forefinger, he dropped his hand and said, quite gently, "Get in the car, Emily, and I'll take you home."

Emily obeyed without another word, and they spent the next long minutes in thick silence, the only noise coming from the muted roar of the Healy's engine.

Eventually Simon heaved a sigh. "Did I frighten you?" he asked, the words vibrating with an uncomfortable edge, even though he again spoke quietly. Emily wet her lips. "A little," she admitted just as quietly. "But I frightened myself more. I've never behaved that way in my life—I've never *felt* like that in my life." She almost smiled. "I've got a reputation of sorts as being disorganized but level-headed. Haphazard perhaps—but sane, calm, and dependable."

Simon snorted.

"Well, I *have* . . . I *am*," Emily retorted. She turned her head away and gazed sightlessly out at the dark, deserted countryside. "Ever since you came into my life, nothing has been the same, including *me*. I wish you'd disappear back into the wilds of Connecticut or wherever you came from and leave me alone."

"I've been on a location in Tennessee, and I'd like nothing better than to get back to the order and sanity of my own life. You've messed my life up as well, Emily Carson," he admitted. Then, after another uncomfortable pause, he added. "I haven't treated a woman like that since I was in my unregenerate teens. If my father were here, he'd likely be tempted to try and mete out the same discipline he did then." He gave a mirthless chuckle. "Especially now that I'm *definitely* old enough to know better."

Emily's curiosity overcame the sinkhole of apathy and depression into which she was sliding. "What on earth did you do—and how did your dad find out?" she couldn't help asking.

"I was seventeen, thought I was God's gift to the female sex, and came on a little too strong for Janie Beth. She told her folks, her dad called mine . . . and I was grounded for two weeks as well as being sole man on the clean-up crew for my dad's contracting business."

He smiled briefly, ruefully. "And in the evenings I had to paint the fence that surrounded Janie Beth's house. She wouldn't speak to me, but her parents let me hear an earful, as did her twitty thirteen-year-old sister. I remember begging Dad to let me out of at least that part of my punishment, but he just smiled, and I painted."

"What a monster of a father you must have."

She could just make out the swift turn of his head toward her before he returned his eyes to the road.

"Not at all," he refuted evenly. "I wouldn't have respected him like I do if he *hadn't* come down on me that hard. I deserved it." There was a fractional pause, then he added, "He disciplined me in love as a father should, Emily; he didn't punish me to vent his own frustration. Didn't your father do likewise for you?"

"I never needed much disciplining, and he quit trying with Jimmy-Joe after he ran away when Daddy whipped him the last time. He was only ten, but he was gone for two days. After that I think Daddy and Mom both decided to pretty much consign him to whatever retribution he might reap if he was caught." She twisted her purse strap round and round in her hands. "But I know he and Mom cared for us as much as they could, in their own way, so don't go feeling sorry for me."

"It would be easier to feel sorry for a Venus fly trap," Simon grumbled beneath his breath.

The next instant they were both blinded by a car with its headlights on the bright setting, hurtling around a curve and approaching them fast—on their side of the road. Simon flattened his hand on the horn and wrenched the wheel hard to the right.

The other car swerved at the last moment and careened by them with inches to spare. It had not slackened speed at all, and they heard the tires squealing in the distance as it tore around another bend.

"Are you all right?"

Emily released her death grip on her purse and wriggled her fingers to restore the circulation. "I think so," she said shakily. "He must have been drunk."

"Or high as a kite on drugs. I was talking the other day to the proprietor at the motel where I've been staying. Apparently the police think there might be a gang operating somewhere in this county. Whatever happened to plain old moonshine?"

"There's a problem everywhere. Two of my boys were caught behind the bleachers last spring. It makes me furious and sad all at the same time to see lives wasted like that."

"I'm sorry about your job. I have a feeling that's probably what sent you off the deep end back at the restaurant, wasn't it?"

"It didn't help," Emily muttered.

A short while later they turned onto the dirt lane that led to her house.

"Is that *another* car coming?" she asked, squinting to catch what she thought had been the flash of headlights down the road and through the barrier of the trees.

"I don't see any lights." Simon pulled into the front yard and switched off the motor. In the sudden silence the quiet ticking of the cooling engine sounded inordinately loud. There weren't even any cicadas buzzing or crickets chirping.

And Ivan wasn't barking a welcome.

"I wonder where Ivan is?" Emily opened the door and got out without waiting for Simon. She put her fingers to her lips and whistled. The shrill sound rent the night, and after a moment she heard the faint barking of her dog. He was across the field, somewhere in the woods the two of them had explored, and Emily pressed her lips together. Some watchdog, but at least he was okay.

"Will you forget that dog for two seconds and listen to me?" Simon had come up beside her, but Emily hadn't noticed because, in spite of the moon, the darkness out here was as total as the blackest hole in the universe.

She wished she had remembered to leave on her porch light, especially when Simon commented on it. Emily ignored him and began making her way to the front porch, barely discernible in the faint light of a grudging quarter moon.

"Emily. . . . I want to apologize."

The words floated across the yard and wrapped themselves around her feet, halting her indignant retreat. For the first time since Emily had walked out on him at the restaurant, Simon sounded like—Simon.

She waited, confused and tentative, listening to his steps swishing through the tall grass and weeds. When he was so close she could feel the warmth of his body, he stopped. Every nerve in Emily's body seemed to tingle with the awareness of his presence.

"Emily—" She heard a thread of laughter in the word, "I still disagree with your description of sparrows, but will you at least forgive me for everything else?"

The last of her indignation softened to a bewildering compliance, and Emily heard herself murmur back in just as whispery a tone, "I guess so." Then, her resolve stiffening slightly, she stepped back away from him and added with a hint of vinegar. "Mabe I better find out what you're asking forgiveness for. Your arrogance, your bad temper, or your—your—"

"My what, Emily?"

Oh, no, there it was again. That wretched note of laughter dancing through otherwise ordinary words, playing a pied piper tune on her heartstrings. Confound the man, anyway. What had he done to her? "Your kiss!" she flung out recklessly as she braced herself for his laughter.

It never came. What did come was a very wet, very dirty Ivan leaping out of the night and practically knocking Emily down. He yapped and whined and panted, his forepaws leaving muddy trails all over her clothes, arms, and legs. His bullwhip tail snapped happily against Simon, who kept dodging about trying to avoid the affectionate welcome.

"Oh, Ivan, bad doggie! Where were you? Stop that—why weren't you guarding the house?" She laughed harder when Ivan turned to Simon, who snarled at the dog to leave him alone. Emily ordered Ivan to the porch. "What's the matter?" she intoned innocently. "Don't you like my dog?"

"Not particularly. He's about as lovable as a dead elephant, and he smells like a sewer."

"He smells like a dog," Emily retorted, stung by the acerbic answer. "He can't help that anymore than you can help smelling like a man!" After one horrible second with those last words ringing in her ears, she added in a much smaller voice, "I didn't mean that the way it sounded."

Simon didn't answer. He had turned away, and he was laughing so hard the sound echoed back from the woods and fields. Emily decided his laughter was one part humor and three parts hysteria, with a dollop of resignation and frustration tossed in for effect. She walked slowly over to the porch steps and sat down on the bottom one. Ivan whined, but she told him to stay. Simon was at least partly right: at the moment he did smell a lot like a sewer.

"I give up," She heard Simon eventually gasp out between chuckles. "I think it's a waste of time trying to accomplish anything with you tonight. We can talk in the morning when I come back to start looking for the will."

The will. In the emotional turmoil of the past hour Emily had virtually forgotten the reason for Simon's presence in the first place.

He must have heard her involuntary gasp. "Try not to worry," he promised in a voice as dark and calm as the night. And try to find it in your heart to forgive me—for everything—Emily Carson."

"Simon. . . ." It was difficult to squeeze his name past the constricted muscles of her throat.

"Will you go inside before I leave and at least turn on the porch light?" His voice floated back across the yard. "With the dog I feel a little better leaving you, but I'd still like to know you're safe inside."

How could someone who had made her angrier than she had ever been in her life turn around and make her feel more protected, and, well, *cared* for than she had ever been in her life? "All right."

She stood listening until the sound of his car faded away. When Ivan poked his nose in her hand and pressed his wet body against her, she cupped his head and held him close. At this moment his presence, smell and all, was all that stood between her and a vast chasm of loneliness.

Chapter Five

Two days later Simon returned, driving—to Emily's outraged disbelief—a pick-up truck which was towing a pop-up style camper.

A wry smile lifted the corners of his mouth. "If your phone were installed, I would have called to let you know," he said, correctly reading Emily's indignation. Stepping past her, he looked around the empty foyer, into the freshly painted but still bare library, and finally back to Emily.

"It really bothers me, you know, you being out here by yourself with no way to call for help. Which is why, of course—" he gestured toward the camper. "This is my 'portable office' that I had one of my guys bring down from Tennessee. I borrowed the truck from the gas station to bring it here so Charlie could take my truck on back to Tennessee."

"You're as bad as my best friend, Barb," Emily groused wearily, at the same time feeling a shameful twitch of relief. "Look, the phone man will be here as soon as he can. Until then, you will all just have to add a few gray hairs to your heads. I've got a few myself after the other night."

"What happened the other night?" The small smile hovering on his lips suddenly widened. "Or are you referring to our cat and dog fight?"

Her cheeks warmed. "I'm referring to the fact that it took me almost forty-five minutes to find Samson, and when I did, he was as strung out as if he'd been tossed between two pit bull dogs, and then I heard—" she skidded to an abrupt halt, not feeling up to facing any more of Simon's bullying concern.

"What did you hear, Emily?" He was looking really concerned now, and Emily grimaced.

"Oh, nothing that out of the ordinary," she tossed out offhandedly. "Just a car that sounded like it was going to stop but changed its mind when Ivan barked."

Simon looked like a lovely white, puffy cloud suddenly burgeoning into a towering thunderhead, and Emily hastened to add, in an attempt to downplay the incident, "I'm sure they were lost and probably needed directions. If they had known Ivan was more of a puppy dog than a watchdog, I'm sure they would have come in and asked for coffee as well as directions."

"It's a good thing I decided to camp out here until I find the will."

He was glowering at her as if Emily were a naughty, rebellious child, and instantly her defenses sprang up. "I haven't granted you permission to move in," she hissed, wanting to gnash her teeth, wanting to kick his shins. "Just because I'm a woman doesn't mean I don't know how to take care of myself. Why do men always have to think like that?"

Good grief! What's the matter with me? Slapping her palms over her flushed cheeks, Emily averted her head and moaned, "Look what you do to me! Simon, I can't *do* this. I'm not constitutionally set up for these kinds of games."

"Neither am I," Simon drawled, looking faintly dangerous. "Let's kiss and make up and start all over." He reached out a lazy arm and folded her into his embrace. "I need to amend your way of thinking about men. *Christian* men, anyway."

"There's nothing wrong with the way I think about men, Christian or otherwise," Emily shoved his chest. He was wearing a creamy yellow, button-down chambray shirt and shorts instead of jeans. He smelled of soap and something minty, and with his green eyes boring into her from close range she realized a few other things about men she hadn't known before. She hadn't realized she could feel this way about one. "Simon, why are you behaving like this?"

His eyes softened, and he dropped a quick, undemanding kiss on her wrinkled forehead and released her. "I don't know," he answered with disarming honesty. "I find you very attractive, but you also frustrate and infuriate me more than any woman I've ever known. And with the situation over the house and Aunt Iris swinging back and forth between us like Edgar Allan Poe's pendulum, my behavior comes across accordingly."

Emily pondered him, nose wrinkled along with her brow as she mulled over the implications behind his words. Men had dated her infrequently over the past years, but usually it was because Emily needed an escort and asked for the date herself. No one had ever mentioned the fact that she was attractive.

She shook her head, and the freshly wound braid swung back and forth along her slumping shoulders. "Let's go find the will," she stated tiredly. "That's about all I can think of right now."

She started up the stairs without a backward glance, but when she reached the top she paused, turning back to Simon. "The next time you grab me and kiss me, you'd better be prepared to nurse a sore jaw."

A dangerous spark glinted in the depths of his enigmatic green eyes. "We'll see," he murmured, and they proceeded in silence to the room at the head of the stairs.

Three hours and three inches of dust and grime later, Emily called a halt. "We've searched every inch and it's not up here. It probably doesn't exist, anyway. Why can't your aunt accept that?"

"You haven't met my aunt." Simon considered the weary, bedraggled young woman in front of him. "Would you give up this house without a fight?"

Emily sighed and admitted painfully, "No. What are we going to do?"

Simon sank down onto the floorboards and leaned back against a wall. His grimy hands worried his matted, damp hair, causing the waves to curl even more wildly about his face and ears. Tracings of dust and perspiration trickled down his face, emphasizing the lines of weariness marring his countenance. He looked up at Emily and sighed. "I'm afraid, Miss Carson, that you're going to have to talk to a lawyer."

Bradley Lauderman's office consisted of two rooms over what used to be Sylvan's only theater. Emily had chosen to go to a lawyer in her hometown because she needed the emotional support of familiar surroundings. Barb's husband, Taylor, had recommended Bradley Louderman, as had her old principal Joe Southers, so Emily was hopeful of sound advice for what she also hoped would be a reasonable price. After her appointment, she planned to run over to the school and throw herself at Joe's mercy, beg him to re-hire her, even as a janitor.

Simon had wanted to accompany her to this appointment. In the last several days, along with searching for the will, he had offered advice on everything from the security of her home to the refinishing of her home to refinishing herself. ("Emily, you can't exist on a diet of cheese crackers and soup—you already bear an uncomfortable resemblance to a starving rock star, especially when your hair looks like that." Emily had thrown the sticky paint rag at him and told him if he was going to criticize the least he could do was shave his head to control his own untidy hair.)

In contrast to his earlier behavior, Simon was now scrupulously treating her like his kid sister. Emily knew he worried about her—and not just concerning her eating habits and casual appearance. The night before her appointment with Bradley Lauderman, Simon had also heard a car idling outside. Peering through the window of his camper, he watched a car door open. When Ivan barked inside the house, it immediately slammed shut and the car left.

Subdued, even surly all morning, he and Emily finally had it out over the matter, with Emily ending the discussion abruptly by bursting into tears. Even now she squirmed when she remembered her behavior. Or at least that's what she kept telling herself. But she had a nagging suspicion that her real discomfort was with Simon's response.

Following her out onto the back porch, trapping her against the railing, he took her chin in his hand and just stared at her in silence for a long uncomfortable moment. "You're the most stubborn woman I've ever known," he repeated, only this time his voice crooned the words instead of shouting. "But you're also a rare and precious jewel, Emily Carson, even though you can't see it."

His thumbs brushed away her angry tears, and then she was free. "God help me," he muttered, fervently then, "because I *can* see it, and that's why you scare me into losing my temper with you." Emily could only stare dumbly.

Simon turned away, so she was not totally certain of his last sentence. "And if someone tries to harm you in any way, God help me for what I would do to them," was what she thought he had said.

That sounded much too romantic and dramatic a statement for a man to make about a woman like her, so Emily tried to shrug the whole incident aside and focus her distracted senses on the encounter with Bradley Lauderman.

Shrugging Simon aside, however, was about like trying to shrug off the Rock of Gibraltar.

Climbing the narrow steps to Bradley Lauderman's office, Emily found that her stomach muscles were clenching and her hands were damp. She opened the dusty, glass-topped door reluctantly, and from the other side of a cluttered desk, a young smiling woman with dark curly hair greeted her.

"Hi. Emily Carson?"

Emily nodded, absorbing the old, sagging chairs, the framed prints of different species of duck hanging crookedly on the walls. Old magazines were scattered on the low table in front of the chairs. Her gaze swung back to the secretary, who had risen from behind the desk. She smiled into Emily's widening eyes.

"I'm due any day and look like a watermelon, I know. But Brad desperately needs the help so I'm hanging in there."

From behind a closed door a man's voice called, "Is that Ms. Carson, Gloria?" The door opened and a tall slender man stepped through. He had a glorious thatch of straw-colored hair and blue eyes that crinkled at the corners. In spite of the fact that it was late summer, his skin was untanned, but he radiated energy and vitality. He held out his arm and shook hands with Emily. "Come on in. We don't stand on ceremony around here. Gloria, can you waddle across the hall and wheedle some coffee from Dave?"

"For you, anything."

As the secretary disappeared, Brad grinned down at Emily. "Dave's a CPA—has an office across the hall. He's so agreeable about sharing his coffeepot, we never got around to installing one of our own." As he ushered Emily into his private sanctum, he winked. "It also cuts down on the exorbitant rates I have to charge my clients."

Emily was charmed by his easy wit and manners. Some of her anxiety began to dissipate, and as she relaxed back into an old but comfortable wingback leather chair she looked around. Brad Lauderman's office was a mess. All four walls were covered floor to ceiling with legal books, documents, and papers. They even surrounded the three metal filing cabinets, one of which had a drawer left open, a file tilted upward at an angle. Emily felt uncomfortably at home.

"Don't look so worried. All lawyer's offices look like this."

She met his teasing eyes with a grin. "Actually, it reminds me of my own place. Organized chaos."

"Exactly." He reached across his desk to a glass jar filled with all shapes and sizes of gum, from sticks to colored balls to Bazooka bubble and huge grape spheres. He caught Emily's rapt interest. "I gave up smoking and got hooked even worse on this." He gestured to the jar and popped one of the smaller balls. Then he leaned back in his desk chair, clasping his hands behind his head and keeping his intent gaze upon Emily. "Now, what's the problem? I've been over all the stuff you had Roger Bates send me. Tell me everything. I don't have to be at court until noon."

Emily took a deep breath. "I better start off by method of payment. If I can't have my old teaching position back, I'll be an unemployed schoolteacher, with the reason I'm here a heavy albatross about my neck."

"That could be a problem, I agree." He sat forward, glancing down at some papers on his desk before looking at Emily again. "Can you type?"

"Yes," Emily answered, though her voice was bewildered.

"Great!" Brad rubbed his palms together, a wide grin splitting his face. "Then I think we might have a solution to both our problems."

An hour later Emily was still protesting, but much less vigorously. Bradley Lauderman wanted her to replace Gloria as his secretary for a couple of months. ". . . By which time you might have found another teaching position, and hopefully the situation with your house will be resolved." He blew a huge bubble, caught sight of Emily's poorly hidden amusement, and sheepishly grinned. "Sorry. I forget sometimes how unprofessional that must look." He swallowed the bubble. "I have warned you, though, that this could drag on for up to six months, depending on a number of factors."

"I know." Emily contemplated her neat but worn taupe pumps a minute, then looked back across the desk in confused indecision. "I still feel uncomfortable with the whole idea of a lawsuit, not to mention working for you while you're more or less working for me."

Brad smiled back in sympathy. "It might raise a few brows about conflict of interest, but we're in Sylvan, not Chicago, and the whole town has known both of us since we were in diapers." He swept a non-professional, frankly masculine survey over her person. "How is it that you and I have missed each other all these years?"

"I was probably still in pigtails chasing after my brother and his friends, making a pest of myself, and you were probably chasing after all the girls in high school making a pest of yourself."

"Hey—I'm not that many years your senior!" He picked up the notes he had taken in the past hour and studied them a few minutes. "If you've given me all the facts, there's a mere six years separating us. Want to complicate our relationship even further by having dinner with me tonight?"

"No," Emily shook her head in mock dismay. "I'm confused enough by this whole mess as it is and besides, I just wouldn't feel . . . comfortable. Mr. Lauderman . . . Brad . . . do you really have to file a lawsuit?"

He instantly reverted to the seasoned professional lawyer. "Yes, Emily, that is the correct legal procedure. As far as I'm concerned you aren't violating any biblical tenets about suing your brother, or whatever the phrasing is. You are merely following legal precedent for the express purpose of determining who has superior title to the property." He stood up, stretching his tall, lanky frame. "Trust me as your lawyer, all right? If you have any more questions about the religious end of it, why don't you talk to Sam Noland? Isn't he the minister of the church you attend?"

Emily nodded and stood up as well. "I don't feel comfortable about working for you either, even if you are deducting your fee out the paycheck." She paused, then leveled a straight look at him. "You still won't be charging me what you normally would, will you?"

"Nope, but at least I'll have a secretary, and that matters a heck of a lot more to me than losing a few bucks." He came around the desk and held out his hand. "Let's shake on it, Ms. Emily Carson."

"But I haven't typed in years, and although I was a secretary for Mr. Evans when he was mayor, I was all of seventeen years old. I've probably forgotten—"

A stick of peppermint gum was thrust into Emily's mouth, and her hand was grasped in a warm, firm handshake. "Chew on that instead of problems that don't exist," Brad admonished her easily. He held her hand a little longer than was strictly necessary, but immediately let go when she tugged. "Set up a time to get together with Gloria and she can show you the ropes. Don't wait too long, though, or you might be winging it as you go."

His intercom buzzed, and he stretched a long arm to take the call. He held his hand over the mouthpiece and finished by saying, "Gloria will set up our next 'business' appointment—or you can do it yourself if she's gone into labor or something."

Emily left the office shaking her head in bemusement, and another hour later she left the building still shaking her head. Gloria had been so relieved she had thrown her arms about Emily and hugged her, then laughed at the awkwardness of her gigantic stomach. She had also asked if Emily had time to learn the ropes now, since she might not, as Brad pointed out, have another opportunity.

The job seemed simple enough. She would basically be fielding phone calls, typing up wills, filing, and a couple of times a week walking the two blocks to the courthouse to file a client's papers with the clerk of the court when Brad was unable to do it. Because she was still trying to restore the house herself, and because he wasn't that overloaded with cases, she would only be working three days a week, leaving her plenty of time to work on her home.

"Since the paperwork from the lawyer who handled the closing on your property indicates that you have good title to the property, keep on with the sanding and painting if that's what cranks your engine," Brad reassured her.

Chapter Six

Emily decided to detour by Barb's house instead of going straight home. She hadn't seen her friend or been able to talk to her in a week, and although she might fuss and worry, Barb was a marvelous sounding board. She also had rock-bed common sense, easing Emily's mind over Simon's ubiquitous presence in her life. Taylor, in fact, verbalized their relief that Emily wouldn't be isolated anymore.

Today, however, when Barb opened the door she gave a relieved shriek, grabbed Emily's arm, and hauled her into the house. "Mark, turn down the stereo!" she yelled, and as they passed the table in the entrance hall, she swiped up a newspaper. "Look at this." She thrust the paper under Emily's nose. "Look at it! I've been out of my mind worrying."

Emily read the headlines, mouth dry. "Car Overturns on County Road—Kills Two Passengers." The subtitle noted that a second wrecked car had been found abandoned near the site of the accident, with several pounds of cocaine and two boxes full of pornography found in the trunk. Identities were being withheld on the dead passengers until more details were known.

The road was the road that led to Emily's house. The time of the accident placed it on the night she and Simon had almost been run off the road.

"That doesn't mean it was right outside my front door, Barb," she began somewhat weakly.

Barb, who had poured herself a glass of iced tea and grabbed a couple doughnuts while Emily was reading, promptly slammed down the glass. "Front door, my Great-Gramma's nightshirt! When are you going to come to your senses, Em? The world is not a safe place anymore, especially for someone like you."

"I can take care of myself."

"That's just the problem," Barb argued, sighing and gulping the tea and doughnuts as she tried to make her point. "You've always had to take care of yourself, and you have no idea how really vulnerable you are. Simon won't be around forever, you know. Someday, something is going to happen and you're going to realize you need other people, and they won't be there—especially when you've isolated yourself out in the boonies."

Emily drove home through a late afternoon thundershower, moody and depressed. Not only was she unnerved by the newspaper article and Barb's consequent flapping, but even more by her friend's observation on her own self-reliance.

Emily had always prided herself on her independence, her ability and determination to do anything she set her mind to, even if she had the knack for bit-ing off more than she could chew. She hadn't really had much choice. It didn't do to try and depend on other people—they only let you down eventually, as she had learned throughout her lonely life. It was simply shortsighted to depend too heavily on other people when the only person you could really count on was yourself.

Sure, God figured in it all somehow, Emily supposed. And maybe in some remote sense He cared about her. But she couldn't worry Him with all her problems when the world had so many worse ones, could she? Wars, famines, diseases—the Lord depended on *her* to keep the oils of her own unremarkable life running smoothly, freeing Him for all the big-time stuff.

It was far better to be kind and friendly to everyone, live by the Golden Rule, but never expect or hope for anything in return. That way, she would not be disappointed and let down when something happened like Simon Balfour appearing out of the blue and threatening to take her house away from her.

A long rumble of thunder pealed across the rain-soaked countryside, and a thin streak of lightning zigzagged across the sky. He makes me feel about like this *storm*, Emily reflected as she slowed down to allow for the torrential onslaught. Telling her God has His loving eye on her all the time, promising he would help find solutions to her problems. Ha! Simon *was* the problem, with his grass green eyes and his silver tongue . . . calling her a sparrow and . . . and kissing her like . . . like he couldn't help himself any more than Emily could control her own response.

I won't be an easy *mark*. I may be easygoing—but I'm not an easy *mark*. She turned onto the dirt lane which, because of the rain, was a sea of mud, and wriggled her tense shoulders. She wouldn't be an easy mark as long as Simon kept his hands to himself.

It was an infuriating admission, but she might as well be honest with herself. She was attracted to the man, regardless of all the circumstances muddying her life as the rain muddied the road. She was almost glad he hadn't found the will yet, not because it meant she would keep her house, but because it kept him near.

Okay . . . she was a borderline easy mark and would just have to try harder.

Pulling into the yard, Emily sternly ordered her heart to be relieved instead of depressed that Simon's car was gone. Ignoring the lack of an umbrella, she slogged up the porch steps, drenched and dreary—and gasped in alarm. Ivan sprawled limply in the corner, not even a flicker of movement from his tail greeting her. He had been sick, and specks of foam lined the corners of his mouth. She rushed to his side, heart hammering. "Ivan, what happened? What's wrong?"

A vet. She needed to call a vet. She was scrabbling frantically in her purse for the key when the brutal fact hit home: she had no phone.

"Ivan," she sobbed beneath her breath. "Lord, please don't let anything happen to Ivan."

Another crack of thunder and a simultaneous lightning flash heralded a fresh downpour. Paying no attention to a note taped to the door, Emily unlocked the house, ran to her bedroom, and yanked off the spread. Halfway down the hall she stopped, remembering how Samson hated storms.

She dropped the spread, ran back into the dining room, and found the cat in his hiding place behind the boxes. Scooping him out, she took him to the kitchen and poured him some milk, spilling half of it all over the counter in her haste. After reassuring him that the storm would pass and begging him to forgive her for leaving him, she dashed back down the hall, grabbing the spread as she ran.

Two hours later Emily drove home alone, having left Ivan overnight at the vet's for observation. Her hands shook when she at last unlocked the door and untaped Simon's note. He'd had to run off to Tennessee again and would be back the next afternoon. He was sorry to leave her alone again.

Alone. Emily wadded the paper into a ball and called for Samson in a voice that did not sound at all like her own. When the cat wandered out to the hall and stroked himself against her legs as if he hadn't a care in the world, Emily finally broke down.

It did not occur to her that *she* might be in danger.

The next afternoon she was getting ready to retrieve Ivan when Simon drove up. "What's wrong?" he asked immediately, looking solid and secure and scruffy in faded cutoffs and a paint-stained t-shirt from Alaska advising "Go kiss a moose."

Under any other circumstances she would have teased him about trying to emulate her own dress style. Unfortunately, not even rage dimmed the intensity of his discerning gaze or the attractiveness of his smile, which was fading fast in light of her awkward silence. "I have to go to town," she answered, nose buried in her purse. "You can come on in and start searching if you want to. I . . . I'll be back in awhile."

Firm fingers lifted her chin. "I asked what's wrong," Simon repeated gently. "You've been crying."

Startled, Emily pulled free, her hands clutching confusedly at her shoulder bag. "How can you tell?" she asked.

Simon stuffed his hands in the waistband of his shorts and contemplated her a moment. "Your eyes are slightly puffy and your nose is still red." His voice suddenly changed, became abrupt, almost cold. "Are you going back to the lawyer? Is what he told you yesterday so upsetting it made you cry?"

"No . . . Brad was very nice. In fact, I'm going to be his—" she stopped, unwilling to go into the details when all she could think about right now was Ivan. She started to brush past Simon. "I'll tell you about it later. I really need to go right now."

"You're going to be his what?"

Hard hands with a grip that was not gentle at all latched onto her shoulders and jerked her around. He held her at arms' length, and the look on his face was indescribable. "Emily, what have you done?" When she looked up at him uncomprehendingly he shook her. "What have you done to keep this house, you idiot?" he repeated, his voice so full of fury and panic Emily's shaky composure erupted as well.

"Let *go*! What's the *matter* with you? Brad said it would be all right since it was Sylvan and not Chicago. I'm sorry if you don't like it but it's really none of your business what I do." She squirmed uncomfortably, then gasped as he thrust her from him, whirled away, and banged his fists on the wall.

Indignation fizzling, Emily took one hesitant step and touched his shoulder. It was like touching one of the sun warmed boulders by a river where she used to vacation as a child. "Simon?" she offered tentatively, wondering at the violent emotion she seemed to generate in him. "There was nothing you could do. It's a job, anyway, and will at least pay the bills. I told Brad I hadn't been a secretary since I was seventeen, but he was desperate because Gloria is due to have her baby any day. I'll be—"

Simon turned back around abruptly and his arm shot out to steady her with an almost convulsive grip. "Did you say *secretary*?" he demanded, a beseeching note beneath the question.

Emily tugged ineffectively at his hand. "Yes." Her own voice reflected her growing bewilderment. "Didn't I tell you?"

Simon released her, lifted a hand to his brow, and closed his eyes. "No," he murmured very quietly, "you forgot to mention that little fact."

"I'm sorry," Emily sighed distractedly. "It's just that I'm so upset about Ivan I don't really know whether I'm coming or going." She paused, gulped, and added, "Speaking of which, I do have to go. Dr. Moffat promised Ivan would be all right, but I won't believe it until he's back here. . . ."

Her voice started to crack and she bit her lip hard. Oh, no. She couldn't break down in front of Simon again. Besides, he didn't like Ivan. He wouldn't understand.

"Ivan? Your dog?" He stepped closer, and Emily tried to smile.

"Someone tried to poison him last night. I got him to the vet in time, but apparently it was touch and go for a while." She swallowed hard. "I'm going to go get him now. Dr. Moffat kept him overnight for observation."

"Ahh. . . ." With heart-stopping tenderness he folded her into an embrace so radically different from his earlier behavior that Emily's defenses collapsed like the walls of Jericho. She clung to him, savoring the heady sensation of leaning on someone else's arms. It wouldn't last but a minute, she knew, but it felt so good. It felt so . . . nurturing. And she needed it so desperately.

"I'm sorry, honey," Simon was whispering into her hair. "I know how much your dog means to you. What a rotten thing to happen on top of everything else." One hand stroked the long braid, her back, and shoulders, while the other held her close. "That's why you've been crying, isn't it?"

Head buried in the soft t-shirt, Emily could only nod.

Simon continued to hold her, his own thoughts whirling and gradually steadying as he was able to accept that Emily was here, in his arms, and unchanged. There were still a lot of unanswered questions, however, and a lengthy examination of his *own* feelings would have to have top priority over the next few days.

Emily amazingly enough had not picked up on his initial train of thought concerning her relationship with the lawyer. Thank heaven for that, Simon told himself with grim amusement. What a fool he would have looked! He had lost control with her at least twice now, and although she was obviously still totally unaware of the effect she had on him, she was not a stupid woman. She was only confused, worried, staggering beneath problems that would have defeated most other people.

Simon tried to serve his Lord in the best way he could, but it did not always come easy. He had accepted Christ as his Savior when he was fourteen, been a model student through high school and college. Then, after Dad retired from his small construction firm and Simon took over and channelled it into one specializing in restoration, he somehow sidetracked onto the road of hard work and "loose women," as Mother had put it.

One day Mom cornered him, sat him down, and looked him straight in the eye. "Son, do you eventually plan to marry and raise a family like your brother and sister have?" she had asked, casually enough so he hadn't immediately bolted.

"Yeah, one day, Mom. I'm too busy right now, you know. Twenty-seven's not exactly over the hill, and I'd like to have a good time for a while yet, I suppose. . . ."

"Hmmmm," Mom replied. "Well, when you do settle down, do you think it would be with a woman like the ones you've been—seeing—over the last few years?"

Not too much seemed to escape his mother, even if he hadn't lived at home since college. "Good grief, no!" Simon had exclaimed ruefully, but with heartfelt certainty. "Not *those* women. . . ."

She had leaned forward then, planting strong, work-roughened hands on her knees and fixing upon him her most serene, impossible-to-argue-with stare. "So what makes you think a pure Christian woman whom I presume *is* your idea of a suitable mate would have anything to do with a man who dates the type of women you do?"

He had never forgotten the lightning bolt of conviction that electrified his senses. It had killed his former lifestyle as dead as the bolt that had struck a white pine in their backyard the previous year. Simon had never viewed women in the same manner since, nor treated them as if they were merely there for his personal gratification.

Over Emily's head he smiled. Emily would doubtless disagree. In the weeks they had come to know each other, he had wrecked her carefully constructed little world, bullied her, lost his temper, kissed her with a ruthless passion she had obviously never experienced, and just now had leaped to a regrettable conclusion for which Emily could justifiably take offense. What a mess!

And now that ugly leviathan of a dog had gotten himself poisoned. Who on earth would do such a thing, when Emily lived in such isolated splendor? And why? Some very unpleasant possibilities were nudging his brain, clamoring for attention and causing the muscles of his jaw to clench. Emily had not exactly made a secret of the fact that she lived out here all alone. And those cars—not to mention his talk with the county sheriff about a crash along Emily's road a few weeks back. He wondered if Emily knew about that.

Unfortunately, poisoning the dog might have been more than an arbitrary, haphazard piece of cruelty. Somewhere out there, somebody just might be planning for one Emily Carson to be his next victim.

Chapter Seven

Surprisingly, Simon went with Emily to pick up Ivan, who was fine, but subdued. Simon spent several minutes talking to Dr. Moffat while Emily paid the bill, made arrangements to bring Samson in to be neutered within the next month, and got Ivan into the car. She couldn't help but wonder why a man who was by and large disinterested in animals would want to talk to a vet. Even after Simon's reply to her query had been an evasive, "Just talking," she was so relieved to have Ivan back, she shrugged the matter aside.

Once they were back at the house and Ivan was ensconced safely in his favorite spot on the front porch, Emily announced that she was going to start painting the kitchen. Simon, as far as she was concerned, was welcome to wear himself out looking for the will wherever he pleased.

"Brad said since the title at present establishes my clear ownership, I can work on the house if I want to," she announced defiantly, expecting a fight.

To her utter astonishment Simon agreed it was probably better that way anyway, but would she promise to break for lunch? He touched the back of his hand to her cheek in a gesture somehow more intimate than a kiss and disappeared upstairs.

For the next two weeks they worked in relative harmony, pursuing their chosen tasks. Their work was interrupted only twice: once by a brief visit from Barb and then by the long-awaited installation of the phone line.

Emily decided Simon must be going over the entire house board by board, and at odd moments when she was particularly tired came to the conclusion he was dragging it out for the sole purpose of annoying her. Several days he prowled outside somewhere, and at other times he worked at a drafting table he'd set up in the library. A couple of times a week he worked outside in the camper in his on-site office, complete with impressive computer, modem, and printer.

Emily had a sneaking suspicion he was also secretly daydreaming about how *he* would restore her house. Her suspicions were confirmed late one Monday afternoon in early September, her third week as Brad's secretary.

It had been a long day, for she was accustomed to standing in front of a blackboard or painting walls, not sitting behind a desk answering the phone, typing, and when she was bored because the phone hadn't rung, updating and reorganizing Brad's files. That day he'd warned her they could expect to hear soon from Iris Bancroft's lawyer, and then the judge could determine the date for their hearing.

As she drove home from work, Emily thought about how she hated the whole process. She felt dreadful knowing she was having to destroy an old woman's dreams, even though Iris was responsible for initiating the whole affair. Of course, from what Simon shared with her, his great-aunt was about as helpless an old woman as Emily was a candidate for Miss America.

Emily hoped the hearing would be soon. Brad was confident of a verdict in her favor, but that was only because as yet, Simon had not unearthed the will.

As the weeks had passed, Emily had grown more convinced the document didn't even exist, and she suspected Simon agreed, though he wouldn't say so. He never mentioned the hassle he endured whenever he called home (always using his credit card).

Emily had come to know whenever Simon's parents had heard from Iris. He never complained, but there would be a certain tension in the grim line of his mouth, and he would work with fanatical single-mindedness until lunch, when he was finally able to shrug aside whatever wounds the woman inflicted with her incessant goading. Privately Emily was grateful Simon had adamantly forbidden his parents from revealing Emily's new phone number under any circumstances.

He had reverted to the calm, courteous stranger she had first met, neither shouting at her and trying to tell her what to do, nor attempting to approach her romantically. When Emily had realized she felt *slighted* by this decorous behavior, she was so angry with her unruly emotions she erected her own formidable barriers, mostly consisting of a combination of offhand aloofness and determined cheerfulness.

Emily's musings were interrupted as she turned into her driveway. Climbing wearily out of the car, she saw Simon sitting on the front porch steps, incredibly enough tossing a stick for Ivan to fetch. While he had never made overt gestures of friendship to the dog, ever since the poisoning episode he had at least been civil, both to Ivan and Samson. Emily smiled as she walked across the yard to them.

Ivan loped across to her side, barking and posturing and as healthy as if he hadn't been inches from death less than a month ago. Emily hugged him and talked doggie drivel all the way to the porch, where Simon had risen to meet her.

"Hi." She always felt awkward and shy around him now, never knowing what to say. "Thank you for playing with Ivan. He gets sort of lonely now that I have to be gone three days a week."

"I know," was the dry retort. "He brought the stick over and whined for ten minutes until I finally gave in."

Emily smiled, hating herself for the warm flush she felt rising in her cheeks. "I'm sorry you think he's a nuisance."

"I'm getting used to both of them," Simon promised, stuffing his hands into the hip pockets of a pair of worn-out cords.

He followed Emily into the house and down to the kitchen. Gesturing her to a chair, he fixed her a glass of iced tea, then sat down across from her and propped his elbows on the table. "The question is, are you getting used to *me*, Emily?"

The question was soft but provocative. Emily searched his face, really looking at him for the first time since the day Ivan was poisoned. The green eyes were narrowed, full of light, and very intent on her reaction, but they revealed nothing. His hair was as wild and unruly, just brushing his ears and neck. Right now it looked as if he had just washed it, and the late afternoon sunlight highlighted the gold and chestnut tones Emily so envied. His tan had faded somewhat, and there were lines scoring his cheeks and forehead she hadn't noticed before. "I suppose so," she finally told him slowly. "Why do you ask?" Simon dropped his gaze a minute, contemplating the table as if it contained some secret message. Then the heavy straight lashes lifted, and Emily found herself unable to avoid the piercing intentness of those eyes. "I want to help you restore the house," he told her, the words slow and deliberate so she could not possibly misunderstand. "Not as the professional, not by bringing in my crew and taking over. Just me, helping you, because I've come to. . . ." He hesitated, as if he were still picking his words carefully. "To care about this place almost as much as you have."

Emily, of course, was not surprised. She was, however, staggered by the tidal wave of relief surging over her. Had she somehow let slip these past weeks how uncertain she was of her ability to complete the project alone, how tired she was of juggling a job along with the restoration? Had the fact that she was still uneasy since the poisoning and thus was not sleeping well become that noticeable?

"Emily?" Simon prodded, reaching across the table and placing his hand over hers. "Please don't fly off the handle or start feeling threatened. You can use the help—you need the help. There's so much I know, so many ways I could help you, show you how to make the work go faster, look more professional." He smiled a little when she bristled. "You've done an outstanding job, honey, but admit it. You *are* an amateur."

"I was going to give in gracefully," Emily grumbled, "but if you're going to adopt that kind of superior stance you can take your help and stuff it in one of the corners you keep poking in for the dumb will." They stared at each other for a minute, then both broke into relieved laughter.

"I was afraid you'd go for my shinbone," Simon confessed between chuckles.

"Well, I'm *still* afraid you're going to bulldoze over my feeble efforts, and then I will go for your shins."

Simon had no difficulty reading between the lines. "Emily," he promised softly, all laughter fading away, "until I find the will, and until the court says so, this house is yours, and Aunt Iris can foam at the mouth all she wants. I only want to help you and enjoy practicing my vocation for the sheer pleasure of doing so. Will you believe me?"

"I'd like to. But Simon, what if you *never* find the will? You've been looking for a month now, and I know conducting business long distance isn't healthy even with all your fancy equipment. How much longer can your great-aunt force you to keep looking?"

Simon stood up, moved around Emily, and drew her to her feet. "I don't care if it takes the rest of the year." His hands moved warmly from her wrists up to her shoulders. "When are you going to realize that's only an excuse to be near you?"

"What do yo mean?" Emily whispered, the question ending in a breathless squeak as he held her close and trailed soft kisses from her temple to her cheek.

"I mean," he murmured, "that I'm tired of pretending that I don't have any feelings. You've flitted around and struggled to feather your nest and chirped on about that lawyer you work for—and not once have you picked up on the fact that I happen to be very attracted to you. *You*, Emily Carson—not the house." He lifted his head, holding his mouth poised just over Emily's. "So . . . what do you have to say about that?"

Just before her eyes closed, Emily watched the teasing green glitter in Simon's eyes flare into something altogether different. Then he was kissing her, not with the almost angry passion of the first time, but with an exquisite blend of tenderness and restrained desire.

They broke apart abruptly when Samson jumped up onto the chair and meowed, causing Simon to start and pull away from Emily. She sank bonelessly into the chair, automatically picking Samson up as she did so.

Simon laughed shortly, his mouth quirked in wry acknowledgment. "You, you striped and whiskered fleabag, you do have some competition for the lady's affections."

"He doesn't have fleas. He's wearing a flea collar," Emily responded with splendid irrelevance. She was spinning, feeling like a playful fall breeze suddenly swirled into a full blown hurricane. Brown eyes wide, dark, and lambent, she gazed up at Simon, struggling to comprehend what had happened.

Simon flexed his shoulders, sighed, and touched her cheek with the tips of his fingers. "Don't look so confused. This has been coming on since the first time I kissed you." He scrutinized her dazed features in something close to exasperation. "Don't tell me you haven't felt the tension between us, Emily, even if I have tried to keep mine under control."

"I felt it," Emily replied very low. "I just had no idea you would feel so . . . so strongly. . . ."

"You really have no awareness of yourself as an attractive woman, do you?" He raked his fingers through the thick waves of his hair in consternation. "You've mentioned as much before, but I suppose I didn't really believe it. I thought the reason you look the way you do was circumstances more than anything else."

Some of the dazed look sparked into resentment. "And what is that supposed to mean? I can't help it if I'm not a nubile teenager with the seductive charms of Aphrodite."

Simon threw back his head and laughed, a deep, attractive laugh designed to capture and hopelessly tangle heartstrings. "Ah, Emily, what am I going to do with you?" He pondered her now with the old teasing affection, and Emily felt fingers of red creeping up into her cheeks. "Put Samson down."

"What?"

Looking as if he were lifting a smelly bag of garbage, Simon reached and gingerly picked up the cat and deposited him on the floor. Then he once again drew Emily to her feet. "You have something far more beautiful than a seductive figure and alluring manner, Emily Carson," he crooned in soft rhythmic syllables, his hands cupping her face, the thumbs gently stroking her cheekbones. "You have character. And purity. And an inner beauty that shines out to any man who is astute enough to see beneath the camouflage." Emily's hands had risen to tug at Simon's, but they fell helpless at her sides as he released her, then gently touched her braid. "This lovely hair you keep bound . . . the style-less clothes that reflect your poor self-image . . . your makeup free face which gazes so guilelessly and fearlessly out at the world and never reveals how lonely or unhappy you are. . . ."

His fingers shushed her as she tried to protest. "You might have convinced yourself and everyone else that you're a contented, quiet lady who could never stir even a ripple of passion in a man, but you're wrong." He smiled into her eyes. "And you know it now, don't you?"

Emily was saved by the bell, literally. The phone rang, and she flung herself away from Simon and scampered down the hall to her bedroom.

"Em? Brad here. Sorry I didn't make it back to the office before you left. I've got the date for your hearing and thought you'd like to know."

The blood pumping furiously through Emily's overheated veins chilled to an abrupt standstill. "When?" she managed to ask, then had to reassure Brad that she was all right, just tired, and no, nothing was wrong before he would answer her question.

Simon was waiting at the entrance to her bedroom, leaning against the door jamb with arms folded across his chest. He was scowling, all teasing and tenderness wiped away. "The lawyer, I presume?" he guessed after she hung up, his voice almost, but not quite, hostile.

Emily nodded. "The hearing is set for this Thursday," she recited, and she looked down at her hands, marveling that they were not quite steady. "Ten o'clock. Your great-aunt's lawyer will have notified her, so I guess I'll see both of you in court, as the saying goes."

Simon stared at her across the room, and it was as if a giant chasm had opened between them. "I guess you will," he agreed evenly.

Emily's chin lifted. "And you'll be flying to Connecticut as soon as possible?"

He sighed deeply. "Yeah. Emily," he stopped, a muscle twitching in his jaw. "I'll call you."

"There's no need—"

"There's *every* need!" He bit out the words, then looked as if he wanted to swallow them back. Turning on his heel, he stalked off down the hall, and a second later she heard the door slam.

Emily sank down onto her bed and buried her head in her hands.

That night Emily jerked awake to the sounds of footsteps prowling around outside the house, then up on the porch. This time, except for Ivan and Samson, she was alone.

At first Emily was so frightened she clung to Ivan, holding the struggling, whining dog to her with her hand clamped over his muzzle so he wouldn't bark. It took several terror-filled minutes to comprehend that insanity, and with a sharp little sob, she let Ivan go.

The dog tore off with a series of roaring barks that would have scared the stripes off a tiger. Emily would not let him outside for fear of what might happen, but at least there were no more footsteps, and after thirty minutes of growling and prowling, Ivan finally settled back down. Emily patted his head and told him he was a good dog, but she didn't sleep at all that night, falling only into a light doze around dawn when the only sound she had heard for hours was Ivan's quiet breathing.

First thing in the morning, she called the county sheriff and explained what had happened. The sheriff dispatched a deputy who tramped around the yard and poked about the porches searching for clues or signs of forced entry. He found nothing. After patting Emily on the shoulder and remarking kindly about women and their generally excitable constitutions, the slightly paunchy, slightly pompous patrolman left. So that day, instead of working on the house, Emily attached a leash to Ivan and embarked on a hike around the parameters of her property. Someone might be using her property for nefarious purposes, and as usual it was up to Emily to take care of the matter.

Gray skies hung like a damp, dirty sheet low and heavy in the sky. September usually wasn't as hot as August, but the humidity was still high enough to be cloying. The air was ripe with the pungent odor of vegetation and wet earth, but at least the wind was in the right direction to keep the paper mill fumes at bay.

Emily marched across the weed-infested field, intent on starting her investigation at a camping site she and Ivan had happened on one day. She kept Ivan leashed because she could not depend on him to stay close enough for her to protect. A detached part of herself laughed at the irony. Ivan was supposed to be protecting *her*, not the other way around! Simon would definitely not understand.

She would not think about Simon right now. She would not. She would concentrate on searching for signs in her woods that should not be there—beer cans, a campfire—Emily didn't know what she was looking for, but she also knew if she stayed holed up in her house like a sniveling coward afraid of her own shadow, she would never forgive herself.

She tramped for hours through underbrush dripping with dew and the rain from two days ago, beneath silent, slender pine trees whose needles carpeted the forest floor. For a while she followed the firebreak, but after sidetracking into the woods to search over the abandoned campsite she and Ivan had discovered in July, Emily struck off into the woods on the other side of the little clearing. Stumbling onto an old logging road made walking easier, but Emily had no idea where it would lead. She checked her watch and decided to follow it no more than thirty minutes, since by then she would doubtless have reached the limits of her property anyway. Someday, God willing, she would have to scratch up the funds to have the boundaries surveyed and updated.

The rutted, overgrown road wound through another quiet glade of pines, then meandered about the edge of a huge cleared meadow. Emily decided it was time to start back just as Ivan growled deep in his throat, then emitted a soft warning woof.

Startled, Emily turned, her eyes scanning the field and widening in astonished disbelief. Ivan barked again, louder this time, and with panicked swiftness Emily clamped her hand around his muzzle.

Unbelievably, parked at the far end of the field was a plane. It was small, without the bright colors tipping the tail or wings or body. There was a van beside it, and several men were taking boxes out of the plane and loading them into the van. For a frozen second Emily couldn't move, couldn't think, couldn't breathe. Drugs. It had to be drugs. It seemed beyond comprehension that she had stumbled onto such a scene, but she had, and all the seeming isolated incidents of the last months blended together to paint a deadly scenario.

Cars slowing and idling outside her house in the dead of night. A crashed and abandoned car full of cocaine and pornographic materials. The footsteps last night. Had her house—abandoned for years—been used as a drop-off point? Storage for their filthy cargo?

Emily had attributed the mess she had cleaned up when she moved in to relatively harmless hoboes. Now she wasn't so sure.

Ivan struggled, whining, and Emily felt the hair rise on the back of her neck. She had spotted the plane—but that meant they could also see *her*.

Emily grabbed Ivan's collar while her other hand stayed clamped about his mouth, then turned and as quietly as she could, crept back into the covering of trees. When the shadows of the pines and a curve in the road provided a modicum of safety, she ran, clenching Ivan's leash in a death grip.

She ran until her lungs ached and a stitch in her side doubled her over so that she had to stop and rest. Ivan whined and licked her face. He wasn't even breathing hard, but sat by her panting easily, tongue dripping, waiting for his mistress to tell him what to do next. For one whirling moment Emily thought she was hopelessly lost, but as her labored breathing slowed, she caught the faint sound of the creek. Still breathing in hard stabbing gasps, she stumbled through the woods until they reached familiar territory.

Her immediate instinct was to grab the phone and call the police. Even in the process of dialing she hesitated, then slowly replaced the phone in the cradle. Was there any chance they'd believe her after the attitude displayed toward her this very morning by that deputy? Even if they did, Emily doubted she could retrace her path to the field. The plane would have left hours ago, and the van with its deadly load would be on its way to ruin more lives.

Emily pummeled her fists on the wall in frustration and despair. What could she do? She had had firsthand experience of what happened when a person got messed up in drugs, for she and a fellow teacher had caught two ninth graders smoking pot under the bleachers the previous spring, and when their lockers were searched, crack was discovered. One of those boys had been an honor student, with his whole life ahead of him. Now—

Emily picked up the phone again, willing to make a fool of herself for the sake of all the other school kids. Then another, even more unpleasant thought struck: If the police went nosing around the area and found nothing, the jerks who were involved with the trafficking would probably know who had set the authorities on their trail.

She spent the rest of the afternoon and evening sanding kitchen cabinets, but the sweaty, backbreaking labor could not drown out the clamoring voices in her head, all telling her to do something different. So she ended up doing nothing at all. She spent another sleepless night—this time with the hammer by her bed as well as Ivan.

At least she had Ivan. When Simon returned, he and his aunt would be guests of Lamar Hansell, Iris's lawyer, so Emily could *not* depend on Simon's help anymore. That was okay by her. She wasn't stupid—and she had Ivan.

Tomorrow at work, maybe, just maybe, she could talk to Brad and ask him for advice.

Unfortunately, no matter what she decided, she still might end up in a burlap sack at the bottom of the creek, and Iris Bancroft could have the property free and clear, will or no will.

Chapter Eight

Wednesday morning, Emily dragged herself to work. Brad, chewing on a couple of sticks of spearmint, barely spared her a second glance.

"Hi, Em. Glad you made it. You need to cancel all my morning appointments. Sorry about this. Re-arrange them for. . . ." he chewed even more furiously as he flipped through several pages of notes, his normally pleasant features distorted in a harried scowl. "For Friday, if you can. If they're going to be dead before then, have them come in as late this afternoon as you can—not before four."

He slapped the papers down and muttered something mildly profane, then apologized to Emily. "I have to go to Albany, Gloria left the reminder on my calendar, but she forgot to tell you so you could remind me of the note she left to remind me."

They grinned at each other. Emily was genuinely fond of Brad, for he was an easy person to like. He had been patient with her rusty secretarial skills, had praised her re-organization of his jumbled files, and never failed to remind her that her own case would turn out all right. Emily waved him out the door.

A little while later the secretary for Lamar Hansell called, and nebulous thoughts of drug dealers and death threats vanished from Emily's mind. Tomorrow. This time tomorrow the waiting and wondering would all be over.

What would the judge decide? Were Iris and her lawyer as confident as Brad that *they* would be the "winners"? How could anybody really win when either Iris or Emily would be devastated, whatever the outcome?

Over the past weeks at odd moments, Emily actually found herself praying for God's help. She even talked to her minister, Sam Noland, as Brad had suggested, marginally relieved when he provided her with some scriptural comfort. According to Pastor Sam, the apostle Paul flat out told the Romans they must submit themselves to the governing authorities—which was what Emily was trying to do now. A lawsuit offered the only alternative to determine legal ownership of the property. Emily's true trial, and manifestation of her Christian faith, would be accepting the outcome graciously.

Brad called at a quarter to five to apologize for not returning in time to go over the procedure for the next day with her. Emily tried to sound offhand, but Brad was too good a lawyer to be misled by her manufactured cheerfulness.

"Don't sound so worried," he counseled her kindly. "It's a fairly straight forward case without the will, Emily. By noon you can go celebrate." There was a pause, then he added hopefully, "Maybe I'll take off a couple of hours and celebrate with you."

Emily found herself wondering what Simon would think about that, so she told Brad with deliberate sweetness that she would love to celebrate with her favorite lawyer. Simon would have his hands full comforting his battle-ax of a great-aunt anyway.

Thursday morning dawned a hot, cloudless day with a brassy sky promising rain by nightfall. Emily dressed carefully, remembering Simon's words concerning her appearance.

Her best, most sophisticated outfit was a suit, bought two years ago for the end-of-the year PTA banquet. A lovely shade of cinnamon, Emily bought it because it fit okay and had been on sale. She never considered the fact that it turned her into a monochromatic symphony, serving to reflect the truth of Simon's favorite nickname for her.

Her suit teamed with a jewel neck ivory blouse, hair carefully brushed, braided and bound on top of her head, Emily dismally surveyed herself in the mirror. She'd wanted to look brisk and businesslike. But her mirror said she resembled a plain brown sparrow.

Would Simon be there? She had been astonished to find a postcard from him waiting in her mailbox yesterday afternoon, since he'd only been gone two days.

"See you Thursday," Simon had penned in a loose but neat script. "Don't worry about Iris. I'll take care of you, too. So will the Lord—go read Psalm 84:3-4. See you soon, sparrow-girl."

Emily tossed the card in the basket with the ones from her mother and forgot about it.

Brad met her on the courthouse steps, told her she looked fine, then spent the next fifteen minutes alternately explaining the procedure and reassuring his apprehensive client.

"You act like you've been indicted for violating the Controlled Substances Act or something," he teased, attributing Emily's sudden jerk of dismay to more nerves. He wrapped a comforting arm around her shoulders, fished in his pants pockets, and pulled out a stick of wintergreen gum. "Here. That ought to help soothe the savage beast within."

The awful moment passed, and Emily managed not to blurt out her onerous knowledge of a plane loaded with some of those controlled substances. Then the door to the waiting room opened, and Mr. Hansell, Simon, and the smallest woman Emily had ever seen walked through.

At first glance, Iris Bancroft did not look as if she could possibly be Attila the Hun in a ninety-five pound package, as Simon had suggested. Silver hair styled in tight curls framed a lined, mahogany-tanned face devoid of makeup save two bright splotches of rouge on each parchment cheek. One gnarled, bony hand supported her slight weight on a cane while the other rested on Simon's bent arm. She was wearing a severely tailored street dress of a soft mauve color that, Emily admitted, was infinitely more becoming on Iris than Emily's own brown suit was on her. The hand-crocheted collar seemed to emphasize her age and fragility until she opened her mouth.

"So you're the unprincipled, land-grabbing opportunist trying to steal my property."

Simon groaned and the lawyer, who had shut the door behind them, smiled in weary resignation.

"Aunt Iris," Simon reminded the woman quietly but firmly, "the matter is going to be decided legally, and name-calling merely detracts from your own credibility."

Iris bridled at the reproof. She removed her hand from his arm and stumped over to where Emily and Brad were standing, flinty gray eyes fastened on Emily.

"I don't care if you're Cinderella," she snapped, her voice raspy, but clear and strong. "That house is mine." She turned and shook the cane at Simon. "You promised you'd find the will and kick the upstart baggage out, and all you've done is let her make mush of your brains." She expelled a forceful sigh then concluded, "I always told your mother you were a stubborn, willful brat. Seems to me you haven't changed much."

"Maybe we should wait in the hall," Lamar Hansell suggested hastily.

Simon came up beside his great-aunt and laid an arm about her narrow, bony shoulders. "That won't be necessary," he promised, green eyes measuring Brad's close proximity to Emily. His mouth thinned, something primitive and raw flashing through his eyes. "Now that my aunt has vented her spleen, she'll behave with the utmost propriety."

Iris snorted, then swatted Simon's arm. "Don't try to put me in my place, nephew. There's not a man alive capable of doing that!"

The two lawyers suppressed smiles, and everyone moved to sit down in some of the uncomfortable, wooden chairs scattered about the room. Brad had not missed the look in Simon's eyes, and he discreetly chose a chair two seats away from Emily. She wanted to swat Simon like Iris had.

They spent a few minutes chatting in restrained, civil fashion, while Iris sat in queenly disdain and ignored them all. But Emily had seen a frightened glitter in her eyes, and when she took a dainty handkerchief from her purse, her hands were trembling. Emily was wretched.

Just before their case was called, Marylou Thomlinson, Mildred Davis's mother and partner, strode into the room, looking like an older copy of Mildred. She had the same brisk energy, the same tall, well-toned body and air of assurance.

"Sorry I'm late," she apologized with a smile encompassing everyone. "Will this take long, Lamar? I need to show a house at noon."

High noon, Emily found herself thinking with crazy humor. All they needed was the music and Gary Cooper. It would all be over by noon.

She only looked at Simon once, as they were all entering the courtroom. He was holding the door for everyone, and as Emily passed through with Brad at her elbow, Simon sliced her a look that would have frozen a welder's blowtorch. Emily couldn't conceal her pained confusion, and his mouth briefly softened. He and Brad exchanged glances, then Brad ushered her to her seat.

What had happened to the Simon who had promised to take care of her?

The procedure lasted only forty-five minutes. The lawyers presented their respective cases, and then the judge retired to his chambers to evaluate the claims before he made his decision. Emily knew he had already studied the case. She just hoped he would make his decision instead of delaying, which Brad had told her was a possibility for which she should prepare herself.

She had *not* been prepared for Marylou Thomlinson's revelations.

According to Mildred's mother, some twenty-six years ago—the very first year she received her broker's license—a man named Harold deCourier had come to see her. He was old and ill, with a very unusual request: He wanted Marylou to handle his father's property—the VanCleef estate—but according to the terms of his father's will, the property could not be sold out of the family for one hundred years from the date of that will.

Harold was, he informed Marylou with touching shame, VanCleef's illegitimate son, which was why his last name was that of his mother. The time limit would now be up in one more year. Twenty-six years ago Marylou had simply signed an agreement, then filed the whole thing in the back of a drawer, figuring she would probably never sell the property so why worry about it?

She had truly forgotten the whole affair. Over the years, the old deCourier place just sat and rotted out in the country. Harold had died years ago. He had never married and left no will that anyone could find, so there the house sat.

Marylou never told Mildred. Why should she, since she never thought about it? Thus, Brad meticulously proved, Mildred sold Emily the property in good faith.

Emily listened in growing horror and consternation, especially since Iris Bancroft turned out to be the granddaughter of Everett VanCleef, and therefore the legitimate heir. At one point Emily glanced toward the older woman, sitting straight and dignified across the room. No emotion showed on the aging, aristocratic face, but Emily still felt like an unprincipled carpetbagger. She couldn't help it. Once Simon had asked if she would give up the house without a fight. She understood now why Iris was just as determined, and the knowledge was suffocating.

The judge returned, everyone rose, and Emily found that she couldn't take a deep breath. Ten minutes later it was over—and Emily had won. Because the will had not been found and because Harold had died without issue, the judge declared Emily's ownership more legally binding than the terms of the agreement between Harold deCourier and Marylou Thomlinson. Lamar Hansell and Brad shook hands, and Lamar went over to console Iris, who was sitting as if turned to a pillar of salt.

Simon bent over her, whispering, but as Emily and Brad started to leave the room, he straightened and met them at the door. "I'd like to speak to you, Emily."

Brad lifted a tawny brow. When Emily nodded and managed to reassure him with a facsimile of a smile, he murmured that he would wait for her in the hall and left.

"I'm truly sorry for your aunt," Emily told Simon. "Seeing her in action, I can understand why you've had such a time of it." She paused, then added painfully, "Why didn't you explain to me?"

"I only found out Marylou's story two days ago. She was in the Mediterranean all summer, remember? Then, too, Aunt Iris believes in playing her cards close to her chest." He regarded her unsmilingly. "Especially now that she knows how I feel about you."

Emily digested those words in stony silence. "And how would that be?" she finally ventured. "From the looks you've thrown my way ever since you walked into the waiting room, I'd about decided I must have turned into the wicked stepmother instead of Cinderella."

A wicked glint appeared briefly. "I did warn you about her tongue, didn't I? At least you haven't had to listen to it for almost three months." The glint disappeared. "What's Lauderman to you, anyway, Emily? Besides your lawyer and employer, that is."

Emily stiffened. "You have no right to ask me such a question. And now that the house is mine . . ." she faltered, her gaze going in spite of itself to Iris, "twice over, I imagine you'll be going back to your own life."

"And prove I'm as undependable, as faithless, as everyone else in your life?" Simon asked, very softly. When Emily's eyes jerked back to his, startled, dark, and vulnerable, he lifted his hand and touched her cheek. "You might have your property, but there's still some goings-on to be cleared up, aren't there? Besides—you haven't learned about God's faithfulness yet. I've decided He's appointed me as His representative in your behalf, so get used to the fact that you'll be seeing a lot of me in the future." He opened the door and held it for her. "See you soon."

Emily ate lunch with Brad, but only because he insisted. Before they parted, Brad grasped her arm and waited until he had her full attention. "Emily, I wouldn't be worth the paper my degree was printed on if I didn't warn you about a couple things."

Alarm filled Emily's face, but she relaxed a little when Brad gave her a wide, sheepish smile.

"Sorry. Maybe I should have phrased it in legal jargon. What I mean is that there is every possibility Iris is going to pursue the will. If it's found, you'll find yourself being served with your own lawsuit."

"Oh."

"And that brings me to my other warning." He loosened his tie, then crammed his hands in his pants pockets. "Be careful with Balfour. The man has his eye on you, Emily, and it isn't just because of your property."

Emily colored. "It's nothing serious, Brad. I'm not the sort of woman to inspire a man to launch a thousand ships for me. And regardless of what you may think, it *is* the house he's interested in." She smiled a little. "He just has a bee in his bonnet about teaching me a lesson about God."

"What?" Brad laughed suddenly, and shook his head. "I've heard a lot of lines, but that one takes the cake. He might talk as pretty as a preacher, honey, but that's not what he's got on his mind. I'm a man, and I know." He eyed her thoughtfully a moment, and shrugged. "I entertained a few thoughts myself until I saw which way the wind blew. Go on home, Emily, but keep what I said in mind."

Men, Emily decided as she drove the twelve miles home, were as undecipherable as they claimed women were. As she turned onto the dirt lane her spirits perked up a little. She was sorry for Iris, bemused and irritated by Brad and Simon, but she finally had a home. A home of her own. And now she could relax and get on with the rest of her life.

She had taken Samson in to Dr. Moffat the evening before for his neutering operation. Now the first order of the day was to call and make sure her cat was okay. Shaking her head and chiding herself for forgetting to go by after she left Brad, she also decided to take Ivan for a walk since she had left him inside this morning.

"Hope he didn't chew up anything else," she spoke aloud, feeling the accumulated hours of worry and tension sloughing off her back as if she were shedding a burdensome extra skin. "Poor baby. Maybe I better let him stay outside again. If he's learned—" The words died in her throat.

Jerking to a halt and flinging herself from the car, she ran to the edge of her yard and stared across the field, horror turning to desperation and spiraling fear. The flames were small as yet, but deadly, creeping with scorching fingers in a steady line across the field toward her house. Smoke curled and billowed in gray swirls, and the air had borne it aloft so that it filled her nostrils with the sharp, acrid scent.

Without wasting another second, Emily whirled and raced for the house. Her fingers shook so badly it took three tries to dial the emergency number. Thank God she had a phone now and Ivan was here in the house, Samson safe at the vet's! She tried to calm the whining, worried dog as she explained the situation in a trembling voice to the calm man at the other end of the line. She managed to give directions, then hung up and began tearing her suit off in a panicked frenzy. The fireman had told her to evacuate and move herself and her car to the main highway, but Emily had no intention of sitting by and watching her property go up in smoke.

Yanking on jeans and a dressy, long-sleeved blouse she normally wore to church, ripping a nail as she struggled into socks and tennis shoes, Emily's mind raced as she tried to figure out ways to cap and destroy the flames. Carrying a bucket would be useless—like spitting in the wind. Should she try digging a firebreak? Starting backfires as firefighters did to combat forest fires? Hose down her yard to dampen everything?

She snatched one of J.J.'s old baseball caps she had saved and stuffed it over her hair to keep the braid up out of the way. Grabbing Ivan, she leashed him and then dumped him in her car in case the worst happened. "You'll be safe here," she patted his head, ran her hand briefly but soothingly over his quivering flanks. "I'll be back as soon as I can."

Stumbling and tripping, she ran across the field with a shovel in one hand and a wet rag to tie across her face in the other, sending up incoherent pleas to God, the firemen, Simon, and anyone else she could think of who might help. There was no way she could put out a fire alone even though she was determined to try.

Sometime later she heard the keening of the fire engines, but she was too busy to be relieved. Smoke stung her eyes and burned her nose, heat scorched and blistered her face and hands as she dug into the earth and flung heavy shovelfuls over the flames; dug and flung until her back was on fire like the field and her hands were raw with sweat and blisters. She was much too preoccupied to notice a sinister figure creeping steadily out from the woods behind her.

The blow caught her at the back of her neck. She went down like a pine sapling felled by a single swipe of the ax. When the fire engines pulled up five minutes later, there was no sign of Emily.

Consciousness returned by degrees, each more uncomfortable than the last. Her first sensation was the awful, searing pain in her head and neck. On the heels of the revelation came the awareness that she was being carried, flung over someone's shoulder like a bag of fertilizer. She tried to move, to scream, then the third realization that she was bound up inside some sort of sack hit her. She was effectively as helpless as a chicken tossed into the gunny sack of a chicken thief.

After awhile, the labored breathing of whoever was carrying her altered to gasps and grunts of exertion, and she decided somewhat fuzzily that he must have been carrying her a long time because she wasn't *that* heavy. She was on the edge of passing out again when she was unceremoniously dumped onto the ground.

"It's about time," a muffled voice complained testily.

"Put a lid on it," was the sharp reply. "She might look like a skinny school brat, but you try carrying her on *your* back for forty minutes."

"Don't see why we couldn't just leave her in the field."

"Because that's a murder rap, you dumb scum! Orca made his feeling plain— or are your eyeballs so fried you didn't catch his reaction after that ballup with Frank and Pete."

"Back off, Gumshoe." The voice came closer, and Emily's heart rose in her throat and tried to suffocate her. "Can we at least have a little fun with the dame? She's not much of a looker, but—"

Emily tried to close her ears to the spate of foul language that followed between the two. She tried to lick her lips, but she was dry-mouthed, parched with fear and thirst and the exertion of fighting the fire. The fire! Oh, please, God, let the firemen get there on *time*.

She wanted to struggle, to free herself from the blinding, scratchy burlap sack that kept her trussed up and helpless. Some deep-seated instinct of survival kept her still, the subconscious voice warning her that movement of any kind would only draw unwelcome attention to her.

But she had to do something. She couldn't just tamely submit to her fate. It wasn't right. It wasn't fair. Never had she felt so helpless, so out of control. Even when J.J. had been at his most rebellious, she at least had been able to talk him into listening to her point of view. And when Mom and Daddy left, she had had the freedom to make a new home. When Simon came and tried to take it away from her she had been able to fight back.

Now she was utterly and completely at the mercy of these thugs, and with that realization she fell into the darkest, blackest pit of despair in the universe. This must have been what Jonah felt like when he had been swallowed by the big fish. What had Jonah done to get out? Emily's conscious mind was coming and going now, flickering in and out like a bad camera reel of a thirties film. Jonah and the whale . . . sparrows . . . Simon called her sparrow-girl because of that song . . . a song about a whale? No, it had something to do with God . . . His eye is on the sparrow. That was it . . . Jonah had prayed and up out of the fish he came. But he was a man and she was just a sparrow-girl . . . God wouldn't listen to her prayers . . . "His eye is on the sparrow, and I know He watches me. . . ."

Help me, Lord. Send Simon before it's too late. . . .

Chapter Nine

Emily was picked up again, roughly, and dumped with scant ceremony into the seat of some kind of vehicle. Through a semiconscious daze, she heard a new voice speaking in a high-pitched whisper.

"Hurry! They got the fire out and now they're looking for the girl!"

"Did you take care of that mutt?"

After a horrible pause the third voice replied in a grudging tone: "Yeah. I . . . took care of him."

Emily didn't notice the bouncing ride or the pounding pain in her head. Tears dripped down her cheeks, soaking her face as, heartsick, she grieved for her innocent pet. He had been slaughtered because she hadn't gone for help when she had the chance.

Ivan was dead, and she was probably next on the list, no matter what that other man said.

After a while, they pulled onto a smoother road, and the bouncing and bumping ceased. The car picked up speed, but Emily had no sense of where they were or which way they were going.

Fortunately, the drive didn't take long. With a squealing of tires and a jolting turn that threw Emily against the door, the car jerked to a halt. Gravel voice— had he been called Gumshoe?—cursed the driver roundly, then Emily heard doors wrenched open and she was hauled out feet first and once again slung over a shoulder.

She sensed the presence of the other two men walking on either side. She could hear multiple footsteps, smell the malodorous combination of sweat, cigarettes, and unwashed bodies.

"This is far enough," one of them finally whined. "It'll take her until tomorrow to find her way back as it is. Let's split, man. I don't like this."

Suddenly Emily was yanked off the shoulder and then held suspended by two hands grinding into her arms like giant metal braces.

"I hope this little scare will teach you to keep your nose out of business that don't concern you. Next time we won't be so *gentle*." There was a harsh bark of laughter. "You might end up in the same shape as your dog." The clamps suddenly released her and she collapsed onto the ground. "Nice meeting you, Ms. Carson. If you value your hide and that pile of bricks, you better not venture too far out of it into the woods anymore."

The sound of footsteps retreated. A short while later the car engine roared to life and gunned off down the road. Emily was alone.

Silence lapped over and around her, gently lifting her up out of the dark hole and tugging at her dazed senses. Eventually she moved her hands and fumbled weakly with the corner of the sack, managing after several abortive attempts to tug it over her head. She winced as the late afternoon sun struck her eyes. How could this possibly still be the same day? Had it only been this morning that she'd learned she was the bona fide, one-and-only legal owner of that . . . pile of bricks? Shock and grief and a residue of terror stiffened her spine, and she forced herself to stand. It took a couple of tries.

"What a mess . . ." Emily mumbled, her voice a quavering husky croak.

In the distance, she heard the faint drone of a plane, the plaintive call of a bird, a car. A car? Feeling like the scarecrow from *Wizard of Oz*, whose stuffing was scattered all over the field, Emily dragged herself a few steps, swaying and dizzy and trembling. They hadn't carried her very far that last time. Hopefully the road was close by.

She fought a stumbling, wavering path through waist high goldenrod and milkweed, and prayed. Even though she was neither starving, nor a prisoner of war, nor dying of cancer, she hoped under these particular circumstances the Lord might incline His ear for a few minutes, if only until she were safely home.

The road proved to be an ancient county road, paved in the distant past with asphalt that was now cracked and crumbling, with weeds encroaching on the edges. If she were lucky, another car might pass by before next week. For the first time since she had been released, Emily's chin trembled. It was one thing to keep your sense of proportion when your life was on the line—it was another thing entirely when you were spared, but then were solely responsible for your continued well-being.

Simon. If only he were here. He would know what to do. He would take care of her. What was she thinking? She could take care of herself, as she had always done. She couldn't depend on anyone, including Simon Balfour. This was the man whose great-aunt wanted her home, who would doubtless be after Simon to keep on looking for the will regardless of this morning's outcome.

Iris Bancroft reminded Emily of the story in the Bible about the widow who kept nagging the judge until he gave her what she wanted, just to be rid of her. From what she had seen and heard of the elderly woman, the judge who this morning had ruled in Emily's favor might eventually reverse his decision just to get rid of Iris.

Simon would have his hands full with his great-aunt. He also had his own life to consider. Surely his team of specialists couldn't do *all* the restoration work in his absence; if they could, they'd go into business for themselves.

Besides, she had made it plain she wasn't interested. All that talk about being God's emissary was nothing but talk, just like Brad tried to warn her. Men were a strange lot, but it was not in Emily to figure them out right now. She had all she could do to put one foot in front of the other and find out if there were a phone or a house at the end of the winding little road.

A sunburned, dust-covered farmer driving a tractor pulling a flatbed of hay came upon Emily a half hour later. He helped her up, and she lay in the warm, sweet smelling hay as the farmer urged the ancient chugging tractor to its limit.

The farmer's wife exclaimed over her, put her on a couch, and nursed her with hot tea. Then she was driven to the county hospital, where an extremely large, comfortable-looking nurse clucked over her smoke- and dirt-laden state. A doctor examined her and harrumphed a lot, but he refused to tell her anything. Emily was wearily trying to remember the name of her insurance agent in Sylvan to tell the nurse when the curtain shielding her from the other cubicles in the small emergency room was flung wide.

Simon erupted into view, his body a coiled spring of tension and his eyes wild. "Emily, are you all right? . . . Emily!"

"Sir," the nurse tried to protest in her best matronly tone, "you can't come in here right now—"

Simon did not budge. "I can and I have." He was at Emily's side immediately, his hand reaching out with trembling fingers to touch her cheek, still red from fighting the fire. "Emily." He couldn't seem to say anything else and stood gazing down at her with red-rimmed eyes. Emily stared back. "Simon. . . . " she passed her tongue over her cracked lips. "How did you find me?"

For a minute his eyes closed as if in agony, and his hands clenched the side of the table with such force the knuckles gleamed white. "I drove out to see you—the firemen were just putting out the last of the flames. Your car was there, but no one had seen you."

He picked up her hand and held it, caressing her fingers, then lifted it to his lips. "We searched everywhere. Someone found an old baseball cap with some of your hairs attached, and your shovel, but that was it." He looked down at her with such naked pain that Emily was shocked out of her *own* pain and exhaustion. "I never want to go through those feelings again. I called the police, Barb and Taylor, Lauderman. . . ."

For the first time, the glimmer of a smile lightened his face. "Do you realize there are probably fifty or so people and officials in two counties combing the woods around your property for you? When the hospital notified the sheriff that a young woman fitting your description had been brought in, I burned up the road getting here."

Emily licked her dry, cracked lips. "I had no idea anyone would go to so much trouble," she whispered.

"How badly are you hurt?" he asked abruptly. "Can I take you home? Are you going to be up to answering some questions from the police—and me?"

"I'm all right. Mostly shaken . . . and a headache. The doctor hasn't really filled me in. . . ." Her voice faded and she bit her lip, her gaze dropping to watch her hands fidgeting with her blouse. "Simon . . . I think I've gotten in over my head this time. . . ."

His hands covered both of hers and stilled the agitated movements. "Whatever happened is not as important as the fact that I've got you here, now, and you're safe." He drew in a deep breath and his hand tightened reassuringly. "Were you assaulted, Emily?"

The question was voiced softly, almost offhandedly, but Emily was not too battered to miss the undercurrents, and suddenly she was as much afraid of what Simon might do as she was of the three thugs who had manhandled her and—and killed Ivan.

"Not exactly," she dragged out unsteadily. "They—I—was being taught a lesson." She tried to take a breath. "Ivan. They . . . they. . . ." She couldn't go on, but Simon didn't need the words spelled out.

"I'm sorry, Emily." Leaning forward, he brushed his lips comfortingly over her forehead. "I wondered when we couldn't find him and hoped he might be with you." He waited a minute, then prodded in a gentle, coaxing tone, "who is 'they,' honey?"

"It would have been nice if you'd waited for us, Balfour."

A short stocky man in a khaki sheriff's uniform strolled over to stand at the foot of the gurney. "Miss Emily Carson? I'm Sheriff Travis Jessup. Mighty glad you're okay, ma'am. Some of my men were getting ready to pen this fella here up in a cage—he was about as uptight as a renegade cougar." He hooked his thumbs in his gun belt and surveyed Simon and Emily. "Care to tell us about it, ma'am? Doc Wilburn ways you're a mite battered about, but nothing near bad enough to stay unless you really want to."

"No." Emily allowed Simon to help her sit up, dangling her legs on the side of the gurney. "No, I don't want to stay here."

Both men waited in taciturn silence while Emily haltingly related her tale of terror. A time or two, Sheriff Jessup inserted a question, but Simon kept silent. His gaze never left Emily, and the hand holding hers refused to let go.

"And then they left and I made my way to the road, and the farmer—I don't remember his name—found me and brought me here."

"The only names you remember hearing are Frank and Gumshoe and another funny sounding name you can't remember?" the sheriff quoted from his notes, watching Emily intently.

Emily nodded wearily, her head throbbing—her whole body was throbbing. Simon's hand held hers in a warm comforting clasp, however, which tightened when the doctor returned.

"She can go," he repeated, albeit reluctantly. "For the first twenty-four hours she probably ought to be monitored, maybe wake her every couple of hours through tonight—just as a precaution." He glanced from Simon to Emily and back again. "I take it this gentleman will see to those conditions?"

"You take it right."

The doctor winked down at Emily, patted her shoulder, and left. Simon held out his hand to the sheriff. "Thanks for everything. I'll get her settled first and then square things away as to addresses and procedures."

"Sure thing, Mr. Balfour. Miss Carson—I'll be in touch." He scratched his chin, looking uncomfortable. "I'm sorry 'bout all this, ma'am. . . ." He touched his hat, gestured to Simon, and walked out.

Simon smiled down at Emily. "I'll be right back. Don't move."

When he came back a few minutes later, he looked grim, but the hands helping her to her feet handled her with exquisite gentleness. "I'm taking you to Barb and Taylor," he said. "They'll put us up until I can call my folks. By the way, we're going down there as soon as you're up to it."

He helped her walk slowly toward the exit, keeping an arm about her shoulders and matching his stride to hers, talking in a soft, steady patter of words. "The sheriff and I decided whisking you off to Florida until this mess is cleared up a little would be our best option. No—don't shake your head at me. It's all been taken care of."

"Barb is something else, isn't she? When I got in touch with her, I thought she was going to come after me with her food processor—then I thought she was going to collar the FBI director himself if she had to hire a private jet to get there to do it."

Emily tried to laugh. That sounded like Barb.

Simon looked pleased. "She got on the phone and inside of thirty minutes had your entire hometown on its way over to start a search." He eased her into the seat of his Jensen-Healy, and they backed out of a parking spot marked "Ambulances Only," then drove slowly off down the street.

Emily leaned back in the seat, her eyes closing against the steady beat of pain, against the rapid tide sweeping her willy-nilly down a stream she was helpless to paddle against. "I can't go to your parents, Simon."

"Just rest, sparrow-girl. Just rest. I've got you now, and everything's going to be okay."

She rolled her had sideways, being careful not to jar the swollen lump. "Do you really think God has His eyes on sparrows?" she mused in a faraway, fading voice.

"I know He does." His hands clenched suddenly on the wheel, and his vice went rough and raw. "I couldn't have stood it otherwise." And on that note silence reigned.

They spent two nights with the Chakensis family. Barb and Taylor wanted Emily to move in with them, but Simon remained obdurate—the next day he was taking her to his parents' home in Florida. Friends dropped in to ask after her and offer aid and comfort, but the bulk of their advice centered around a central theme: under no circumstances should Emily return to her house.

The police had been unable to find any sign of her abductors, although after hearing Emily's story about the plane, they combed the woods, looking for the open pasture. Emily had not talked to Sheriff Jessup since the day after the fire, so she had no idea if they had found any clues or not.

"I suppose there's at least a smidgen of good in being knocked out and hauled around like a sack of dirty laundry," she commented over supper that evening. "At least my story is taken a little more seriously. Now I'm not just a neurotic woman living alone and scaring myself to death with my imagination."

Simon paused in the act of taking a bite of his mashed potatoes. "Has someone been giving you that impression?"

"Not since I was bashed over the head," Emily provided hastily. Simon was becoming more and more possessive, and it was downright uncomfortable, if not awkward. She had never had anyone fuss over her before, treating her as if she were fragile and needed protecting. Part of her responded as a desert flower responds to spring rains, but the rest of her remained a wary, prickling cactus.

"The man who came out after I heard someone walking around outside the house one night treated me more or less like a feebleminded ninny." She abruptly became aware of three sets of eyes boring holes of recrimination into her and ducked her head guiltily. She had forgotten that they hadn't known about that incident.

"You heard someone walking around outside and didn't say anything?" Barb's voice ended in a shriek, and Mark and Lara put their hands over their mouths and giggled.

"Calm down, honey," Taylor remonstrated his wife before turning to his children and adding sternly, "You two go take your baths and get ready for bed. You've got school in the morning."

"Em, why couldn't you be back teaching? Dump that house and come back here where you belong, where you'll be safe."

Emily very carefully laid her crumpled paper napkin by her plate and rose. "I have a very good job as Brad's secretary," she responded in a colorless monotone, "and as for belonging—I feel more at home in that house with Ivan and—" She stopped as a rush of emotion threatened to engulf her. "Excuse me," she muttered, and fled out into the backyard.

Simon followed her a little while later. She was sitting in a rope swing with a board seat Taylor had rigged for the children, her feet idly scuffing the dirt patch beneath it where all the grass had been worn away. She was staring fixedly into space with a closed, blank expression, but the hands clasping the rough hemp rope as if she were clutching a lifeline betrayed her inner turmoil.

Without a word, Simon gave her back a gentle push and began swinging her, his hands warm and firm.

"I could accept it better if they had at least left his body," Emily offered almost inaudibly. "At least I could have buried him and grieved and gotten it over with."

"I know." His hands kept up the gentle pushing, but each time they pressed into her back for that brief instant of contact, they somehow conveyed a message of caring sympathy.

Emily closed her eyes a few minutes to try and savor the early evening and relax. Last night the wind had changed, bringing in a cool front and the deep blue skies of approaching fall. The breeze riffling through her hair with the motion of the swing smelled of dry leaves and smoke and mid-September. In front of her, the sun had just slipped over the horizon, leaving behind a pastel watercolor sky of pale orange and pink and blue.

Life should have been serene, like a happy child tossing tiny pebbles into a placid pool. But it took everything Emily had to keep from bursting into tears.

"Sunset's beautiful, isn't it?" Simon observed as if he knew Emily needed to changed the subject. "I think sometimes that God reveals Himself the most dramatically in sunsets and sunrises, don't you?"

"I suppose."

"But I've also found He can reveal Himself just as dramatically in other ways—sometimes to my cost."

Emily swung up and back, up and back, and then gave in. "What do you mean?" she asked.

She heard Simon chuckle softly. "Sometimes that still small voice we Christians are supposed to cultivate is more of a first sergeant's shout when I'm not listening like I should." He gave her braid a gentle tug as he pushed her away. "Like when I lose my regrettable temper, or when I'm so blind with worry I forget."

"Forget what?" Emily found herself persisting.

Simon stopped the swing and his hands closed over hers. He turned her, swing and all, to face him, holding her not only with his hands but with the compelling message in his eyes. "When I forget the faithfulness of God," he declared with the strength and depth of a mountain stream. "When I try to control all the circumstances, forgetting that He's promised to stay with us at all times—good and bad—so all I really need to do is trust Him to deliver."

Chapter Ten

Sheriff Jessup met them at Emily's house early the next morning before they took off on the short drive to Florida.

"Got a few leads," he informed them after inquiring after Emily's health and shaking Simon's hand. "We found the field they were using as an airstrip, but needless to say we found nothing else useful. We'll stake it out awhile just in case, though." He glanced around the library. "You did a nice job on this room, but why don't you clean up that window?"

"I'm saving it for last." Emily shrugged self-consciously. "It was sunbeams hitting that window and reflecting on my windshield that brought the house to my attention, and when I discovered the window, I knew I had to have this place."

She sighed. "But it's been a lot harder and more tedious then I dreamed it would be," she slanted a quelling look at Simon, "and imagining how beautiful my window will look when it's cleaned up is all that keeps me going sometimes."

"You've done a first-class job," Simon assured her. He nodded toward the window. "I've been itching to get my hands on it myself. "I've restored period homes all over the South and have never come across a lead glass window of this caliber in a private residence. I'm pretty sure it's a Tiffany or LaFarge, but since Emily hasn't given me permission to check more closely, I have to suffer in silence." He smiled at Emily's look of astonishment, but now was not the time to pursue the matter.

"Have you found anymore about the low-life creeps who assaulted Emily?"

The sheriff nodded in satisfaction. "Her hearing the name 'Gumshoe' was a piece of luck for us. We've been in touch with the DEA and the FBI, and they both had this character on file." He contemplated his scuffed up shoes a minute, hand stroking his chin.

"I wasn't too wild hearing that—means this is more than a bunch of locals out to make a few fast bucks. Gumshoe is a former private investigator, hence the nickname. His real name is Henry Parskoni. He apparently lost his license because of his cocaine habit—he's street smart and a real cynical son of a gun. He's also careful. I'm surprised he let the mention of his name slip by."

"What about the other guy Emily mentioned?" Simon asked.

"Nothing yet. But we do think we've tied this incident to the wreck that resulted in two casualties back in July."

"My mailman said there was a second car involved, and you had found some drugs inside it."

"Yes'm." He hesitated, then added, "High grade stuff—and two boxes of the most disgustin' porno books and magazines I ever had the misfortune to see." He shook his head slowly, looking every inch the world-weary, battle-worn officer of the law fighting a war he couldn't win. "Whole darn country's straight on a road to hell, if you'll forgive the expression, ma'am. It's the tip of the iceberg down here, since we suspect this area might be one of the drop-off points of a pipeline from South America. We figure on average, we only manage to seize about fifteen percent of this garbage before it hits the streets." For a minute the three of them struggled with the weight of their helplessness, then Sheriff Jessup put his hat back on and moved briskly toward the front hall. "Well, I'll be going now that I've apprised you of the situation. Let me know twenty-four hours before you bring her back, and I'll assign some men to her."

"Thanks," Simon said. He looked as grim as the sheriff.

Emily hastily tossed some clothes in the suitcase Simon had brought in from his car. Barb had packed her some things the other day, but Emily, who had never given much thought to dressing herself up as long as she was fairly neat and clean, found herself wondering what Simon's parents would think of her. Probably a mousey, colorless woman Simon had taken under his wing for incomprehensible reasons of his own.

As she knelt on the floor of her closet, she tried to bolster her drooping spirits. Why not just look at the experience as an all-expense paid vacation to Florida with a very attractive man? It was too bad she didn't have an address for Mom and Daddy—she could have sent them a postcard.

She pushed her clothes aside and tugged at a box of summer clothes and other stuff she had never unpacked. A corner of the box seemed to be stuck on something, and she pulled harder, wanting to finish and be on her way so she wouldn't have to think anymore about her motivation for giving in to Simon so easily.

There was an ominous sound of ripping wood, and with a muttered exclamation, Emily peered behind the tangle of clothes into the dark interior of the closet. Wonderful. One of the cardboard flaps on the box had caught on a loose panel or something in the wood. She carefully edged her fingers behind the flap and in between the splintering panel to try and disconnect them.

"Just what I need. Something else to repair!" Emily grumped aloud, stifling a sigh of frustration as she tried to feel what was going on. The closet didn't have a light in it, and she didn't feel like searching for a flashlight. With a sudden spurt of impatience, she tugged at the wood and the cardboard flap, scraping her knuckles as she did so.

A tearing, rending sound announced that the wood, as well as the flap, had pulled free of the wall. Emily yanked the box of clothes out of the closet and shoved the clothes on hangers out of the way. She was planning to stuff the displaced panel back, when her fingers encountered something cold and metallic in the space behind it.

The realization of what she had uncovered struck her a stunning blow, and with shaking hands she withdrew what turned to to be a metal strongbox. She backed unsteadily out of the closet and stood, black spots dancing before her eyes.

With a feeling of sick foreboding, she laid the dusty coffer on the floor. Incredibly, it wasn't locked, and after only a slight hesitation, it opened quite easily. Inside was a faded manila envelope, so old it was closed by old-fashioned strings tied around a button. Inside the envelope was a folded sheet of paper, with the heading "Last Will and Testament of Everett VanCleef" written in an elaborate, bold script across the top.

"What's taking so long?" Simon appeared in the doorway. "Emily? What's the matter? What's that?"

He crossed to her side, studying her face, but his face dropped to her hands when she mutely help up the will. "Oh, no," Simon breathed, a stillness coming over his body. "Why now?"

With careful fingers, he lifted the will from Emily's trembling hands and began reading aloud, his voice a somber, expressionless baritone. "'I, Everett Peter VanCleef, being of sound mind and declaring this instrument to be my last will and testament, dispose of my properties as follows. . . .'"

"Simon," Emily sighed in a wisp of an undertone, "I feel sort of funny. I think I'd better sit—"

She swayed, then Simon's arm was around her, and he was guiding her over to the bed. They sat down together, and his hand moved to the back of her neck. Pressing with gentle insistence, he made her lower her head almost to her knees.

He kept her there a few minutes while he massaged her neck, being careful with the still tender bruise where she had been hit. "Easy, easy, love," he quieted her with his voice and hand. "I'm sorry . . . so sorry. . . ."

There was the sound of rustling paper and then his other hand slid beneath her chin and lifted her back up. Emily was incapable of hiding the shock, the inertia of shattering defeat that revealed itself in her stricken eyes.

"I can't bear it," she choked out, her voice still nothing but a thready wisp. "I've lost everything. Everything. I can't bear it anymore."

"Shh . . . shh. You haven't lost everything, I promise."

Emily very carefully removed herself from his hold and stood up. "Brad warned me if the will were found Miss Bancroft would have a good chance of winning a second lawsuit." Her unseeing eyes fastened on her shoulder bag lying in a jumbled heap on the bed beside the half-filled suitcase. She picked it up, rummaging inside until she found the huge old brass key.

"Here," she held it out to Simon. "Take it. I quit. I can't handle any more. I hope you enjoy restoring it." Her voice drifted off, then resumed in a vague, dreamy tone. "I wonder if Brad could use a full time secretary. . . ." She looked around. "I'll try and move my stuff out as soon as I can."

Simon stood up, and with utmost gentleness took Emily by the shoulders and walked her down the hall into the kitchen. She looked, Simon found himself thinking in agony, even worse than when she had told him about Ivan. *Lord, what can I do? She needs You now more than ever—because I don't know if she'll ever trust me again.*

Sitting Emily down in the kitchen chair, Simon fixed her a glass of water and told her to drink it. After pawing through the largely empty cupboards, he finally unearthed a half-empty box of animal crackers. "I want you to eat these while I finish packing your suitcase," he instructed Emily as if he would a child.

Emily looked at the cookies and water. "All right, Simon," she said apathetically, her entire posture speaking so wrenchingly of defeat that it was all he could do to keep himself from grabbing her and wrapping her in a fierce embrace.

He strode back to her bedroom, shoved in the suitcase what few clothes remained to be packed, and slammed the lid shut. If she needed something else, he could buy it for her later, but right now he was determined to clear out and get Emily on the road to Florida.

He glanced around the bathroom, then prowled the downstairs to make sure everything was secure. Jessup had promised to keep an eye on the premises while they were gone, the vet was caring for the cat, and the post office was holding her mail. All Simon had to do was keep Emily from giving up completely.

He laughed a bitter, mirthless laugh. Might be too late for that, he thought, and he couldn't blame her. Why had she had to find that blasted will? For two cents he'd burn the thing and be done with it, but he knew that evasion and lies and pretense were never the answer.

Jaw firming in renewed determination, he returned to the kitchen. "Come on, honey," he glanced at the barely touched water, the box of crackers still in the exact position he had left them. "We'll eat on the way." He put his hand beneath her elbow and tugged her up.

Looking neither at him nor around the house, Emily followed blindly. She was a lifeless, broken doll and her once vibrant, spunky personality lay in a crumpled heap somewhere deep inside her. She allowed Simon to lead her outside and down the steps, then over to the midsized sedan he had rented to make the trip more comfortable.

Emily slept most of the trip.

Nathaniel and Katherine Balfour had built a beach-front home years before on a tiny strip of a peninsula at the bottom of Florida's panhandle. Simon spent the bulk of the six-and-a-half hour drive praying while he drove, watching Emily as much as he did the road.

She still looked pole-axed, a docile, passive zombie. Simon would have preferred tears, or even her unpredictable, almost humorous display of temper rather than this present lifeless state. Right now she reminded him of a snuffed out candle.

Barb and Taylor had shed a goodly amount of insight into Emily's complex personality, her paradoxical blend of reckless confidence and the easygoing phlegmatic woman so astonished by her own capacity for passion. As far back as they could remember, Emily had had to pretty much play a lone hand. Her parents should never have had children, Barb contended forcefully, because they were both basically selfish people.

"They never neglected their kids or abused them exactly," she admitted. "It was more like they were just going through the emotions of being parents, just waiting till Emily and J.J. were old enough to take care of themselves." She smacked her lips fondly at Taylor, who shook his head at her and returned the blown kiss. "I mean, they dropped her and J.J. off at church, but never went themselves. And if Emily was receiving an award at school or something, her mom would slip in long enough to see Emily, then disappear before it ended so she wouldn't have to go backstage and be around all the other kids. Emily said once that kids make her mother nervous."

"You're making her sound like a cold-hearted monster," Taylor remonstrated mildly.

Barb shrugged her plump shoulders. "You weren't as close to Emily as I was. She used to come over to our house after we became best friends in high school and just sit in the kitchen listening to Mama and me yak. She'd get the most wistful look on her face. Mama used to cry after she went home because she felt so sorry for her."

"I suppose work was sort of a substitute for her," Simon finished, his own heart wrenching as he thought of what Emily had become, and what she could have been had anyone taken the time and care to let her know she was special and loved.

"In a way," Taylor put in, his expression thoughtful. "I also think it was just as much an escape. At home she had indifferent parents and a wild, rebellious younger brother she spent most of her youth keeping out of trouble. At least at work she could be validated somewhat."

Breaking away from his silent reverie, Simon woke Emily as he turned onto the narrow road that ended at the gate of a state park encompassing the northern half of the peninsula. His parents lived a few miles south, and as they would be arriving in less than fifteen minutes, he knew Emily would need some time to compose herself. He also needed a few quiet moments to determine how best to proceed with their relationship.

He pulled the car to the sandy shoulder of the road and shut off the engine. He had known since the day she was abducted that he was more involved emotionally with Emily Carson than he had even been with another woman—but he was uncertain about the future.

Was he ready to make the kind of commitment required to keep from destroying her? He knew things had reached a point where he would either have to back out of her life completely and take that risk—or be prepared to be bound to her the rest of his life. Did he love her? As if with a mind of its own, his hand slid across the back of the seat to trace a smoke-light path across the crown of her head.

This morning at Barb and Taylor's house—another age ago—she had meticulously woven her hair into a neat French braid, and Simon had overheard her anxiously asking Barb if she looked respectable enough to meet his parents. His finger smoothed the silky soft layers, and he had to fight to keep from awakening her with a kiss.

Respectable! *God, I really need your guidance now. If this woman is the one You have chosen to be my mate, I need to know—I need a little more confidence not only with my own feelings, but hers.* He knew Emily still didn't place much trust either in the Lord or him. Actually, she didn't trust *anyone.* And yet he knew that at one time she had accepted Christ for her eternal salvation.

She stirred, head rolling toward him slightly so that the still neat braid slid over his hand and spilled down the seat. Simon fingered the plait, wanting to bury his face in the softness with so urgent a need he had to force himself to move away from Emily completely. He had felt desire before, knew how powerful the sexual drive could be. But never had he felt the tremendous pull when tenderness was coupled with that desire. He wanted Emily with every drop of warm red blood in his body, but he also wanted to protect her, to shield her, to convince her that his feelings for her were more than raw passion.

He flexed his tense shoulders and drew a deep breath. He would definitely have to talk things over with his own parents, who thankfully were the loving, supporting parents God intended a mother and father to be. He bowed his head a minute and sent up his fervent petition, then slid back across the seat.

"Emily." He gave her shoulder a gentle squeeze. "Wake up, love. We're almost there."

Emily lifted heavy-lidded eyes and blinked slowly, dazedly. Lifting her hands, she rubbed her eyes with her knuckles like a sleepy little girl, stretched, and winced at the stiffness of her muscles.

"Here," Simon offered, turning her with careful hands, "I'll massage some of the kinks out for you."

"Where are we?" Emily croaked, her voice still blurred with sleep.

"We're about five miles from my folks' home. You've been asleep over four hours."

"Oh." She sat up straight and twisted back around to face him. Her eyes were wide, very dark. "I wish I could just sleep forever."

Simon scowled. "I made a promise to myself that I wouldn't lose my temper with you anymore, Emily. But if you make any more statements like that, I'll be tempted to change my mind.

"I wasn't talking about suicide," she refuted with indifferent flatness. "I just don't have the energy to face anything or anyone right now."

Simon relaxed, and he gave her braid a tug. "My folks aren't 'anyone,' so you won't be having to face anything except a quiet, deserted beach and the tide tickling your toes. *And* some good Southern cooking to put meat back on your scrawny bones." He re-started the car and drove slowly along the winding asphalt, rolling the window down so they could smell the sea breezes.

"Simon?" Emily ventured in a small voice a few moments later when he turned onto a bumpy lane of shifting white sand and gravel.

He turned his head, his ear caught by the soft uncertainty of her tone. "What, honey?"

"Do you think they'll be angry with me for buying your great-aunt's house and causing so much trouble?"

He winced. "Emily," he ground out with commendable restraint, "*You* are not causing the trouble. You're an innocent victim, on all levels, and nobody blames you for anything. And my parents will love you—exactly as you are."

She turned her head aside, gazing out at the gnarled scrub oaks and pine scrubs and the dunes. It was a surprisingly wild and desolate stretch of land for Florida, but Simon had a feeling right now it matched Emily's mood exactly.

Moments later, his mother threw her arms around him and covered him in flour and laughter and kisses. A spare woman with gray-brown hair and Simon's green eyes, she apologized unrepentantly as Simon tried to fend her off. "I'm making biscuits, but I guess I forgot in the emotion of the moment."

His father hugged him as well, then clasped his hand in a firm handshake. "You're looking good, son." He looked Simon up and down, then his shrewd hazel eyes moved to Emily.

Although not a large man, Nathaniel Balfour had the wiry toughness honed by a life spent outdoors working at physical labor. He was almost bald, and wrinkles crisscrossed his tanned face, giving him more of the weathered look of a farmer instead of the carpenter he had been.

Emily stood quietly off to the side, watching with reserved solemnity while the wandering son was welcomed home. When Simon finally reached to tug her over, he could feel her stiffness, sense the awkwardness as if he were inside her skin.

"You would be Emily." Nathaniel Balfour stepped over to her and held out his hand. His wife elbowed in between and gave Emily another floury hug.

"Don't be so formal, hon," she admonished her husband with a wink to Emily. "Emily will get the wrong impression." She lifted the hem of the faded apron she wore and wiped some flour off Emily's arm. "Emily, welcome to our home. We want you to make it yours for as long as you like." She beamed at Simon with maternal indulgence. "Simon has kept us informed of your miserable state of affairs, and Nat and I feel what you need is a nest right now where you can feel safe and spoiled."

"You can also see if you can put a pound or two on her," Simon chimed in, reaching out a long arm and catching a stiff Emily next to him. "That way when I hold her I know it will be a woman instead of a baby bird."

Emily blushed, and Katherine Balfour gave a delighted peal of laughter. "What a silver-tongued wretch you are," she chided him. "Come on, Emily. I'll show you to your room before I get back to my biscuits. Simon, you and your father can bring in your cases. Supper's at seven, so you should have time to take her for a short walk down the beach."

Chapter Eleven

Emily followed Mrs. Balfour down a long cool hall, feeling off-balance and strangely shy. This was not the kind of greeting she had steeled herself for, and Simon's parents were . . . were as nice as Simon himself could be when he chose.

"I hope this will be all right," Mrs. Balfour gestured to the small but light and airy room.

Emily nodded and smiled, but couldn't think of a thing to say. The Balfour home was beautiful but not as elaborate as Emily would have expected. Built on stilts, with a rustic cedar exterior, wraparound porches, and a gable roof with one side extending over the back porches, it was a house to be lived in rather than showcased. Simon had mentioned that his father had built it all himself, disdaining his eldest son's offers of help.

Though not a luxury resort, the house exuded a quiet charm, a welcoming comfort that seemed to reach out gentle hands and tug at Emily's bruised and battered heart. She turned to Simon's mother, struggling to find the words, and found the older woman studying her with such a wealth of compassion that Emily's eyes misted.

Horrified, she walked over to the window and looked out, saying the first thing that occurred to her. "What a wonderful view."

Katherine joined her and laid a work-roughened hand on her shoulder. "Emily, I have three children, and I love them all dearly. They live separate lives with their own families now, but whenever they have a problem, or just need to get away from things, they come here." She patted Emily's shoulder once more and then moved away.

"There's a phrase in the Bible I've always loved—the one hanging on the wall over there." She waited until Emily turned and found the small framed verse on the wall behind the rocker. "'He reached down from on high and took hold of me; he drew me out of deep waters,'" she quoted with lilting softness. "Simon has shared with us some of what you've been going through—I hope you won't mind. Nat and I both pray your being here will help you to feel the Lord drawing you out of those deep waters."

She walked out then, quietly shutting the door behind her, leaving Emily alone.

For a long time Emily stood at the window and watched the waves lifting in white foamy crescents, then ebbing away from the clean sandy shore. If there were any peace this side of heaven, surely one could find it here.

If God were truly in His heaven and all was right with the world everywhere else, would it be asking too much for Him to make things all right in her own little corner of the world? A tear slipped out and dribbled forlornly down her cheek. Simon's parents seemed so nice . . . so much like, well, like a mother and a father ought to be. No wonder Simon was so confident, so sure that God was taking care of things. He had grown up with a family who seemed to demonstrate that kind of love every day.

From down the hall, Emily could hear the sound of their voices, the deeper bass of Simon's father softening the lilting mezzo-soprano of his mother. And Simon's voice, a mixture of rich black coffee and golden honey and Samson's soft fur. They were a unit, complete within themselves and safe from the isolation of not belonging.

Emily turned away from the window and sat down in the rocking chair, listening to the soothing rise and fall of their voices and the murmur of the sea. *I want to belong, too*, she finally admitted to herself. *God, I want to have a home and family, too.*

A soft but peremptory knock on the door interrupted her solitary reverie.

"Emily?" Simon's voice sounded from the other side. "Let's go for that walk on the beach. There's time before supper."

They strolled around the porch and down a boardwalk that ended at some dunes covered in grass and sea oats. The sand was cool and soft, sifting between Emily's toes and over her ankles as they wandered barefoot down to the deserted beach.

Waves lapped lazily, lifting in slight swells and then sliding onto the smooth shore like a wet, glistening sheet. The setting sun cast a silver sheen over the rippling surface of the waters, and the rest of the world was bathed in the opalescent flow of a September twilight.

"I love to come here," Simon admitted reflectively. "It doesn't seem to matter how majestic the mountains or how serene the woods—there's just something about the rhythm of the sea and the canopy of the sky that draws me closer to God."

He drew Emily's hand through his arm and hugged it to his side. "There's a verse—I think in Psalms—that talks about God wrapping Himself in light. That's what this scene reminds me of."

"It *is* peaceful." She closed her eyes, swallowing against the hard lump rising in her throat.

Simon paused, lifting his hands to cup her face and study it, patterns of green light shifting through his eyes like the waters of the sea. "Emily, share your pain with me. I want to help—please don't shut me out."

Emily tried to back away but was helpless against the strength of those gentle hands, the power of those eyes. Her feet sank into the damp sand as her heart sank into the shifting sands of Simon's moods. He was in turn tender and sensitive, tough and obdurate, wildly passionate. And running through it all, like the sunlight invading the surface of the water, was his abiding faith in God.

How could she fight against something her soul yearned for so deeply, something she found as impossible to believe in as the pot of gold at the end of the rainbow?

"Why do you have so much faith in God?" she blurted out, searching his face with haunted eyes.

Simon's fingers began caressing the shadowed hollows and soft curves of her face. "Because He loves me," he replied simply. "Loved me so much he was willing to sacrifice His only Son. He loves you just as much, Emily. Believe that."

"I know." She swallowed, trying to ignore the absent stroking of his fingers. "But it's hard to understand how someone like . . . well, like *me* rates anything beyond salvation. I'm not important. The world wouldn't come to an end if I did—and God has so many more important things to take care of than to be bothered with my small problems." She put her hands up and pried his away, moving back a few steps. "Besides, if He really cared about me," she said in a moment of honest revelation, "I wouldn't be having all the problems I do."

"Is that how you see God?" Simon questioned casually, without any hint of censure. "As the benign big genie in the sky doling out favors to His children to prove He loves them?"

"Of course not!" Emily flung back, stung in spite of his non-threatening tone.

"Is that what your parents did for you?" he continued, still in the same gentle cadence that nonetheless trampled her abraded feelings like the hooves of a galloping horse. "Gave you all the things you needed—but never gave themselves?"

He saw too much. Somehow he knew too much. Maybe he's picked Barb's and Taylor's brains. Emily turned on her heel and fled, walking down the beach and leaving a trail of damp footprints behind. How dare he pick and probe her psyche! With each word, he undermined the girders she had so painfully dragged into place over the years to protect herself. And in another minute, he'd have her bawling all over him like a whining baby.

She stepped on a broken shell and staggered, almost falling from the sudden pain. Glancing back, she saw Simon following her, but without any pretense of haste or pursuit. It was as if he knew she had no place to go.

Stunned by the raw finality of that thought, Emily sank down in the sand, heedless of the grittiness and dampness. She couldn't escape from him. She couldn't escape from the person she became when she was around him. She ceased to be the detached, easygoing creature whose feelings were buried so deeply no one ever guessed at the depths or intensity. Instead she became hypersensitive, vulnerable—and ridiculously easy to provoke.

Simon sat down beside her. She could feel his eyes moving over her, but she kept looking out at the water struggling to withdraw into herself and become as insignificant and unnoticeable as a shell fragment. "Remember the other night when I was pushing you in the swing?" he asked, the question so unexpected Emily's head swiveled toward him, her braid swishing across her back and flipping over her shoulder.

"Yes. Why?"

"We were talking about the sunsets then, too." He smiled, a slow smile with the warmth of a golden sunset reflected in it. "Like I said, there's something about being out here that brings me closer to God, and I want you to feel it, too." He relaxed back on his elbows, lifting sand and letting it drift through his fingers. "I believe I mentioned something about how the beauty and inevitability of sunrises and sunsets reminded me of the faithfulness of God."

Emily watched her toes, caked with sand, digging into its coolness as if to hide. "So?" she muttered.

"You never read the verse I asked you to read, did you?" Simon countered without heat. "If you had, you'd understand the point I'm trying to make."

"And what point is that?" Her determined show of indifference was a mistake. With a fluid swiftness so abrupt she didn't have time to react, Simon reared up and grabbed her shoulders, pinning her with his eyes. "No more," he blazed. "I won't let you withdraw anymore, Emily." He leaned forward, his breath fanning her cheek, and the words had no place to go but straight to her heart.

"You've been keeping God at a distance because you're so afraid. You're afraid He doesn't care enough about you to risk trusting Him, just the way you're afraid of me. You bottle up your emotions and give the world the tame, placid version of Emily Carson, and I won't let you get away with it anymore."

"Simon—"

"Well, I'm only a man, and someday I will let you down, or unintentionally hurt you, or fail you because I'm a fallible human being. But God won't ever do that—He can't. It's not possible. Your problem is you just won't accept God's love for you—personally. And it's robbed you of all the confidence and peace to which you're entitled. It's robbed you of joy."

"I don't—"

"You might restore that house and *think* you're happy, satisfied, and secure, but it's a lie. Until you let God restore the joy of your salvation, you'll stay as empty and feel as abandoned as that old place was for fifty years." He leaned closer, and in the rapidly approaching night, his eyes seemed to burn with a fire so bright the sea and sky and sand receded into a single swirl of darkening shadows.

"You've got to open up and allow yourself to believe in that faithfulness because it's as real, as inevitable, as wondrous as the sunset. He's not the one trying to take your house away, or burn it down, or destroy innocent animals, honey. That's all man's doing. God is there, hand stretched out, just waiting for you to take it so He can carry you through.

He released her abruptly and sat back. Then, with a significance that took Emily a moment to grasp, he slowly held out his hand.

Emily sat in the sand, motionless, though her insides were as unstable as a vial of nitroglycerin. Simon was telling her something so significant, so life-changing, that she simply couldn't grasp it. And with his own outstretched hand, he was creating a vivid picture to illustrate the words he had just spoken. What would happen if she put her hand in his? Beyond that, if she symbolically put her hand in the Lord's as Simon wanted her to do?

And what would she do when Simon inevitably let her down, as he had warned her he would?

The silence between them stretched taut, shimmering like a hovering knife blade between Simon's hand and Emily.

She knew that if she refused this outstretched hand, her relationship with Simon—however uncertain it was right now—would be irrevocably altered. Like footprints washed away by a relentless tide, so their relationship would be washed away, the only thing left an impersonal, smooth expanse of beach as untouched, unmarked as before.

Emily had tried to convince herself that she was satisfied with being alone. She had created her world and populated it with people and activities to keep her busy. She had been a comfortable Christian, content to sing in the choir on Sunday mornings and praise the Lord for His goodness. At Easter she had even sung a duet from Handel's "Messiah" proclaiming that He would feed His flock like a shepherd. She had thought she believed it.

She realized now that her faith wasn't the size of a mustard seed. It wasn't even as large as one of these minuscule grains of sand. She also realized that the world she had created for herself would never satisfy her again.

Slowly, heart pounding, Emily lifted her arm and held out her hand. Her fingers trembled.

Hard, warm fingers closed around hers and drew her to her feet. Unnoticed, the last glimmer of sunlight slid into the ocean, and the deep blue sky darkened to the dusky purple a shade away from black. "For a minute," Simon breathed as he drew her into his arms, "I was really afraid." His had descended and his lips brushed the delicate lobe of her ear. "Ah . . . Emily. Shy and wary—my stubborn sparrow struggling so hard to build her nest . . . what am I going to do about you?"

"Hal-loo down there, you two!" Nat's voice caught on a sudden breeze and swirled down to them, breaking the mood instantly. "Dinner's on! Come and get it!"

Simon's arms tightened around Emily momentarily, then she was free. "It's just as well," he murmured as they brushed sand off their clothes and then picked their way across the drifting sand to the boardwalk. "Much more time out here with you and I might have gotten carried away. And if my dad found out about that, this time I might have to paint all your porches and be grounded forever."

A smile tugged reluctantly at Emily's lips, then withered. "You'll probably be painting them anyway," she reminded him, dullness coating the words.

He took her arm firmly as they began walking back down the boardwalk and up the stairs to the house. "We'll talk about it tomorrow."

Two days rolled by along with the undulating tides. Emily was stuffed morning, noon, and night with every kind of delectable meal Katherine Balfour could devise. In between she lolled about on the beach or in a huge old rocker on the porch. Nathaniel taught her the rudiments of chess and took her on long walks along the largely deserted beach.

To Emily's consternation and utter bewilderment, Simon left the house the first morning after they arrived. Katherine explained kindly that there had been some sort of emergency at one of his jobs—they had called after Emily had gone to bed and Simon hadn't wanted to disturb her. She was to sleep in, rest, and be as lazy as an old hound dog napping in the sunshine. He hoped to be back within three days.

Emily accepted this development with equanimity. It was awkward, though, feeling as if she had been beached with Simon's parents like a piece of driftwood, but by lunch of the first day their natural warmth and genuine interest in her helped soften the awkwardness. She still couldn't talk too much about herself, or about the house and her abduction, but she did relax enough to fall back into a facsimile of her former serene, mild-tempered persona.

By suppertime the second night, she was calling the Balfours by their first names without any self-consciousness. She was even sharing in their evening devotionals, luxuriating in their naturalness, their faith that was as much a part of their lives as breathing.

And they included her as if she belonged.

Emily woke on the third morning with a smile on her face for the first time in six months. That morning Nat was going to take her surf fishing, and then Katherine was going to show her how to make the famous biscuits all the men in the family raved about. The first evening Simon had scarfed down four and would have buttered up and downed a fifth, but Nat swiped it right as he was reaching for it and ate it himself, his eyes twinkling at Simon like a cat lapping a saucer full of spilled cream.

With a single-mindedness developed from childhood, Emily managed to lay aside all the worries waiting for her in Georgia. She coveted the time spent with these two people who had welcomed her as if she were their own, coveted it with the greedy desperation of a pearl merchant whose oyster bed was going dry. Because, for all she knew, this would be the only time in her life when she would ever truly feel like a member of a family.

At odd moments, thoughts of her own family intruded, marring the brightness of the day as tarnish on fine old pieces of silver. Emily quickly banished them. She had long ago accepted things the way they were and saw no need to dwell on what hadn't been and could never be. But that was no reason to look this particular gift horse in the mouth.

She stretched beneath the covers, then kicked back the sheet in a sudden burst of energy. Nat had told her the earlier they got down there, the better the fishing would be, and Emily didn't want to keep him waiting. She opened the room-darkening shades covering the windows and gasped in dismay.

It was a little past seven, but there was no sun today. A glowering, slate-colored sky brooded over choppy, restless waters. The sea oats on the tops of the dunes waved wildly in response to a whipping wind, and Emily dropped into the rocking chair and plunked her head on the heels of her hands in dejection. So much for a lovely, relaxing day.

"Doesn't look good," Nat confirmed when Emily dragged out a little while later. Katherine's normally pleasant face wore a concerned look today as she poured her husband a second cup of coffee. "What's the weather report now?" she asked, since he had just come back from the den where the television was.

"They're still calling it a tropical storm, since it hasn't turned into hurricane force yet, but if and when it does, we better get the boards up. It's stalled off the Keys, and there's no telling which way it will come."

Emily sat down and thanked Katherine for her cup of coffee. "Have you had many bad hurricanes here?" she asked.

"We've been luckier than a lot of folks," Nat answered and smiled comfortingly as he glanced up and caught the worry in Emily's face. "The last really bad one was a couple years ago. We lost a window and the boardwalk, but the house stood."

"Thanks to you." Katherine laid her hands on her husband's shoulders and kissed his cheek. "Over the years some of the other homes have crumbled like matchsticks from the worst hurricanes. But when Nat builds a house, it's for keeps."

Emily watched the love flow between them and felt a queer wrenching in her heart, a plaintive cry echoing in the barren wasteland of her soul. Nobody had ever looked at her like that or offered the almost worshipful support Katherine and Nat gave to each other. Unwillingly her thoughts strayed to Simon, but there was about as much future in daydreaming over him as there was daydreaming about her house. Both of them were slipping out of her grasp, and Emily years ago had given up trying to hold on to will-o-the-wisps.

After breakfast, Nat and Katherine moved to the den to monitor the weather reports. Emily decided to walk down to the beach since it wasn't raining yet. Somehow the bleak uncertainty of the day matched her mood.

Katherine gave her a Windbreaker to wear because the temperature hovered in the sixties and, with the wind swooping about in erratic gusts, Emily would appreciate something to cover her arms. She gave the younger woman a hug as she held the screen door for her.

"Don't wander too far. Things can deteriorate pretty fast in conditions like this." She smiled into Emily's downcast face. "Of course, thanks to the capriciousness of nature, things could also clear up and this could turn into a mild breezy day. You just have to take each moment as it comes and trust in the Lord to see you through regardless."

Emily knew she wasn't just talking about the weather. "I'm trying to believe that," she confessed sadly. "But it's awfully hard right now."

"I know." Her lined face bathed in concern, Katherine leaned suddenly and pressed a kiss to Emily's cheek. "And we do care, Emily. Not just because my son is fond of you, but because you're *you*."

A lump formed in Emily's throat and stuck. "Thank you," she whispered, and fled.

Chapter Twelve

Emily walked over an hour, head down against the wind, hair hopelessly tangled as it was whipped and tugged about her back and in her face. She didn't care.

Hands stuffed in the pockets of her jeans, she watched her feet scuffing in the sand and walked. There was no one out this morning, not even the elderly couple she and Nat had met and chatted with on previous mornings.

Beside her, the Gulf of Mexico churned, and on the horizon a lumbering trawler plowed through the heaving water like a dinosaur in a pond shrugging aside a spring zephyr. Emily paid neither the Gulf nor the ship the slightest attention.

The storm in her soul already blew at hurricane force, and she was so caught up in its fury, she was unaware that she was no longer alone on the beach. Only when her downcast eyes fell upon an extra pair of sneakers did she lift her startled gaze and bump into Simon's solid chest.

His hands fastened loosely on her forearms to steady her. "Hello, Emily," he greeted her, his face solemn. The wind was having a heyday with his hair, too, whipping it wildly about so the waves tumbled all over his ears, neck, and forehead. In contrast, his mouth remained a straight, unsmiling line.

Emily couldn't help it. She stared up at him, revealing all the confusion and wariness and hopeless longing. Simon groaned deep in his chest, jerked her against him, and kissed her.

"Why did you do that?" Emily gasped out when at last he lifted his mouth and set her a little ways from him.

"Because I wanted to. And don't ask me why, or I'll do it again just to shut you up." He snuggled the two unzipped panels of her Windbreaker beneath her chin, the knuckles of his hands brushing the soft underside of her throat.

"What gives you the right—" Emily sputtered, indignation and alarm kicking through her, but her protest was abruptly silenced as Simon carried out his threat. When he lifted his head this time, Emily was clinging to his neck and shoulders, legs weak as water.

"You are the most baffling, frustrating woman I've ever known." His fingers danced across the surface of her skin, skimming an electrifying message over her windstung face and the little pulse hammering in her throat. "And for some reason I'm attracted to you more strongly than I've ever been to another woman. You, on the other hand, seem to think you're about as desirable as lukewarm cream of wheat."

"It's the truth," she slurred the words.

Simon administered a brief but firm shake. "Stop it!" he demanded, temper whipping through the words like the wind was their hair. "Look at me, Emily!"

She opened her eyes, hands moving to push against his chest in an effort to be free. "What are you trying to do to me?" she wailed, struggling to cope with the extreme shifts of his moods. "You cuddle me up, then tear me down. You kiss me, and then you yell at me. You tell me you find me attractive, and then you treat me like a scummy rag!"

Simon was not fooled by Emily's display of temper. He might have succeeded in riling her enough to momentarily break her out of her misery and depression, but he had also confused and frightened her. That, of course, made him a stupid, insensitive jerk. *Help me, Lord.* If he weren't careful, he could lose the battle altogether, and hence the war.

There was something else he had to tell her, and because he'd been stalling, he had ended up muddying the issue by dragging feelings into it. But when he'd seen her walking out here looking so lost and alone, he couldn't stand it, especially when she looked at him with those huge dark eyes. God knew how desperately he was trying to control his feelings, but it was getting harder. When she found out his news, she probably wouldn't let him any closer than a mile.

"Emily," he allowed with a sigh, "I know I'm a first-class heel, even though all I wanted was to jar you out of your depression. I can't apologize for kissing you, but I will admit to lousy timing." He waited, but when Emily refused to respond, he took a deep breath and took the plunge. "There's something I need to explain, and after you hear what it is, maybe you'll understand why I'm behaving the way I am."

"That's a first-class excuse," Emily finally retorted, the words muffled because she had her hands over her face now.

Simon groaned. "Emily, are you crying on me?"

"No! Yes. What if I am? I feel like a yo-yo the way you're acting. It's . . . humiliating." She faltered, caught her breath on a sob, and tried once more to move around him.

"Emily . . . please. I'm sorry. Don't go in yet." He waited in agony, his eyes on her bent head and the rigid line of her back. After a long, painful moment, she slowly turned around, but she still wouldn't look at him. Simon allowed his pent-up breath to escape in a long sigh, and with a hesitant gesture of repentance, he reached and brushed his fingers across her cheekbone.

"I'm not providing you with a very loving example of God's faithfulness, am I?" he observed, chagrin coating the words. "Unless you keep in mind that at least I do keep coming back, even if it's only to confuse you more."

Almost, she smiled. She lifted her head and faced him with an expression as blank as a sheet of fresh typing paper. "What else did you want to tell me?"

His eyes flickered briefly, but he didn't sidetrack this time. "I have something to tell you about Aunt Iris, and it isn't very pleasant, though I doubt it will come as a surprise."

"She's suing me." She made the statement matter-of-factly, but Simon knew her better. He opened his mouth, but Emily interrupted. "Why didn't you just tell me, instead of . . . initiating that . . . display a few moments ago?"

Simon buried his hands deep in the hip pockets of the chinos he was wearing and gave her a candid answer. "I couldn't help it. You looked so lost and alone, and I was about to make it worse. I wanted to wipe away that lost look and wake you up to how I really felt. I know I'm coming across irrationally, and I do apologize for it." He dropped his gaze to his feet, then lifted it back to Emily's coffee-dark eyes. "But with God as my witness, I'll never *deliberately* hurt you. Never. Can you try to believe that at least?"

After lunch Simon announced their decision to return to Georgia.

"Emily is going to need to talk with her lawyer, and I'm going to see what's happening with the sleaze balls trespassing on her land." He watched Emily grimly, hating the whole mess with a vehemence bordering on homicidal.

"Wouldn't it be better if she stayed with her friends?" his father commented.

Simon nodded his head at Emily, his expression remote. "You try to convince her. I gave up an hour ago." A muscle in his jaw quivered as he battled his frustration. "For two cents I'd leave her here, but knowing her, she'd simply hike down to the main road and hitch a ride."

Emily smiled across the room at him. "You're just a poor loser," she stated with false sweetness. "It may not be my home much longer, but while it is I plan to live in it. No slimy low-lifes are going to frighten me away, and—"

"The next time they might do more than frighten you," Simon interrupted harshly. "Why do you insist on being so pigheaded, woman?"

"Simon," his mother interjected, doubt and dismay so blatant Emily turned her head away. "How about our tagging along with you? We could stay at Emily's—"

"No!" both Simon and Emily chorused in emphatic agreement.

"We don't need to go providing them with any more ammunition," Simon stated flatly. "I've talked to the sheriff. He promises around-the-clock protection, for a while anyway—as long as he can. But I don't want you two involved. It's bad enough having Emily in the thick of it."

"I can take care of myself."

Simon sliced her an impatient look. "Like you did the day you landed in the hospital?"

Emily slumped in defeat. "I'll go make sure my bag is packed," she mumbled, walking past Simon with downcast head.

His father waited until Emily shut her door, then motioned for Simon to follow him into the kitchen while Katherine followed Emily. "Don't you think you're being a mite bossy?" he observed mildly, and Simon flushed.

"I can't seem to help it. She won't listen to reason. I know she's hurting, not only over the drug issue, but now this confounded lawsuit." He slammed his hands down on the counter, rattling the dishes drying in the drainer next to him. "Why did she have to find the will? It's almost impossible to get through to her now. She's clammed up inside herself so tightly and so blindly that she has no idea of what could happen to her all alone in that big old mausoleum." He whirled and faced his father. "I'm beginning to hate the place, you know. Hate it because it's going to cost me the woman I—"

He stopped, stunned, and then groaned aloud covering his eyes with the back of his hand. "I'm in love with her," he confessed, and dropped his hand to stare across at his father. "If something happens to her—if Aunt Iris takes the place away from her—I don't know if I'll be able to stand it."

Nathaniel laid his arm around his son's shoulders. "I know . . . I know. You're just going to have to do a lot of praying—and as much protecting as she'll allow." He grinned a little bit. "But if you'll take the suggestion of the old man who reared you and suffered through your wild youth, try honey instead of vinegar. Emily might not be a militant feminist, but she's been on her own too long to fall tamely in line with your commands."

"If I try that approach I doubt I could maintain my Christian code of ethics, Dad," Simon responded dryly. "And Emily's . . . untouched."

Nathaniel lifted an eyebrow. "That's refreshing—and a relief from a parental point of view. I thought she looked—I guess 'unawakened' would be the word."

"And you don't know how badly I'd like to awaken her." Simon examined his fingernails, then met his father's smug expression. "That's right—gloat. You and Mom have been trying to marry me off for ten years now."

He contemplated his hands as if wondering whether he'd like to wrap them around Emily to caress her—or throttle her. "I suppose you realize that persuading her to marry me will be about as easy as the Arabs and Jews negotiating a truce in Jerusalem.

"I trust you'll control yourself, son, and remember your Christian convictions, regardless of your feelings."

"I'm not going to seduce her, Dad, if that's what you're getting at." Simon straightened, giving his father the sort of stark honesty he had given him all his life. "I do want to make love to her, because I love her—even if I only acknowledged it this moment. But it's because I *do* love and desire her so much that I can wait. Do you have any idea what it means to me to know that if she'll marry me, I'll be the first—and only?"

"I know. I pray God will grant you that chance, if Emily is truly the woman He has picked out to be your mate." He cleared his throat, and his eyes were damp. "She's a pretty special lady. Your mother and I would love to have her as a daughter."

"Thanks, Dad." Simon squared his shoulders and moved toward the hall. "I better see what's keeping her and Mom. There's no telling what Emily may try. Being around her is like trying to catch hold of fog."

"Knowing your mother, she just might succeed. And then present your elusive lady to you for Christmas."

Chapter Thirteen

The nearer they came to the Georgia border, the more nervous Emily felt. Simon was strangely pensive and even more strangely non-aggressive. He hadn't tried to talk her out of going to the house anymore, and he hadn't badgered her about how to handle the lawsuit and what she ought to say to Brad. If she hadn't been so worried about the future, Emily would have been hurt.

As it was, she found herself wishing Simon would at least talk to her, even if it was only about the weather, which was gray and drizzling and miserable. When she was looking out the window, all her mind did was scrabble frantically around the problems she faced, without offering any solutions. "Simon?" she finally asked, almost whispering.

"Hmm?"

"If I admit I'm a little bit scared, will you jump down my throat and say 'I told you so'?"

His hands tightened on the steering wheel, and he shot her a brief look that encompassed a galaxy of emotions. "Have I been that terrible, Emily?"

She puzzled at the hint of hurt, the nuance of despair. "You haven't always been sweet and understanding."

He scowled at that. "What do you expect when you insist on modeling yourself after a sitting duck?"

"Nothing, I suppose." She choked down the hurt and resumed contemplating the countryside.

A few minutes later Simon pulled off into a deserted roadside picnic area. A misting rain slid down the windshield, blurring the surroundings now that the wipers were no longer swishing back and forth. The atmosphere inside the car thickened until Simon commanded very quietly, "Come here, Emily," he pointed to the space beside him.

"Why?" Emily responded warily, her body stiffening with suspicion and a strange sort of excitement.

"Because I've decided to try my hand at being sweet and understanding for a change. Now come here."

"I didn't mean to hurt your feelings," Emily grumbled, but she undid her seat belt and slid over.

"That's better," he murmured huskily. "Now . . . put your arms around me and kiss me."

"What? What's that supposed to prove?" She floundered about, looking everywhere but at Simon.

He uttered a low laugh, picked up the end of her braid, and began winding it around his fist until she was forced to move right against him, their faces inches apart. "No problem," he breathed. "I don't mind kissing you. . . ."

His mouth closed over hers, kissing her with tender thoroughness and consummate skill. Emily's arms crept up over his shoulders and clung to him as she gave herself up to the incandescent cloud of feelings. She could feel Simon's heartbeat thundering, its wild cadence matching hers, and she marveled that she really did seem to affect him so strongly.

After awhile his hands released her and gently removed her arms from around his neck. "Now, relax and let me give you the reassurance you're so desperate for."

He held her head against his chest and stroked her hair, all the passion wiped away as if it had never been. "I'm trying, you see," he murmured above her head, "to teach you that you *can* trust me, at least physically."

Emily gradually relaxed, and at last closed her eyes with a low murmur of contentment. If only he would be like this all the time. If only she *could* trust him. She stirred restlessly, and his arms tightened.

"Be still," he coaxed. "Be still and rest, sparrow-girl. It's going to be all right. Everything is going to be all right. Because regardless of how things turn out, regardless of how you feel about me—God will be there, taking care of you." He paused, then added in such low tones that Emily wasn't sure she heard, "And so will I."

The next morning when Emily called Brad to tell him she'd be in to resume her secretarial duties, he did not try to hide his relief. He did tell her that they would also take the time to have a lawyer-to-client chat, but she was not to worry about a thing.

Emily wondered if Simon would fuss about her going back to work so soon, but he smoothly agreed with her decision, pointing out that she would be a lot safer thirty miles away in Sylvan anyway. Emily sourly reminded him that she was not a two-year-old who needed coddling and then clamped her mouth shut. She was feeling raw after a crying jag the night before. Somewhere inside her lived a two-year-old whose feelings were bruised because Simon had made no effort to console or coddle her.

She drove the miles to Sylvan in uneasy silence. It was really no wonder Simon acted so unpredictably around her. She pushed him away with one arm and clung with the other. Heat stole into her cheeks as she relived her unbridled response in the car coming back from Florida. Simon must think her a totally desperate woman willing to take any crumbs he cared to toss her way—and if the price was patting her shoulder and telling her things would be all right . . . well, he *had* come through with his end of the bargain.

It was no use. She was mooning and pining over him like the girls in her eighth grade classes pined over a high school junior. The only difference was that the girls had a better chance of landing a date with the junior than Emily did landing Simon Balfour. In spite of everything he kept telling her, he was still out of her league. Way out.

"Things are never that bad." Brad greeted her glum countenance with a cheery welcome smile that didn't try to hide his open relief. "Here. Have a stick of strawberry gum—a gal I met in Albany gave me a couple of packs."

"No thanks." She tried to produce an answering smile as she put her purse under the desk, but it wavered. "Brad, I'm scared."

Brad's cheerfulness disappeared behind his bland lawyer's mask. "Let's just take things one at a time, all right? You worry about secretarying and let me worry about the legal matters."

That, unfortunately, was easier said than done, as Emily found out when she was sitting across from him later that afternoon. Brad did not try to confuse her by spouting off legal terminology, but he did not mince words either.

"As I warned you, Ms. Bancroft has filed in probate court to prove the validity of the will I gather it was your dubious honor to find." He chewed a few moments on his third stick of the strawberry gum, drumming his fingers on his desk. "It was in a safety deposit box hidden behind the closet wall in your bedroom, Lamar told me."

Emily nodded. Her own hands were clenched tightly between her knees, and despite the pleasant coolness of the day, she could feel perspiration dotting her brow and dampening her palms. "Simon dropped it off at Mr. Hansell's office on our way to Florida. He figured the sooner we got it over with, the better."

"Hmmm," Brad replied unhelpfully. "Well, they certainly didn't let any grass grow under their feet, which I suppose isn't surprising after meeting Ms. Bancroft." He gave a reluctant grin. "Formidable woman, isn't she?"

"I don't stand a chance," Emily declared miserably.

"Now, now, don't insult your lawyer," Brad chided, but he didn't disagree with her. "I've got about three weeks to dig up some other court decisions that will support our position. You concentrate on being my secretary and keeping yourself safe." He looked across at her. "Are you staying with Barb and Taylor?"

"N . . . no." She couldn't sustain the alert look of suspicion that entered his face, and dropped her gaze. "I'm staying at the house. Sheriff Jessup has assigned two men to guard the place, and I know the DEA is also—"

"Emily, that's insane!" Brad jackknifed up out of his chair, raking his fingers through the thick thatch of blond hair. "Where is your Sir Galahad, anyway? Or has he kissed you off now that the will has been found?"

Emily found herself unaccountably angry at the disparaging reference to Simon, and caution was thrown to the winds. "He most certainly has *not* 'kissed me off!' In fact, he's promised that as long as I live in the house, he won't leave until the men who abducted me are behind bars." The words resounded off the filing cabinets and hovered in the air like a burst of fireworks on the Fourth of July. Emily watched with dismay the incredulity and disillusionment wash over Brad's lean, attractive face.

"Not only does that make you a sitting duck for another abduction, or worse, but under the present circumstances, Balfour's presence could be construed as even more of a conflict of interest than your working for me."

"I don't know why the two of you insist on behaving like snapping turtles," Emily muttered, exasperated. "The main reason he's staying is because he's doing most of the restoration work now—and yes, it's because I gave him permission."

Brad sat back down and casually propped his feet on the desk, crumpling several papers in the process. "Snapping turtles, huh?" He contemplated the ceiling with a bland expression Emily hated. "Are you telling me Balfour has been suggesting libelous interpretations of my actions toward you—with no evidence to substantiate his claims, I might add?"

"Quit talking like a lawyer!" Emily retorted

Brad burst into laughter. "Boy, have you got it bad! Do you leap as hotly to my defense with Balfour?"

Emily gave a disdainful sniff. "I have better things to do than sit around while you mock me. If our—consultation—is finished, I'm leaving. I need to go by the grocery store."

For a laid-back lawyer, Brad could move with startling speed, blocking the door before Emily had taken more than two steps. "Come down off your high horse, Emily. I was only teasing you, and you know it."

"Sounded more like harassment to me."

Brad folded his arms across his chest. "Stop talking like a lawyer," he mimicked.

Giving up, Emily finally laughed. She returned to retrieve her purse, aware that Brad was still watching her even as he stepped aside. Emily did not trust the look on his face at all—it reminded her of Simon. "See you day after tomorrow," she tossed out lightly.

"Okeydokey." Just before she reached the bottom stair he called to her. "Emily?"

She twisted her head around. "What?"

"Be careful with Balfour, will you? I don't trust him."

Emily's face closed up like elevator doors. "Neither," she enunciated carefully, "do I."

Chapter Fourteen

The court date was set for the first week in November. Emily told Simon, and he watched her carefully circle the date on her wall calendar hanging in the kitchen.

Autumn arrived and the last of summer withered with the last of the honeysuckle and wisterias. Some of the bronze mums Emily had planted back in July bloomed, and Simon helped arrange them in a jar on the kitchen table. The monthly missive from Emily's parents showed a dramatic New England fall, and Emily taped it on the wall above the mums. Simon tactfully made no comment.

He spent most days working on a different area of the house from Emily, though any time she asked for help, he willingly obliged. Most of his evenings were spent in his portable office.

One week he'd had to spend in Tennessee, tying up work on the eighty-year-old stone cottage. The two deputies had been re-assigned due to lack of funds and staff, but Sheriff Jessup arranged their return while Simon was gone. Emily, quieter with each passing week, barely protested. Without telling her, after returning from Tennessee, Simon renegotiated the dates for his next job, postponing work until after Christmas.

Two days before the hearing, he was on the side veranda, applying a wood preservative to the yellow pine floorboards he had replaced. He was enjoying himself so much that it was almost easy to forget the reason he was able to do the work in the first place. Everett VanCleef certainly had built this place to last, for there was surprisingly little deterioration even though the house had been unattended for almost fifty years.

Simon had repaired mortar joints in the bricks, and with Emily's permission had hired a local carpenter to help replace a sill and several of the joists under the porches which had succumbed to rot. But other than three windowsills on the north and east side of the house that had also needed replacing, the exterior wood structures were fairly sound. Yep, Everett sure had wanted this house to last, and considering the terms of his feudal will, it shouldn't have been too surprising.

The will.

The hearing, now only two days away.

Simon plopped the brush down and sat back on his heels a minute, tension curling his spine. That blasted will!

Every time Simon caught Emily in the library, gazing at the leaded glass window with agony in her eyes, it took every ounce of self-control to keep from cleaning the window himself, then falling at Emily's feet and confessing his love. More than anything on this earth, Simon wished for providential blessing to restore both woman and window to their light and beauty.

If I keep a lid on my temper and try extra hard to wait on You, Lord, is there a chance? And no, I'm not trying to bargain. I just can't help wanting to know, wanting -"

"Simon. . . ."

He jerked out of his prayerful reverie with a start, lifting his head to where Emily was standing just outside the french doors leading onto the veranda. In one swift, encompassing glance, he marked the colorless complexion and the way she was clutching the front of her sweatshirt with her hand. His eyes zeroed in on the hand, which was covered in blood.

He was by her side in two swift strides. "What happened?"

"I was trying to replace that broken pane—the one you picked up at the store yesterday for me. . . ." She gasped a little as Simon gently pried loose her hand and exposed the wound.

"Easy, love." It was a nasty cut, a diagonal slash across the back of her wrist, and it was bleeding heavily. "Here—hold it up—that's it. . . ." He whipped his handkerchief out and placed it directly on the cut, applying a firm steady pressure and talking to her in a low, soothing voice. "It's okay, Emily. It's okay. Come on, now, and let's get you to the bathroom and clean you up. At least it's the back of your wrist instead of the front." He gave her what he hoped was an encouraging smile. "You could have been a first-class klutz and gone for the artery."

"You're so reassuring," Emily muttered faintly. "I'm bleeding to death and all you do is make disparaging remarks about my abilities." For some reason— probably because she was tired and worried and still insecure—she took offense at his teasing remark instead of responding to him in kind.

After sitting her down, Simon lifted her chin with his free hand. "I wasn't denigrating your work," he promised softly. "You've done a great job, and I'm proud of you."

Her head lifted. "You are?"

Simon gazed down into her incredulous, suddenly smiling eyes. *Lord, I love this woman.* His fingers stroked a tender path across her soft lips. "Yes," he affirmed deeply, "I am. Now take a deep breath and lean on me. This is going to hurt."

He wouldn't allow her to work any more that day, bullying her into sitting on the veranda in a deck chair Barb had donated so she could watch him work. Emily submitted both to his doctoring and gentle dictatoring with such a hazy, dreamy acquiescence Simon wanted to shout aloud his feelings. She *was* softening, responding to him now. Soon, very soon he would confess his love, and pray she would reciprocate. *I can't wait much longer, Lord.* He refused to speculate about the aftermath of the hearing.

They whiled away the afternoon in rich harmony, with Simon savoring every moment. As he worked, he shared stories of various homes he had restored and the sometimes hair-raising tales of the owners he'd had to contend with. Emily countered with similar hair-raising stories of her life as a junior high teacher, relaxing into the serene, warm, and compassionate woman she was when she wasn't feeling threatened.

Early Wednesday morning, Simon drove Emily to Sylvan to spend the day and night with Barb and Taylor, while he flew to pick up Iris. Emily had withdrawn again, treating him to the remote, polite facade she'd perfected since the trip to Florida. Simon hung onto his temper, but it was an effort. The thirty-mile trip seemed twice that long because of the grim silence that hung between them. Finally they reached Barb and Taylor's home.

"Heard any developments on the drug ring?" Taylor asked in a low voice while Barb dithered over Emily's bandaged wrist.

Simon shook his head. "Last week a plane was sighted taking off from a field two counties west of here, and a Customs agent managed to track it until bad weather closed in and they lost it. Nothing else has turned up so far, and we don't know if it's the same people or not."

He didn't tell Taylor (who would tell Barb) that a weekly check by Sheriff Jessup of the woods surrounding Emily's property had turned up evidence of a recently used campsite. That in itself was ominous but inconclusive, so Simon had chosen not to burden Emily or her friends with the information.

She wouldn't appreciate his decision, he knew. Abruptly, Simon wanted to pound his fist through a wall. He interrupted Barb by stepping in front of her and turning to Emily. "Walk me back to the car?" He cupped her elbow and smiled at Barb.

"Trying to flaunt your power?" Emily observed snidely once they were outside, and Simon counted to twenty.

"I know you're feeling pretty defensive and vulnerable right now," he returned, very quietly, "but I wish you'd try trusting me for a change instead of automatically assuming the worst."

Emily flicked him one look of shattering pain. "I can't trust you. I won't." Her chin jutted. "And if your great-aunt wins tomorrow I'll pack my bags and you won't see me for the dust."

The chill of her pronouncement rang in Simon's ears long after he drove off, and he knew the look on her face would haunt him the rest of his life.

Taylor took the day off so he could drive with Emily and Barb to Timmons. It was a muggy day, so hot and close the crispness of autumn might have been a dream. In the deep south, summer and fall often waged a contest throughout November, with the dreary dripping rains of winter finally ending the battle.

Barb had taken Emily in hand, forcing her to choke down half a grapefruit and a slice of cheese toast for breakfast and then picking out what she should wear to the hearing. Emily had brought along the brown suit and cream blouse she'd worn the first time, but Barb regarded the outfit with disdain.

"You don't need to look like you're going to prison, and that's about what all those neutral shades do for you." She began plundering her closet, muttering imprecations since her dress size was at least two sizes larger than Emily's. "Haven't you listened to anything I've tried to tell you over the last couple of years about your needing to wear brighter colors?"

"I'm not auditioning for a beauty contest, Barb." Emily sat listlessly on the edge of the bed, brushing out her hair with halfhearted strokes. Her bandaged wrist made this awkward, and the cut throbbed a little. "I frankly don't care how I look."

Barb ignored her. "Here—try this blouse. You'll have to wear the suit, but we can at least liven it up a little. With the jacket on and the way this blouse is supposed to drape in folds, no one will notice that it's a little big."

Emily eyed the brightly patterned blouse swirling in vivid shades of burnt orange, red, and sienna. When she put it on with her brown suit, the difference was startling. Emily glanced in the mirror and shrugged. "It's okay, I suppose. Thanks, Barb."

She sat in the back seat as they drove to Timmons, ignoring the glances Barb kept casting over the seat and the looks Taylor sneaked in the rearview mirror. She was clammy and cold in spite of the sultry day, and wondered if she would ever be warm again. Brad had tried to reassure her yesterday before she left the office, but he was not hopeful and was too good a lawyer to lie. Emily could feel the shroud of hopelessness bearing her down, down into a cold pit of nothingness.

All her life she had wondered why she wasn't loved, what lack in her existed that kept her parents from loving her enough to provide her with the love and security her soul needed and craved. J.J. had fought his way to recognition, but all it had earned him in the end was trouble until he grasped the life ring of the Air Force Emily had tossed to him so desperately. He had never bothered to toss her anything in return, and Emily had learned to go her own way because no one would ever care enough to help her out.

And now, just when she had finally found something to call her own, something that needed to be needed—just like herself—it was going to be yanked away from her. *God,* she found herself praying, *God, what am I going to do? What's the matter with me? This is even worse than being held upside down in a bag, not knowing if I was going to live or die. I don't have a choice now—I have to keep on living, but Lord, I feel dead inside.*

"When hope within me dies . . . I draw ever closer to Him. . . ." The single line of melody whispered across her heartstrings, so faint and haunting that for a moment she actually caught her breath, straining to hear. "From care He sets me free. . . ." The music was stronger now, and the words plucked a little louder, sounding in her head like chimes. "His eye is on the sparrow . . . and I know He watches me—His eye is on the sparrow, and I know He watches me."

The song. Simon had told her she reminded him of that song—that's why to this day he sometimes called her sparrow-girl. It aggravated her, infuriated her, irritated her—but not until this moment did she feel the comfort and reassurance the nickname also offered. Emily had only been concentrating on the unflattering ramifications of being a sparrow—plain, brown, and not worth looking at twice.

Simon had tried to tell her differently, but she hadn't listened. She closed her eyes, bowing her head to force out all the other intrusive sounds. She wanted to listen now. She pictured the battered hymnbook Mrs. Jenkins had given her and tried to focus on the page on which the song was printed. There was something about being afraid, about clouds. Why had she just stuffed the book in a box of other forgotten paraphernalia when she moved out of the apartment? The words were hovering on the tip of her tongue, so close she could—

That was it! . . . draw ever closer to Him . . . From care He sets me free. . . ." *Lord, I would give anything—including that house, if I could draw closer to You and know You cared about me. Simon claims You do, and he certainly acts like he's got an inside track to Your ear, but then he's been a lot more faithful to You over the years than I have.*

The haunting melody deepened into the baritone chords of Simon's voice reciting another Bible verse. What was it? Something about salvation restoring the joy. . . .

"Emily? You okay? We're almost there." Barb's voice intruded suddenly, shattering the melody Emily was straining to hear.

Emily lifted her head and forced a smile. "I'm okay, Barb. Believe it or not, I was actually praying."

Barb looked abashed. "I'm sorry, Emily." She reached a hand over the seat to Emily, and after a brief hesitation Emily's lifted in response. "Everyone has been praying for you, even the kids." She squeezed Emily's hand, then let it go as Taylor slowed to pull into the diagonal parking space in front of the stately, columned courthouse.

They were a little late, and when the three of them walked inside the same drab waiting room as before, it was already crowded with people. Their case was not the first one on the docket this morning, and there were a half dozen or so other equally nervous individuals all waiting their turn.

Everyone else blurred in Emily's eyes when she caught sight of Simon. For the past three months, they had lived like friendly next-door neighbors who worked together, and for most of that time Emily succeeded in regarding Simon in that light.

Now—with a single glance—everything had changed. He was sitting beside Iris, looking so solid and capable and masculine next to Iris's petite fragility that Emily's mouth went powder dry. He was wearing a charcoal pinstripe suit with a mint green silk shirt and coordinating tie, the effect lending him an aura of leashed power and raw elegance Emily had never really noticed. The thick waves of his rich, nutmeg-brown hair radiated health and vitality, and the same sizzling life leaped out of his eyes when he saw Emily.

Something sizzled in Iris Bancroft's gray eyes as well, but it was the cold sizzling of steam rising off frozen steel, and it was also frankly triumphant. Her snappy cardinal red suit, tailored gray blouse, and matching gloves made Emily feel like a frumpy dowager instead of the other way around.

Simon started across to meet her immediately. Brad, talking in the corner with Lamar Hansell, also caught sight of her. He excused himself, a grim, determined look behind his deceptively lazy, charming demeanor.

"How are you doing? Did you sleep at all?" Simon was asking her in a husky undertone, his gaze moving over her face, her hair, dropping to the suit and Barb's blouse. "That's a pretty blouse—lots better than the one you wore the last time."

Emily bit her lip to keep from smiling. He was trying so hard, "It's Barb's. You'll have to tell her you approve of her taste better than mine."

"Emily." Brad was at her elbow. "We need to discuss a few things."

For a spine tingling moment the air froze into an aura rife with unspoken threats and warnings. Emily glanced from Brad to Simon, trying to comprehend why the hairs on the back of her neck were tingling, and why Simon looked, well, almost primitive, as if he were about to rip Brad apart like a ravaging wolf devouring a piece of raw meat.

Feeling uneasy, uncertain, she shifted her gaze over Simon's shoulder and met head-on the frozen glare of Iris Bancroft. But there was an arrested gleam there as well, an almost reluctant dawning of awareness Emily didn't understand any more than she did Simon's behavior.

Then the moment passed as Brad tugged her away and Taylor moved up beside Simon, asking him a question and forcing the younger man's attention.

"Brr," Brad shivered as he led Emily over to the only two vacant chairs left in the room. "Your watchdog is growling awfully noisily for someone who only wants to restore your house, Ms. Carson. He almost acts jealous, if you ask me."

"I thought you had something you needed to talk to me about," Emily reminded him, faint color staining her bleached-out cheeks.

Brad smiled a little, but took the hint. He dropped down in the chair beside her, glanced off to the left, then deliberately lifted Emily's hand and held it comfortingly between his own. "Emily, you know this doesn't look good, but I wanted to remind you that we still have the option of filing a countersuit ourselves if the judge decides in the plaintiff's favor this time."

Emily shook her head. "I can't take any more, Brad." She looked up at him hopelessly. "I know you've done the best you could—probably better than any other lawyer could have done—but if this goes the way I think it will, I'm throwing in the towel." She swallowed, then finished in a tone so low Brad barely heard. "Simon will do a better job on the house with me gone, anyway."

Brad cursed softly but succinctly, then issued a gruff apology when Emily winced. She found herself noting with stunning irrelevance that Simon had never once used foul language or curse words in her presence. He liked ordering her about, lost his temper with her—even yelled at her, but never had he blasphemed or employed gutter language to vent his anger and frustration. He wasn't perfect and was honest enough to admit it, but Simon Balfour was a committed Christian to the core. She might not ever be able to trust him—but she *did* trust his faith.

"Emily!" Brad was jiggling her hand, and she looked at him, eyes wide and startled. "It's time to go. They're calling our case."

He kept her hand tucked in his elbow as they all moved toward the door. Simon shot Brad a murderous glare and Brad merely deflected it with a provocative grin, but dread had reared up and grabbed Emily's throat and she didn't notice anything.

She remained a motionless statue as the court was brought to order and the case presented. The judge retired once again to his chambers. No emotion ruffled the barren desert of her countenance when, as predicted, the judge returned to set aside his prior decision, determining that the validity of the will should prevail over Emily's later title.

Voices gusted around her like breezes, but she sat unmoving, feeling as if layers of clear polyurethane were being applied around and around her. She was present, but unreachable. Barb's arm was around her, and Taylor was patting her shoulder. Brad said something, but he was talking to Mr. Hansell now and whatever he told her slid right off.

He came back a minute later and took her hand. "Listen, Em, I know what a blow this is. Why don't you hang up secretarying for me awhile and try to just rest—get your perspective back. Gloria will be able to come back in a week anyway, and I can manage until then." The voices around Emily rose suddenly, as if someone were arguing, and a warm, strong hand on her arm was urging her to rise.

"— just leave her alone!" Barb was snarling. "Go gloat with your old biddy of a great-aunt!"

"I don't think you understand." The hand tightened, and Emily found herself standing. "I'm not asking your permission."

She was being led down the short aisle and out of the courtroom, and because it was Simon, her senses swam into a sharp stabbing moment of focus. "Please leave me alone," she stated clearly.

"Not on your life."

"Wait a minute, Balfour!" That was Brad's voice coming closer again. "I need to—"

Simon halted, jerking around with Emily following like a boneless rag doll. "You don't need to do anything but back off," Simon suggested so quietly, so deliberately, that Brad did just that. "Whatever formalities need to be handled you can either handle yourself or wait. I'm taking Emily some place private, and I'm taking her now."

Emily wanted to summon up the energy to fling aside his hand and unleash the temper she had discovered she had after she met Simon. It stayed locked up somewhere in the frozen storage area of her heart, though, and she ended up allowing herself to be hustled out of the courthouse, down the steps, and into Simon's Jensen-Healy without even lifting her little pinkie.

"What about your great-aunt?" she inquired with polite detachment.

"Lamar is taking her to his home. We'll pick her up later." He drove several blocks to a small park and playground, parked, got out, and came around and helped Emily out. Keeping her hand firmly in his, he walked her over to a wooden park bench placed between two towering pines.

He sat down, then joined her, turning so he could watch her, his hands reaching out to grip her shoulders. "Emily," he sighed her name almost as if in prayer. "Emily, you don't have to lose the house. You don't even have to leave it." He shook her gently, forcing her eyes to focus on him so he knew she was taking in his words. "Emily—sparrow-girl— I want you to marry me."

Chapter Fifteen

Emily was staring at him blankly. "You want me to marry you?" she parroted in a dull monotone. "Why? The house belongs to your great-aunt now. You can restore it however you like. Why marry *me*?"

"Because I'm in love with you!" he all but snapped. "Why else would I ask you to marry me?" His hands slid down her arms, back up to cup her face. "Did you hear me? I love you."

For a brief instant something stirred inside her, as if a flickering spark buried so deep under the ashes was struggling to re-ignite. Then she shook her head, lifting her own hands to gently but firmly remove his. "You don't love me—you just feel sorry for me." She forced a painful smile. "It's okay, Simon. I'll be okay after awhile, but I appreciate the gesture."

She made as if to rise, then a startled gasp escaped her restricted throat when Simon jerked her completely off her feet and into his lap. He wrapped her in a firm embrace, his face thrust inches away from hers.

"I do not feel sorry for you, woman!" he growled. "I said I love you, and that is *exactly* what I meant. I've never told a woman that before, and I hadn't planned on telling you yet. But now that I have, you better believe it, or we'll have the first shotgun wedding in America where the bride*groom's* father is holding the shotgun instead of the bride's!"

"Nobody loves me like that," Emily whispered. "They never have—why should you?"

He groaned, and began covering her face with kisses. "You are loved, Emily Carson," he promised fervently, feverishly. "You are lovable, and you are loved. By me, by all your friends—by your heavenly Father." His mouth found hers, and he kissed her long and deeply. "Marry me, Emily. Marry me, and we'll restore the house and our lives together."

"No." She began shaking her head, and couldn't seem to stop. "No. You don't really love me, and I won't trap us both. Leave me alone, Simon, please. Take me back and leave me alone." When his arms merely tightened, she began to struggle, but the efforts were weak, sluggish, as if all her batteries had run completely down. "Let me go," she whimpered, perilously close to breaking.

Simon released her, watching with tortured gaze as she scrambled up and backed away, hands shaking as she straightened her rumpled suit and hair. His hand lifted, reaching out, pleading. "Emily—please try to believe me. I love you. As God is my witness, I love you as much as a man can love a woman. Love, Emily. Not pity."

The tears began then, a slow, hot trickle that slipped over the pooling rims and slid down her ashen cheeks. "I wish I could believe you," she sighed in a choked undertone. "I've always wished I could believe you." Lifeless, defeated, she stood in front of him, inches away, the tears falling unheeded. She might as well have been on another planet."

"We'll discuss it later." He took out a handkerchief and wiped his face, looking exhausted—but determined. "Let's go fetch Aunt Iris."

"I'd rather not. She won't want to be anywhere near me."

"You leave Aunt Iris to me."

"I suppose you expect to be tossed out on your ear," Iris Bancroft announced in a reedy patrician voice, setting down her glass of iced tea and fixing Emily with a penetrating gaze. "You look like you're facing a firing squad."

"Aunt Iris—"

"Stay out of this, boy. You've caused me enough trouble in the last months to put me on digitalis." Her ivory-handled cane thumped on the Oriental rug of Lamar Hansell's study. "I heartily disapprove of your actions, but of course you're aware of that, I dare say."

"You've made it pretty clear," Simon returned calmly. "But what you don't seem to understand is that I love Emily, and I'm going to marry her."

Iris surveyed him archly, the merest suggestion of a smile softening the severity of her lined, narrow face. "I understand quite well," she refuted, and emitted a disdainful sniff. "Just because I never married myself doesn't make me blind, deaf, and dumb. You've been pie-eyed over this girl for months, and after seeing her at court today, it's plain as spring water she's just as pie-eyed over you."

Emily flushed, wondering if it were possible to feel any worse. "Miss Bancroft—"

The older woman shushed her. "I've come up with the perfect solution," she announced, bracing her gnarled hands on the arms of the chair and leaning forward. "I've gotten too old for Connecticut winters, and although I can't say I'm overly fond of the South—such dreadful humidity!—I must confess it's likely to be easier on these arthritic old bones. I plan to move into," she paused, shooting Emily a shrewd, calculating glance, "into *my* house, and it will become my winter residence. Emily will remain living there until the two of you marry— I'm getting too old to live alone anyway. After the wedding Simon can either find me an acceptable cottage nearby, or have one built."

She lifted her chin to an imperious angle and regarded the two stunned individuals before her. "The house will be my wedding present to you both. Well? Are you both agreeable to that?" She examined Emily closely a minute. "I admit to being somewhat set in my ways, and I can't abide laziness and stupidity. But I daresay we'll get along fairly well—you're a teacher by profession, I understand."

"Yes, ma'am." Emily found her way to a worn wingback sofa and sat down. "But you hate me. . . ." She shook her head in bewilderment. "I took your house away. . . ."

Iris hooted in derision. "Balderdash! I was mad, girl, but I'd never met you. How could I hate you? The past few weeks, if you must know, I've reluctantly had to accept the fact that I maintain a grudging respect for you."

She marked Simon with an old-fashioned look. "Anyone who can catch and keep this footloose young devil has to have something besides a pretty face." She lifted her cane and pointed it at Emily. "You hide the looks you have, but it didn't fool me. And it obviously hasn't fooled my grandnephew. Well, Emily Carson? Is that a deal?"

Emily looked at Simon, who had started grinning, a wide grin that spread from ear to ear. She looked at Iris, whose stern, glacial demeanor was dissolving into wrinkles and twinkles right before Emily's disbelieving eyes. She looked down at her lap, trying to comprehend what was happening. *Dear God,* she found herself pleading silently, *what do I do now?* The cold, choking panic spread, freezing her veins. Her heart.

She couldn't trust these people. She couldn't. One day they would decide she wasn't worth their while and would leave her stranded and alone again. "It won't work," she said, her voice small but set. "I can't do it."

Simon's grin faded and his green eyes narrowed to slits. "What do you mean by that?" he questioned, very softly. Iris's back stiffened, but she held her tongue.

Emily made a short, jerking gesture with her arm. "I can't marry you."

"You love me, Emily. You can deny it until the cows come home, but you love me as much as I love you. If you'd stop being so blasted defensive and prickly, you'd admit I feel about as much pity for you as I do the characters who hauled you off in a gunnysack." His nostrils flared when Emily shook her head. "I'm not above trying a little kidnapping of my own."

"Leave the girl alone," interrupted Iris sharply, surprisingly. "She's been through enough and doesn't need your bullying and browbeating."

A long, painfully tense moment followed. Simon measured both the truth of his great-aunt's words—and Emily's infuriating mind-set. Throat tight, a muscle twitching in his cheek, he faced Emily down until she turned her head away.

A childhood memory came to Simon suddenly, wrenchingly: He'd caught a fledgling blue jay and wanted to keep it for a pet in the new birdhouse he'd just built. To make sure the bird didn't escape, he held it tightly in both hands and ran all the way home.

Excited, breathless, he called for his brother and sister, but when he carefully opened his hands to show them the bird, it was dead.

"I only wanted to keep it safe and give it a home," he'd sobbed to his father.

Dad laid a comforting hand on his shoulder. "Son, sometimes the best way to help a fledgling bird is to just let it go, so it can learn to fly on its own."

"All right," Simon said now, his voice raw because he couldn't hide his pain. "All right, Emily. I'll leave you alone, give you some time." He reached out and brushed a tear from her cheek with trembling fingers. "But try not to take too long, sparrow-girl. I'm not as strong as you think."

They arrived back at the house a little before five o'clock. Simon muttered something about working in his portable office a little while. He shot Emily a brief glance and disappeared inside the camper.

The sultry day was finally cooling from a tentative afternoon breeze. Emily changed into some light cotton slacks and a three-quarter raglan sleeve pullover, then wandered around the house like a displaced ghost. Pausing in front of the stained glass window in the library, her fingers gently traced along a dust-covered fragment molded into the likeness of a flower. Someday it would be a rich sunset hue . . . but she wouldn't be here to see it.

She meandered out onto the front porch, moodily scanning the burned field behind the house. Though still charred and blackened, nature was already healing the wound, covering the area with weeds and autumn wildflowers. Somewhere in the woods came the faint, far-off sound of a dog barking.

A dog? When this house was the only property for two miles in every direction? The faint sound echoed again. Emily froze, not moving, not breathing, her entire body straining to hear.

There! Over in the direction of the old campsite she and Ivan had discovered. Was it possible that they hadn't killed him? Could it be? If they hadn't really killed Ivan—

Even as her brain formulated the thought, her feet were in motion, flying down the steps and across the yard. "Ivan!" she screamed with every ounce of breath in her body. "Ivan! Where are you?"

From behind she vaguely registered Simon's voice shouting her name, telling her to wait, to stay away from the woods. She ignored him. Didn't he understand? She had to find out, *had* to see if she had heard a dog and if it had been Ivan.

She no more thought about drug rings or nefarious criminals or what had happened the last time she strayed into these woods than she heeded Simon's frantic yells for her to come back. Heart in her throat, she ran all the way across the field and plunged into the woods, calling Ivan's name as she fought her way through the underbrush.

She was halfway down the old logging road before Simon caught up with her. He snagged her shoulder, jerked her around, and held on grimly as she fought to free herself. Sobbing, pummeling, kicking, she finally managed to wrench loose. "I have to see!" she cried frantically. "Simon, I heard a dog bark—it might be Ivan. I have to see!"

"Emily—honey, it's too dangerous. It's almost dark, and the woods are probably full of stray dogs." He advanced upon her cautiously, keeping his voice low and reasonable. "Come on, now. Let's go back to the house. You know you don't need to be out in these woods until the police—"

"I don't care!" she flung back. Her hair had tumbled out of its neat bun and spilled about her face and neck and down her back. Emily swiped at it, then turned away. "I have to find out!" she repeated, her voice breaking. She ran off, down the trail, with Simon at her heels.

Moments later she burst into a clearing, lungs on fire, eyes blurred with tears so that for a moment she had no awareness beyond her furiously pounding heart. Then Simon was there, his arm going about her shoulders and holding her to him in a bone-crunching hug.

"You don't listen too good, Ms. Carson," a gravelly voice chided from just behind her. "And now we got ourselves a problem."

Chapter Sixteen

It was two hours later, more or less. Though Emily knew it must be dark outside, with a blindfold covering her eyes, her mouth gagged, and her hands tied behind her back, her only certainty was the knowledge that she and Simon were still alive.

The van in which they'd been traveling had stopped. With cautious, surreptitious movements she wriggled her body, trying to loosen stiff, numbed muscles. Trying, less successfully, not to worry about Simon.

She couldn't hear anything but the sound of her own harsh, raspy breathing. Was he conscious yet? She remembered seeing two men coming toward them, remembered Simon trying to thrust her out of the way. Her frightened gaze caught a blur of movement and she had tried to call out to Simon.

She was too slow, too late. Something hard struck the back of his head, and the arm holding her had dropped away.

Emily had gone a little crazy then, but recalled little except Gumshoe yelling hoarsely for them to either tie her up and gag her, or he'd take care of her the same way. Before the pimply-faced young man and swarthy looking Latin-type had succeeded, Emily managed to scratch deep furrows across the young man's cheek, and the other guy would wear bruises on his shins for days.

Suffocating terror roared back through her. Emily choked back a sob, repeating in her mind like a litany: They weren't dead yet. The probability nonetheless loomed before her like a mushroom cloud, and so, ever since they had been tossed into the back of what felt like a stripped-to-the-bones van, Emily had been praying.

She prayed because she had no other hope, because Simon was unable to do so, and until he had groaned and moved awhile ago, she hadn't even been certain he *was* alive. She must *not* think about the feelings she had endured then.

In her head, she sang all the songs she had learned in choir over the years, and whenever the fear threatened to choke her and send her back into a nether world of screaming phantoms and leering demons, she thought of sparrows and all the verses Simon had quoted with such deep faith over the past months.

Simon . . . Simon, please be all right. Lord, please let Simon be all right. Help us, please. Give me the strength to endure . . . God, please let me know You are there.

No legions of angels descended to set them free, and no fiery chariots swept down to burn their unsavory abductors to a crisp. But a small, steady voice had surfaced from the deepest part of her being. *I'll never change. You'll always have Me, and I will always be with you, my child. Just like salvation—My love is forever.*

Emily hung on to the Voice—and waited.

The van doors opened with a screeching jerk. Ungentle hands hauled them out, and a minute later she was unceremoniously dumped onto some sort of hard floor.

"Tie 'em both good," a voice grunted nearby. "And make sure this shack burns long enough to destroy any evidence."

"Alright, alright . . . whadya think I am—a dummy? And I know it has to look like an accident, right?" That was the young, pimply-faced man, the one who promised Ivan had been taken care of.

Heart racing, Emily struggled impotently against the bonds. This couldn't be happening, it wasn't real—

"Hurry it up, you two! I want to get outta here." Emily felt a rough rope passed around her middle, then her back was against Simon's and she realized they were being tied together. Bile rose in her throat, and in spite of the last hours of steadfast prayer, a strangled sob escaped.

Incredibly, she felt the muscles in Simon's back constrict, press harder against her, and his elbows, locked with the rope to hers, moved with the slightest of gestures. He was conscious! He was even aware of what was going on and was trying to reassure her.

Confidence and renewed determination flooded through Emily, spilling new life into her numb limbs and floundering heart. She couldn't see, she was afraid to try and speak, she could barely move—but now she could hope. *Thank you, Lord! Oh, thank you! Now please get us out of here.*

The smell of burning wood and sound of crackling flames jarred Emily momentarily out of her euphoria. She began to struggle convulsively until the urgent pressure of Simon's back and arms once again calmed her.

"That'll do it. Now let's split." A harsh guttural laugh grated their ears. "So long, lovebirds. You won't be gettin' in the way anymore, will you?"

A door slammed, and they were alone with the gathering strength of the fire radiating heat and terror.

The minute the door shut, Simon began speaking. His words were barely legible, hard to hear over the fire, and Emily realized he'd been gagged as well. But she responded to his voice like a morning glory to the sun.

"Prss magain' muh back," he ordered, and she understood immediately what he was trying to do. It had been a game growing up—sitting back to back and seeing if you could stand up without using your arms. Little did she suspect then how useful such a game could be. Without hesitation she matched the pressure against her back, bent her knees, and as she felt Simon rising, tried to counter with a similar move.

"Muh ft . . ." she croaked, tumbling sideways because her ankles were bound.

After a heart-stopping moment, she managed to regain her balance, and they stayed upright.

For another moment they stood motionless, recovering breath and gathering wits. "Jus' relak. Truh to jus' come wif me," Simon managed, the crackling flames and growing smoke fumes rendering comprehension almost impossible.

He seemed to be trying to edge in the direction of where they had heard the door slam, and it took only one step for Emily to realize they hadn't bound his feet like they had hers, probably because he had been unconscious at the time.

Simon seemed to realize about the same time that hers *were* bound, since she had had to hop instead of step. He moderated his step so she could hop without falling. Sweat poured down her body, soaking into her clothes, and she couldn't seem to stop the tremors in her arms and legs. But she stayed upright, close to Simon, and hopped.

Behind them the fire roared as it engulfed something even more flammable. Suddenly Simon ran into the wall, and she heard his muffled groan. Tears sprang to Emily's eyes. This was her fault. Simon was hurt, and might die— and it was her fault, just like Ivan's death had been her fault.

Simon turned so that their hands could just touch the coarse, unfinished boards that made up the walls of the shack, already hot to the touch. Choking, gagging, Emily prayed.

Then she heard the doorknob rattle, and her bound wrists twisted along with Simon's as he struggled to turn the knob and open the door. When she felt it opening and pushing her almost off balance again, she sobbed against the restraining gag, feeling the inrush of cool air against her face, in her hair.

Simon did not waste time trying to talk anymore. Instead, he encouraged her through a series of firm but urgent tugs to follow him. As they jerked and hopped out the mercifully unlocked door, the sound of crashing wood exploded behind them and part of the ceiling collapsed.

With a sucking roar of redoubled intensity, the triumphant fire devoured the interior of the shack. Emily felt the heat of it blasting her, searing her as Simon all but dragged her on his back the last few feet.

They were still too close to the burning structure when she lost her balance again and tumbled sideways, throwing Simon off-balance too so that they both fell to the ground. She heard him grunt in pain, and frantically struggled to get back up with him before he passed out. Too close—they were too close to the shack, and the flames and heat could still accomplish their deadly mission. And it was her fault.

Once again the firm, steady pressure of Simon's back quieted her, guided her. "Easy, love," she thought he said, and in mere seconds they managed to regain their feet. With Herculean effort, Emily managed to keep from panicking again, blindly obeying the largely unspoken communication of the man to whom she was literally bound.

The analogy burst into her soul like the consuming brightness of flame. She was trusting this man with her life, not knowing where he was going, and she was unable to either see him or give him much aid on her own. He wasn't leaving her behind because it was her fault, or trying to make her feel guilty. He was only working to save her life.

And *that* was the way she should trust God, whom she could neither see nor hear. Nor did she know exactly where He was leading her. She certainly couldn't offer Him much aid on her own. All she could do was surrender, no longer resisting.

Just as she knew Simon would give his life to keep her from all harm, was struggling to do that right now—so she realized, truly understood for the first time in her life, how much God cared for her. Cared for her so much that he sent His beloved Son to die for her, even though the fault was hers—not His.

She, Emily Carson, did matter after all. And there *was* Someone who loved her . . . who had always loved her. Loved her as she yearned to be loved. *Oh, Lord, she prayed in everlasting gratitude, thank You. Thank You for restoring the joy of my salvation—thanks for Your faithfulness in spite of me!*

After awhile she came to the more fundamental awareness that Simon was fumbling with the cords that bound their wrists. For several frustrating minutes he worked in silence, but it was no use. He muttered something unintelligible. "Muh fingehs . . . too big. . . ."

Emily moved her raw, throbbing wrists back together and found his fingers with her own. She pressed, trying to tell him to let her try. His fingers brushed against her wrists and jerked, and Emily knew he was probably feeling the rawness and seeping blood.

"Ahm okay." She gagged again, so she quit trying to talk, focusing every atom of her concentration on working the knots in the slender cords free. Her back and shoulders burned, and behind them she could hear the snapping, crackling flames, smell the charred wood and choking smoke.

"Oo can do it. Take ur time. At's it." Simon coached her, soothed her, encouraged her as if they had all the time in the world.

I can do it, Emily ground out to herself. *I've done it before.* This was no different from the time J.J. and his stupid little friends tied her up when she was eleven and left her in the woods. She escaped then, and she could do it again.

This was no different, yet it was. Then, she'd been alone. Now Simon was with her. And not only Simon she thought with growing excitement. *I can do it, because You're with me,* she prayed. *With Christ I can do all things.*

A minute later she succeeded in loosening the knot, and with a violent tug, Simon came free of the bonds. He worked with savage speed to untie the rope that bound him and Emily together.

"Almost home free, love," he enunciated clearly, directly in her ear, and Emily knew then they would be. He twisted and dropped a kiss on the top of her head as he swiftly untied the gag and tugged off her blindfold.

Two minutes later they were both free, and fell into each other's arms.

They were sitting beneath a pine tree, for Emily's leg had given out, and Simon was running his hands over her the same way she was doing him. "It takes more than a knock to to keep me down," he consoled her with a white-toothed grin, barely visible in the flickering light of the fire. "I'm okay, honey. Stop shaking now—I'm okay." He laughed a little. "I'm more worried about you than you are me, so how about if you reassure me for a minute?"

"I'm fine—just sore, mostly on my wrist where it was cut. And my jaw and shoulders hurt."

He lifted her wrists and rubbed his thumbs gently over the raw, blistered skin, then tilted the bandaged one up toward the fire to try and examine it better. The thick gauze bandage she had taped there that morning was crumpled, but at least it had been thick enough to protect the wound.

"What about the fire?" Emily asked, and they both turned to gaze at the remainder of the shack.

"It looks like it's just going to burn itself out, fortunately."

Even as he spoke, the two remaining walls toppled into the center of the fire, sending an explosion of sparks and flames shooting into the night. The build-ing had been placed in a clearing, so there were no trees or even protruding branches close enough for the fire to refuel itself with a roar into new life.

Simon put his arm around Emily, and she dropped her head onto his shoulder. They sat beneath the pine and watched until the flames died, first to flickering tongues, then to a glowing pile of embers and a wavering column of smoke.

"We were supposed to be in there," Emily spoke at last into the night, and a spasm shuddered through her weary frame.

Simon hugged her harder. "I know," he agreed quietly. "But we weren't." He cupped her face and kissed her very tenderly. "Let's thank God for our lives, then see about finding shelter for the night."

They bowed their heads, and Simon offered an eloquent prayer of thankful-ness that melted Emily's heart completely. How could she have been so blind not to know she was head over heels in love with this man?

She rubbed her damp cheek against his shirt, basking in the steady beating of his heart. Her fingers crept up to softly touch his beard-roughened cheek. "Simon? I've been praying—a lot—these past hours and you know what? Never has God been so real to me I felt—really *felt*—His power and presence surrounding me, sustaining me . . . us. And everything you've been saying all these months suddenly made perfect sense."

Incredibly, his chest heaved, and a sob of utter relief seared her ears. Then his arms hauled her up and he kissed her, words and tears all mixing up together. Emily eventually managed to wriggle a hand between to cover his mouth.

"You haven't let me tell you something else," she laughed, breathless, her own eyes aching with tears of joy.

"What's that?"

"I love you with all my heart, Simon Balfour . . . and if you still want to marry a plain brown sparrow who doesn't feel insignificant anymore . . . she's yours."

"Oh, God, *thank* You!" Simon vowed, passion and relief making his voice shake. "Yes, yes, yes, you impossible woman—of course I still want to marry you."

"Even though I almost killed us both?"

He kissed her. "Hush. I love all of you, Emily Carson—including the impulsive, unthinking woman who has a thing for ugly animals."

Emily dug an elbow into his ribs. "Just for that—I'm only marrying you to stay in the house."

Simon grabbed a fistful of her hair and wrapped it around her throat. "That was *my* line, remember?"

Emily pulled his head down, and for the next few minutes neither of them said anything. Eventually Simon lifted his head, his fingers smoothing her face. Cradled in his arms, surrounded by enveloping darkness, Emily knew she had found a home at last.

"Simon?"

"Hmm?"

"Let's make sure we clean the window before the wedding, okay?"

"No-o problem."

Epilogue

The day after Thanksgiving, Emily, Simon, and Aunt Iris were sitting on the front porch, rocking in three of the huge wicker rockers Simon bought from the couple in South Carolina whose old country inn he would be restoring after Christmas. The sun had finally broken through the storm clouds which had dumped an inch of rain Thanksgiving day.

Emily rocked in blissful contentment, holding her husband's hand and watching the sunbeams streaming down into the dripping yard. "It was nice of Sheriff Jessup to phone the good news yesterday, even though it was Thanksgiving," she mused dreamily. Simon squeezed her hand.

"Without bail," Simon added. "All of them, including Gumshoe." His gaze moved lovingly over Emily, causing her to blush. "God sure moves in mysterious ways—using a murdering drug dealer to finally convince my wife," he leaned over and kissed Emily, "that she couldn't live without me—or the Lord."

Iris snorted. "If you two are going to start acting like a pair of billing and cooing doves again, I'm going back inside."

Simon chuckled and stood. "Don't move. Emily and I will go for a walk."

"Simon—it's too wet."

He ignored her laughing protests and hauled her into his arms, carrying her. "There. Quit complaining, sparrow-girl. I want to watch the sun shining on our window."

"Oh." Emily relaxed, hugging him. "In that case. . . ."

He carried her out into the yard, finding just the right spot to best savor their pride and joy.

"I like the purple iris best," Emily announced after a few minutes of rapt contemplation. "It's incredible the way the sun makes all the colors so rich and alive—Simon? What is it?"

He had cocked his head in a listening stance, turning his face to the field behind the house. He wasn't even looking at the window. In exasperation Emily twisted her head. "What are you doing?"

"I thought I saw—" he stopped, then gently set Emily down. "Yes. There, near the edge of the field. Something moved."

"Probably a rabbit."

"Nope, too big. Didn't you say you'd seen some deer—" his voice died, the hand loosely clasping Emily's waist suddenly jerking her hard against him.

Emily peered across the field, and then she heard it: a weak but very definite "woof." And saw, very briefly, a large bony head. "Ivan. . . ."

They tore off across the field, oblivious to the wet scratchy weeds and soggy

They tore off across the field, oblivious to the wet scratchy weeds and soggy earth, coming to a breathless halt to stare in disbelief at the animal whining weakly at their feet. Dropping to her knees, Emily gathered the gaunt, filthy dog into her arms, sobbing. "Ivan, Ivan. . . . You're alive!" Ivan's bullwhip tail thumped weakly.

Simon was shaking his head. "I don't suppose we'll ever know what the old boy endured—or why they didn't kill him instead of dumping him somewhere. It's probably taken him all this time to find his way home."

Emily looked across at him, eyes swimming in tears. "He came home," she repeated, so choked with happiness and tears she could barely speak.

Simon grinned. "Well, I guess I'll have to change my way of thinking about ugly smelly dogs, now, won't I?"

He knelt, his hand coming down to join Emily's, stroking Ivan's floppy ears and filthy head. Then he gently elbowed Emily aside and lifted the dog into his arms. Ivan licked his face feebly—and Simon didn't even grimace. "Come on, you ugly, overgrown moose," he said, "let's go home."

And they made their way back across the field, to the welcoming, beckoning house.

Heartstrings

Irene B. Brand

Chapter One

From her vantage point on Pinnacle Rock, Veevie Wooten saw Evan Sullivan as he parked his truck at the base of the mountain. Steadily climbing, it would take Evan half an hour to reach her. Relaxed, Veevie leaned against the gnarled oak tree that through the centuries had forced its way through the rocky base to wrap strong tentacles around the cliff.

The sun shone unseasonably warm for mid-October and Veevie cast her sweater aside. Appalachia had its faults but from this spot it was hard to find them. A dense, almost unbroken forest cover blanketed the rugged landscape. Wispy haze lent mystery to the colorful hills swaddled in the yellow, red, and brown leaves of autumn. Sun filtered through the branches of the old oak, and the girl arched her back to take full advantage of the warm rays that turned her auburn hair into a kaleidoscope of burnished hues.

"Wish I had a dollar for every time I've looked at that old mountain," she murmured aloud. "Sixteen years of seein' the same view, and I ain't tired of hit yet."

Veevie refrained from glancing to her left. She knew what she'd see if she looked that way. *A naked mountain, that's what it is*, she thought, and she shook her head in disgust.

"Shameful people, to tear away the mountains for a handful of coal," she muttered.

Her thoughts echoed Grandpap's sentiments, but how could she help it? She'd always lived with him.

Veevie scanned the length of the Mill Creek Valley that snaked its way between two high mountain ranges. Dilapidated buildings of the Miller coal mine remained at the head of the hollow where two streams tumbled down the mountainside to form Mill Creek. A lake that had formed behind tons of mine debris sparkled in the sunshine. At the mouth of the creek, a few buildings of the Sullivan No. 2 mine protruded above the treetops.

Until a few years ago, scores of miners had lived in the valley, but when the Miller mine closed, they'd moved on to other towns. Grandpap had bought his house from the coal company, as had a few other miners, but Mill Creek now had less than fifty residents along its eight-mile journey to the Guyandotte River.

Evan's step startled her. He climbed the ledge to sit beside her. "What a sour face! Aren't you glad to see me?"

She moved close to him. Veevie hadn't seen him since the first of September when he'd gone away to college, and she yearned to feel his arms around her.

"Hit's been long, Evan. I've missed you." She fondled his curly brown hair and blended into his arms. Without looking, Veevie could feel Evan's ever-present smile, one that crinkled his gray eyes and lit up his strong features. She'd missed Evan's smile most of all, or at least she thought that was what she'd missed until he lowered his lips to hers.

Veevie squirmed in his embrace as Evan's lips traced a path to her ear lobe.

"I've missed you, too, Veevie. Happy sixteenth birthday."

"I was afeared you wouldn't come, Evan."

"I promised, didn't I?" he said, with a slight frown, and Veevie wondered what she'd done to vex him.

He drew a small box from his pocket.

"Oh, Evan, you didn't need to bring no present. Just havin' you is all the birthday I want."

But she took the box with eager fingers. "Oh," she gasped when she saw the ring.

"It's an opal. That's the October birthstone." When tears clouded her green eyes, he continued, "It's not an expensive ring since I don't have much money now. But one of these days I'll buy you lots of jewelry. Until then, that ring will be a reminder that you belong to me."

His lips cut off her words of thanks, but Veevie soon broke their embrace. "Hit's purty, Evan. I'll keep hit always. How long will we have to wait?"

"Too long," he whispered. "My father has big plans for me, and marriage isn't one of them."

A hawk soared high above them, screeching its displeasure at a flock of blackbirds chattering among the trees. Wispy clouds floated across the blue sky. The sun's heat radiating from the rock made Veevie drowsy.

Her contentment fled at Evan's next words. "I have bad news for us, Veevie." She roused, frightened. "What?"

"Dad has decided that I need to change schools. I'll be leaving the state university at midterm. I've been accepted by the engineering school at the University of California at Berkeley. I'm going there in January and Dad wants me to continue through the summer."

"So you won't be workin' at the mine next year?"

"No, he thinks I've had enough on-the-job experience. The other things I need to know are in books, he says."

"But, Evan, don't you ever think for yourself? You're almost twenty years old. Shouldn't you make some decisions on your own?" She knew she had no right to question, but the fact that he was leaving scared her. *Had his father found about about her?*

"Dad doesn't force me into anything. I want to learn all I can about mining—after all, I'll be managing the company someday. It will be only a few more years."

"Morgantown was far enough away. Hard to tell when I'll see you again."

He lifted her hand and kissed it. "Oh, I'll be home sometimes on vacations. Logan County isn't so far from Charleston. I'll see you as often as I can." He put his arm around her. "You know I've loved you for over a year. I'm not going to change. We can't be married until I'm through college, but do we have to wait for everything?"

"Yes, we do," she said, and her voice trembled. "I've told you before that I won't shame Grandpap like my ma done. It's bad enough that he's had me on his hands—I ain't takin' no chance of givin' him another kid to raise." She looked at him, and her voice mirrored the pleading in her sea-green eyes. "Please, Evan, don't ask me. I ain't strong enough to hold out against you forever. Don't ask me no more."

He sighed guiltily and looked away.

"All right, Veevie. I guess I respect you more for saying no."

"I'm glad somebody respects me. Not many folks do. Hit's all right to buy liquor from the local moonshiner, but decent folks won't get too chummy with his granddaughter." She tried not to sound bitter but the look of compassion on Evan's face told her she hadn't succeeded.

"It has never made any difference to me, Veevie. You know that."

"I know, Evan, you've never shunned me, and that's why hit's hard to deny you anything."

Evan looked away from her across the mountain and she followed his gaze. Without glancing her way, he said, "Veevie, as my wife, you'll live in the city and meet lots of important people. Why don't you start grooming yourself for that? And can't you learn to speak the English language correctly? You shouldn't say 'hit', and 'ain't'—you know better."

"Hit's the way I've talked all of my life."

"Is there any reason you can't change? For me?"

"You're ashamed of me, ain't you, Evans?" *Why hadn't she realized that before*? He'd never wanted to see her out in public. She'd met Evan last summer when he'd come to Logan County to work in the new mine his father had opened at the mouth of the hollow. They'd seen each other often, but all of their meetings had either been here on the pinnacle or at her home.

"No, I'm not ashamed of you."

Veevie's day was ruined, and she slid off the rock and started down the path.

"I didn't want to hurt you, Veevie, but if you come out in my world talking as you do now, you're going to be hurt a lot more."

Veevie thought that instant she'd return his ring, but she had to have some remembrance of him. He tagged behind her down the narrow path until they reached his truck.

"You're angry with me now, Veevie, but you think about what I said. You're a smart girl, and there's no need for you to bury yourself in these mountains. Plan to go to college as soon as you finish high school."

Veevie couldn't answer him. It seemed as if a giant hand had clamped around her throat. She wanted to hurl angry words at him. "Maybe I don't want to be in your world," her mind thundered, but her rebellious heart whispered, "Oh, yes, you do. Admit it, life without Evan will be pointless."

She woodenly received his kiss. "Wear the ring, my little sweetheart. Let it remind you that I love you. I'll be back someday, and we'll meet on Pinnacle Rock."

Like a wild deer, she darted away from him and into the woods. She couldn't watch him leave for in her heart she believed she'd never see him again. Her heartstrings, which had seemed so full and vibrant a few hours ago, were now tuned to the breaking point.

Veevie heard shouting when she entered the clearing and she rounded the corner of the cabin on a run. Grandpap stood on the porch, a leveled shotgun in his hands.

"I ain't sellin' my land to no strippin' company," he thundered. "Get off my property."

"Now be reasonable, Mr. Wooten," the man at the foot of the steps pleaded. "We've an option to buy much of the other land in this valley, but your property is the key to the whole area."

Veevie ran to the man, grabbed him by the arm, and propelled him toward the truck standing beside the road.

"There ain't no reasonin' with Grandpap when he's holdin' a shotgun, Mister Man. I don't know what you've said to rile him, but you'd best be gettin' away from here."

The man shrugged his shoulders in defeat, mumbling, "There's nothing on earth more cantankerous than an ignorant mountaineer."

The engine of the pickup roared as the man raced recklessly down the dirt road.

Veevie followed John Wooten into the log cabin and watched as he placed the gun on a rack above the mantle. He gasped for breath and lowered his body weakly into a rocker by the fireplace. In his youth Grandpap had been tall and brawny, but sickness had taken its toll and he was only a shadow of the man who'd cared for her when she was a child.

"Grandpap, you ought not to get upset like that. What was the ruckus about?"

The old man spat contemptuously into the open fireplace. "That skunk works for a company that's tryin' to buy up land in Logan County. I ain't sellin' no mineral rights to 'em."

Fortunately, Evan's father operated deep mines; otherwise, Grandpap would never have let him come to see her. Grandpap had been a coal miner for years until black lung disease had forced his retirement, but he'd always hated strip mining and what it was doing to the mountaintops of West Virginia.

"And don't you sell to 'em when I'm dead and gone neither," he hurled at Veevie.

"I won't, Grandpap, but don't talk about dyin'."

"We've got to talk about hit, and I aim to do that in a little bit, soon's as I get my breath. Why didn't Evan come by?"

She refused to meet his eyes and busied herself sweeping the ashes off the hearth.

"Didn't he show up?"

"Yes, he came, but I don't think he'll be back. He's ashamed of me."

"Did he say so?" Grandpap shouted in a voice still strong in spite of black lung.

"No, of course not." She wouldn't let Grandpap bad-mouth Evan even if she were mad at him. "But why wouldn't he be ashamed of me? Look at me."

"I've been a-watchin' you grow up for sixteen years, and you're a right purty girl in my book."

"Maybe, until I open my mouth." Veevie had never smiled much because she wanted to keep her crooked teeth covered. That had been bad enough, but now she realized that her speech was as ugly as her teeth.

"You want to get your teeth fixed? Ain't there braces or such that will straighten 'em? All you have to do is ask me. I've got some money."

"Moonshine money!" Veevie said bitterly.

"I've got money that didn't come from my still. All I've made from the liquor I added to my black lung pension to keep food on the table. I don't keep anything from hit."

He motioned her to a chair beside him. The house was too hot for Veevie but Grandpap needed the added warmth.

"Hit's time we had a little talk, girl. I ain't goin' to live much longer, and I want you to know what's what."

She started to protest, and he held up his hand. "Don't argue. You've got to face facts. Black lung works slow, but hit's a relentless foe. I want you to know how I've provided for your future."

He chewed slowly on his tobacco and spat into the fire.

"I've been layin' aside a nice little nest egg in the bank at Logan, and I've got a lawyer down there takin' care of my money. Hit all goes to you when I'm dead." Grandpap paused to catch his breath. "Last summer, when Cousin Bea was visitin' from California, I asked her if you could come and live with her when I die. She's a refined woman and can shape you up where you lack manners and right talkin'. There'll be plenty of money for college if you want to go."

"But that means I'd have to leave the mountains!"

"Hit'll be best for you to leave here and make somethin' of yourself where nobody's ever heard of the Wootens. I want your promise—will you do hit?"

She nodded slowly but her heart would not consent.

"As far as that's concerned, you'll still have this place. Your money'll be in a trust fund, and I've made arrangements that the taxes will be paid on this land until you get yourself settled. Hit'll always be here so you can come if you want to, but I don't want you tied to the place. After a few years, you can do what you want to with hit, but I'm hopin' you won't sell hit to no coal company that'll strip the land."

"I promise to do what you want me to, Grandpap."

He ruffled her hair, as near as he ever came to affection. "All right, that's enough of this funeral palaver. Let's go talk to Ivy about gettin' your teeth fixed."

John Wooten's cousin, Ivy Fisher, and her husband Ben lived a mile away but Veevie had to hustle to keep up with Grandpap's long-legged gait.

"You talk about dyin' and then outwalk me. You're good for a long time."

John stubbornly shook his head but said nothing. When they reached the Fishers' ramshackle abode John explained to Ivy the reason for the visit.

"There's a man in Logan can do hit, and Ben can drive her in tomorrow to see about hit," said Ivy.

As John sauntered out to the potato patch to see Ben, Ivy called to him, "I'm fixin' supper for you, so don't figure on rushin' back up the creek."

When John was out of hearing, Ivy turned to Veevie. "What's brought on this sudden fit to have your teeth fixed?"

Ivy Fisher, in her midfifties, had wiry silver hair that crowned an angular face with chin and jaws sharp enough to cut paper. Veins were prominent in her thin neck. What Ivy lacked in beauty she made up for in a personality that was pleasant and outgoing. She mothered both Veevie and John, and Veevie often brought her problems to the older woman.

"Evan hurt my feelings, and I let Grandpap find out about hit. He thinks fixin' my teeth will make me feel better, but that won't heal the hurt that Evan is ashamed of me."

"Hit's never a good idea to marry up, Veevie. I feared you were headed for a fall when you started courtin' Evan. Mine owners and miners just don't mix."

Veevie had heard that all her life, but she'd thought that she and Evan could overcome the barrier.

Before she could answer, a knock sounded at the door.

"Come in," Ivy called, and Miss Amelia Dixon entered.

"Pardon my laziness, Miss Amelia. I didn't know hit was you, or I'd have come to the door," Ivy apologized.

"No matter," Miss Amelia said as she smoothed back the iron gray hair from her face. Ivy scurried out of her chair and urged the short, lean woman toward the best seat in the room. As a missionary, Miss Amelia had become a fixture along the creek during the past ten years as she worked with the children, visited in troubled homes, and helped the elderly. She seemed to have an unusual knack of knowing when trouble came. Had she divined that Veevie was downhearted today? Veevie thought her romance with Evan had remained a secret, so she doubted if Miss Amelia even knew of Evan's attentions.

It appeared Miss Amelia had only wanted to talk to Ivy, but when she left the Fisher household, she asked Veevie to walk to the car with her.

"I've been missing you at church, Veevie. Has your faith faltered?"

"No, I don't think so," Veevie said, "but sometimes my family background stands in the way. I often think hit's better for the other kids if I stay away. I'm an embarrassment to them."

"Don't be foolish, Veevie! That's your imagination—the youth at the church have been kind to you."

Kind to me, but they've never accepted me for what I am, Veevie thought, but she didn't want to hurt Miss Amelia, so she said nothing.

"I want you to come back on Sunday," Miss Amelia insisted.

"All right, I'll plan to come. Thanks for bein' concerned about me."

"God is concerned about you, too, Veevie. Remember His words, 'The Spirit itself beareth witness with our spirit, that we are the children of God: And if children, then heirs; heirs of God, and joint-heirs with Christ.' I can understand why you're self-conscious about the circumstances of your birth, but that shouldn't stand in the way of your spiritual growth. If you're a child of God, your natural birth doesn't matter. I'm expecting great things of you, Veevie."

"I'm glad your grandfather lived to see you graduate from high school," Bea said. The cabin hadn't yet lost its funeral smell from the flowers the neighbors had brought to Grandpap's wake, and the sight of his emaciated body lying in the coffin still haunted Veevie.

Listlessly she helped her cousin close the house. She didn't want to leave home, but she'd promised her dying grandfather more than once that she'd go to California with Bea. Veevie knew she could get a job and support herself here, but before he died, Grandpap had made her promise again. "Go to Bea's for a while. See somethin' of the world. There's a lot more to life than you'll ever find in Logan County."

Veevie closed her suitcase and stood for a moment looking around the cabin. Cousin Bea had agreed with her that it was best to leave the house as it was while Grandpap had lived. Ivy and Ben had promised to look after the place for her.

"I want to walk around a little, Cousin Bea."

"Don't be too long. We should arrive in Charleston before dark. Our plane leaves Yeager Airport at nine o'clock in the morning."

"I won't be gone more than an hour or two. I want to say good-bye to a few places."

After a brisk climb, Veevie stood on Pinnacle Rock and glanced out over the creek valley. She hadn't seen or heard from Evan for over two years, but when she stood here on their rock, she felt as close to him as if he held her in his arms. Just one small note after he went away to college in California, and that was it.

For two years she'd devoted every thought and act to becoming the woman he wanted her to be. She had excelled in her school classes and had spent hours with the missionary learning proper conduct. This contact with Miss Amelia had also introduced Veevie to an inner spiritual strength that saw her safely through days of prejudice at school and the trying hours of Grandpap's slow death. She had made her life over for Evan, but he apparently didn't care anymore. She had hoped he'd read about Grandpap's passing and would come to comfort her, but she'd looked for him in vain.

Admit it, Veevie! Admit the reason you don't want to leave here is because you keep hoping he'll come back to you. Could she leave Appalachia without trying to see him once more? Veevie pondered the question as she hurried down the mountain.

Veevie and Bea arrived in Charleston by midafternoon. When they entered the motel room, Veevie still hadn't decided what she should do. She twirled the opal ring on her finger, watching the rainbow hues catch the sunlight. She hadn't removed it since the day Evan had placed it there. When Bea went into the bathroom, Veevie found a telephone directory in the nightstand and her finger hovered over the names until she found Sullivan Mining Company.

She lifted the receiver. She didn't even know whether Evan had come home or if he were still away at school.

She dialed the number rapidly before Bea returned. "I want to speak to Evan Sullivan, please," she said with bated breath when the receptionist answered.

"Mr. Sullivan is on another line at the moment. May I take a message?"

As Bea was opening the bathroom door Veevie replaced the phone receiver. *I have to see him*, she thought desperately.

"Cousin Bea," Veevie said. "There's an old friend of mine here in Charleston I want to contact. Do you mind if I leave for a little while?"

"No, go ahead, I want to rest anyway. Do you want to take the car? I won't turn it in until we reach the airport."

"No, thanks. The office is on Kanawha Boulevard, just a few blocks from here, I think. I'll ask directions, and if it's too far to walk, I'll take a taxi."

Having funds was still a novelty to Veevie. *Grandpap hadn't been funning when he said he'd accumulated a nest egg for her*, she mused. He'd left plenty of money to make her independent so she could pay her way with Cousin Bea.

The motel clerk directed Veevie to the Sullivan Mining Company and she walked quickly along the street until she came to the stone building front on the Kanawha River. Her steps slowed as she entered the imposing edifice and the movement of the elevator made her stomach churn as the cage lifted rapidly to the sixth floor. She checked the doors until she found one marked, "Evan Sullivan, Vice-President."

Taking a deep breath, she gingerly opened the heavy door. Veevie expelled the breath that she didn't even know she was holding when she entered the reception room. The blond secretary looked up expectantly.

"I'd like to see Mr. Sullivan, please, Mr. Evan Sullivan."

The woman looked at the book in front of her. "Do you have an appointment?"

Veevie shook her head.

"Mr. Sullivan is a busy man and he rarely sees anyone without an appointment."

Veevie's thoughts exploded inside her. *I have to see him. After coming this far, I have to see him. If she won't let me go in, I'll jump over her desk and rush through his door.*

"I want to talk to him," she demanded, staring at the woman, although her heart hammered in her chest.

The secretary said haughtily, "May I have your name and the nature of your business with him?"

"Tell him Genevieve Wooten would like a few minutes of his time."

The woman pushed a button on the intercom.

"Yes?" Evan's voice sounded in the room, and Veevie held on to the desk to steady herself.

"A Genevieve Wooten is here to see you, sir."

Did he hesitate? It seemed so to Veevie, and her heart skipped a few beats before he answered, "Certainly. Send her in."

Veevie's hand shook so much she could hardly open the door. Evan stood to greet her. "This is quite a surprise, Veevie. Please sit down."

Fortunately, a heavy walnut desk separated them or she'd have run into his arms. For a moment his presence overwhelmed her to silence, then she whispered, "You've changed so much, Evan. I hardly know you."

His curly hair was the same, as were his gray eyes, but a close-cropped beard made him look much older, more mature, more unattainable.

His smile was as ready as always. "You've changed quite a lot yourself. What brings you to Charleston?"

Oh, Evan, have you forgotten everything? Didn't your promise mean anything?

She lifted her hand to the desktop, hoping he'd see the opal ring and remember, but her hand stopped suddenly when she saw the smiling portrait of the woman in a gilded frame. Veevie stared at the picture and then shifted her eyes to Evan who refused to meet her gaze.

The telephone rang but Evan didn't answer it. The intercom buzzed and the secretary's voice sounded, "Your wife is on the phone, Mr. Sullivan. She wants to know what time you'll be home for dinner."

Veevie scrambled to her feet and bolted from his office, not heeding his repeated calls to come back.

Chapter Two

The driver braked suddenly when he saw the S-curve warning sign, and the occupants of the huge bus slid sideways in their seats. Lounging in her private compartment at the rear of the bus, Genna Ross seemed unperturbed by the dangers of the narrow, winding road. She laughed at the expression on the face of her manager, Jim Slater.

"Relax, Jim. People drive over these roads every day."

The bus careened wildly, and Jim grabbed a book to keep it from falling off the table. Jim was a slender man of thirty-five, and the expensive cut of his tailored suit showed off his well-knit physique. His neatly trimmed blond hair and full beard emphasized the blue of his eyes.

"Whatever possessed you to accept an engagement in such a Godforsaken place is more than I can imagine. Why didn't you let me check into the details first? After all, it's my job to manage your affairs. And to think you're doing this as a benefit!"

"Jim, did you ever see anyone die from black lung disease?"

"No," he answered carelessly.

"Well, I have, and it's not an easy death. That's the reason I'm giving a concert for miners with the disease. And remember, it is *my* affair."

As Genna looked out the window she realized she wasn't as calm as she appeared. How many people would identify country singing star Genna Ross as Logan County's own Veevie Wooten? Ten years had seen many changes: A new hair color, expert grooming, and the weariness of fame had changed the wildflower into a greenhouse orchid. *Would anyone recognize her*? Surely not Evan Sullivan, should she be unfortunate enough to encounter him.

She had refused an invitation to sing at the Civic Center in Charleston, much to Jim's displeasure, simply because of Evan. But in spite of the pain it might cause her, she longed to return to Logan County, and the invitation had presented too great a temptation. The chances of seeing Evan in the small town where she'd attended high school were slim.

"And why are you taking two weeks off after the concert without telling me where you're going?"

"Quit crabbing, Jim! Look on it as a bonus. You only had to reschedule three engagements and you receive two weeks' vacation in the bargain."

"But why be so secretive about what you're going to do?"

"There are times when I'd like to forget that I'm Genna Ross, when I just want to be myself. I can't do that if you're following me around trying to make me famous."

"That's not the real reason I want to be around you, Genna. You keep leading me on but you never let me come too close."

Genna's green eyes glittered angrily, and she clamped her mouth on an angry retort. Swallowing once, she said calmly, "Be fair, Jim. I've never led you on, never once have I given you any reason to believe you're anything except a manager to me. I hope we've become friends, but it will be nothing else. You must make up your mind to that."

Jim picked up her latest album lying on the table between them. " 'A One-Man Woman,' " he read the title song. "That song made you rich. Why can't I be that one man? I've wanted you long enough, and you don't seem to want anyone else. Are you in love with somebody—is there some lost love you're yearning for?"

Genna didn't want to quarrel with Jim but she didn't like his prying. Now that she'd achieved fame, she couldn't hide her Logan County background much longer. Not that she was ashamed of her youth, but thinking about home always brought back Evan's memory. Why couldn't she forget him? At least if this visit unearthed her past, no one would ever know about Evan, since for his own reasons, he'd kept their meetings secret.

"Jim, I've appreciated all the things you've done for me, but as far as I'm concerned, the time has come for us to go separate ways. I'm willing for you to leave whenever you want to."

His face paled at first, then broke into an angry frown. "Are you really serious? Don't you realize that I've made you a star?"

Genna laughed. "Oh, is it your voice and body that fans come to hear and see? Excuse me, I thought it was mine."

"Joke about it all you like, Genna, but our lives are too closely entwined to consider separation. I didn't intend to make you mad, but I don't like the idea of being told I'm fired."

"I'm willing to forget it if you are, on the condition that you realize I'm the one who makes the final decision on everything. You don't own me or my career, Jim. Remember that."

Not giving Jim a chance to reply, Genna moved out of the room toward the front of the bus. Cary Mullins chatted with the driver. The three band members slumbered in their seats. Lori Blair, Genna's secretary, pored over the latest issue of *Country Lanes*.

" 'One-Man Woman' is still on the Top 10, Genna. Congratulations!"

Genna nodded her thanks and went to sit beside Cary who had been with Genna for five years as her makeup artist, hair stylist, and masseuse. Cary had become, however, much more valuable than her job description. Of all the people in her employ, Genna had the greatest regard for this woman.

Cary gave her employer an understanding smile and gently massaged the muscles of Genna's neck. Like a kitten being stroked, her long slender body relaxed under Cary's skillful hands.

"Ah, Cary," she sighed contentedly, "what would I do without you?"

"Jim been badgering you again?" the stocky African-American woman asked.

"Uh-huh. The pressure of these tours is bad enough without having constant company. I have half a notion to sell this bus and travel by plane. Too much togetherness isn't good for us."

Jim strode down the aisle and sat on the seat opposite her.

"I've been talking to the editor of one of the state's major newspapers. He'll be at that high school for an interview at seven o'clock, so you'll need to have her ready by then, Cary."

Genna's muscles tightened under Cary's hands.

"No interview, Jim. I'm here to give the benefit show, but I don't have any other obligation to the town. It isn't as if they were doing me a favor."

"But, . . ." Jim began.

"Call and cancel the interview. I'm tired, and a two-hour show is all I'm going to do tonight. Cary, please order food brought to the motel after the show. We'll eat together."

Jim stomped angrily down the aisle, and Cary lowered an eyelid at Genna as Lori followed him.

"Going to sympathize with him, I suppose. I wish the two of them would make a match of it. Then maybe he'd leave you alone."

"She's willing, but he isn't," Genna answered. "It takes two to make a match, Grandpap always said. Most of the time I don't pay any attention to Jim. Guess I'm just irritable today."

Coming home shouldn't have made her irritable, but ten years was a long time, and she couldn't help worry about what this return might do to her career. She hoped her fame was strong enough that her public wouldn't mind if they found out that she'd been the illegitimate granddaughter of the local moonshiner. That didn't bother her as much, however, as the possibility of resurrecting memories of Evan. After all these years, she could still close her eyes, feel the sensation of his lips on hers, and revel in the closeness of his embrace. Genna had planned this homecoming as a sort of catharsis. If he'd cast a spell on her, maybe a visit to old surroundings would expunge it. *But what would happen if she saw him?*

When they entered Logan County Genna strained her eyes to see Pinnacle Rock but unshed tears clouded her vision. She almost cried again when they entered the small town of Woodville where she'd attended high school. Many of the stores were closed and vacant company houses loomed on the hills. The whole place had a neglected look. Genna had heard that mine mechanization had meant a loss of jobs for miners and that the population had decreased accordingly.

The manager of the motel rushed out to meet them and showed Genna to what was obviously the best room in the building.

"We're delighted to have you, Miss Ross. Not many people of your fame would take time for us. Anything I can do for you, let me know."

"My friend, Cary, will want a room that adjoins mine, and she'll be ordering food for us. Otherwise, I'd like not to be disturbed to allow time for me to rest before the concert."

Jim followed Genna into the room and looked disgustedly at the faded draperies, the none-too-clean carpet, and the meager furnishings. He turned on the manager but Genna headed him off.

"I'll be very comfortable here, sir. I appreciate your hospitality."

After the manager left, Jim angrily poked his fingers into the lumpy bed. "This is nothing but a hovel."

"I've slept in worse places, and it wouldn't have helped my popularity if you'd thrown a fit about the room. He's offering the best he has."

"I'm going to sleep on the bus."

"Help yourself. That will save me some money for your lodging." Cary laughed when Jim exited angrily and slammed the door.

"I'm glad you don't allow him to run over you, Genna. He's getting too big for his britches, as the old saying goes."

Genna soaked in a tub of hot water then relaxed under a massage from Cary. She slipped into pink slacks and a matching floral blouse for the ride to the auditorium. Her stage garments would be at the schoolhouse. The chauffeur, Lance, waited at the door of the motel with her Mercedes.

"Thanks for bringing the car, Lance," Genna said as she and Cary settled into the back seat. "I want to use it for a few days' vacation. You can travel back to Nashville on the bus, but I suppose Jim told you that."

Easing the car away from the motel, Lance said, "He told me. I'll be glad to drive you around on a trip if you like, Miss Genna."

"Thanks, guy, but I want you to have some free time, too. Why, are you afraid I'll wreck the car?"

He grinned. "No chance of that; I've seen you drive. I sometimes wonder why you need me."

"She wants you for a bodyguard, you big hunk," Cary assured him.

"She may need one tonight. Lots of people are ganging into that little auditorium." He wheeled the white Mercedes into a small lot behind the building and parked at the same spot the school bus had stopped years ago to unload its passengers. Passing through the door into the hallway behind the stage, Genna marveled to herself, the place even smells the same. *I feel as if I've been transported back into time. I'll bet if the bell would ring, I'd dart into Room 55 for my English class.*

Jim cut short Genna's musings when he hurried toward her. "You have thirty minutes before the first show starts."

Genna dressed in sequined mauve pants and a matching silk blouse and sat on a dressing stool so that Cary could style her hair and apply her face. Observing her image in the mirror, Genna thought there was little chance that any former classmates would recognize her. Heavy shadow made her sea-green eyes appear dark and sultry, and not since her rise to stardom had the natural auburn hair appeared. Cary worked diligently to keep Genna's hair in the honey-blond tones her fans loved.

Because she'd lived so long with Bea in California, the news writers had yet to piece together her ragged past. *Give them time*, she thought, but at least her physical appearance wouldn't give her secret away. Before she returned to the circuit, she intended to visit Grandpap's old house and find her graduation picture to compare the changes time had made.

Genna stood offstage and listened to Jim launch into his flowery introduction. Genna seldom suffered stage fright, but tonight she felt a slight quickening of her pulse. If she only knew who would be in that audience, she'd feel better.

She raced onstage, blowing kisses to the crowd and waving to them. A sea of faces greeted her, and as their adulation soared around her, she thought of the time she'd tried out for the senior class play, and was turned down. A part in that play would have meant much more than all of their cheers tonight.

Forcibly, she pushed the past aside, signaled her band, and launched into the show as she would have in any other place.

> *I'm a one-man woman*
> *From morning till night,*
> *In the dark times of life*
> *His love brings me light.*
> *And if he will open his heart's closed door*
> *I'll be a one-man woman forevermore.*

That song had become her trademark in the past six months. She tried to believe that she didn't have Evan in mind when she wrote the lyrics, but here in these old surroundings she admitted she still loved him as much as she once had. With pathos marking her words, she sang:

> *No other man will claim me for life,*
> *No other man can make me his wife,*
> *Only one man will win my heart . . .*
> *For I've been a one-man woman right from the start.*

It didn't help to remind herself that Evan already had a wife. That fact was etched indelibly in her soul and mind.

During the intermission Genna mingled with the crowd, signing programs and shaking hands. No one showed any sign of recognition, nor did she meet anyone who seemed familiar to her. Hordes of people still waited to shake her hand when Jim propelled her toward the dressing room. She took five minutes to drink a cup of hot tea and change into another garment.

Cary had a blue gingham pioneer dress and a matching bonnet ready for her to wear. She tied the string loosely to let the bonnet dangle over Genna's shoulders. Onstage again, Genna sat on a high stool and reached for a dulcimer. The beginning of her last act always featured mountain folk songs that she'd learned from Grandpap and his neighbors. Tonight as she sang these simple, well-loved tunes she hoped her audience would be pleased.

> *Poor little turtle dove, setting on a pine,*
> *Longing for his own true love as I did once*
> *for mine,*
> *For mine, as I did once for mine.*

The applause convinced Genna that she'd chosen well, and she continued her repertoire, ending with the ballad that Evan had loved because it reminded him of Scotland, his ancestral home.

> *A bonnie, wee lassie whose name it was Nell,*
> *Lived in a house where her grandmother*
> *dwelled.*
> *The house it was small, and the windows*
> *no less,*
> *Having four panes, one needed a glass,*
> *That nice little window, the cute little*
> *window,*
> *The sweet little window where grand-*
> *mother dwelled.*

After she answered her second curtain call, Genna ran offstage where Cary waited with a lightweight coat. They hustled down to Lance and the waiting car and were gone before the crowd began to leave the building. Jim and Lori would supervise the band as they packed up the equipment and stored it on the bus.

"Oh, but I'm tired, Cary. I must be getting old. These engagements exhaust me."

"You put so much of yourself into it. I watched from the wings, and you've never done so well. Seemed as if a new Genna was out there on the stage."

"Or an old Genna," she murmured.

The next morning Genna waved to her crew as they pulled out of the parking lot. She slid behind the wheel of the Mercedes and followed them for several miles. She hoped to give the appearance that she was traveling with the bus. She didn't want any fans following her, nor did she want Jim and Lori to have a clue to what she planned to do during her self-imposed leave. She spent the morning driving around the area seeing old places. When she went by the Sullivan No. 1 mine, she was surprised to see that it was closed. Most of the company houses were boarded up, and the company store, while still in operation, had few customers. In her childhood the store had always been crowded. She looked in dismay at the strip mines in the area. When she came to the crossroads that led to her childhood home on Mill Creek, she turned the car back toward the town of Logan. Too many memories in one day was more than she could handle.

She registered for a motel room under the name Genevieve Wooten and telephoned Ivy and Ben. Overjoyed to know she was in town, they would be glad to have her stay with them for a few days.

"Thanks, but if the old house is still livable, I'll hang around there."

"We've kept it just like when you were here, Veevie. You'll feel right at home," Ivy assured her.

She telephoned the attorney who handled all of her affairs in Logan County and made an appointment to see him the next day. When hunger pains made Genna realize that she hadn't eaten since breakfast, she left the motel to look for a cafe. It had been years since she'd had to think about her personal needs.

"I'll starve to death without Jim and Cary to wait on me," she said to no one in particular.

Leaving the restaurant, Genna paused with her hand on the car door. She heard heavy footsteps behind her and a sudden silence as if someone had stopped close by.

"Veevie?"

Genna gripped the side of the car for a moment, but she ignored the voice and slipped under the steering wheel, keeping her back to the speaker. She didn't have to look to know it was Evan.

He stepped closer to the car.

"Veevie?" he said again, and she steeled herself to look at him.

"Are you speaking to me?" she said, without a hint of an Appalachian accent. Her speech teacher at college had made sure of that. "My name is Genna."

She could tell by the expression on his face that she had almost convinced him he'd made a mistake. Almost, but not quite.

"I'm sorry," he said slowly. "I thought you were a friend I'd been expecting to come back to Logan County someday. Your walk and posture resembled hers, but I can see now that you don't look like her."

"Sorry to disappoint you," Genna said as she started the car's engine. She had to escape his piercing gaze.

"Did you say your name was Genna?" Evan asked, apparently reluctant to have her leave.

Genna nodded.

"Genna Ross, by any chance?"

Genna hesitated, but nodded again. She couldn't keep both identities from him.

"My daughter is quite a fan of yours, Miss Ross. She made me bring her down here from Charleston so she could hear your concert last night."

"Oh, were you at the concert?" Her heart pounded. She thought that he might hear her sing someday, though she always figured that she'd know when he was in the audience. If he had been there, he would surely have recognized the folk songs, for she sang those just as she had when she was a teenager.

"No, unfortunately, I didn't attend. I had several business deals to handle, but my daughter was very disappointed that she didn't get to meet you personally. Would you be kind enough to give me your autograph? It would make her day."

Genna reached into the backseat of the car for a large poster advertising her concert. She slashed Genna Ross in large letters across the bottom of it. Handing it to him, she said, "There, that should make her happy."

As she pulled away from the curb, she couldn't resist a peek through the rearview window. Evan stood on the sidewalk gazing after her.

Chapter Three

Delivery trucks crowded the streets of Logan at the early hour when Genna, dressed in blue sweats, slipped out of her motel room. She wiped dew from the windows of the Mercedes and drove northward a few miles through the fog to Chief Logan State Park. Stepping out of the car she sniffed the air delightedly.

Too many years in the cities, she mused. *Why did I wait so long to come home?*

Other joggers and walkers greeted her with a wave and a frequent, "Good morning!" This was Appalachia, this was home. She hadn't jogged alone in years. Although often irritated by Jim's watchdog mentality, she'd had to admit that it wasn't wise for her to run alone in the cities where they usually stayed. But for now it was good to be alone, if only just to think. During this early morning run, however, she simply concentrated on the little brook meandering through the park, the maples and poplars along the pathway, and the chatter of songbirds.

The hour she spent among God's creation seemed to awaken Genna to her spiritual needs. She remembered some words Miss Amelia used to quote: "Exalt ye the Lord our God, and worship at his footstool; for he is holy." In the last few years Genna had neglected her relationship to God. Now in the country, could she find the closeness to Him she'd once known? With Miss Amelia's help, she could. She'd be sure to visit the missionary.

The carefree run, and a brisk shower when she returned to the motel, gave Genna a vigor she hadn't known for months. Without Cary to style her hair, Genna blew it dry and let it hang loosely around her shoulders. She pushed aside most of her makeup and brushed a bit of gloss on her lips. Except for the change in hair color, she didn't look so different from Veevie Wooten. If she walked the streets of Logan looking like this, there were sure to be people who would recognize her.

Once she stepped out of this room as Veevie Wooten, it wouldn't be long before someone would also identify her as Genna Ross. The background she'd shielded so long would become common knowledge. If Evan had recognized her yesterday when he hadn't even attended her concert, many country music fans would be bound to put the two identities together.

But she'd come too far to go back now. She went to the cafe beside the motel and ordered a full breakfast. She felt as though she'd need the bacon, eggs, and hash browns to make it through the day. Coming home wasn't as pleasant as she'd anticipated.

She covered the miles from Logan to Mill Creek in less than an hour. *Guess my modern car goes a lot faster than Ben Fisher's truck*, she thought.

When she turned off the main highway to take the Mill Creek road, Genna slowed down, partly because of the rough road but also because she wanted to see everything. The Sullivan No. 2 mine was still operating, obviously the interest that kept Evan in the area. Along the seven miles between the mine and the Fisher house, Genna counted only twelve residences that seemed to be occupied. Sadly she shook her head, remembering the many neighbors they'd had when she was a child.

Ivy and Ben lived in the same spot, but she was delighted to see a new mobile home instead of the rickety house they'd had in the past. She had paid them well for taking care of her place, so perhaps she'd contributed to their improved status. Not much else had changed though, she decided, when a beagle bounded off the porch to greet her. Ben wouldn't do without his dogs.

Ivy ran out and hugged her. "Law, Veevie, but you've changed. And what's happened to your hair?"

"Now, Ivy, it costs me a lot of money to have hair this color. Don't tell me you don't like it!"

Ben joined his wife and shook Genna's hand. "It's purty," he said. "Reminds me of that singer, Genna Ross."

Even though Ben must be in his early sixties, he was a stalwart man with a winning personality. A man of unhurried calm, he'd always displayed a sense of humor.

Genna threw her arms around him. "Oh, Ben, you remind me so much of Grandpap."

"Come on in, Veevie," Ivy invited.

"Say, I like your new home. You people are more prosperous than you used to be."

"After Ben lost his job in the mine, we had some hard times, but he took up carpentry and he's made a good livin' at that."

"Tell me the news," Genna invited. "What's going on around here?"

"I suppose you noticed the empty houses as you came up the creek."

"Yes. How long has Sullivan No. 1 been closed?"

"About five years. There ain't as much demand for coal as there once was. Our governor and senators are always tryin' to find new markets, and they've found some, but not enough to save the Sullivan mines. All of them have closed down except Sullivan No. 2 at the bottom of the hollow."

Genna's pulse quickened. "Then I don't suppose you see much of the Sullivans in Logan County."

"Evan Sullivan is around once in a while, seein' as he's still got some business interests here. That boy has had all kind of bad luck. I feel kinda sorry for him. He was always a good sort," Ben said.

"What's happened to him?" Genna asked, trying to sound casual in her questioning, but Ivy cast a speculative glance in her direction.

"First of all, his father died and left the business to him just about the time the mines began to close. Then, two or three years ago, his wife was killed in a car wreck that left him with a kid to raise," Ben said.

Genna's hands tightened on the arms of the chair. She wanted to hear more, but emotion choked her and she changed the subject.

"What about the old home place? Do you think it's good enough for me to spend a few days there?"

"Hit ain't no mansion, Veevie. Never was, you know, but if you want to batch a little, no reason you couldn't," Ben said. "Still just got three rooms."

"You'd best eat with us, though," Ivy invited. "You're nuthin' but skin and bones."

"Unfortunately, I weigh more than I used to."

After lunch, Genna said, "I'll go up to the cabin now, if you'll let me have the key."

"You'd better not take that fancy car up there," Ben said. "Since nobody lives beyond here, the road ain't maintained. You can borrow my truck."

"My car isn't as fragile as you think. I'll drive slowly." She felt suddenly reluctant to visit her old home, and she went first to the family cemetery in the hollow behind the house. Ben had kept the small plot mowed, so Genna had no trouble finding Grandpap's grave, or that of her mother.

She stepped up on the front porch at last, and her hand trembled as she fitted the key into the lock. She'd had the lock installed before she left for California; the door had never been locked in Grandpap's day. Nothing had changed inside the house, except for its emptiness. Genna sat in Grandpap's old chair and the tears flowed, taking with them much of the bitterness she'd harbored.

Going to the car, she put on her jogging shoes. Stuffing a package of cheese crackers and a can of cola in a sack, she headed toward Pinnacle Rock. Beset by greedy briers and fallen logs, she had a hard time keeping on the path. Loose rocks rolled under her feet, causing her to stumble. No one had traveled that way for a long time. Panting from exertion, she eventually came to the huge boulder. Even here changes greeted her. The oak tree had finally succeeded in cracking the rock and a large portion of it had tumbled down the mountainside. The rest of the rock looked as if it would endure forever.

She gasped audibly when she looked at the mountains across the creek. Brown and barren, strip miners had denuded the mountaintops of their crowning foliage. Of all the changes in her life, this one seemed the hardest to take. She had dreamed about this spot all of the years she'd been away, believing that despite the world's mercurial nature, Pinnacle Mountain and its surroundings would remain the same.

She lay back against the rock and sobbed as the past pulled at her heartstrings.

What had the Psalmist said? "I lift up my eyes to the hills—where does my help come from? My help comes from the Lord, the Maker of heaven and earth."

As much as she loved the hills, she knew that they were temporal things and no strength could be gained from them. She'd long known that only God could supply her needs, but she'd allowed herself to lose contact with Him.

A sound behind her startled Genna out of her reverie and she turned quickly, swiping at her eyes.

Evan Sullivan looked at her reproachfully. "So it was you. Why did you lie to me?"

"I don't remember our conversation exactly, but I don't believe I lied. I am Genna Ross now."

She turned away from him, overcome by sadness and yearning. She still longed for him, and having learned this morning that he no longer had a wife made a difference. But she mustn't forget how he'd wronged her years ago.

Without an invitation, Evan climbed to sit beside her on the rock. "You've come a long way, Veevie, from the last time I saw you here. I'd like to hear about it."

"Grandpap knew that he wouldn't live very long after he contracted black lung, and he made provisions for me. He made me promise lots of things before he died, and one of them was that I'd go to live with my Cousin Bea in California. Grandpap never spent much money, and when the mines were going strong he'd made good wages. He put his savings in a trust fund for me. I didn't want to leave the mountains, but I was alone and didn't have much choice."

"It was several months before I heard your grandfather had died. I would have helped you if I'd known."

Genna stared at him with hostile green eyes, and Evan's face flushed.

"When I got to California, even though I'd graduated from high school, Cousin Bea hired a tutor for a year to take off my rough edges. You'll remember, I had lots of them; you'd pointed that out to me."

Genna ignored the plea in Evan's eyes and continued, her voice growing more harsh the longer she spoke.

"She knew that I'd never make it through college without learning better grammar and some basic subjects I'd not had. I went through four years of college, and right from the first, I excelled in drama. I starred in several college productions, and in my senior year, a talent scout spotted me and thought I had the capability to achieve success as a singer. He was right, and in about six months, Genna Ross was born. My advisors considered 'Veevie Wooten' a handicap, so I adopted a stage name. Genna is a derivative of Genevieve as Veevie had been."

"I'm not a country music fan, so I haven't followed your career, but what puzzles me is why no one in Logan County guessed who you are."

Genna shrugged her shoulders. "I've not kept in touch with anyone here except Ben and Ivy, and I've never told them about my career. Cousin Bea died the year I graduated from college, so her family didn't know what I was doing. A lawyer in Logan has handled my trust account, and I contact him periodically. In all my local business transactions I use the name Genevieve Wooten."

"Looks like you covered your tracks very well," Evan observed."

Genna nodded and set the crackers and drink on the rock. "Want to share my snack?"

"Kinda like old times, don't you think?" He smiled, but Genna ignored his comment.

"I've been surprised myself," she continued. "It would be like some magazine writer to uproot my past, but I haven't given them any leads. By the time I'd started my career, I'd lost my mountain talk. A few good drama teachers had taken away my Appalachian colloquialisms, so I couldn't be traced to the hills that way."

"Then why come back now? If you stay around here, your past will be revealed."

"When I received the invitation to perform that benefit show, I remembered how Grandpap had suffered from black lung. I decided to come back for that, and the nearer the time came, the more I longed to be home again. Afterward I sent my crew back to Nashville. I wanted to be alone."

"But what if you're recognized? Are you ashamed of what you used to be?"

She turned on him angrily. "I was never ashamed of what I was. I've never been ashamed of Grandpap. It was the dread of seeing you, Evan, that prevented me from returning, kept me from revealing my roots. But now that I've been unfortunate enough to encounter you, I'm going to burn all of my bridges behind me. I'm ready to reveal my dual life. My fans won't hold it against me that I'm a moonshiner's granddaughter, that I used to say 'hit,' 'ain't,' and 'you-all.' "

"That's a strike below the belt, Veevie. I suppose you still haven't forgiven me?"

"I suppose I haven't. Would you expect me to?"

She stood up. "Time to get off of this mountain before nightfall. As you probably discovered, the trail isn't in good shape. Nobody else has wanted to use it, I guess."

"I came up here for several years, hoping you'd come back, but I finally gave up."

Without answering, she started down the mountain with Evan following silently behind her. His truck was parked beside her Mercedes at the cabin.

"Veevie, I wish you'd give me a chance to explain. I wanted to ten years ago when you ran away. I tried for months to trace you, asked everyone in Logan County I could think of."

"You must not have asked the right persons. A few people knew where I was, but it was too late to explain then anyway."

"Will you listen to my explanation now?"

"Come in, if you want to. Sorry I can't offer you any food. I brought only a few things with me and I won't be here long. Let's sit on the porch."

They sat silently for several minutes. The sun's orb hovered over the mountain peak and long shadows fell across the yard. Genna heard a fish flip-flop in Mill Creek. A robin hopped pertly through the grass, only to stop abruptly before pulling a struggling worm from the ground.

Genna wished that her heart would stop racing as she gazed intently on her stage-perfect manicure. She couldn't look at Evan. *Why couldn't she overcome the attraction this man held for her?* But Genna was an actress, and she willed her hands to relax on the chair arms as she rocked serenely in Grandpap's old rocker.

"Do you know that my wife is no longer living?"

"Cousin Ivy mentioned that this morning. Otherwise, I'd not have listened to you at all."

"When I left you on your sixteenth birthday, I had no idea but to come back to see you, but all kinds of things happened. I went away to school and didn't come home very often."

"Had your father learned about me, and that's the reason he kept you away?"

"Probably. But the longer I went without seeing you, I began to forget, and I started dating Marsha. She was the kind of woman Dad thought I should marry, and before I knew it, I was engaged to her. By that time, Dad wanted me in the business with him, and we married and moved to Charleston."

"So you patterned your life the way your father wanted it?"

"I suppose so. Gradually, my memories of you faded into the background. My marriage wasn't happy, but I blamed no one but myself. Marsha hated the hills. The only happy part of that marriage is my child, Michelle. I didn't love my wife, but I love my daughter."

"Is that your explanation then? All you have to say for yourself?"

"There isn't much else I can say except to ask your forgiveness. The need to do that has haunted me for years."

"Forgive you? Yes, I suppose I do. I forgive you for marrying someone else. You had a perfect right to do that, but I do think you could have told me and not left me to find out in a most embarrassing manner. The least you could have done was to have told me."

Genna tried to control her voice, but in spite of herself, all of the bitterness came rushing out unharnessed.

"I was ashamed to write to you, Veevie. I thought that you must have found out some other way. You didn't write to me or make any move to keep in touch. I wrote you one letter after I went to California, but you didn't answer it."

"No, because I didn't want to annoy you with my lack of education. I spent two years trying to make myself suitable for you. Grandpap used his precious money to straighten my teeth. I studied hard, had Miss Amelia, the missionary, help me with my grammar, tried so hard to be the kind of person you wanted. Even after a silence of two years, I hoped you hadn't changed, that you still wanted me. Then I came to your office to be confronted with the truth."

Evan left his chair and wandered to the edge of the porch, putting his arm around one of the posts. His other hand nervously jingled the change in his pocket.

"Put that way, the bald truth sounds pretty bad, and I don't blame you for feeling bitter, Veevie. I've never blamed you. Right from the first, I've placed all the blame on myself, but that doesn't make my guilt any easier to live with."

Genna rose slowly, finding she had to lean against the rocker for support.

"Evan, I thank you for the explanation. You've done what you wanted to do and I really think that's all we have to say to each other. I don't have any desire to resurrect the past. In a few days I'll be leaving here, and I don't know when, if ever, I'll return. I have a busy winter concert schedule."

He turned toward her and, thinking she might never see him again, Genna looked intently at the close-cropped beard and the gray eyes that seemed hooded with grief. His youthful face had haunted her for years; this time, she'd have the picture of a mature Evan to carry with her.

"You may not have anything more to say to me, my dear, but I haven't finished. The love I had for you when you were a girl has never changed. It was only after you were gone that I realized how much I cherished you, how much I'd lost. Ten years of loneliness hasn't cured me of that. I'm not sure anything will ever change the way I feel about you. Good night, Veevie."

Genna sat on the top step of the cabin porch for a long time after Evan left. The sound of katydids droned in her ears and lightning bugs flitted through the darkness. Dry-eyed, she finally trudged into the house and prepared for bed, but she lay until morning without any thought of sleep. Evan wasn't the only one who realized how much had been lost.

Chapter Four

"Okay, Cary. I'm awake," Genna mumbled, but the pounding on the door continued. She blinked her eyes a few times and realized that she had awakened at the old homestead.

Struggling out of the feather bed, she threw a robe over her gown and rushed to the door. A burly man wearing a hard hat was poised on the edge of the porch. He turned, bug-eyed, when Genna appeared.

Genna's eyes swept the yard crowded with two dump trucks, an end-loader, and a bulldozer. Several men stood beside her car peering at the interior. She stared at a sign nailed to a porch post.

CONDEMNED. NO TRESPASSING, STAY OUT!

"What do you mean by putting that sign on my house?" she shouted. Reminding herself of Grandpap, she tore the cardboard off the post and threw it on the ground.

"Ma'am, we were told this house was vacant, but I wondered what that Mercedes was doing out here in the yard."

"Don't evade the question. Why did you nail up that sign? What's all this machinery doing on my property?"

"I'm a foreman for the Keystone Mining Company. We're starting to mine in this hollow. This house is in the way of our operations and we have to destroy it to make a road for our mining equipment."

"Over my dead body, you'll strip that hollow." She ran back into the house and returned with Grandpap's shotgun. "Or over your dead body! This property will never be strip-mined. Move that equipment out of here immediately!"

"Now, ma'am, listen to reason."

Genna lifted the gun and fired into the air above the man's head.

Good old Grandpap! He always kept a shell in this gun. Genna rubbed her arm where the gun had kicked her. *I'll sure get chewed out by Cary if that leaves a bruise,* she thought.

The workers scattered like quail and the foreman jumped inside a pickup. "I'm going to get the sheriff. You ain't got no reason to shoot at me. This property was sold for back taxes."

Genna darted into the house, threw on a sweatshirt and a pair of jeans and picked up her purse, then ran across the yard to the Mercedes. As she dashed away, she called out the window. "I'm going to call the sheriff myself. Don't touch one thing on this property or you'll live to regret it."

At a speed too fast for the unimproved road, she rushed the mile to Ivy's house. Ben must have seen her coming and he met her on the porch.

"What's up, Veevie?"

"There's a group of miners up at the house saying they've bought the property and are going to start stripping there. I want to call my lawyer. Let me use your phone."

"He won't be in his office this early."

"I'll call him at home then. I promised Grandpap that I'd never let his property be strip-mined." Her fingers trembled until she had trouble dialing the numbers.

"Mr. Blankenship," she said when a sleepy voice answered the phone. "This is Genevieve Wooten, and I'm in trouble." Breathlessly, she explained about her early morning visitors.

"That's impossible, Miss Wooten. I've paid those taxes faithfully from your trust fund, just as you instructed me."

"Then will you take steps immediately to stop them? Bring the sheriff out here and halt these workers until we can find out the mistake. Grandpap will turn over in his grave if they lift one shovel of dirt."

"I'll be out in an hour. Can you keep them from starting until then?"

"Yes. I've already peppered one of them with a shotgun blast. I figure there's some more shells around someplace."

"Veevie," Ben said when she hung up the phone, "you don't mean you shot at them fellers. That old gun of your grandpap's always hits the mark." Ivy pushed a cup of coffee into Genna's hand.

"I shot over his head." She sipped a little of the coffee and handed the cup back to Ivy. "Come with me, Ben. I may need some help until Mr. Blankenship arrives. I took them by surprise, but if they use force, there isn't much I can do against five men."

"Yeah, I'll go. Wait'll I get my gun."

Genna looked in the mirror over the couch. Her disheveled blond hair scattered over her shoulders and her sleepy eyes looked small without makeup. No one could possibly mistake her for Genna Ross the way she looked now, she thought wryly.

Ben climbed into the passenger seat of the Mercedes and held on to the dashboard when Genna lurched out of his yard.

"Do you always drive this fast, Veevie?"

The goldenrod blooming along the road turned into a blurred yellow streak as she floored the accelerator.

"Only when I'm in a hurry. Lance would have a fit if he saw me treating the car this way, but he didn't pay for it."

"Who's Lance? Did you get married while you've been away?"

"No, I'm not married. Lance is my chauffeur."

Ben whistled. "You got a chauffeur? You've gone up in the world since we've seen you."

"I've gone up far enough that I don't intend to let some thief steal my property."

The five men were huddled together in front of a dump truck when Genna rounded the bend. By the time she stopped her car, they were in the vehicles with the windows closed. Genna pecked on the window of the foreman's pickup. He lowered the window a crack.

"My lawyer and the sheriff are on their way out here. Don't you make a move until then," Genna cautioned him.

Ben settled himself on the porch step, his rifle over his knees. "Go freshen up, Veevie. I'll stop the critters if they try any funny stuff."

Genna hurried inside and twisted her billowing hair into a barrette. Noting from the window that Ben still had things under control, she sat at the kitchen table in an attempt to still her trembling knees.

A sweet roll and a container of orange juice wasn't much of a breakfast, but it did soothe her spirit. When she went back to the porch, she picked up Grandpap's gun and joined Ben on the steps.

They stayed seated when a sheriff's car drove in behind the mining equipment. George Blankenship stepped from the car with a deputy sheriff behind him and together they approached the house.

"You two are looking warlike."

The Keystone foreman ventured out of the truck. "That woman shot at me. I want her arrested."

"You can't have a woman arrested for protecting her property," Blankenship said, looking sternly at the man. "Where's your deed for this property?"

"I can't carry a deed around in my pocket. The Keystone Mining Company has bought up the land on the east side of the mountain, and I was sent to start work. Here are my orders and the survey of the land."

After flipping through the papers the foreman handed him, Blankenship said, "This property is included in your orders all right, but somebody has made a mistake. I've paid the taxes on this place for ten years and I have the receipts to prove it but they're in the bank vault. I can't get in there on Saturday, and the courthouse is closed too. I did contact the county judge, however, and he issued a temporary restraining order to stop this work for a week until we get the matter straightened out."

The Keystone employee appealed to the deputy. "Does that mean we can't work today?"

The deputy nodded. "Not today, not for a week."

"Can we leave this machinery here until then?"

"No," Genna said. "I came home for a visit to enjoy myself. I can't do it if I see that machinery. Move it now."

The man swore under his breath and turned on his heel. After a conference with his men, he motioned them to follow him and they rattled noisily down the road.

"Thanks, Mr. Blankenship. I'm sorry to bother you, but you know what Grandpap thought of strip miners. I sure am glad that I happened to be home. What next?"

"I'll arrange a meeting with the management of the Keystone Mining Company to prove we're in our rights. These men," he motioned to the departing workers, "can't make any decisions. They're only following orders. Will you be around a few days?"

"Yes, at least until we get this straightened out."

"I'll set the appointment as early in the week as possible."

"Leave word with Ben; I'll check there."

Watching Blankenship and the deputy leaving, Ben laid his gun aside. "Well, you won that round."

Genna didn't answer, but she felt Ben's keen glance on her. He smiled slightly. "Veevie, I've been puttin' two and two together, and though Ivy says I'm crazy, I've come up with an answer. How far wrong would I be if I added Veevie Wooten and your sudden appearance back in Logan County, and came up with the answer, Genna Ross?"

Genna stretched her long legs and looked out over the hollow, peaceful once more now that the mining equipment was gone.

"I'd have to give you an A plus, Ben."

"Just what I figgered. Ivy and me went to that benefit show over in Woodville three nights ago. All the time you was performin', I thought you seemed familiar, 'specially when you sung them mountain songs. 'Course I'd seen you on television a few times and then your picture is always on your records. I knew hit was farfetched, but when you showed up here a couple days after the concert, I thought hit had to be you. Why haven't you told us? People in Logan County would have been mighty proud to know one of our own had gone to the top. How come you changed your name?"

Genna shrugged her shoulders. "Many singers take stage names, and I liked the sound of Genna Ross. I've always kept my real name on legal papers, and I use it when I correspond with Blankenship. He knows my professional name, but I suppose he guarded that as an attorney-client confidence."

"We won't say anything if you don't want hit known. I thought maybe you was kinda ashamed of your kin here at home."

"No, that isn't true. I don't intend to hide my past any longer. Reporters love this kind of story. Once they learn about my rags to riches background, they'll spread it everywhere and I'll get lots of free publicity. I knew when I came back here my roots would probably be revealed, but Ben, I was homesick."

He patted her on the shoulder. "Becomin' rich and famous hasn't made you happy then?"

Tears glistened in her eyes, and she wiped them away angrily. "No, it hasn't.

Someplace along the way I've lost more than I've gained. I don't know that I'm searching for happiness, but I would like to know serenity and peace of mind again. I believe I could find it here."

"Why don't you stay with us a while? These old hills have helped more than one person get a right outlook on life."

"Ben, I can't stay long this time. I've a full schedule for the next six months. My business manager had a fit when I told him I was taking this two-week vacation. Last night when I couldn't sleep I made some decisions. I'm coming back home."

"Good for you, Veevie, or should I call you Genna now?"

"I don't much care. Last night I had a longing to be here in the springtime—to watch the serviceberry trees herald the coming of spring, to walk in the woods and see the blooming dogwood, the redbud blossoms, to listen to the whippoorwills."

"Hit's a good time to be in this hollow."

"I'm booked through next March, but I'll tell Jim not to schedule anything for the spring months. The first of April, I'm coming home for an extended stay." She patted the post beside her. "Do you think we could make this old cabin more livable—add a bathroom, put in central heat, and the like?"

Ben walked around the house with her and helped her make plans. "I wouldn't want to change the structure of the house, but I could insulate it and put vinyl siding on the exterior, and maybe panel the three downstairs rooms. There's pretty kitchen paneling available now, as well as woodgrains for the other two rooms. We could put in electric baseboard heat too."

"Yes, but I'd still want to retain the old fireplace. I spent some cozy times in front of it with Grandpap." *And Evan, too,* her conscience tormented her.

"Here in the back, you could build a new room for a bath without changing the looks of the place."

They wandered back to the spring house and Genna stuck her head into the damp interior. She filled a tin cup full of the cold liquid that had dribbled into a tank imbedded in the dirt floor.

"Don't suppose I'd have any trouble with the water supply?"

"Nope, that water has been seepin' out of Pinnacle Mountain since I first remember. Hit'll always be there."

"If the Keystone Company doesn't ruin it when they start stripping the east side of the mountain," Genna added bitterly.

"Might happen," Ben agreed, "but let's hope not. You could put a little pump here in the spring house, and with a few feet of pipe laid underground you'd be in good shape."

"I'd keep most of the old furniture, but I'm going to discard that feather tick for a waterbed. It will take fifteen minutes every morning to get the kinks out of my back after a night spent in that bed."

Ben laughed. "Years ago when we didn't know any better, we thought a feather bed was a luxury. I slept on a cornhusk mattress when I was a youngun. You keep wantin' to revive the past, Veevie, but all of it wasn't good."

"I'm finding that out the more I remember."

"Want us to do this remodelin' for you next winter while you're gone—have it all ready when you come in the spring?"

"No, I think not. I want the fun of doing it myself."

"I'd better head back down to the house or Ivy will think we've been hauled off to jail."

"I'll drive you, but I don't want to be away from here too long—I still don't trust the Keystone Company."

"I think that restrainin' order will hold them off all right, but I can see your point. If you're gone, I'll keep an eye open. They won't bring that equipment up this creek without me seein' them."

"Ben, I've been wanting to ask, is the missionary Miss Amelia still around here? I don't want to leave without seeing her."

"Yeah, she's still rattlin' around these hollers in her old VW visitin' saints and sinners alike. You'll find her in the same place."

After leaving Ben at home Genna drove on down the hollow to Miss Amelia's small cottage.

Of all the former places and people Genna had seen so far, Amelia Dixon had changed the least. Short and lean as ever but still spry, Miss Amelia was blessed with the keenest blue eyes Genna had ever seen. Amelia said warmly, "Veevie! I thought you'd never come to see us again. Come in."

The living room was cluttered with the many items Miss Amelia had accumulated through the years. Genna walked around the room, touched the keys of the upright piano, and moved her hands along the replica of the praying hands on the mantle. On the end table beside Miss Amelia's recliner the familiar, well-worn King James Bible had been replaced by a modern translation—the only evidence of the passage of time.

Perhaps sensing that Genna was having trouble controlling her emotions, Amelia allowed her to browse in silence.

With a wistful smile, Genna sat on the stool beside Amelia's chair. "So at last I've found something that's unchangeable. Miss Amelia, I feel as if I've come home at last."

"When you've changed so much, you have no right to expect everything else to remain static. You've been gone a long time. Are you home to stay, Veevie?"

Genna shook her head and, at Amelia's invitation, launched into a full description of her life in California and her rise to fame. She paused only when Amelia handed her a cup of hot tea.

But Amelia, like Ben, had read the hidden meaning of Genna's story. "So you've acquired everything but happiness?"

With eyes downcast, Genna nodded. "Can you give me words from that to fill the void I have?" She motioned to the Bible. "You always used to do that. More than once I've come here disheartened and you said the magic words that perked me up again."

Miss Amelia's hand moved toward the Bible, but first she lifted Genna's head, forcing her to look into her eyes. Genna flushed, happy that she had nothing to hide from that piercing gaze.

"So you've stayed decent then? I had to know."

"Yes," Genna said simply.

"Forgive me for being rude, but out in the world where you were, it must have been quite a struggle to live morally pure."

Genna shook her head. "On the contrary. Not once during the building of my career have I ever felt any temptation to do otherwise. I've had many offers, but the temptation wasn't there."

Genna had phrased those words carefully. They were true during the building of her career, but Evan had tempted her. She had never forgotten her feelings for him and no one since Evan had rekindled them.

"So much for your morality—what about your spiritual life?"

Miss Amelia had always been one to drive right to the heart of a matter; Genna complied with a direct answer. "I haven't been to church since Bea died, Miss Amelia. When we're out on tour, usually we travel all day on Sunday. Weekends are the busiest time for us. I'm not using that as an excuse. It was just easy to stop going."

"Yet you're looking for that which is unchanged, when the greatest change in you is the neglect of your faith." Genna nodded. "And I seem to remember that someplace in the Bible, it says, 'I am the Lord, I change not.'"

"Yes, that's in Malachi. Seems to me, Veevie, that all you've achieved has been a gift from God, and I feel He must be disappointed in how you've neglected Him. If you don't have time for spiritual growth, you're too busy."

Genna nodded. "I know. I need one of your down-to-earth sermons. I think that's one reason I had to revisit the hills. It's as though I'd lost something that I can only regain here, but I can see now that I won't find it right away. I took a long time going away from the Lord; I have to work my way back. Will you pray for me?"

"I always do, Genna." She smiled as she took Genna's hand. "It's going to be hard to remember the new name."

"Doesn't matter. It's rather nice to hear Veevie again."

"Let's pray now before you go." Genna knelt beside the chair and felt the missionary's hands on her hair. The years retracted and she was a teenager again, hurt by Evan's rejection, suffering from insults by her peers, longing for a day of reckoning. That day had come now, she supposed, but somehow it wasn't as sweet as she had thought it might be.

While she still knelt, Miss Amelia said, "You wanted a Bible verse: 'Do not conform any longer to the pattern of this world, but be transformed by the renewing of your mind. Then you will be able to test and approve what God's will is—his good, pleasing and perfect will.'"

Genna's eyes misted when she stood up.

"Go to church with me tomorrow," Miss Amelia invited.

Genna hesitated a bit. *Was she ready for that*? But she agreed. "Where will we go?"

"To Bethel, of course. You'll see a few people you know, but there are some changes too."

A brick church, complete with factory-built pews, had replaced the small wooden structure with its rustic hand-hewn benches. A carpeted area housed a pulpit and a communion table. The old upright piano had been abandoned for a spinet. Nothing seemed familiar to Genna as she prepared her heart for the pastor's message. His text from Isaiah 58:12, however, proved significant: "Your people will rebuild the ancient ruins and will raise up the age-old foundations."

Her foundations hadn't been destroyed, but she needed to rebuild her spiritual values. While the pastor talked, she tried to reason out those foundations that had once sustained her spiritually.

Ben hailed her when she approached the Fisher home after leaving the church. She pulled over and he stuck his head into the car window. "Ivy's got a picnic lunch packed. Go home and change your clothes and we'll come for you in the truck."

Genna hurried into her jeans and sweatshirt and waited on the porch when Ben drove into the yard. When Ivy scooted over and made room for Genna, Genna said, "No, I want to ride in the back. It will be more like old times."

She stepped on the bumper and jumped into the pickup bed, dodged a weed trimmer, picnic basket, and thermos jug, and leaned back against the truck's cab.

"Hold on," Ben called. "We're goin' to the head of the holler, and hit's a rough road."

A haze hung over the area, a sure sign of Indian summer, and a flock of bluejays began squawking their displeasure at this human invasion of their sanctuary. Not many vehicles traveled this old road anymore, Genna surmised, although it had been a busy area when the coal mine at the head of the hollow had operated.

That had been the mine where Grandpap had last worked, but it closed about the time he'd had to retire. A few more years and there would be nothing left of the thriving coal operation of twenty years ago.

Ben gunned the engine and the pickup climbed steadily along the side of Pinnacle Mountain. Genna strained her eyes to see the rock outcropping where she and Evan had met on Friday but they were too close to the base of the mountain. Ben stopped the truck near the edge of the lake. Even here decay had set in. The picnic tables were barely visible in a field of blooming sunflowers, wingstems, and goldenrod.

"Doesn't anyone use this anymore?"

"There's no one around to use it. Very few young people live on Mill Creek now and them that do have cars. Hit's more fun to go to Logan or to stay home and watch videos than to come skatin' or swimmin' at this old dam," Ivy said.

Ben took the weed trimmer from the truck. "I'll cut the weeds away from one of the tables. We don't want a rattler picnickin' with us, or if he does, I want to see him first."

"We knew the place had run down, but we thought you might enjoy a picnic like we used to have."

"We did have some good times, Ivy, and I want you to know I appreciate how good you were to Grandpap and me. You helped us pass many a lonely Sunday by bringing us here on picnics."

Genna walked around the lake on a deer trail while Ivy and Ben prepared the lunch table. Runoff water from the mountain had collected through the years behind an impoundment that the mine company had built out of refuse from the mine. At this point Mill Creek was formed by two mountain streams, and the mining company had dammed the left-hand fork by dumping slag from the mine. For every load of coal they removed from underground, the miners also brought out slag—a mixture of shale, clay, and mine dust.

The miners needed a place to dispose of this refuse, and since a supply of water was required to clean the coal, the impoundment served two purposes—disposal for the slag, and from that, collection of the water they needed.

Genna paused on the crest of the fifteen-foot-high impoundment. While the mine operated, the water had been too dirty for any recreational purpose; once the mine had closed, however, the impurities had settled to the bottom. Although the coal company, which still owned the site, had put up No TRESPASSING signs, local residents had eventually built picnic tables on the sides of the lake. Most residents were afraid to swim in the water, but in winter, skaters had often built bonfires on the banks and spent many a cold evening sliding over the frozen lake.

Ben joined Genna. "I wish they'd destroy this thing—let the water out gradually. I've been afeared of it ever since that Buffalo Creek disaster a few years ago."

Genna remembered distinctly that February day in 1972. A forty-five-foot-high impoundment had broken at the head of Buffalo Creek spilling a twenty-acre lake down the valley. Several towns had been destroyed with a loss of 125 lives. Ben, who'd helped with the rescue efforts, had never forgotten those shattering days, and the memories caused him to be wary of the hundreds of other such impoundments scattered throughout mining country.

Genna glanced at the water behind them. "There's not as much water here as in the impoundments on Buffalo Creek."

"No, but the conditions are the same. This dam rests on a spongy base of silt and sludge, and though the water looks clear enough now, there's all kinds of junk on the bottom of that lake—metal and wooden refuse from the mines. In winter, when we've had lots of rain, this whole dam is squishy."

"Who's responsible for maintaining it?"

"The mine company still owns the land, but hit's hard to get them to do anything. We've approached the state and federal agencies, but hit's one of those situations where people pass the buck. I am goin' to call someone about that soft spot over there." He motioned toward their right, where oozing water had soaked one portion of the dam.

Genna locked her arm through his. "It won't collapse today," she said brightly, "so let's enjoy our picnic."

"That's what everybody says—just keep puttin' hit off another day. One of these days hit'll be too late," Ben grumbled. His face etched in worry, he good-naturedly let Genna propel him toward the picnic table where he helped himself to Ivy's spread of fried chicken, baked beans, and potato salad.

Chapter Five

The next morning, still wallowing in nostalgia, Genna climbed the narrow steps to the loft room that had been her bedroom when she was a girl. She removed the curtain from the one small window and lighted the oil lamp on the dresser. Ivy must clean the room often, she thought, as the feather tick on the twin bed was neatly fashioned and not a speck of dust or dirt was evident.

Genna pulled the curtain away from the closet. The clothes she'd left behind when she went to California still hung there. She lifted the white dress she'd bought to wear to the senior prom, hoping Evan would come back and serve as her escort. She'd never worn the dress. She smiled wryly as she compared these garments with the designer clothes she now wore.

In a dresser drawer Genna found some pictures she'd cherished years ago. The top photo of a smiling brunette elicited a delighted response. "Angela Minton! I haven't thought of her for years."

Angela had been Veevie's only close friend. Her father had worked at the Miller mine and then had moved on to work for the Sullivans when they started mining operations in the county. Angela had been Veevie's confidante, and the only person to whom she'd revealed her love for Evan. Because Angela's father had once been in prison, she was outside the pale of society, too, so the two girls had comforted one another. They'd corresponded for a year or so after she left, but she hadn't had any contact with her friend for a long time.

When Genna went to the Fishers' for lunch, she asked, "What ever happened to Angela Minton? I found a picture of her today and it sure brought back memories."

"It should have," Ben said. "A feller would be hard put to find two more giggly girls."

"She lives in Woodville," Ivy answered, ignoring Ben's comment. "She's Angela Keefer now."

"Maybe I'll go and see her this afternoon."

"She works someplace, so you'd better wait until after supper."

Genna contemplated a visit with her friend most of the afternoon. Following Ben's directions, she drove into Woodville about four o'clock and found Angela's residence. The one-story frame house was freshly painted white and green shutters framed the windows. The grass had been cut recently and flowers were attractively grouped around the yard.

Angela wasn't home yet so Genna rolled down the window of the car and waited. She'd been there about an hour when a blue Chevrolet pulled into the driveway. The woman who emerged looked inquiringly at the Mercedes parked in front of her house.

It's Angela all right, Genna laughed to herself, as she hurried from her car to Angela's side. "Do you remember me? I'm Veevie Wooten."

"You can't be," Angela said. "If you tell me you're Genna Ross, I'll believe that."

Genna could tell that Angela wasn't joking; she really didn't recognize her childhood friend.

"Don't you remember the time we stayed all night with Ben and Ivy, and after they went to sleep, we slipped out and went skinny-dipping in the creek?"

Angela laughed. "You must be Veevie! We didn't tell anyone else about that. Come on in."

"Are you too busy for us to talk over old times this evening? I could go buy a pizza for dinner."

"I have to leave around seven o'clock, but we can visit until then. While you go after the pizza, I'll change my clothes and make a salad. Iced tea sound good to you?"

"Yes, that's fine. Is your tea as good as what Ivy used to prepare when we went on picnics?"

"Probably not. I've learned that most foods don't taste as good as they did when we were children."

When Genna returned with the pizza, she said, "Angela, I must tell you the truth first. When you said I was Genna Ross, well, you were right."

Angela set down the pitcher of iced tea with a thud. "I didn't see how I could be mistaken. I saw your show last week, and I recognized you instantly when you got out of the car. I've thought of you so often, Veevie, and wondered what had happened to you."

She burst into laughter when she brought the rotary cutter to divide the pizza.

"What's so funny?"

"I suddenly remembered what they wrote about you in the class prophecy—that in ten years, you'd be working as a waitress in Bob's Bar and Grill."

"If I remember, you didn't receive a glowing prophecy for the future either."

"No, I was to marry a miner and have five children."

"Well, how far wrong is that prediction? What have you been up to since I've seen you?"

"After our graduation, I was at loose ends for a while. I wanted to go to business school but Dad was out of work and we had no money. But Miss Amelia, bless her heart, scurried around and secured some grants for me and I went to college, majoring in business administration and music."

"I remember that you always played the piano for our sing-alongs with Miss Amelia."

"She'd given me enough lessons that I had sufficient background to enroll in advanced music classes."

"What are you doing now?"

"I give private piano lessons and play the organ at the Methodist church. To make a living, I'm the business administrator at the hospital."

"No husband?"

"My husband died two years ago with cancer. We had no children. Now tell me everything about yourself."

Since it was apparent that Angela was interested in her career, Genna talked at length about her accomplishments.

Once Angela interrupted with a smile. "I don't hear anything about any romantic attachments—hasn't the great Genna Ross broken lots of hearts?"

Genna bit her lip and shook her head.

"You've never gotten over Evan, have you?" Angela said keenly. "The way you loved him was almost an obsession. I didn't think you'd ever forget him. By the way, have you seen Evan?"

"Yes, unfortunately! He's the reason I haven't come home before this. I thought I could avoid him this one time, but as luck would have it, I've seen him twice."

"Hey, I just thought of this—that's the reason you wrote 'One-man Woman.'"

"Yes, I had him in mind when I was writing. The same way with a new song to be released soon, 'Why Do I Love Him?' I hoped writing about him would make the past go away, but you can see it didn't work." Suddenly Genna glanced at her watch. "It's half past six, Angela. I've got to go or you'll be late for your appointment."

"Why don't you come with me? Miss Amelia and I are going to a little church up in Pickett Hollow for an evening service. The congregation doesn't have a preacher, so Miss Amelia goes up each Monday evening for Bible study. I go along to provide the music."

Genna glanced down at her jeans. "What about my clothes?"

"Everybody dresses casually these days. I'm wearing slacks, too."

Miss Amelia arrived in her VW about fifteen minutes later, and she smiled when she saw Genna and Angela together.

"Just like old times. I meant to tell you Sunday that Angela still lived in the area. I'm going to expect a song out of you, Genna."

"I don't know what it would be. I never sing church songs."

"High time you did then," Miss Amelia said crisply. "You can find something in one of the hymnals."

Genna took the back seat and watched with interest as Miss Amelia drove north out of Woodville. After a couple of miles, she left the paved road and wound her way up a small creek valley. Fifteen minutes later, she stopped beside a white frame church perched on the side of a hill.

When they entered the building, Genna was taken back to the sanctuary of her childhood. The room was sparsely furnished with a few wooden benches and an old, battered pulpit. When Angela ran her hands across the stained keys of the old upright, Genna noted the piano was sadly in need of tuning.

The congregation was small, but what they lacked in numbers, they made up in enthusiasm. Genna joined them in their joyful singing of hymns she hadn't heard for years. "I Saw The Light," "When The Roll Is Called Up Yonder," and "Sweet By and By" rolled off her tongue as easily as if she'd sung them yesterday.

Knowing that Miss Amelia intended for her to sing during the testimony meeting, Genna leafed through the pages of the tattered hymnal. When the missionary introduced her, Genna had decided on "Where Could I Go?"

She gave the words a Genna Ross flavor and the worshipers sat spellbound. She tried her best not to make it a performance but strictly a song of worship. On the way home Genna sat quietly remembering the words of the chorus. The Psalmist had lifted his eyes to the hills, but where could she turn for help? The song had given her the answer.

> *Where could I go, oh, where could I go*
> *Seeking a refuge for my soul.*
> *Needing a friend to save me in the end,*
> *Where could I go but to the Lord?*

When Miss Amelia stopped at Angela's house, she held Genna's hand for a minute. "Thanks for singing tonight. You have a great talent, but have you ever considered you might not be using it in the right way?"

No mistake this time—someone was pounding on the door.

"Veevie!" Ben's yell pierced her semiconscious state. "You awake?"

She threw on a robe and made an attempt to open the bedroom window. It squeaked from disuse, but she finally forced it up a few inches.

"Here I am, Ben. What do you want?"

He sauntered off the porch toward her. "Blankenship phoned. The hearin' with Keystone is at eleven o'clock. He said to meet him at his office. Had your breakfast yet?"

"No," Genna answered groggily.

"Ivy said for me to fetch you down to eat with us."

"One of her breakfasts sounds better than anything I have here. Wonder if she'd mind if I shower down there?"

"Nope. Come down when you want to."

She forced the window back into place and checked the few clothes she'd brought with her. The skirt and blouse she'd worn recently needed laundering.

Wrinkling her nose, she murmured, "Nothing suitable for a judge's office. He'd probably cite me for contempt of court if I show up in sweats or jeans."

Mired in indecision, she finally put on the shirt and jeans she'd worn yesterday. Walking to the car, she shivered in the brisk air. The maple leaves in the yard showed a tinge of yellow in the morning sun. She had to halt the Mercedes at the road's edge to permit the passing of a low-bed truck hauling a bulldozer. At first she thought it was more Keystone Mining equipment heading her way, but the truck bounced on up the road and around the bend.

When Genna pulled up at Ben and Ivy's her concerns about the bulldozer were behind her.

Ben greeted her with an update. "I called the company about that leak in the sludge pond, and those fellers are aimin' to fix hit, I reckon."

Genna passed on into the kitchen. "Is there any place in Logan where I can buy dress clothes? I didn't plan to be here except a few days and I brought only casual things. Who'd believe I'd become involved in a lawsuit!"

Ivy placed grits and bacon on the table and returned to the stove for the biscuits. "There's some good stores in Logan along that second street back from the river. You recollect where it is?"

"Yes. I'll go early and try to find a suit. I need more clothes like I need a hole in my head, but I want to look respectable."

Ben drew up his chair and dropped his head for a quick blessing. Reaching for a biscuit, he said, "I hope you ain't expectin' to win against a coal company—hard to do in Logan County."

"I'll win this one. They have no legal right to take my property," Genna said defiantly.

"Might take a lot of money."

"I've got a lot of money."

"Well, good luck to you then," Ben said.

Genna enjoyed the short drive into Logan. She smiled when she thought how these curving roads would have frustrated Lance, but she was in no hurry. She stuck her head out of the window occasionally to look straight up at the mountain tops. Huge rock outcroppings crisscrossed the forested peaks.

The first store she entered she found a navy blue suit with a rose silk blouse that instantly transformed her into a businesswoman. She wasn't so lucky at the shoe store across the street, but she finally settled on a pair of navy high-heeled sandals. It had been so long since she'd chosen clothing by herself that she felt odd handing money to the aged salesman.

She became aware that several pairs of eyes behind the counter were watching her keenly.

"Aren't you Genna Ross?" one young saleswoman said. "I went to your concert the other night."

"Yes," she answered slowly.

"We thought you'd already gone," the older man said. "Are you going to have another appearance in the area? My grandson wanted to hear you sing."

"No, I have some business to transact here this morning, but I plan to leave in a few days."

After accommodating a shy request from the young woman for an autograph, as well as one for the salesman's grandson, Genna excused herself quickly. She knew she would have to hurry to make it to the law office on time. George Blankenship was waiting for her, as she suspected, his briefcase in hand.

"We're to meet Sullivan and his lawyer at the judge's chambers. I have all of the tax receipts and a copy of your deed. Whoever drew that mining plat made a mistake."

Genna heard only one thing he said. "Sullivan?"

"Yes, Evan Sullivan bought the Keystone Mining Company a few months ago, although it's not generally known. He was forced into strip-mining when several of his underground mines played out."

Genna's throat and tongue felt suddenly parched. She swallowed with difficulty. Her knees trembled, and she took the lawyer's arm for support as they climbed the steps to the second floor of the courthouse. She didn't want to make an enemy of Evan, but still she felt angry. *Didn't he remember how Grandpap had felt about strip miners? He seemed to have forgotten other things, but surely he could have remembered that.*

At the end of a narrow hallway, Blankenship stepped aside to allow Genna to enter the room first. Evan and another man, presumably his lawyer, stood facing them. Genna took one quick look and lowered her eyes. She breathed a prayer of thankfulness for the slight warning that Evan was her adversary.

Blankenship shook hands with Evan and his lawyer. "Gentlemen, this is my client, Genevieve Wooten, whose stage name is Genna Ross."

"I've met her," Evan said stonily. His unfriendly voice startled Genna so much that she felt faint. *Had she come back to Logan County for this?*

A door at the rear of the room opened and the judge entered. He motioned them to be seated and joined them at the table.

Turning to Blankenship, he said, "I've studied the case slightly, but you may present your client's position now."

Blankenship stood. "I represent Genevieve Wooten who owns fifty acres of land that once belonged to her grandfather. Mr. Sullivan's firm, the Keystone Mining Company, has erroneously included this property in its operations on Mill Creek. Apparently, he had bought some land for nonpayment of taxes and thought the Wooten land was included."

"When that plat was drawn, my client didn't know that Miss Wooten still owned the land in question, Your Honor," asserted Keystone's lawyer.

"I have affidavits and receipts showing that the taxes on that property have never been in arrears," Blankenship continued. "Even if Mr. Sullivan owns the land adjoining the Wooten property, we want his operations delayed until a survey is made of the line and a fence built to avoid any infringement on my client's property."

"But that will take months!" Evan exploded. His lawyer placed a hand on his arm.

"We are willing to concede," his lawyer stated, "that a mistake was made by the Keystone Company in mapping the property to be mined. We apologize to Miss Wooten and are willing to pay for any inconvenience we may have caused her. The mistake occurred because the Wooten land had at one time belonged to the coal company from which my client bought the property." Addressing Blankenship, he said, "We are willing to buy her acreage."

Blankenship looked at Genna, and she shook her head. "The property is not for sale," Blankenship answered.

"Then would you consider granting a right of way through your property? That hollow is the key to the whole area. If we have to start operations from the east side, it will cause weeks of delay."

"No right of way, and the fence has to be built," Genna said weakly, but she turned to Evan, her voice pleading. "Don't you see? I promised Grandpap. You know how he hated strip-mining, how he hated to see the mountains scraped bare. He made me promise that I'd never let that happen to his land. Don't you see?" she repeated. "He's the one who gave me a chance in life. I have to do this." Genna could feel Blankenship's stare but she needed to make Evan understand why she couldn't give in.

Evan jumped to his feet. "All I can see is that you've finally found a way to get even with me. All right, have your revenge, I hope you enjoy it." He kicked his chair away from the desk and headed for the door.

Genna and the two lawyers stared silently after him until the judge rapped on the table.

"Mr. Sullivan, do you want to be cited for contempt of court? Come back here and sit down. These proceedings will close when I say so."

Evan stopped in his tracks. Genna heard him returning, but she didn't look at him.

"I apologize, Your Honor."

"I'm unable to give a decision immediately without studying the facts, but on the surface, it appears that the plaintiff is in her rights. Both parties will be notified as soon as possible. In the meantime, the Keystone Mining operations in the vicinity of Mill Creek will be halted." He stood up and left the room without further comment.

"Evan," Genna whispered, but he didn't look her way. With a face as white and as stony as Pinnacle Rock itself, he rushed through the doorway.

Genna followed Blankenship silently back to his office.

"I'm sure you have nothing to worry about. The judge is fair, and there couldn't possibly be any decision except in your favor," Blankenship said as he sat behind his desk. Genna leaned against a chair, wanting to leave Logan County behind her as quickly as possible. First she would need to settle with the lawyer for his fee. She'd telephone Ivy and Ben that she was leaving and then head for Nashville. Perhaps the fast pace of her personal appearances would deaden the gnawing pain pulling at her heartstrings. She felt the blood drain from her face at Blankenship's next words.

"I feel sorry for Sullivan though. This will probably ruin him."

"What do you mean?"

She eased into a chair, unable to stand any longer.

"He's had his share of reverses—costly strikes and the closing of his bigger mines. He's invested a great deal of capital in this new mining enterprise and his notes are due soon. He has to mine coal or he won't be able to meet his payments. This delay may force him into bankruptcy."

Suddenly, without warning, Genna laid her head down on the desk top and sobbed.

"I supposed he had plenty of money. The Sullivans were always considered rich. I don't want to cause him to lose his business."

"What can you do unless you allow him to strip your property?"

She shook her head. "Anything but that. Can't you contact his lawyer and find out the amount of his debts, or at least what he needs for these next payments? I'd gladly pay off the loans without having him know. If you can make arrangements, I'll have my accountant in Nashville wire the money to you."

"If I can't manage without Sullivan knowing, what then?"

"Then try to persuade him to accept for old times' sake. He was once a . . . friend of mine. I don't want him hurt. I'm going to leave today, but I'll telephone on Friday to see what you've managed."

Genna hurried to the Mercedes, looking up and down the street to be sure she wouldn't encounter Evan. She received a jolt when a young man shoved a video camera in front of her. "We've been waiting for you, Miss Ross," his companion said. "How about an interview?"

"Why not?" Genna shrugged her shoulders. She no longer had a need for anonymity in Logan County.

"It's a surprise to all of us, Miss Ross, that you're from this area. When did you leave here?"

"When my grandfather died about ten years ago. This is my first trip back."

"You've always kept your past a secret—that's been one of your charms. Why did you return now?"

"I wanted to do that benefit show because my grandfather had black lung disease. I'm not ashamed of my roots, although I don't suppose it would have helped my career to advertise that I was an illegitimate child raised by my grandfather, the local moonshiner."

The cameraman kept his instrument tightly focused on Genna's face, as the reporter hurriedly consulted his notepad.

"But why are you revealing this now?"

"I don't much care now who knows. Please excuse me." Still distraught, she slipped into the car, and turned the ignition key.

I wonder how long it will be before Jim finds out? she thought with the first traces of amusement she'd felt all day.

Chapter Six

Even after hours in a Nashville salon transforming herself from Veevie Wooten to Genna Ross, Genna knew the process wasn't a success. She wasn't the same woman she'd been when she departed two weeks ago. In late afternoon she telephoned her staff to set up a dinner meeting. By the sound of Jim's voice Genna knew the media had done their job.

Jim was waiting for her when she entered the lobby of her hotel apartment. "Our table is ready," he said stiffly, holding the door open into the private dining room the hotel had reserved for them. "Lori and Cary are waiting for us."

Genna silently preceded him into the room. The sight of Cary was a balm for her troubled mind, and she bent to kiss her on the cheek. She squeezed Lori's hand.

"Hi, gang! I've missed you. Have you slave drivers scheduled lots of work for me now that my little vacation is over?" she asked brightly.

"There's a recording session at ten in the morning," Jim said as he held her chair. "They're going to use your new song, 'Why Do I Love Him?' as the title number on the new video."

"Oh, that's great!"

They talked of trivia while the waiters brought their food, served family style. When the four of them were alone again, Jim blurted out, "Genna, I'm your manager, but you'd never know it by your actions of the last week. If you have any startling news to release, I'd appreciate if you would tell me first."

"You can believe this or not, I don't care, but I had no intention of revealing anything when I left you in Woodville. I only intended to visit my old home place and see two cousins who had no idea I was Genna Ross. Then things just went haywire and people began to recognize me."

"You should have known they would," Lori said, her brown eyes sparkling angrily as she flipped back her long black hair.

She's getting as bad as Jim, Genna thought. *When will these two people realize that they're working for me?*

"Why are you so upset, Jim?" Genna asked, ignoring Lori. "Are you mad because I hadn't told you all, or because you think my past will hurt my success?"

"It won't do you any good."

"I'm not so sure about that," Cary commented quietly. "I thought Lori said the video sales had boomed since that news hit the national networks."

Jim gave her a dirty look.

"Oh, well, forget it!" Genna said. "If there is any harm, it's too late to undo, and I don't want to talk about it. My childhood wasn't so happy that I like to recall it, so let's finish our meal without an argument. Seems like that's all we do anymore."

The next day after two hours in the recording studio for her new video, Genna stopped at a deli for a sandwich and an iced tea.

"To go," she told the young clerk, who looked at her with admiring eyes. When Genna left the store she caught sight of Jim a block away running to catch up with her.

"Wait up," Jim called, "I'll grab a sandwich, and we'll go over your contract with Soundtone Recordings while we eat."

"No, Jim, I need a break from shop talk."

"You've been gone for two weeks. What more do you want?"

"I need to be by myself for a while. I'll be at my apartment at two o'clock. Why don't you come by then?" She exited through the sliding door into the parking garage.

Dodging the noonday traffic, she was soon on Interstate 40 heading eastward. She rolled down the window and let the wind blow freely through her hair. Even though the recording had gone well, she'd been under stress and found it difficult to relax in Nashville where so many people knew her. Those few days in the mountains had given her a taste of solitude, and she missed it.

Genna left the interstate at the first interchange beyond the city's limits. She drove aimlessly for a half-hour on a state highway then turned off on a narrow road. She passed many small farms, admiring the fields of ripened corn that awaited the picker. As she approached a small brick church situated on a knoll above the road, she noticed a picnic shelter on the oak-shaded lawn nearby and she pulled into the vacant parking lot.

She nibbled at her sandwich while enjoying the antics of two squirrels. They scurried around the lawn collecting acorns that they then carried to some secluded spot in the high trees. Genna tried to interest them in bits of her sandwich, but the squirrels sniffed indifferently, swished their tails, and hurried off to gather more nuts. The squawking bluejays greedily grabbed the tidbits the squirrels rejected.

After disposing of the paper bag in a trash can, she wandered into the tiny church cemetery, still loathe to return to Nashville. Glancing at her watch, she knew she had to leave or be late for her appointment with Jim.

She had just reached the car when a huge bus drove into the parking lot. "CAROL SUE AND THE HOSANNAS" was brightly painted across both sides of the bus.

Carol Sue? The name sounded familiar and Genna hesitated. The bus door opened and a spritely brunette hurried down the steps.

"Hi," she called to Genna, as she breathed in the air scented with drying hay from the nearby fields. "What a beautiful day!"

"And what a beautiful woman!" Genna laughingly answered.

The woman flashed her a smile. "Thanks." She eyed Genna keenly. "Should I know you?"

"Maybe. Genna Ross sound familiar?"

"Sure. I saw your picture in the recording studio this morning. You were recording in Studio B. I was across the hall."

"Let's hope our tapes didn't get mixed up."

"Yes, let's! I'm afraid my public might be disillusioned if 'One-Man Woman' became crossed with 'Amazing Grace.'"

"Oh, so you're a gospel singer. I remember you now. Aren't you the rock star who turned to gospel music a few years ago?"

"Yes, and those few years have been the happiest time of my life. I'd like to tell you about it sometime."

"I'd love to hear it," Genna said earnestly, stirred by the radiance of her brief witness.

"Are you coming to the concert tonight? I always give a testimony sometime during the evening."

"Where is the concert? Here?"

"Yes," Carol Sue said with a grin, "and from the size of this building, we may have to hold the concert in the parking lot."

With her heart still heavy and her thoughts still clouded, Genna sped back into town to keep her appointment with Jim. As usual, he had a list of schedules for her to look over.

"I've got two surprises for you," he said, smiling suavely. "Wait until you see your December schedule."

"Europe!" Genna exclaimed, excitement brightening her eyes. "You managed it at last."

"Yes, your last concert stateside is in Columbus, Ohio, November 29th. After that, we'll be flying to London for a week's tour in the British Isles."

"And I'll have appearances at several American military bases on the continent, I see."

"We'll finish the last concert December 20th, in plenty of time to be home for Christmas."

"I see this schedule goes through March 31st. Don't make any other commitments after that for two or three months. I'll do the fairs in August and September, but nothing in the spring months."

"Why not?"

"I have other plans."

"I'm waiting breathlessly."

Genna stood up indicating the interview was over.

"The other surprise can wait. I can't stand too much good news at once. Is there anything else you need to discuss with me?"

His eyes glittered angrily, and he obviously struggled with an angry retort.

"Yes, I'd like to discuss dinner tonight. Any objections to going out with me?"

"None at all. In fact, I even have a place I want you to take me after we've eaten."

"Just using me for a chauffeur?"

"Forget it then. I don't need an escort. I'll go alone or ask Lance."

"No, no, I'll take you."

"Good. I'll be ready at five o'clock. If you'll excuse me, Lori is due in a few minutes, and we have a lot of correspondence to deal with."

"I just can't figure you out. You've been different ever since we played that one-horse town in West Virginia. Have you found another man?"

"Honestly, Jim, I haven't found the first one yet!" *Must she tell him in plain English that she was tired of his possessiveness*? He was a good manager—why couldn't he be content with that?

Genna assessed Jim's potential a few hours later seated across from him in the seafood restaurant. He was on his best behavior and Genna sincerely wished she could care for him. Had Evan thwarted her ability to love? Now after ten years, did she truly love Evan or was she still in love with what they once had?

"Since you've told the press about your childhood, I can't see any reason why you can't share it with me," Jim commented.

Genna shrugged her shoulders. "Not really so much to tell, I reckon. I was an illegitimate child, and my mother died giving birth to me. My grandparents took me in and raised me."

"Unwanted child and all that, huh? A real tear-jerker."

His tone offended her, but she tried to push aside her resentment. "No, I can't say I ever felt unwanted. They were good to me, and Grandpap was especially loving after my grandmother died. He saved enough to provide me with an education when I went to California to live with my cousin."

"What about his being a moonshiner?"

"Lots of people make moonshine in Logan County—a perfectly respectable occupation, some think."

"You know the more I hear about this, the more I think it would make a great book and movie. People love to read about and see these heartbreaking, rags to riches stories."

"No, Jim. I would never agree to it, so let's say no more. I don't want my family's name dragged through the mud. No book. No movie."

"Okay, okay! It was just a thought." He threw up his hands. "Where are we going tonight?"

"To a gospel concert by Carol Sue and the Hosannas."

He uttered a loud guffaw. "You've got to be kidding." A quick glance at the expression on her face told him she had never been more serious. "Wait a minute. Are you getting religion? Is that what's wrong with you?"

Nettled, she replied, "There's nothing wrong with me. And I've always been religious."

"Oh, I know you've always been straight enough, but don't spring any of this spiritual jazz on me."

Genna gathered her purse. "Unless you want dessert, let's go. The concert starts in less than an hour, and we have several miles to drive."

The little brick church was crowded with people but Genna and Jim managed to wedge into a seat near the front.

Because Genna seldom attended concerts other than her own, she immediately became interested in the audience and the effect the music had on them. The audience seemed to have come from all over as most people were strangers to each other. Thankfully, she and Jim didn't create any undue interest.

Other than the type of music, she couldn't see that the concert differed much from hers. Three women, the Hosannas, sang background music to most of the star's songs. Carol Sue was dressed in sequined garments, and her band was much like the one that traveled with Genna. The big difference was in the message of the music.

When Carol Sue sang about the cross and the love of God, Genna traveled back to her childhood. There was Miss Amelia, sitting at the piano of Bethel Church, a group of children gathered around singing. She remembered especially the lyrics, "What a friend we have in Jesus, all our sins and griefs to bear."

Had that been why she'd been able to stand Evan's unfaithfulness and the loss of Grandpap? When Carol Sue sang, "He was there all the time," Genna wondered how ever-present God had been in her life. All the time when she shifted from West Virginia to California? All the time when she went to college? All the time when she was on her rise to fame? Had He been there all the time, and she hadn't been conscious of it?

Genna realized her palms were moist and she suddenly felt faint. *He'd been there, and she hadn't recognized Him.*

During intermission Genna visited the women's room while Jim searched for some refreshments. Returning to the church's sanctuary, Genna came face-to-face with Carol Sue.

"So you did come!"

"Yes, and it's a great show." The lights blinked that intermission was almost over and Carol Sue turned to leave. "Let's talk sometime," she called over her shoulder.

The second half started with several numbers from Carol Sue's latest album. When it was time for the inspirational closing, the lights dimmed and Carol Sue stood spotlighted, the three Hosannas humming softly in the background.

"As you know, I had a startling run of successes in the rock music field," she began. "My career started at sixteen, and by the time I was twenty, I'd reached the top. There was nothing wrong with my rock music. It was clean, and it appealed to a vast audience. I enjoyed doing it, but one day something happened to me. I met my Master face-to-face."

A chorus of "Amens" amid wild applause interrupted her testimony. Jim glanced at Genna, a hint of exasperation on his face. "Let's get out of here. These people are nuts."

She silenced him with a brusque wave of her hand.

"And once I'd met the Master, everything I'd achieved paled into insignificance. For two years, I've been singing to praise Him, spreading His name around the world. I have a new audience, a new set of fans, but more importantly, I have a peace in my heart that the world can't take away. The Bible promises, 'And the peace of God, which transcends all understanding, will guard your hearts and your minds in Christ Jesus.' I've found that peace, and I pray that you will too."

I had that peace once and I want it again, Genna thought. *The resentment I've harbored against Evan has been a barrier to my spiritual growth.*

She shook her head and tried to concentrate on the woman on stage. As the lights brightened, Carol Sue said, "We have a special guest in the audience tonight, and if none of you has met her, this would be a good time. Genna Ross, will you come forward, please?"

Genna felt Jim physically sinking into his seat, and he mumbled through clinched teeth, "Now look what you've done." She blithely ignored him and made her way to the stage amid a wave of applause.

"How about doing a number with me?" Carol Sue whispered as the applause faded.

Startled, Genna said, "Carol Sue, what would we sing? I don't know any of your favorites."

"Think of something you know and we'll give it a try. You sing the lead, and I'll fill in on the harmony."

Again, Genna thought of Bethel Church and Miss Amelia's favorite chorus, "I've Got the Joy, Joy, Joy, down in My Heart."

Genna hummed a measure of the chorus. "Do you know that one? The second verse fits in with what you've said tonight."

Nodding, Carol Sue said a few words to the band, and the two women swung into the old chorus.

" 'I've got the peace that passeth understanding down in my heart, down in my heart, down in my heart. I've got the peace that passeth understanding down in my heart, down in my heart to stay.' "

Carol Sue held up her hands to acknowledge the enthusiastic applause. "Thanks, folks. Maybe we can do this again sometime." She hugged Genna. "Let's keep in touch."

Jim hardly spoke all the way back to Nashville, and Genna was too involved in the new sensations of her spirit to even care. Finally, she broke the silence by laughing.

"It isn't funny, Genna. Things like this can ruin your career."

"Oh, be realistic, Jim. I had no idea this was going to happen. I met Carol Sue today and she invited me to the concert. I went out of curiosity. I didn't suppose she'd even know I was there, but I happened to meet her during intermission."

"As your manager, I'm supposed to keep things from 'happening' to you, but I can't do it when you're determined to go your own way. We need to be in control of your future, not just let it run along haphazardly."

"Jim, for the first time in years, I'm beginning to think that I'm not in control of my future. There may be something more ahead than I know about."

"What do you mean by that?" he demanded.

"I don't know myself. When I have it figured out, I'll let you know."

"Please do," he said sarcastically.

When they reached the door of her apartment, she looked at her watch. "There's time for you to come in and tell me about the second surprise you mentioned."

Genna filled two glasses with soft drinks and set a tray of veggies and crackers on the coffee table. Jim picked up his glass and drained it and asked for a refill before he removed some brochures from his jacket pocket and handed them to Genna.

"A representative from this company approached me last week with the proposition to produce a new line of jewelry known as the Genna Ross Collection. What's your opinion?"

Genna smiled. "I'm certainly willing to talk to them about it but I'll reserve my final opinion until I know more details. Why don't you make an appointment with their representative?"

Since Genna had worn the firm's jewelry, she had no reluctance to put her name on their products. The company had been in business for over fifty years and had earned a well-deserved reputation of quality workmanship. As they discussed the idea, Genna and Jim agreed that the project would be advantageous. The ease of their conversation reminded Genna of the working relationship she and Jim had once had, and perhaps could have again.

Before she prepared for bed, Genna opened the safe in the bedroom where some of her jewelry was stored. Her hand trembled when she sorted out a tattered cardboard box from among the many velvet containers. She lifted a white opal ring from the box and held it to her lips. It had been months since she'd looked at the ring, the gift from Evan on her sixteenth birthday. She had worn the ring on a chain around her neck until three years ago when its fragile band had broken in two. The ring had been repaired, but Genna had not worn it again. Although the gold needed to be polished, the opal still displayed its rainbow of colors. She slipped it on her finger and slid the band back and forth enjoying the brilliance of the fiery stone. Genna had never owned another opal.

That night Genna went to sleep with the ring on her hand. Memories of Pinnacle Mountain filtered through her dreams, the wind shifting the leaves, dappled rays of sunshine painting the rock where she and Evan sat.

When she met with the jewelry company's representative two days later, Genna liked his proposition. She would have final approval on any new item added to the line, and she'd receive a ten percent royalty on all sales.

"I've been thinking about this," Genna said, "and I do have one stipulation to make before we proceed any further. I want an opal on every piece of jewelry that bears the Genna Ross name."

"But opals are out of fashion now," Jim objected. "Very few people buy them."

"The Genna Ross name will sell them. Besides, it's a lovely stone that should be revived."

The representative was silent for several minutes and then smiled shrewdly. "Miss Ross, you've just come up with a great suggestion. We haven't been able to agree on a name for the line yet, but I can see great possibilities with the opal as our centerpiece. It will run the price up higher than we had anticipated— we'd buy only the best gemstones, the black opals of South Wales and the white opals of Australia and Europe." He paused for effect, then added excitedly, "We could call the line 'Opal Fire.' I can't speak for all of the management, but with your permission, I'm going to recommend it."

After he left, Jim looked at Genna. "How did you come up with that idea?"

"I've always liked opals."

"You don't *have* any opals."

"Not any you've seen, but I'll wager I'll be wearing lots of them now. 'Opal Fire'—I like that name."

Chapter Seven

"Our last stop before Europe," Cary said as she arranged Genna's hair for the performance that night at the municipal auditorium in Columbus, Ohio.

"I'll be glad for a few days' rest before we head overseas. This has been a rugged year in many ways."

"But a good year, too, dear," Cary reminded her. Besides Genna's sold-out concert tour, advance sales of the Opal Fire jewelry collection had already exceeded a million dollars and the line wouldn't be ready for distribution until March.

Genna felt like someone with a split personality. Onstage, she was still Genna Ross, the country western sensation, but during her quiet times, Veevie Wooten, the simple country girl, was dominant. On those days she longed for the quietness of the hollow on a dew-spangled morning, the exhilarating walk to Pinnacle Rock, and the comfort of being with her own kind. Could a mountaineer ever be completely happy away from the hills? When the land of your birth tugged at your heartstrings, would you ever feel in complete harmony elsewhere?

This latest bout of melancholy had been sparked by a dated communique from George Blankenship. Blankenship had written six weeks earlier, and although the letter had been forwarded twice, it had reached her only yesterday.

"I want you to know I have used your money to bail out the Keystone Mining Company," Blankenship had written. "The gift was offered anonymously, per your instructions. The surveyor marked the boundary between your land and that purchased by Keystone. A fence has been built around your farm. The mountain is being stripped now, and I can understand your loathing of the project. Although Sullivan has guaranteed to reclaim the land, as of this letter the mountain is nothing but an eyesore."

New thoughts of Evan had surfaced with the letter as well as the debut of her new song that night, "Why Do I Love Him?" Every time she sang the heartwrenching lyrics, Evan's face floated across her thoughts. Not coincidentally, the Columbus concert was scheduled for the same day as the release of the video and album based on the song. When Genna ran onstage to the thunderous applause of her fans, the band gave the cue and she swung into the lyrics.

> *When he's unfaithful, or cold or far away,*
> *I still love that man of mine.*
> *Even though my heart, he once betrayed*
> *I'll love him for all time.*

Why do I love him?
I don't always know,
But it isn't any secret that . . .
He's the dawn of my morning,
The heat of the noonday sun;
He's the warmth of late evening,
My strength when the day is done.

Genna's eyes misted at the applause of the enthusiastic audience. Amid the chanting demands for an encore, her heart cried, "Oh, Evan, Evan!"

After intermission, dressed in the garb of a mountain woman, Genna picked up her lap dulcimer and, as usual, presented a selection of mountain folk songs. When the last echoes of applause had died in the back rows, Genna's next selections surprised even herself. Almost as if her fingers moved of their own volition, she swung into a medley of hymns beginning with "Amazing Grace" and "What a Friend We Have in Jesus." Although the band faltered a time or two, they were good at following her lead. By the time she concluded with "God Be With You Til We Meet Again," the band's accompaniment was as polished as ever.

Jim might quarrel with her, but her audience, after its first startled silence, interrupted her singing time and again with applause. *I'll make this a part of every concert,* she thought, feeling in her heart that this was right for her.

Ater the third curtain call, she finally surrendered to the demands of her insistent fans with a stirring rendition of "One-Man Woman."

Blowing kisses at the crowd, she escaped at last to her dressing room.

"Did you hear the concert, Cary?" Genna asked as she began removing her stage makeup.

"Yes, it's one of your best. I liked the gospel music and so did the audience."

"I haven't seen Jim yet, but I can guess his reaction."

"He'll like anything that will roll in proceeds at the box office and increase his bonus. Jim has two great ambitions in life—to become a rich, rich man, and you know what the other is."

"The first ambition he may achieve; the other, he won't."

She disappeared into the shower, and came out with a belted pink terrycloth robe. She relaxed on Cary's padded table for her postconcert massage.

"I've never bothered you with questions, Genna, but I wonder why he won't?"

"Won't what? Oh, you mean, Jim's ambition? I. . . ." A knock on the door interrupted her.

"Who is it?" Cary asked.

"Message for Miss Ross," a male voice answered.

Cary shielded Genna behind a slightly opened door. A hand holding a small envelope reached through the opening. "I'm to wait for an answer," the voice said.

Genna glanced at the writing before she opened the envelope. The script had a slightly familiar look.

> *Veevie (you're still that to me),*
> *I attended your concert tonight.*
> *May I see you?*
> *Evan*

Genna suddenly felt unbearably warm and her hand trembled as she handed the note back to Cary.

"That's the reason."

Cary scanned the message. "I don't understand."

"That's the reason Jim will never realize his ambition."

"Oh," Cary said softly.

"But you needn't advertise that fact. Where's a pen?"

Silently, Cary found one in her purse. Genna paused indecisively for a few moments before she scribbled, "Yes. My dressing room, five minutes."

She scrambled off the table and glanced in the mirror. Her hair streaming down her back and her face devoid of cosmetics, she looked like the Veevie of long ago.

"We don't have much time," Cary said. "What clothes do you want to wear? Do you want me to do your hair?"

Genna wrapped the robe closely around her. "There's no time for my hair. Let me just slip into the pants and sweater I wore here tonight." With years of experience as a quick-change artist, Genna was ready when Evan knocked softly two times.

Cary opened the door and slipped into the adjoining room as he entered. Facing Evan from across the room, the distance seemed as wide as an ocean to Genna.

After a long silence, she spoke first. "And I always thought I'd know if you ever attended one of my performances!"

"I was traveling through town on my way home from Detroit when I heard the announcement of your concert on a local radio station. Impulsively, I decided to attend. At first I thought I'd go on and not let you know I'd been here. I was afraid you'd turn me down if I asked to see you."

With her throat tight and painful, Genna shook her head and whispered, "Never."

"I won't stay long. I just wanted you to know I thought you were great. No wonder Michelle raves about you. I'll have to listen to your tapes; she has enough of them."

"Is that the only reason you came?" The strength of his presence overwhelmed her. Genna Ross had fled; she was all Veevie Wooten now, a woman who loved this man wholeheartedly.

"I forfeited my right to anything more a long time ago."

With her eyes never leaving his, she began to sing softly.

> *No other man will claim me for life,*
> *No other man can make me his wife,*
> *Only one man will win my heart . . .*
> *For I've been a one-man woman right from*
> *the start.*

In two quick moves, Evan crossed the room and gathered her into his arms. His heart beat rapidly, keeping time with her own pulsebeat.

"My Veevie, I wouldn't presume, wouldn't dare to hope, that you were singing about me after what I've done to you."

He lowered his head until she could feel his warm breath on her face. A knock sounded at the door.

"Who is it?" she demanded irritably.

"Jim and Lori. Are you ready for dinner?"

She drifted out of Evan's arms whispering, "Do you have to leave right away?"

"I'm driving home tonight, but I can delay a few more hours. I want to talk to you, Veevie."

Genna opened the door and Jim and Lori breezed in. They stopped in surprise at the sight of Evan. Genna Ross wasn't in the habit of admitting fans to her dressing room.

"Jim, Lori, meet a friend of mine, Evan Sullivan. Evan, this is my manager and secretary."

If he ever had any good manners, Jim forgot them now. "Where in thunder did you drop from? I've never heard of you."

Evan's face flushed angrily, but without waiting for him to answer, Genna said, "Evan is an old friend, and we have lots to talk about. I'm having dinner with him so the two of you can go ahead without me."

She stood by the door they hadn't bothered to close and motioned them out.

Jim paused in the doorway. "What time will you be back? I have some details about Opal Fire to discuss with you."

Just to annoy him, she said, "We can talk after breakfast."

He exited without another word and Genna said, "Pardon me for inviting myself to dinner, but sometimes Jim's protective role is a bit hard to take."

Evan rubbed his chin. "I'm not sure protective is the right word, but I'll be delighted to take you to dinner."

"Good. I'll tell Cary where I'm going."

In the adjoining room, she quickly summoned Cary with a look of excited desperation. "Think you can do my hair real fast, Cary?"

"He can wait a few minutes," Cary said with a laugh.

"Maybe, but I can't. I've waited twelve years for a date with him."

Cary brushed her hair, and with a few quick turns of the curling iron brought the unruly tresses under control. "Please pack my things, Cary, so they can be stored on the bus. I'll see you at the hotel."

"My car is down the street in a parking garage," Evan said when she joined him. "Do you have any place in mind to eat?"

"No, you choose. I eat very little on a concert day so I'm ravenous now."

She'd forgotten how broad and powerful he was. As a young man, Evan had been tall and slender, but the years had fleshed him out until he seemed to dwarf her. Strength seemed to radiate from him.

When he left the traffic behind, heading westward, he said, "I've wanted to apologize for the way I treated you the last time we met, Genna. Guess I'd better get used to calling you that," he added slowly, "but I like Veevie better."

With a smile, she touched his arm. "Do you mean you like Veevie better than Genna as a person or as a name?"

"I thought Veevie was more approachable. I was never afraid of her—I'm uncomfortable with Genna."

"I haven't changed that much, Evan. The outside trappings are different but inwardly I'm much the same."

He squeezed her hand. "I hope so. I'm sorry I was so belligerent that day in Logan, but I was on the brink of ruin, and I couldn't stand to think that you'd be the one who would finally send me there. Maybe I deserved it from you, but it hurt to think you were being vindictive. Since then, I've had time to appreciate your side of the case."

"Evan, I had no idea you owned the Keystone Company until a few minutes before we came to that courthouse. I had no choice anyway—you know how Grandpap felt about strip-mining."

"Yes, I remember. But I was so excited about seeing you again, and then to find out that you were the party opposing me was more than I could take."

"Are things going better now?"

"Yes, I had a surprise reprieve, and now that I've started more mining operations, I'm coming out of the financial slump. That worry is over, but I have another one facing me."

"Oh?"

"The union at the deep mine is pushing for benefits that I can't afford. The miners' contract runs out in January, and I'm sure they'll strike. If they wait for me to meet their demands, they might as well."

"I'm sorry, Evan. You've had your problems."

"And they all started when I lost you."

"I hardly think it's accurate to say you lost me. You simply shoved me away."

"Ouch! I know that's true, but I tried to explain to you about that."

"Regardless, I don't want to talk about the past, Evan. It's too painful. Tell me what you're doing now. Tell me about your daughter."

"Michelle is eight years old now, and we're great friends."

"Do you have any help with her?"

"Yes, I have a housekeeper. I'm gone too much to have Michelle at home alone. Mrs. Gilley is about fifty years old and has a solid head on her shoulders. She's able to command Michelle's respect and friendship."

"That sounds like a good combination."

"Michelle is going with her maternal grandparents to Florida for the Christmas holidays, and since that will leave me footloose, I've decided to take a vacation. Anything's better than spending Christmas alone worrying about the strike."

"Where are you going?"

"To the Holy Land. All my life I've dreamed of being in Bethlehem on Christmas Eve. I want to walk out in the open and see the stars as they must have shone the night Jesus was born."

"That sounds like a fine vacation. Circumstances aren't quite so tense in the Middle East now."

Evan slowed the car. "I don't know much about this area, but that sign indicates the next interchange has some restaurants. Shall we stop there?"

"Sure. I don't care where we eat."

The area didn't offer much choice, but they finally decided on a steakhouse. Evan bowed his head over the food, and Genna prayed, too. It had been a long time since she'd been so thankful.

"Considering all the things that have happened to you, I'm surprised you ever thought of me. Why didn't you forget me entirely? You had every right." Evan looked deeply into her eyes.

"I tried to, Evan. I didn't like to live with resentment, but more than that, I didn't want to hold on to a dream."

"Do you still feel that way, Genna? Haven't you ever forgiven me?"

"I think so, Evan. The trouble is that I'm afraid of love now. I don't want to be hurt again."

He squeezed her hand. "I'm sorry for what I did. Is there any way I can make it up to you now?"

"Not unless you can help me forget the past."

"We can do that by talking about the present. What are your plans?"

"The greatest thing for me in the future is a trip to Europe during December. Jim has tried to arrange an overseas tour for a long time. We leave New York next week, and that will give me time to rest a bit after ten days of nightly performances."

"You like this life style?"

"Yes, it gets in your blood. You live from one concert to the next. It's been good therapy for me."

They left the restaurant shortly before midnight. "I wish you didn't have that long drive. I shouldn't have asked you to stay, but a few minutes together didn't seem like enough."

He drew her close to his side when they entered the car. "This evening has meant more to me than you'll ever know. Thinking about it will keep me from going to sleep."

The return drive passed quickly and they were back in the city sooner than Genna anticipated. She wasn't ready to say good-bye yet. What about the future? Or was there any future for them?

Evan walked with her to the door of her room. "Genna, is it possible for us to forget the past and start over? I don't want to walk away without some plan to see you again. Is there still a place for me in your life?"

"I hope so, Evan. I hope so," she whispered. "Why don't you telephone me before we leave for Europe? I'll be at the Roosevelt Hotel in New York next week."

"Depend on it."

They faced one another as if yearning for a youthful love that they would never share again. Genna felt like a teenager waiting for her first kiss. Would Evan make the first move? She doubted it, but she couldn't.

She extended her hand, but Evan ignored it and drew her into a tight embrace. She nestled against him breathing in his presence. In his arms, she sensed the fragrance of the wild plum trees blooming in the creek valley. She smelled the smoke from the coal burning in Grandpap's fireplace as she and Evan had stared into the embers and dreamed of the future. So much of her past belonged to Evan.

Genna lifted her lips and Evan needed no other invitation. The past receded and she was overcome by new sensations. Nothing she'd ever experienced before with him compared to the longing she now felt. The youthful Veevie had never known what it was like to have every nerve flaming at the touch of his lips. The adult woman Genna wasn't sure she liked her reaction. She would never allow Evan to hurt her again, but in his arms she was vulnerable.

Genna pulled away quickly. "It's time for you to go."

Evan laughed huskily and his voice was unsteady. "Yes, I guess I should. I'll call you next weekend. Good-bye, Genna."

Chapter Eight

Sensing Genna's reluctance to be alone with Jim, Cary stayed close to her the next day. But Jim wasn't to be thwarted so easily. When the bus entered Pennsylvania and picked up speed on Interstate 80, Jim made his move. "Genna, I want to talk to you alone." Sluggishly Genna left the seat beside Cary and strolled back to the office where Lori was typing fan letters for her signature. "Would you excuse us now, Lori?" Jim said.

Lori gave him a resentful look and left without a word.

"Now, who is the big guy?" Jim said as soon as they were alone.

Genna eyed him levelly as she answered, not once diverting her gaze. "I told you who he was, Evan Sullivan, an old friend."

"How old? How long have you known him? It must have been before I knew you."

"Jim, I'd lived more than twenty years of my life before I met you. I knew hundreds of people in that time. Is it necessary for me to report on everyone?"

"I'm not interested in anyone except Sullivan. How long has it been since you've seen him? Is he the reason you've changed and become so secretive lately?"

Genna glared at him, her thoughts churning. She wasn't going to submit to this third degree. Jim must be out of his mind to interrogate her in this manner.

"I don't want to fight with you, Genna."

"Then don't do it. You're the antagonist. There's nothing in our contract that says you have control over my personal life, or my professional life for that matter. You work for *me*. Do I have to keep reminding you of that?"

"If you wreck your career—all we've worked for—because of some local yokel, I'll be hurt too. That gives me some right to question you."

Genna laughed at his preposterous statement. "Jim, you've gone from the ridiculous to downright insulting. Stop being foolish. We'd better go over my tour schedule again. If you spend the next three days in Massachusetts with your sister, we won't have another time."

The expression in Jim's eyes was pleading, but Genna ignored it. He didn't resume his interrogation, but his manner remained stiff and unyielding during the rest of the trip.

During their few days in New York, Cary and Genna slept late, breakfasted at leisure in the hotel's coffee shop, lunched in exotic restaurants, and shopped in elegant stores. The Madison Avenue stores were decorated for Christmas and Cary soon became caught up in the infectious spirit.

"Don't buy all of your presents here, Cary," cautioned Genna as Cary's legion of shopping bags threatened to overwhelm passersby. "Remember, you'll have three weeks in Europe. You'll want to buy some things over there."

"But we're always rushed on these tours. You know how Jim exacts every bit of publicity he can. We'll be busy all the time. By the time we return to the States, all of the merchandise will be picked over. I'm looking out for my grandkids now."

"Maybe you're right," Genna conceded, as she and Cary entered yet another fashionable emporium. Ben would like the binoculars she found in an interesting high-tech store, but Ivy would probably shake her head over the shirtwaist silk dress and leave it hanging in the closet. At least, she'd have the exclusive store box and wrapping to show the neighbors.

Even though Genna hummed Christmas carols along with the melodies wafting from loudspeakers throughout the stores, inside she didn't feel like celebrating. Since Bea's death, Genna had spent Christmas alone. The holiday was an unhappy time for her and she was always relieved when it was over. Maybe the European tour would be a help this year.

"What are you doing for Christmas, Genna?" Cary asked one morning at breakfast. "My daughter told me to invite you to spend the holidays with us in Nashville."

Genna shook her head. "Thanks, but I won't do that. Christmas is a family time, and you need to be away from shop talk for a week. I haven't really thought about it. I may stay over a week in Europe. If you're right about Jim keeping us busy, I won't have any time to sightsee, and I'd hate to come home without visiting some of the great landmarks."

"Alone?"

"I'm a big girl, Cary. I don't need anyone to stay with me. You make your plans to go home and forget about me."

Evan's call came two days before they left, much to Genna's relief. Her old fears about him had returned. Genna cuddled the phone lovingly under her chin and for a few minutes they talked of trivial matters.

"What are your plans for Christmas?" he asked.

"I don't have any. My last concert is on the 20th so the band and my staff can arrive stateside in time for Christmas. I may stay in Europe for a few days. I have to be home by January 2nd, Jim has a concert planned in Boston."

"Maybe I shouldn't ask, but will you meet me in Israel for a few days?"

Genna gasped. "Oh, I don't know, Evan."

Insistently, he continued. "I'm going on a group tour, and we'll be in Tel Aviv from the 21st until the 27th. From there we will visit Bethlehem. I'd like to see the Holy Land with you."

"It may be too late to make arrangements."

"You could stay in the same hotel where the tour group is based, and you might even be able to join the tour for a few days. I'm traveling with Watoga Tours. We'll leave Israel for Athens on the 27th, but we could spend some time together before you have to fly home."

"I'll have to think about it, Evan. Let me telephone you tomorrow."

"But tell me, Veevie," he persisted, laughing at his choice of names, "do you want to go? To me, that's almost as important as if you do go."

Genna's answer came after only a slight hesitation.

"Yes, Evan, I want to go very much."

"Good. I'll wait for your call. I love you, Veevie," he whispered softly before he replaced the phone.

Genna lay back on the bed, not realizing that she hadn't replaced the phone receiver until the recorded operator's voice startled her.

Genna considered having Lori check on travel arrangements, but on second thought, she decided to do it herself. She'd prefer that Jim didn't know where she was during that time, and what Lori knew, Jim knew.

The next morning she telephoned Watoga Tours' local office. The salesperson who answered readily said, "Yes, we'll be pleased to have you join our tour at Tel Aviv for three days. Would you like for me to arrange your air passage too?"

"That would be a help. I'll arrive in Israel from Frankfurt, Germany. Will you deliver my travel documents to the Roosevelt Hotel?"

In less than two hours, the woman contacted Genna to assure her that all the scheduling had been completed. Trying to stifle her excitement, she telephoned the news to Evan.

"I'm all set," she said. "I'll be on the Lufthansa flight arriving in Tel Aviv from Frankfurt at 10:30 A.M. on December 22nd. I can join your tour that afternoon."

"Great! That's the best news I've heard in months. It will be good for us, Genna."

"Do I pretend not to know you?"

"Of course not. What gave you such an idea?"

"It might be embarrassing for your tour companions."

"I don't know any of the other people on the tour, but it wouldn't matter anyway. You wouldn't embarrass me."

"Not even if I said 'hit,' 'ain't,' and things like that?"

When he remained silent, Genna wished she'd kept her mouth shut. "No matter what you say," Evan said evenly.

Jim had booked a concert for every night in the British Isles, leaving only one free day before they flew to Germany. His good mood was a reflection of the great reception Genna had received, so he amicably agreed to go with them on a day's tour. "But with only one day to see England, how can we possibly make a choice?" Lori moaned.

"Why don't we all write down the place we most want to see within a day's drive of London? We'll mix them together, draw out one choice, and that's where we'll go," Jim suggested.

Cary's choice of Salisbury Cathedral was the winner and no one seemed disappointed. They rented a van large enough to accommodate their party and hired a guide to ride with them. Though it would rush them to make their nine o'clock flight from Heathrow Airport, they agreed to see Stonehenge as well while they were in the vicinity.

Long before they completed their eighty-mile drive from London, the spire of Salisbury Cathedral greeted their view. The landscape of grassy uplands and rolling plains was mostly devoted to farming and pastureland. Flocks of sheep dotted the green fields.

Their guide, a thirtyish, vivacious English woman with a cockney accent kept up a running commentary as they traveled through the countryside. The driver of the van, Genna's electric guitarist, had no trouble adhering to the left side of the traffic as they entered the little town of Salisbury. They took turns exclaiming over the many Tudor-style inns and tearooms lining the streets. "No place else in England will you find a purer example of the pointed, early English style of architecture than here at Salisbury Cathedral," their guide began when they reached the grounds of the cathedral. "Construction on this edifice started in 1220 and it took thirty-eight years to complete. Workers completed the spire in the fourteenth century.

"I would suggest you visit the cathedral's octagonal Chapter House noted for its fine sculpture dating from the thirteenth century and see one of the four remaining copies of the Magna Carta in the library. Take a look also at the clock in the north transept, reportedly the oldest working mechanism in Europe."

The guide handed brochures to all of them, and when the others walked toward the entrance, Genna took Cary's hand. "Let's walk on the lawn first."

Jim seemed eager to join in step. "I'll go with you."

"No, we'll catch you later." He frowned but didn't tag along as Genna feared he would.

The cathedral sat on a wide, rich lawn atop a level plain beside the gently flowing Avon River. Genna wrapped her coat more closely around her as a keen breeze blew across the plain. The stone of the cathedral had a yellowish sheen in the bright light.

"Hard to believe this building has been standing over 700 years," Cary commented as they walked back toward the cathedral.

Genna smiled. "I feel quite insignificant when I consider the magnificence of the building."

"Don't I hear organ music?"

"I hope so. I'd love to be here during a service."

They hurried into the north transept, pausing to look at the clock the guide had mentioned, and then moved in the direction of the nave. An organ recital was in progress and they quietly slid into a pew. Genna glanced around, amazed to see hundreds of people sitting in rapt attention as the strains of the mighty organ vibrated throughout the building.

When the music ended in about fifteen minutes, Genna realized how absorbed she'd been in her own thoughts. Again and again she felt confronted with the question, "Where do I go from here?"

After traveling the nine miles north to the renowned Stonehenge, the bus stopped near the large oval of lintels and pillars made from rough-cut stones. Reported to be England's most important ancient monument, Lori was unimpressed with the moment of unveiling. "Fiddle! I thought these things were huge!"

All were irritated because a fence separated them from the famed spot. Nonplussed, the guide said, "You have to use your imagination to realize that these pillars represent a major engineering feat. Most of these stones, some weighing tons, were moved here from some great distance, probably from Wales, 3500 years ago during a time when the ancients had no heavy equipment to help them."

"Why are they considered so important?" one of the young band members questioned. "I've never heard of the place."

"Some historians associate this site with the Druids, while others think it was an astronomical calendar capable of predicting eclipses. But whether it was an ancient burial ground, sun-worshiping temple, or a human sacrifice site, it's still an important remnant of ancient history," the guide said crisply.

"If you say so," the young man said and entered the bus for a nap while the others circled the strange assortment of stones, many of which had toppled from their original spots.

"You're *what*?" Jim shouted. It was the final night of their tour, and he was in her room at Frankfurt.

"I'm not going home with the rest of you tomorrow. I want to do some sightseeing before I go back to the States."

"If you think I'm going to leave you over here alone, you're crazy. Or will you be alone?" he asked suspiciously.

She laughed. Even Jim's churlishness couldn't dampen her pleasure when she was on her way to spend a few days with Evan. Her evident happiness had radiated through her singing and every show had been a beautiful experience.

"No, I won't be alone. I've arranged to go on a tour, so I'll have a guide. I won't get lost."

"But why do you do these things without consulting me?"

"Note how you're reacting now that I have told you. That's the reason. I avoid unpleasantness as long as possible."

"Won't you tell me where you're going?"

"No, you wouldn't approve of that either. If there's any necessity to phone me, Cary has my itinerary."

"Why don't you make Cary your manager? She seems to be the only one who has your confidence."

Genna laughed again. "Thanks for the suggestion. I may do that. Now run along, Jim. I have to dress for the concert."

The next day Genna deliberately delayed her departure from Frankfurt until she was sure that Jim and the rest of her staff were on their way home. Now she had two hours to wait at the hotel before taking a taxi to the airport. Too fidgety to stay in the room, she checked out and asked the clerk to store her luggage while she shopped.

She wanted to buy Evan a gift, but she had no idea where to find it. She turned right at the hotel's entrance because she thought she'd seen some shops in that direction. Two American servicemen immediately fell in step with her.

"Hi, Miss Ross. We saw your concert last night. It was great," one of them said in a voice marked by a deep southern drawl. His buddy towered over the southerner by at least a foot. She stopped. "Thanks, guys. Now, you just run along and do whatever you intended to do. I don't need an armed escort this morning."

They grinned at her. "Maybe you do," the southerner said, "and we aren't kidding," he added, his face sobering. "Lots of people here resent Americans, and there are always terrorist groups around. You wouldn't make a bad hostage, ma'am."

"Well, come on then. Tell me where I can find a gift for that special guy in my life." She made the statement to discourage the soldiers, but it had the ring of truth.

The tall soldier moaned. "Might have known there would be a special guy. There's a jewelry shop close by. It's too expensive for us, but you probably could buy something."

Genna laughed. "I don't care how much it costs, but he probably would."

Once inside the store, the choice wasn't hard to make. She had eyes for only one item. "I'll take the black onyx ring with the diamond in the center." It was a massive ring of white gold, but it wouldn't look too large on Evan's brawny hand.

The soldiers escorted Genna back to the hotel. "Sure nice to run into you, Miss Ross. Hope we can catch one of your concerts when we're back in the States."

She signed two of her cards. "If you ever do, use these as free tickets for you and your family with my compliments, and be sure and let me know you're there."

"You're the greatest, Miss Ross. And a Merry Christmas to you."

Intending to escape her fans for three days, Genna had registered for the tour as Genevieve Wooten. By the time she settled into the first-class section of the jumbo jet, however, Genna wondered if that were possible. During check-in procedures and the hour's wait in the airport, numerous people had approached her asking for autographs and even handouts; many others simply stared at her in perplexity. Fortunately only Genna and an elderly German couple who didn't speak English occupied the compartment so Genna had a peaceful flight.

Genna awakened with a start when the pilot's message sounded. "Arrival at Tel Aviv in fifteen minutes. Flight attendants, please ready the cabin for landing."

Genna rushed to the restroom and tried to repair her makeup and straighten her hair. Her suit looked as if she'd slept in it as she had! At least she'd have time to shower and change clothes before she saw Evan. The brochure indicated he would be on tour this morning.

Moving slowly with the crowd up the ramp to the passenger area, she heard a shout, "Veevie!"

She waved to him as he pushed through the crowd, his arms cradling an enormous bouquet of red roses. Dropping the bouquet on a chair, he pulled her into his arms and squeezed her until she was breathless. The scent of rose petals swirled around them.

"I was so afraid you wouldn't come," he finally whispered.

"Why? I told you I'd be here."

"Just a worrier, I guess. Anyway, I'm so glad you are. Let's go find your luggage. We don't want to waste a minute of our time together."

"Have you been having a good time?"

"Wonderful," he answered as he guided her through the terminal and down to the luggage area. "We toured Galilee yesterday and took a boat ride on the Sea of Galilee, but it was a calm trip, nothing to remind us of the time Jesus stilled the waters."

"I supposed you'd be on tour this morning; I didn't expect you to be here."

"The others are visiting the ruins of Qumran this morning, but I skipped it."

"Skipped it! Why, Evan, that's where they discovered the Dead Sea Scrolls. That was one of the highlights of the trip."

"Maybe, but having you here is a highlight for me. I had to see you the minute you arrived. Besides, tomorrow we'll be doing sightseeing around Jerusalem. You know, if we return in time, we'll go with the group this afternoon to Masada."

Genna rubbed her face against the sleeve of his coat. "Thanks for being here, Evan. It's nice to be wanted."

"You are."

The tour members greeted Genna warmly, not recognizing her as a singing star, and accepted at face value Evan's explanation that she was a friend.

The tour of Masada took more time then Genna had envisioned, but she felt swept up immediately into the drama of the story. Some of the ruins, the guide explained, dated to 76 B.C., but most of the fortress had been built by Herod the Great. The story of the 960 Jews who had committed mass suicide rather than submit to the Romans stunned Genna, but their courage inspired her to stand firm in her faith against Jim and others who might criticize her.

The evening was free, and after a meal with the others at the hotel, Genna and Evan strolled through the bazaar section of Tel Aviv.

"Help me buy some gifts for Michelle," Evan said. "You should have good ideas."

"I don't know much about children, but I'll help."

They held hands and swung their arms rhythmically. "I feel like a boy myself," Evan admitted. "Do you realize, Genna, that we've never had any fun together?"

"Except tonight. Everybody's supposed to be kids at Christmas. Shall we?"

Evan accepted the challenge. They walked from booth to booth buying trinkets for Michelle.

Arriving back at the hotel, they parted in a happy mood. Evan was right; they'd never had any fun before.

The tour guide briefed them at breakfast. "A full day ahead of us, folks. We'll spend the day looking at sites around Jerusalem, and tonight we'll attend services in Bethlehem Square. If any of you wish, we can arrange for a trip to Shepherd's Field about midnight."

"I'd like to go," one woman said, "but how safe is it?"

"As safe as you are anywhere in Israel, I think."

"Evan, let's go," Genna said softly. "It will be wonderful to be on the hillsides around Bethlehem on Christmas Eve. The manmade places are interesting, but I want to see the stars and imagine that I can hear the message the angels brought to the shepherds."

He nodded. "That's what I wanted to do when I booked this tour."

The bus labored up the steep road until they came to the Mount of Olives. While Evan took pictures of Jerusalem and the Kidron Valley, Genna tried to recall some of the things that had happened on this site.

In her imagination, she, too, went to sleep while Jesus prayed alone. From this point, Jesus must have mourned over the Jews' failure to accept Him as the Chosen One. She stood with the apostles and watched Him ascend into heaven with the promise that He'd return again. She strolled beneath eight old olive trees, the remains of a grove destroyed by some unnamed Roman conqueror. Perhaps this very grove of trees had shaded Jesus, she thought solemnly.

Leaving the mount they drove through the Golden Gate, a replacement of one through which Jesus traveled during His triumphant journey into Jerusalem. She held tightly to Evan's hand as they walked along the Via Dolorosa, partly because of the rough street, but mostly because she wanted to share his quiet strength as she contemplated the road that Jesus followed to Calvary.

Would she have been as brave as Simon of Cyrene, who at this point was commanded to carry the cross? Was it here that Jesus told the women of Jerusalem not to weep for Him but for themselves? At the Church of the Holy Sepulchre, she bowed her head wondering if Jesus had really lain there.

Visiting the scenes of His sacrificial suffering seemed to give more emphasis to his birth as they at last entered the old square of Bethlehem to participate in the service at the Church of the Nativity. Genna refused to let the sight of many soldiers guarding the area spoil her worship. God's Son, born as a tiny baby, might not have been pleased with the ostentatious splendor of the church, but on this night of nights, Genna ignored the trappings man had added and envisioned a beautiful peasant woman and her newborn child.

Darkness had completely fallen when they left the church, and a few of the more adventurous tourists followed their guide to the countryside. The stars overspread the sky like a tablecloth. Genna backed up to Evan and he pulled her close for warmth. The few tourists who had braved the danger and the cold to come to Shepherd's Field clustered around a huge bonfire on the land that was reportedly still on the records as belonging to Boaz. Was she standing where Ruth had once gleaned in the field of the man who would become her husband? Although Genna knew that God as Sovereign of all the world was as close to her in Nashville as any place, why then did she feel so much closer to Him here?

Softly, Genna began to sing, "It Came upon the Midnight Clear." One by one the shivering group joined in singing many of the traditional carols, ending with the popular spiritual, "Go Tell it on the Mountain."

Two men presented short sermons. One spoke in Arabic, which was translated by a missionary from the United States, and the other man spoke in English, his message in turn translated by a Christian Arab. A group of native girls passed around cookies and hot chocolate.

As they walked reverently back to the waiting bus, Genna whispered to Evan, "It may have been 2,000 years ago that Jesus came to this place, but tonight He was born for me. I feel my life is now on a new course."

Puzzled, Evan decided to discuss this further with Genna when they reached the hotel. The first floor coffee shop stayed open all night and Evan and Genna sought a quiet corner. After ordering hot tea, Genna sensed the questions on

Evan's lips. "What I meant about having a new course charted for me . . . for the past few months, I've been wondering if I'm using my talents the way I should. I've made lots of money, I have thousands of happy fans, but I'm afraid my music hasn't done anything to glorify God." Pausing to sip her tea, Genna raised her hand to stifle Evan's comments and continued.

"I met Carol Sue, the gospel singer, in Nashville last fall. I attended her concert, and she called me to the stage to sing a duet with her. It was a new experience. Since then, I've occasionally added hymns to my repertoire, and most of my fans have appreciated it." She laughed wryly. "But I'm afraid Jim hasn't."

Evan cleared his throat. "Genna, I don't have any right to ask, but is there anything between you and Jim?"

"Nothing on my part. Jim would like there to be more, but I've told him repeatedly that there never will be. He's a good manager, but the past few months have been stormy between us. I'm not sure I can tolerate him much longer. He's convinced I can't make it without his help, but I think I can. If I should make the transition to gospel music, I'm sure he'll leave me. If I haven't already answered your question, I'm ready for him to resign."

"Is there any hope for us, Genna? Can we truly start over again?"

"It's more complicated than that, Evan. I'm planning to spend this spring in Logan County. I've already told Jim to leave my early summer free. I want to be in the mountains when the redbud decorates the mountainsides, when the dogwood and rhododendron bloom. I'm planning to remodel Grandpap's old house into a vacation retreat. I can't see any reason why we can't forget the past and start over, but it may not happen right away."

Evan lifted her hand and kissed it, his eyes saying more than his lips. "If you're living in Logan County, I'll be parking on your doorstep so much you'll get tired of me."

"I doubt that, but you may get in the way from time to time. Don't worry, if you do, I'll let you know," she said teasingly.

"I'll not interfere, I promise."

"I'm expecting the hills and Miss Amelia to help me decide about my future. I need to meet Michelle, get to know her. She needs to know me. Many things have to be settled before we can make any real plans."

Evan kissed her hand again before he released it and leaned back in his chair sighing deeply. "I know. I've been trying to push my problems out of my mind on this tour, but every night when I'm alone in my room, I start worrying. I'm facing that strike when I return home, and it's apt to become violent. Considering that I might be teetering on financial ruin, we can't make long-range plans anyway."

"That wouldn't matter to me."

"No, but it would to me. A man has to retain his pride, even if he loses everything else. I'd hate to think that the woman I love is a great success in her profession and I fail in mine."

A tremor of distress flitted through Genna's mind. *What would he say if he knew she was the one who'd bailed him out of his former crisis?*

"Evan, let's not spoil our last few hours together by discussing our problems." She reached into her purse. "Here's your Christmas present."

"Sweetheart, this is beautiful," he said as he unwrapped the sparkling ring. He slipped it on the second finger of his left hand. "A bit too small for that finger," he said, "but I can have a jeweler change that at home."

He reached into the pocket of his coat. "I have something for you, too, but I'm afraid it doesn't compare with your gift." Genna's fingers trembled as she opened the blue velvet box to reveal a string of beautifully matched pearls.

"I bought those in Egypt a few days ago."

"You probably don't remember the only other gift you gave me," she said. She reached for the chain around her neck and pulled out the ring he'd given her years ago.

He stared at it. "No, I hadn't forgotten, but I supposed you'd thrown it away years ago."

"I couldn't bring myself to throw away the ring or to forget your promise that someday you'd buy me something better. I had to wait a long time, but that day has come at last."

"I've heard Michelle talk about a new line of Genna Ross jewelry that features opals . . ." he said musingly.

He pulled his chair close to hers. No other guests shared the room with them and even the waiters were out at the moment. As he caressed her lips with his, he whispered, "I'll be waiting impatiently until the dogwood bloom."

Chapter Nine

The Genna Ross Opal Fire jewelry collection was ready for distribution in mid-March and the company feted Genna at a gala reception in her Nashville hotel. More than a dozen locked cases of the new jewelry were on display in the lavishly decorated ballroom.

The invitation list included all country music stars who made their home in Nashville, as well as jewelry salespeople from around the country. As she stood in the receiving line greeting friends and strangers, Genna looked up with delight when she saw Carol Sue.

"We're still going to have that talk someday," the gospel singer said, "but you're too busy tonight."

"Yes, and I leave tomorrow for another round of concerts."

"Congratulations on your jewelry. I've ordered several sets."

After the well-wishers left, Genna took time to examine the collection. She ordered watches for both Lori and Cary. The goldtone metal case and adjustable bracelet were enhanced by an opal-studded watch face.

Most of the jewelry was designed for women, but she searched for something to send Evan. She finally decided on a masculine cluster ring that combined New Zealand white opals and rubies. The way Jim looked at her when she chose the ring, he obviously thought the gift was for him.

He followed her to the apartment after the reception, and though she was too tired for further conversation, she couldn't wait any longer to discuss her future. Her relations with him had become more and more strained during the winter months, and she dreaded the emotional strain that would necessarily result from their parting. Only one thought propelled her to begin: Three more appearances and she was heading for home and Evan.

"Jim, I think it's only fair to tell you the career change I'm considering. I know you'll disapprove, but you can make your own plans accordingly."

"What have you done now that you haven't told me?"

Genna stifled her anger and answered evenly, "Nothing, but I'm telling you now what I may do. I'm seriously thinking of going into gospel music."

She had expected a verbal onslaught, but hardly the look of horror that crossed his face. Never before had she seen Jim speechless.

"You have to be kidding," he sputtered out finally.

"No, I'm not. This summer will be a decision time for me in many ways. If I'm convinced that this is God's will for my life, in the fall when I start touring again, it will be as a gospel singer."

"You're talking like a fanatic, Genna! What does God have to do with your success? I've made you a great star, and I won't let you throw it away. Think of the rest of us."

"There's no reason you can't continue as you have. I'll need a manager, a secretary, and a band, no matter what I sing."

"You'll lose millions of dollars!"

"I don't care."

"Well, I care. I won't let you do it."

Jim's emphatic statement indicated that the matter was closed, but Genna simply smiled at him.

"I've been wanting to tell you," Jim continued, "I've talked to a publisher who wants to do your life story. They've had a ghost writer following your concerts and checking into your past. They're ready to run the story. All you have to do is sign the contract."

A hot flush of anger flooded Genna's body. "I told you I didn't want a book," she shouted angrily. "How dare you set someone to investigating me! I've seen you at work too long. No book, and that's final. Remember this, Jim. If a publisher runs that book without my permission, I'll sue them and fire you."

The heated exchange only heightened Genna's desire for the mountains, and she thought about home all the next day as they traveled to her next appointment. When they finally checked into their hotel for the night, she sank into a soft chair and closed her eyes. In her mind she climbed to Pinnacle Rock and smelled the warm scent of the earth as the March sun warmed it; a few serviceberry trees were putting forth their white blossoms.

"Oh, Evan," she whispered, "why aren't you a letter writer?" They had contacted each other infrequently during the winter months. She hesitated to telephone him during the day at the office, and her evenings were fairly occupied with her concert tour.

The newspapers had been full of the strike against the Sullivan Mining Company. Pickets had been up for months, and Genna knew this posed a severe drain on Evan's already strained finances. She wanted to send him some money, but she didn't dare interfere again. Once a picture had appeared in a Chicago paper showing Evan crossing the picket line while his workers shouted obscenities at him. He looked as if he'd aged years since Christmas. Since that time he'd been sequestered in the mine buildings.

Finally the desire to talk to him became so strong that she dialed the number of Sullivan Mine No. 2. He answered the phone.

She drew a breath of relief. "Evan, I've been so worried about you. Are you all right?"

"Physically, yes, but not mentally."

"Are you busy now? Do you have time to talk?"

"Nothing but time. I'm a prisoner in my own office. I'm afraid to leave for fear they'll wreck the whole operation."

"Isn't there anyone with you?"

"I have a security force protecting the place. I'm hoping that the strike will soon be over; we have meetings scheduled between management and union representatives almost every day."

"It's almost time for me to come home. I hope you aren't still having trouble then. I want to spend some time with you, Evan."

"And I need you. We'll arrange to be together somehow."

"Is there anything I can do? Maybe I shouldn't mention it, but I could help you financially. I know this strike must be a drain on your resources."

"No," he said determinedly. "I won't have that between us. We have enough of the past to overcome, Genna. I won't be dependent upon you."

Genna's hands trembled. *What if he found out she'd helped him once? Would that destroy all they'd gained so far?*

"How's Michelle managing in this situation?"

"She's all right. I'm happy you've been writing to her. I want the only two women in my life to like one another."

"I'm looking forward to meeting her."

A thud sounded on the line, accompanied by a scrambling noise, and Genna heard the clatter of the phone as it fell.

"Evan! Evan!" she screamed over and over. The line went dead. She frantically dialed again and received a busy signal.

Cary entered the room. "It's time to dress, Genna." Then she noted Genna's agitation. "What's the matter?"

"I was talking to Evan, there was a shot and the line went dead. He's in that miners' strike, you know. I have to find out what happened to him. Get the travel agency on the line, I'm going to Evan."

"Genna Ross has never run out on a concert before. You'd better think twice."

"But how can I sing when my heart is in shreds?"

"That's where the acting comes in. You've been talking about your renewed faith in God. Now's the time to trust Him. Maybe the telephone line was cut by the shot. When you panic like this, you're listening to the devil instead of to God."

Genna blinked back the tears. She needed Cary's common sense to calm her hysteria.

"You're scheduled to go home in a week, aren't you?"

At Genna's nod, she continued, "Then settle down. After tonight's show, try to telephone and see what has happened."

Genna never knew how she made it through that night's performance. In spite of the praying she did, it was the hardest show of her career. She trembled all over when she finally reached her room at the hotel. She submitted to Cary's ministrations, which usually soothed her tired mind and spirit, but nothing seemed to help.

One thought occurred to her but she quickly dismissed it. It was past eleven o'clock, and Ben and Ivy would long since have gone to bed. There was nothing they could tell her now, and there was nothing she could do but wait until morning. After a sleepless night, Cary greeted her with a breakfast tray and a suggestion.

"Why don't you call the coal mine again? By now the telephone line may have been repaired. Evan may even answer your call."

"Cary, I don't know what I'd do without you. I'm going to miss you this summer."

After trying for two hours without success to reach anyone at the mine, she finally received an answer.

"This is Genna Ross. May I speak to Mr. Sullivan?" she asked, her voice trembling in spite of herself.

"I'm sorry, ma'am. He isn't here."

"Can you tell me where he is? We were talking by phone last night and suddenly the line was dead. I'm concerned about him."

After an uncomfortable hesitation, the man said, "He's in the hospital."

Genna gasped, and her heart pounded until she could scarcely breathe.

"He was shot in the back last night. He's in stable condition, but he will be in the hospital for several days."

After she found out the name of the hospital, Genna thanked the man and hung up. Relieved to know that he was alive, Genna searched out Cary to tell her the news. Cary handed her a newspaper before she got a word out.

"We could have found out about him by reading the paper. Here's an account of the whole thing." Genna grabbed the paper and hurriedly scanned the article.

The reporter concluded, "The only good thing to be gained from the heinous attack on Sullivan seems to be that the tide of public opinion has swung toward the mine management. Even union officials have condemned the wounding of this man who has done so much for the Appalachian coal miners."

Remembering that Angela Keefer was the business administrator at Evan's hospital, Genna put in a call to her.

"Calm down, Genna," Angela's voice reassured. "I don't think he's on the critical list. Hold on a minute while I make some inquiries." Genna drummed her fingers on the table earning her a resigned glance from Cary, but the minutes seemed interminable until Angela spoke again.

"I talked to his doctor, and Evan is in no danger of dying. The bullet has already been removed, and fortunately it missed any vital spot. Go on with your tour, he's in good hands."

Genna wilted with relief. "You're a good friend. Don't tell anyone I telephoned, but I had to know."

Before she left the hotel to travel to her next concert, Genna wired a huge bouquet of flowers to Evan at the hospital. She wanted to talk to him but decided that would have to wait until she could see him. *In less than a week, in less than a week,* the wheels of the bus seemed to say, and they would be together.

At the end of the last scheduled concert, Genna kissed Cary good-bye and shook hands with Jim and Lori and the members of her band. She wondered fleetingly if they would ever be together again. Jim had orders not to make any more appointments for her until she contacted him. She had given her employees a three-month paid vacation; before that time elapsed she would have her decision made. With a light heart Genna headed for the mountains.

"Yes, Mr. Sullivan is still a patient in the hospital," the nurse on duty told her. "Room 135."

Feeling as if she were on wings, Genna swept down the hall. Ever since his hospitalization, she had envisioned herself as his private nurse. The strike had been settled and the miners had agreed to a new contract. That would relieve Evan of his worries, and they could have a few months to find each other again.

She knocked on the closed door and it opened slightly. A youthful face peered at her. "My daddy is asleep. What do you want?"

So he didn't need her after all. This was the other woman in his life.

"Is that you, Michelle? This is Genna Ross. May I come in, please?"

The door swung open and gray eyes so like Evan's peered up at Genna. "Gee, Miss Ross! You're more beautiful than your pictures. Come in."

Genna forgot Michelle when she saw Evan lying on his back in the hospital bed. The intravenous tubes leading down to his arm brought home to her the certainty of his accident.

"Is he all right?" she whispered to Michelle.

"The doctor says so, but he lost lots of blood."

She couldn't stay here any longer without doing something foolish, so Genna backed toward the door. She wanted to throw her arms around him, she wanted to cry, but she couldn't do anything except stare at him. Michelle's presence was a problem. *What had he told her about them?*

"I'll come back when he's awake."

"But he'll want to see you," Michelle cried loudly, and Evan opened his eyes.

A smile lit his face, and he didn't look nearly as ill as Genna had thought at first. He held out his hand to her, and Genna reached for it blindly, blinking back the tears. She was conscious of Michelle's eyes upon them.

"Are you all right, Evan?"

"Doctor says I can go home in a few days. Are you home to stay?"

"Perhaps until the end of summer, or at least long enough to remodel

Grandpap's house and make those important decisions I told you about. Our tour schedule has been so heavy that I haven't had time to think."

"You look tired, Genna. Time you had a little rest."

"You have a good nurse, I see," Genna said with a smile in Michelle's direction.

"The best. She says she's going to take care of me after I go home, but I say she's going back to school. We'll see who wins."

Leaving the two of them together, Genna felt a pang of jealousy. Michelle fit into his life as she never could. Already Genna missed the excitement of the tour circuit, and she hadn't been away from it a week. Could she bury herself here in Logan County even for Evan? Would he expect her to give up her career? That was something they hadn't discussed, but it would have to be settled.

When Genna passed the Sullivan No. 2 mine, she noticed many cars near the entrance. Ben and Ivy would know what was happening, Genna thought, as she made her way down their winding dirt road.

"You came at a terrible time," Ben said. "There's goin' to be big trouble at the Sullivan mine, so I hear. I feared you'd be mixed up in hit when you came along the road."

"What do you mean?"

"Best I can hear, the miners are intendin' to wreck hit tonight. I'm glad Sullivan's in the hospital; leastways, he won't get hurt again."

"But I thought the strike had been settled."

"The miners ain't happy with the contract agreement. They're disregardin' union orders and have walked out on a wildcat strike," Ivy said.

"What are they going to do?"

"I ain't for sure," Ben said.

Genna headed for her car. "I'm going down there."

"No, Veevie, no!" Ivy called, running toward her. "It's no place for a woman."

"Maybe not, but it might be the place for Genna Ross. I have many fans in this county, perhaps they'll listen to me."

She was already guiding the Mercedes out of the yard when Ben jumped in beside her. "If you're goin,' I'll go along. Veevie, why can't you get Sullivan out of your system?"

"He's an old friend."

"Not old enough for you to risk your life to save his property."

They heard sporadic shots before they arrived at the mine. "What's your plan?" Ben shouted at her.

She had the window down, and at the speed she was traveling the noise in the car made it difficult to carry on a conversation.

"I don't have one."

"Just like a woman. We're goin' to get into a mess of trouble."

"No one asked you to come along." When their way was blocked by a barrier of vehicles, Genna hurriedly parked the Mercedes. She heard shouting from the mine buildings and she ran toward the commotion, Ben at her heels. More than a hundred miners were crowded near the fence surrounding the mine; facing them was a much smaller force of security men.

Evan would have been the target of this confrontation, Genna thought, as she prayed her thanks that he was still in the hospital. She edged her way to the front of the crowd wondering what she could do. Spying a dump truck turned on its side in front of the gate, she whispered to Ben, "Help me up on it."

A miner at the fence held a microphone and she grabbed it from his hand as Ben hoisted her to the truck bed. Although she hadn't sung without music since she was a girl, she swung into her song as readily as if she had the band as a backup. As she sung a few verses of several hymns, the shouting lessened and the miners left the fence to crowd her improvised stage.

"It's Genna Ross," a young miner shouted.

"That's right," she called back with a smile. "Have a favorite song you'd like to hear?"

"What about 'One-Man Woman?' "

She sung his request, and then another and another until she sensed their anger abating. Finally when she held their attention, and she said, "Men, I grew up in this county in the home of a coal miner, and he taught me that miners didn't want women meddling in their affairs. But I can't stand aside tonight and watch you destroy yourselves and this business. Think how many of you have worked for Sullivan Mining. Consider the people in this county who've had only good from your employers.

"Stick with the bargaining table a little longer, guys. Evan Sullivan is fair. He'll give you everything he can, but his back is to the wall. Too many mines in this state have closed. If you destroy this one, you'll never have a chance to work here again."

"She's right, men, let's go home and sleep on it."

The crowd dispersed quickly, and a miner helped her off the truck. If it hadn't been for Ben's steadying hand, her shaky legs wouldn't have carried her back to the car. She'd saved Evan's mine for him again, but this time he might find out. She didn't need his thanks, but she did need his pride as a man. There would be no hope for them if that were gone.

Chapter Ten

Genna walked hesitantly up the hospital steps. *How would Evan react to her?* Any hope that her appearance at the mine two nights ago would escape public notice had died an unmerciful death. Emblazoned across the local newspaper the next morning was the headline, GENNA ROSS SAVES SULLIVAN MINE FROM DESTRUCTION. In smaller type another headline stated, Sullivan Remains Hospitalized. A picture on the front page showed Genna with microphone in hand atop the makeshift stage.

If Evan had been grateful, he could have let her know. She had waited two days to go see him, but finally reasoned he wouldn't know how to contact her by phone.

She took a deep breath and stopped at Room 135. She walked in the open door. A stranger was in the bed that Evan had occupied.

"I'm sorry," she apologized. "I was looking for Evan Sullivan."

"He went home yesterday."

"Oh, I see. . . ."

She walked down the hallway and stopped briefly to gaze out a window at the narrow, crowded streets below. Why hadn't Evan contacted her before he left? She couldn't erase the question from her mind. He could have reached her through the Fishers if he'd tried. She'd give him a few days of convalescence and then she'd telephone him.

In a way Genna was relieved to have their meeting postponed. The rest of the day she spent in Logan talking to contractors and buying supplies for the renovation of Grandpap's home. She had looked the place over with Ben and they had agreed that part of the back porch could easily be converted into a bathroom. Genna eagerly planned the way the old home would look. Before she went home, she applied for a telephone installation.

For a week Genna did little except roam the woods around her cabin. She climbed each day to Pinnacle Rock, and each time was rewarded with a more breathtaking canvas of nature. The dogwood trees bloomed in increasing white profusion, giving a hint of summer to the otherwise sleeping woodland.

At first she was jubilant seeing the places she'd thought about each spring for years, but how different it was from what she'd always envisioned! Since Christmas she'd thought of Evan's presence beside her as she visited the places of her memories. Try as she might, she couldn't recall the pleasures of youth.

What had Evan said? "We'll have to start over again." Perhaps he was right. Her beloved mountains had not brought the healing she needed in her heart.

Another week passed before she finally had a telephone. There was still no word from Evan, and she had waited as long as she could. She wanted to hear from him even if he didn't want to hear from her. Impulsively, she telephoned his home in Charleston.

The woman who answered the telephone identified herself as the housekeeper, Inez Gilley.

Genna stated her name and said, "I want to inquire about Mr. Sullivan."

"He's doing quite well, thank you."

"Has he been able to leave the house?"

"He's taken a few short trips in the car."

She certainly wasn't getting much information. "Is Mr. Sullivan at home now? I'd like to speak to him if he is."

"Just a minute, please." It seemed like hours before the woman returned. "Mr. Sullivan is resting at the moment. He doesn't want to take any phone calls."

"Oh . . . well, thank you very much. Would you tell him I have a telephone installed at my summer home now?"

"I'll tell him," the woman said and severed the connection.

Where could she go when her heart was breaking? The one person who came to mind was Miss Amelia.

Every time she entered Miss Amelia's living room and sat on the stool beside her chair Genna felt like a child again. Miss Amelia took her hand, and after they sat in silence for several minutes, she asked, "Genna, what makes you so unhappy?"

"I'm not supposed to be unhappy. I'm the great Genna Ross," Genna said bitterly, "and that means nothing because I can't have Evan Sullivan. Am I just being stubborn, Miss Amelia?"

"No, you're following what your heart desires, but you don't have your priorities in the right place. Tell me, Genna, why did you leave your career this spring?"

"To remodel Grandpap's home. To see if Evan has any place in my future. To assess what I'll do with my singing."

"Why?"

"Why what?"

"Why did you find it necessary to evaluate your career?"

Genna hesitated a long time. The mantle clock ticked away the minutes. It was easy enough to say these words to Jim and Evan, but when she said them to Miss Amelia, Genna had the feeling that she was committed. A statement to Miss Amelia was almost as binding as one she'd make to God.

"I think God is calling me to use my voice for some kind of Christian service." And then a sudden thought shook her. "Have you been praying for that?"

Miss Amelia smiled slightly. "Yes, my dear, I have. I've always lived by Jesus' words, 'Seek ye first the kingdom of God and his righteousness; and all these things shall be added unto you.' Once you acknowledge God's leadership in your life, you'll realize your other desires."

"Does that mean Evan?"

"Not necessarily. Evan may not be in God's plan for you, and you'll give him up if that's the case. You'll cease tearing your emotions apart because of Evan."

"But I love him so much," Genna sobbed, and she lowered her head to Miss Amelia's knees. Genna was conscious of a trembling hand on her head, and she looked up into Miss Amelia's face. Tears lined the wrinkled cheeks.

"Oh, Miss Amelia, did you have to make a choice like this too?"

"Yes, Genna," she replied hesitantly. "Before I came to the mountains, I loved this young man very much, but he made it plain that if I married him, I couldn't be a missionary. In other words, it was God's will for my life or him. Believe me, I wrestled with the problem much as you are doing."

"But you let him go?"

"Yes, and once the decision was made, I wasn't sorry. I've never looked back. I've been happy."

"How am I going to know God's will?"

Miss Amelia picked up the Bible. "The answer is here, Genna. I can't tell you. If you seek God's will, you'll find it."

Genna studied the Bible for days, no nearer a decision than she'd ever been. It was hard to get her mind on her meditation when the papers and television were full of news about Evan. The wildcat strike had been settled and the miners were back at work.

When she heard on the radio that Carol Sue and the Hosannas were scheduled for an appearance in Roanoke, Virginia, she decided to pay a visit to Ivy and Ben.

"Want to take a little trip with me?"

Ben rolled his eyes heavenward. "In that high-powered car?"

Genna couldn't decide if Ben were joking about her fast driving or if he really were afraid of the speed.

"I'll promise to keep to the speed limit. I want to see the Carol Sue concert in Roanoke, and it will be good for you to have a little vacation. We'd be gone only two days."

When they agreed, Genna telephoned for reservations and they left early the next morning. As she shared Ben and Ivy's first view of the Blue Ridge Mountains, Genna forgot her own turmoil over Evan. After they'd settled into a motel, Genna telephoned the hotel where Carol Sue reportedly had registered. She asked for the singer's secretary.

"This is Genna Ross, and I'd like to make contact with Carol Sue. I'm here in town and, if she has time, perhaps I could pick her up after the concert tonight and we could go out for a light meal." Genna gave the number of her motel and asked the woman to telephone Carol Sue's answer.

Within fifteen minutes the phone rang and the secretary said, "You may pick Carol Sue up here at the hotel at ten-thirty tonight."

While Genna watched the concert, she kept trying to put herself in the place of Carol Sue. Could she possibly present a concert that was entertaining yet at the same time spiritually stimulating? Carol Sue had a rare gift that Genna Ross might not have. When they left the auditorium, a peaceful hush seemed to have settled on the huge crowd and talking was at a minimum. Ben echoed Genna's sentiments when he said, "I feel just like I've been to church."

Genna took the Fishers to their motel and returned to the downtown area. Carol Sue waited for her in the lobby.

"It's great of you to take time for me," Genna said. "I know how tiring a concert can be, and you did a super job tonight."

"But you also know it's necessary to unwind, so I'm pleased you telephoned."

As Genna maneuvered her way into the traffic lane, she explained, "I've wanted to talk with you for months, but it seems our paths didn't cross. I'm spending the summer at my Appalachian home, and when I knew you were this close, I decided to come to see you."

They left the windows down and the cool wind ruffled their hair as Genna drove at moderate speed down Interstate 81. After about ten miles, she exited and pulled into the lot of a small drive-in restaurant.

"Shall we order and stay in the car to eat? We'll have more privacy that way."

"That's fine. If we go inside, there's bound to be someone who would know one of us."

"Yes, but we'd be panicking if no one wanted to talk to us," Genna countered lightly.

After they received their order at the drive-in window, Genna locked the doors and drove to a secluded but well-lighted section of the parking lot.

"Since I saw your concert last year, I can't put out of my mind that I should be doing something similar."

"I've thought the same thing. Genna, you're a natural for gospel music."

"Would you think I was competing with you?"

Carol Sue laughed. "Of course not. I have more invitations than I can possibly fulfill. There's a need for both of us."

"I've been adding a few gospel songs to my concerts, but this overriding feeling keeps occurring that there should be a change in my repertoire. God knows what He wants me to do, but He hasn't revealed it yet, though I feel pressured to make a decision soon."

"If I were you, I'd stop the agitation and just put yourself at God's disposal. When He has a new place for you, He'll reveal it. In the meantime, why not go on as usual?"

"Sounds reasonable," Genna agreed. "I have several fairs scheduled for August and September, and I'm looking forward to those. I know my manager is desperate to arrange my winter's schedule, but I can't give the word."

"Gospel singing has been a great challenge to me, and you probably would like the change, but don't do anything until you know that it's right for you. I feel in my heart that God has some great plan for your life, and when the opportunity comes, you'll know what it is."

Genna left Carol Sue at the hotel with a lighter heart, and the next morning the feeling of peace was still with her. Taking their time, Genna and Ivy and Ben spent the day driving along the Blue Ridge Parkway. At almost every turnout where they stopped to view the Shenandoah Valley, Ben scratched his head and muttered, "It's a big old world when you see hit from here, ain't hit?"

Genna laughingly agreed it was, but wondered what Ben would think of the world if he'd ever seen it from an airplane. Genna didn't head toward Logan County until it became too dark to see, and they arrived on Mill Creek at a late hour.

"Way past my bedtime," Ben said as he crawled out of the car, "but I had a good time, girl."

A few weeks later, when Genna was returning from Logan where she'd gone to order some supplies, she saw Evan's truck at the mine. She went on by for a mile, then turned and drove slowly back. All she could do was try. She had to see him at least once more before she put him out of her life.

Just as she pulled in the parking lot she spied Evan a few feet away walking toward his truck. He wouldn't have a chance to avoid her now.

"I'm glad to see you're back at work, Evan. Are you feeling all right now?"

"Yes, thanks," he answered gruffly without looking at her.

Her eyes smarted and she blinked rapidly but she held back her tears. The years in drama school paid off as she said without a tremor in her voice, "Seems to me when we parted at Christmas, I heard something about us starting over again. Have you changed your mind about that, Evan?"

"This is no place to talk," he muttered, still not meeting her gaze.

"You don't seem to want to talk elsewhere, but I'll be at home this evening."

"I'll be there at seven o'clock."

Three hours until seven o'clock, but she supposed she could survive. She spent the hours praying, and by the time Evan arrived, she had chosen her words carefully. She knew now that she had to sing, and if Evan couldn't accept her and her successful career, she'd have to give him up. God had given her the talent to sing and she couldn't shove it aside, not even for Evan. When he drove into the yard, she whispered, "All right, Lord. Not my will, but yours be done."

She took Evan on a tour of the house, which didn't take long, and they seated themselves on the porch. The June night was aburst with lightning bugs, singing insects, and the fresh smell of the yellow rambler rose at the end of the porch.

When the silence lengthened between them, Genna said at last, "I think I have the right to know why you've changed toward me."

He turned angrily toward her. "As if you didn't know! How do you think I feel to be obligated to the woman I love? Genna, why did you go to the mine that night?"

"If I hadn't gone, you wouldn't have a mine left."

"I'll admit the truth of that, but that doesn't make it any easier to take."

"Would you have preferred to have your operations wrecked? To have no place for the miners to go now that the strike is over? What's bothering you, your pride? I have reason to remember that your pride has always stood in your way; you were always concerned with what people thought about the Sullivans."

The words were bitter in her mouth. *Would she never forget Evan's rejection of her on Pinnacle Rock?*

Evan continued as if he hadn't heard her. "And then to find out that you were the one who'd given me the money to save the mining operations! I thought the accountant had secured a loan until I asked him the other day about paying it back. When I found out he didn't even know where the money had come from, I stormed into Blankenship's office and demanded the truth. Genna, why did you meddle in my business?"

A lump rose in Genna's throat, but she swallowed convulsively and said, "Let me ask you again. Would you have preferred to lose your business rather than to accept help from me?"

He turned away, and Genna continued. " 'Pride goeth before destruction, and an haughty spirit before a fall.' Maybe this isn't the time to remind you of that, Evan, but you're being foolish. I had the name and the voice to convince those miners to avert a problem that would have ruined you and them. I had the money to save you when I wouldn't let you strip my property. I felt responsible for that problem because of the promise I'd made Grandpap. Was the only reason you liked Veevie Wooten because she had nothing? Yes, Evan, Veevie Wooten would be completely dependent on you. But I'm not Veevie Wooten anymore, not the crooked-toothed, ill-spoken, plain girl of the past. I'm Genna Ross now, and nothing can change that. I came back this spring hoping to revive the past. The first thing I learned is that one can't erase twelve years."

"I know," he said. "I wish I could."

"I thought we could when I came home. But this month I've wrestled with my problems, and I've reached an answer. I won't let you hurt me again. If you want to accept me as I am, money and career, then we might be able to begin again. If you expect me to be Veevie Wooten, I'm sorry but I'm not giving up everything I've gained for you. I'm ready to forget that we once meant something to each other."

"Do you really mean that?" he asked, surprise in his voice.

"I really mean that. If you need to think about it, all right, but I don't intend to waste any more time grieving over what we lost. I'm going to make a new start, with or without you."

He reached for her and pulled her into his arms. "Then make it with me, Genna. I don't want to lose you again. Forgive me for being angry."

Genna stifled the tears welling up from her heart. *She couldn't give in yet.* "But how do you feel about my career? One of the things I've had to deal with this month is what direction my work will take. God wants me to continue singing, not in the same way, perhaps, but for His glory. How will you feel about that? Will you accept that my life won't always be subject to what you want?"

"I'll admit that won't be easy. I want to marry you, Genna, I want you in my life always. I won't like it if you're gone for weeks at a time. I'd want us to be together, but if you'll marry me, I'll accept you as you are."

She kissed him lightly on the cheek. "I won't want to be away from you either, but it may come to that. God hasn't revealed what He wants me to do, but I'm expecting an answer soon. I had to acknowledge that He came first in my life, even before you, Evan, as much as I love you."

"But you will marry me?"

"Let's give ourselves a month. That's when I have to notify my band about my plans. We can see each other as often as possible, and I can spend some time with Michelle, too. I guess I want to see how I like having to share you with someone else. I need to know that from the outset."

Evan smiled and drew her close again, his hand caressing the waves of her hair. As she returned Evan's embrace, Genna realized, perhaps for the first time, that she embraced her future as well.

Chapter Eleven

Genna held the letter from Cary for five minutes before she opened it. She corresponded regularly with Cary, but none of the other letters had filled her with such dread.

A newspaper clipping fell out into her lap when she opened the envelope. The headlines of the article said it all: GENNA ROSS LIFE STORY TO BE PUBLISHED BY GARNER PRESS. Before she read the article, with trembling fingers she scanned Cary's note. "I doubt you've been reading many newspapers this summer and perhaps you missed this. Did you know anything about it?"

According to the article, the book had been written by Joe Bagley, a ghost writer, who did biographies of many famous people for Garner. Genna assessed the situation trying not to lose her temper. She mustn't act rashly. Maybe the publisher was putting out an unauthorized biography, but Garner was a reputable publisher. She doubted they'd act in an unethical manner.

She quickly contacted George Blankenship by telephone.

After he heard her story, he asked, "What exactly do you want me to do?"

"I'd like for you to call the publisher, as my attorney, and inquire where they received the permission to do my life's story. When I have that information, I'll decide what to do next."

Blankenship obtained the information quickly and got back to her within an hour. "Your manager, Jim Slater, signed the contract authorizing the book."

"But I told him not to do it. I don't want the book."

"How much authority have you given him as your manager?"

"I'd have to check the contract, but I feel sure I gave him only authorization to book my personal appearances and schedule recordings."

"Perhaps the best thing to do is to let the book be published. If you make too big a fuss, they'll probably publish anyway. Even if you sue them, all the publicity will make people more determined to read the book."

"You may be right, but I don't think a company like Garner would want to be on my blacklist. Will you write a letter to them, saying that I had not authorized the publication, and that my manager knew I didn't want a book?"

Now that her relations with Evan were mending, she didn't want anything to smear their youthful romance. She'd read too many biographies, written to be made into movies or to make money for recording companies, where the truth was stretched to make a sensational story. Even if the book related accurately her romance with Evan, he wouldn't like it.

Blankenship heard from Garner Press within a week, and he contacted her by phone.

"They said they were very sorry that Miss Ross was displeased about the book. They had been led to believe that you were agreeable to the publication. They will halt printing until your personal approval is given, but they asked if you'd be kind enough to read the proofs to see what you find objectionable."

"Yes, I'll read the proofs," Genna told Blankenship. "If they'll agree to my edited copy, I'll let them go ahead; otherwise, I'll take other legal action. May I have an appointment to see you tomorrow? I have some other work that can't wait any longer."

Within a week she had to notify her staff about contracts, and she'd made her decision. Jim and Lori had to go, and since she didn't know what type of singing she'd be doing, she had decided to terminate the contracts of the band too. If she sang only folk songs and gospel music, she could do very well with a pianist. She would keep Cary on the payroll for at least a year.

The next day when Blankenship read copies of the contracts, which had been forwarded from her accountant in Nashville, he assured Genna that her intentions were legal. Just as she thought, the contracts could be terminated with a month's notice and two months' pay.

"Since I want to be fair, pay them three months' salary. My accountant will take care of the details, but I'd like you to write the letters."

The proofs of her biography came in the mail the next week, and Genna spent two days going over them. Obviously, the author had visited the area, and the book would contain photographs of her birthplace, the schools she'd attended, and even the little Bethel Church. Several of her childhood acquaintances had been interviewed, including Angela Keefer, but not a word was mentioned about Evan. They'd kept their secret well, and she breathed a sigh of relief.

Actually the book didn't say much about her girlhood years. The author had picked up her story when she started drama school in California and followed carefully her rise to fame. The manuscript was well written and factual with only a few exceptions, and within a few days she sent the proofs back to the publisher with her corrections and approval.

As soon as Blankenship mailed the letters to her staff, Genna telephoned Cary.

"I wanted you to know in advance about it, Cary."

"But why are you keeping me? What are we going to do?"

Genna laughed. "I don't know. God hasn't told me that yet, but you'll draw your salary until I know. Whatever I do, I want you with me."

Genna had expected Jim to telephone, not to appear at her door. When he stepped up on the porch one afternoon in late July and knocked on her screen door, for a moment she was relieved the door was locked.

At a loss for words, at last she unlocked the latch and said, "Come in, Jim." *Perhaps she owed him something,* she thought.

He surveyed the room. "So this is where you've been wasting your time. Quite a step down for Genna Ross, isn't it?"

His comment gave Genna time to control her emotions, and she laughed. "You should have seen the house before I remodeled it. That's been one of my projects this summer."

"Genna, you can't do this to me," he said as he sank heavily into Grandpap's old rocker.

"But I have done it," she replied. "You can't say I hadn't warned you. I'd hesitated to fire you, but when you went ahead with that book contract without my consent, that was the last straw."

"That was too great an opportunity to lose. Garner Press does biographies of only top stars."

"I had already told you I didn't want any book, Jim. When I told the editor that you had no right to sign that contract, he agreed they wouldn't publish the biography. However, I've read the proofs and didn't find them objectionable, so I've given my consent."

"That didn't do my rating with Garner any good."

"You should have thought of that before you double-crossed me."

"Are you still planning on becoming the next Carol Sue?" Jim could not contain his old teasing nature, despite the tone of the visit.

"I don't think so, but I'll be going into some kind of Christian singing."

"Have you hired another manager yet?"

Genna shook her head. A strong breeze swept down the hollow and rattled the windows of the cabin. A cardinal's clear call sounded from the maple tree in the front yard, while a woodpecker drummed on a distant dead bough. She tried to detach herself from the room. Change had always been hard for her, and Jim had been part of her life for five years.

"Then why can't I continue as I always have? I'll not disregard your wishes again."

"It's too late, Jim. You were a good manager until you let your personal feelings get in the way. You're either critical or jealous of every move I make, and I'm tired of it. I'm sorry, because we did make a good team once, but no more."

"If you'd have married me, we would have made a better team."

Genna shook her head. She had been expecting Evan, and she heard his footsteps on the porch. He'd been away for two weeks and had no idea about her biography. When he entered the room, she couldn't help comparing him to Jim. Evan represented the security she had always needed. Jim would always remind her of those exciting days of reaching stardom, but also of the misery and bitterness of the years when Evan was only a memory.

"Jim, if you remember, you met Evan Sullivan in Columbus last winter. Evan and I haven't made final plans, but we're sort of engaged to be engaged." She walked to Evan, and he drew her close in the circle of his arm. "I don't know whether this will make you feel better or worse, but I've loved him since I was sixteen years old, and I'll never stop loving him."

Jim scrutinized them closely. He swallowed hard, and finally said, "I hope you'll be happy." He left the room without another word. Secure in the warmth of Evan's embrace, for the first time, she felt sorry for Jim.

Early the next morning, Blankenship telephoned. "There's a man here who wants to talk business with you, Genna. Is it all right if I send him out?"

"Let me come to your office. When discussing business, I'd prefer to have an attorney present. Is this business anything I'll be interested in?"

"I rather think so." Blankenship sounded excited, and Genna agreed to be at his office within the hour.

The large, florid man in Blankenship's office introduced himself as Lowell Graham. "Miss Ross, we're looking for a place to build a year-round resort in West Virginia, and we think that mountainous area near your home would be ideal. What we have in mind is to build a place that we can tie to the name of a well-known person similar to Dollywood in Tennessee. If you'd allow us to name the resort for you, and you'd make frequent appearances at the hotel, we'd have a winner. The natural area is great for this. We'd appeal to the skiers in winter but plan other activities throughout the year. What do you say?"

"If I'd allow my name on the resort, I'd want some control over it. Are you selling stock in this venture?"

Graham smiled. "We do hope for some local monetary investment. We'd welcome Genna Ross as a stockholder."

"You should know that I am thinking of changing my musical repertoire from country music to gospel."

"Surely you would consider singing the folk songs you've included in the past."

"Yes, at times, but my primary thrust will be gospel music. I'll be touring some, so I couldn't be at the resort every day."

"We're intending to make so much money that you'll want to stay here all the time," Graham said with a smile.

"Logan County could use a boost to its economy now, and what's good for the resort will be good for our area."

"We'll give you several names to choose from, but we're favoring Gennaland."

"I'm going to be on concert tour for the next two months, but I'll notify you of my decision."

Genna broke the news to Evan as soon as he came to see her that night. "What do you think of the idea?"

The eagerness in his eyes warmed Genna's heart.

"I know I shouldn't be selfish, and I'm trying to let you decide your own career without any influence from me, but it would make me happy to know you'd be working nearby instead of traveling so many months out of the year."

"Funny how we have the same idea! Yet one thing bothers me—do you believe a resort will ever be successful here?"

"With the Genna Ross name on it, I feel sure it will. That's the reason the promoters want a large name. They like this area, and then to find that you live here cinched the proposition for them."

"Will they be able to find enough land?"

He smiled. "I had a visit from the agent too. They want to buy the property I'm stripping up here on the mountain. It will be a good way to reclaim the area when I've finished. They plan to put a ski lodge on the eastern slope of the mountain; this side wouldn't be changed at all."

"What else do they plan beside the lodge?"

"They want to develop a golf course if they can locate enough level land and to build a tramway across Mill Creek Valley. They're either leasing or buying some of the old Miller property. And, of course, they'll have swimming facilities, tennis, and other recreation at the lodge."

"Good! They'll be doing what I want done, preserving the mountain beauty that I cherish. You know, Evan, if we're married, we can't very well live in this cabin."

"How long before you have to give them an answer?"

"I've put them off until after I've finished my fall concerts. In the meantime, Blankenship is looking into the financial condition of this company."

"What does he think about the resort?"

"He's as excited as he ever gets about anything. He believes it will be a boost to the county's economy."

"It will surely boost my economy. They've offered a lot more for that land than I paid for it. With my finances on a solid footing again, at least that won't stand in our way of happiness."

She kissed him tenderly. "Evan, I'm beginning to believe nothing can stand in the way of our happiness now."

Now that Genna had terminated the contracts with her band, she had a short time to arrange for musical accompaniment for her upcoming state fair concerts. With Lori gone, she would also need a secretary.

Lunching with Angela one day, Genna said, "Here's where I miss Jim. I need a pianist part-time and a secretary part-time, and I haven't had to worry about hiring before. Jim did that. I really don't know where to turn."

"Do you want two different people, or would you be happy if one person could fill both needs?"

"I'll have to settle for what I can find, I suppose, but I'd like to find one person who's a trained musician and also has business experience. Do you know where I could find such a person?"

The amused expression in Angela's eyes baffled Genna for a moment, and then she shouted, "Would you?"

The other diners in the restaurant looked at Genna, and she flushed and lowered her voice. "I would love to have you, but I wouldn't have considered asking you to give up your job."

"I have a good income from my husband's insurance, and I'd enjoy leaving Woodville occasionally. I haven't traveled much, and I think it would be fun to do concerts with you. Don't worry that it will inconvenience me. I'd love playing while you sing, and I'm sure I could handle your scheduling and other business."

"It sounds like a great idea, but let's not decide until we've practiced together. Shall we try out some music tonight?"

After a few practices, Angela could follow every tempo and inflection of voice that Genna introduced. After renting office space in Logan, Genna set Angela to work in her dual role as secretary.

The first of August they joined Cary in Nashville, and the three women spent the next two months traveling by plane and rental cars to the fairs. Finding this way of travel most satisfactory, Genna placed the big bus on the market.

By the time the tour ended, Genna had made her decision, convinced that God had made plain His will for her life. She would spend most of her time singing at the resort, booking only occasional appearances away from home. She telephoned her decision to Lowell Graham, and he told her that he'd start immediately proceedings for building the resort.

She wrote Evan a letter, telling him of her plans and her love for him. Tears flowed freely when she wrote the last paragraph. "The past is behind me now, Evan. We've waited a long time and I'm ready to marry you. I love you."

Chapter Twelve

Soon after Genna returned from her fair concerts the weather turned unseasonably cold. With two nights of frost the turning of the leaves from green to autumn hues was evident. Ben stopped Genna one day when she was returning from her office in Logan.

"I'm goin' to cut a bee tree tonight. Want to come along?"

"Well, Evan is coming to see me this evening. Will it be all right for him to go too?"

"Sure thing. Ivy's goin', so we'll make a party of it."

"It may turn into quite a party if those bees are still active. Aren't you rushing it a bit?"

"After these two big frosts, they won't sting."

"Uh-huh," Genna said unconvincingly. Bee stings or not, she didn't want to miss this nostalgic adventure. One of her earliest memories was tagging along with Grandpap when he climbed the mountains to cut a tree where the wild bees had stored a supply of honey. The hoard from two or three of these trees had kept honey on their table throughout the winter.

Genna telephoned Evan as soon as she arrived at the cabin.

"Sounds like fun," he agreed. "There's supposed to be a full moon tonight. . . ."

"It won't be a romantic walk, I warn you. From my experience, the tree will probably be on the steepest side of the mountain, and our only interest will be in keeping the bees from stinging us."

Evan laughed. "Nonetheless, I'm game. I like anything if I'm in your company. Love you."

"Me, too. See you soon after dark."

Bundled into heavy coats and gloves as protection against the sharp cold, they walked to meet Ivy and Ben at their house. As they started up the mountain trail, Evan asked Ben, "Why do you go at night, and why does it have to be a cold one at that?" He pulled the coat collar around his neck.

"If it's not chilly, the bees will sting you. They're sluggish when it's cold. You cut at night because the weather is colder then."

"I always thought it was to keep the bees from seeing you," Genna said.

"They don't need to see to find you," Ivy commented.

They walked single file in silence, the only sound the rhythmic crunch of their feet on the frosty turf. Genna and Evan carried flashlights, but they were hardly needed. Evan's predicted full moon peered over the mountain and bathed the area in a subdued light.

Ben had his hands full with a crosscut saw and an ax and Ivy carried two buckets. Since only Ben knew the location of the tree, they followed him through the woods. Their destination was a steep point, and when they paused to catch their breath, Ben pointed out some landmarks.

"There's your house, Genna, and ours is right here below us. That's Sullivan No. 2 to the left." Genna had left her porch light on so it was easy to find her house and of course many lights surrounded the coal mine.

Shining his flashlight on the side of a huge tree, Ben said, "See the hole next to that lower limb. That's where the bees go in and out." The tree, which Ben said was a black oak, was about fifty feet tall and the first limb was twenty feet above the ground.

"Ever use a crosscut saw?" Ben said to Evan.

"No, they didn't teach that in engineering school."

"You'll not learn any younger. Be a good experience for you." Ben circled the tree. "First, we have to decide where we want hit to fall. Stuck up on this point like hit is, hit's bound to go downhill whatever we do. Stand back now."

Ben picked up the ax and began to chop the tree trunk about three feet above the ground. When he'd made a sizable gash in the bark, he picked up the saw and said to the two women, "Stand a fur piece off for the tree might buckle and fall backwards. Be ready to run if hit does.

"You take one end of this saw," Ben instructed Evan, "and we'll pull hit back and forth steadylike. When you hear the tree creak a little, help me pull the saw out, then run out of the way. I'll push the tree over if hit's still standin,' but chances are the weight will pull hit down even if hit ain't sawed all the way through."

With a smile in Genna's direction, Evan did as he was told. The tree was about ten feet in circumference, and from Genna's observation, she thought Evan was doing a fine job. Unimpressed, Ben ordered, "Here now! Quit jerkin' on that saw. Do you want to break the teeth outen hit? Pull steady." Evan followed his instructions, and Ben gruffly added, "That's better."

"Come down here, Ivy," Ben called, "and hold the light. I want to see how much farther to saw." Ivy scurried toward the tree and flashed a beam on the trunk and Ben decided he had a few more inches.

The only sound in the forest was the rhythmic hum of the saw as it bit farther and farther into the tree trunk, scattering sawdust at the feet of the two men. Genna saw the top of the tree jerk, followed by a sharp snapping sound.

"Quick, pull out the saw and run!"

Ben was close behind Evan when he reached the women. The old tree hovered between the heavens and the earth for a few moments as though reluctant to give up its commanding position in the forest. At last the pull of its enormous weight was too strong to be withstood, and with a final shudder, it left the spot it had occupied for centuries, crushing the underbrush and smaller trees in its path. The noise of the crash was deafening, but after the tree settled to its final resting place, a strange hush settled over the forest.

Genna broke the quietness by saying softly, "There's something a little sad about it, isn't there?"

"I know," Ivy agreed. "I feel bad every time one of these trees is cut, especially when you realize how many years it's been standin.'"

Ben, practical as always, said, "This is nature's way. That tree had outlived hits usefulness. Hit was dyin,' or the bees couldn't have found a place in hit. God planned nature this way. The dyin' tree made a home for the bees, and the bees provided food for man. Veevie, I'm expectin' you to help me take the honey."

The tree had been so tall that its uppermost branches had landed on the other side of a small gully forming a bridge from one side to the other. A low, humming sound came from inside the tree, and Ben whistled. "Boy, listen to that buzz. The fall stirred 'em up. Ivy, fill up the smoker and light hit. We're goin' to need hit."

"Explain to me what's going on," Evan said.

Ben pointed to an item shaped like a coffeepot with a set of bellows on one side that Ivy had pulled from a bucket. She stuffed the top of the pot with rags and ignited them with a match.

"That's a smoker," Ben explained. "We'll use it to blow smoke in that hole. As soon as the smoke dulls the bees, I'll cut the trunk of the tree where they have their hoard, and we'll lift out the honey."

Ben took another apparatus from the bucket and pulled it over his head. Genna laughed when she recognized it as the same kind of garb Grandpap had worn: nothing but an old straw hat with some cheese cloth draped over it. Ben tied it around his waist with some heavy string and pulled gloves on his hands.

"There's another one," he said to Genna. "Put hit on. You can hold the bucket."

"Just like I used to do for Grandpap," Genna said excitedly.

Ben found a foothold under the tree and puffed smoke into the hole. The bees hummed angrily, but the noise soon ceased. Using the ax, he cut a slab off the trunk and straddled the tree near the cut he'd made. He motioned for Genna, and she moved to his side carrying a bucket.

Three layers of comb had been made, and Genna saw the bees working sluggishly in and out of the waxy openings filled with amber honey. Using a butcher knife, Ben soon filled one bucket with honey and Genna handed it to Evan who brought the other bucket. When it was filled, Ben laid the slab back over the opening.

"I'm leavin' a third of the honey to keep the bees alive through the winter."

"Will they make honey in this tree again?" Evan asked as they gathered up the buckets of honey and the equipment to head for home.

"Not likely," Ben answered. "Come spring, they'll move on to another tree."

Genna felt the frigid air seeping through her heavy coat. Her breath rose before her face and her hands felt numb. When they reached the Fishers' house, Ivy said, "Let me put some of this honey in a dish and you can take hit home with you."

The cold air urged them along, and Evan and Genna made record time to her cabin. Though it was almost midnight, Genna said, "If you're not afraid to try some of my cooking, come on in, and I'll make some biscuits to go along with our honey. That climb made me hungry."

Evan entered the house and helped her remove her coat. "Sounds fine to me, but I'm surprised you can cook."

With a saucy look over her shoulder as she entered the lean-to kitchen, she said, "I'll admit I haven't done much, but Grandpap taught me to make biscuits a long time ago. Ivy has been a good teacher this summer."

"Want me to make some coffee?"

"Yes, the automatic brewer is there on the shelf, and the coffee is in the fridge."

The biscuits and coffee were ready in a half-hour and they soon consumed a large portion of the honey Ivy had given them. When they finished, Evan said, "When we're married, Genna, every night will be like this night . . . good companionship and the thrill of being together. I'm ready whenever you are."

"I'm ready too. Let's set the date for early spring."

"Do you think hit will ever stop rainin'?" Ben asked as he sloshed through the water that had collected in Genna's front yard.

Genna met him on the porch, glancing anxiously toward the muddy water roiling down Mill Creek. "The weather report warned of flash floods."

"There ain't no letup in sight near as I can tell," Ben grumbled as he warmed himself in front of her small fire. "You sure are cozy here. I bet Grandpap wouldn't know the place if he'd come back. Hit helps to have money, don't hit?"

Genna smiled at him. "Yes, it does. I've lived in both extremes, never having enough money, and then having more than I needed. I've leveled off this year. The royalties from my recordings have rolled in steadily, so I've done very well for having worked only part-time since March."

"Hit's sure good you're goin' to stay here, girl. We like havin' you around, and you'll get all the singin' you want at that resort, time hit opens up."

"They plan to have it finished by next fall. I have agreed to make some personal appearances this winter and next spring, too, but I won't be gone much."

"How about you and Evan? Anything goin' to happen there?"

Genna nodded happily. "Next spring. We want to give Michelle time to get used to the idea, and Evan needs to feel he's on his feet financially. He's too proud to live on my income."

Ben nodded sagely. "Sure, don't blame him. A man likes to provide for his own. So hit looks like things are coming up roses for you."

"I'm almost thirty years old, Ben, so I'm a little late trying matrimony. I hope I can stay hitched, as Grandpap used to say."

Rising slowly from his chair, Ben said, "Better late than never."

"Don't go yet."

"Yeah, got to. I'm goin' to take a look at that dam at the head of the holler. I keep my eye on hit whenever we have lots of rain. I'm afeared of hit."

"Wait until I put on a coat and I'll go with you. I've been in too long today, I've got cabin fever."

Ben's truck churned through the mud as he guided the vehicle up the hollow and the side of the mountain to the sludge dam.

The water was already within an inch of the top. "What if it runs over the fill?" Genna asked, panic in her voice.

"Tain't runnin' over that worries me. I'm afeared the whole thing is goin' to bust one of these days, just like that one at Buffalo Creek several years ago. If hit does, there won't be nothin' left of Mill Creek, 'cept a memory. I wish I'd raised more ruckus about it, but hit's easier to let things go sometimes. I don't worry about hit until hit starts rainin.' "

"It's not your place more than any other person's. But I had no idea this lake got so full when it rains. I've only been up here in the summertime and usually the water level is low then."

Ben was unusually quiet all the way back to her cabin. "Why don't you come and bunk with us tonight, Veevie? You're awful close to that creek, and here on the level, you could get some high water."

She laughed at his fears. "You sound just like Grandpap. He was always predicting we'd get washed out of this hollow sometime and we haven't yet."

"John Wooten was a right smart man, Genna. He had a good head on him. Better come home with me."

Genna laughed away his fears, but she couldn't clear her mind of worry. She kept the television on to see the occasional flood warnings, and she paced nervously as the rain continued pounding on the roof. She walked out on the porch several times and strained her eyes to see the water. With an occasional flash of lightning to aid her vision, it did seem as if the water were closer to the road each time she looked.

Suddenly the night was shattered by a blast as loud as a dynamite charge. The sound had come from the hollow, and Genna knew her fears had been realized.

The dam had collapsed!

Gratefully she saw headlights coming up the road, and she laughed nervously. "Good old Ben. Coming to check on me again. I'm getting out of here."

Rapid steps crossed the porch and the door was shoved open. "It's me, Genna," Evan said. "We've got to get out of here. I was coming to check on you, and I heard that blast. I'm afraid the dam has burst."

Genna grabbed his arm. "Listen," she whispered.

After the first blast, quietness had settled around the homestead, broken only by the heavy rain pelting on the galvanized roof. Then they heard a sound resembling the roar of a train coming down the hollow. Evan raced out on the porch and she followed him.

For a moment, Evan was stunned. "Look at that wall of water!" Genna strained her eyes and the lightning flashes illuminated a wall of water about eight feet high mixed with rocks and other debris rolling toward them. Trees snapped like matchsticks as the deluge of water continued unhindered. The destructive wall weaved back and forth from one side of the hollow to the other. When it changed course and headed toward the house, Evan grabbed her arm. "Let's head for the mountain. Even now, we may not make it."

The wall of water hit the front porch and shook the house as soon as they left. Water tugged at Genna's feet, and she slipped backward, but Evan pulled her with him until they reached the cemetery knoll.

"Higher," he gasped. "Nothing can stop that water."

Genna never knew how they were able to climb the mountain, she only knew they had never stopped. Whenever she stopped for breath, Evan would beg, "Hurry, sweetheart."

The batteries in Evan's flashlight were weak and the light flickered often. It was better than nothing, but most of the time Genna stumbled along the darkened trail. Once when she started to slip, she grabbed at a tree for support and the swinging branch struck her sharply in the throat. She cried out but Evan was ahead of her and didn't hear.

The path they followed seemed familiar, and she realized Evan was on the Pinnacle Rock trail. Rain poured over her head, drenching her clothes. When they came to a rock overhang about halfway up the mountain, Evan stopped. "Let's stop here and rest. We'll have some protection from the rain."

He flashed his light around the rocky ledge to be sure that it was free of animals, then he sat down, his back against the wall, and pulled Genna into his arms.

"I'm afraid to imagine what happened to the rest of the valley," Genna said, shivering.

Evan drew her closer and wrapped his jacket around both of them. "Nothing could survive that onslaught of water. Anyone or anything in its path will be destroyed."

A sudden thought occurred to her. "The mine, too."

He laughed wryly. "Yes, this will finish me. I don't know whether to be happy or sad as much trouble as I've had at the mine the last few years. I'm wiped out."

"You still have your strip-mining."

"No, I sold that land to the resort company today. That's what I was coming to tell you."

"Then at least we'll have that to look forward to."

"But most important, we'll have each other. If I hadn't arrived when I did, I might have lost you too. That's a loss I couldn't handle, Genna."

"I love you, Evan," she whispered.

"What's the matter with your voice? You don't sound like yourself."

"A tree limb hit me in the throat and I've felt numb ever since. It's an effort to talk."

"We'll stop talking then. Try to rest if you can."

The rain had lessened somewhat by daylight. Genna was drowsy and Evan shook her gently awake.

"Do you feel like walking on to the pinnacle? I'd like to see the damage."

Genna opened her mouth to speak but no words came out. Evan looked at her in consternation. She tried again, but no words, only a squeak.

"Sweetheart," he said, "can't you talk yet?"

She shook her head.

"We'll have to get you to a doctor."

She framed the words with her lips. "How? We'd better see what the valley looks like."

Silently, Evan took her hand and helped her up the mountain trail. Standing beside Pinnacle Rock, Genna gasped in disbelief. The valley was devastated. They couldn't see an undamaged building and the winding road and the bridges that had crossed Mill Creek were gone. The old mining structure at the base of the mountain had been swept away in the deluge; even the lake where they'd picnicked last summer was empty. The water and heavy debris had roared down the valley leaving behind only a heavy layer of mud.

Mill Creek was overflowing its banks. Genna strained her eyes to see Grandpap's cabin, but she couldn't tell if anything remained. The tipple and the buildings of Sullivan Mine No. 2 had collapsed under the onslaught of the wall of water and debris. For a half-mile on each side of the river, trees and under-brush had been swept away.

"I can't believe this," Genna whispered.

"It's bad enough what's happened to the property, but what about the people? What about the people?"

"Is there any way we can get to Ben's?"

"We can go around the mountain. Are you up to walking?"

Genna merely nodded.

By noon they came out on the point where Ben's trailer had been. Genna felt faint. Half a dozen large trees had been deposited at the site. She turned away with a sick heart, and Evan's arm comforted her.

She roused herself when she heard a shout.

"Look!" Evan said. "There's Ben up there, waving to us."

Genna started running toward the spot, but Ben called, "Stay there, we're comin' down."

"Thank God," Genna whispered. "At least they escaped."

Ben lumbered into the clearing, Ivy at his heels. He grabbed their hands. "I was never so glad to see anyone in my life. I felt sure the water had got you." He turned to Evan. "What'd you make of that? Ever see anything to beat that water?"

Evan shook his head. "Never. Of course the dam must have burst, but I couldn't believe how fast that water traveled."

"Why, hit was more than six feet high, just pushin' everything in front of hit. If hit had to happen, I wish hit'd been in the daylight, so we could have seen."

Ivy reached them by now, and Genna hugged her. "Oh, I'm glad I still have you. Everything else is gone."

"What's wrong with your voice?"

Genna shook her head, and Evan answered, "While we were climbing the mountain last night in the dark, a tree branch struck her in the throat. She hasn't been able to talk well since. It seems as if her throat is paralyzed."

"What'll that do to your singin'?" Ivy asked.

Genna turned startled eyes toward Evan. It was the first time she'd considered that the freak accident might have ended her singing career. The flood and its aftermath had towered over her personal problems.

"You suppose there's any way we can take her to a doctor? My truck was up at her cabin, but that'll be gone now," Evan said.

"There's no road left to travel on. One of us could try to walk out to telephone for help, but hard to tell how far we'd have to go. I figger there'll be people checkin' on this today or tomorrow. Better wait hit out, rather than for us to leave the women to fend for themselves. Ivy and me spent the night in that little barn." Ben motioned toward a little building high on the mountain. "Nothin' to eat, but at least hit was dry."

Late afternoon Ben heard the sound of an engine. A civil defense helicopter hovered over the area and Ben and Evan rushed out of the barn to wave their arms. The pilot signaled that he'd seen them and started to descend seeking a spot wide enough to land. He was more than a mile from the barn when he landed in a field swept level by the flood.

"Come on, Genna," Evan said. "Let's see if he'll take you to the doctor. I'm worried about you."

Genna didn't argue. She was getting worried herself; she couldn't make a sound now.

Evan recognized the pilot as a member of the National Guard. The man grabbed his hand. "Boy, is it good to see somebody alive. This whole creek is wiped out. For eight miles, I haven't seen a living soul or animal—nothing."

He willingly took Genna into the chopper and since there was room for him, Evan went too. The man had brought a box of food that he left with Ben and Ivy.

"We'll be all right, so don't worry about us, Genna. Get yourself to a doctor," Ivy said.

Evan stayed with Genna all through the long examination. The doctor shook his head as a preface to his diagnosis.

"Frankly, I don't know what to tell you. Loss of voice might have come from the blow, or from the shock you'd had. At this point, all I can suggest is complete bed rest and no effort to talk at all. If you want to communicate, write on some paper."

Evan accompanied her into the hospital room before he left. She reached for the pad of paper the nurse had left and wrote, "I love you, Evan." He gathered her into his arms, tears in his eyes, and kissed her.

"I'll be back tomorrow. You'll be all right, sweetheart."

When he came the next day, his face was grave.

"I don't know if I should tell you this, but I know you're wondering. Mill Creek is a wasteland. Twenty people are missing or dead, and one of them is the missionary Miss Amelia."

Tears seeped from Genna's eyes. *Was she to have nothing of the past left?*

"The only good news is that your cabin is somehow still standing. The water went through and drenched everything and took the porch, but it seems as if the main wall of water didn't hit the house. You'll have a job on your hands, but I think it can be restored."

"Your mine?" She formed the words with her lips.

"Nothing left."

Within two weeks Genna's voice had returned slightly and the doctor allowed her to leave the hospital. A specialist had been called in from Johns Hopkins University School of Medicine for consultation.

"It may be, Miss Ross, that you can never sing again. At any rate, I would strongly advise you not to try for several months. After that, you can probably handle short engagements, but the long concert tours you used to take are probably a thing of the past."

The diagnosis was a blow to Genna, but perhaps this was God's answer. At least she would have the resort, she told herself with no particular comfort. She refused to let her mind dwell on the possibility that her career was ended.

The year was almost past and Genna sat on the reconstructed porch of her cabin. In spite of the worry over her voice and the postponement of their wedding, royalties from her book and a contract for the movie rights had brought in more money than she'd earned on concert tours. Michelle had spent several weeks with Genna and she was reconciled and eager for Genna and Evan to marry.

Evan had started an engineering consultant firm, and his first job had been on the resort hotel that had progressed on schedule. Due to open in a month, Genna had agreed to have her show billed on opening night, but here she sat afraid to open her mouth.

Many of the residents of the creek who'd survived the flood hadn't been able to handle the trauma of its aftermath. A few had sold their property to the resort company and moved away. Ben and Ivy had kept their land, but when they replaced their mobile home, they'd moved it to a high spot on the mountain far above the level the deluge had reached.

When Genna finally moved back into the cabin after it was refurbished, she often left her bed during the night to peer out the window to see that her home wasn't threatened. When it rained at night, she didn't go to bed at all. But as the months passed, her worries had calmed and she felt that she was about back to normal, if she only had the courage to sing.

Evan was coming this evening so that they could make final plans for their wedding. Miss Amelia was gone, so she couldn't go there to calm her spirit. Changing into hiking shoes, she headed once again for Pinnacle Rock.

As she gazed out over the valley, she saw the few houses rebuilt since the flood. A tramway had been constructed from one mountain range to another and would be opened to the public next week. On the eastern mountain, she could see the tower of the ski lift soon to be open.

The hills hadn't changed. Mill Creek valley might be level as a floor, but the hills were still there. The land could be stripped for coal and reclaimed, resorts could be built, but the mountains remained. Yet she remembered the Psalmist's true source of strength: "My help comes from the Lord, the maker of heaven and earth."

Murmuring a prayer for courage, Genna opened her mouth and she sang, "Praise God from whom all blessings flow." Her voice seemed as strong as ever. Tears stung her eyes and slid over her cheeks. "God is so good," she murmured.

She wanted to share the good news with Evan as soon as possible, and she headed off the mountain. She saw him coming up the path and she began to sing. "'He touched me, O, He touched me, and O, the joy that floods my soul.'"

Evan threw back his head and laughed exultantly. He drew her into his arms and swung her around as if she were a child.

"Am I to understand that you are practicing for the new Genna Ross Show?"

"That's right! My theme is going to be 'He Touched Me.' Can you think of anything more fitting?"

While she stood wrapped in his arms, Genna's thoughts quickly scanned the past fourteen years. She'd started out at this point in Evan's arms, and now she had come full circle. The way back had been a long one, full of frustration and disappointment, and many times her heartstrings had been stretched to the breaking point. If she and Evan had married when she was eighteen, what would her life have been like? Probably happy enough, but could the youthful Veevie ever have loved Evan as much as the mature Genna? Neither Genna nor Evan would ever doubt the power of a love that had persevered through the long years of separation.

Before Evan's lips claimed hers, the words of "One-Man Woman" came back to Genna with more poignancy than at any time in the past.

> *And now that he's opened his heart's closed door,*
> *I'll be a one-man woman forevermore.*

A Matter
of Choice

Susannah Hayden

Chapter One

The alarm clock buzzed loudly for the second time on that gray, drizzly, early March morning. Stacie Hanaken groaned, rolled over, and stretched her slender arm to hush the abrasive intrusion on her sound slumber. Her limbs heavy with sleep, it seemed an extraordinary effort to reach as far as her bedside table to find the right button.

When the irritating buzz finally stopped, she pulled her head out from under the pillow and squinted with one blue eye at the large red numbers of her digital alarm clock—and then sat bolt upright. Could it possibly be that late? Stacie rubbed her eyes with the heels of her hands and looked again. There was no question she would be late for work if she wasted even one more minute. Quickly she threw off the covers and scurried toward the bathroom.

On her way to the shower she grabbed bunches of her thick, coppery hair and twisted them into a haphazard knot on the top of her head. Her hair, the color of a shiny new penny, was the first feature most people commented on. It hung smooth and silky to the middle of her back with a controlled wavy fullness which no hairdresser had ever been able to duplicate for her envious friends. Nevertheless, Stacie occasionally thought of cutting it short into a style which would look more mature. After all, she was not a college girl anymore; she was a career woman who had just accepted an exciting promotion.

Brad had always liked her hair long; she supposed that was why she never gave in to the urge to cut it. She enjoyed having long hair but lately had come to think of it as more trouble than it was worth. Like today; it needed to be washed, but she did not have the time. Stacie stopped for a moment at the shower door and put the final pin in place. As she checked to be sure her hair was securely off her neck, she could almost see Brad's face next to her own in the mirror. She still could not believe that he had actually broken their engagement!

They met when Stacie was in her third year of college and Brad was a carpenter working for a contractor who was building a new dormitory on the campus. It was love at first sight, and everyone agreed that if two people ever belonged together, it was Brad and Stacie. To support herself, she worked nearly full-time in the college personnel office while she also carried a full load of course work. She typed papers for other students, babysat the children of her professors—whatever she could do to be able to stay in school and graduate with her class. She turned down promising dates over and over again for the sake of her schoolwork and her dream of becoming a social worker.

On that crisp fall day with red and gold leaves swirling in the breeze and crunching underfoot, Stacie rushed to the administration building to deliver a completed project. Impulsively, she took a shortcut through the construction area and literally stumbled over Brad's shiny red toolbox, nearly sending 200 sheets of neatly-typed pages flying all over the campus. Brad caught her elbow just in time to steady her, and when she looked into those dark eyes, darker than any she had ever seen, she knew she had just met—or was about to meet—an exceptional man. His matching dark brown hair curled softly at his temples and brushed the top of his collar in the back. He smiled in an amused way at the pretty coed he had just caught hold of; she felt a firm strength in his arms and an immediate comfort in his presence.

Brad invited her to dinner that night, and again for the next night. Stacie accepted, forgetting all about using her schoolwork as a reason not to date. Although he had not finished college himself, Brad admired Stacie's motivation and determination to earn a college degree in spite of the fact that it was an uphill battle for her and that most of her classmates had easier circumstances. Then, when she landed a job in the public service office of the small town of St. Mary's where they lived, he beamed with pride and threw a party to celebrate. On the eve of her graduation and the beginning of her career, he tenderly asked her to be his wife and, without a moment's hesitation, she joyfully accepted. For a long time, she had been hoping he would propose, but when the actual moment came, she still found it hard to believe that someone as wonderful as Bradley Bauman Davis truly wanted to spend his life with her.

Stacie shook herself out of her reverie and turned on the water. She stepped into the steamy shower stall and turned the water up as hot and hard as she could stand it hoping that both the heat and pressure would get rid of her nervous tension. Often, as now, she would sing or pray aloud as she stood in the shower, soothing body and spirit at one time.

Today, however, it was not working. All she could think about was Brad and how much she had missed him in these last two months. He was a man of contagious ambition and surging leadership, two qualities about him which she had soon come to love. He was quick to assess a difficult situation and make practical suggestions which invariably led to solving the problem. Somehow it always seemed natural for other people to follow his directions and it seemed natural for him to step in where leadership was lacking. Between the two of them, Stacie and Brad had the energy, initiative, and determination for any task which might come up. They both looked forward to spending many years together as a loving, united team.

It was with happy anticipation that Stacie had phoned Brad one day two months ago to suggest they have a celebration dinner. When he asked what they would be celebrating, she smiled to herself and told him he would just have to wait to find out. She would not satisfy his curiosity until they were face-to-face over a table at O'Reilly's, eating identical corned beef sandwiches.

Stacie arrived at the restaurant and saw Brad's secondhand truck, with its once-bright red color sadly faded, parked near the door. Grimy as it was, she could not resist dragging her fingers lightly across the hood. She loved to be near something that belonged to Brad almost as much as she loved to be with Brad himself. Her mouth turned up in pleasure, she pushed open the door and glanced around the cozy dining room. When she found him sitting at the table with a puzzled look on his face, she unashamedly kissed him and tousled his curly hair.

"What was that for?" Brad asked, pleased but still curious.

"That, sweetheart, was a celebration kiss." Stacie took off the light gray jacket she was wearing and hung it over the back of her chair before sitting down. She reached for Brad's hands. "I have some terrific news!"

Brad was clearly intrigued and amused by her enthusiasm. "Well, I guess you'd better clue me in, so both of us can go around grinning like Cheshire cats."

"Do you remember meeting my boss, Jack Rogers, at the company party?" Brad nodded, and Stacie continued. "He came into my office today and offered me a promotion."

"That's wonderful, Stacie! You've been there only eight months. I know you do a great job, and I don't know anyone else as dedicated as you are, but a promotion . . . that's great news!" He leaned across the table, kissed her, and then, as he often did to her, he affectionately thumped her nose with his index finger. "Tell me more. What's the new job?"

"You know I've been working on that research project on homeless people in the state . . . studying causes and possible solutions. Now I'm going to get to do something besides just paperwork!" Her eyes were bright with excitement. "They want me to be the assistant director of a new shelter for the homeless. It's not supposed to open for about six months so I'll have some time for training first."

Brad leaned back in his chair and looked at her proudly. "You'll be perfect for the job . . . you're so organized and you really care about what you're doing." He stopped and tilted his head in a questioning way. "Isn't there a homeless shelter already here in St. Mary's? This is not a very big town. Are there really enough homeless people to need a second one?"

"That's the rest of the news," Stacie said. "The job is not here in St. Mary's. The new shelter will be in Thomasville."

Stacie was too excited to admit to herself that Brad tensed up at the mention of Thomasville. Eager to give him more of the details, she kept talking. "The agency has been wanting to do this for a long time. Thomasville is a good spot for a new shelter because there aren't any within miles of there. I'm still in shock that they asked me—"

Brad cut her off abruptly. "But Stacie," he said with his voice low and the proud smile gone from his face, "that's nearly 200 miles from here."

She hardly knew what to say. When she spoke, her voice was barely audible. "Yes, I know where Thomasville is. I've lived in this state all my life." Stacie looked down at her lap and twisted the corner of her napkin between her fingers until it was shredded. It was obvious to her now that Brad was not reacting the way she had hoped . . . and expected.

After an excruciating and long silence, during which they hardly moved a muscle, Brad said, "Well, it's very flattering that they thought of you for this position. It's too bad you can't accept."

Stacie jerked her head up and, with her mouth open in disbelief, stared at Brad. "I haven't given them an answer yet. Of course I wanted to talk with you. But it's the kind of job I've been preparing for and praying for . . . I can't just dismiss it without serious thought."

When the waiter came and said his familiar hello, Brad and Stacie ordered the corned beef sandwiches and sauerkraut that they usually relished. But neither of them ate much—or said much—and the evening ended early.

Remembering that she had overslept, Stacie abruptly shut off the shower and stepped out of the stall. As she wrapped her flannel robe around her, she wished she had thought to start the coffee before getting in the shower; now there would be no time. When the pins were out of her hair and it cascaded gracefully, she started brushing it and thinking about what she should wear to work. Was her pink blouse clean? It would go well with her new linen navy suit and the navy pumps which were so much more comfortable than those brown shoes that hurt her feet.

The drizzle had turned to a steady rain, and Stacie grimaced at the thought that she would need her khaki raincoat and umbrella. She moved to the closet and methodically removed the clothes she would wear that day. Once dressed, she added small gold earrings and a simple gold chain. Although she still did not feel enthusiastic about leaving the apartment, a glance in the mirror told her that she appeared ready. She blew out a sigh and straightened her slouched shoulders, determined that people would not know the depth of her pain simply by looking at her. A guarded, private person, Stacie had not talked very much about her engagement to the people she worked with. Some of them had noticed her suddenly bare ring finger, but few realized the connection between her promotion and the broken engagement.

Accepting Brad's marriage proposal was the easiest decision Stacie had ever made but agreeing to take the new job was the most difficult decision of her life.

Stacie was convinced that God wanted her to work at the new shelter in Thomasville but she could understand Brad's reluctance for her to accept it. He had his own contractor's business now, and the St. Mary's area was bursting with potential new growth. There would be plenty of work there and he would make a very comfortable income for them to live on. He insisted that if they got married he would provide for them, and it made sense for him to do that in St. Mary's.

The night Stacie told Brad she had decided to accept the promotion there was a twisted knot in her stomach. Unspoken tension hung in the air, and she had been dreading this moment more and more as it got closer. But she knew she had to do it. She picked up their dishes from the small table in her apartment and carried them to the sink. Slowly she walked back into the living room where Brad was waiting for her.

"This is very hard for me, Brad," she started, not even able to look him in the eye. "I love you with all my heart, and I really thought the Lord had brought us together. We've had two incredible years, and I can't live my life without you. But I also think the Lord wants me to take this job. It's such a strong feeling—I can't explain it completely, but I know I can't just ignore it."

Out of the corner of her eye, Stacie could see Brad shift his position so he could look at her when he spoke. "I love you, too, Stacie. You know I do. But I just don't see how I can pick up and move to Thomasville and start all over again. I've worked so hard to get a business going here."

"So what do we do now?" Stacie could hardly hold back the tears; she knew what his answer would be.

"We can't get married and live 200 miles apart. If I'm going to provide for us, I have to live here." Even though he held his voice steady with conviction, Stacie could hear the sadness in Brad's words.

They sat together on the couch in Stacie's apartment—the country-blue and gray-plaid couch with the ruffle around the bottom that they had picked out together as their first piece of furniture. To her surprise, Brad reached for her and drew her close. All they could do was hold each other and share in their mutual pain. Clearly, Brad did not want her to move away, but just as clearly, she had to do it.

Devastated by the impasse they had reached, Stacie hoarsely asked, "Do you want your ring back?"

Brad gently lifted Stacie's left hand and wrapped his fingers around hers. "No, it's your ring. It no longer means that we're getting married, but it still means I love you, and I don't think I'll ever stop." He moved his hand to her chin and lifted her face, streaked with tears. Putting his lips softly on hers he kissed her long and slowly and then picked up his jacket and left without speaking again.

Now, Stacie stood staring at that same couch. They had bought it together just after having announced their engagement. It was supposed to have symbolized the beginning of their life together, and they had spent many evenings on it, resting in each other's arms as they talked of their future together. They had thought about other furniture, the fine home Brad would someday build for them, their work in the church, her work in the community. Brad supported Stacie's desire to continue working at St. Mary's public service office and he had always seemed to understand how important it was for her to be helping other people. Only on that painful night did she at last realize that his understanding had limitations.

Standing immobilized in her living room, Stacie put her fingers to her lips and could almost feel the tenderness of Brad's kiss and his work-calloused hand under her chin. How she loved him! *Would she really be able to move to Thomasville and start a new life without him?* Brad was the first and only man she had ever loved, and it was incomprehensible that she should ever care for anyone else with the same passionate intensity. She really believed she was following the Lord's will by taking this new job. *Did this mean she would always be alone, always longing for the touch and companionship of the man she loved? Had she made a horrible mistake when she accepted the new job?*

The phone jangled loudly and Stacie jumped involuntarily. She glanced at her watch and thought that it was too early in the morning for someone to be calling, but she crossed the room and picked up the phone on the second ring.

"Stacie?"

"Oh, hi, Megan." Stacie was relieved to hear the voice of her best friend and relaxed into the tufted blue chair next to the window.

"I hadn't talked to you all week, so I wanted to see how you are. I hope it's not too early to call."

"You know you can call any time, Megan. But I'm fine, really. You don't have to keep checking up on me." Stacie instantly regretted the sarcasm in her own voice. She fingered the edge of the white eyelet curtain and looked with growing dread at the downpour outside the window.

Megan, in her characteristic way, ignored the edginess in Stacie's words. "Well, I happen to know you are not so fine as you say, but we don't have to talk about that now. I also wanted to know if you're planning to go to Bible study tonight."

"I suppose I should. I've missed the last two weeks. But it's so hard. . . ." Stacie knew Megan would understand how difficult it was for her to go to Bible study when she knew Brad would be there. Yet, the group included her closest friends and she did not want to drop out completely.

"I'll pick you up and we'll go together," Megan said, her voice deliberately cheerful.

"Thanks, Megan. I'm sorry I snapped at you. You're my best friend in the world, you know that."

"See you tonight, friend."

Megan hung up, but somehow just hearing her voice had made Stacie feel better. Sensible, solid, faithful Megan, her roommate from college and the dear friend who was supposed to have been her maid of honor in another few weeks. Stacie had been so pleased that Megan and Brad got along well and that neither of them had resented her intimate relationship with the other. She smiled as she remembered how they would often join in teasing her about some peculiar habit or when she said something that did not come out quite right. She had been blessed with these two people who cared deeply for her and had grown fond of each other as well.

Stacie now had only two minutes before she absolutely had to leave. She snapped on the radio, and as she gulped down a glass of orange juice, she heard the announcement that the rain was not expected to let up until sometime the next day.

"Ugh!" she said aloud and reluctantly got out the umbrella from the small closet next to the door of the apartment. She picked up her briefcase and purse and, making sure to lock the door behind her, hesitantly ventured out into the rain.

Chapter Two

Somehow Stacie muddled through the day at work—and even managed a reasonable degree of productivity. Her tiny office, once part of a larger suite that had been subdivided, was packed with the evidence of her hard work. The bookshelves overflowed with college textbooks, government reports, census data, and papers by national experts that predicted sociological trends. Snapshots splattered the walls—pictures of her during her internship in Chicago and photos of the St. Mary's shelter and the people who stayed there, some of them for months at a time. On the corner of her desk was the stack of bulging case files that she was handling.

Stacie felt that if she could not find satisfaction in her work, then there really would be no point to sacrificing her relationship with Brad. So, at the office, she was meticulously attentive to the tasks before her. Easily she could have closed her office door and allowed herself to lapse into isolated self-pity—everyone would have thought that she was just hard at work preparing for her transfer to Thomasville. But, instead, she propped the door open first thing in the morning and made sure she kept herself busy. While working, she could hear the rapid clicks of computer keyboards, the hum of the photocopier, the bleeps of the new telephone system. Periodically, she would smell the inviting aroma from the coffeepot in the back room and would go out and refill her large mug.

The reports spread across her desk were overwhelming. Accurate records on homeless people were difficult to keep, but the studies showed a definite increase in the number of women and children who suddenly were without a place to call home. Since the new shelter in Thomasville would be a haven specifically for women and children, Stacie had buried herself with information about other programs which were effective in helping these one-parent families find jobs and establish new homes. She continued to handle some of the routine work of the shelter in St. Mary's, but most of her time was now devoted to preparing for the move to Thomasville. The building would be ready when she arrived, but it would be up to the new staff to devise a program to attack the problem.

Lunchtime came. Stacie made sure to save the notes she was collecting on her computer and pushed her chair back from the desk. On Tuesdays and Thursdays she spent her lunch hour working as a volunteer in the food line that was offered by her agency. A look out the window told her she would still need her umbrella, so, disgruntled, she took it off its hook and left the office.

Around the corner at the shelter, the lunch crowd was already gathering. Stacie pushed open the door and was nearly run over by a four-year-old boy, exuberantly charging at her.

"Joey!" she said, laughing. "Slow down." She stooped to give Joey a quick hug. "How's my favorite boy?"

"I'm hungry!" Joey reached around Stacie's neck with both arms and squeezed.

"Then you came to the right place." She stood up and took hold of his hand. "Let's go see what's for lunch."

Stacie got Joey settled with his mother and his baby sister and then took her place behind the serving table. Mounds of tangled spaghetti noodles filled several serving platters and steam rose from the pots of sauce nearby. The line of hungry people moved steadily. Stacie was always amazed at how many people came for this meal, even in a town as small as St. Mary's, and that many of them would not have another meal until the next day.

Joey and his family had been coming to the shelter for several weeks. The energetic little boy with blond hair and blue eyes chattered constantly and was a favorite of everyone who worked in the lunch line. As she served the meals, Stacie could not resist looking over at Joey every few minutes. He seemed to sense when she was looking and gave her a friendly wave every time, sometimes loudly calling out "Hi, Stacie!" before his mother hushed him. His blue pants were too short and the knees were looking worn; the thin gray sweater he wore was too big. Stacie often thought how easy it would be to feel overwhelmed by the impossible task of solving the problems of all the people like Joey's family. But she was not discouraged. Helping even one family, or even one little boy, was a start. She knew there were many more little boys like Joey in Thomasville.

When she got home from work, Stacie was exhausted. The rainy weather had put her in the mood for a bowl of hot soup for supper, a favorite and frequent meal choice in the evenings. She took a container of homemade beefy vegetable soup from the freezer and emptied it into a pan on the stove. As she stood and stirred it, waiting for it to thaw, she worked at changing mental gears from the demands of the office and the emotions of the shelter to the challenge of attending a Bible study where she would see Brad. It would not be the first time they had seen each other since her decision to move away, but she was not sure it would be any easier than the other times.

As she sat and ate, alone, she worked hard not to think of all the suppers she and Brad had shared at that little table. Homemade beefy vegetable soup was actually his favorite, and for a long time after their breakup she had not been able to bring herself to eat any of the supply in her freezer.

Stacie considered calling Megan and saying she could not go, but resisted the urge. Instead, she changed into comfortable jeans and a bright blue sweatshirt and sat in the chair by the window to listen for Megan's familiar toot of the horn. Her friend was prompt, as Stacie had expected she would be.

"You sure you're up to this?" Megan asked as she pulled away from the curb.

"I have to be," Stacie replied. "I can't give up my whole life just because of what happened with Brad. I'll be lonely enough when I move away; I don't want to feel that way now." She looked at her friend—an easygoing kindergarten teacher with her brown hair tied in a casual ponytail and baggy clothes hiding her athletic build—and was stabbed by the realization of how much she would miss Megan. Thrown together as roommates by the routine workings of college administration, Megan and Stacie had cemented their relationship by suffering together through term papers, bad dates, final exams, and career choices. They both had been ecstatic to find jobs in St. Mary's where they could be near one another. In a few months though, Stacie would be leaving behind more than Brad when she moved to Thomasville. And, without Brad, she would feel Megan's absence even more acutely.

"I think it's Brad's turn to lead the discussion tonight," Megan said softly, "so I'm sure he'll be there."

Stacie turned her head away and looked out the window; trees and telephone poles whizzed by. True to the forecast, the drizzle had not let up all day, and the view was gray and shrouded in the early evening dusk. "There will be twenty other people there," she said. "I probably won't even have to talk to him. Just stay right with me, please."

"I won't leave your side." Both Megan's tone and words were very reassuring.

Brad's shiny new blue work van, a symbol of his business success with his young company's colorful logo emblazoned on both sides, was already parked in the church lot near the door. Brad had wanted to trade in his old pickup for a long time. Apparently, business was finally good enough that he had done it. On the one hand Stacie was glad for his success; on the other hand, the sleek new van was a visible and indisputable argument that his business was going well enough to make moving away seem foolish.

Megan purposefully pulled her small used and dented car into a space at the far end of the lot, and the two young women walked together into the church building. The lounge where the group of young adults met every Thursday evening was filling up, and the room buzzed with clusters of conversations about college courses and career challenges. Megan gave Stacie a characteristic cheerful smile and nudged her toward one of the groups.

They chatted amiably with several other people, but Stacie had to work hard to concentrate on the conversation. Someone asked her about her new job but, as she answered the question, she was not sure her thoughts were coming out coherently. Out of the corner of her eye she saw Brad sitting on a couch talking quietly with a couple of women from the college. She knew it was ridiculous and chastised herself immediately, but, involuntarily, jealousy welled up inside her. Although his dark head was bent in earnest, attentive conversation, she saw his eyes flicker briefly when she looked in his direction. Immediately, she turned away; still, his face floated before her, his familiar and attractive features replacing those of the young man who was talking to her.

She was startled for a moment when she heard Brad's voice urging everyone in the room to take their seats and get comfortable so the Bible study could begin. As always, the others accepted his leadership and lowered themselves into the menagerie of donated couches and chairs scattered around the room. Stacie and Megan sat together on a small, tattered, beige love seat, their Bibles poised in their laps, awaiting direction from Brad.

Brad read the passage and launched into a preliminary explanation of several verses before asking some questions for the group to discuss. While he spoke, Stacie could legitimately keep her eyes on the Bible in her lap, but, during the discussion, it was more difficult to keep from looking at Brad. Mechanically, she turned her head from side to side as people around the room joined in and tried to follow the flow of the discussion. She used to be one of the most vocal participants in these stimulating talks, but tonight she could barely make sense of the main points people were making. Periodically, Stacie sensed Megan glancing at her and forced herself to smile or nod so her friend would know she was all right. Stacie knew she had been right to come. Although the people in the group were stunned at their broken engagement, they respected and cared for Brad and her and did not want either of them to drop out of the group.

When the meeting was almost finished, Stacie noticed Pastor Banning slip into the room and sit in a chair near the door. After the closing prayer, Brad motioned for the pastor to come up and address the group. Pastor Banning walked around to the front of the room to explain his purpose.

"Several of you have told me you would like to take on a special project as a group," he said, "and I think I have just the thing for you to do. I met a woman last week who could really use your help."

He went on to explain that there was an old youth camp, the old Family Homestead, about twenty miles out of town owned by a woman named Margaret Barrows. For many years she and her husband ran the camp, but when he became ill, she closed it to take care of him. Recently, he passed away, and the elderly Mrs. Barrows wanted very much to see the camp restored and back in operation. She had enough money available for the restoration if she could find donated labor. There would be cleaning, landscaping, painting, and construction work to be done but, if the group would take on the project, perhaps the camp could be ready before summer.

Stacie was caught up in the enthusiasm pulsing through the group. If the goal was to refurbish the camp before summer, she could help before moving away for her new job. She did not mind strenuous physical labor—in fact, she enjoyed it. At the mention of construction work, attention had shifted noticeably to Brad. Everyone seemed to assume he would head up the work project and he seemed to have already accepted the assignment. Megan looked questioningly at Stacie.

"It's okay, Megan," Stacie whispered. "I want to do this. It sounds like there's a lot to be done; I want to help."

Someone started circulating sign-up sheets for various tasks, and Stacie and Megan both signed up to go out the next weekend to scrub the cabins and do odd jobs. Long after the meeting was officially over, the group's members stayed in the lounge planning work dates and making lists of the supplies they would need. Stacie was pulled out of her self-consciousness and listened carefully to the suggestions Brad was making. Without realizing the moment of the shift, she had begun to participate fully in the zealous planning.

Knowing that tomorrow was a workday, Stacie at last suggested to Megan that they should leave. Megan nodded her agreement and they gathered up their books and notes. They were almost to the door when someone called Megan's name.

"I'll be right there, Stace," Megan said, and turned her attention away.

Stacie leaned against the wall contentedly. Despite Brad's involvement, she thought this work project would be just what she needed. It would provide a distraction from the intensity of her job and the physical exercise would be invigorating. How could anyone resist the chance to work on a summer camp for kids—certainly she could not.

"Hello, Stacie."

Stacie was jolted out of her musings by the sound of Brad's voice. Instinctively she looked around for Megan, who had her back turned. She felt awkward, but there was no way out.

"Hello, Brad." Scrambling for something to ease the tension she suddenly felt, she offered, "I saw your new van; things must be going well."

"Yes, the business is going well; there is plenty of work for all of us." As always, Brad's tone was even and controlled, and, without hesitation, he looked directly into Stacie's eyes.

"I'm glad. I know how your men depend on you." It was not for his own sake alone that Brad was reluctant to leave St. Mary's. He had three people working for him fulltime who would lose their jobs if he closed his business.

Brad nodded. "This is a busy time of the year, you know, getting ready for the summer. When the nice weather gets here, we'll be swamped."

"Are you sure you have time for the work at the camp?" Stacie asked, half hoping that he would answer negatively.

"I'm sure I'll have some very long days, but I really want to do this."

"Me too." For a fleeting moment, Stacie wondered if Brad was also looking for a distraction. *Was it really feasible for them both to be involved in the same work project? Was it as hard for him to be together as it was for her?*

Their conversation seemed to have come to an awkward end, and Stacie wished Megan would hurry.

"Stacie. . . ." Brad moved a step closer. "Stacie, I miss you. . . . Couldn't we talk some more about this? If there's any chance you'll change your mind. . . ."

"It's not that simple, Brad," she said, looking away. She wanted desperately to step back from him, but she was already leaning against the wall and had nowhere to go.

"I can make a good living for us here, Stace, and you'd be free to get involved in any social projects you want. It wouldn't even matter if you got paid. Wouldn't that make you happy?" Brad was gently stroking her forearm with one finger, and she was tortuously tempted to look at his pleading face and surrender in agreement to what he offered. Nonchalantly, she moved her arm out of his reach and took a small step to the side.

"Brad, I miss you, too." She still avoided looking at his face. "I don't understand what's happening any more than you do, but I know God wants me to take this job." She spoke with conviction in her voice because she felt it in her heart.

"It doesn't have to be this way, Stacie."

"I don't have any choice, Brad."

"Ready to go?" Megan's lighthearted voice was a welcome interruption.

"Whenever you are," Stacie answered, turning toward Megan and giving Brad a clear signal that their conversation was over.

"I'm sorry about that," Megan said when they got outside the building. "I said I wouldn't leave your side, and then off I went the first time someone called my name."

"It's okay, Megan." It was drizzling again, and Stacie pulled the hood of her jacket up over her head. "After all, you can't run interference between Brad and me indefinitely. It's been two months since we broke up."

"What did he want?" She unlocked the car and they got in.

"He wants me to change my mind."

"Why doesn't he change his mind?" Megan asked innocently as she turned the key in the ignition.

Stacie shrugged. "He's got good reasons, sensible reasons. Brad has a thriving business with people who depend on him, and I just have a dinky, little, non-profit job."

"Don't talk that way!" Megan said sharply, and then added more softly, "Your reasons for going to Thomasville are just as good as his reasons for staying in St. Mary's."

Stacie appreciated Megan's support. Most people could not understand why Stacie would give up Brad for the job in Thomasville, and she seemed unable to make them understand that it was not a choice she wanted to make. Megan, however, understood that Stacie simply could not make the obvious, easy decision unless she was convinced it was also the right decision. They drove several blocks in silence and pulled up in front of Stacie's apartment.

"Are we still playing tennis on Sunday afternoon?" Megan asked.

"Sure, if the rain stops," Stacie answered. "The forecast calls for rain all weekend."

"Well, if you don't play you can always come over and help me clean out my refrigerator instead," said Megan.

Stacie laughed. The chaos of Megan's refrigerator had been a standing joke between them for more than a year, and the simple reference to it conjured up reassurances of the depth and solidity of their friendship.

Stacie let herself into her apartment and reached for the light switch. With her fingers poised to flick it on, she changed her mind and set her things down in the dark. Her feet took the familiar path to the couch where she stretched out and stared up at the shadows on the ceiling.

Could Brad be right? she wondered. *Am I misunderstanding what God is saying to me just because this job is what I've always wanted? After all, Brad is what I've always wanted, too, and what he says makes a lot of sense. How can I be so sure about two things that are completely incompatible with each other? Is this some kind of a test?*

She lay in the dark for a long time. Obviously, there were no easy answers, and she struggled with the polarity of her emotions until she lapsed into an exhausted sleep. It was several hours later when she roused herself and moved to her bed for the rest of the night. All too soon the alarm clock was buzzing once again.

Chapter Three

"Hey Stacie! The doughnuts are here."

It was a Friday morning ritual at the office: enormous frosted doughnuts from the Swedish bakery across the street and freshly brewed, raspberry cream gourmet coffee. Today's goodies were supplied by Marsha, the receptionist.

Stacie put down her pencil and looked up from the report she had been immersed in for the last two hours. It was not very interesting reading, but the report had been issued by the governor's office and she had to know what it was about. Why couldn't government people write in plain English? she always wondered. How could their programs ever work if nobody could understand them? Even though she was not in the mood to socialize, she decided she would go have a doughnut; maybe the break would perk her up a little bit.

The little room the agency used for breaks and lunch was already full. Friday, when there were doughnuts, was the one day of the week that everyone managed to get away from their desks for a few minutes in the morning. Glancing around, Stacie saw that she was the last staff member to arrive.

"There are still three doughnuts left," Marsha said, pointing to the top of the filing cabinet where the box sat. "You were a little too pokey this morning."

Stacie smiled and inspected the open box. Three golden glazed doughnuts lay flat in the bottom, daring her to select just one. She picked up a doughnut with one hand and a napkin with the other and turned around to look for a place to sit. Marsha motioned to an empty chair next to her; Stacie complied and sat down beside the stout, middle-aged woman who colored her hair a very strange shade of orange.

"Are you making any progress with that report?" Marsha got the question out just before filling her mouth with another bite.

"Slowly but surely," Stacie said. "There is a lot of good information in it, but it's hidden behind a pile of words that doesn't really mean much." She took a careful bite of her doughnut, trying not to get a ring of glaze around her mouth.

Marsha was licking her fingers now. "Well, you've got the circles under your eyes to prove that you've been trying to read it." She smiled slyly at Stacie. "Or did you have one of your wild nights last night?"

To Marsha, who lived alone with her three cats and went to bed at nine o'clock every evening, anyone who didn't go straight home from work every night and stay there until morning was having a wild time. In Stacie's mind, going to a Bible study at the church was hardly having a wild night, but she merely smiled and let Marsha continue with her fantasy of what Stacie's life was like. She got up and poured herself a cup of steaming coffee and took a cautious sip. "Mmm, I like this flavor, Marsha," she said.

"You say that every time I get it."

"That's because I like it every time." Stacie took another bite of her dough-nut. "Is it my turn to buy next week?"

"Check the schedule by the water cooler," Marsha directed.

"I'll do that." Stacie took her doughnut and coffee and started back to her office.

"Oh!" Marsha's tone made Stacie turn around and look, questioningly. "I for-got to tell you. When Jack was here for his coffee he was looking for you. You should probably check with him. I don't know what he wanted."

"Thanks, Marsha. I'll check it out."

Stacie normally met with the agency's director on Wednesday afternoons and their last meeting had been routine. She wondered why he would be looking for her on a Friday morning. The first thing she had to do was finish the doughnut and clean up her sticky fingers. She crammed the last of the pastry into her mouth just as she sat down in her chair. In the middle of her desk was a note from Jack Rogers that had not been there when she left a few minutes ago. The note said he wanted to see her.

With her napkin, she dabbed at the corners of her mouth and wiped her fin-gertips. From the center desk drawer she pulled out a small mirror and looked at her image. The evidence of the doughnut was gone, but Marsha was right about the circles under her eyes. If only Marsha knew the truth of what Stacie's life was like right now, she might not make those frequent remarks about wild nights.

Standing up, she straightened her skirt and brushed crumbs off the sleeve of her blouse. Jack wanted to see her right away; no matter how tired she was, there was no point in putting it off. Stacie went to the end of the short hall, turned right, and knocked on the first office door.

"Come in!" said a voice.

She turned the knob and pushed the door open. "You wanted to see me?"

"Yes, Stacie, come on in." Jack Rogers motioned for her to sit in one of the blue chairs across from his wood-grain desk. As always, his office was immac-ulate and meticulously neat. Each file folder had its proper place, every book was on the right shelf, and the trash can was neatly tucked out of sight. Whenever Stacie went to Jack's office, she felt guilty for the clutter that char-acterized hers. At thirty-five, Jack had a lot of responsibility and was obses-sively productive; he also managed to be very tidy about everything he did.

"I just read your last memo," Jack said as Stacie got settled in the chair. "You've got some great ideas for the new shelter. It's obvious you've put a lot of energy into your thinking."

Stacie was grateful for the compliment but felt awkward receiving it. "The project is an important one," she said, taking the focus off herself.

"It's time to get some numbers together. We'll have to restructure the inside of the building we have and we need to know what that's going to cost." Jack tapped the end of his pencil on the edge of the desk. "I think it would be good if you went to Thomasville next week. Have you met the director you'll be working with?"

Stacie shook her head. "I've seen some of his correspondence, and we've spoken on the phone once, but I haven't met him in person."

"Dillon Graves is a good guy. You'll like him. Very capable." Jack swiveled his chair and leaned back thoughtfully. "I'll ask Marsha to check with him about his schedule. Maybe you can work something out for the end of next week. The two of you can go through the building together and sketch out how you think it should be arranged. Then we can get estimates from local contractors and go from there."

Stacie nodded. "Sounds good. I don't see a problem." She stood up to leave.

Jack reached back to the credenza behind him and picked up two large computer reports. Pushing them across the desk toward Stacie, he said, "I know these are no fun, but you'd better look at these when you're done with the one you have." He smiled at her. "Speaking of contractors, I ran into that friend of yours. Bill—is that his name?"

Stacie's heart started to beat faster. "Brad."

"That's right, Brad. Didn't I meet him at the Christmas party?"

"Yes, we came together." Stacie was nearly choking on the words.

"Nice guy. Too bad he doesn't live in Thomasville. We could use him there."

Not wanting to stand there and talk about Brad, Stacie picked up the reports and said brightly, "I'd better get my nose back to the grindstone."

Stacie let the heavy reports fall with a thud to her desktop—which did not look anything like Jack's. There were many things about Jack that Stacie admired. He was very efficient, understood the seriousness of the problems he faced every day, and dealt fairly with his staff. But, for a person whose job was to help people, Jack Rogers had an incredible capacity to ignore the personal lives of the people he was with the most. When Jack met Brad last Christmas, it was common knowledge that Stacie was engaged to him—even Jack knew what the diamond on her left hand meant. Now, he did not remember Brad's name and called him "that friend of yours."

Jack's confidence in her as an assistant director meant a lot to Stacie. But now she realized that he had no idea what price she was paying to accept the position he offered. She wondered if it had ever even crossed his mind that her engagement might complicate her decision about the new job. Hadn't he even wondered what happened to Brad?

The new reports would have to wait until she finished plowing through the one she had left open on her desk. With a soft groan, she picked them up and looked around for a better place to put them. There was an open spot on the top of the bookcase, so she put them there. Has Jack always been so neat, she wondered, or is it only because he has a big office?

She had never had a chance to finish her raspberry creme gourmet coffee, and now it was cold. Stacie thought about going back to the break room to see if there was any hot coffee left but decided against it. She still had more than eighty pages to get through before the end of the day.

Her phone rang. She picked it up and said mechanically, "Stacie Hanaken."

"Don't sound so excited," the voice said facetiously.

"Hi, Megan. It's been a hard day, that's all."

"More government reports?"

"Right. Reading this stuff is like chewing sand."

"Let me make you a better offer. Let's go to Katie's Kitchen for dinner. My treat."

"Oh, I don't know, Megan. I'm pretty tired."

"Come on, Stace," Megan pleaded. "I don't want you going home and having soup from your freezer again, and sitting there all alone for the whole evening."

"Soup is nutritious." Stacie defended her eating habits.

"So have soup at Katie's Kitchen. Just get out of your apartment tonight." Megan sounded insistent, so Stacie relented.

"All right, we've got a date."

"This is a great table," Megan remarked, looking around. "It's away from the kitchen and sort of out of the way. I like it." The table for two was set with a crisp, crimson tablecloth and matching napkins. A low, burning candle glowed softly in the center of the table, next to a slender vase holding one rose.

Stacie hung her purse on her chair and sat down across from Megan. "I haven't been here too often. I like all the plants."

"I'm surprised you haven't been here more. It strikes me as the kind of atmosphere you would really like. And the food is great."

Stacie looked at the wall behind Megan and nodded. Throughout the restaurant there were pictures of historic Victorian houses, each of which was matted in soft blues and pinks and framed in oak.

"You're right. I do like it. I always have. But Brad didn't care for this place very much. . . ."

"Oh." Megan did not need to use a lot of words to let Stacie know she understood.

Stacie changed the subject. "I kill everything I bring into my apartment. I hope that my being this close to all these gorgeous plants won't hurt them!"

Megan chuckled. "You were never any good at basic science. Plants need water, my friend. You always forget that."

To her own surprise, Stacie found herself laughing, too. "Maybe I should visit your kindergarten class the next time you have that 'plant-a-seed-and-see-what-happens' project.

A wide shadow crept across their table and their bantering came to a halt. "Good evening, ladies," said a dour woman whose face was surrounded by wisps of grayish hair that had come loose from her ponytail. She hardly moved her mouth as she delivered her dry, unenthusiastic speech: "My name is Rita, and I'll be your server tonight. Here are your menus. The specials are marked on the back. I'll be back in a few minutes to take your order." As she slapped the menus down on the table and disappeared, Megan and Stacie laughed even harder.

Rita was back almost immediately; Stacie and Megan had barely recovered their composure enough to tell her what they wanted to eat. She set a basket of warm rolls between them and left just as abruptly as the last time.

In spite of Rita's making it known that she was having a very bad day, Megan and Stacie were enjoying themselves. It had been a long time since they had been out to dinner together, and they found it as pleasant as it always had been. They sipped their iced teas and generously spread real butter on their homemade rolls.

"This is so naughty," Stacie said, eyeing the warm roll in her hand as the butter was starting to drip down toward her wrist. "You should have seen the doughnut I had at work this morning."

"Aw, live it up for once," Megan said. "There's always next week for dieting." She took an enthusiastic bite of her own roll.

"Speaking of next week, Jack Rogers wants to send me to Thomasville. I'm supposed to meet—" Stacie broke off abruptly.

"Stace? What's the matter? Are you all right?"

Stacie forced herself to swallow. "I'm fine, Megan." She took a sip of her tea. "No, I'm not fine, Megan. Don't turn around, but Brad just walked in."

Megan's eyebrows moved together in a puzzled look. "I thought you said he didn't like this place."

Stacie nodded. "That's what he always told me. But he's not alone, and maybe *she* is more persuasive than I am."

Megan was fidgeting in her chair, working very hard at not turning around to stare. "She who? Who is he with?"

"Jenna."

"Jenna!" Megan was appalled. "Brad came here with Jenna McLean? She can't be more than nineteen years old."

"She's a nice girl, actually."

"Come on, Stacie, you don't have to say things like that to me. How could he give up someone like you to go out with Jenna McLean?"

"We broke up, Megan. I have no claim on Brad."

"Has he spotted us?"

Stacie shook her head. "I can see him through the branches of that rubber plant behind you but I don't think he can see us."

"Do you want to leave?" Megan prodded.

Stacie thought for a second and then said, "No, we've already ordered. Besides, we would have to walk right past them to get to the door."

"You don't have to put yourself through this, Stace. We can go eat soup at your place if you want."

"I want to stay, Megan," Stacie said definitively. "Let's change the subject. Tell me what you know about this camp we're going to be working at."

"Well, I went there two summers in a row when I was in grade school. I remember it as being a pretty neat place to go."

"Were the Barrowses there?"

"Yes, and they seemed ancient then," said Megan. "I can only imagine what Mrs. Barrows must look like now."

"To a kid, everyone is old. Maybe she wasn't as old as you thought."

"Maybe. I can remember. . . ."

Stacie heard very little of what Megan said for the next few minutes. The branches and leaves of the rubber plant were spaced perfectly for her to discretely view Brad and Jenna across the room. She simply did not have enough willpower to stop watching the two of them, with their heads leaning close together over one menu and shy smiles passing between them. Jenna tossed her head, laughing at something Brad said, and her blond, wavy hair floated gracefully through the air and settled back on her shoulders. With a demure smile, she reached out and laid her hand lightly on Brad's forearm. He responded by placing his other hand over hers and looking directly at Jenna with a wide smile on his face.

Stacie could see their lips moving in a conversation which obviously delighted them both. It was unlikely that they would notice her, tucked away at a secluded little table. In fact, they seemed so completely absorbed in each other that they were noticing very little of what happened around them.

Brad tipped his head back in laughter again and then lightly thumped Jenna's upturned nose with his forefinger, before leaning over to kiss her.

"Stacie? Stace, are you all right?" Megan's voice pulled Stacie out of the fog she felt swirling around her. "You look pale, Stacie. Are you feeling all right?"

"I'm okay," Stacie answered, in a whisper.

Megan twisted in her chair and looked through the leaves of the rubber plant. It took her only a moment to know what was upsetting Stacie. "Have you been watching them?" she scolded.

"I couldn't help it," Stacie answered pitifully. "We broke up. There's no reason he shouldn't go out with whomever he wants. But I can't help feeling jealous. The way he is with her—that's the way we used to be together." Stacie's eyes were filling with tears. "Maybe you and I should trade places so I'll have my back to them."

"I have a better idea," Megan said determinedly. "When that waitress with the sparkling personality gets back, we'll tell her we want our food to go."

"Don't be ridiculous, Megan. We came here to eat, so we'll eat."

"Don't give me an argument, Stacie. You always do things the hard way. You don't have to put yourself through this. We're leaving."

A few minutes later, Megan guided Stacie's elbow right past Brad and Jenna's table without stopping, and without even looking at them. Whether Brad saw her or not, Stacie did not know.

Chapter Four

Megan eased her small car down the narrow road and followed the circle around until she came to a stop in front of a small stone cottage. "It sure looks different from what I remember," she said to Stacie, her only passenger. Looking around, they could see that they were the first of the church group to arrive at the camp.

Stacie glanced at her watch: 9:37 A.M. "We're early. What do you think we should do?"

"We could see if Mrs. Barrows is in the house, or we could just get out and look around." Megan opened her door and stuck her head out. "At least it stopped raining."

They got out and surveyed their surroundings. The cottage was about twenty feet ahead of them. Paint was peeling off the black shutters, and the flower beds were overgrown with a tangled mess of weeds. The walk leading to the house had large gaps where the stones had given way to the soft mud and sunk several inches into the ground.

"Are you sure this is where she lives?" Stacie was doubtful. "It's hard to tell if anyone is here."

"From what I remember, this is the place." Megan turned and looked in the other direction. "We used to play softball in that field over there. It looks like an enormous weed patch now. And, if you follow the road around the circle a little farther, you get to the cabins, girls on one side of the road, boys on the other." Megan gestured to a small dilapidated shed behind the house. "There used to be some equipment stored in there."

Stacie inspected the dubious building from a distance. "If all the buildings look like that, we have our work cut out for us." One wall had definitely separated from the roof, and the glass in the single window had been shattered. The wood around the door frame was half-rotted, making Stacie think the shed would collapse if anyone unknowingly leaned against it. She turned her attention back to the house. "Should we ring the bell or wait for the others to get here?"

"We might as well let her know we're here. Maybe we can get started on something." Megan gingerly led the way along the mud and stone path and rang the bell.

Almost immediately the door opened. "Come on in, girls. I heard your car pull up." Margaret Barrows took Stacie by the wrist and literally pulled her into the cottage. Her grip was firm and her smile sincere.

Somehow Stacie thought an elderly, widowed woman would be small and frail, but Margaret Barrows was five feet, eight inches tall and looked robust. One shoulder hunched slightly as she moved quickly around on her long legs. Her gray, curly hair framed a face with wide cheekbones, and silver glasses highlighted her blue eyes.

"Please, sit down," Mrs. Barrows said. "I'll get you some juice."

Megan protested. "No, please, we don't want you to go to any trouble. We know we're early, but the others will be here soon, I'm sure."

"I'm sure they will, dear." Mrs. Barrows smiled indulgently at both Megan and Stacie. "But until they arrive, you just sit down and make yourselves comfortable. I'll be right back." She disappeared through a swinging door and Megan and Stacie were left standing awkwardly in the living room.

Stacie shrugged her shoulders. "I guess we should sit down. She means business about the juice."

Megan smiled and relaxed. "Okay. She's the boss."

They sat side by side on the couch and found themselves looking across the room at a wall filled with framed photographs. Many of the pictures were black and white. Quite a few were poses of happy, smiling campers from over the years; others were of family members, Stacie supposed. One face appeared over and over again, and she felt as if she were watching a young man age gradually as her eyes moved from the left side of the wall to the far right. Obviously, he was someone important to Mrs. Barrows.

"You have quite a collection of photographs," Stacie said when Mrs. Barrows come back into the room.

"Every face up there is special." Mrs. Barrows set a tray down on the coffee table in front of Megan and Stacie. Two tall glasses were filled with ice cubes and apple juice, and there was a plate laden with bran muffins and banana bread. "I thought maybe you'd be hungry, too."

Stacie and Megan looked at each other and smiled, silently wondering what to make of Margaret Barrows.

"David always liked to have banana bread around," Mrs. Barrows explained. "I can't seem to break the habit of making some every week."

"David was your husband?" Megan ventured.

"For sixty years." Mrs. Barrows looked fondly at the last photo on the wall. "That one was taken before he got so sick." She gestured toward the tray. "Please, help yourselves to something to eat."

Stacie obediently reached for a slice of banana bread; Megan chose a muffin. Contented, Mrs. Barrows lowered herself into a recliner across from them. "Tell me about yourselves. I don't even know your names."

This put Stacie and Megan at ease, and, in between bites of delicious, home-baked bread, they did not hesitate to tell their hostess about their jobs and interests. Megan was in the middle of an outrageously funny story about one of her kindergarteners when they heard the sound of cars pulling up in front of the house.

"Looks like the rest of the crew is here." Mrs. Barrows stood up and went to the window. Stacie and Megan were right behind her.

"That looks like everybody," Stacie said. Including the two of them, there were nine volunteers from the group who had come to spend the day working. From the grubby way they were dressed, no one would have ever guessed the responsible, professional jobs that most of them held. Brad had come in his new van. He dropped down from the driver's seat and went around to the other side of the van to open the door. Before Stacie could even see who it was that had come with Brad, she knew it was Jenna McLean. Stacie sighed as quietly as she could. This was going to be harder than she thought.

Mrs. Barrows was already out the front door and striding across the weedy lawn toward the motley-looking group. Enthusiastically, she shook the hand of everyone who had come.

Megan took one last swallow of apple juice and said, "We'd better get out there before all the good jobs are gone." Reluctantly, Stacie followed her outside.

Mrs. Barrows was already in the middle of her exuberant instructions. "I have plenty of buckets and brushes for scrubbing the insides of the cabins. That shed behind the house has a couple of lawn mowers in it. If you can't find the gasoline, let me know, it might be in the basement. There should be a weed trimmer in there, too. If you need water, there is a big reel of hose around the side of the house."

Stacie could not help but smile at the contagious enthusiasm of Mrs. Barrows. It was obvious she had a good idea of what needed to be done and was well prepared for the work crew.

Megan nudged Stacie's elbow. "Can you believe her?" she whispered. "Most people her age would be happy just to settle back and enjoy their retirement. It's incredible that she has the energy to get this place going again."

Stacie nodded. "It'll be great when it's all done."

Mrs. Barrows clapped her hands sharply. "Okay folks. Let's get to it!"

Soft laughter rippled through the group, but they immediately complied. Brad and a couple of the other men headed for the shed to see about the lawn mowers. Several of the women started unwinding the long hose so that the buckets could be filled. Stacie stood still for a moment, unable to fight the habit of watching Brad as he walked away. A slight movement in her peripheral vision caught her attention, and she realized she was not the only one watching Brad. Jenna was standing right where Brad had left her.

Stacie immediately moved into action. Since Brad was apparently going to work on cutting the grass she would simply opt for an indoor job, and she probably would not run into him all day. Maybe Jenna would stay outside, too. She snatched up a bucket and headed for the water hose. Megan and Mrs. Barrows were already walking side by side toward the first of the cabins and Stacie decided to join them. She squirted some soap into the bottom of the bucket, squeezed the nozzle of the hose to fill it, and followed the others around the circle road.

The inside of the cabin was musty with layers of dust. Mrs. Barrows produced a broom from one corner and batted at the cobwebs hanging from the ceiling. Megan managed to pry open the windows and found a rock to prop open the door so the fresh air could circulate. Stacie pushed up the sleeves of her oldest sweatshirt, gripped a brush, and plunged her arm into the soapy water. The others had gone to work on the next cabin up the road, so Megan, Stacie, and Mrs. Barrows were on their own.

The day passed more quickly than Stacie had expected. After a couple of hours, everyone stopped for a quick picnic lunch and then got right back to work. By the middle of the afternoon, Megan, Stacie, and Mrs. Barrows were able to move on to another cabin to begin the process all over again.

Mrs. Barrows was very appealing, Stacie decided. She was not the doting grandmotherly type that Stacie had expected. It was true that Margaret talked a lot, but it was fun to listen to her stories about the campers she had known over the years. When she found out that Megan had been to the camp as a child, Mrs. Barrows squealed with delight and launched into a whole new set of stories from Megan's era. More than once, Stacie and Megan had to put their brushes down and compose themselves to keep from collapsing with laughter.

"Knock, knock." Stifling their giggles, the three of them turned to see Brad standing in the doorway. Stacie had not seen him since that morning.

"I don't mean to interrupt your fun," he said with a sparkle in his eyes, "but Donna wants to talk to Megan." He looked directly at Megan now. "She wondered if you could come out to where she's working."

"Sure." Megan plopped her brush in her bucket and wiped her hands on her jeans. "It's probably about Sunday school tomorrow. I said I would take her class."

Brad stepped aside to let Megan through the door, but he made no move to leave himself.

Out of the corner of her eye, Stacie tracked Brad. She dipped her brush in the water again and vigorously attacked the dirty wall in front of her. Gray water spattered back at her face, making her blink involuntarily, but she kept at her task, rubbing the wall as hard as she could. With the bright sky behind him, Brad's muscular form stood silhouetted in the doorway.

Mrs. Barrows picked up her bucket and moved it farther down the wall. "Pretty soon we'll need clean water, Stacie."

"Yes, I suppose so," muttered Stacie without looking at either the water or Mrs. Barrows, but only at the wall. Her elbows bobbed up and down with her effort.

"I'll just go get some right now." Mrs. Barrows dropped her brush and bent over to grip the bucket handle with both hands.

"Please, let me go," Stacie offered, politely. *Oh, please let me go!* her mind screamed.

"Nonsense, I can manage just fine. I'll be right back."

She was gone. There was no one to shield Stacie from Brad, who had moved to let Mrs. Barrows pass and then stepped into the cabin instead of out, as Stacie had hoped.

Brad turned his head from side to side. "Looks like you're making good progress in here."

"Yes, I think we are."

"The lawn is almost under control out there."

"That's good."

"I understand there's another set of cabins, too."

"So Megan told me." Stacie wished Brad would leave, so she certainly was not going to encourage any conversation with him.

But Brad was not easily dissuaded. He walked over to the window and knocked on the loose frame. "Looks like I'd better put this on my list of things to fix."

Stacie scrubbed even harder and wondered how long Mrs. Barrows would be gone.

"That beam doesn't look too secure, either." Brad looked up at the ceiling above Stacie's head. He was behind her now, so she could not see him, but she could sense him, and she knew he was coming closer. Casually she stepped to the side and started scrubbing a new spot.

"Can't you even talk to me, Stacie?" She knew Brad was trying to get her to look at him, and she refused.

"Here we go, clean water." Finally, Mrs. Barrows was back. "I put extra soap in it this time, too. Maybe that will speed things up."

Stacie forced herself to brighten up. "I'm sure it will. We'll be done soon, anyway." She stepped away from Brad and took the bucket from Mrs. Barrows. She jostled it just a little, and the water sloshed over the side and left a soapy puddle at her feet. Keeping her distance from Brad in a way that she hoped would give him a clear signal, she set the bucket down and resumed her work.

"Mrs. Barrows, I see some things that need fixing around here," Brad said. "Maybe I'll take a look at all the cabins and make one master list of what needs to be done."

"Oh, that would be wonderful, Brad." Mrs. Barrows was more than pleased at

Brad's suggestion. "David used to take care of all the building problems. I'm afraid I'm not much use in that department."

"Well, don't worry about it," Brad reassured her. "I'll make sure everything is in tiptop shape." He smiled at Mrs. Barrows and looked over at Stacie. "I suppose I'd better get back outside. Just let me know if there is anything I can do for you, Mrs. Barrows."

"What you're already doing is wonderful, all of you. How can I tell you how much I appreciate it?"

"We're glad to help." Brad wiggled his fingers in a good-bye wave and left.

Once he was gone, Stacie slowed her scrubbing speed considerably and started breathing more deeply. Mrs. Barrows wordlessly picked up her own brush and also started in again. All day long they had bantered back and forth and laughed until their sides hurt. The quiet between them now felt very strange to Stacie, but she didn't know what to say. After a few minutes, Mrs. Barrows broke the silence.

"Are you and Brad friends?"

"Sure," Stacie answered quickly—perhaps too quickly. "We're all friends; everyone in the group likes to be together."

Mrs. Barrows scratched at a stubborn spot on the wall. "You didn't say a word to Brad. I got the feeling that you didn't even want to be here with him."

Stacie did not answer. She could not; the words just did not come.

"Maybe we should take a break, Stacie," Mrs. Barrows said gently.

"No, I'm fine. We'll be done before too long." Stacie started scrubbing harder again.

Mrs. Barrows put her hand over Stacie's and took hold of the brush. "I insist. The dirt has been here a long time; a few more minutes won't make a difference. Let's go up to the cottage and have tea."

Stacie didn't have the strength to argue.

Once again Stacie found herself in the quaint living room gazing at the wall of pictures. Mrs. Barrows swooped up the tray Stacie and Megan had left that morning and vanished into the kitchen. In a few minutes, Stacie heard the comforting whistle of the teakettle and knew that she would have only a few more minutes alone. It was obvious that Mrs. Barrows had detected something was wrong, even though she had known Stacie for less than a day. The question now was, how much should Stacie tell her?

"Here we go. I brought sugar and lemon so you can fix your tea just the way you like it. We should probably let it steep for a few more minutes."

Stacie was admiring the white porcelain teapot with a pattern of blue windmills. "What a beautiful teapot," she said sincerely. "The windmills look so delicate, and there's so much detail."

"David gave me that for our fortieth wedding anniversary."

"It's a beautiful gift. It sounds like he was a thoughtful husband."

Mrs. Barrows tilted her head and smiled. "We had our tough times, but he was a good man. I was very happy being married to him."

Stacie felt a lump forming in her throat. She had hoped to say something like that about Brad someday, but now she did not know if she would ever feel that way about any man.

"When I think of how close I came to not marrying David. . . ." Mrs. Barrows shook her head.

The question hung in the air, so Stacie had to ask it. "What do you mean? Did you have doubts about whether you should get married?"

"It's a long story, but there was another young man before David. I was very young, and there were a bunch of us who ran around together. I was madly in love with one of the boys before I met my husband. But David—David was in a class by himself—and there was a spark between us right from the start. Still, I felt a sense of loyalty to Henry. When he asked me to marry him, I said yes, and convinced myself that what I felt for David was just puppy love and I would get over it. When I think of what I would have missed if I had not married David . . . let's just say I'm awfully glad I did."

Stacie's eyes were filled with tears, and she could barely hold back the sobs.

Mrs. Barrows poured a cup of tea and handed it to Stacie. "Now, dear, why don't you tell me just what is going on between you and Brad."

Chapter Five

The view outside the window was a shapeless rush of colors as the train rumbled down tracks that had been in use for half a century. For a midwestern spring, the day was fairly bright. Every now and then, when the train slowed down enough, Stacie could see flecks of green dancing on the brown branches and knew that the spring rains were doing their work. April would be brighter and more colorful than March had been and spring would burst forth with its yearly reminder of the wonder of life.

Stacie had anticipated leisurely enjoying the countryside from the comfort of her reclined seat on the train. But she had not expected the lulling sensation brought on by the steady motion of the train and, after the first fifty miles, she found herself struggling to stay alert. She knew she needed to rest because she had not been sleeping well. Still, she felt she ought to be doing something more productive with her time, even on a train.

When Jack Rogers first suggested that Stacie should take a trip to Thomasville, she assumed she would drive the 200 miles to her future home. When Megan made a casual comment about a childhood train ride, Stacie remembered that the railroad still operated a regular schedule between St. Mary's and Thomasville. Impulsively, and not characteristically, she called Dillon Graves to ask him to meet her at the train station.

Stacie forced herself to sit upright in her seat and took a professional magazine out of her briefcase. For a few moments she successfully concentrated on the lead article, but her mind began to wander. Although more awake now, it was still very hard for her to focus her thoughts. The photograph on the page in front of her blurred and somehow transformed itself into a picture of Mrs. Barrows, with her soft gray curls and bright eyes, handing Stacie a cup of steaming tea.

Even though she had known Margaret Barrows for only a few hours last Saturday afternoon, Stacie had unplugged her emotional dam and, while they shared a pot of tea, confided the whole story of her relationship with Brad. After spending so much of the day laughing with the older woman, Stacie took comfort in also sharing her tears. Now it was Thursday, and Stacie was plodding her way through her problems in the real world. Although talking with Mrs. Barrows had not given Stacie any immediate answers about her feelings for Brad, she had begun to feel less like an emotional blob and a little more like her old self.

As the train rocked rhythmically back and forth, Stacie turned the page of the magazine and made another stab at reading. The article was about a new program for developmentally disabled children in a suburb of Chicago, and for more than a week Stacie had been looking forward to having time to read the entire article. One paragraph at a time, she made her way through the description of the unique program, with its advantages and disadvantages.

"Next stop, Thomasville." The conductor's garbled voice barely came through the static of the speaker at the front of the car, but Stacie already knew that they were getting close to the station in Thomasville. She closed her magazine and put it back into her briefcase, then laid her head back to look out the window and enjoy the last few minutes of the scenery.

To Stacie, Dillon Graves was only a voice on the phone or a signature at the bottom of a letter. She had never even seen a photograph of him, so she did not really know who she was looking for when she got off the train and scanned the old wooden platform. It was the middle of the day when she arrived and there were not many people around, so she thought surely it would be obvious who Dillon Graves was. One man sat on a bench reading a newspaper; he did not even look up when the passengers stepped off the train, so obviously he was not Dillon. The only other man she saw looked much too old; Jack had said that Dillon was thirty-two.

Stacie picked up her small suitcase and decided to go inside the station; it was empty except for the ticket agent. Trying to look hopeful but wondering if she had made a mistake, Stacie found a wooden bench that looked fairly clean and tentatively sat down.

"Stacie?"

She jumped at the sound of a smooth voice over her shoulder. Fumbling with her briefcase, she said, "Yes, I'm Stacie. You're Dillon?"

"That's me." He smiled at her and put out his hand.

Stacie stood up and shook the soft hand of Dillon Graves. He was tall, several inches taller than she had imagined, with tightly-curled blondish hair which was boyishly long in the back. He wore clean but faded jeans and a beige tweed jacket over a yellow shirt which was open at the neck. On his feet were well-worn sneakers. Stacie was awkwardly aware of the crisp linen jacket and pants she had chosen to wear that day; she felt drastically overdressed, compared to Dillon.

"Let me help you with your bag." Dillon reached down and picked up the small suitcase. "Is this all you have?" he asked, his lips turned up softly at the corners.

"Yes," Stacie answered. "I'm staying only until Sunday." Afraid she would stare at his freckled face, she tried not to look directly at him. His appearance and clothes—everything about Dillon was different from the professional, methodical administrator she had pictured. But she liked him instantly.

Dillon gestured toward the doorway. "There's a nice park near here. I thought we could get some meat and bread from the deli next door and have a little pic-nic while we get to know each other."

"I'd like that," Stacie said with enthusiasm. "I'm starving."

"Great. You wait here while I put your things in my car. I'll leave it parked; we can come back for it later."

Stacie watched Dillon's lanky strides as he went to the parking lot and his ten-year-old compact car that needed a paint job. He opened the back door and set her things inside. Even from a distance she could not help responding to his warmth. Although they had spoken on the phone several times, Dillon was brand new to Stacie. She liked the fact that he did not know about her personal life or history and felt that this was a chance to be anybody she wanted to be, to explore a fresh start in a new place.

"Ready?" he said when he got back to where she was standing.

"Absolutely."

She walked comfortably alongside of Dillon. When they came around the side of the station, Stacie saw what looked like the main street of the town. There were a few antique shops and specialty stores, several century-old, limestone buildings which housed the city offices, and the small park that Dillon had mentioned. Already Stacie liked Thomasville; it seemed quaint and tidy and appealing. She knew though that there must be another side to life in Thomasville, or the agency would not be setting up a homeless shelter there. But what she had seen so far she liked very much.

"Here's the deli." Dillon's voice interrupted her mental evaluation of the town. "What do you like to eat?"

"Oh, anything would be fine."

"Come on. You must have some preferences."

Stacie relaxed and smiled. "All right. I'd like roast beef on a hoagie roll."

"We should be able to manage that," Dillon said, pulling open the door and holding it for Stacie. "They make a mean German potato salad here, too."

"Sounds great."

Dillon ordered the sandwiches, salad, and soft drinks to go. When their lunch was ready, they took the sacks and crossed the street to the park. Just as they got situated and unpacked the food, the wind gusted and they grabbed their napkins and cups, just in time. Instinctively, Stacie pulled up the collar of her jacket.

"Are you cold?" Dillon asked. "We could go back to the deli and sit inside."

Stacie shook her head. "The sun feels good. It's been such a rainy spring at home . . . I would hate to miss out on such a pretty day." She took a bite of her sandwich, trying not to embarrass herself by dropping food on her lap.

Dillon sipped his drink. "How long have you lived in St. Mary's?"

Stacie thought for a quick moment while she chewed. She decided she could answer that question without opening up the conversation to everything that had happened to her during her years in St. Mary's. "I've been there about five years," she said brightly. "I went to St. Mary's College and then was lucky enough to find a job that would let me stay there."

"Sounds like you like it a lot."

Stacie tilted her head thoughtfully. "I guess I really do. I'm going to miss it when I move here."

Dillon waved his hand down the main street. "This is a great town, too. You'll see."

"You seem pretty confident."

Dillon smiled that warm smile of his. "I guess I'm prejudiced. My family lived here when I was in high school and I've always loved it. When I had the chance to come back for this job, I couldn't pass it up." He picked up his sandwich and pondered where the next bite should be.

"Did you always want to be a social worker?" Stacie asked.

Dillon shook his head. "No. In college I wanted to be a psychologist. But somewhere along the line I decided that if people didn't have a safe place to live there wasn't much point in trying to help them handle their emotional problems. So I got involved with a couple of homeless shelters, first as a volunteer and then on the staff."

"And now you're here," Stacie summarized, "ready to open a whole new center. I'm sure your psychology background isn't wasted in a job where you have to deal with people all the time."

"It comes in handy," Dillon agreed. "I have run into some real characters, but I'm sure you have, too."

"Jack said you already have a contract on a building," Stacie said. "Is that working out all right?"

Dillon swallowed a mouthful of roast beef and shook his head. "We've had some problems. It's a bit complicated because the building is owned jointly by several people, and we have to get them all to agree to the sale. But I'm hopeful. In fact, they've already given me a key. When we're done here, I'll take you over and show you around."

"One more bite." Stacie pushed the last of her potato salad into her mouth and started collecting sandwich wrappings and napkins. "Ready when you are."

They strolled back to Dillon's car, their conversation becoming increasingly excited as they talked enthusiastically about the new project they would be sharing. Stacie decided that, as much as she loved St. Mary's, moving on to a new place would be good for her. Away from everything that was familiar, she felt invigorated with the potential of what lay ahead of her. It was already clear that working with Dillon would be a comfortable distraction from what she was leaving behind. Getting the new shelter set up would be challenging and time consuming and she would have little time on her hands for wishing she were back in St. Mary's.

Dillon unlocked the door on the passenger side and let her in. When he was settled in the driver's seat and had pulled out of the parking lot, he started pointing out features of Thomasville. "Like a lot of midwestern towns, Thomasville was built up along the railroad so that it would be easy to get supplies in. But, by the turn of the century, it was clear that Thomasville would never be the booming metropolis the founders thought it would be."

"From what I've seen so far, it seems like a nice town," Stacie said. "Why is there a homeless problem here?"

"A lot of people have been asking that question. The most obvious answer is the high unemployment in surrounding rural areas, especially since the manufacturing plant outside of town shut down three years ago. Some of those people have never been able to find another job."

They rode in silence for a few minutes, each of them absorbed in thoughts of the seriousness of the problems they would encounter.

"Have you started looking for a place to live yet?" Dillon asked.

"No. I was hoping to get a few leads this weekend. But I still have plenty of time until I'm scheduled to move."

"I'll keep my eyes open for you. I found an apartment in a nice building for a reasonable rent." Dillon looked over at Stacie and added, "I'm just sorry there aren't any vacancies right now."

"Me, too," Stacie blurted out before she realized what she had said. She was caught off guard by his remark and regretted answering so quickly. She hardly knew Dillon Graves; why should she be sorry that she could not live in his apartment building? Yet she was.

"The building is just up in the next block," Dillon explained. "I have to warn you that it needs a lot of work. I don't suppose you know any trustworthy contractors."

Stacie looked up at Dillon abruptly. Why would he ask her if she knew any contractors? From his expression she decided that the question was sincere and merely professional. She shook her head and answered truthfully. "I'm afraid I don't know anyone around here."

"Well, I have a couple of leads, so I guess we'll start collecting bids."

Contractors. Until Dillon said that word, she had not thought of Brad all day; it would be too easy to fall into despondency about what she was sacrificing in order to come to Thomasville. Instead, she resolved to concentrate on the good things that awaited her here in this new place.

They parked on the street in front of the old wooden building and Dillon unlocked the front door. He held it open for her, and Stacie cautiously stepped over the threshold. The floor creaked and felt strangely soft.

"Are you sure this is safe?"

"I wouldn't have brought you here if it weren't," Dillon assured her. "It's already passed city inspection, and, once the improvements are made, you'll forget it ever looked like this."

"I can't see anything. Aren't there any windows?"

Dillon chuckled. "They've been boarded up for years. Unfortunately, the light switch is across the room."

Stacie felt the firm touch of his hand on her elbow as he guided her through the shadows. Obviously, Dillon knew exactly where he was going, and Stacie was surprised at how easy it was to trust him. She was also surprised at the pleasure she felt from such a simple gesture as his hand on her elbow. *Did it mean anything? Couldn't he have crossed the room by himself and turned on the lights? Was he looking for a reason to touch her? Or was it all her imagination?*

"Here we are." The switch clicked and the room filled with light. Dillon's hands were in his pockets. The moment—if there had been one—was gone.

"I think this will be the reception area, with the registration desk over here." Dillon paced around the room while he talked. "We'll widen the hallway back there that leads to the kitchen and dining room and have the sleeping rooms upstairs. Full capacity will be about sixty-five people."

For the next two hours, Stacie attentively followed Dillon around the building soaking in the information he had already gathered and asking questions to decide how she could help. More than once he stopped in mid-sentence to ask what she thought about something, reminding her that as assistant director her opinions would be an important part of making decisions when the shelter was functioning.

When the tour ended, the afternoon was nearly gone. Dillon told Stacie that he had made several appointments with city officials for the next day, and he wanted her to come to the meetings with him. "We'll get our business taken care of, and then maybe we can find something fun to do on Saturday."

"That would be great," Stacie heard herself saying, as if it were someone else speaking the words.

"Unfortunately, I have a commitment tonight, or we could have dinner together," Dillon said apologetically.

"Don't worry about me," Stacie answered. "I brought plenty of work along with me." Once again she was not sure what he meant by his comment. *Had he wanted to have dinner together to talk more about remodeling the building? Or did he have something else in mind?*

"Then I'll just drop you off at your motel and come back for you at about nine tomorrow morning."

"That should be fine."

For supper, Stacie had soup and salad at the little coffee shop across the street from her motel. By then it was already dark and she did not want to be out walking alone. After her active day and the hours of Dillon's company, her small motel room seemed strangely quiet and still, and, for a few minutes, she sat motionless on the end of the bed expecting something, she didn't know what, to happen. She was used to being alone in her own apartment but alone in a motel room, she felt isolated and lonely. Luckily, she had brought plenty of work along with her, mostly things to read, so she would have no trouble passing the evening.

She decided to treat herself to a long hot bath before delving into a stack of journals and newsletters from other shelters. Stacie wished she had brought along some bubble bath to soak in. Still, it would be a luxury to relax in the tub without any deadline for when she had to get out. She piled her thick hair on top of her head and lowered herself into the bath. With her neck leaning against the back of the tub, she closed her eyes and gradually relaxed. In a matter of moments, she was very near sleep.

Stacie knew that she was not sleeping, but she was not really awake either. Behind her closed eyelids, discordant images crashed into each other: Brad renovating the new shelter; Dillon visiting her apartment in St. Mary's; Brad's long and gentle kiss on the night they broke their engagement; Dillon's mysterious grasp on her elbow as he steered her across the dark room; Megan's face rising through clouds and looking from Brad to Dillon and back again; Mrs. Barrows and her pots of tea and pictures of David lining the wall; dinner with Dillon at a fancy restaurant in the middle of the park; Brad tilting his head back in laughter at Jenna McLean's humor; living next door to Dillon; the pain in Brad's voice as he said "Can't you even look at me?"

Water splashed out of the tub and onto the floor as Stacie stood up abruptly. This bath was not turning out to be very relaxing after all. She dried herself off, got dressed for bed and sat on the end of the bed to consider the rest of the evening. After what had happened when she almost dozed off in the tub, she was hesitant to try sleeping; besides, it was too early to go to bed. But she knew she would not remember anything she read if she tried to work tonight. Restlessly, she flipped on the television, something she rarely did at home, but she was desperate tonight. Scanning the television guide, she reluctantly admitted that there was nothing on that she wanted to watch, so she shut the set off.

If Dillon had not had a commitment for this evening, she could be enjoying his company right this minute, relishing an interesting appetizer instead of fearing disturbing dreams. *Would she have gone to dinner with him,* she wondered, *if she believed that his interest was personal and not professional?* Five days ago she had told Mrs. Barrows that she still loved Brad; now she was wishing that Dillon had not dropped her off at her motel and gone on with his life. Those two facts simply did not make sense when placed side by side.

Something was wrong—or something was changing.

Chapter Six

Stacie decisively pressed the print button on her desktop computer and sat back in her chair to relax for a few moments. For several weeks, ever since her trip to Thomasville, she had been spending a lot of her time trying to clear up projects that needed to be done before she could move. Jack Rogers told her not to worry about most of the things, but her own conscience demanded that she do her best to get everything done.

The laser printer, stationed outside her office door in the reception area, sucked another piece of paper through its mysterious insides, and clicked as it spit the page out the other end. Stacie listened for the familiar series of sounds three more times before getting up and going out to the printer to retrieve her report.

"Got a wild weekend planned?" Marsha popped her head out from behind her desk, a stack of folders on the corner of her desk nearly obscuring her.

Stacie shrugged. "Nothing too exciting. I'm going to spend Saturday out at the camp again."

"Haven't you been out there an awful lot lately?"

"It's been a couple of months since we started on the project," Stacie said, "but things are coming along."

"Are they going to be ready for campers this summer?"

"Absolutely. The owner hopes to start advertising soon, and camp can start before the end of June."

Stacie collected her report and ducked back into her office. Before she even sat down, Marsha was standing in the doorway. Stacie had not thought Marsha could move that fast.

"Almost forgot to tell you that Dillon Graves called while you were out to lunch."

Stacie looked up, her interest piqued. "Did he say what he wanted?"

"He asked to talk to Jack. Actually, he sounded upset." Her message relayed, Marsha turned and sauntered back to her chair.

Stacie had been in contact with Dillon several times a week ever since they met. She appreciated that he included her in decisions about setting up the office and the sleeping rooms and his cheerful voice on the phone was always a welcome interruption. After spending three days with him, he was no longer a faceless mystery; in fact, every time they spoke, she could picture his freckled face and crinkled smile.

Beyond that, she was unsure what to think of Dillon Graves. He had a face now, but he was still a mystery. When they were together, she almost believed that he was attracted to her and, to her own surprise, she responded warmly. But their contact in the weeks since their weekend visit had been strictly professional, and now Stacie thought she had probably been mistaken about him all along. Her dilemma was that she still felt herself responding to him personally. Relating to him about the work they had in common was comfortable, but she was curious about what it would be like to see him every day. Would it be easier to figure him out when they were working together, or would she still find herself wondering what he was thinking and feeling?

It was strange that Marsha said that Dillon sounded upset. Although Stacie had to admit that she did not know Dillon Graves very well, she had a hard time picturing him getting upset easily. Either Marsha was inferring something that was not there, or something drastic had happened; Stacie could not imagine what that could be.

The report now lay on the desk in front of her, waiting to be checked for mistakes. Stacie spread the four pages out across the desk and started reading slowly and carefully. She was halfway through the second page when she intuitively sensed someone in the doorway. It was Jack Rogers.

"What's wrong, Jack?" she asked, instantly knowing he was upset; Marsha must have been right about Dillon.

Jack closed the door behind him and sunk heavily into the faded gray chair against the wall across from her desk.

"Dillon called. The deal is off."

"What?" Stacie's mind churned faster than she could speak. "The shelter—doesn't Dillon want to run the new shelter?"

"The deal for the building is off," Jack clarified, pressing his lips together in disgust. "It's owned by a group of people and one of them doesn't want to sell. And the way their partnership is worded, that's all it takes to call the whole thing off."

Still in shock, Stacie did not know what to say. "But I thought we had a contract. . . ."

Jack shrugged. "It was contingent on the agreement of all parties concerned. And one party does not agree."

"Why not?"

"Who knows? Maybe she's not happy with the purchase price we agreed on; maybe she doesn't like the thought of destitute people wandering around her prestigious building; maybe she's on a power trip."

Stacie stared bleakly at her bookcase and the stack of resources she had already organized to take with her. "This is ridiculous." She forced out a heavy sigh. "What happens now?"

"Well, I've been on the phone all afternoon with several of the board members. The consensus is that we should go ahead and try to open a new shelter anyway. But it may not be in Thomasville."

"But Thomasville needs a shelter."

Jack nodded. "I know. But so do a lot of other places. Like Weston."

"Weston?"

"That was our second choice all along. One of the board members has a building that he can make available almost immediately."

"But what about approval from the city and all the homework that we've already done in Thomasville?" Stacie asked.

"We'll just have to do it all over again."

"Is Dillon willing to go to Weston?"

"I think so, Stacie. Are you?"

Weston was only thirty miles from St. Mary's. It would be a much easier move and from a personal standpoint, it made more sense than moving to Thomasville. "I guess so," she said. "I'm committed to doing the job, so I guess it doesn't matter where."

"Good. That's what I wanted to hear." Jack stood up, looking noticeably calmer. "I'm sorry about all the last minute scrambling this will mean, but you and Dillon will have to go to Weston and work on things."

Stacie nodded. "I guess we'll start by looking at the building and go from there."

"Then I'll leave it up to you to get in touch with Dillon and arrange things. I think you should do it as soon as possible, though. Next week maybe?"

"Of course."

"You're kidding! Weston?" Megan looked at Stacie incredulously and set her hamburger down on the plate in front of her. "That's so much closer to St. Mary's." Her delight was obvious. "For my own sake, I'm glad. It won't be so hard to see you."

Stacie turned the catsup bottle upside down and thumped the side of it; she had been meaning to buy a new one for at least two weeks but had not gotten around to it. "I'm glad about that part, too."

Megan's expression turned serious. "You don't sound excited."

Stacie did not answer; she just kept waiting for the catsup to crawl down the side of the bottle and onto her plate.

"What about Brad?" Megan prompted.

"What about him?" Stacie answered a little too abruptly.

"Well, if the whole reason you two broke up was because you had to move two hundred miles away, then maybe. . . ."

Stacie shook her head. "I don't know, Megan. Lately I've been thinking there had to be more to it than that."

"What do you mean? Brad would take you back in a second."

"Sure, now that he could have what he wanted all along. I don't want him to 'take me back,' Megan. I don't know how this change affects my relationship to Brad, but if we're going to get together, we'll have to have a better understanding about what we both want. Maybe we didn't know each other as well as we thought we did."

"Aw, come on, Stace." Megan crossed Stacie's small, tidy kitchen to get a napkin. "You two had a great relationship, and it doesn't have to be over. You can both have what you want this way. Brad works on jobs all over the county, so whether he lives here or in Weston won't matter."

"Can we change the subject, please?" Stacie bit into her hamburger and then said with her mouth full, "Are you going out to the Homestead tomorrow?" She knew Megan did not want to let go of talking about Brad, but Stacie just did not feel up to it. And she was not sure Megan would understand her confused feelings about Dillon, so she did not want to discuss him, either.

"No, I can't go tomorrow," Megan answered. "But some of the others are going. Brad is going, for instance."

"Megan!"

Stacie finally succeeded in getting Megan to talk about something else, but her own mind brimmed with the exact questions her friend had raised. *What did this change mean about her engagement to Brad? Should she tell him right away and expect to pick up where they left off? Should she wait until the move actually happened and see how he reacted?* It had been more than four months since the night they broke their engagement. Maybe they had drifted far enough apart in that time that they did not belong together anymore. And, although she knew she still had strong feelings for Brad, Stacie also felt a lively spark when she thought about Dillon. *What did that mean?*

"Thanks for meeting me here," Stacie said as she fumbled in her jacket pocket for her keys.

"No problem," Dillon answered. "Weston is so close to you that it makes sense to go together from here."

Stacie locked her apartment door and dropped her keys back into a pocket. "Then, let's get going."

The drive to Weston took just under an hour. This time it was Stacie who was familiar with the local area and could point out the interesting buildings and places shrouded in legend. When she pulled her car into the parking lot of the building they had come to see, she was impressed.

"From the outside, it looks like a great building," Stacie commented as she slammed the car door.

Dillon was scanning the neighborhood. "Great location. It will be easy for people to find, and it looks like it's right on the bus route."

"Let's check it out," she said.

They got out of the car and approached the front door of the building. Dillon produced a key Jack had from the owner and turned it in the lock. They stepped inside to a room filled with daylight streaming through the large front windows. Despite this, Stacie remembered her cautious steps in the darkness of the Thomasville building and the way Dillon had confidently guided her across the room.

"Ah, this time the light switch is right next to the door," Dillon said, as if remembering the same moment. Although it was not really necessary, Dillon flipped the switch and fluorescent lights hanging from the ceiling started to hum and flickered on. It was obvious that the building had been an office complex. The large reception area with worn gray carpeting was the focal point for four modest offices. At the rear was a hallway leading to another large room, this one with exposed cement floors and utility shelving on the walls.

"Must have been a warehouse," Dillon speculated.

"We could section off a portion for a supply room and convert the rest to a place to eat," Stacie said, pacing the length of the room. "We could seat about sixty people in here, I would think."

Dillon was nodding. "Apparently there are more offices upstairs."

"Sleeping rooms."

"Right. But for how many beds?"

"Let's go up and take a look."

It took only a few more minutes for Dillon and Stacie to be satisfied that the building would be adequate.

"I think we can tell Jack that this will work out, if he can come to an agreement with the owner," Dillon said. "Now, all we need is a contractor."

Stacie resisted the urge to mention that she knew a contractor. "I guess we'll have to start all over again with getting bids."

"We've lost a lot of time, and it might be hard to find someone who will do indoor work during the good summer weather."

"If we can find a contractor, how soon can we open?"

Dillon tilted his head in thought. "Maybe by the fall. We'll have to see how much red tape the city will make us wade through."

"On to city hall, then."

After a quick lunch, they spent the rest of the day collecting the names of all the city officials they would have to contact and finding out what Weston's city council would need to know about their plan before approving it. Their vigorous conversation flowed with ideas, and Stacie filled page after page in her notebook.

It was almost supper time when they headed back to Stacie's car and started the drive back to St. Mary's. The hour passed quickly—too quickly. Even though it was work that brought them together, Stacie had thoroughly enjoyed the day with Dillon. She was invigorated by being with someone who shared her vision, and she especially appreciated Dillon's mild-mannered approach to getting things done. He did not get ruffled; he just kept working at one task after another until he was satisfied with their progress.

When they reached the city limits, Stacie toyed with the idea of asking Dillon to come to her apartment for dinner. Mentally, she inventoried her refrigerator to see if she had the fixings for a meal. She could offer something simple, like pasta and salad. But would she be crossing over an invisible line if she invited Dillon home to dinner? Their hours together had been filled only with business. Although Dillon was warm and congenial toward her, how could she know that he did not relate to everyone with that same warmth? She decided against asking him if he was free that evening and took the exit off the highway that would take them to his hotel.

She pulled into the parking lot and slowly maneuvered to the main entrance. "How's your room here?" she asked pleasantly.

"Not too bad. It could use a fresh coat of paint, but it's clean and quiet."

"It's an historic building, you know," Stacie pointed out knowledgeably.

Dillon smiled curiously. "I can tell by the plumbing."

Stacie burst out laughing and Dillon joined her.

"Have a nice evening, Stacie. I'll see you at the office in the morning."

Stacie did not immediately pull away from the curb; she watched, mesmerized, as Dillon pulled open the oversized door and was swallowed up by the mammoth building. She had a twinge of regret at not having invited him to dinner, but it was too late now.

Dillon was around the office most of the next day. There was no desk for him to use, so he sat at a small wooden table across from Marsha in the reception area. Stacie had offered to share her limited space, but Dillon insisted that he would be disturbing her too much and that he was getting along just fine at the table. Marsha scowled at him from time to time for tying up her phone, but Dillon just flashed his irresistible smile and gradually won her over. Before the day was out, Marsha was offering to help Dillon with his calls.

They had agreed the day before that Dillon would set up the appointments they needed and Stacie would work on pulling together a proposal for the city council. She could use the Thomasville proposal as a guide, but many of the details had to be changed. Fortunately, Dillon had put his original proposal on computer disk, so it was fairly easy to work on the revisions. By the end of the day, Stacie had a draft completed and a list of additional information about Weston she would need to have before she could finish the job.

She was packing up her briefcase, getting ready to go home, when Dillon knocked on her door frame. "I think we're all set for three appointments in Weston next week," he said.

"That's great."

"Took me all day to get that far; those city people don't want to be pinned down."

Stacie smiled. "The important thing is that you got the appointments."

"I suppose so."

"Will you be staying in St. Mary's until next week? Or are you going home and coming back again?

Dillon shrugged. "There's really nothing that I have to be in Thomasville for. In fact, I should start looking for a place to live in Weston. Maybe I'll spend a few days doing that."

Stacie nodded at his sensible plan. "I'm sure Jack would like to have you around here for a while, too."

"I like hanging around here. I've finally got Marsha softened up. How tough can things be when I've accomplished that?"

They both laughed.

"Well, I see you've got your briefcase ready, so I guess you're on your way home," Dillon said. "You're not taking work home, are you?"

"Just a little," Stacie said apologetically, fingering the strap on her briefcase and looking away from Dillon. "Stuff to read mostly."

"I have a better idea."

Stacie glanced up. "What's that?"

"Let's have dinner together."

"Well, I. . . ." Inside, Stacie was leaping at the invitation. Outwardly, she did not want to misinterpret it.

"You've lived here for six years. Surely you know some good restaurants."

"As a matter of fact, I do," Stacie answered, more composed. "We've both been so busy today that we haven't had much chance to talk about how things went yesterday. Dinner would be a good chance to do that."

Dillon leaned against the door frame and smiled with one side of his mouth. "That wasn't exactly what I had in mind."

Stacie's heart was beating faster and she fumbled for words. She decided to change the subject. "Well, I'd like to go home and freshen up. Can I meet you somewhere in about an hour."

"I'll pick you up, and then you choose the restaurant."

Stacie nodded awkwardly. "Fine. Do you remember how to get to my apartment?"

"It isn't hard. I'll see you in an hour."

Three hours later Stacie and Dillon were walking up the sidewalk to her apartment building, acting out the best jokes they knew and laughing conspicuously. If neighbors looked with disfavor on the disruption of the quiet spring evening, they did not notice. Stuffed with Italian food, they were experimenting with Italian accents in their conversation and gesturing wildly as the owner of the restaurant had done all evening. When they got close to the building, Stacie put a finger to her mouth. "Shhh. We'd better quiet down. I've got some older neighbors who go to bed pretty early."

"I know it's a work night, Stacie, but I hate for this evening to end."

"I had a great time, Dillon. I haven't laughed that much in weeks." They were standing outside her door now. She reached into her pocket for her keys. "I should have left the porch light on. I can barely see the keyhole."

"I'm glad you left it off."

That strange remark caught Stacie's attention and she looked up at him.

Dillon put his fingers lightly on her chin. "I'm glad you left the light off because it makes it easier to do this." He bent his head to kiss her and Stacie forgot all about looking for her keys.

Chapter Seven

"Stacie! I found them!" Margaret Barrows leaned precariously out the window of the dining hall and hollered in the direction of the shed.

Stacie popped her head out of the musty shed, wiped the stray copper lock of hair off her forehead, and squinted back at Mrs. Barrows. The older woman gestured for Stacie to return to the building which housed the somewhat dilapidated kitchen and rustic dining room.

"They were here all along," Mrs. Barrows said once Stacie was within easy hearing distance. "I can't imagine how we missed them the first time we looked." She held the door open for Stacie and pointed toward the kitchen.

Stacie, her hair braided down the back of her neck to keep it out of the way while she worked, went into the kitchen and stooped to look inside one of several cardboard boxes tucked away in a corner cupboard. There were all the plates, cups, and bowls which Mrs. Barrows had lost track of during the years the camp was idle. The beige plastic dishes were tightly stacked, but Stacie estimated that there were place settings for close to one hundred campers. "Do you think this is all of them?" she asked.

"Oh, I think so, yes, that looks right." Mrs. Barrows glanced at her wristwatch. "They'll all need to be washed, but let's take a break first. I made some lemonade this morning." She smiled affectionately at Stacie. "My dear, will you help me pour? It's quite warm today; I'm sure everyone will want some."

"Of course." Stacie brushed her hands together to loosen some of the dust and then followed her friend up the small hill to the cottage. As always, she was amazed at the vigor which the kind, gray-haired woman displayed. Margaret Barrows roamed the camp with the energy of someone half her age—or less—Stacie thought, especially when she was having trouble keeping up with her. More than once Stacie had been out of breath as she trailed behind Mrs. Barrows along the woodsy paths leading to the cabins and outbuildings dotting the landscape of the Homestead.

By the time they got to the cottage, Stacie was ready for some lemonade. They took two glass pitchers brimming with refreshment and a stack of clear plastic cups and went to the shaded redwood picnic table outside the back door.

"Would you do the honors?" Mrs. Barrows asked, nodding her head toward the huge gong hanging from its own stand out in the yard.

"With gusto!" Stacie took the oversized mallet from its hook and swung. The gong reverberated so loudly that it would be impossible for anyone at the camp not to hear it. Sure enough, in a few seconds, workers began to straggle out of the various buildings and amble toward the picnic table.

The mid-May weather was more like the end of June. Finally, the spring rains had ended, and the earth at the camp turned from mud to dirt. Only last weekend the group had come in jeans and sweatshirts; now, most of them were in shorts and T-shirts, with sweat beading on their foreheads. Lemonade poured steadily out of Stacie's pitcher; she hoped that there would be enough to go around.

"That looks good, Stace." It was Brad's turn to come to the table.

Stacie had a fleeting, irritated thought that Brad could just as well have gone to Margaret's end of the table. But she dutifully surrendered the last of the lemonade in her pitcher and smiled as pleasantly as she had to all the others.

"What are you and Mrs. B. up to today?" Brad seemed determined to make conversation. He propped himself casually against the end of the table.

"Washing dishes." Stacie's answer was blunt and she glanced around the yard distractedly.

"Washing dishes?"

"Yes. Hundreds of them."

"Oh, you mean the camp's dishes," said Brad. "I thought they were lost."

"We found them. Now we're going to wash them."

"I see." Brad tilted his head straight back and tossed the contents of his glass down his throat. He set the empty cup down on the table. "I'll see ya, Stace," his said, his tone noticeably muffled.

Stacie did not return his farewell. Glad he was gone, she turned her attention to collecting the glasses left abandoned on the picnic table. She stacked them, tucked them under one arm, and picked up the empty pitchers. She was ready to return everything to the kitchen and get back to work.

"I suppose you know that you were quite rude to Brad."

Mrs. Barrows's direct tone caught Stacie off guard. Like a scolded schoolgirl, she could not even offer a defense. "Well, I, I. . . ."

"You were a snob." Margaret took the glass pitchers out of Stacie's arms, pivoted on her left heel, and went through the back door.

"Why does he always talk to me?" Stacie pleaded pitifully, following Mrs. Barrows and setting the glasses in the sink.

"It's a fair enough question, my dear, given your history with Brad, but you needn't whine when you ask it."

Stacie looked at Mrs. Barrows with wide eyes. Had she really been whining?

"Let's leave these until later and get back to work on that stack in the dining hall." Mrs. Barrows held the door open for Stacie. "But don't think that I'm going to forget what we were talking about."

In the dining hall kitchen, Stacie wordlessly plugged the sink, turned on the hot water, and squirted detergent into the running stream. As the deep porcelain basin filled with suds, she lifted the plates out of their boxes and stacked them within easy reach.

Mrs. Barrows slipped a faded, yellow gingham apron over her head and tied it in the back. From a drawer she produced a stack of flour-sack dish towels. "Now, what's going on, Stacie?"

Stacie wanted to tell Mrs. Barrows how confused she was, but she didn't know how to start. Distressed, she plunged her hands into the water and began wiping plates.

"Really, Stacie, I don't think you're being fair to Brad. He cares about you very deeply, I'm sure of it."

"Mrs. Barrows, he's the one who wanted to break our engagement."

"You know very well that he didn't do that lightly. So that's no reason to be dismissive when he speaks to you."

"I just wish he wouldn't talk to me at all. It would be so much easier." She handed Mrs. Barrows the first of the plates to be dried.

"Stacie, pardon me for being so abrupt about all this, but I don't think you're telling me everything there is to tell."

"What do you mean?" Stacie focused her eyes on the dusty dishes.

"You've been acting strangely for the last couple of weeks."

"What do you mean?" Stacie repeated.

Mrs. Barrows put down her dish towel and turned to face Stacie. "You don't have to talk to me if you don't want to, Stacie." Her tone softened. "But you know that I want to listen if you need to talk."

They resumed their task and worked in silence for several minutes. Finally, Stacie spoke. "I'm not moving to Thomasville, Mrs. Barrows."

"Now we're getting somewhere. I knew something had changed. What happened?"

Stacie shook her head in frustration. "The building contract didn't work out. So my boss and the board of directors decided to try another location."

"Well, are you going to tell me where?"

"Weston."

"Oh, Stacie—that's so near. Aren't you delighted?"

"I suppose I should be."

"But you're not."

Again Stacie shook her head. "I was sort of looking forward to a chance to start over in a new place without all the baggage I'm dragging around here."

"By 'baggage' I suppose you mean Brad," Mrs. Barrows said.

Stacie nodded. "Megan thinks this should solve all my problems with Brad. Weston is close enough that we could live either here or there and both do our jobs."

"So?" Mrs. Barrows carried a stack of dry dishes to the cupboard and set them in their place. "You don't agree, do you?"

"Megan's idea is too much like a fairy tale; it has such a happy ending."

"Why shouldn't you have a happy ending, Stacie, dear?"

"Well, I guess I'm not saying that I don't deserve a happy ending. But I'm not sure that getting back together with Brad is the right happy ending."

Mrs. Barrows pinched her eyebrows together. "I think I need a bit more explanation. You told me just a few weeks ago that you still love Brad. Have your feelings changed?"

"I'm not sure." Images of Dillon Graves and Weston and an Italian restaurant filled Stacie's mind. She brushed these thoughts away to try to concentrate on her discussion about Brad. "I've been thinking a lot these last few months. And it seems to me that maybe our relationship was not so strong as we thought it was. If we had really been committed to each other, wouldn't we have been able to work something out? Was calling off the wedding the only option we had?"

"Do you believe in the goodness of God?" Mrs. Barrows asked.

"What?" The question seemed to Stacie to come out of nowhere. "Of course I believe in the goodness of God."

"You've had a tough life, Stacie. Your father left when you were eight; you're mother died when you were nineteen. You worked hard against the odds, to get through college. And then Brad failed you."

A tear escaping from one eye, Stacie's hands fluttered uselessly in the dishwater.

"Stacie, dear, you do deserve something good. Maybe working in Weston so you and Brad can be together is something good that God wants to give you."

"But you don't understand, Mrs. Barrows. There's more to it than that."

"If you want to tell me. . . ."

"I met somebody else. At least, I think I have."

Mrs. Barrows waited patiently for Stacie to continue.

"His name is Dillon, Dillon Graves, and he's going to be the director of the new shelter." She sighed deeply. "I'm not sure I understand what's happening between us, because it's been so fast. At first I thought I was imagining things; he's nice to everybody, not just me. But a couple of nights ago we went out to dinner, and we had a great time. It was obvious that his interest is not just professional." Stacie thought of his kiss outside her apartment—definitely not professional interest.

"And you share his 'interest?' " Mrs. Barrows prompted.

More composed, Stacie resumed her washing motion. "I'm not sure. I like him a lot, I feel very comfortable with him, and we have a lot in common. But I was with Brad for so long. I'm not sure how I feel about getting involved again."

Mrs. Barrows voice was soft. "Maybe that's because you are not yet uninvolved with Brad."

Stacie shifted her weight to look at her companion. "But it's been five months, Mrs. Barrows. It's over between us."

"I've heard you say that several times. Yet, you also say you love him."

"I do! That's why I'm so confused. I think I love Brad, but if I really do, why do I feel so attracted to Dillon?"

Mrs. Barrows slung her dish towel over her shoulder and reached out to hug Stacie from behind. "I can't answer all your questions, Stacie. But I can remind you of the goodness of God—and the love of God. And I can tell you again how close I came to marrying the wrong man. Oh, I suppose I would have been happy with Henry, but it would never have been the same as it was with David."

"In any event," Stacie said with forced cheer, "my confused feelings are no excuse for being rude to Brad. It's handy to blame this mess on him, but it's not really his fault."

Mrs. Barrows gave Stacie's shoulder one last squeeze and grabbed a fresh dish towel. "When are you going to tell Brad about Weston?"

"Megan thinks I was crazy not to have called and told Brad everything the moment I found out."

"I think we've established that Megan is a romantic at heart. I want to know what you think."

"I'll have to tell him. I can't keep it a secret from everyone forever. Pretty soon everyone in the group will know and it wouldn't be fair for Brad to find out from the grapevine," Stacie said.

"Have you got a spare minute, Mrs. Barrows?"

Stacie's heart nearly skipped a beat when she realized that she was not alone with Mrs. Barrows any longer. They had been so engrossed in their conversation that they had not even noticed the creak of the screen door when it opened or the slap that it usually made when it shut.

Even before she turned around, Stacie knew she would see Brad standing at the door.

"What do you need, Brad?" Mrs. Barrows said cheerfully.

"We'd like your opinion on a landscaping problem, if you don't mind."

"I'd be glad to come take a look, but I'm sure whatever you all decide would be perfectly fine." Mrs. Barrows wiped her hands dry and casually tossed the towel on the counter. "Where have you been working today?"

"Out behind the old barn. Some of the guys are worried about the slope back there. Does it get pretty muddy when it rains?"

"Yes, we have had a problem in the past. I'm not sure there's much that can be done about it. . . ." Their voices trailed away as they went out the door. This time Stacie did hear the harsh slap when Mrs. Barrows let go of the door; why hadn't Brad fixed that spring yet, she wondered.

The plates were clean and dry, but the bowls and cups were waiting. Stacie looked at the grayish-brown concoction in the sink and decided it was time for some fresh water. Blindly she reached through the dirty liquid and pulled the drain plug. At first she thought it was not going to drain, but finally she detected some reluctant circular motion in the water. When the basin was empty, she started the process all over again.

While she pushed herself through these motions, Stacie's heart was still in her throat. *How long had Brad been standing there? How much had he heard?* He had spoken only to Mrs. Barrows, without acknowledging Stacie's presence at all. Stacie thought that could have been because she had been so short with him during the lemonade break; but it also could have been because he had heard her talking about Dillon. In her anxiety, she was washing dishes rapidly and piling them high in the dish drain. Out of necessity, she stopped washing and started drying with the dish towel Mrs. Barrows had discarded on the counter. Now, she felt even more pressure to decide what to do about telling him the news concerning Weston. She had do something soon; but she simply was not ready to have an emotional encounter with Brad.

The door creaked and slammed, and Mrs. Barrows returned. "I see you got along well enough without me," she said crisply.

"I changed the water," Stacie replied matter-of-factly, without looking at Mrs. Barrows. "The sink didn't seem to be draining very well. Maybe you should have somebody take a look at it."

"I'll be sure to do that." Mrs. Barrows cautiously approached Stacie and stood next to her to resume drying the dishes. After a moment of awkward silence, she spoke. "I don't think he heard anything, Stacie, if that's what's bothering you."

Stacie laughed unexpectedly. "How do you always know what I'm thinking?"

Mrs. Barrows shrugged. "Perhaps because we are so much alike."

"He would never say anything, you know," Stacie said.

"I suppose not. So why not ignore the fact that he was here and continue with the plans you were making to tell him yourself?"

"I just don't want him to think my working in Weston instead of Thomasville will automatically change anything between us."

"Maybe it won't," Mrs. Barrows speculated, drying the last dish. "Then again, maybe it will. You will think about it, won't you?"

Chapter Eight

Stacie looked at the clock again, the fourth time in the last ten minutes. It was eight minutes until the time the meeting was supposed to start, so she decided to make the coffee.

Megan had given her a coffee bean grinder last Christmas, and Stacie had taken up the pleasure of having gourmet coffee for special occasions, attributing this indulgence to the influence of the receptionist at work on Friday mornings. She took out a small bag of French-vanilla coffee beans, carefully measured enough for one pot of coffee, and dribbled them into the top of the grinder. Following the instructions precisely, she pushed the button and counted to thirty before releasing it. Satisfied that the beans were ground finely enough, she pulled a filter from the cupboard and finished getting the pot set up. Glancing at the clock yet another time, she went ahead and turned on the coffeepot.

While she waited for the coffee to brew, she reached up into the cupboard above the refrigerator and took down a small oak tray and some simple, white porcelain mugs. From the basket of napkins which always sat on her kitchen counter, she selected four, each bearing the message, "Welcome Friends," and placed them neatly between the mugs.

Stacie carried the whole tray out to the living room and set it down in the center of the coffee table. Although she had done it earlier, she could not resist the urge to punch up the throw pillows on the couch and straighten the stack of magazines on the end table. It was three minutes until starting time. Where was everyone?

As the coffee dripped steadily into the pot, Stacie wondered how she had gotten herself into this predicament in the first place. Weeks ago at church she had signed a sheet saying she was willing to work on a camp publicity committee, and somehow she found herself hosting a meeting with three other people, one of them being Brad. At least Jenna was not coming, Stacie thought with relief. The other two committee members, Donna and Paul, were creative people with lots of good ideas, in Stacie's opinion, and she expected to enjoy working with them. *But why was Brad involved? Wasn't it enough that he was in charge of the work at the camp?*

Guilt overwhelmed Stacie for the umpteenth time. Despite her intentions and her promises to Mrs. Barrows, she still had not brought herself to apologize to Brad for her curt behavior, and she was certain that that would hang in the air between them tonight. But with Paul and Donna there, they would be forced to focus on the real reason for the meeting, which was not to resolve their personal problems but to plan a publicity strategy to find children who wanted to go to camp.

As she went to make sure the porch light was on, Stacie caught a glimpse of herself in the mirror next to the door. Her pink top made her cheeks look rosy and highlighted her blue eyes. Her full, coppery hair hung loose in a casual style well past her shoulders. She squinted into the mirror and wondered what she would look like if she were ever brave enough to cut her hair. She knew she was attractive, but she also thought her long, girlish hair made her look too young. Maybe she should look at some magazines, she decided, to see if she could find a hairstyle she liked.

The ringing phone jolted her out of this vain consideration; she crossed back to the kitchen, picked it up, and said hello.

"Hi, Stacie, it's me, Donna."

"Hi, Donna. Where are you?"

"I'm sorry to be calling at the last minute, but I'm not going to make it to the meeting tonight."

"Is everything okay?"

"Well, I had car trouble on the way home from work and finally had to have the car towed. I'm still at the garage. I called someone to come and get me, but I don't know when that will be. I hate to miss the first meeting, but. . . ."

"Don't worry about it," Stacie said, forcing herself to be lighthearted. "We'll just assign all the jobs to you. Isn't that what happens when you miss a meeting?"

What Stacie was really thinking about was that now there would be only one person, Paul, to act as a buffer between her and Brad for the rest of the evening. She really could sympathize with Donna's problem, however, and chastised herself for even allowing her thoughts to stray from Donna's very real circumstances to her own selfish concerns. "I'm sure we'll have other meetings," she said. "I'll let you know if we decide anything tonight."

She hung up the phone just as the doorbell rang. For some reason, she had imagined that Paul would arrive first, so, when she opened the door and saw Brad standing on the step, she was taken aback for a moment.

"Am I the first to arrive?" Brad asked.

"Yes, yes, you are." Suddenly Stacie realized she had positioned herself firmly in the doorway. Quickly she stepped aside. "Come on in and sit down." Stacie swallowed hard as she followed Brad into the living room. This was not going to be easy.

"I wonder where everyone is." Brad looked questioningly at Stacie and sat down on the couch.

"Donna just called," she explained. "She can't make it. Car trouble."

"That's too bad." Brad shook his head. "She really needs a new car. I wish there were some way I could help her get a good deal on one."

"Anyway, that leaves you and me and Paul. He should be here any minute."

Stacie felt awkward standing up, but she was not sure where to sit. If she sat on the couch next to Brad, that might make things worse. If she sat in the chair across from him, he would have more opportunity to give her that piercing look which always weakened her, and that would not be any good. Finally she decided not to sit at all.

"How about some coffee?" she offered.

"Great. It smells wonderful. French vanilla?"

Stacie nodded. "It should be just about ready. Excuse me."

As she grabbed the handle of the coffeepot and checked to be sure that no loose grounds had worked their way down into the coffee, she kept her eyes off of Brad. In selecting French vanilla, she had suppressed the knowledge that it was Brad's favorite; now she wished she had chosen anything else, even just normal coffee.

Back in the living room, she picked up a mug and filled it with steaming brown liquid. The light scent escaped the pot and perfumed the air pleasantly. She had to admit it did smell appealing. She set the pot down next to the mugs and compelled herself to sit down in the chair across from Brad.

Brad looked at the wall behind her. "That picture is new, isn't it? The one with the carousel?"

"Yes, it is." Stacie was glad for an impersonal topic of conversation. "I found a whole set of prints in a shop. I loved them all, but I had to be realistic; I could afford only one."

"Well, you chose well, I'm sure. The colors are perfect with the other things you have."

"Thank you." What else could she say? All of her furnishings, most of them acquired during their engagement, had definitely been influenced by his tastes. The colors, the styles, the assortment of things were all choices they had made together in expectation of furnishing a home of their own some day. When they broke up, she offered to give him whatever he wanted from the collection, but he had refused to take anything. This was the first time he had been at her apartment since that painful night.

She stood up. "I fixed some stuff to nibble on. Why don't I get it for you."

"Well, I had a big supper. . . ."

Already on her way to the kitchen, Stacie was not deterred. "I'll just set it out, and maybe we'll feel like having something after we get started."

"I wonder what's keeping Paul."

Yes, Stacie thought. *Where are you, Paul? Please get here soon.*

The tray she carried to the living room had three kinds of crackers and two kinds of cheese meticulously arranged in a circular pattern. She forced herself to smile as she set it down in front of him. "Maybe Paul will be hungry when he gets here."

The phone rang again, and Stacie's stomach instantly soured. Hesitantly, she picked up the receiver. It took only a moment to find out that her intuition was right; Paul was not coming, either. She was going to be alone with Brad.

"Paul?" Brad questioned.

Stacie nodded.

"Not coming?"

"Nope. Too tired. He's working twelve-hour shifts, six days a week."

"Plus helping out at the camp," Brad pointed out. "He hasn't missed a weekend since we started."

Stacie nodded her understanding of Paul's situation, but she did not know what to think about her own.

As if reading her thoughts, Brad stood up, "Well, I guess I could leave and we could try to set this up for another night."

To her own surprise, Stacie disagreed. "I don't think we should put it off any further. We're weeks behind already and we really should have started on publicity at the same time we started the refurbishing project."

Brad shrugged his shoulders. "I think you're probably right about that. I suppose I can stay, if you want to give it a try."

"I'm not sure if our ideas will be as good as the ones Donna and Paul have," Stacie said, "but I'm willing to work at it if you are."

Brad gestured toward the couch. "Let's get started, then."

Stacie picked up the clipboard she had gotten out in anticipation of this meeting and settled into one corner of the couch. With one foot tucked underneath her, she stuck the end of her pen between her teeth while she reflected for a moment. "Maybe we should start by making a list of all the ideas we have, and then go back through them and see which are the best."

"That sounds like a good plan." Brad leaned back comfortably. "Let's see, I think Pastor Banning has some children in mind from the neighborhood that he'd like to see go to the camp."

"Do you know who any of them are?"

"No, but we could get a list of names from him and then check with their parents."

Stacie dutifully made the first entry on her list.

"We could make up a bulletin insert," she suggested, "and distribute it to all the churches in town. A lot of church camps are filled up by now, so there may be some children who will be surprised to find out there's still a chance to go to camp this year."

"Good thinking."

"And I know a few children from the shelter downtown. If we could figure out a way to cover their costs, I'm sure they would love to go."

"I hate to see money be a problem for any child. We'll work on scholarships.

Go ahead and write down their names," Brad said, pointing to her clipboard.

"What about newspaper ads?"

"That would be a good way to let the community know what's going on out at the camp," Brad agreed. "But it could be expensive. Will we be able to afford it with the budget we're working with?"

Stacie twitched her nose. "It would probably blow everything we have, which isn't very much."

"Well, write it down anyway, just in case."

As she wrote, Stacie gradually brightened. "Hey, what about the religion page?"

"What about it?" Brad tilted his head to listen.

"The paper runs a religion page every Saturday. We could ask the religion editor if he would be interested in a human interest story."

"Hey, I think you're on to something here." Brad, sitting at the other end of the couch, twisted to face her.

"It would be completely free publicity. We've done stuff like this for the shelter. The paper could send out a reporter, or we could find someone to write the story, get a few good photos. . . ."

"They would have to agree it's a great story."

"And Mrs. Barrows is certainly an interesting human," Stacie observed.

"Quite so, my dear, quite so," Brad said.

Stacie laughed out loud at his perfect imitation. When she regained control, she said, "It would certainly be more worthwhile than some of the stuff that gets published in that paper."

"Absolutely. The editor will jump at it."

"Okay." Stacie turned back to her list. "Have we got any other ideas?"

"Let me see. . . ." Brad casually reached for a cracker and popped it in his mouth. "We could put posters in the store windows downtown."

"Or hand out flyers at the grocery store," Stacie added, also reaching for a cracker with a dab of cheddar cheese on it. She put her clipboard down on the couch and reached for the coffeepot.

Brad picked up the list and looked it over. "I think we've already got some good ideas here. Do you think Donna and Paul are still willing to help out, even though they couldn't come tonight?"

Stacie was quick to reassure him. "I'm sure they are. Well, realistically, Paul may not have much time to give, but I know Donna really wants to do this."

"She's pretty artsy. Maybe she could work on the things that need to be printed and we could do some of the other legwork."

Stacie craned her neck to check the list again herself. "I could call the newspaper and see if they're interested."

"And check on the children from your shelter."

"Right." She scooted toward the center of the couch and put her hand out for the clipboard. Brad moved it so she could see better, but he did not let go of it.

"So I should talk to Pastor Banning," he said, "and arrange to visit with the families of those children."

"You always do a good job with visiting people."

They sat side by side on the couch now, their shoulders rubbing lightly against each other and their heads nearly touching as they bent over the clipboard together. Absorbed in their planning, Stacie, surprisingly, had easily put aside her discomfort at being alone with Brad. After only a few minutes, several promising ideas had emerged. It crossed Stacie's mind that they would have to check with each other to see if they were really finding any campers, and she had some trepidation about continued contact with him. But, for the first time since their breakup, she felt comfortable in his presence. Maybe it would be possible for them to find a way to be friends.

Brad leaned back again, and his hairy, muscular forearm brushed against her elbow. She liked the way it felt—and then immediately berated herself for responding to such a casual sensation. The inconsistency between thinking about being friends and the urge to respond to an accidental touch was bewildering. Nonchalantly, she moved away from him and refilled her coffee mug.

Brad picked up a few more crackers with his fingertips. Stacie took a swallow of coffee and listened to the crunch of the defenseless wafers against his teeth.

"Well, I guess one of us has to get in touch with Donna and see if she would be interested in doing these flyers," said Brad.

Stacie nodded. "I promised I would let her know what we decided. I'll call her."

Instinctively, Stacie thought that now that their business was done, this lull in their conversation was probably a good time to tell Brad about the change in plans for the new shelter. If she could bring herself to do it now, she would not have to make a special point about it later when the news hit the church grapevine. But first she would have to apologize. She was not sure which option was more difficult.

"Well, I guess there's not much more to be done tonight," Brad said, stretching his arms and stifling a yawn.

"I'll bet you're tired." Stacie weakly stated the obvious. If Brad left now, her chance to do this casually would be gone. But could she keep him here until she mustered up the courage she needed?

"I guess I'll be going, Stace." Brad stood up.

"Brad, please sit down."

He looked at her questioningly, but he complied.

"I need to say a couple of things." All the words which she had rehearsed to herself disappeared. "I'm not sure where to start. Yes, I am. I have to start with apologizing for the way I've been treating you lately."

Brad listened without speaking.

"I mean, you've been trying to be nice to me, and I've been really mean. Like last weekend at the camp. Please forgive me."

His hand moved slowly across the couch cushion between them, and he wrapped his fingers lightly around hers.

"I . . . I understand what you've been feeling, Stace. People are not always themselves when they're in pain."

Her mind told her to extract her hand from his, but she made no move to do so. "I was dreading having you here tonight, but it's worked out all right, don't you think?"

He smiled and nodded. "It's been fine." He paused long enough to catch her gaze directly. "I've missed this place. I've missed you, Stace."

She broke from his gaze and looked down at their joined hands. The enormous lump in her throat made it hard to talk. "I've missed you, too, Brad," she admitted in a fragile voice barely above a whisper.

Brad moved over next to her and wrapped her in his arms.

"Brad, please, there's more I need to say."

"Shhh. Something tells me we'll have plenty of time for talking. Let me just enjoy holding you for a few minutes."

Instinctively, she returned his embrace. Mentally, she did not want to, but her heart gave her no choice. He slipped his hand around the back of her neck, under her hair, and urged her to turn her face to him. When she did, her lips met his.

Stacie had no further thought of resisting and she returned his longing kiss with all the fervor of the kisses during their engagement. The hand behind her neck began to move through her hair, while the other caressed her shoulders. Her own arms were now locked around Brad's waist. It was all very familiar. Her mind ceased to fight with her heart as she moved her hands up his back.

The phone rang.

Until that moment, Stacie had not realized how fast her heart was beating. She drew back from Brad's kiss.

"Let your machine pick it up," he urged, not releasing his hold on her shoulder.

The phone rang a second time. The interruption had brought Stacie to her senses, and she was grateful for the opportunity to disengage and regain her perspective.

"I'd better answer it," she insisted. "It could be Donna," she added, although she did not think it likely.

Brad let go and she got up and answered the phone on the third ring.

"Hello. . . . Oh, hi, Dillon. How are you?"

Stacie was mortified. Why had she let Dillon's name slip out of her mouth? She felt caught. She was going to have to be rude to either Brad or Dillon, and given what had just transpired, she was not ready for them to be aware of each other—not like this. She lowered her voice as much as possible and carried the phone around the corner into the kitchen.

"I just wanted to see how you're doing," Dillon was saying.

"I'm doing fine," she said, "just fine." If she told him anything different, this whole situation would explode in her face. "Actually, I'm in the middle of a meeting with the camp publicity committee." She tried to make her tone sound light and wished that there were some people noises in the background. "Maybe we could talk another time?"

Dillon agreed to call in a few days, and Stacie hung up the phone. Her heart was pounding and she steeled herself to return to the living room and face Brad. If only she had let him go when he said he wanted to. None of this mess would have happened.

"Hi," Brad said simply when she returned to the room.

She forced herself to smile. "Hi."

He did not say anything else, but she sensed he was expecting her to offer some explanation. "That was somebody from work."

He poked out his lower lip and shrugged one shoulder. "I never heard you mention anyone named Dillon before. Somebody new?"

"Yes." She studied his face, trying to figure out just how much she would have to tell him. "Actually, he's the director of the new shelter. I'll be working for him pretty soon."

"Oh." The silence hung thickly between them. "Isn't it a bit strange for your boss to call you at home on a Friday night?"

Stacie racked her brain for a believable explanation which had some semblance of truth. She could not come up with one fast enough.

"You're involved with him, aren't you, Stacie."

Stacie sighed and looked away, not answering. How could she? She was not sure herself whether she was involved with Dillon.

"Stacie, how could you kiss me like that a few minutes ago?" Brad's face was pale and pained. "How could you let me hold you like that without letting me know about him?"

At last Stacie defended herself. "There really isn't anything to let you know about. We've been out a few times, that's all."

"What do you mean, 'out a few times?'"

"Why are you grilling me? Dillon is a friend." She started getting sarcastic. "I suppose you'd say the same thing about Jenna."

"Why are you bringing Jenna into this?"

"I saw the two of you at Katie's Kitchen that night. It looked to me like you were enjoying her company quite well."

"I only went out with Jenna because you didn't want me anymore."

Stacie could hardly hold back the torrent of tears. "I never said that! I never said I didn't want you. You're the one who broke our engagement, or don't you remember that detail? You wanted to call all the shots."

Brad was silent. She could see he had clamped his jaw shut to control his words. Why hadn't she done the same? Never during their entire relationship had they ever shouted at each other like this. How had they moved so quickly from their closeness on the couch to barking at each other across the room?

"Good night." Brad left, and Stacie let the tears flow.

She collapsed on the couch and hugged a throw pillow to her chest where only a few minutes ago she had held Brad. There was no question in her mind now that she still loved him, despite her confused feelings for Dillon. Poor Dillon was getting caught in the middle of something he did not know anything about.

Stacie reached up to click the lamp off and then picked up a box of tissues from the end table. Deep sobs welled up inside her, building up force until she was crying hysterically. Using one tissue after another, she blew her nose and wiped her eyes until she got herself under control, at least outwardly.

Inwardly, she could not have been more out of control. She thought about calling Megan, but she had never told Megan about Dillon. She could call Mrs. Barrows, but then she would have to admit she still had not told Brad about moving to Weston. The plain fact was that she was too exhausted to make explanations to anyone, so she suffered alone. When she was done crying, she pulled the afghan off the back of the couch and huddled in the dark.

The hours passed silently and painfully. Finally she slept, too spent even to fight the disturbing images of her dreams.

Chapter Nine

Stacie was beginning to be annoyed by insistent thumping. Foggy from her fitful sleep, she was not sure where the noise was coming from, but she knew she did not like it.

There it was again, only louder this time and more like pounding. As her irritation rose, an excruciating pain pierced her left temple.

"Stacie! Are you in there?"

Sprawled on the couch, the afghan long ago fallen unnoticed to the floor, Stacie reluctantly opened her eyes at the urgent sound of Megan's voice. What was Megan doing here? What time was it? What day was it?

"Stacie, open this door right now or I'm going to call the police."

More banging. Stacie could hear Megan jiggling the doorknob. She almost believed Megan would call the police. Somehow she had to conquer the dry lump in her throat and make her voice work to let Megan know she was all right, at least physically.

"I'm coming," she croaked.

"Was that you, Stacie? You get over here and open this door."

Stacie pulled herself up on the couch and repeated, "I'm coming," this time a little louder. Leaning heavily on the coffee table, still strewn with last night's cold coffee, stale crackers, and dried cheese, she heaved herself up and lurched toward the door. She aimed at just enough furniture to support herself as she navigated across the room. With the door open, she held her hand to her aching head while Megan charged into the room.

"What took you so long to come to the door?" Megan demanded. "You had me worried sick that something terrible had happened to you." She paused and took stock of Stacie's unkempt and pained appearance. "Are you going to tell me what's going on?"

"Just let me sit down," Stacie groaned. "I've never had a hangover, but if it feels any worse than my head does today. . . ." Her voice trailed off, leaving the thought unfinished. She collapsed into the armchair and leaned her heavy head to one side, seeking support. "I'm always glad to see you, Megan, but what are you doing here?"

Megan's forehead scrunched up in a question. "It's Saturday."

That bit of information was not helpful to Stacie.

"The camp? Remember?" Megan prompted. "I came to pick you up so we could ride out together."

"Oh, yes. Saturday." Stacie's eyes were closed and it was hard for her to breathe. "Can you get me something for this headache?"

"Of course," Megan generously agreed. She shook a finger at Stacie. "But when I get back, I want to know why you have this headache and why you look like such a wreck."

Megan disappeared down the hall into the bathroom. Stacie could hear her rummaging around in the medicine cabinet, looking for some pain reliever, and then running water to fill a cup. In addition to the agonizing headache, Stacie's neck was strangely stiff from sleeping in an awkward position on the couch. Wincing with pain, she turned her head from side to side. Then, with extreme effort, she lunged from the chair back to the couch so she could be prone again.

Her mission accomplished, Megan returned with two white tablets and a small cup of water. Stacie propped herself up on one elbow just long enough to swallow the pills. She handed the empty cup back to Megan. "Thanks. I hope that helps."

"You look like you collided with a train, Stacie." Apparently Megan was not in the mood for an indirect route to the information she wanted. She propped herself on the edge of the coffee table, pushing away last night's tray. "Just exactly what went on here last night?"

Stacie pushed her hair back off her face, not sure what to say to her blunt friend.

"Does this have anything to do with Brad?" Megan probed suspiciously.

"It has everything to do with Brad," Stacie admitted. "We had a terrible fight."

"I thought you weren't even speaking to him. How could you have a fight?"

"We managed somehow."

Megan picked up the cold coffeepot. "I'm going to make some fresh coffee while you pull yourself together," she said in her sternest tone. "I want the whole truth and nothing but the truth."

Stacie nodded. "Coffee would be good."

While Megan clanked around in the kitchen making a fresh pot of coffee, Stacie tried once again to sit up, this time with more success. The horror of the night before was still fresh, but she was reconciled to the reality of a new day. At the very least she had to sit up.

Megan returned with a glass of orange juice in her hand. "I thought this would get you going while we wait for the coffee."

"Thanks." Stacie took a long, welcome sip, and the lump in her throat diminished slightly. "Don't look at me that way, Megan. I will tell you what happened. Just give me a chance."

Megan kept silent, but her impatience was evident. Finally, Stacie started to talk. "Brad was the only one who showed up for the meeting last night. It was awkward, but we got through it. We even had a few good ideas. But then. . . ."

"Then what?"

Stacie looked away. "We started kissing."

"That's good, isn't it?" Megan said hopefully, trying to catch Stacie's eye.

Stacie studied her orange juice. "I'm not sure it was very smart, but I couldn't help it. It was too much like the old days when he was here so much."

"So how did kissing turn into fighting?"

"Is the coffee ready?" Stacie glanced toward the kitchen. She wanted coffee, but more than that she wanted time to figure what to say to Megan about Dillon. She had talked about Dillon in a general way, but never so that Megan would think there was any attraction between them. Now she would have to admit the truth.

Megan handed Stacie a mug of steaming coffee. "Well?"

"Well . . . the phone rang, and it was Dillon."

"So?"

"So, I haven't told you everything about Dillon. It wasn't a business call. We've been out together a couple of times."

"I see." Megan's jaw was firmly set. She reached up and nervously tucked her brownish hair behind one ear. Her gaze did not leave Stacie's face.

"I'm sorry I didn't tell you sooner, but there really wasn't anything to tell. We enjoy each other's company, but I'm not sure if it means anything."

"Apparently Brad thought it meant something, right?" Megan knew Brad almost as well as Stacie did, so it was no surprise that she could predict his response.

Stacie nodded. "Right. He gave me the third degree, and I lashed back about seeing him with Jenna that night. You can fill in the rest."

Megan leaned back on the couch, cradling her mug. "Did you get any sleep at all?"

"Some. But I don't know if I'm up to going out to the camp today."

"I understand. Mrs. Barrows will understand, too."

Stacie shook her head. "No, Mrs. Barrows will have a thousand questions that I'll have to answer eventually, just like you did."

Megan smiled at the comparison. "We're good for you, Stacie. You know that. Otherwise you would just shrivel up and never talk to anyone."

"You're probably right about that." She set her mug down on the table. "Maybe if I take a shower, I'll feel better."

"You don't have to go today, Stacie. Brad will probably be there."

"At the moment, I don't even care. Besides, he was so mad last night, I doubt he would come anywhere near me today." She turned to look at Megan. "Will you wait for me?"

Trying vainly to control her wild hair, Stacie shuffled off to the bathroom and turned on the shower. When ready, she stepped gratefully into the steaming spray. The moist heat was therapeutic for her stiff neck and, in a few moments, she felt much better physically. Her emotional numbness persisted, but at least she was moving around more normally.

By the time she had finished showering and put on fresh clothes, she detected the smell of bacon and eggs coming from the kitchen. Megan was hard at work putting breakfast on the table. She looked up from setting the plates out and greeted Stacie as she entered the room. "Hi."

"What's all this?"

"No point in going out to the camp without eating. We're getting such a late start, we'll probably miss lunch."

"Sorry about that," Stacie said sheepishly. "I didn't know I even had any bacon."

"Well, you did, and it wasn't green or moving, so I used it. So here's breakfast. Eat." Megan scratched Stacie's back affectionately and smiled. "Remember when we were in college and I broke up with Doug?"

Stacie laughed. "Now there was someone who looked like she had collided with a train."

Megan agreed. "Yep. You took such good care of me. I thought there was never going to be any life after Doug, but you pulled me through."

"Aw, you're like a cat. You always land on your feet. Not like me; I roll over and play dead."

"Well, not this time. Not if Mrs. Barrows and I have anything to say about it." She gestured toward the table. "Let's eat while everything is hot."

The eggs were cooked over-easy, just the way Stacie liked them, although she knew Megan would have preferred scrambled eggs. The whole wheat toast already was spread with butter and orange marmalade, and the bacon was fried to a perfect crispness. Megan kept Stacie's juice glass filled throughout the meal.

They abandoned their earlier conversation and instead reminisced lightheartedly about Doug and other college friendships. They lingered over their empty plates for long after the time they should have been in the car and on the road. Normally it would have been easy for Stacie to feel guilt-ridden about her failure to be at the camp first thing in the morning, but Megan had a way of giving her unspoken permission to indulge herself in little pleasures. When she finally did carry her dishes to the sink, she took the opportunity to pour herself another cup of coffee, glad that it was just plain coffee—no gourmet flavored beans, especially no French vanilla, just plain, grocery-store coffee. It would be a long time before she would want any more French vanilla coffee. Maybe she would even give the bag of beans to Marsha at the office.

Megan insisted on washing the dishes, giving Stacie a few cherished minutes, to sit quietly and alone in the living room. Looking around at her familiar things in this comfortable setting, she had an urge to start packing right away. She would not move to Weston for several more weeks, but a flash of insight told her that she should get out of this apartment where she had spent so much time with Brad. Maybe in a new city, in a new apartment, she would get him out of her system once and for all. Maybe she would even give away some of the things they had selected together and really start fresh. Perhaps then she could be sure she would never give in to him the way she had last night, knowing that the bigger question between them had not been resolved.

Despite her resolve to stay awake, Stacie dozed off during most of the forty minutes it took to drive to the camp. The indulgent morning with her best friend had purged her of the emotional tangle of the night before, and she was relaxed, even carelessly limp. Her half-dream state brought her images not of Brad or Dillon but of the caring hands of Megan pouring juice and turning eggs, and of Mrs. Barrows with her comforting trademark pot of tea. Only when the car came to a stop and Megan turned off the engine did Stacie revive and look around. "We're here already? Did you take a shortcut I don't know about?"

Megan flashed a broad false smile. "Don't try to be cute, you lazy bum. Nap time is over; we're here to work."

"Absolutely. I'm ready to roll up my sleeves and dig in."

They got out of the car and proudly surveyed the progress that had been made in recent weeks. The lush green lawn was neatly trimmed; bark chips layered two inches deep kept the weeds under control around the edges of the parking lot. The shed had been scrubbed and painted with a sturdy outdoor finish, and the rustic pine of the dining hall gleamed through its large windows. The narrow circular road leading to the cabins was clear of debris, and freshly-painted markers pointed to the various trails.

Stacie turned to Megan with satisfaction. "This place is really shaping up."

"Sure is. It looks even better now than I remember it as a child."

"I've lost track of what we're supposed to do today," said Stacie.

"Well, I think the insides of the cabins are ready for painting. But since we're so late, maybe we'd better check in with Mrs. Barrows."

Together they started for the cottage, hoping to find Mrs. Barrows there. They were almost to the door when they had to stop abruptly—Brad had appeared from around the back of the house and stood directly in their path.

"Good morning, Brad," Megan said with an even, cheerful tone.

"How ya doin', Megan?"

"Pretty good. What's going on here today?"

"A lot of painting." Brad spoke to Megan but looked at Stacie. "If you're looking for Mrs. Barrows, she's up in the first girls' cabin."

"Great. Maybe we can help up there," Megan answered.

Now Brad spoke to Stacie, oblivious to Megan's presence. "Can we talk for a few minutes, Stace?"

The question was simple and reasonable. Even a few days ago, Stacie would not have wanted to have a private conversation with Brad. Now she thought she really had nothing to lose. Brad had spoken only a few words, but they were enough to let her know that the anger of last night had dissipated for him as it had for her. The emotional calm that she had achieved during her pampered morning was unruffled, and she agreed to his request.

Megan excused herself gracefully and walked up the road toward the cabins, leaving Stacie and Brad standing alone outside the cottage.

"Maybe we could walk for a bit," Brad offered, gesturing toward a trail. "Have you been on the path to the duck pond?"

Stacie shook her head. "No, but I'd like to see it."

They sauntered in silence for quite a while. The spring foliage, fuller and greener than even a few days ago, proliferated along the path. Sunlight filtered through the leaves and left delightful patterns of shadows and light. Chipmunks, tiny and quick, darted between the trees faster than Stacie could turn her head to watch them. The path was level for the most part and quite easy to hike. Stacie had never been this far in; the wet spring had made the trails so muddy that it had not been very appealing to explore them. Today, with a foretaste of summer, the path boasted its best flora and fauna. Even though she was with Brad and could easily have felt awkward, the shared silence let her soak up every detail of the walk.

After about a mile and a half, they came to the duck pond. The swampy patch of land, too wet to walk across, was just barely too large to walk around. According to camp legend, occasionally there were ducks there; Megan said she had seen some one summer years ago. Today there were none, but Stacie did not really mind.

"There's a good sitting log right over there." Brad's observation was the first interruption to the silence of the last thirty minutes.

"Thanks. I'd like to sit and look around," Stacie said. "It's really beautiful here. I was wishing we had brought some bread crumbs along, but since there don't seem to be any ducks, I guess it doesn't really matter. I wonder how complicated it would be to get some ducks and bring them here before camp starts." Stacie realized that she was prattling but could not seem to stop herself. She knew Brad had not brought her up here to talk about ducks, but, sitting next to him on the log, she was suddenly nervous.

"Stacie, I want to apologize for last night."

She had not expected that. She picked up a stick and began scratching in the dirt without saying anything.

"I had no business raking you over the coals about having a boyfriend. It's just that I never expected you to be interested in somebody else so soon."

"Well, I. . . ." Stacie felt she should say something, but she was not sure what.

"Let me finish," Brad persisted gently. "It's just that I'm still insanely jealous, I guess. I love you, Stacie. It's hard to think about you with another guy. Now I know you think I've moved on because you saw me with Jenna. I want to explain about that, too."

"Brad, I'm sorry I threw that in your face. You don't owe me an explanation." She really did not want to hear about his relationship with Jenna, any more than she wanted to discuss her friendship with Dillon.

"But I want to explain," he insisted. "I went out with Jenna because she kept asking me out. As soon as she found out that we had broken up, she swooped in and circled around me. I tried to care about Jenna, but it just didn't work." Brad shifted his weight to turn toward Stacie, who was still scratching in the dirt. "Stacie, honey, Jenna doesn't hold a candle to you. I love you. I know you don't want me to say that, but I have to. I don't want you to think that I could leave someone like you and take up with Jenna McLean."

"I don't know Jenna very well, but she seems very nice."

"Oh, sure, she's nice. But she's not you." He put his hand on her forearm to stop her nervous action.

"Brad, please," she said, pulling her arm away but not looking at him. "Let's be careful. Last night things got out of control, and I don't just mean our tempers."

Brad shook his head. "I don't think so. I think what happened between us meant something to both of us. If I could get you to look at me, I would dare you to deny that."

Stacie said nothing. She couldn't deny it, and Brad knew it. It would be an outright lie to look him in the face and say that feeling his arms around her and returning his kiss had meant nothing to her. Although skittish at first, her response had been genuine and without regret—until the phone rang. *What turning point would they have come to if the phone had not rung? Or if it had been anybody other than Dillon?*

Not answering Brad would leave him with only one conclusion: that she agreed with him. She did nothing to dissuade him. When he leaned over to kiss her, she did not resist. While she did not respond with the abandonment of the night before, clearly she was responding, so he moved closer and wrapped his arms around her.

This time, although craving the moment, Stacie kept her head. She broke off the kiss and pulled away. "Let's take it easy, Brad. We're on rocky ground, and I don't know if we should be doing this."

"I love you, Stacie."

She looked him squarely in the eyes. "I know, but that doesn't mean everything is okay between us. We can't just pick up where we left off as if the last five months never happened."

It was Brad's turn to sigh and look away. "We'll work on it, Stace. Somehow we'll work it out."

Was this the moment to tell him that she only had to move to Weston, not Thomasville? Or would that seem like a quick fix to a bigger problem? She decided she would tell him. Even if she harbored fears about resuming their relationship, Brad was entitled to know. *But how should she start?* She could not just blurt it out.

While she struggled for the words, Brad interpreted her silence in his own way. "Well, I guess we should head back." He stood up. "The guys will be wondering where I am."

The moment was gone. Stacie comforted herself with the thought that at least they were on speaking terms. There would be another opportunity to tell him about Weston, perhaps when she was more sure of where their relationship stood.

Brad offered his hand and she accepted it to pull herself up off the log. But he did not let go of it, and she did not object. Once again they walked the trail in silence. She stopped several times along the way to gather a bouquet of wildflowers; each time Brad offered his hand again, and each time she accepted it.

When they came to the clearing where the cottage and dining hall stood, Mrs. Barrows was there. As soon as Stacie saw her, she gently but quickly dropped Brad's hand and used both of hers to hold the wildflowers.

"There you two are," Margaret Barrows said in a playfully scolding tone. "All this work to be done around here, and the two of you are off picking wildflowers."

Stacie smiled. "I'm sorry I didn't come this morning, but the day is not over. I am fully at your disposal for the rest of the afternoon."

Mrs. Barrows continued her scolding. "It's practically time to start fixing supper. Those flowers had better be for me."

Stacie laughed and held them out. "There is no one else so deserving."

"Since I have no peace offering, I'd better get back to work," Brad said sheepishly, glancing up the road toward the cabins. "I wonder if they need more paint up there." He headed off to the shed to gather his supplies.

"Well," Mrs. Barrows said, "you have quite a selection of flowers here. Let's get them into some water, shall we?" When she looked at Stacie, her eyes were full of questions.

But Stacie was not ready to talk. She was pondering this new plane in her relationship with Brad and trying to decipher what it might mean for the future.

"Enjoy the flowers, Mrs. Barrows," she said cheerfully. "I think I'll go see what Megan's up to."

Chapter Ten

The pages of the worn brown hymnal rustled as Stacie found number 367 and stood with the congregation for the last hymn. When the organ introduction ended, she opened her mouth and sang with gusto.

By the time she arrived at the church this morning, the pew where Megan sat was too full to accommodate another person, so Stacie had taken a seat near the back with the other latecomers. She often sat near the front with Megan, especially since breaking up with Brad, because she disliked sitting alone. But, actually, she preferred sitting toward the back where she could survey the whole congregation: the graying heads of the pillars of the church; the squirming children anxious to escape; her friends from the college and career Bible study. For over five years she had been coming to this church every Sunday and Thursday. Ironically, she was the one who had first brought Brad to this church where he had quickly become a leader.

If she moved to Weston, it would be a long drive to come back here every week, but she hoped to stay in touch with the people. What kind of church would she find in Weston, she wondered. Did Dillon even go to church? They had never talked about it. When she was with Brad, it was easy enough to convince herself that her attraction to Dillon was merely an infatuation; but would she feel that way when she moved to Weston and worked with him every day? She chastised herself for letting her thoughts wander to Dillon.

The organ shifted into somber concluding tones and the congregation sang a muted "Amen." With a twinge of guilt, Stacie realized she had not absorbed a single word of the hymn she had just sung. Actually, her mind had wandered more than usual during the entire service. She had taken notes on the sermon to force herself to pay attention, but even then she had lost the thread of logic somewhere after point two. Now she squeezed her eyes shut and focused on the prayer and benediction intoned by Pastor Banning. And then the organ brightened up and burst into a triumphant exit march.

The 263 people attending church that morning flowed into the aisles and moved slowly en masse out to the narthex. If Stacie had moved a little more quickly, she easily could have been out the door and into the sunshine, ahead of the crowd. But she was in no particular hurry, so she sauntered along listening to snippets of pleasant, Sunday-after-church conversations and returning the greetings of the people around her. Before long, she was happily trapped in the center aisle among the throng waiting to shake the pastor's hand. When she spotted Donna clear across the sanctuary in a side aisle, she remembered the publicity meeting. In all the emotional upheaval of the weekend, Stacie had forgotten about her assigned tasks. Donna was edging her way past people in a hurried way and would be gone long before Stacie could escape the crowd, so she settled for making a mental note to call Donna before the day was over. She had no plans for the afternoon; surely she would find a moment to do it.

"He's not here."

Stacie recognized Megan's voice, even in a whisper behind her, and turned around to greet her friend. "Who's not here?" Stacie asked in a full voice.

"You know very well whom I'm talking about," Megan persisted in whispering. "Where is he?"

Stacie shrugged. "How should I know? I hadn't even noticed he was missing."

"So you're going to play dumb, heh? I'll drag it out of you."

"Drag what out of me?" Stacie said with dry amusement.

"Everything." Megan widened her eyes dramatically. "I want to hear everything. You thought you were off the hook because Julie rode home with us last night, but today we will be all alone."

"What are you talking about?" Stacie laughed, moving a few steps up the aisle. "Did we have plans that I forgot about?"

"We have plans you never knew about," Megan corrected. "It's all been decided, so don't argue with me."

"I wouldn't dream of it," Stacie said with mock fear. "But would it be too much to ask exactly what has been decided?"

"We're going on a picnic, the first of the season," Megan informed her. "I have a cooler packed in the trunk of my car with everything we need." She gripped Stacie's elbow playfully. "So don't try to escape.

"Is this an elegant tablecloth-and-crystal picnic, or will I be allowed to change my clothes?"

"Well, if you promise to hurry," Megan reluctantly conceded.

They reached the end of the aisle. Without really stopping, Stacie absently extended her arm to shake the pastor's hand. He held onto her hand to get her attention.

"I wonder how the publicity meeting went the other night," he said. "Is there anything I can do to help?"

"Thanks for asking," Stacie answered. "Actually, Brad is supposed to get in touch with you for some names."

"I don't see him here this morning," the pastor said scanning the crowd.

Stacie was glad he did not ask her where Brad was; she really did not know. The fact was that she was curious herself, although she was reluctant to admit it. "I'm sure he will follow through, probably in the next couple of days."

Not wanting to hold up the exit line any longer, nor talk further about Brad, Stacie smiled graciously and stepped aside; Megan was not far behind.

"March straight out to the car, young lady," Megan commanded. "Let's not waste a moment of this glorious afternoon sunshine.

The end of May was turning out to be unbelievably like summer. Knowing that midwest weather could change in the space of a few hours, people all over St. Mary's were taking advantage of every gorgeous moment of the day. Swings filled with children squealing delightedly as they soared high above the sand-pits, and the slides were slick from steady use. Softball fields were full of makeshift teams, and kites sailed through the air in scattered open fields. In neighborhood backyards, winter-white legs extended on chaise lounges in eager anticipation of the sun's rays. Three-year-olds determinedly peddled tricycles on the sidewalks, while six-year-olds tenaciously balanced atop two-wheelers.

Megan steered through the residential streets and out to the main highway, then picked up speed. They both rolled their windows down and let the wind whip through their long, loose hair.

"Where are we going?" Stacie howled above the gushing wind. The wind and sun felt wonderful, but it was nearly impossible to converse in the moving car.

"You'll know when we get there!" Megan called back. "I promise you'll like it."

"I hope you brought a lot of food. I'm ravenously hungry."

"All your favorites, I assure you."

Stacie turned her eyes back to the scenery outside her window. The trimmed lawns of the town gave way to split log fences around farm acreage laden with promising summer crops. Scattered tender green sprouts stood in bold relief to the black earth which nurtured them. The sky above them was a shining blue and boasted high, luminous, white clouds. Brown cows with random blotches of white sedately swung their tails at the swarming flies and chewed cud with an unbelievably slow but steady rhythm. Shirtless, a farmer sat high atop his tractor tilling a fallow field.

Spontaneously Megan broke out into an old camp song and, laughing, Stacie enthusiastically joined in. Songs they had not sung in ten years rang through the air. They could barely hear themselves above the roar of the wind, but they kept singing. When they had exhausted their supply of camp songs, Megan started in on her repertoire of kindergarten songs, and Stacie laughed even harder as she did the motions to "The Eentsy, Weentsy Spider" and "I'm a Little Teapot."

Stacie gave herself fully to the release and exhilaration that such silliness brought. Twice in the last two days she had given in to kissing Brad—and enjoyed it, wanted it—and twice she had regretted it. She had known all along that they still loved each other, so really nothing had been resolved. The only change was that she had somehow gotten past wishing Brad would go away and leave her alone. She would not have to be rude to him in order to protect her wounded feelings from further attack. For weeks, even months, she had been in a complete funk because of their broken engagement. But she had come out of that dark tunnel now. She did not know what the future held for them, but she was ready to stop being a wounded wimp and take control of her life once again. And singing silly songs was helping.

She grinned at Megan at the end of the second round of "Twinkle, Twinkle, Little Star," completely relaxed. Undoubtedly, Megan had brought her out here to get her to open up and talk, and she would oblige her soon enough. For the moment, it was enough just to be together with no sense of responsibility or time constraints.

Megan followed the car and made a left turn into a state park.

"I haven't been out here in ages," Stacie said with enthusiasm. "I wonder if the wildflowers are blooming on the hillside yet."

"That's exactly what we're here to find out." Megan passed the arrows pointing to the hiking trails and the picnic area and continued down the road she knew would take them deep inside the park where not many people bothered to go. Finally they parked the car and started walking up the hill on a narrow footpath, Megan's cooler suspended between them. They both knew where to go. They had come to a spot which had been a favorite during college, a place where they came when they wanted to be alone. All along Stacie had suspected this was their destination, and now she was delighted to be right.

Megan was well prepared. She had even brought the proverbial red and white checkered tablecloth, which she spread on the ground at the top of the hill. Stacie sat down, waiting to be further pampered.

Megan reached into the cooler and pulled out a plastic container. "Chicken pasta salad," she announced, and reached in again. "Watermelon. Iced tea, lemon only. And of course, chocolate chip cookies."

"A perfect menu," Stacie said, reaching for the plastic picnic plates. I couldn't have done better myself."

Megan confessed that the chicken pasta salad was a new recipe, so they analyzed it as they ate. The watermelon provided ample seeds for a vigorous spitting contest, and the cookies were gooey and soft, just the way Stacie loved them. Satiated, they stretched out on the tablecloth and lay flat on their backs.

"This was a great idea, Megan," Stacie said with gratitude. "You can kidnap me anytime if we can come here."

"Well, you've been under so much stress the last few weeks, I figured you could use a little diversion."

"Mmmm." Stacie had her eyes closed contentedly. "Megan, tell me the truth. Do I bring all this on myself?"

"Define 'all this,' please."

"You know what I mean. You think I should just tell Brad about Weston and then marry him and live happily ever after. Do you think I make myself miserable because I don't take the easy way out?"

"Don't you want to marry Brad and live happily ever after?"

"I always thought I did." Stacie rolled her head and looked at Megan, who was staring up at the clouds. "But suppose I did marry him. What about the next time something like this happens? Will we be able to resolve it any better than we did this time?"

"You guys had a great relationship, Stace." Megan said emphatically. "I think you gave up too soon. Look what happened. If you had gone ahead with the wedding, you still would have found out you were moving only to Weston and everything would have worked out."

"It seems so simple when you say it." Stacie propped herself up on one elbow. "Why isn't it so clear to me?"

Megan shrugged one shoulder. "Maybe you're too hurt still. Brad let you down in a big way when he made you choose between the job and him. Maybe you don't trust him anymore."

"You're so wise, Megan," Stacie said, twiddling a blade of grass between her thumb and forefinger. "I do feel that way. But I also feel guilty."

"Why?" Megan's wide eyes looked at Stacie.

"Because I hurt Brad by the choice I made. Supposedly I loved him. How could I not choose to be with him?"

"As I recall," Megan said dryly, "God had something to do with your decision."

Stacie nodded. "At the time I really believed that, and I guess I still do." She flopped back down on her back. "So why would God make me choose between the job and Brad?"

"These are deep questions, my friend," Megan answered. "But I'm not so sure God is asking you to choose anymore."

Stacie did not respond. She lay still and felt the warmth of the sun through her eyelids. The soft earth beneath her conformed to her body, and the thick pad of grass cradled her form. She could not have been more comfortable home in her own bed. In the air was the exhilarating fragrance of spring. The wildflowers they had come to see dotted the meadow below them and perfumed the hillside and the very atmosphere around them shouted that winter was over.

More than anything, Stacie wanted to know that her own winter was over. It was possible now to be in Brad's presence and not be consumed with the hurt and guilt which had wracked her spirit during the spring months. Her downward, inward spiral had led to nothing but aggravation and, in that darkness, Dillon had been a luminous beacon. Dillon, knowing nothing of her past, beckoned her into the future. *He would never be Brad, but could she be happy with him?* She thought of Dillon's pleasant face and gentle demeanor and concluded yes, he was a fine man and they could have a promising future if she gave him the right signals. *So why had she been kissing Brad during the last two days?* She kissed him because she loved him, undeniably and passionately. But her questions about the strength of their relationship were deep; she was serious when she asked Megan what would happen the next time a similar problem came up. Blind love does not solve everything; life is not a fairy tale.

She sighed and readjusted her position. Glancing over at Megan, she decided her friend had dozed off. Stacie was physically relaxed, but her mind was racing too fast to sleep. She sat up and rummaged in the cooler for another chocolate chip cookie.

"I know exactly how many cookies are left, so don't think you can pull anything over my eyes."

Stacie laughed at the sound of Megan's voice.

"I thought you were sleeping."

"Maybe I was. But I know the sound of a chocolate chip cookie hunt when I hear it."

Stacie handed a cookie to Megan. "There are only four left. We might as well finish them off."

Megan took a bite and chewed. "When was the last time you looked at the clouds, Stace?"

"What do you mean?"

"Look up there. The clouds are so puffy and white today. When was the last time you saw shapes in the clouds?"

Stacie shook her head. "Not for a long time." She settled back and looked up. "I used to lie in the backyard with my mother and tell stories about the clouds when I was little."

"Tell me what you see today."

"Come on, Megan. I just see clouds."

"Look again. Don't stop with the obvious." She pointed straight up. "See that one? It's a charging unicorn."

Stacie squinted at the bright sky. "I guess if you use your imagination, it could be a unicorn."

"Don't be such a fuddy-duddy. Why do you think God gave you an imagination in the first place?"

"All right. I'll try." She surveyed the sky and selected a cloud. "That one over there is a dollhouse with a pointed roof."

"I can see that," Megan encouraged. "Try another."

For a long time they lay side by side on the checkered tablecloth picking out images in the sky. After a while they launched into adventurous stories about their imaginary pictures. Megan's stories always had a happy ending; Stacie's stories always had a complication.

They lapsed into a contented, companionable silence. The afternoon was waning, but they had an unspoken agreement that they were not ready to go home.

"You know," said Megan lazily, "Mrs. Barrows usually has tea about this time of day."

One corner of Stacie's mouth turned up slightly. "Yes, it is about teatime, isn't it."

"We came pretty far south on the main road. If we just cut over to the east, we could be there in twenty minutes."

"But she won't be expecting us," Stacie protested.

"Can you honestly say you think that would matter to her?"

Twenty minutes later, they pulled up in front of Mrs. Barrows' cottage at the Homestead. With girlish giggles, they got out of the car and knocked on the front door.

Mrs. Barrows opened the door. "Why, Stacie and Megan, what on earth are you girls doing out here on a Sunday."

Stacie and Megan looked at each other and grinned secretly. "We were in the neighborhood, so. . . ." Megan said.

Margaret Barrows waved her hand in the air. "Nonsense. There is no neighborhood around here, and I don't work on Sundays. You came 'specially to see me. Well, I'm delighted. Please do come in. We must have tea." She ushered them into the living room. "I don't know what you two have been up to, Stacie, but perhaps you'd like a napkin to wipe that bit of chocolate out of the corner of your mouth."

Stacie's fingertip flew to her mouth and immediately detected the telltale evidence of her indulgence. Laughing, she explained, "We were having a picnic. Megan kidnapped me."

"And brought you here as a hostage?" Mrs. Barrows questioned.

Stacie shook her head emphatically. "No one would have to hold me hostage to get me to come here. I hope you don't mind the intrusion. Are we interrupting something?"

"Just finished a letter to my sister. You're just in time for tea, but I suspect you had already figured that out." She glanced at them sideways and disappeared into the kitchen.

Megan and Stacie settled comfortably into their places on the couch. On other occasions they had tried to help Mrs. Barrows fix tea and she had always chased them out of the kitchen, so today they did not even try. They were content to sit and soak up the atmosphere of care and love which exuded from the photographs lining her walls.

"Did you girls go to church this morning?" Mrs. Barrows called out from the kitchen.

"Yes, we did," Stacie answered.

"Someday I hope to come into town and visit your church to thank everyone for their hard work." She came back into the room with a tray filled with the teapot, cups, and pastries. "It means so very much to me to be able to open the camp again, although it will never be the same without David." She poured tea and offered cups to Megan and Stacie.

"Everyone has had a great time with the project, Mrs. Barrows," Megan said. "That's thanks enough."

"I would still like to come." Mrs. Barrows gestured toward their cups. "You girls enjoy your tea; then we'll talk about why you really came to see me."

Megan and Stacie looked at each other.

"We just came because we enjoy your company," Stacie offered weakly.

Mrs. Barrows shook her head. "Are you sure you don't want to talk about yesterday?"

Stacie blushed.

"I saw you and Brad coming out of the woods, you know," Mrs. Barrows said. "It looked to me as if it were more than a casual stroll."

Stacie set her teacup down gently and tried to think of what to say. "Nothing has really changed, Mrs. Barrows. I'm just not angry with Brad anymore. After all, you were the one who told me I was being unfair and rude to him. I apologized for that."

"Did you tell him you are moving to Weston?" Mrs. Barrows, as usual, was eager to get right to the point.

Stacie looked away, so Megan answered in a chastening voice. "No, she hasn't told him. She doesn't think it will change anything between them."

"I will tell him," Stacie said in her own defense. "I was going to tell him yesterday, but the time was not right."

"More likely you were too frightened," Mrs. Barrows observed. "You're not prepared for how he might respond to the news, are you?"

"I . . . I'm just not sure of what I want," Stacie fudged.

"The Lord works in some strange ways, my dear. Open your eyes and look around you." She leaned forward and took Stacie's hand. "One thing I know for sure: Brad wants you, but he's just as confused as you are."

"But Brad always knows exactly what he wants. He never gets confused."

"Things are not always what they seem to be, Stacie dear."

Chapter Eleven

Stacie woke the next Saturday to the furor of the rain pelting her window and the entire apartment building shuddering in the wind. The brooding, dark morning sky had made her sleep later than usual, even for a Saturday, until the roar of the storm invaded her unconsciousness and commanded her attention. She got out of bed and went to the window to peer out. The storm was relentless. Pulling her summer robe off its hook in the closet, she wrapped it around herself and padded out to the kitchen to make a pot of coffee.

She was supposed to go out to the camp today to paint. Since it was indoor work, there was no reason to be discouraged by the weather, but she could not help feeling disappointed. The camp was such an invigorating place to spend a day when the weather was nice. Even if the rain let up, after the torrent unleashed last night the pleasant winding walking paths would be reduced once again to slippery trails of mud. Nevertheless, her mood was brightened by the thought that she could see Mrs. Barrows regardless of the weather. The transformation of the run-down structures into solid, safe buildings and the change of the landscape from weed patches to rolling lawns was extremely satisfying, but for Stacie, the highlight of the project had been her growing fondness for Mrs. Barrows. It was hard for her to believe this wise woman and dear friend was a complete stranger only a few weeks ago. She smiled contentedly as she waited for the coffee to brew.

Glad that it was Saturday and she did not have to fight traffic to get to the office on time, she sat with her feet propped up on the coffee table, sipping her steaming coffee and leisurely flipping through some magazines that had been left unread for weeks. She still had about two hours before she had to leave for the camp, so there was plenty of time to indulge in small pleasures. After a second cup of coffee and a piece of toast, Stacie headed for the shower, where she stood for a very long time under the dense, steamy spray.

At last she emerged, put on her robe, and looked at herself in the mirror. Despite the coffee and magazines and long shower, her face was rippled with strain. The last encounter with Brad had certainly not cleared up any of the confusion she was engulfed in. To complicate matters, Brad had not called all week. There was no objective reason to think he would; nevertheless, she had been reluctantly hopeful.

In the week since she had seen Brad, Stacie had lost a lot of sleep wondering if she should have told him about the job change. Should it make a difference at this point, she wondered. Although he continued to profess his love for her, Brad still had not shown any softening of his position. It was so tempting to let herself surrender to his caresses and live happily ever after married to Brad. But would she be happy? If she took the easy way out and went running back to his arms now—she quickly dismissed the thought. Perhaps she would tell him she would be working in Weston instead of Thomasville, but not yet . . . not until she was completely sure of what the experience of the recent months meant about their relationship.

And what about Dillon. Sweet, charming, attentive Dillon. When she was with Dillon, Stacie almost felt that she could leave her past behind her and start all over again in a new job in a new city with a new relationship. She felt no pressure about anything from Dillon; he was simply comfortable to be with. As much as she would miss her friends in St. Mary's when she moved, Dillon could make the change much easier if she would let him.

Stacie towel-dried her hair and began brushing it. The wind which had awakened her earlier persisted, and once again she went to the window and stared out. She thought to herself how truly odd this weather was. It was not a typical late spring thunderstorm; there was something eerie about the way the sky looked.

Back out in the living room, Stacie snapped on the television. The usual Saturday morning cartoons dominated the stations, but she kept flipping channels, hoping to find a weather report. Suddenly, the set started beeping to signal the beginning of an emergency report.

Please be advised that there is a tornado warning currently in effect for all of Grundman County until 10:00 A.M. We have received a confirmed report that a tornado has touched down about twenty miles south of St. Mary's in a rural area of Grundman County. An abandoned church camp is said to have the only structures in the immediate area of touchdown. The extent of the damage is not known. We repeat, there is a tornado warning currently in effect for all of Grundman County until 10:00 A.M.

Stacie was already on the phone, dialing. To her horror, Mrs. Barrows did not answer. The possibilities raced through Stacie's mind: Mrs. Barrows could be outside or in the bathtub, or the phone lines could be down because of the storm. Or she could be hurt. After twelve haunting rings, Stacie instinctively dialed Brad's number.

"Hello." His voice sounded muffled.

"Don't they know that camp is not abandoned!" she said, half hysterically. "Mrs. Barrows is out there!"

"Stacie? Is that you? What are you talking about?"

She realized that Brad was probably sleeping late and maybe had not even noticed the rain.

"Brad, there's been a tornado! The guy on television said it touched down in Grundman County at an abandoned church camp. That has to be the

Homestead—but they think no one lives there."

"Did you try calling?"

"Of course!" She was impatient with his rationality. Did he think she was a thoughtless idiot? "There's no answer."

"I'm on my way. I'll pick you up in ten minutes."

Stacie hung up the phone and ran to the bedroom to dress. She hurriedly pulled on last night's clothes and twisted her wet hair into a haphazard ponytail. With a rubber poncho pulled over her head, she was out on her front step with an umbrella—which was useless against the wind—when Brad pulled up in his van. He leaned on the horn and stretched across the front seat to throw open the passenger door, and Stacie dashed to the street and hurled herself into the van. She was not sure the vehicle had even come to a complete stop; all she could think about was the danger that Mrs. Barrows might be in.

Normally it took at least forty minutes to drive to the camp, but today the roads were slick and visibility extremely poor. Stacie looked at her watch. It was a little after nine; there was still a danger that the tornado could strike again, and she was leading Brad straight into the heart of it.

"Tell me exactly what they said on television," Brad said, and this time Stacie took comfort in his ability to stay in control and think on his feet.

"It wasn't much. I guess St. Mary's is not in danger, but there's a tornado warning for Grundman County. They said there was a touchdown at an abandoned church camp twenty miles south of town, but no one knows what damage was done."

"How long is the warning in effect?"

"Until ten o'clock. About another hour."

"They may not let us through, Stacie."

"What do you mean? They who? We have to be sure she's all right." Stacie was beside herself with fright. Brad reached over and took a firm hold of her hand.

"It'll be all right, Stace. We'll get to her. But if there's been any damage the county sheriff may have the road to the camp blocked off." He squeezed her hand, and she clutched his arm with her other hand. "We'll get through somehow."

Stacie was beginning to get a grip on her emotions. "Maybe there's something on the radio now," she suggested with surprising calm.

"Good idea." Gently, Brad extricated his hand from her grip so he could work the knobs of the radio. Most of the stations had music or talk shows, but at last he found some news. They impatiently sat through a report of the actions of the state legislature and the governor's vacation plans before finally hearing the information they sought.

A second tornado touchdown has been reported in rural Grundman County, this one allegedly tearing the roof off of a farmhouse and damaging a cornfield. This touchdown is unconfirmed. A church youth camp believed to be unoccupied may have sustained an unknown amount of damage earlier this morning. In addition, the sheriff's office is reporting that the main roads into Grundman County from the north are subject to flash floods and there may be a power line down. Please avoid driving south into Grundman County. We repeat, avoid driving south into Grundman County.

"Keep going, Brad," Stacie said determinedly, looking directly south.

"I never said I was going to do anything else." Brad looked at his watch. "It's going to take us at least an hour to get there, even if we don't hit a roadblock."

Torrential rains washed across the road with tidal wave force; the wipers running on high speed could hardly keep the windshield clear enough to see the road ahead of them. Brad had both hands tightly on the steering wheel now and was leaning forward, intently focused on staying safely on the pavement. Stacie looked at her watch at least every two minutes as they crept along. They were out of town now and headed into Grundman County. Just as the radio report had said, water swept across the road in many places, and she could not help being frightened by the number of small cars already abandoned along the side of the highway. Brad's van was heavy and high, and so far she felt safe—both in the van and with Brad.

Brad was concentrating much too hard to attempt conversation, but every few minutes, he would say, "It's going to be all right, Stace," and each time she believed him a little more. She prayed silently for Mrs. Barrows and for their own safety as they tried to reach her. Turning her head, she looked at Brad, whose gaze did not leave the road in front of him. In spite of all her confusion about their relationship, she had not hesitated to call him when she needed help. She did not know what the future held for them, but she knew that she loved him and that he loved her. Stacie never had a moment's doubt that he would respond instantly and unquestioningly to her plea simply because she asked.

They came to the narrow, twisting road which would lead them to the camp. There was still another five miles to go, but they were encouraged to have made it this far. Abruptly, Brad slammed on the brakes, and Stacie felt the rear end of the van swing sharply to the right on the slick pavement. A county sheriff's vehicle sat squarely across the road, blocking any further progress. Brad rolled down his window as the officer approached the van, and Stacie sat forward to hear the conversation.

"You'll have to go back, sir," the officer said. "The creek has risen and the road is flooded just ahead. For your own safety, I have to ask you to turn around."

"What about the camp, officer?" Brad asked calmly. "Do you know how bad the damage is?"

"Not yet. Our emergency crew will get there as soon as possible to assess the damage."

"Sir, are you aware that the camp is not unoccupied? A friend of ours—an elderly woman—is living on the grounds while the camp is being refurbished."

The officer clearly was startled. "Our information was that no one was living there. I'll radio the station immediately and tell them what you said so they can send help. But you'll still have to turn back."

"Of course. Thank you, officer."

Brad obediently rolled up his window and began to negotiate a turn in the cramped roadway.

"Bradley! What are you doing?" Stacie demanded. "We can't leave until we know Mrs. Barrows is all right."

"You heard the man. We have to turn back."

"I can't believe my ears. I would never have thought you would give up so quickly—not when we're this close." Stacie slumped in her seat with disgust and frustration.

"Who said anything about giving up?" Brad said, the van now squared away and headed back toward the main road.

Stacie was confused now. Brad looked at her and winked. Then she started to smile.

"You sly old dog—you know another way, don't you?"

"You guessed it. There's a supply road I used just last week with a truckload of lumber. It's pretty rough, but it'll get us into the camp." He pressed his foot to the accelerator and the van picked up speed.

In only a few minutes he found the turnoff for the supply road. The van bounced from side to side as it hit one pothole after another, but they were making progress. The narrow dirt road was pure mud in places, and even Stacie could feel the tires slipping. Brad doggedly continued; Stacie's knuckles turned white from clenching the dashboard. Even with a seatbelt on, she felt like she could be thrown from her seat with the next lurch.

Without warning, they stopped. "What happened?" Stacie asked urgently, although she already knew the answer.

"There's a tire spinning. We're stuck in the mud, Stacie."

"We're so close! Why is this happening?"

"I can't answer that, but we can't just sit here." Brad looked out the window at the unrelenting downpour. "I'll get out and see what I can do. You sit over here, and when I give you the signal, accelerate."

Stacie thought of Mrs. Barrows and needed no further urging to spring into action. Brad opened the door on his side and hopped down to the mud. She slid over to his seat and twisted around to see what he was doing. She felt the van bouncing as Brad put his weight on the rear bumper and jumped. At his signal, she put her foot on the gas and pushed down gently. The tire continued to spin and Brad was sprayed with mud. The van did not move.

Taking her foot off the pedal, Stacie turned around for Brad's next signal. He spread his feet, gripped the bumper squarely with his hands, then tilted his head at Stacie. Once again she accelerated. This time, the van inched forward until finally she no longer felt the stubborn drag of the mud. Brad charged along the side of the van and jumped in, smearing mud all over Stacie before she could get out of the way. It was with overwhelming relief that Stacie surrendered the steering wheel to Brad.

In another twenty minutes they were at the rear entrance of the camp. Stacie looked at her watch—it was 10:45 A.M.—nearly two hours since the tornado had struck the camp. The rain was letting up at last, but there was no telling what they would find.

"We'll start with the house," Brad said, barreling through the camp road and pulling to a sharp stop in front of the small cottage where Mrs. Barrows lived. Simultaneously they jumped out of the van and ran for the house, calling out her name as loudly as they could.

Stacie tried the front door. "It's open!" she called and pushed her way in. There were only five rooms and it did not take her long to determine that Mrs. Barrows was not in the house. This meant she was out on the grounds somewhere. Stacie ran out the front door, calling for Brad. "She's not here, Brad. She's hurt, I just know it."

"We'll find her, Stacie. She might be fine, just out looking at the damage for herself." Stacie knew he was right—it was completely possible that this is exactly what had happened. But somehow she didn't think so.

"Let's get back in the van," she said, suddenly feeling in control. "Take the outer circle first, past those old cabins we were supposed to paint today."

Brad nodded and complied immediately. The camp road was not built for vehicular traffic, so they had to go slowly. They both looked around carefully for any sign that Mrs. Barrows had been this way recently. They circled around the barn—fortunately there were no animals at the camp yet—and on past the prayer chapel and the open playing field. Constantly they called out her name. The storm had dissipated to a drizzle, making it easier to see and hear, but there was no response to their persistent shouts. Hoping that Brad had been right—that Mrs. Barrows was simply out looking over the grounds now that the storm had passed—Stacie anxiously looked for her friend to peek her head out from around the corner of some building and signal to them that she was safe. But it did not happen, and the further around the circle they went, the stronger was her sense of foreboding danger.

"Stacie, I don't see much damage," Brad said at long last. "There's some fencing missing, but the buildings all seem to be standing."

"So far," Stacie said stubbornly. She had to see for herself that Mrs. Barrows was all right before she would relent.

"Oh no!" Fear was evident in Brad's voice now.

"What?" Stacie cried out in alarm.

"One of the cabins—it's just gone!"

She could see he was right. They were approaching a cluster of four cabins—but only three were standing, surrounded by randomly scattered debris of lumber and bits of furniture.

"We were going to work up here today, Brad," Stacie said, almost choking on her words. "She might have been up here this morning getting things ready."

Brad halted the van and they got out once more.

"Mrs. Barrows! Margaret! Are you here?" they called out.

The silence which answered them was ominous.

Stacie reached for Brad's hand as they began to pick their way through the rubble between the cabins. They looked closely at everything they kicked out of the way. Gradually, they began to bend over and throw aside larger pieces of wood and clear the debris until they could see the ground beneath the piles.

Suddenly, Stacie screamed. Brad was instantly at her side and saw what she pointed to.

Margaret's legs were visible from the knees down beneath a pile of mangled residue of the cabin—but they could see no more of their friend than this. Frantically, they began pulling off the broken chairs and twisted metal bed frames and furiously cast these aside until they could determine what was preventing Mrs. Barrows from standing up.

A beam covered most of her frail body, a large, heavy, long ceiling beam which seemed to be the only piece of the cabin left intact.

Stacie covered her open mouth with one hand and clutched her stomach with the other as Brad began to heave away the last loose pieces. After a split second, she recovered her senses and knelt at Margaret's head and looked carefully at the colorless face.

"She's breathing, Brad, but she's unconscious!"

"Don't try to move her," Brad cautioned. He looked up at Stacie and then at the beam. "I don't think we can move this, Stace," he said mournfully.

"We have to try."

"Of course we'll try. But I really think we're going to need help."

Together they tried to find a point of leverage and lift the beam off of Mrs. Barrows. Brad's muscles rippled with perspiration as he pushed and pulled to the extent of his strength. With growing dread Stacie realized they could not budge the beam even an inch; it was futile to think they might, and they were wasting precious time trying.

"You're right, Brad, we need help. At least we know she's alive. I could kick myself now, but I didn't think to check to see if the phone was working when I went through the house."

"We've got to get through to the sheriff's office and tell them to get medical help out here immediately. I'll take the van and go back to the house. If I'm not back in a few minutes, it means the phone is dead and I had to go find that officer at the roadblock."

Stacie nodded at the sensibility of his plan. Tears were streaming down her cheeks. She was terrified, but she had with her the one person she most wanted to be near in a crisis. Even when he left her alone with the unconscious Mrs. Barrows, she knew she would draw strength from him.

Brad came to where she sat on the wet ground near Margaret's head and squatted down next to her. "Will you be all right?"

"I have to be," she responded, almost on the verge of sobbing. "Hurry, Brad. Go, and hurry back."

Chapter Twelve

Stacie dared not touch Mrs. Barrows. Every muscle in her body screamed to reach out and wrap itself around the woman lying unconscious in the rubble. But she held back, anxiously waiting for Brad to come back with medical help who would know whether Mrs. Barrows could be moved safely. Although Margaret was already drenched, Stacie pulled off her rain poncho and gently spread it over the still form. Desperately she wished she had some warm blankets to wrap around Mrs. Barrows. She knew there were some in the cottage, but she was afraid to leave her helpless friend alone long enough to run for them. Stacie whimpered as she watched vigilantly for any sign of consciousness. There was none.

Stacie rummaged through her pockets and came up with a tissue. Delicately, she wiped the grime from Mrs. Barrows's face. For the first time, she noticed that the older woman's glasses were missing. Stacie instinctively glanced around to see if they were in sight, but it was hopeless to try to find them. Undoubtedly they were broken anyway. Without them, Mrs. Barrows did not look herself. Instead of her bright blue eyes, Stacie saw only sagging, still eyelids. Her colorless skin made Stacie gasp in a moment of fright. She bent her head close to Mrs. Barrows's mouth to listen. The shallow sound she heard brought instant relief; Mrs. Barrows was not breathing deeply, but she was breathing. Without disturbing her position, Stacie reached for a wrist and felt for a heartbeat. Once again she was relieved.

She looked at her watch. How long had Brad been gone? Only five minutes—it seemed so much longer. Cold and wet, she crouched and tried to keep warm. Was it only six days ago that she and Megan had indulged in their spontaneous picnic and descended on Margaret for tea? She had been her usual vivacious self, fussing over the teapot, insisting that they eat pastries, and offering advice they did not even know they wanted. Despite her age, Stacie had never once thought of Mrs. Barrows as fragile or delicate. But now there was no strength left in her. In fact, she looked as if she might slip away at any moment. The stark contrast between that delightful day last weekend and the dreadful sight before her was too much for Stacie and her whimpers swelled to sobs.

The sound of groaning startled her. She looked down to see Mrs. Barrows trying to turn her head.

"What . . . happened. . . ." the older woman sighed.

"Shhh," Stacie soothed her, stroking her forehead. "Brad went for help."

"Stacie . . . is that you?" Mrs. Barrows still had not opened her eyes, and her voice was barely audible.

"Yes, it's me." Stacie was encouraged that her voice had been recognized. "Just lie still until Brad gets back." The control in her voice did not betray the magnitude of her relief that Mrs. Barrows had risen to consciousness and was able to speak coherently.

"I came out . . . to the cabins . . . paint . . . storm . . . happened so fast."

"Please, Margaret, don't try to talk. Please just be still until we get some help." Stacie wiped her face off again. "I'm sorry I don't have anything to keep you warmer."

"How . . . did you get . . . here? The road. . . ."

"Yes, the road was flooded, but Brad knew another way in. We had to see if you were all right."

"I . . . I. . . ." Mrs. Barrows was drifting away.

"Margaret! Mrs. Barrows! Don't go to sleep. I think you should try to stay awake."

"Can't. . . ." To Stacie's dismay, Mrs. Barrows lapsed into unconsciousness again.

Brad had been gone more than ten minutes now. That meant the phone in the cottage was not working and he had gone out to the road. Maybe he could not even get through; they had barely been able to drive in on the back road.

"Dear Lord, please let him get through," Stacie prayed aloud. Wiping streaks of tears from her face, she continued to pray steadily, never taking her eyes off of Mrs. Barrows.

It was another ten minutes before Stacie heard the roar of the van's engine coming down the camp road. Brad screeched to a halt and leaped out. As he ran toward Stacie, he called out, "How is she? Is she still alive?"

Stacie choked on a sob and nodded vigorously. "Yes. She was conscious for a few minutes. I tried to keep her awake, but. . . ."

She stood up and threw her arms around Brad's neck, clutching tightly. He stroked the back of her head to soothe her.

"Did you find anyone to help us?" she asked.

"Yes. But I had to go all the way out to that trooper who wanted us to turn around." He held her close. "He used the radio to call for help. The paramedics are on the way."

"The road—"

"It's muddy, but it's clear," he assured her. "Stacie, you're shivering. Sit down over here and try to keep warm."

She did not want to let go of him, but she obeyed his instructions, shaking both from chill and fright.

"I've got a couple of old blankets in the van. Will you be all right while I get them?"

She nodded tearfully, and he ran back to where he had left the van. She watched him go, admiring his strength in contrast to her own collapse at the sight of Mrs. Barrows under the beam. It was so typical of Brad to be unruffled no matter how severe the problem.

Throughout the two years they dated and the months of their engagement, Brad had always been a rock. In some ways Stacie knew she had depended on him too much. He was quick to make decisions, while she could spend weeks weighing the pros and cons of every little choice. She had to admit that his decisions were usually good ones. Maybe it had been a good decision to break their engagement instead of facing the dilemma of a marriage spread out over 200 miles.

Stacie thought of herself as intelligent and competent. Obviously Jack Rogers and Dillon Graves saw her that way as well. Her work was compassionate and insightful, and she had a way of helping people feel at ease. She was a great organizer and threw herself wholeheartedly into everything she did. But when it came to Brad, her mind turned to mush; she could not think clearly or define her feelings for him.

Brad returned with two tattered blankets; Stacie jumped up to spread one over Mrs. Barrows. She tucked it in around her bony form as snugly as she could without causing movement. As Stacie stooped and lightly stroked the hair of her newest friend, Brad crouched beside her and wrapped a torn army blanket around her shoulders. Instantly she felt warmer, though she knew the dampness of her clothing would soon seep through the green wool. She let her weight rest against his chest and welcomed his arms around her. Together they silently watched Mrs. Barrows for any sign of change, for good or for worse.

The screeching siren announced the arrival of the ambulance. They both jumped to their feet and hurried up to greet it, waving their hands wildly to show their location as it came around the circle. The siren went silent and two paramedics jumped out of the front seat.

"We almost didn't find this place," the driver said. "That supply road is not on my map. Whoever gave directions did a great job."

Stacie looked at Brad and could not help feeling proud. Without his clear thinking, it could have taken much longer for help to arrive.

The paramedics, garbed in blue uniforms and yellow slickers, were already at work on Mrs. Barrows.

"Vital signs are good, all things considered," remarked one as he set up the radio to communicate with the hospital. "She seems to still have circulation to the legs. That's good. We'll get an I.V. started and then we'll see about getting this beam moved."

"The fire department is right behind us," said the driver. "They'll wrap a chain around this thing and lift it off in no time."

As if fulfilling his prediction, another siren screamed into the camp as a red fire truck lumbered through the narrow road. Three more men in yellow slickers jumped down and went into action. A small crane on the back of the truck wheeled around and the men churned chain off an enormous spool. Brad moved quickly to help fasten it around the beam, while Stacie held her position next to Mrs. Barrows's head. Faster than Stacie could have imagined, the beam rose in the air, swung around, and crashed into the pile that had been the cabin. Stacie was horrified at the sight of Mrs. Barrows's crushed legs. Obviously, they were both broken; she had known all along that they must be, but it was terrifying to see that it was true. Mrs. Barrows was probably unconscious because of the pain.

The paramedic, expertly slid a stretcher under Mrs. Barrows, still unconscious, and hoisted her into the ambulance. The driver turned to Stacie as he raced around to the front seat. "Are you coming along to the hospital?" he asked.

"Yes!" she cried, and immediately lurched toward the back of the vehicle, still clutching the army blanket around her shoulders. She looked at Brad over one shoulder.

"Go ahead," he said, helping her into the ambulance. "I'll bring the van in and meet you at the hospital."

She nodded as the second paramedic jumped in and swung the doors shut, harshly leaving Brad on the outside.

The siren shrieked again as the ambulance plowed through the mud and began its journey to the hospital in St. Mary's.

Stacie stopped for a moment to lean against the wall in the emergency room. It was the middle of the afternoon, and she was sore and tired and emotionally worn out, not to mention sopping wet. Her clothes, muddy from her vigil at the side of Mrs. Barrows, stuck to her body, and she longed to peel them off and step into a hot shower. She had been at the hospital for more than two hours. As soon as the doctor took a look at Mrs. Barrows, he had shooed Stacie out of the examining room and left her to wait for what seemed an eternity before finally reporting on Margaret's condition.

Stacie still had not connected with Brad. Surely he had followed the ambulance to the hospital, just as he said he would. Probably he had not been allowed beyond the waiting room of the emergency room. Since she was not immediate family, even Stacie had been only grudgingly tolerated outside the examining room. She rubbed her eyes with the dirty heels of her hands and decided to find Brad. If he were waiting someplace where they could not tell him what was happening, he would be worried sick.

After pausing to get a drink of cold water from the fountain, Stacie pushed open the doors that led to the reception area for the emergency room. To her amazement there were four people there from the church, among them, Megan.

Megan spotted Stacie and quickly crossed the room; the others were not far behind. "What's going on?" she asked. "How is she?" She put her arm around Stacie's damp shoulders.

"She's in bad shape, but they think she'll be all right. Both of her legs are broken, and some ribs are cracked." She looked wearily around the group. "The main thing is that she is still unconscious. Except for a few minutes after we first found her, she hasn't regained consciousness at all. They're not sure why." The ponytail she had pulled her hair into so many hours ago had given way. Now, she pressed a damp strand of hair back from her face, but it refused her effort and drooped down over one eye. "There's nothing we can do. I'm sure they'll let us know if there's any change."

Stacie still carried her rain poncho and Brad's two blankets. She looked around. "Where's Brad? Isn't he here?"

Megan took the damp pile out of Stacie's arms. "He's around here somewhere." She tried to fold the blankets a little more neatly and then stacked them on the floor. "You need some dry clothes, Stacie. Why don't you let me take you home to change."

Stacie shook her head defiantly. "No. I'm staying."

Megan backed off. "Okay, then how about if you give me your key and let me go to your place for some dry clothes. I can be back in half an hour."

This time Stacie nodded and dug in her jeans pockets for her apartment key. Gratefully, she handed it to Megan.

"I'll get a towel, too," Megan said sensibly. "You can clean up in the ladies' room."

Megan left and Stacie sank into the nearest chair, exhausted. Others from the group tried to talk to her, but she did not feel much like having a conversation and left many of their questions unanswered. She dared not lean her head back against the wall for fear of falling asleep, which she did not want to do until she knew Margaret was all right. Where was Brad, she wondered again.

Then she saw him. He came in from the hall with a cup of coffee in his hand—and Jenna McLean at his side. Stacie turned her head and looked away. She remembered Brad's explanation of Jenna's attentiveness, and she believed him completely, but she was not much in the mood to encounter it firsthand.

Brad came directly across the room and stood in front of Stacie. Setting his coffee cup down, he reached for her hands and pulled her to her feet. He was as muddy and damp as she was, but neither of them cared. She fell into his embrace and buried her head against his chest, oblivious to the surprised audience around them. They stood like that for several minutes, not wanting to let go of one another. Finally, Brad steered her toward a sagging couch where they could sit together and continue to comfort each other.

Out of the corner of one eye, Stacie could see Jenna McLean sitting by herself, swinging one foot in a nervous rhythm. But she knew the truth about Jenna now and did not feel threatened by her. It was up to Brad to make Jenna understand where things stood between them, and Stacie instinctively knew not to get involved.

No matter what the future held for the relationship between Brad and Stacie, she was glad he was there in that room at that moment. If he had not been home this morning when she phoned, she would have panicked. He had been a tower of strength all day, and she did not want to suffer through this ordeal without him.

But she could not think beyond the moment. She blocked out the larger questions which plagued her recently; this was not the time or place to try to sort them out.

Megan returned with a plastic bag containing a complete change of clothing. Insistently, she pried Stacie away from Brad and escorted her down the hall.

"Come over here, Stacie," Megan instructed, turning on the water and splashing her hand under the hot water. "This won't be the same as a real bath, but you'll feel better."

"The only thing that will make me feel better is hearing that Margaret is okay," replied Stacie.

Satisfied with the water temperature, Megan pulled up the stopper and let the sink fill up. "If it weren't for you, she might not even be alive, Stace."

"Why is she still unconscious?" Stacie stepped up to the sink and splashed hot water on her face and arms while Megan took the dry clothes out of the plastic bag.

"At least her vital signs are good, right?"

"I should have tried harder to keep her awake."

"You did everything you could, Stacie. Stop beating yourself up." Megan handed Stacie a towel and the clothes and told her to change in one of the stalls.

Cleaner and dryer, Stacie did feel a little better. Brad sat where she had left him, still damp but not seeming to care about his own condition. She sat down beside him and willingly took hold of his hand. Megan bundled up all the wet clothes and blankets and said she would take them out to her car.

"She's like a mother hen, the way she looks after me," Stacie commented.

Brad smiled slightly. "It comes from hanging around five-year-olds all the time like she does. She can't stop taking care of people."

Momentarily relaxed, Stacie leaned her head on Brad's shoulder.

Jenna nonchalantly wandered across the room and sat across from them. Stacie smiled pleasantly but decided not to say anything.

After a few minutes, Jenna spoke. "Brad, maybe you'd like to go get something from the cafeteria. I'll bet you haven't eaten all day."

Brad's response was even and firm. "No thanks, Jenna. I'm fine for now." His fingers tightened their hold on Stacie's.

Stacie sensed the disappointment Jenna was feeling but returned Brad's warm grasp. She felt a twinge of guilt, since she knew that she was relying on Brad's stamina for the moment without being sure what their relationship would be like tomorrow or next week. But she needed Brad right now. Besides, Brad had already told her that he was not interested in Jenna McLean.

More than once during the afternoon, Stacie found herself checking her watch against the clock on the waiting room wall, thinking surely that time was standing still. The minute hand circled slowly around its route, dragging the hour hand with it. Megan made several trips to the cafeteria for coffee and kept everyone well supplied. Despite Brad's rebuffing, Jenna stayed with the group, and Stacie believed she was sincerely concerned about Mrs. Barrows. What she could not believe was how slowly time was passing. Every magazine in the room had been passed around to each of them at least once. Every crack in the paint, every flaw in the furniture became all too familiar to Stacie. Other people waiting for other patients came and went, and the vigil for Margaret Barrows continued.

Every time the automatic emergency room doors swished open, Stacie's heart skipped a beat. When Dr. Pressman finally appeared, she was instantly on her feet.

"How is she, Doctor?" she asked, hardly giving him a chance to speak. "Is she conscious? Can I see her?"

"Slow down, Stacie," the doctor said, holding his hand up in the air. "She's better and yes, she is conscious. I'm sure now that she is out of the woods. At her age, we'll have to keep a close watch on how the broken bones heal, but she seems to be in good health generally, so we have every reason to believe she will heal completely."

The group gave up a mass sigh of relief, and Dr. Pressman continued his report.

"She's resting comfortably, and she asked about you, Stacie, but I must insist that she be allowed complete rest tonight." He looked around at the group. "Obviously you all care about her a great deal, but the best thing you can do now is go home and get some rest yourselves, especially you, Stacie. Come back tomorrow—just one or two at a time, please."

With that, Dr. Pressman turned around and disappeared into the emergency room once again. The group looked at each other and slowly started for the door. Stacie looked from Brad to Megan, grateful that they were both there.

Brad put his arm around her shoulders. "Come on, Stace. I'll take you home."

Stacie did not resist the suggestion. Megan walked out with them, and when they reached her car, Stacie gave her a quick hug, gathered her wet clothes, and whispered thanks before continuing on to Brad's van.

The once, shiny van was splattered with mud, both inside and out. It was starting to drizzle again, but not hard enough to wash off the dirt, only enough to smear it around. Stacie could hardly see out her side of the windshield, so she was not surprised when Brad took the time to clean it off properly. She leaned her head back against the seat and watched absently as he worked. Before today she had never even been in Brad's new van. For months, she had listened to his plans to buy one and looked at brochures and reports with him. But he did not buy it until after they split up, so this was the first time to share his fulfilled dream. She was sorry it was under such oppressive circumstances. She scanned the dashboard and saw that it had all the features he wanted, with plenty of room in the back for transporting tools and supplies for his work. He had made a good choice, she decided.

Brad climbed into the driver's seat and smiled at her while he turned the ignition key. They did not speak much during the ride home, but even the silence between them was comforting. The scenery around them however, was alarming. Apparently no buildings in town had been affected by the tornado itself, but the fierce winds had ripped trees from their roots and strewn them around the neighborhoods. Large branches of older trees hung precariously, ready to fall with the next storm. At this point in the day, Stacie was too numb to absorb the impact the storm had had on the town itself.

Parked in front of her apartment, Brad came around and opened Stacie's door. As he walked her to the door, he said, "I'm glad you called me this morning, Stace. The way things have been between us, I didn't know what to expect."

Stacie shrugged. "What we've been going through is inconsequential compared to what happened today. Mrs. Barrows is all that matters."

Brad nodded. "I won't argue with you there." He paused, and she thought he was going to kiss her, but he didn't. He just squeezed her hand and said, "Good night, Stacie. I'll call you."

"Good night, Brad," she murmured, surprised. She had imagined he would come into the apartment with her, but he had already turned to walk back to the van.

She let herself into her apartment and immediately went into the bathroom to start a proper bath. She rummaged under the sink and came up with a couple of ounces of bubble bath and poured it under the running water. She watched, mesmerized, as the foam multiplied and swelled to an inviting crest. When she shut off the water, she also shut off the light and lowered herself into the tub in the dark. She could not remember the last time her entire body felt so sore. Perhaps it was when her mother died. Stacie, who was nineteen at the time, had been frightened then, too, but she had not had anyone like Brad to lean on. She had been on her own with her grief then, and she never wanted to do that again. She never wanted to be that alone again.

Obviously she loved Brad. But what she and Megan had talked about last weekend was haunting her. *Could she trust Brad? Could she love him unreservedly, or would she always be afraid that she would come second to his other goals?* Stacie consciously set these thoughts aside for another time. In contrast to the taxing day, she was starting to relax in the hot bath and gave herself over to enjoying it completely.

Chapter Thirteen

Stacie's arms were so full she almost could not get the door open. Unsuccessful at using her elbows to open the door of the hospital gift shop, she turned around and backed into it, giving it a shove with one hip. The glass door finally opened and Stacie entered the main lobby, her arms laden with books and a potted Swedish ivy plant.

In the lobby, she stood still for a moment to get her bearings; for some reason, it was easy for her to get turned around in this hospital. She always had to concentrate on following the blue floor stripe down the gray-tiled hall to the elevator. Cautiously, she balanced her load in one arm so she could free up a finger to push the button of the elevator. While she waited for the muted ding to announce the arrival of the elevator, Stacie relaxed. The appealing color scheme of the hospital—gray, blue, and mauve—was very restful.

Every day for the last ten days, Stacie had stopped by the hospital on her way home from work. Despite assurances from the doctor, she wanted to see for herself that Margaret Barrows was getting better. An eighty-three-year-old woman with two broken legs was not something to take lightly. Nearly every night, images of Margaret lying cold and still in the rain haunted Stacie's sleep. So every afternoon she went to the hospital to see that Margaret was really warm and lively, just the way she had always been, even though she was confined to a bed.

Stacie rode up to the fourth floor and found room 477. Before entering, she paused to listen for voices. She heard only the quiet background sound of the bedside radio so she knocked briskly and went in.

"Hello, Mrs. Barrows. How's my favorite patient today?"

"Quite chipper, thank you." Margaret inspected Stacie's full arms. "What in the world have you got there?"

Stacie lifted the plant a little higher. "I went in for a magazine and came out with three books and a plant." She shrugged her shoulders. "I'm an easy target when it comes to greenery. I thought you might enjoy having it here in your room."

"That's very thoughtful, dear, and the plant is lovely. I'm not quite sure where you are going to put it, though."

Stacie was already scanning the room. In typical hospital fashion, the furnishings were sparse, but the heating vent running across one end of the room doubled as a countertop. The limited space was already cluttered with nearly three dozen cards from well-wishers and a bouquet of cut flowers that were starting to wilt. Stacie cleared a space for the plant by moving the vase to one side and rearranging several of the cards.

"Everyone has been so kind," Mrs. Barrows said. "Especially you, Stacie. You needn't come absolutely every day, you know."

Stacie turned to the bed and took Margaret's hand. "Stop scolding me!" she said in mock irritation. "I will be here every day whether you like it or not."

"It just so happens that I do like it," Mrs. Barrows assured her. "May I change the subject? I understand things are going well at the camp. I had a note from Donna about the publicity."

"Yes, she's coordinating the registrations. We've had a good response from the other churches. The weekend camps are filling up quickly and we have the counselors lined up, so we think it will work out."

"What about someone to cook? I'm afraid I won't be of much use in the kitchen for quite some time."

Stacie squeezed Margaret's hand. "Megan's working out a schedule for people to take turns cooking. Don't worry; the kids will not go hungry."

"In one of those upper cabinets in the dining hall, there is a cookbook I used to use. It might help Megan if she could see it. Feeding sixty kids at a time is not easy, you know."

Stacie nodded. "I'll look for it. But please don't worry about it. We'll be ready on time."

"Will you be there for opening day, Stacie?"

"I think so. I don't start working in Weston until the next week." She propped herself on the edge of the bed more securely. "Weston is not that far away; I'm sure I'll make it down a couple of times during the summer."

"You just missed Brad, you know."

Stacie smiled. "You're changing the subject again. We were talking about the camp."

"You were talking about Weston," Margaret corrected her, "and I have the distinct feeling that you still have not discussed that with Brad."

"Why don't I get you some fresh water." Stacie picked up the brown plastic pitcher and stepped toward the sink.

"You can waffle all you want, Stacie Hanaken, but you can't change the facts." Margaret's voice was very stern. "You haven't spoken to him about it, have you?"

Stacie abandoned her diversionary tactic and set the pitcher back on the night stand, still empty. "I just never think it's the right time."

"You just never have enough courage."

Stacie had no answer. As usual, Margaret Barrows went to the heart of the question. At least half of the time when Stacie came to the hospital, Brad was there, too. Several times they had walked out to the parking lot together. They were comfortable with each other, even affectionate, but they had not talked about anything other than Mrs. Barrows or the work at the camp. On the days when Stacie pulled into the parking lot and saw Brad's van parked, her hands got clammy and her heartbeat quickened. Inwardly, she scolded herself for acting like a schoolgirl with a crush, but she could not deny that being near Brad made her feel something that no one else in her life evoked. Secretly, each time she came, she hoped to find him visiting Margaret.

Yet, she kept him at arm's length. She avoided talking about her job or moving to Weston. And if she sensed that he was about to say something that probed their relationship, she quickly steered the conversation to lighter subjects and focused her attention on anything other than his gaze. Sometimes she could feel him watching her when they were together at the hospital; and she could nearly feel the sensation of his arms around her and the closeness they had shared on the day of the tornado. But she drew very clear boundaries around their relationship.

What was she afraid of? Clearly Brad wanted to reestablish their relationship and clearly her feelings were equally strong. *So what was holding her back?* Only a few weeks ago, she found it difficult to be around him. Now she looked forward to seeing him, but she did not dare let him know. *Why couldn't she abandon her hesitations and at least tell him about Weston?* That would be a starting point to find out if their relationship had a future. *But was she ready to find out about the future?*

"I'm sure you think I'm a crabby old woman who doesn't know how to mind her own business."

Margaret's words brought Stacie back to the present conversation. "No, of course not," she was quick to answer. "I always appreciate your advice."

"Forget the advice. Let me remind you of a story I'm sure you already know—Abraham and the sacrifice of Isaac."

"I'm not sure I follow," Stacie said cautiously.

"Think of yourself as Abraham and Brad as Isaac. I'm sure you will see my point."

Stacie pondered this silently. God asked Abraham to sacrifice Isaac his son, and Abraham was obedient enough to do it. In the end, God gave him back Isaac the very thing he was supposed to give up.

"It's time for your pills again, Mrs. B."

Stacie looked up to see the head nurse breeze into the room with a small paper cup in her hand.

"I feel absolutely fine," Mrs. Barrows announced. "I don't believe I need any pills today."

The nurse rattled the pills in the cup. "Doctor's orders, Mrs. B. When the doctor does his rounds in the morning, you can talk to him about it. Until then. . . ."

"You do what the doctor says," Stacie warned, shaking her finger. "I'm going to sit right here until I see you swallow those pills."

"Oh, all right." Obviously, Mrs. Barrows was outvoted. "But I feel so much better. I fail to see why I am even here."

"Mrs. B, in case you haven't noticed, you have two broken legs. And your ribs are pretty banged up, too." The nurse softened a bit and added, "Actually, we all agree that you are doing very well. I think the doctor might be ready to release you soon, but we're concerned because you live alone out in the country. Maybe a few weeks in a rest home—"

Margaret cut her off. "Oh, that does not sound appealing in the least. I may be an old lady, but I'm as sensible as I ever have been. I've already worked it out so I won't be alone when I go home."

The nurse lifted an eyebrow in interest. "Oh? Perhaps you should talk to the doctor about it tomorrow, then." She handed Mrs. Barrows the little cup with the pills. "In the meantime, you must take these."

Mrs. Barrows grimaced, but she took the pills and swallowed them. Satisfied, the nurse left them to their conversation.

"You know, Stacie," Mrs. Barrows said, "I spent a lot of time waiting around this hospital when David was ill, but, before now, I've never been a patient. I don't care for it very much. I am not accustomed to people fussing over me all day long."

"They're just following doctor's orders and taking good care of you," Stacie reminded her. "Now tell me what you meant when you said you would not be alone when you went home."

"Bradley! I thought you had gone." Mrs. Barrows left Stacie's question unanswered and looked past her to the doorway filled with Brad's tall frame.

"I left my jacket." He gestured to a chair where his blue windbreaker was slung carelessly over the back. "Hi, Stacie. I thought you might be here. I came a little earlier today, so I missed you."

Stacie smiled warmly at Brad. He was in his work clothes and no doubt had come straight from his construction site. But he had made an effort to clean up. His T-shirt was neatly tucked into his jeans and his wavy hair was freshly combed. He needed a haircut, but Stacie found the ragged look appealing. Even when he was dirty and tired, she wanted to be near him. She followed every movement he made as he swept up his jacket with one hand and turned to look at her. Out of the corner of her eye, Stacie could see Mrs. Barrows looking back and forth between her and Brad. The color rose in Stacie's cheeks. Neither she nor Brad spoke, but they looked steadily at each other with slight smiles on their lips.

"They'll be bringing my dinner very soon," Mrs. Barrows said. "I'm sure the two of you could use a cup of coffee at the very least. Why don't you go down to the cafeteria and see what you can do to remedy that?"

Mrs. Barrows made no attempt to hide her pleasure at seeing the two of them together. Her directness momentarily embarrassed Stacie, who broke her gaze on Brad and instead glanced nervously out the window. She fumbled for words. "Oh, I'm sure Brad is busy. He's already late because he forgot his jacket. . . ."

Brad was chuckling. "Don't waste your breath, Stacie. The only way she'll be satisfied is if we agree to go down to the cafeteria together. So just give in and agree."

Stacie relaxed and laughed, too. "All right. But just coffee—you know what the food is like down there." She leaned over and gave Mrs. Barrows a quick kiss on the cheek. "I'll see you tomorrow."

Brad and Stacie walked down the hall together toward the elevator.

"I've been meaning to call you, Stacie," Brad said apologetically. "But I've been so busy since the weather got nice. There's a lot of outdoor work to be done this time of year."

"I'm sure you're swamped with work. At least everything is under control at the camp, so you don't have to worry about that." She pushed the elevator button and absently looked up at the numbered lights above the door.

"What I mean to say," Brad said, groping for words, "is that I was hoping we could spend some time together before you move away. I know you want to take things slow and easy—and that's fine—but I'd like to know where things stand."

The doors slipped open and they stepped into the empty elevator.

"I'm sorry to be causing so much confusion. . . ." One level of Stacie's mind was concentrating hard on keeping up with this conversation; at another level, she grappled with how to tell him she was not moving very far away. If she had any hope of having what she had sacrificed, then surely this was the moment.

Brad was talking, and she was missing part of his words. She snapped back to attention. "I've done my share of confusing things," he said.

The elevator came to a smooth stop on the first floor. Stacie saw the white block letters directing them to the cafeteria, and she wavered for a moment.

"Brad, I don't really want any coffee. Would you mind if we just walked for a bit?"

Brad lifted his wrist and looked at his watch. "I have a meeting in a few minutes, actually. How about if I walk you to your car at least."

Stacie nodded. She wanted to tell him about Weston. His being in a hurry would make it easy to let the moment pass and keep putting it off, but in the elevator she had resolved to do it now. He held open the outside door for her. By the time her shoes hit the sidewalk, she had decided she could not wait any longer.

"Brad, I'm not moving to Thomasville."

Her abrupt words had a jarring effect. Brad stopped in the middle of the doorway and looked at her, bewildered.

Quickly, she continued her explanation. "I'm still taking the new job, but the location has changed. We're going to open a shelter in Weston instead of Thomasville."

"I see." Brad continued walking.

Brad's terse reply surprised Stacie. She waited for him to say more, but he gave no indication that he would say anything. Along with Megan and Margaret Barrows, Stacie had always supposed that when she told Brad she was not moving to Thomasville, he would be enthusiastic and want to resume their engagement. Mentally, she had prepared herself to remind him that this one change in her job did not resolve all their problems. Although she had procrastinated about having this discussion, she had played it out in her mind over and over again, always assuming Brad's response.

But she had been wrong. Brad did not say any of the things she thought he would say. Her carefully prepared defenses were unnecessary. She had supposed that he would take her in his arms and tell her he loved her, but he made no move even to touch her hand.

After an awkward silence, Stacie changed the subject. "My car is over this way."

Brad walked stiffly beside her. She spotted his van, so she knew that he was going out of his way to walk her to her car. When she first suggested that they take a walk, she had imagined a more extended conversation—and some reaction to her news. She did not know what to make of his silent response.

She opened the car door and turned to him, determined to make one last attempt. "I'll still be around for a couple of weeks. We could get together. . . ."

Brad nodded but still did not say anything.

"Well, you'd better get to your meeting," Stacie said awkwardly. "Good night, Brad."

"Good night, Stacie. Have a nice evening." His tone was courteous and warm, but there was no spark. Stacie might as well have been a salesclerk in the local department store.

Chapter Fourteen

Stacie closed the folder and pushed it to the corner of her desk. Three more awaited her attention.

All afternoon she had been making her way through a stack of case files, updating the information and writing brief notes so the new caseworker would know the status of each file. There was not much to say really. Especially in recent weeks, a lot of her time had been spent on research and reports; she missed being actively involved with families in need. Working in Weston would put her in direct contact with as many as twelve families at a time, and she was looking forward to that dimension of the job. She still had a lot to learn, but she was eager to start learning it by actually doing the work of helping families get back on their feet.

She stretched her arms out in front of her and yawned. Since leaving Brad in the parking lot four days ago, she had felt unsettled and had not slept well. The lack of sleep was catching up with her but it was Friday, and she looked forward to sleeping late tomorrow morning. She patted her open mouth with the fingers of one hand as another yawn forced itself out.

"I saw that."

Stacie flinched, startled by the voice in her doorway.

"What's the matter, Stacie? Are you working all night or something?"

"Dillon! Marsha didn't tell me you were coming." Stacie's mind scrambled for an explanation of his presence.

"That's because Marsha didn't know. It was kind of an impulsive thing." He lowered his slender frame into the chair across from her desk and gave her a friendly look. "Besides, I didn't come to see Marsha, as charming as she is. I came to see you."

Stacie looked at him quizzically. "Have I forgotten a meeting or something? Sometimes my brain doesn't work too well on Fridays," she said apologetically.

"Nah, no meeting. I just wanted to see you."

Stacie reached into her desk drawer for the file on the Weston building. "I'm sure there are some things we need to discuss. I'm still waiting to hear from a couple of people—"

"It's Friday afternoon, Stacie." Dillon interrupted her. "I didn't drive 200 miles on a Friday afternoon to talk about the building."

"Excuse me?" Intuitively, Stacie was on guard.

"When I phoned you a couple of weeks ago, you said you had some people at your place and couldn't talk."

Stacie nodded. "Yes. That was the night we were planning publicity for the camp."

"But you never called me back. I've left several messages on your machine."

Stacie looked away. How could she possibly explain to Dillon everything that had happened in the last few weeks—or even in the last few days. The truth was that she had not thought about her personal relationship with him very much lately.

"This may sound like a trite excuse," she began, "but I've been taking care of a sick friend. Mrs. Barrows, the woman who owns the camp, was injured when a cabin collapsed. She's eighty-three years old, and I've been really worried about her."

"I'm sorry to hear about that." Dillon looked genuinely sympathetic. "I hope she's getting better. But you look like you could really use a break, some time to relax. How about spending the day with me tomorrow?"

Stacie ran her hand through her hair, stalling for time. There was not much to be done at the camp anymore, but she had been planning to spend Saturday alone, catching up on her reading and writing long overdue letters.

Dillon sensed her hesitation. "I know it's short notice, and you probably have a thousand things you could be doing with a day off. But I'd really like it if you spent it with me."

What was really holding her back was too complicated to explain. In the past, being with Dillon allowed her to detach from the pressure she felt about other things in her life. He was completely separate from her existence in St. Mary's and he had no idea what her life was really like.

Against her better judgment, she said, "Okay, sure. It would be nice to get away from things."

"They're forecasting nice weather; maybe we could go to the zoo," Dillon suggested.

Stacie nodded. "I haven't been there for a couple of years. That would be great."

Dillon stood up. "Looks like you've got a lot of work to wade through, so I'll get out of your way. I'll let you sleep in tomorrow and pick you up in the late morning, if that's all right."

"That would be perfect," Stacie answered, smiling.

After Dillon was gone, Stacie had a hard time concentrating. It was a good thing the day was already nearly over. She did not make much progress with the rest of the files and was relieved when 5:00 P.M. finally came.

At home, she dropped her briefcase on the coffee table and plopped down on the couch, wondering what in the world she had gotten herself into now. *Why had she accepted a date with Dillon? Weren't things complicated enough with Brad right now?* She reminded herself that Dillon did not know anything about

Brad; and she had certainly acted interested in Dillon the last time they were together. She really did enjoy being with him, but the change in her relationship with Brad during the last three weeks certainly affected her perspective. And this was all at Dillon's expense. He was entitled to some explanation. Once again she was being unfair to someone she cared about.

It's not really a date, she told herself; it's just two friends going to the zoo to enjoy a nice day. The zoo would be a public place with a lot to see and do; maybe being with Dillon would help her sort things out once and for all.

The next morning, the sun woke her up much earlier than she would have liked, but she indulged in the luxury of lying in bed in that half-awake state where her problems did not seem real. Periodically, she would turn over or bury her face in the pillow at a new angle. Burdened with the dilemma of what to do about Dillon, she had not slept well—again.

Eventually, she got up and made coffee. Leisurely, she looked at the morning newspaper. It was past 9:00 A.M. before she decided to get started on some of the things she wanted to do before Dillon came. Dishes had been stacking up in the sink for three days, and she could not remember the last time she had dusted and vacuumed. She certainly did not want anyone to see the apartment looking that way, and, if she hurried, maybe she could get a load of laundry done before he arrived. She decided to get the work done first and then shower and dress properly. Revitalized by coffee and toast, she shifted into an active mode. She pulled on some comfortable sweats, tied her hair back with a ragged ribbon, and got started.

She cleared up the dirty dishes, inventoried her refrigerator, and made a grocery list. She had just gotten the vacuum cleaner out of the closet when the doorbell rang. Without even thinking about who it might be, she went to the door and pulled it open automatically.

"Dillon!"

He looked at her, amused. "You didn't forget our date, did you?"

"No, of course not," she said, stepping aside so he could come in. "I'm sorry. . . . I wasn't. . . . What time is it?"

Dillon started to laugh, and Stacie flushed with embarrassment.

"I guess I should have been more specific than 'late morning.' Or maybe I'm an alien from another time zone."

Stacie decided to relax; being caught vacuuming in her sweats was not the end of the world.

"It's only 10:00 A.M.," she said in mocked irritation and shook a finger at him. "That's mid-morning, not late morning."

"Shall I go away and come back in an hour?" he offered.

"Don't be ridiculous," Stacie said, reaching for his wrist and moving him toward a chair in the living room. "But you'll have to amuse yourself out here while I get changed. Maybe you can get the vacuuming done." She left him and cheerfully disappeared down the hall.

The opportunity for a long, hot shower was gone, but Stacie went into the bathroom to wash her face and brush her teeth. Then she went to her closet to select some fresh clothes. Suddenly, she burst out in laughter when the whirr of the vacuum cleaner filled the apartment. The moment of embarrassment had completely passed, and she was beginning to be genuinely optimistic about the day for the first time. If he could put her at ease so simply, it was bound to be an enjoyable, relaxing day.

And she would not have to think about Brad. She could revel in the marvelous weather, take snapshots of the animals, and dream with Dillon about the new shelter. Brad had not called in the four days since their last casual meeting. Somehow she had thought that the news about working in Weston would have been enthusiastically received by Brad. His withdrawal had shocked her, and every day that went by without a phone call befuddled her more.

Dillon and Brad were so different and seemed to want different things from her. Sometimes it was hard to figure out what she wanted from herself. Yes, she needed to get away from all of this.

She pulled on some gray cotton slacks that she would have ironed if there were more time, put on a red shirt, and then scrounged around in the closet for some comfortable walking shoes. Her hair could hang loose, she decided after brushing it thoroughly. Pulling a white sweater off a hanger, she was ready to go.

It was a perfect day for the zoo. The sun was shining, but it was not uncomfortably hot, and it was too early in the summer for the bees to be as bothersome as they would be in a few weeks. Stacie had not been to the zoo since she had come with Megan's Sunday school class almost two years ago. Even before they arrived, she cautioned Dillon that the zoo contained more than they could comfortably see in one day. As soon as they were inside the gate, Dillon stopped to study the map.

"What's your favorite animal?" he asked.

Stacie laughed. "I never really thought about it. Elephants, I guess."

"Then we go this way." Dillon pointed confidently to the left. "On the way there we can see the monkeys and the birdhouse. Oh, and the snakehouse."

Stacie grimaced. "I'll pass on the snakes, if you don't mind."

They strolled side by side along the blacktop path. Stacie's camera, hanging casually around her neck, gave her something to do with her hands when she started to feel nervous about being with Dillon. But it was not long before she relaxed completely and started really enjoying the day.

She stopped every now and then to snap a photograph and although she was taking pictures of the animals, she always managed to capture a child in the frame as well. As she had expected, the zoo was swarming with families. Some of the children were cranky and hungry—it was almost lunchtime—but most of the ones Stacie noticed were fascinated by the animals, and she was delighted by watching them. Her zoom lens allowed her to capture their expressions without disturbing their natural reactions.

"I didn't know you were a photographer," Dillon said after she clicked a shot of twin girls surveying the African elephants.

Stacie shrugged. "It's just a hobby. I like photographing children."

Dillon raised an eyebrow. "Maybe we could get some of your shots blown up and hang them at the new shelter."

"I'm not sure they'll be good enough for that," she said hesitantly.

"You never know until you try."

"Some of the families that come to the shelter might be there awhile," Stacie said. "I'd like to organize an outing for the children. If we could find transportation, we could bring a group here."

Dillon nodded in agreement. "It would be a real treat." He scanned the menu of the concession stand they were approaching. "Are you hungry? It looks like they have your basic hot dog or your basic hot dog."

Stacie smiled. "What's a trip to the zoo without a hot dog?"

With their hands full of food, they found an empty bench and claimed it. They sat contentedly munching and watching the streams of people pass by. Intermittently, they chattered about the animals, zoos they had visited when they were children, plans for the Weston shelter, and favorite childhood pets. Dillon had Stacie nearly hysterical with laughter by recounting the antics of the puppy he got for his tenth birthday. Eventually, Dillon consulted the map again, and they resumed their leisurely tour of the zoo.

Stacie had to admit she was having a wonderful time. Just like the other times when she had been with Dillon, he had a knack for making her relax and enjoy herself, free of the weight of her personal problems. Purposely she had kept Dillon separated from the rest of her life. Other than knowing a little about the work she was doing at the camp, he did not know any of the people or experiences that were important to her. He did not know about Megan nor about how involved she was in her church; he certainly did not know about Brad. When Dillon and Stacie were together, it was almost as if those other things did not exist, and in those brief times, she found welcome respite.

But she knew this was not real. Sooner or later, the two worlds would have to meet.

Her feet ached at the end of the day. Unquestionably she was relaxed and had relished every moment of the day. Dillon put his arm around her shoulder as they walked up the sidewalk to her door, and for the first time all day she felt reality striking. She had willingly held his hand on and off all day, because she had a genuine affection for him, but she was unsure how to handle what was certain to come next.

She knew Dillon expected that she would invite him in. It was not even supper time yet, and they could easily spend the evening together as well. It was an awkward moment when they reached the door for she knew he was waiting for her to give some signal about whether the date would end or not.

Stacie pulled her keys out of her pocket and turned to Dillon. "I had a wonderful time," she said, and then laughed. "That sounds trite, I know, but I did have a nice day."

"Let's not wait so long before we do something together again," Dillon said. "Of course, after we're settled in Weston, it'll be a lot easier to see each other."

Stacie nodded but did not say anything.

Dillon seemed to understand that she was not going to ask him to come into the apartment. "Good-bye, Stacie," he said, and then he leaned down to kiss her.

She turned her face up to his like she had in the past, but pulled away after only a brief kiss.

"What's wrong?" Clearly, Dillon was puzzled.

"I'm sorry, Dillon."

"Sorry about what? Don't you feel well?"

"I've really enjoyed the time we've spent together," she said, looking down at her hands and twisting her keys between her fingers. "When I'm with you, it's so easy to relax and be myself."

"But?" he asked.

"But . . . I don't think it's a good idea for us to keep seeing each other—personally, I mean."

Dillon was bewildered. With a sigh, he leaned against the brick building and searched her face for some explanation. "This doesn't make any sense, Stacie. I thought we were both enjoying each other."

"We were!" She was quick to reassure him. "I like you a lot. But I just don't think. . . ."

"I get it," Dillon said with a flash of insight. "There's another man." It was a statement, not a question.

Given Brad's reaction at the hospital four days ago, Stacie was not sure how to answer Dillon. But at that moment, she realized that what Brad felt did not matter so much as what she felt. She enjoyed Dillon—there was no question about that. But she loved Brad.

Chapter Fifteen

"There you go, Mrs. Haskins," Stacie handed the plate to the middle-aged woman with wispy brown hair. "Enjoy your lunch." She smiled mechanically, as she had for all the other people who had come through the lunch line that day. As soon as Mrs. Haskins turned her back, Stacie's smile disappeared.

Stacie automatically scooped up another serving of tuna casserole and stood poised to plop it on a plate. After a moment she realized no one was there to receive it. It was after 1:00 P.M., and the line had trickled down. She studied the tangled mess of noodles balanced on the oversized serving spoon; a pasty mixture held the strands together, the bland whiteness broken up only by an occasional bright green pea or a glimpse of tuna. Actually, it did not look too bad, as far as tuna casserole went. Now that the line was finished, Stacie could sit and eat if she wanted to. But she did not have much of an appetite.

Tired, Stacie sat down on the three-legged wooden stool behind her. Cheap, bent flatware clanked and scraped against plastic dishes as the crowd of about forty chased after every morsel of their daily hot meal. Two large coffee urns were nearly ignored; only the very faithful were drinking coffee in the June heat. Stacie picked up a wet rag and absently wiped a spot off the table where there was nothing to be wiped. If she could just keep busy, she told herself, she would not have time to feel sorry for herself.

Dillon had been in the office most of the morning, working at his little table in the reception area and using Marsha's phone. It was a good thing Stacie did not know beforehand that he was going to be there; she would have been unbearably nervous about going to work. As it was, she simply followed her usual routine and went to the office, where there was plenty to occupy her mind and hands.

Every time Dillon spoke to her, Stacie's heart raced. Her throat throbbed with a rapid pulse and her ears seemed to clog up. Dillon, on the other hand, remained calm and cool all morning. Cordial as always, he interacted freely about their project. Never once did he hint at what she had said Saturday or make any reference to their personal relationship. To her surprise, he seemed to accept easily his own insight that there was another man who had a hold on Stacie's heart. But, one morning of being in the same building would not tell the whole story. Stacie could not help wondering what it would be like to be with Dillon everyday. *Would she regret her decision not to get involved with him? If he gave her another chance, would she take it?*

Stacie had let Dillon believe that, yes, there was another man. *But was there?* Brad had let another weekend go by without phoning her, and once again he had not been in church. Normally, he hated to miss even one Sunday, so missing two Sundays in a row meant something was wrong. And Stacie felt responsible. She had willingly given up Dillon—and had no regrets—but apparently she did not have Brad, either.

Scanning the room, Stacie saw that most of the people were finished eating. The cart outside the kitchen door was accumulating a stack of dishes as people cleared their own tables. Most of them would spend the rest of the day outside in the fine weather; a few would linger around the shelter during the afternoon lull and eventually settle in for the night. With a few exceptions, Stacie would see them all again when she came back to help on Thursday. These were the people she had dedicated her life to; these were the people who needed something which she could give. Some of them had been eating and sleeping at the shelter for months and they were very familiar to her.

Still, she did not know them, and they did not know her. She knew their circumstances, and she worked hard to help them get back on their feet. If she did her job well, then they moved on and others drifted in to fill their places around the lunch tables. *Would her whole life be that way*, she wondered, *full of people who floated in when they needed her and moved on when they did not? Would there ever again be a man in her life who wanted something other than hot food and low-cost housing? Would she ever be close to someone who saw past the job that she did to the reason why she did it?*

Rising abruptly from the stool, Stacie shook off her musings and concentrated on the task of cleaning up. She wheeled the metal cart, laden with tottering plates and cups, into the kitchen.

The phone in her office rang for about the tenth time that day. Normally, Stacie did not mind interruptions, but at this rate, she would never get through the stack of work she had assigned herself for the day.

"Stacie Hanaken," she mumbled into the receiver.

"Hi, Stace."

Stacie dropped her pencil and sat up. "Hi, Brad." He had not said enough for her to judge his mood, but she cautiously asked, "How are you?"

"I'm fine."

"Busy, I suppose."

"Yes, there's plenty to do." Brad paused and got to the point. "Stacie, I just called to let you know they're finally going to let Mrs. Barrows out. I'm going to take her home this afternoon. Maybe you'd like to come along."

"Absolutely! What time?"

"Can you meet me at the hospital at 4:00 P.M.?"

Stacie looked at her watch, and then at the pile of work on her desk, and then back at her watch. "Four o'clock is fine."

"I'll see you then."

Brad hung up and left Stacie sitting in the chair listening to silence on her end of the phone. Slowly, she replaced the receiver in the cradle and sank back in her chair.

It was a few minutes after 5:00 P.M. when they arrived at the cottage. Brad maneuvered the van as close to the door as he possibly could. Mrs. Barrows sat sideways on a bench in the back with her legs, in casts, propped straight out in front of her. As soon as the engine was turned off, Stacie released her seat belt and squeezed through the front seats to get to Margaret. Brad already had the wide door of the van open.

"I think I can just lift her out, Stacie," he said.

"Don't talk about me as if I weren't here," Mrs. Barrows chided. "I've got two broken legs, but my ears are fine."

"Yes, ma'am," Brad answered, putting his face close to hers with a grin. "May I help you out of the van?"

"Yes, you may. I'm hardly in a position to quibble about your offer, am I?"

"Stacie, I took the wheelchair out of the back. Why don't you make sure it's locked open, and I'll just lift her down into it."

Immediately Stacie hopped out of the van and stood behind the wheelchair. She positioned it close to the van door and carefully checked to be sure the chair's wheels were locked.

"Okay, Mrs. B.," Brad said, "on the count of three. One, two, three."

With a smoother motion than Stacie would have thought possible, Brad whisked Mrs. Barrows out of the van and into the wheelchair.

"Well, that was certainly a fine job, Bradley," Mrs. Barrows commended. "I didn't feel the least bit insecure."

"Now we'll get you in the house and make sure you have everything you need," Stacie said. When they arrived, she had noticed a small gray car parked across from the cottage, but she could not quite remember who it belonged to. Obviously, someone was there to care for Mrs. Barrows—but who?

She unlocked the wheels and started pushing. The front door of the cottage was only a few yards away, but the stone path was not conducive to a smooth wheelchair ride. Stacie could see Mrs. Barrows literally bobbing up and down with the bumps.

"Stacie, dear," Mrs. Barrows said mildly, "who issued you a driver's license for this contraption? Rather a rough ride, don't you think?"

Stacie laughed. "Sorry. I'll get better with practice, I'm sure."

The front door opened up just then, and Stacie saw who it was had arrived in the gray car—Jenna McLean.

"Jenna, honey, how kind of you to be here so early," Mrs. Barrows said cheerfully. "I wasn't expecting you until later."

"I wanted to be here when you got home."

"I hope I haven't inconvenienced you too much. You're being very sweet to come stay with me for a few weeks."

So it was Jenna McLean who would be taking care of Mrs. Barrows. It had not occurred to Stacie that Jenna could do this, but it made perfect sense. She was a college student with no classes during the summer weeks, and she was going to be a camp counselor on the weekends anyway.

"Hi, Stacie," Jenna said, putting her hands on the handles and pushing the chair into the middle of the living room. "How's our patient?"

"She has been quite cooperative," Stacie reported lightheartedly, "and I'm sure she will thrive in your capable hands."

"I'll do my best," Jenna said.

Stacie had been momentarily flustered when she realized that Jenna would be caring for Mrs. Barrows, but she quickly came around to appreciating the sacrifice Jenna was making of her summer vacation in order to do it. Jenna would do a good job. Despite her schoolgirlish approach to Brad, Jenna seemed sincere and obviously had genuine affection for Mrs. Barrows.

"Why don't I fix us all some tea," Stacie suggested.

"Be sure to put fresh water in the kettle," Mrs. Barrows instructed. "The tea bags are on the shelf next to the sink. I'm sure there's no fresh cream after all this time away—"

"Mrs. Barrows, please relax," Stacie laughed. "I'm quite experienced at brewing tea, I assure you. I'm sure I can find everything I need."

Amused, Mrs. Barrows retreated. "Very well. Get on with it, then."

Stacie swung open the door to the kitchen and looked around. Jenna had come early enough to tidy up and make the kitchen sparkle. The copper teakettle gleamed on the back burner of the stove. Stacie lifted it and filled it with water. The old gas stove had to be lit with a match, but it took only a moment to find one. She leaned against the counter and watched to make sure the flame caught properly.

Satisfied with her success, she turned her attention to finding mugs and the blue and white porcelain teapot Mrs. Barrows always used when she served tea. Stacie thought it was a nice twist to be able to make tea for Mrs. Barrows, who always insisted on fussing over everyone who came into her home. Her injuries would force her to accept the attention she deserved from other people, and that was a thought which pleased Stacie.

With the swinging door shut, Stacie could hear only muffled voices from the other room interspersed with brief outbursts of laughter. No doubt Mrs. Barrows had found yet another story to tell to her captive audience, and they relished it. Although curious about the story, Stacie savored the moments alone in the kitchen. The ride from the hospital had been tense—both because she was concerned that Mrs. Barrows was not comfortable and because Brad spoke to her only in limited ways. She even wondered why he had bothered to invite her along. Now she heard him laughing freely with Jenna and Mrs. Barrows and became even more convinced that she was the cause of whatever was disturbing him.

The kettle whistled. Stacie quickly turned off the gas and poured the steaming liquid over the tea bags in the porcelain pot. The familiar tray that Mrs. Barrows always used was nearby, and Stacie arranged the pot and four mugs on the tray, with sugar and lemon, and carried it into the other room.

"There don't seem to be any fresh pastries around," Stacie teased, "so we'll have to make do with just tea."

"I suppose it will be quite some time before I can do any baking," Margaret lamented.

"It's the perfect opportunity for me to learn," Jenna said enthusiastically. "You can let me be your hands and feet for a while, and maybe I'll pick up a few tips."

Mrs. Barrows tilted her head toward Jenna. "I'm a very strict instructor, you know."

"And I'm a very quick learner," Jenna answered right back. "And we'll have lots of time together."

Stacie felt a pang of jealousy. It was silly, of course. It was impossible for her to leave her job all summer and spend it with Mrs. Barrows, as appealing as that sounded. The important thing was that Mrs. Barrows had someone to look after her, and Jenna was a perfect candidate.

"I'm afraid I have to spoil the party," Brad said, swallowing the last of his tea. "I have to get back to town." He turned to Jenna. "Do you have everything you need?"

Jenna nodded. "I stopped at the grocery store on my way here."

"Call if you need anything at all."

Again, Jenna nodded.

"Ready, Stacie?" Brad asked her, without really looking at her. Suddenly, she realized that was what she had found so strange about his behavior all afternoon. For as long as she had known Brad, he had always looked her directly in the eye, even when she tried to avoid his gaze. Now he seemed not to look at her at all. In fact, he seemed more interested in Jenna. *Or was it her imagination?*

"I'm ready when you are," Stacie said, awkwardly bumping the coffee table with her knee as she stood up.

The ride back to town was very quiet. From the start, it was evident that Brad was not in the mood for conversation—not with Stacie, anyway—and there was no point in pushing him. She knew him well enough to know that when he was ready to talk, he would. She only hoped it would be soon. For weeks she had treated him this way and he had every right to be cool toward her. But deep inside, she clung to the belief that his true feelings were much different, and eventually they would surface.

Brad brought the van to a slow stop along the sidewalk outside Stacie's apartment. He made no move to get out, but she had not supposed that he would.

With her hand on the door handle, Stacie said, "Thanks for including me in taking her home, Brad."

Brad shrugged and looked out the window. "We were together when we found her; it seemed logical to take her home together."

Logical. Stacie repeated the word in her mind. It was a word distinct from feeling, divorced from emotion. Logical. Brad had called her because it was the logical thing to do.

"Well, good night, Brad."

"Good night, Stacie."

Before driving off, Brad courteously waited until she reached her door and unlocked it. With the door half open, she stood under the dim porch light and watched him pull away.

Had he pulled away from her completely? Would the image of his new van disappearing into traffic linger in her mind? She had hoped for so much more.

Chapter Sixteen

The morning was getting away from Stacie much too quickly. For weeks she had looked forward to opening day at the camp but now that it had come, she did not feel ready.

For one thing, the opening of the camp meant that soon she would start working in Weston, and she had done nothing about finding a new apartment. Several trips to, the grocery store had yielded dozens of boxes suitable for packing. A few of them now contained some books and magazines or miscellaneous dishes wrapped in towels, but most of them lay in a flattened pile in the living room, daring Stacie to begin packing in earnest. If she had been moving to Thomasville, she would have been ready but Weston was close enough that she did not really have to move until she was sure she wanted to. Never had it occurred to her not to move nearer her new job—until it came time to pack. She was reluctant to read the apartment listings in the Weston newspaper. For the time being, she decided she would make the long drive back and forth.

Stacie haphazardly slapped butter on her toast and hastily crammed it into her mouth, chasing it with a swallow of orange juice. That was all the breakfast she had time for now and she knew there would be plenty to eat at the Homestead later this morning.

The phone rang, just as she forced the last lump of bread down her throat. "Hello," she said.

"Good morning!"

"Hi, Megan. Ready for the big day?"

Megan laughed skeptically. "Time will tell how prepared we are." She paused to get to the real reason for her early morning call. "Stacie, I've got so much junk to take out there, I'm running out of space in the car. And I promised Donna I would give her a ride, her car's in the shop."

"Again?"

"Yep. I don't think there will be room for all three of us."

Stacie moaned. "So I have to drive out there by myself?"

"I'm sorry. We could caravan if you'd like."

"No, go ahead. I need a few more minutes to get ready, anyway." Stacie glanced at the clock. "I'll see you out there in about an hour." Disappointed, she hung up the phone. But she did not have time to wallow and she immediately moved on to the next task.

Four gallons of red fruit punch concentrate sat on her kitchen table. She would have to lug those out to her car, to begin with, and they were heavy enough that it would take two trips. Without further procrastination, she loaded up her arms and started out the door. She was nearly out when the phone rang. With her foot propping the door open and her arms full, she hesitated only a moment before deciding to let her answering machine pick up the call. Whoever it was would have to wait until she lightened her load a little.

Outside, she crinkled her face at the weather; it was not the bright, sunny day they had all hoped for. She would definitely have to take a sweater out to the camp for the opening ceremonies. The sky was gray and cloudy, but it was just possible that the rain would hold off long enough for them to enjoy their festivities. The ceremony would be brief, just Pastor Banning making an introduction and Mrs. Barrows welcoming the campers and their families. After that, the picnic would start and everyone would be free to roam the acreage as they pleased.

Stacie made one more trip to the car with the rest of the punch concentrate and a sack of plastic silverware. As an afterthought, she put in the only lawn chair she owned and slammed the trunk closed.

By the time she got back inside, the light on the answering machine was blinking. She whizzed by the machine and snapped on the play button on her way to the closet for a sweater. She stopped in her tracks when she heard the voice on the phone.

"Hi, Stacie. Megan said you'll be driving down by yourself. I thought maybe you'd like to ride with me instead. Maybe you're already on your way, and that's why I got your machine, but just in case I'll stop by on my way out of town." Click. The message ended.

Stacie slowly retraced her steps to the phone in disbelief. *Why would Brad suddenly call on the morning of opening day, after days—almost weeks of an impenetrable silence? Had Megan put him up to this? Worse, had Megan contrived the whole thing? Had Donna's persistent car trouble become an excuse for throwing Stacie and Brad together?*

She looked at her watch. If she hurried, she could be ready to leave in ten minutes, and maybe she could be gone by the time Brad arrived. On the other hand, she was curious about why he suddenly called and sounded so pleasant. If she left now, she would never know the answer.

In shocked slow motion, Stacie went to the bedroom and picked up her hairbrush. She tugged it through her thick hair until both her hair and her emotions were under control, and then pulled her hair back and off her neck in a sleek, silky ponytail. Her crisp white shirt and blue walking shorts looked very sporty and camplike. When the doorbell rang, she knew she would answer it.

"Hi, Brad. Sorry I missed your call."

"That's okay. I saw your car and figured you were still here." He smiled nervously. "I don't have anyone else riding with me. If you want to, maybe. . ."

Stacie had never known Brad to leave a sentence hanging in the air that way. She nodded awkwardly herself. "Sure. I've got some things . . . in my car. . . .

That's where I was when you called. . . . I'll just get my keys." Self-consciously, she left him standing in the doorway while she fetched her keys from the kitchen counter.

When the trunk sprang open, Brad immediately reached in for the load. The early summer sun had already bronzed his face and arms, evidence of his hard work. Stacie involuntarily admired his muscles, bulging slightly, as he efficiently transferred the punch concentrate from her trunk to the back of his van. She followed meekly with the lone lawn chair—feeling silly with only one now that she was not alone.

In a few minutes, they were on their way. Brad sat comfortably in the driver's seat, and Stacie, on the passenger side, tried to keep from staring at him while she wondered what this was really all about.

The gray clouds lost their innocence and spat a mist at the earth below. "Wouldn't you know it," Brad said, "rain for opening day."

Stacie shrugged one shoulder. "It's not really raining. Maybe it will clear up before we get there."

"I hope so. I don't think everyone will fit in the dining hall." He flicked on the windshield wipers. "Maybe this will help a little."

"I haven't had a chance to tell you how nice the van is," Stacie said. "I'm glad it all worked out for you."

Brad smiled but kept his eyes on the road. "It sure makes my life a lot easier. And having the logo on the side is worth a hundred billboards." He started chuckling. "One guy said that he called my company because he'd seen one of our vans—made it sound like we had a whole fleet out there. I guess because I get around to so many places, he thought there must be more."

"Then things are still going well."

"Just great." Brad sounded genuinely enthusiastic. "The guys I have working for me are doing a terrific job. Lon's wife just had a baby, and he brings new pictures all the time. I keep threatening to put an extra bolt in his neck to make sure his head stays attached."

Stacie sat and listened to Brad ramble on about the projects he was working on. Although she was interested in everything he had to say, she could not help thinking that this was not the reason he had come by to drive her to the Homestead. One moment, she enjoyed their casual conversation; the next moment, she desperately wanted him to get to the point. But she said nothing of how she felt.

"Look!" Brad said, leaning over the steering wheel and pointing forward. "Isn't that an incredible rainbow?"

Stacie leaned forward and immediately caught his enthusiasm. "I can see the complete arch—and it looks like it's coming down right in the middle of the Homestead."

Brad looked directly at her, for the first time all morning, and grinned. "Do you suppose Mrs. Barrows has a secret she hasn't told us about?"

Stacie joined right in. "Something about little green people with funny accents who keep the camp going?"

They watched, spellbound, as the road they followed seemed to lead them straight to the end of the iridescent arch of colors. By the time they reached the Homestead, the mist had gone—and with it the rainbow.

The grounds of the camp were so crowded that there was hardly a suitable place to park the van. Nevertheless, Brad confidently backed into a tight space Stacie never would have attempted to put her car into, much less a full-size van. Somehow she scrounged up the determination not to squeeze her eyes shut as he maneuvered into the spot at the beginning of the circular road. As soon as they were out of the van, the crowd swallowed them up. Stacie turned to say something to Brad, but he was gone.

She scanned the lawn for him and spotted him, but he did not look back at her, and she knew she was on her own. Still befuddled about why he had offered her a ride, Stacie retrieved two gallons of punch concentrate from the back of the van and started toward the dining hall. She ducked to avoid being attacked by a soccerball in flight and gave it a swift kick as it rolled across her path. The scene before her was a whole new place—the kind of place Margaret Barrows had been describing to her all through the spring weeks. Children, parents, and counselors in distinctive T-shirts swarmed the central lawn. Megan was busy passing out photocopied maps showing the camp buildings and trails. Pastor Banning was putting the finishing touches on a makeshift platform for the opening ceremony. With the rain gone, the day could not be more perfect.

Jenna emerged from the cottage, capably steering Mrs. Barrows and her wheelchair across the lawn.

"Stacie, dear, isn't it a marvelous day?" Margaret's eyes were bright and nearly twinkling with pleasure.

"Absolutely perfect," Stacie answered, leaning over to kiss a pink cheek. "Everything looks great. Are you all set for your part?"

"Nothing will delight me more than officially reopening the Homestead."

"Here, Stacie," Jenna offered, "let me take that punch concentrate for you."

"Thanks, Jenna," Stacie said, grateful to be relieved of her load.

Mrs. Barrows gestured for Jenna's attention "You tell the girls in the kitchen that there's a big tub on top of the refrigerator that would be perfect for mixing the punch. And the wooden ladle with the long handle—"

"Please, Mrs. Barrows, relax!" Jenna rolled her eyes, then looked at Stacie. "She's been like this all morning. She refuses to believe that everything is under control."

Stacie clicked her tongue. "Whatever shall we do with her?"

"Oh, hush, both of you," Mrs. Barrows scolded.

"I'll be back in a few minutes." Jenna gripped a gallon in each hand and meandered toward the dining hall.

"In all the confusion this morning, I seem to have forgotten my watch." Margaret fidgeted in her chair. "What time is it, Stacie?"

"Just past 10:30 A.M. If Pastor Banning is ready, we should all be set to start at 11:00 A.M."

"I feel so useless, stuck in this silly chair," Margaret said, her frustration evident in her tone. "There's so much to be done."

Stacie put her hand on Margaret's shoulder and squeezed. "Everything is going according to plan. Just relax and enjoy the day."

"I thought you were coming with Megan," Mrs. Barrows said, abruptly changing the subject as she so often did.

"I was planning to, but I ended up riding with Brad."

"Oh?" Mrs. Barrows said hopefully.

"He called me this morning and offered me a ride."

"That's wonderful. It's always a pleasure to see the two of you together. Where is he now?"

Stacie shrugged. "I don't know. He's been acting strangely all day. As soon as we got here, he disappeared."

"Have the two of you sorted things out?"

Stacie lowered herself to the grass and crouched beside the chair. "I'm not sure. I can't figure Brad out today. I mean, he hasn't really talked about what was bothering him; but something is different, that's for sure."

"Perhaps I'll have a word with him today," Mrs. Barrows determined.

Amused, Stacie shook her head. "When he's ready to talk, he will."

Stacie believed what she said to Mrs. Barrows; she just hoped it would not be too long before Brad was himself again and gave some clue about what he was thinking. Stacie flinched as a badminton birdie whizzed by her left ear, keeping her from sinking into an ill-timed, reflective mood.

"Maybe we'd better check in with Pastor Banning," Stacie said, rising to her feet and releasing the brake of the wheelchair. She carefully maneuvered the chair across the lawn, trying to hit as few bumps as possible.

Outside the dining hall, a makeshift platform stood. It was constructed of odds and ends of lumber left over from the repair work Brad had done and was decorated by some of the children with bright crepe paper and balloons. Pastor Banning had insisted on including a short ramp off the left end so that Mrs. Barrows could be wheeled up to her rightful place.

"Good morning, Stacie," Pastor Banning greeted her enthusiastically.

"Everything looks terrific," Stacie said, gesturing widely. "Are you about ready to start?"

"I think so. Why don't you go ring the gong?"

"Gladly."

Stacie swung the mallet as hard as she could, several times in a row, and then watched, satisfied, as the attention of the crowd turned toward the platform. No doubt the campers would soon be scrambling over each other for the task of ringing the gong. Low, deep reverberations hung in the air as Stacie replaced the mallet on its hook.

It took only a few seconds to return to where she had left Mrs. Barrows—and she was surprised to see that Brad had taken her place behind the chair. Wordlessly, she stood next to him and looked up as Pastor Banning cleared his throat and started to talk.

"Greetings to all of you on this beautiful day that the Lord has given us," he said, sounding as if he were in the pulpit on a Sunday morning. "I am sure that each of you is enjoying your visit to the Homestead just as much as I am. It gives me great pleasure to present to you the woman who has made this camp possible for all of the children who are here today. Please welcome Margaret Barrows."

Pastor Banning started the applause which welcomed Margaret to the platform. With a broad smile on his face, Brad wheeled her up to a central point and returned to stand beside Stacie.

"When I closed down this camp several years ago," Mrs. Barrows began, "so that I could care properly for my husband, I did not know if I would live to see the day it was open again. I only wish David could be here beside me today. The Homestead was his dream to begin with; I was fortunate that he allowed me to share it with him." Her eyes filled with tears, and her voice had a faraway quality. "For fifty-three years I experienced the goodness of God through the love of David Barrows. He was steadfast in the lean times, a solace in sorrow, and always the spark of joy in my life. I wish you all could have known him."

Stacie's mind told her that Mrs. Barrows was talking to the whole crowd; her heart was hearing words meant just for her. She glanced up at Brad out of the corner of her eye—and felt the color rise in her face when she saw his gaze fixed on her. She turned back to listen to Margaret.

"I could tell you hundreds—thousands—of stories of this place in the years gone by. But the important thing is that you are here today, and hundreds of new stories will be told after you have gone because you were here. Welcome to the Old Family Homestead."

Stacie vigorously joined the zealous applause which followed Margaret's speech. In the midst of the crowd's response, she felt a touch on her shoulder. She turned her head slightly, and Brad grabbed both her hands before she could speak.

"I'm no David Barrows," he said, "and I don't know if I'll ever deserve to have anyone say those things about me. But if it happens, I want you to be the one, Stacie."

"Brad, I—"

"No excuses this time, Stacie, for either one of us. Let's get married."

Stacie gently pulled one hand away from Brad and fingered a gold chain around her neck. In a moment it was clear what was hanging from the chain: the simple diamond in a plain gold setting sparkled in the sunlight. She held it up for him to see, and he wrapped his hand around hers.

"I see you two have finally patched things up," said a cracking voice from the platform. "Bradley, you put that ring right back where it belongs."

"With pleasure!" Brad said, slipping the ring off the chain and onto Stacie's finger.

Passage of
the Heart

Passage of the Heart

Kjersti Hoff Baez

Chapter One

Jamie squinted at the midwinter sun and pulled her sweater tighter around her slim shoulders.

"I should've worn my coat," she murmured. "Grandma's going to throw a fit when she sees me without it."

The January air was appropriately cold. An occasional gust of wind reminded the young woman she was no longer in California. The rolling foothills of the Catskills surrounded the tiny train station liked a rumpled quilt.

Jamie sighed. She was really here. Her father's speech still echoed in her mind: "You've got no discipline. You're hanging around with the wrong crowd. Arrested twice for drunken behavior, and now you've flunked out of college."

Her parents had given her two choices: Go to community college and live at home (under their rules), or spend a year with Grandma Kate.

"Maybe Grandma's principles will rub off on you," Dad had said.

Jamie rolled her eyes at the thought of staying at home. After being away at school for two years (well, almost two), she wasn't about to endure the humiliation of living with Mom and Dad. And community college! She rolled her eyes again. Staying with Grandma Kate wouldn't be much better, but at least she'd be away from home.

Running her fingers through her rich brown hair, Jamie straightened her shoulders. "Besides," she said aloud, "I'm almost twenty-two. I don't need Mom and Dad breathing down my neck."

"Here, here!" said a deep voice behind her. Startled, she turned around and came face to chest with what looked like an overgrown cowboy. Looking up, she saw two pale blue eyes twinkling down at her. She gulped.

"You certainly are the picture of independence," he grinned.

"Uh, ehem, I uh . . ." Jamie realized how idiotic she must look, shivering like a child with several suitcases cluttering the platform at her feet.

"You must be Jamie Carrigan. Mrs. K. couldn't come for you on account of her car not working so she sent me. My name is Judah."

He held out his hand to welcome her to Caderville, but Jamie was reluctant to respond. She didn't like feeling idiotic, and this tall oaf made her feel like a fool. She made up her mind she wasn't going to like him.

"Thanks for the fanfare," the young woman said sarcastically, "but could you please just take me to my grandmother's? I'm tired and I'm freezing."

"It's no wonder. Where's your coat?" The man didn't wait for an answer but reached down to pick up her suitcases. He loaded her belongings into a beat-up red truck. Jamie followed in silence and climbed into the cab.

Judah threw the truck into gear and they made their way through the small town of Caderville. He rambled on about what a wonderful person Mrs. King was and what a great man Mr. King had been, but Jamie wasn't listening.

"Where in the world did you get a name like Judah?" she interrupted. "Sounds like something out of the Middle Ages."

"Actually, it's found in the Bible, ma'am."

"I know. I wasn't born yesterday, for Pete's sake." She sighed in disgust. Hopefully she wouldn't have anything to do with this guy after he dropped her off at Grandma's. "So why'd your parents give you a name like that?"

"Well, ma'am, actually my parents didn't name me. I was found in a box on the steps of Hillside Church on a Sunday morning. The sermon that day happened to be about the Lion of Judah so the pastor's wife named me Judah. She and the Reverend adopted me."

"Oh."

Touché, Jamie thought to herself. *Instant replay of me playing idiot. I think I'll keep my mouth shut.* She settled into her seat, determined to keep quiet.

Through the window of the old truck, Jamie reacquainted herself with the terrain of her mom's home state. The naked trees colored the hills pewter, and bands of evergreen crested the tops with a dark forest green. She caught glimpses of the river, a silver ribbon that flowed through the valley. Whenever Ellen Carrigan spoke of her childhood home, it was with real tenderness. "Must be heaven overflowed one day and a piece of it settled down in the Delaware Valley," she would say. Jamie had to admit the foothills did have a beauty of their own.

Caderville was nestled in the valley and was scarcely big enough to call a town. The well-preserved buildings that lined Main Street greeted Jamie like an entourage of friendly old faces. She studied each one carefully to see if anything had changed.

Oh, wow, a movie theater, she said lamely to herself.

Judah broke the silence as if he had read her mind.

"It's new," he said pointing to the theater. "A man from New York moved up here and renovated the old Macintosh building. Caused a lot of excitement."

"Yes, how terribly exciting," said Jamie. "Where I come from, we have five theaters."

Judah whistled and shook his head in disbelief.

"Who would want to go the movies that often?" he asked.

Jamie looked at him in sheer amazement. *He's from the Stone Ages. I just know it. Somehow an alien ship transported him from the age of the dinosaur and dropped him in the twentieth century. Why Caderville? she thought. Why me?*

"What do you do for excitement?" she asked. "Watch the grass grow? Catch wart toads and have frog races?"

Judah smiled. "Mostly I work," he said. "But there are plenty of fascinating things to do around here, if you look. And I do have some hobbies I enjoy."

Let me guess, thought Jamie. *You rope grasshoppers, sit around a campfire, and count the stars.*

She looked at the dark haired, blue-eyed, Neanderthal cowboy. The less she knew about him the better, so she dropped the conversation. Hopefully she wouldn't run into him very often while she stayed at Grandma Kate's.

Judah turned the truck down a dirt road and drove a mile out of town. A mailbox with King painted on it in red letters stood resolutely at the head of a long driveway. Jamie turned to look at the sloping yard and old farmhouse. Despite the fact that only boredom awaited her in Caderville, it was always nice to visit Grandma Kate. There was something comforting about her that Jamie couldn't explain.

Snow graced the yard with a sweeping whiteness that dazzled Jamie's eyes. The white house with the black shutters bid welcome to Jamie, saluting her with a customary wisp of smoke from the chimney. Jamie knew that meant a fire in the fireplace and cocoa in a mug.

"Stop the truck," she exclaimed to its driver, momentarily forgetting to act like an adult. He obeyed and she leapt from the truck, running through the ankle-deep snow. She raced toward the house as another, younger Jamie had often raced. Young woman met with child, and with one burst of excitement, Jamie reached the front door with its iron clacker. The red door flew open, and there stood Katherine King.

"Grandma!" Jamie shouted, grabbing the woman in a bear hug.

"Good heavens Jamie, you'll break my neck!" Kate protested with a smile. "And where in the world is your coat?" She held her granddaughter at arm's length. "Have you lost your mind? It's January, dear. Around here that means snow, cold. Or have you forgotten?"

Jamie sighed. "Oh, Grandma. It's in my suitcase."

"Well at least you brought it!" she exclaimed. "My how you've grown. Why, you're a beautiful young woman! Even prettier than the pictures you sent me!"

"Oh Grandma," Jamie blushed and walked through the foyer to the living room. A fire was crackling cheerfully in the large, stone fireplace. Jamie hurried over to enjoy the warmth. She let the heat from the fire soothe away the cold in her hands and feet. Then she flopped down on the green, overstuffed sofa in front of the fireplace.

"This is great," she sighed happily. "I'm so glad to be here." Her earlier misgivings disappeared, chased away by the comfort of her grandmother's home.

"And I'm glad you're here! I'm glad Judah was able to pick you up. Let me give you a proper introduction." She turned to call to him, but he was gone. Jamie's suitcases were assembled neatly in the foyer.

"I don't know how he does that," Kate said, half to herself. She looked out through the open door and caught a glimpse of red as Judah's truck bounded out the driveway. "Here one minute and gone the next."

Jamie let go a sigh of relief. *Good-bye and good riddance,* she said to herself.

"Come and have some dinner," Kate called to Jamie from the kitchen. "Then we'll see about getting you settled in your room."

Jamie pulled herself away from the comfortable sofa and followed her grandmother into the big country kitchen. The aroma of roast beef and gravy tantalized Jamie's appetite. She sat down across from her grandmother and fingered the lace tablecloth that covered the table with soft whiteness.

Kate smiled at her granddaughter and bowed her head to say grace. Jamie bowed her head too, but she didn't hear the heartfelt prayer of thanks for food and family. Her mind wandered to the prospect of spending a whole year in the boondocks. She glanced over at her grandmother. *As long as she doesn't try pushing her God stuff on me we'll be fine,* she thought. *Maybe this year won't be so bad.*

A firm "Amen" tugged Jamie back to the table. As the two women enjoyed their meal together, evening stole silently into the valley. Faint pink reflected on the snow as the sun fell behind the hills. The blue of evening took its place. Muffled laughter rested lightly in the night air, a token of life from within the country home.

Chapter Two

"Rise and shine, Sleeping Beauty," a voice called up the stairs. "Rise and shine!"

Jamie groaned and turned over in her bed. "It must be the crack of dawn," she muttered, looking over at her nightstand. The brass alarm clock with its old fashioned bells seemed to grin at her. "Eight o'clock," it rang. Hardly the crack of dawn.

"Oh, shut up," Jamie said to the clock.

She rolled out of bed and went to the window. Sun and snow dazzled her eyes for a moment. The barn across the way stood comfortably in the snow. The worn boards of the old building had long since faded to gray. Here and there a sliver of red stole some light and reflected stubborn fragments of its former glory. Jamie smiled. She remembered how years before the barn had often beckoned her to come exploring. To her surprise, today was no different. She felt drawn to it.

Jamie pulled on a pair of jeans and an evergreen sweater and ran down the stairs. She grabbed her jacket from a hook in the foyer.

"I'll be there in a minute!" she called to her grandmother.

"Jamie, breakfast is—" Kate stopped in mid-sentence and went to the window to watch the young woman run through the snow. "Some things never change." She smiled to herself. Memories of pre-breakfast trips to the barn by a little girl in brown braids prompted the old woman to laugh. How good it was to have family in the house again!

Jamie slowed up as she approached the large doors at the front of the barn. She grasped the metal rings that served as handles and pulled open one door. The smell of hay and manure permeated the air. "I love that smell," she said aloud. "Good grief. What would Cassie say to that?" She thought of her sophisticated friend and college roommate and laughed. Cassie wouldn't be caught dead in a barn.

Despite the brightness of the morning, it was dark inside the barn. Dust danced on the fleeting shafts of light streaming through the small, grimy windows. Jamie squinted to get her bearings. A gentle lowing in one of the stalls caught her attention.

"Azalia! How are you, old girl?" Jamie scooped a handful of grain from a nearby sack and offered it to the old cow. She petted the animal's soft brown coat.

"What's new, sweetie?" she asked, gently pulling Azalia's head toward her. The cow looked at her with sad brown eyes.

"Yeah, right. What could be new around here!"

A jealous snort erupted from an elderly russet horse in the next stall.

"Merlin, I haven't forgotten you!" She rubbed the old horse's nose and hugged his neck.

Jamie looked around the rest of the barn.

"And where are your reckless cohorts this morning? Napping, I suppose, instead of hunting for mice." She searched for a sign of the barn cats, but to no avail. Then a movement from a far corner of the barn alerted the explorer to another's presence.

"What in the world?"

Jamie walked quietly over to the other side of the barn. Hidden in the shadows of an old stall stood a magnificent black horse. Even in the dimness of the stable, Jamie could see the lustre of the animal's shining coat. She stepped closer to the stall.

"Grandma didn't say anything about you," she said in amazement. Reaching over the wooden slats of the stall, Jamie put forth her hand to pet it.

Suddenly, the horse jerked away from her and snorted loudly. It angrily reared up. Jamie almost fainted with fear.

"Don't touch, him!" a voice yelled at her from behind.

Someone grabbed her and pulled her away from the agitated horse. Jamie started to scream, but then she realized who had her by the arms. It was Judah.

"What the—"

"Calm down," Judah said sternly. He let go of the frightened girl and talked soothingly to the black horse. It responded to Judah immediately and whinnied softly.

"Are you crazy?" He turned to Jamie. "You could have gotten hurt." His tone softened when he saw how shaken the young woman was. "Shadow doesn't care for strangers. He's a little jumpy."

"Jumpy!" Jamie exclaimed, catching her breath. "More like crazy! I won't go near that animal again."

She looked over at the black stallion. It stood calmly surveying Jamie as if she were the animal in the stall.

"Wait a second," Jamie turned to Judah. "What is that animal doing here anyway? Grandma never said anything about a horse, and besides, she couldn't handle a thing like that." She pulled her long brown hair back with an angry motion and looked at Judah defiantly. "And what, may I ask, are you doing here?"

"So many questions." Judah walked to the horse. " 'That animal,' as you call it, happens to be mine. He's one of my hobbies." He rubbed Shadow's nose affectionately and pulled two lumps of sugar from his jacket pocket. "He loves this stuff," he said over his shoulder.

"So what is your horse doing in my grandmother's barn?" Jamie demanded,

·knowing she didn't want to hear the answer.

"Mrs. K. lets me board him here, and in exchange I help her out around the farm. I take care of the cow and the horses and clean out the chicken coop and fix things that need fixing. My regular job is in town. I'm a mechanic." He leaned against the stall and grinned. "That answer your questions?"

Jamie looked with exasperation at the tall cowboy.

"Great," she said curtly. "Just great."

She turned in a huff and walked stiffly back to the house. She knew Judah would be following her, and she fumed.

"Of all the rotten luck. I thought I was rid of this guy, and now I find out he practically lives here."

Jamie threw open the back door of the house that opened to the kitchen. Grandma Kate greeted her with a cheery smile.

"Well, dear, I see you met up with Judah this morning. How nice! Judah, why don't you join us for breakfast?"

Jamie shot a pleading look at Kate, but Kate was oblivious to it. She set another plate on the table. Jamie and Judah sat down across from each other while Kate brought on the pancakes and sausage.

"Isn't this nice," the woman exclaimed as she busied herself around the table. "I love it when I can cook for someone besides myself!"

Judah and Jamie ate in silence. Kate brought out a book from the sideboard and opened it with loving hands.

"Today's passage is found in John 7:14-24. Mr. King always used to say if you didn't start the morning with the Word, you'd be running on empty all day."

Jamie squirmed. Reading the Bible and praying and all that kind of thing was okay in the privacy of your home, but not in front of other people. She looked over at Judah, certain he would have a smirk on his face. To her surprise, he was leaning forward with anticipation.

"Read on, Mrs. K."

Kate read the passage. Her voice carried with it a gentleness born of love and a conviction born of faith. As she finished reading, she repeated verse twenty-four.

" 'Stop judging by mere appearances, and make a right judgment.' Isn't that the truth? So many times we jump to the wrong conclusions just because of outward circumstance. It's a shame."

"It's not only a shame, but it can also be a deadly trap," said Judah seriously.

Jamie rolled her eyes. Not only was he an overgrown cowboy, but he was a fanatic to boot!

Judah and Kate didn't seem to notice Jamie's exasperation. They continued to discuss the Scripture. Jamie waited for Sunday school to end.

Finally Judah changed the subject. "Your car's running fine now Mrs.K. It was just the carburetor."

"Oh that's just fine, Judah," said Kate. She got up to clear the plates. "Now what do I owe you?"

"Nothing at all," said Judah.

"Don't be ridiculous. I'll send a check to your boss."

Judah shook his head and smiled at the old woman. "I learned a long time ago not to argue with you."

Jamie helped her grandmother clean up the kitchen. Judah, never one to sit for very long, got up and threw his jacket on.

"I'll double-check the animals. It's cold out there this morning." As he closed the door behind him, a rebel gust of cold air threatened the warmth of the country kitchen, but it was no match for the wood stove in the corner.

"We'll drop Judah off at the garage on our way to the drugstore," said Kate to her granddaughter. "Mr. Wheelock is expecting you today."

"Well, Grandma, I guess we're not wasting any time." Jamie grinned. "Don't I even get to goof off one week before I start working?"

Kate patted her on the cheek."I didn't want you to get bored, my dear."

Bored! Jamie thought to herself. *How could I be bored in Caderville?*

"Besides," said Kate lightly as she pulled on her boots. "Your dad said you did plenty of goofing off last semester."

Jamie winced. Grandma Kate was sweet, but she was nobody's dummy. It wasn't going to be easy to have some real fun without her finding out about it.

Judah stuck his head in the door. "Car's all warmed up and ready to go."

"Just a minute," protested Jamie. "I don't even have my makeup on." She hurried up the stairs to her room and quickly applied mascara and lipstick. She pulled her hair back in a clip and glanced over at the brass clock. It seemed to say, "Hurry up, hurry up."

"Oh shut up," she muttered.

She bounded down the stairs, plucked her coat from its hook, and followed Kate out the door.

"By the way, Grandma," she said as they walked to the car together. "Why didn't you tell me about that horse in the barn? It almost—"

"Oh yes, Shadow. Isn't he the sweetest animal? He's always begging for sugar and nuzzling my hand. Isn't he a beauty?"

"Yeah right," mumbled Jamie. "That 'sweet animal' almost killed me."

"What did you say dear?" Kate asked as they got into the car.

"Nothing," said Jamie.

Judah drove the women to the garage and let himself out.

"You drive carefully, now," he said to Kate as she took the wheel. "And nice seeing you again, Princess."

Jamie turned beet red. "The name's Jamie, if you don't mind."

The man just smiled and turned back to the garage.

"See you later," he called over his shoulder.

"Not if I can help it," Jamie said under her breath.

"Jamie! I heard that! Don't you like Judah? He's such a nice young man." Kate turned to study her granddaughter's face.

"He's not my type," Jamie responded.

Kate said nothing more on the subject and drove to Main Street where the drugstore was located. Situated between a flower shop and a dry cleaner, it looked like something out of an old magazine. The front window framed a small counter and soda fountain. A handful of patrons clad in winter coats grasped coffee mugs and nodded to one another in conversation. A bell jingled when Kate opened the door. The gleaming wood floor added to the old-fashioned air of the place.

A ripple of "Good morning, Kates" erupted from the counter as the pair entered the drugstore. Kate showed off her granddaughter before going to the back of the store. Ben Wheelock was busy behind the divider that separated the pharmacy from the rest of the store. Jamie could see his gray head just over the top of the wall, customary pen tucked behind his ear.

"Ben," Kate called to the pharmacist. "Jamie is here, and she's raring to go."

Ben hurried out from behind the divider and took Jamie by the hand. "Welcome back to Caderville, young lady. Glad to hear you'd be willing to work for me. I could use the help."

"Thanks for hiring me," Jamie responded. She had always liked Mr. Wheelock. He had been kind to her when she was a child, and he had a good sense of humor.

"Besides," said the gray-haired man. "I've been thinking about settling down, and there's a shortage of eligible women around here."

"You old coot! You'd be robbing the cradle!" Kate scolded.

"I could never compete with the loves of your life," interjected Jamie, in mock despair.

"Who? Who are they?" asked Ben. "Do you know something I don't know? Who?"

"Why, the fish, of course!" Jamie grinned.

Kate let out a whoop and slapped Ben on the back.

"She's got you dead to rights, old man. You're more at home in the river than the parlor."

While they were laughing, the door to the store opened. A gust of cold air wrapped itself around Jamie's ankles and sent a shiver up her spine. The trio looked to see a blond man in a brown leather jacket walk in. Ben Wheelock stiffened.

"Mind shutting the door, Braxton," snapped the pharmacist.

"Oh yeah," said the young man. He turned back and flipped the door close.

"Sorry, Wheelock." Approaching them once again, he let loose a low whistle. "And who do we have here?" he asked, eyeing Jamie.

Jamie looked into the handsome newcomer's eyes. They were steel grey. An odd feeling stirred within her. She couldn't tell if it was fear or excitement or both.

Chapter Three

This guy is a knockout, Jamie thought to herself.

Kate moved instinctively closer to Jamie as if to protect her. "This is my granddaughter," she said coldly.

The threatening look in the grandmother's eyes spoke volumes to the young man. This attractive young woman was off limits.

Jamie couldn't understand why Mr. Wheelock and Grandma were acting so strange. It wasn't like either of them to behave that way. They were being downright rude!

"My name's Jamie," she said with a smile.

The young man bowed gracefully, taking her hand.

"Chad Braxton, at your service," he said. He kissed her hand.

"Who said chivalry is dead?" Jamie asked with a grin.

"Ah, fair maiden! Your sensitive heart has found me out! 'Tis but a rumor that chivalry is dead. It lives on in my heart." Chad ignored the stony looks from Kate King and the pharmacist. "Dost thou think you could join me at the Pheasant Inn for a meal this fine day?"

"Alas, I cannot join you in such sweet repast," said Jamie, striking a dramatic pose. "There are chains around my hands, my feet."

"What be those chains," Chad asked with mock concern.

"Work," she said flatly.

The two would-be actors broke into laughter. Ben and Kate were not amused.

"Is theres something I can do for you, Braxton?" the pharmacist interjected. "If not, I have business to attend to."

Jamie swallowed her laughter. Chad shrugged his shoulders.

"I just came in for some antihistamines."

"Right this way," said Ben.

The young man made his purchase and turned to leave. "See you around, Jamie," he said with a smile.

As the door closed with a jingle, Jamie turned to Kate and her boss.

"What in the world is wrong with you two? Who is that guy, and why were you so mean to him?"

Ben took his glasses off and carefully wiped them with his handkerchief. "He's a troublemaker, Jamie. Nothing but pure trouble."

"He's an idiot," snorted Kate.

"Grandma!" Jamie gasped. "I've never heard you call anyone an idiot before. What in the—"

"Well, there was that one time a few years ago," said Ben to Kate. "That guy that ran for mayor. You called him an idiot, as I recall."

"Oh yes," Kate mused. "I did. He lost, too, thank goodness."

"Then there was the time—"

"Will you two stop that and answer my question?" an exasperated Jamie interrupted. "Who is Chad Braxton?"

"He's the oldest son of the man who renovated the old Macintosh building. Made it into a theater." Kate put her hands on Jamie's shoulders. "Chad Braxton is a mean, disrespectful young man. He's headed for trouble and will end up nowhere. I would much rather you stayed away from him."

Jamie didn't say a word. She concluded that this Braxton guy must be a lot of fun to be around, especially if Grandma and Ben Wheelock didn't like him. They were such sticks-in-the-mud. Perhaps this year wouldn't be so boring after all.

"Come along, Jamie." Ben changed the subject. "It's time I showed you the ropes around here. It can get pretty busy, and I want you to be ready for it."

"I'll leave you two to your work," said Kate. She kissed Jamie on the forehead. "I'll pick you up around four o'clock. Is that about the right time, Ben?"

"For today, yes. After she gets the hang of it, I'll need her until five."

"Okay. See you later!"

Jamie spent the rest of the day learning the routine of the pharmacy. She was in charge of the cash register and the soda fountain. At noon, she ate at the counter with Mr. Wheelock, but her thoughts were with Chad Braxton. She wondered if he had gone to the Pheasant Inn after all.

He certainly seems like an interesting guy, she mused. *I must tell Cassie about him. She'll be green with envy!*

The jingle of the door interrupted her thoughts.

"Hello, Princess," a deep voice sounded across the room.

Jamie scowled. "The name's Jamie, cowboy." She got up from her stool and busied herself behind the counter, determined to ignore the dark-haired man.

"All right, all right. Jamie. How's it going?" Judah asked.

"Just fine," said Jamie tersely.

"I see you two have met already," spoke Ben Wheelock. "And you really appear to have hit it off." He laughed and turned to Judah. "How did you manage to offend my employee?"

"Oh, I don't know," Judah smiled. "I guess she just doesn't like country boys."

Jamie turned around, brandishing a soup spoon. "I'll thank you both to stop talking about me behind my back," she said, her voice tinged with irritation.

"Sorry, Jamie, but we couldn't help it," replied Judah. "Now that you've turned around, though, that won't be a problem."

Ben started to laugh, but one look at Jamie's frown changed his mind. "See here, young man. Stop teasing my employee. That is my job, and my job alone. After all, I've known her since she was a little girl."

Ben smiled at Jamie. Never able to resist the old man's charm, she smiled back. "I'll go check the shelves," she said, leaving the two men at the counter.

Judah turned to Ben. "So what's new, Ben?" He lowered his voice. "I thought I saw Chad Braxton come in here this morning. Did I see right?"

Ben scowled. "Yes, it was him. Prowling around like the king of the forest."

Judah's jaw tightened. "I don't trust that guy."

"Well neither do I," replied Ben. "but it's a free country. Nothing you can do about it. He's evidently here to stay."

Judah glanced over to see where Jamie was working. She was dusting the shelves in the back of the store. Her long brown hair looked rich against the evergreen of her sweater. Her cheeks blushed with the effort of her work.

"Ehem," Ben cleared his throat to get Judah's attention. "He met her, you know. Braxton met Jamie."

Judah got up from his stool. "Maybe I better talk to her."

"Are you crazy?" Ben stopped the young man in his tracks. "Obviously Jamie is less than thrilled with you. You would only make her mad. Besides," he whispered. "Katherine said something to her already, and I think she's going to have a heart-to-heart with her later."

Judah nodded in agreement. "You're right as usual, Ben. I've got to get back to the garage anyway. I'll see you later."

Jamie watched Judah leave. She had seen the two men in tight conversation and had caught them looking in her direction. Resisting the urge to go over and set them straight, a determined look came over the young woman's face.

"Tonight I'll settle this Jamie-sitting-service thing once and for all, and that will be the end of it."

Chapter Four

Dinner at the King house that evening was unusually quiet. Kate realized Jamie had something on her mind. After dessert, the two settled in the parlor in front of the fireplace. The yellow flames of the fire decorated the room with familiar coziness. The two women faced each other on the green sofa.

"Now, Jamie," Kate began, "I can tell you have something on your mind. I do too."

"I know, Grandma," said Jamie softly. "But do you mind if I go first? I think it would save us a lot of trouble if I told you first how I feel."

Kate nodded.

"I know you want to talk to me about Chad Braxton. I know Ben Wheelock wants to talk to me. Even that Judah guy is hovering around." Jamie took a deep breath and continued. "Do you remember when I was twelve years old and Billy Ritchfield wanted me to go for a walk with him?"

"Billy Ritchfield." Kate smiled. "I remember him. He was a little snake in the grass. I didn't trust him for one minute."

"I know," Jamie responded. "You kept quoting a Proverb, something about the folly of fools'."

" 'The folly of fools yields folly.' Proverbs 14:24," quoted Kate. She laughed. "Now there's a tongue twister if I ever heard one. Try saying that one five times fast."

Jamie smiled. "Grandma! Don't try to change the subject. Now you remember that I did as I was told—"

"Most of the time," interjected Kate.

"Grandma! Be serious." Jamie cleared her throat. "You remember that I did as I was told and did not go on that walk with Billy."

"Good thing, too! That rascal went and played around that old abandoned well at the Chamber's place. Fell and broke his leg, as I recall."

Jamie sighed. "Yes, Grandma, he did. The point is, I obeyed you." She took her Grandmother's soft hand into her own. "But I was a child then. I needed you to guide me. That was fine, then. But I'm not a child any more."

Kate's eyes misted over for a moment. "You're right my dear. You are no longer a child. You must make your own decisions."

"Exactly," responded Jamie with relief. "I knew you would understand what I am trying to say. And I hope you will do me a favor."

"Of course, Jamie," said her grandmother.

"Please tell Mr. Wheelock and that Judah guy to back off when it comes to my personal life. They'll listen to you." Jamie got up and walked over to the mantel of the fireplace. "I don't want to hurt Mr. Wheelock's feelings. And as for Judah—" The young woman's voice became agitated.

"Yes dear?" Kate said sweetly.

"Oh nothing. Just please do me that favor, will you?"

"Okay, Jamie, I'll tell them." responded Kate. She got up and joined her granddaughter at the mantel. Jamie's face was flushed with the heat of the fire, and her eyes sparkled with the reflection of the flames. Looking into Jamie's face, Kate King realized this was no longer a twelve-year-old girl. A young woman stood before her. Perhaps this young woman still had a lot to learn about life, but it was time for her to learn it on her own.

"Jamie, I know sometimes you feel that I am preaching to you. But I want you to know I want only the best for you. I care about you."

The young woman smiled. "I know, Grandma."

"Ben cares about you, too. We all mean well," she said. "Now let me say this: I realize you think my faith in God is old-fashioned and the Bible out of date. I hope one day you discover what I did when I was young—that God is real and His Word holds the key to life."

Jamie looked away from her grandmother. She was embarrassed that Kate knew her so well.

"It's all right, dear," Kate gave Jamie a hug. "I love you no matter what."

Jamie returned her hug and sighed with relief. The Big Conversation was over. She flopped back down on the sofa.

"Now about Chad Braxton," Grandmother King spoke briskly.

"Grandma! You promised!"

"Okay, okay," Kate laughed. "I'll go make some hot chocolate."

Jamie leaned back on the sofa and stared into the fire. The illusive blues and greens melding in the flames triggered memories of other winters spent in Caderville. She could see her grandfather in his chair by the lamp, wearing his cherished brown sweater.

"Jamie girl," he used to say, "you're just like your grandma. She used to sit and stare into that fireplace for hours—"

"Hours, my foot," Kate would retort.

"For hours," Grandpa would continue. "She used to say she could see things in the fire, like princes fighting emerald dragons, all dressed in golds and blue satin." Then he would laugh with affection. "She certainly has an imagination."

"Had to have an imagination to marry you!" Kate would tease. Then the two would laugh, their laughter intertwining in the shared joy of each other's company. Even Jamie the child discerned the special love between her grandma and grandpa.

"Jamie, here's your cocoa," Kate nudged her granddaughter and brought her back to the present. "Where were you just now? Miles away?"

Jamie smiled. "Not miles. Just years."

Kate handed Jamie her a cup of cocoa. "Scalding hot, just the way you like it."

"Grandma," Jamie asked after they were both settled with their cocoa, "do you still miss Grandpa a lot?"

Kate smiled at her granddaughter. "Of course I do, dear. Your grandfather was my best friend. There are so many things I miss about him. I miss the sound of his voice. And the way he used to laugh and laugh at his own jokes, remember?" Tears formed in Kate's eyes. "I especially miss the way he used to look at me. He didn't have to say a word. His eyes were saying, I love you. Do you know, he always made me feel beautiful? Even when I turned old and gray?" She smiled and wiped her tears. "Good memories warm the heart!" she said.

A harried knock at the door momentarily startled the two women. Katherine answered the door with Jamie close behind. It was the Reverend Thomas Jacobsen.

The reverend extended his hand to Kate. "Hello, Katherine. Sorry to bother you so late in the evening," he said.

"Come right in Thomas, and tell me what's the matter. I can tell by the tone of your voice something's wrong."

"It's Sadie Atkins. She fell down, and they're trying to convince her to go to the hospital. But you know Sadie."

Kate grabbed her coat and quickly put it on.

"Let's go. If there's anyone more stubborn and independent than Sadie, it's me."

"Thanks, Katherine," said Pastor Jacobsen. He extended his hand to Jamie. "Nice to see you again, Jamie. Sorry I don't have time to stop and visit. Hopefully I'll see you at church?"

Jamie smiled at the reverend. "Nice to see you again, Reverend Jacobsen."

"I've asked Judah to drive us," said the pastor. "That road up to the Atkins' place can be treacherous at night. He's waiting out in his truck."

Kate turned to her granddaughter. "You don't mind if I leave you here alone, do you Jamie?"

"Of course not, Grandma," Jamie replied. "You'd better hurry."

The pair rushed out the door. Jamie watched as they got into Judah's truck. She could see his outline in the cab. He honked the horn to say hello, and she reluctantly waved to him.

"Well, I shouldn't be rude, after all," she muttered.

Closing the door behind her, Jamie followed the aroma of her cocoa back into the living room. She turned on the black and white TV that stood in the corner. The reception wasn't too good, but there was nothing else to do.

"Why she doesn't buy a color TV is beyond me," Jamie said aloud. "You'd think it was a sin to watch television."

She settled for an evening game show and prepared to be bored out of her mind. During a commercial that proclaimed how natural it was to dye one's hair, the phone rang. Jamie picked up the phone in the study adjoining the living room.

"Hello?"

"Ah, fair maiden, is it really you?" a husky voice intoned.

"Chad?" Jamie asked, trying to conceal the excitement she felt.

"The very same. Chad Braxton, at your service," he said jovially. "And what are you doing this evening? Anything exciting?"

Jamie sighed. "If you call watching a game show exciting, I'm delirious with the thrill."

Chad laughed. "Actually, I don't care much for TV."

"Well, you and my grandmother have something in common," Jamie said.

"I'd have to disagree with you there," Chad spoke seriously. "I don't think your grandmother likes me at all."

The silence at Jamie's end of the line betrayed the awkwardness she felt. She didn't know what to say.

"It's okay," said Chad quickly. "I understand your grandmother. I don't mind. People like her don't see eye to eye with people like me."

Jamie felt a tinge of defensiveness rise up within her.

"What do you mean, 'people like her'?" she pointedly asked.

"Whoa, calm down. I don't mean it in a bad way," said Chad. "You're grandmother is a devout Christian, right?"

"Yes," Jamie replied.

"Well, I'm not. I believe in doing what you feel is right for you, not what someone or some book tells you to do," Chad explained. "You know what I mean?"

"Yes," responded the young woman wholeheartedly.

"Sounds like you feel the same way," said Chad.

"Don't get me wrong," Jamie said quickly. "I respect my grandmother's beliefs. And I wouldn't let anyone badmouth her. But I just don't relate to her way of looking at life. That's all. We all have to make our own decisions."

"Here, here!" exclaimed Chad. "Now enough of this serious stuff. How about going to the movies with me Friday night? My Dad owns the theater so we can get in free."

"Well, I certainly wouldn't want you to spend any money on me," Jamie teased.

"Ouch, my heart," Chad cried. "You have pierced me through. Just for that, I shall have to take you out to dinner first."

"That sounds wonderful," Jamie replied. "I accept."

"I'll pick you up at seven. And it will be the Pheasant Inn, so dress accordingly."

"Okay," said Jamie. "See you tomorrow."

"Good night, fair maiden," said Chad.

"Good night, Chad," Jamie fairly whispered. She hung up the phone and hugged herself in excitement. Up the stairs she ran to get ready for bed. She donned a soft flannel nightgown and curled up on her bed. Looking at the clock, Jamie realized it was getting late. Her grandmother wasn't back yet.

"What are you going to tell her?" the clock's gentle ticking seemed to ask. "What are you going to say about Chad Braxton?"

"I'll simply tell her the truth," said Jamie aloud. "Now that we've had our heart to heart talk, it won't be hard to be open with Grandma." She stopped and sat up. "I'm talking to a clock. I must be more tired than I thought. It's time for lights out."

Jamie turned out her lamp and rested her face in the plump softness of her pillow. As she drifted off, she heard her grandmother come in the front door.

"Good night Judah," Kate called into the night.

"Good night, Mrs. K.," a strong deep voice replied.

"Good riddance," Jamie mumbled, trying to dismiss his intrusion. But the young woman fell asleep with the sound of Judah's voice resting on her mind.

Chapter Five

"Jamie," Judah called to her. "Are you coming with us?"

Jamie turned to look at Judah. He was carrying a Bible the size of a refrigerator box. Kate stood next to him. She held out an iron chain to her granddaughter.

"Here, honey," she said. "This will look just lovely on you!"

Jamie dutifully lowered her head. Katherine draped the chain around Jamie's neck. It suddenly became very heavy. Jamie began to choke.

"Grandma, why are you doing this?" She tried to lift her head, but it was no use. The chain became heavier and heavier.

"It looks lovely, dear," Kate smiled.

"Help me, Grandma."

"Come along now," spoke Judah. "Time to go."

Jamie struggled again to lift her head. "Help me!" she cried out. "Help!" But Kate and Judah turned away and started down a road without her.

"Help!"

Suddenly Jamie woke up. Her sheets had become tangled around her neck. Her grandmother burst into the room.

"What in the world? Are you all right, Jamie?" Kate sat on the edge of the bed. "You were calling for help!"

Jamie pulled the sheets away and sat up. "It was just a nightmare, Grandma."

"Good grief," said Kate. "You scared me half to death."

"Me? Scare you? You were the one terrorizing me in my dream!" Jamie exclaimed.

Kate let out a laugh. "That's funny! Was I chasing you with old Mr. Spoon in my hand? Remember Mr. Spoon?"

"Yes, when Mom and Uncle Frank were kids, you used to threaten to spank them with that old wooden spoon. I've heard the stories." Jamie lay back on her pillow and closed her eyes. "What time is it, anyway?"

"We might as well get up," said Kate. "It's almost seven. What time does Ben want you at the pharmacy?"

"Eight o'clock," Jamie said. Her eyes flew open. "Eight o'clock!" she exclaimed. "I've got to shower and wash my hair and blow dry it and do my makeup and eat breakfast in less than an hour!" The young woman flew out of bed and into the bathroom.

"The last time I saw you move that fast you were ten years old," Kate called after her granddaughter. "Remember? The time you threw a rock at that bees' nest?"

"Thanks for reminding me," Jamie shouted from the shower. "I can still feel those stings. And all you and Grandpa did was laugh!"

"You would have laughed too! John had to put you in the mud hole to soothe the stings. What a sight! Covered with mud except for your eyes."

"What did you say?" called Jamie.

"Nothing," replied Kate. "I'll go make breakfast."

As Jamie dressed, she thought about the nightmare. She realized how restricted her grandmother and Judah's beliefs made her feel.

"It's amazing how our dreams can express our inner feelings," Jamie said thoughtfully as she looked at herself in the mirror. "I'm glad Grandma and I had that talk last night. Hopefully things will be different now."

Jamie hurried through breakfast. Kate dropped her off at the pharmacy, promising to return at five. The day went smoothly. Jamie soon knew the routine. She chatted with the customers, kept track of the cash register, and served up snacks and coffee at the soda fountain.

"You're a regular pro," beamed Ben Wheelock. "Where have you been all my life?"

Jamie brushed off Ben's praise with a smile.

"It's my job," she said. "Besides, my boss is a real tyrant. I have to do well, or else!"

"Very funny, young lady," grinned Ben. "Now get back to work, or else!"

On her break, Jamie pulled on her coat and took a walk down main street. She found herself drawn to the old Macintosh building. It had been beautifully restored, the original carvings repaired and repainted. The marquee was tastefully designed in wood and glass, with old fashioned letters announcing the next movie. The raised numbers 1874 on the crest of the building looked as if the years had never passed. Jamie closed her eyes for a moment and imagined it was 1874. There were horses and carriages and ladies in long dresses and street lanterns glowing in the night and—"

"Beautiful, isn't it?" observed a voice from behind.

Jamie nearly jumped out of her skin.

"Y . . . yes," she stammered.

A man with a round, kind face greeted the young woman with a smile. He stretched out his hand. "Braxton's the name. Joseph Braxton."

"Mr. Braxton," Jamie said. "You must be Chad's father."

"Guilty as charged," replied the man. "He's my oldest. Then there's Jason, Adrian, and Luke."

"Wow!" exclaimed Jamie. "Four boys! How does your wife manage it?"

"A well-developed sense of humor," replied Mr. Braxton, "and Valium."

Jamie laughed. "My name's Jamie Carrigan. Katherine King is my grandmother. I'm spending the year with her."

"Katherine is quite a lady!" said Mr. Braxton. "She certainly can hold her own in any discussion." He rubbed his hands together. "Here we stand, in the dead of winter, shivering like a couple of kids at the pool on a windy day. Would you like to come in and see the place?" He put his key in the lock and opened the door.

"Oh, no thank you. I'd love to, but I have to get back to the pharmacy. I'm on my break," said Jamie.

"Okay, then," Mr. Braxton replied. "Don't let me keep you. Come by any time and I'll give you the grand tour!"

He disappeared into the theater, and Jamie made her way back to the pharmacy. *I'll be there Friday,* she said to herself. Jamie frowned. *I haven't told Grandma yet. She's not going to like it, but I guess she'll get used to the idea.*

Lost in her thoughts, Jamie ran right into someone.

"I'm sorry," she said, blushing with embarrassment. She looked up into the person's face. It was Judah.

"You!" she cried. "Why don't you watch where you're going?"

Judah's face suppressed a smile. "I guess I wasn't paying attention. I'll try to be more careful next time. Anyway, it's a good thing we bumped into each other."

Jamie smirked. "Yeah, right."

Judah ignored Jamie's reaction. "Your grandmother called me. She asked if I could drive you home after work. Says she's up to her elbows in apple pies. She's baking a bunch for the church bake sale Friday night." Judah looked into Jamie's eyes. "You going?"

"Home? Of course I'm going home. I'm through here at five. Try to be on time."

"No, I mean are you going to the bake sale?" asked Judah.

"Why in the world would I be going to a bake sale?" Jamie rolled her eyes. She stopped and stared at Judah. "Don't tell me you're going? You? The star mechanic and wild horse tamer? A bake sale?"

Judah looked puzzled. "Why not? I go every year. I help deliver the goods to the shut-ins."

Jamie tried not to laugh. "You're just a saint, aren't you? Underneath all that tall, dark, and ruggedly handsome exterior, you're a regular Mother Teresa."

The young man's face reddened for a moment. "You really think so?" he asked.

"What? That you're like Mother Teresa? Without a doubt—"

"No, I mean ruggedly handsome," Judah grinned.

It was Jamie's turn to blush. "I've got to go. I'll be late. Ben will throw a fit."

Hurrying away, Jamie gritted her teeth. "What did I say that for? Open mouth, insert foot. I hope he doesn't take me seriously."

Ben Wheelock was waiting at the door of the pharmacy, pencil behind ear, foot tapping the floor.

"Miss Carrigan, you are five minutes late," he said sternly. "I don't pay you to wander the streets of Caderville."

"Sorry, Mr. Wheelock," Jamie said. She hung up her coat. "It won't happen again."

"See to it," Ben replied.

Jamie busied herself behind the cash register. The afternoon was a busy one. A steady flow of customers gave testimony that the flu season was in full swing. By the time five o'clock rolled around, Jamie was exhausted. Ben came out from behind the partition wiping his brow.

"What an afternoon, eh Jamie?" He smiled at his assistant. "Weren't bored, were you?"

"If I never see another bottle of cough syrup, I'll be happy."

The door swung open and in walked Judah. His face still sported traces of grease, and he was wearing his work overalls.

"Look what the cat dragged in," hooted Ben. "What's the matter, Judah? Fall in the tar pit?"

Judah pulled a handkerchief from one of many pockets and tried to wipe his face. He only made it worse.

Jamie hid behind her boss. "Save me, Mr. Wheelock! It's the creature from the Black Lagoon."

"Very funny." Judah stuffed his handkerchief back into a pocket. I didn't have time to change. I didn't want to be late picking you up."

"Let's leave before anyone sees us," said Jamie, half seriously.

"Kate baking pies for the sale tomorrow?" asked Ben. "I better get there early if I want to get one. They sure go fast. You're going to the sale, right Jamie?"

The young woman was about to give a speech about everyone in Caderville expecting her at the bake sale when someone ran into the store.

"I was hoping I wouldn't miss you!" Chad Braxton said, catching his breath. "I just got in from school. We still on for Friday night, Jamie?"

"We certainly are," Jamie said clearly. "You said seven, right?" She watched to see Ben and Judah's reaction. Ben was fuming, and Judah's black eyes smoldered. *Touché,* thought Jamie. *They got the message.*

"Yep." Chad noticed the grease-laden Judah standing next to Jamie. "My, my. Was it a bad accident? Any other survivors?"

Judah clenched his fist and took a step toward Braxton.

"Calm down, old man! It's just a joke," laughed Chad. He peered into Judah's face. "You're a mechanic down at DiLoreto's garage, aren't you? I think you worked on my BMW."

"Judah Weston." Judah held out his hand. Out of habit, Chad shook his hand, only to find his own now covered with grease.

"Wonderful," he muttered. A trace of anger flared in his eyes, but Jamie intervened.

"I better be going, now," she said hurriedly. "Grandma will be wondering where I am."

"You're right," said Judah. He held open the door for her. "Let's go."

"I'll see you tomorrow," Jamie called to Chad.

Chad watched Jamie leave with Judah.

"I'm closing up shop, Braxton." Ben pulled the shade on the front window. "If you don't mind."

Braxton left the shop in time to see Jamie get into Judah's red truck. She saw Chad through the window and wistfully waved good-bye. Judah jerked the truck into gear and pulled abruptly away from the curb. Looking into his rearview mirror, he glared at the sight of Chad standing beneath the street light, arms crossed, a confident smile on his face.

The air in the cab was thick with tension. Jamie spoke up to avoid any discussion of the young Mr. Braxton.

"It sure gets dark quick around here," she commented. The sun had already set, and the shadows of evening laced the road in front of the truck.

"Winter is kind of long here," said Judah quietly. He glanced over at Jamie, feeling suddenly idiotic about the way he looked. "Sorry I look such a mess," he said apologetically.

"Don't worry about it," Jamie responded nonchalantly. "Don't give it a second thought." *I certainly won't!* she thought.

"And listen, I'm going to talk to Grandma about driving her car to work. I can always pick her up on my break if she needs to do anything. That way you wouldn't have to bother picking me up."

"Okay."

The ride out of town to the King house was quiet from that moment on. The moon was rising, a sliver of light in the black winter sky. The edge of town gave way to country road. The hills that sheltered the valley glistened in the moonlight. Jamie loved the way the snow sparkled, as if strewn with millions of tiny jewels.

Judah turned up the King driveway and dropped Jamie off at the door. The young woman gingerly walked through the snow away from the house lights, so she could get a better look at the expanse of stars overhead.

"It still takes my breath away," she said to herself. Because Caderville was so far from any big city lights, the night sky was especially dark. The panorama of stars that glittered in that canopy of black was a wonder to Jamie. "It's as if I could see every star," she whispered.

As Judah's truck pulled out of the driveway and on to the road, he stalled it on purpose. He wanted one more look at the warm lights of the farmhouse. He needed to think about what was going on inside his head.

"Why do I get so angry lately, whenever I see Chad Braxton around?" he said to himself. "I've always known he was a jerk, but today I almost punched his lights out! Why am I so jumpy?"

He looked out toward the house. The answer to his question was standing in the field, head back, soaking in a miracle of creation. Judah hadn't expected to see her, and he sucked in his breath. He suddenly had the urge to jump out of the truck, run to Jamie, and throw his arms around her.

"I've gotta get out of here," he mumbled. "I'm going crazy." His hand was shaking as he tried to turn the key in the ignition. "Get a grip on yourself, Weston," he ordered. After what seemed like an eternity, the engine kicked in.

Judah looked up for one more view of the lone figure in the field. She was gone.

Chapter Six

"What in the world were you doing, Jamie?" Kate exclaimed as Jamie came in the front door. "You'll catch your death of cold out there, and you with no boots on!"

Jamie hung her coat up and gave her grandmother a hug.

"Sorry I'm a little late," she said as she headed for the living room. Jamie sat down in front of the fire and pulled off her shoes. Her feet were cold and wet. The heat from the fire warmed away the chill.

"I suppose you were stargazing? Like mother, like daughter. Ellen used to drive me crazy, standing out there at all hours, staring at the sky. Moonstruck, starstruck, I do declare!"

Jamie slipped her feet into a pair of fleece-lined suede slippers. "What's for dinner?" she asked, heading for the kitchen. The sight of the kitchen shocked the unsuspecting granddaughter. Flour was everywhere, apple peelings draped the table and counters, and pieces of dough were strewn about.

"Don't look so alarmed, dear," spoke a frustrated Kate. "I baked six pies today. No wonder it looks like a bomb hit." She picked up an apple peel and threw it in the garbage can. "I just know I'm going to dream about apples tonight."

They cleared the table, and Kate took a pot of stew from the stove. Jamie retrieved the blue and white bowls from the cupboard.

"Those bowls have been in this house since I was a child," said Kate. "Your great-grandmother brought them here from England. They were part of a wedding present from her mother. I still have most of the set."

Jamie had heard the story a thousand times, but she never tired of its telling. It was so romantic, the young English bride coming to America to marry her Scottish groom. Kate still had a trace of an accent now and then, especially when she was angry.

"By the way," Kate said. "You'll want to dress warmly tomorrow night. The church basement is kind of damp and drafty."

Jamie took a deep breath. "I'm not going to the bake sale. I'm going to the movies with Chad Braxton."

It was Kate's turn to be shocked.

"But I thought you'd go with me to church," she said, incredulous. "Everyone's expecting us, and it's always such a nice affair."

"It's not that I don't want to be with you, Grandma, but Chad asked me to the movies before I knew anything about a bake sale."

Katherine's lips formed a straight line at the mention of Chad Braxton. "That man is nothing but a—"

"Grandma," Jamie gently interrupted, "remember our talk last night?"

Katherine stopped and grew thoughtful. She studied Jamie's face. "Okay, you win. But I would rather you didn't develop a relationship with that Braxton. There are plenty of other young people in this town."

"Like Billy Ritchfield?"

"Billy's grown into a real nice fellow. Why, he even sings in the choir."

"Oh, brother!" Jamie sighed.

"Why don't you join the choir, dear?"

"Grandma!"

"Oh, yes, I forgot. You couldn't carry a tune in a bucket. Poor dear," Kate patted Jamie's hand and wiped an imaginary tear from her eyes.

Jamie giggled. "You are cruel, Katherine King. I'm calling the hot line. Granddaughter abuse."

They laughed together and finished their meal.

Later that night when the last light was extinguished, virtual silence filled the farmhouse. The clock on the mantel kept a solitary rhythm that dotted the air with the passage of time. The occasional creak of a floorboard and the knocking of the hot water pipes filled the darkened rooms with comforting familiarity.

In contrast to the lovely quiet was the loud cacophony of thoughts that filled the minds of the two women in the house. Each lay upon her own bed, wide awake and filled with anxious thoughts.

Jamie traced the events of the day in her mind, focusing on the troubling spots. How could she have told Judah he was handsome? It had just sort of slipped out. *I guess he is handsome, in a way,* she thought. *But he's certainly not my type. I hope he forgets I said that. All I need is him following me around!* She thought of Chad, so definitely charming and attractive. *What should I wear?* she agonized. *The Pheasant Inn is so formal. Good grief!* She sat up in bed. *What if I can't find anything to wear?* Dropping back on her pillow, Jamie recalled the scene in the drugstore when Judah and Chad looked as if they were about to slug each other. And Grandma's warnings concerning a relationship with Chad. Like a runaway carousel, her thoughts went round and round, not stopping until she fell asleep, exhausted.

Kate lay awake, worrying about her granddaughter. She worried about Chad Braxton and his influence on Jamie's life. She could tell Jamie was interested in that young man. There was something about him that wasn't right. Almost as if he seemed dangerous. *Maybe I'm overreacting,* she thought. *But maybe I'm not.* Anxiety threatened to overwhelm her, but this grandmother had a weapon with which to fight. Climbing quietly out of bed, the silver-haired daughter of God got down on her knees. She took her burden to His throne and left it there. When

Kate King lay her head back on the pillow, sleep came on the wings of His peace.

Chapter Seven

The interior of the Pheasant Inn exuded a pleasing warmth as the handsome couple entered the foyer. Polished mahogany beams and shining brass lamps radiated elegance at every turn. A baby grand tucked in the corner sprinkled the air with music.

"No wonder people come from all over the county to dine here," whispered Jamie. "I'd forgotten how beautiful this place is."

"I do have good taste, don't I?" remarked Chad.

"And so modest, too," chided Jamie.

Chad laughed. "You certainly know how to hurt a guy."

A waiter dressed in black and white escorted the couple to a table near a window. Gazing out toward Caderville and the valley beyond Jamie enjoyed the sleepy gleam of lights and a glimpse of borrowed silver whenever the river reflected the moon.

"Speaking of hurting a guy," Chad continued as the waiter handed them menus, "I thought your grandmother was going to kill me when I came to pick you up. If looks could kill, I'd be at the morgue even as we speak. Only I wouldn't be speaking if you get my meaning. I'd be—"

"All right already, I hear you!" Jamie sighed. "She's just set in her ways." Jamie fingered the long-stemmed glass of water the waiter had set before her. "I wish she didn't see me as a little girl."

"Well I certainly don't see a little girl sitting across from me," Chad said soberly. "I see a captivating woman. That dress is fabulous."

Jamie tried hard not to blush. Her black off-the-shoulder silk shift was simple but elegant. She had spent an hour trying on everything in her closet before coming to a decision. From the look in Chad's eyes, Jamie knew she'd made the right choice.

"So," said Chad, "tell me about yourself."

"What an original line," Jamie smirked.

"Sorry!" Chad laughed. "So. Tell me about yourself."

"I'm from California, and I'm taking a year off from school to spend time with my grandmother."

"You mean you flunked out, got into some trouble, and your father sent you here to rehabilitate."

Jamie's mouth dropped open. She felt both anger and amazement. How in the world did he know that about her? Was it written all over her face—"delinquent drop-out?"

Chad patted her hand reassuringly. "Don't look so shocked. I'm pretty good at people analysis. And don't feel insulted. You are in the company of someone who managed to flunk out of college *twice.* I'll probably be forty-two by the time I graduate."

Jamie let out a nervous laugh. "It's nice to know we have something in common. What are you doing now?"

"I go to SUNY at Lamberton. Know where that is?"

Jamie nodded. "About ninety minutes from here, isn't it?"

"Yeah, but I only go part time. I work at a stockbroker's office the rest of the time. After all," he grinned, "I have to be able to support my habits."

A tingle ran down Jamie's spine. "And what, pray tell, are your habits?"

Chad mocked a sinister grin. "Oh, evil things—fifty dollar ties, hundred dollar wine, and million dollar women, like you."

Jamie laughed. Chad Braxton was totally charming. She felt at home with him. Here was someone who understood where she was coming from and didn't condemn her! In fact, she bet he'd been through some of the things she had experienced.

While they enjoyed their meal, Jamie and Chad talked about college and shared their various escapades. Anyone observing the two young people could see they were thoroughly enjoying each other's company. Laughter periodically erupted from their table as they swapped war stories.

"And then there was the time I got arrested," drawled Chad. "TWI."

"TWI? What—"

"Talking while intoxicated."

"That's against the law?" Jamie giggled.

"It is if you're doing it in class." Chad shook his head. "My professor did not appreciate it."

Jamie frowned. "They can't arrest you for that."

"Well, I did take a swing at the guy when he insisted I leave. I felt rather insulted."

"Oh boy," said Jamie. "That brings back fond memories. My friend Rochelle and I had one too many brews and decided to referee the football game. When we refused to get off the field, they called the police. It was humiliating."

"Getting arrested is humiliating."

"No, I mean the football game. We lost 34-0. Rochelle and I were only trying to help."

They collapsed with laughter. In the midst of their revelry, Jamie pushed back the memory of the dirty jail cell. She ignored the memory of her father's face when he had come to pick her up. And most of all she shoved away the remembrance of her mother's tears in the late hours of the night. Tears for Jamie.

After dinner, Chad and Jamie hurried to the theater to catch the late showing. Mr. Braxton greeted the couple at the door.

"Miss Carrigan! How nice to see you again!" Joseph Braxton beamed. "So glad you could come this evening. I'll have to give you the grand tour—"

"Cut the hospitality speech, Dad," Chad snapped. "We'll miss the beginning of the movie."

Chad's father turned red, seething with anger and embarrassment. But he said nothing. Jamie felt embarrassed herself.

If I ever spoke like that to my Dad, he'd have my head, Jamie thought. She shot a troubled look at Chad as he stood at the concession counter. Suddenly an old conversation with her mother popped into her head.

"When you start dating, Jamie," Ellen Carrigan had said thoughtfully, "watch and see how the man treats his parents. That will be a real indicator of how he'll treat you if you ever marry him."

"Oh, Mom," Jamie had protested, "you are so old-fashioned. People don't think about things like that anymore. They go by being in love. If you're in love, you marry the guy, no matter how his family life is. You're not marrying the family, are you?"

Jamie shook her head as if to shake off the memory of her mother's words. They made her feel uncomfortable. *Besides,* she thought, *I just met the guy, for Pete's sake. It's not like we're engaged!*

Mr. Braxton voice broke through Jamie's thoughts. "Don't mind my son, Miss Carrigan. He's just an overgrown adolescent. He doesn't know the meaning of the word manners." He glared at his son, but Chad brushed him off.

"Lighten up, Dad."

"Enjoy the movie," the owner called after the couple. Jamie smiled and, popcorn in hand, followed Chad to the dark showing room.

The Friday night movie was the latest horror flick. Suspenseful scenes and grisly surprises pulled screams from the audience. Jamie had neglected to tell Chad that she hated horror movies. They gave her nightmares. She sat terrified and tense, which Chad thought was hilarious.

"I hate that!" she said when the heroine went down into the cellar by herself. "That is so stupid! Why do they always go down by themselves to investigate? For Pete's sake, what's she going to do when she gets there? Fight the monster with her flashlight?"

"Shh," someone hissed from behind Jamie and Chad.

"Jamie, calm down," whispered Chad, trying hard not to laugh.

"Well don't you think that's 'e dumbest— Yep, there she goes. It's got her. She'll be dead as a doornail in a minute. Yep, there it goes. She's dead."

"Do you mind?" inquired a man seated to Jamie's right.

"Sorry," she whispered. "Look! There goes another guy. Same thing. Would you look at that?"

"Jamie, loosen up! It's just a movie!"

"Shut up. I'm scared to death."

At that Chad put his arm around her. "Poor baby," he crooned into her ear. His breath tickled her and she trembled. She didn't protest his nearness. It felt good to be close to him. All negative thoughts from the scene in the lobby disappeared.

Finally, the last victim was maimed, and the evil perpetrator was banished by the hero. Or was he? Somewhere, as usual, an odd egg lay in a corner, under a bush, portending evil and Horror Movie Part II. Jamie sighed with relief as the credits rolled and the dim lights in the theater came on.

"Are you okay?" Chad asked dramatically. "Will you need a therapist?"

"Probably," responded Jamie. "I'll have nightmares for the next two weeks."

"Oh, dear, and it's all my fault. Maybe I should stay with you tonight."

"Yeah, right." said Jamie as they reentered the lobby. "You and my Grandmother can sit up all night and hold my hand."

"I forgot about your grandmother," Chad sighed. "Well, it's the thought that counts."

Chad's father weaved his way through the milling crowd and approached the young couple.

"Miss Carrigan, you look a bit green," Joseph Braxton commented. "Enjoy the movie?"

Jamie thought of Chad's arm around her. "As a matter of fact, yes."

"Next we're showing 'Driving Miss Daisy.' I think that will go easier on your stomach."

"I'm not so sure about that, Dad," Chad teased.

"Your taste in movies is abominable," responded the elder Braxton.

"Good night, Dad," Chad said. "We've gotta go."

" 'Good night, Dad?'" Joseph gasped. "He's actually being polite! Jamie, you must be a good influence on Chad. Please, spend as much time as you can with him," he added with a grin.

Jamie straightened her back resolutely. "I shall do my best to rehabilitate the cad. I mean Chad."

"That's not fair!" protested Chad. "That's two against one."

"As I recall, those are your favorite odds," replied the father.

"Good night, Dad."

Mr. Braxton put on a serious face. "Good night, Son," he said solemnly.

Jamie laughed, and Chad threw his empty popcorn box at his father. The two threw on their coats and ventured out into the cold.

At the door of Katherine's house, Jamie and Chad stood shivering in the night air.

"I had a great time," Jamie said.

"As did I, fair maiden," spoke Chad elegantly. "I hope to make this a habit, you know."

Jamie smiled. "You and your habits! I don't know if I like the idea of being someone's habit."

"Well," said Chad diplomatically. "Why not make me one of yours?"

"I'll think about it," responded Jamie, playing hard to get.

"Now if there's anything more maddening than a woman who plays hard to get, I don't know what it is." He put his arms around Jamie. "As for playing games," he said, "I always play to win."

Somewhere in the back of her mind Chad's words disturbed her. But the little alarm that had been triggered was silenced when Chad pulled Jamie close and kissed her lightly on the lips. She was taken by surprise, not that Chad had kissed her, but that she had let him. She pulled away and looked into Chad's silver- grey eyes.

"I don't think I should . . . we should . . . uh . . ." She stumbled for words, her head spinning. "I'm not really interested in a heavy relationship, you know what I mean?"

Chad smirked and ran a hand through his blond hair. "Lighten up, Jamie. It was only a kiss!"

Jamie turned beet red. "Oh, yes. I was just kidding."

Chad pulled up the collar of his coat. "Look, I gotta go. I'll call you, okay?" He smiled and tapped her on the nose with his glove. "See you later."

Jamie watched the dark blue BMW pull out of the driveway and disappear down the road. She felt like a complete fool.

"What has gotten into me?" She said to herself. "One minute I'm ready to melt in his arms, the next I'm babbling like an idiot." She looked up at the January moon and sighed. "I guess I'd better slow down and take it easy. Besides, you never know what a day might hold."

Jamie turned and put her hand on the brass knob of the front door. It felt cold and sent a shiver up her spine. She smiled as she closed the door behind her. "It's definitely going to be an interesting year."

Chapter Eight

"The sermon this morning is entitled 'The Sparrow and the Promise.' Please open your Bibles to the Gospel of Matthew, chapter ten. We'll begin reading at verse twenty-six." Pastor Jacobsen cleared his throat and began to read: "'So do not be afraid of them. There is nothing concealed that will not be disclosed, or hidden that will not be made known. . . . Do not be afraid of those who kill the body but cannot kill the soul. Rather, be afraid of the one who can destroy both soul and body in hell. Are not two sparrows sold for a penny? Yet not one of them will fall to the ground apart from the will of your Father. And even the very hairs of your head are all numbered. So don't be afraid; you are worth more than many sparrows.'"

Jamie looked around at the little Baptist church. The bright winter sunlight merged with the stained glass windows and passed through, scattering a riot of holy colors around the sanctuary. Reds, blues, and greens shimmered on the pews and worshippers. A rich blue-purple spilled onto the faded red carpet in a pulsing circle of tinted light. The faded brown covers of the hymn books belied the lively songs tucked between them. Jamie picked up an "I Wish" card from the holder in front of her. She scanned its contents. A check beside the appropriate square would bring about the desired result—a visit from the pastor, prayer, a favorite hymn sung. Jamie sighed.

I wish, she thought, *I were back in bed.*

Snatches of the sermon penetrated her wandering mind.

"God even knows the number of hairs on your head!" Pastor Jacobsen exclaimed. "Although, that's not such a feat in some cases, eh Clarence?"

Clarence Sunderman, the grocer, nodded his balding head. Laughter rippled through the congregation. Jamie smiled. Caderville Baptist may be boring, but it did have a sweet way about it.

Jamie returned her attention to the windows. Despite its humble size, Caderville Baptist Church had impressive stained glass windows. There were seven in all, three along each side wall and a large one above the pulpit. The wealthy logger William Cader, who made his money in the 1850s when logging on the Delaware River was a thriving business, donated the money for the windows when the original church had burned down. Kate had told Jamie the story of the original church. Rumor had it that the new young preacher, with his passionate preaching and loving manner, ("Didn't hurt that he was good lookin' too," Grandpa had interjected), had stolen the heart of one of the young women in the valley. Her fiancé, a logger, hadn't taken too kindly to losing his girl, even to a man of the cloth. So one night when it was customary for the preacher to be praying in the church, a mysterious fire had been started. The wooden church had burned to the ground. Not a trace of the preacher could be found. It had been assumed he was dead until the next day when it was realized that Emily was missing too. Months later one of the faithful parishioners (they said it was Sadie Atkins' grandmother), had received a letter from some far-off place like India. The two young lovers had married and were serving together as missionaries.

It could never be proven that the logger had burned the church, but everyone knew it was him. His boss, William Cader, had somehow felt responsible and put up the money to rebuild. His crowning donation had been the windows. Each one portrayed a scene from the Gospels, with the glory of the resurrection depicted in the soaring window over the pulpit. Jamie's favorite window was of Christ in the storm-tossed boat. His hand upraised, he was rebuking the winds and waves. The deep blues and greens swirled around him in raging beauty, while Christ, robed in glowing white, stood like a peaceful commander, strong and in control. It was a magnificent work of art.

"That which is hidden will be revealed. Our hearts are open to Him who created us. In the hidden places of the heart we need to grow and discover the depth of God's love. Even the sparrows are watched over by the Lord. How much more does God watch over us?" The sermon was reaching its climax. "Hidden places of the heart." The words tugged at Jamie for a moment, but she shrugged them off. "Don't be afraid of those who can hurt us or even kill us. The physical realm is not the bottom line. The eternal realm is, and we can have eternal life now if we will trust in the Lord."

Jamie looked at her watch. Almost time for lunch.

"Katherine," Reverend Jacobsen called from the pulpit, "why don't you come up and lead us in singing hymn number forty-two, 'The Lord is Watching Over Me.'"

Jamie tried to look attentive since the pastor was looking in their direction. Kate got up and joined the pastor at the pulpit. As her clear voice began to sing, the congregation and pastor joined in. Jamie fumbled through the words, catching on to the chorus. "The sparrow does not fall alone, and neither then shall I; the Lord is watching over me, my hope shall never die."

As the service concluded, the pastor gave one last announcement. "Don't forget to join us today for the ice skating party. We're going up to Blueberry Lake this afternoon at two o'clock. The folks from the church at Hillside will be joining us. Hope to see you there!"

Amid the hellos and good mornings, Kate and Jamie made their way to the front doors of the church. A voice called to Jamie over the friendly hubbub.

"Jamie Carrigan!" A young man hurried over to catch her before she left. She turned to see a man in a gray suit grinning from ear to ear. "Remember me?"

For a moment Jamie drew a blank, but there was something about that mischievous grin. "Billy Ritchfield!" She held out her hand to him. "How's your leg?" she laughed.

"Very funny," Billy replied. "It's good to see you, Jamie. Are you going to go ice skating?"

She hesitated momentarily, but her grandmother jumped right in. "Of course, she's going," Kate said. "She'd love to go."

"You'll have to excuse my grandmother," Jamie spoke up in exasperation. "She still thinks I'm twelve years old."

"Mrs. King, the last time I asked Jamie to go somewhere, you wouldn't let her." Billy grinned. "Will you give me another chance?"

Kate laughed and slapped the young man on the back. "Of course, Billy." She bowed low. "You have my permission," she said formally.

"Grandma!" exclaimed Jamie. "I can speak for myself!" She turned to Billy. "I'd love to go."

"I'm just teasing, Jamie," smiled Kate. "Get cold, baby."

"You mean 'chill out' Grandma," corrected Jamie.

"Whatever. It will be cold, by the way. Better get home and break out the long underwear!"

Jamie rolled her eyes and followed Kate out the door. "I'll see you there, Billy," Jamie called over her shoulder.

After a warm lunch and a search for the long underwear, Jamie was ready to skate. Katherine drove her granddaughter to Blueberry Lake, ten miles from Caderville. It was situated on a small, elevated plain in a cluster of hills north of the town. One side of the lake was laced with trees, and the other was dotted with summer cottages. A meadow on the eastern curve climaxed into a ridge overlooking the lake. When Jamie arrived, people were already gliding across the ice.

"I have to drive over to Lamberton and see Sadie at the hospital," Katherine reminded Jamie. "I'm not sure when I'll be back, so you'll have to get a ride home, okay?"

"No problem," replied Jamie. "Sure you don't want to stay?"

Katherine laughed. "My skating days are over. I've had my share of it though," she continued. "Your grandpa and I used to sneak up here at night when the moon was full and skate all alone, just the two of us. That was before we were married."

Jamie gasped. "Before you were married! You sneaked out of the house! And on top of that you skated, without a chaperone! Why Grandma, you wild thing you!"

"Never you mind," Katherine scolded. "Take this thermos of cocoa and have a good time. Maybe Billy can drive you home." She raised her eyebrows and smiled sweetly.

"Thanks. For the cocoa I mean, not the matchmaking advice." She leaned over and gave her grandmother a kiss. "Is anyone going with you?" Jamie asked as she got out of the car.

"I'm picking up Louise Hanson on the way."

"Good. I'll see you later!" Jamie waved good-bye and headed for the shore of the lake.

There were almost thirty people gathered for the party. Jamie scanned the crowd for Billy. She finally spotted him. He was wearing a glaringly orange parka and a purple woolen cap.

"Billy," she called. "Over here!"

Billy located Jamie's voice and hurried over to where she stood. "Glad you could make it, Jamie. It's a perfect day for skating."

Jamie had to agree. The sun was bright and the air briskly cold, but there was no wind to make it feel even colder. Jamie pulled on her skates and followed Billy to the ice.

"I must warn you that I haven't skated in a couple years," said Jamie, her ankles wobbling in the snow.

"No problem!" responded Billy. "I'm not exactly a professional myself."

"Well, at least I won't have trouble finding you in the crowd," Jamie teased.

"I know, I know," sighed the young man. "You could see me a mile away on a dark night in Transylvania. My mother bought this coat for me for Christmas. If I don't wear it at least once she'll never forgive me."

"Never mind," said Jamie. "You'll be the light of the party!"

"Haw, haw, haw," groaned Billy. "Come on, let's skate!"

He grabbed Jamie by the hand and pulled her onto the ice. After a few faltering steps, Jamie regained her bearing and was gliding around with the best of them. She weaved in and out among the crowd. The various colored coats of the skaters created a rainbow of moving color on the sparkling ice. It was invigorating.

"Wait up," Billy called to Jamie. "I can't keep up with you."

Jamie slowed down and took his arm. "Too many lemon meringue pies?" she asked innocently.

"So I've gained a few pounds. I'm still in shape."

"In the shape of what?" Jamie laughed and skated away, with Billy in hot pursuit. She turned to look back at her pursuer and promptly forgot to watch where she was going. The inevitable occurred. Jamie bumped into someone and nearly sent him flying.

"Mr. Wheelock!" Jamie cried. "Are you all right?" She reached out her hand to steady the man.

"Jamie Carrigan, I declare, you almost knocked me into the next county," Ben

Wheelock scolded. "Where in the world were you going in such a hurry?"

Billy skated to the rescue. "It's my fault, Ben. I was chasing her."

"You young people are all alike. Not a grain of sense in your heads. Why, at your age I was—"

"I know, you were done with college and working in a pharmacy," Jamie interrupted.

"I've told you that story before?" The pharmacist adjusted his cap.

Jamie nodded. "At least twice."

"Probably more like fifty times," mumbled Billy.

"What'd you say, Billy?" Ben asked.

"Pretty nifty times, back then, huh?" answered Ritchfield hastily.

"You bet. Back then, men were men, and women were women."

"You mean women were slaves," Jamie smirked.

"Oh, fiddlesticks. I'm going back to my skating. I'm pretty good, you know. Good day, and watch where you're going," Ben grinned and left the two with a semi-graceful turn of the skate.

"He thinks he's God's gift to the skating world," a voice sighed behind Jamie and Billy. "But actually he's an accident waiting to happen."

"Reverend Jacobsen! Good afternoon," said Billy. Jamie smiled and shook the pastor's hand. "Last year," the pastor reminisced, "he knocked over Violet Cranberry. She fell right on her . . . ahem . . . behind. Couldn't sit in church without a pillow for weeks. I don't think she ever forgave him. No sir. When Ben Wheelock dons his skates, I stay as far away from him as possible." Jamie laughed and thanked the pastor for the information.

"Any time," Thomas replied.

"Oh, Thomas!" Ben's voice called. "I need to talk to you."

"See you later," the pastor whispered hurriedly. He dug his skate into the ice and fled from the pharmacist.

Billy shook his head and watched as Ben tried to catch up with the pastor. "Those two are a riot," he said affectionately.

Jamie studied Billy's face. "Tell me, something, Billy. I never figured you to be the churchgoing type. Why do you go?"

The question caught the man by surprise, but he gladly answered. "I never thought I was, either. You remember how wild I was when I was a kid? Well, I was even worse as a teenager. Almost messed up my life real bad. But Pastor Jacobsen took an interest in me. And his genuine caring for a misfit like me really grabbed me. So I figured I'd try what he was preaching about. I found out it's real."

"What's real?"

"God's love," he said simply.

"Wait a minute!" hushed Jamie. "I think I hear violins! Or is it an organ?"

"Lighten up, Jamie," Billy chided. "You were the one who started this conversation."

Jamie shrugged. "You're right, I'm sorry. It's just that I hear enough of this from my grandmother. Let's change the subject."

"No problem," Billy replied. "How about we go find that thermos of cocoa? I brought some doughnuts to go with it."

Jamie looked puzzled. "How did you know I was going to bring cocoa?" Her eyes narrowed. "Grandma! That sneaky—"

"Jamie! Lighten up!" Billy laughed and skated back toward shore.

"I'll be there in a minute," Jamie called. "I want to skate a little more."

Almost half of the small lake was swept clean for the party. Jamie skated around the outer rim, taking in the scenery. The sky was a bright blue, a stunning contrast to the pewter hills and snow-laden fields. Here and there á bird flitted across the lake and disappeared into the trees. Despite the talk and laughter from the party, Jamie could hear the beautiful winter stillness in the hills. She remembered the winter day her grandfather had taken her to the lake. They had climbed the ridge, and he had told her to listen.

"Listen to what, Grandpa?" ten-year-old Jamie had asked. "I don't hear anything."

"The silence, child. The winter silence. It only comes in the winter. It wraps these hills in a special quietness, like a blanket. You can almost hear the mountains dreaming, dreaming of seasons gone and the spring to come. Listen, child. You'll hear it."

Jamie smiled at the memory. How right Grandpa had been.

"Princess! Fancy meeting you here!" Judah Weston approached Jamie on his black leather skates.

"Judah! What are you doing here?" Jamie tried not to sound exasperated.

Judah looked down at his feet. "I think these are skates. I guess I'm skating."

"Marvelous."

"Seriously, I'm here with the group from Hillside Church. That's where I go to church."

"Oh," said Jamie. "Isn't that special!"

"You are the sweetest girl I've ever met!" Judah drawled. "You know how to make a guy feel real comfortable."

"Sorry," Jamie replied, "I didn't mean to. Especially in your case." She turned to head back to the shoreline.

"Nice seeing you," Judah grinned, "and don't go too near the edge over there. It might be a little thin."

"Thanks for the warning," Jamie called over her shoulder.

She hurried away, totally aggravated. That man always made her feel like a little kid. What did he know about the ice anyway? She continued her tour of the rim and approached the edge near one of the docks. Suddenly, she heard a crack and her left foot fell as the ice broke. She let out a yell, and her other foot broke through. As the icy water hit her legs, she panicked. Abruptly the water reached her waist. She felt the bottom and tried to keep her footing. Her legs buckled beneath her.

"Help!" she screamed. "Help me!"

The next thing she knew, strong arms pulled her out and dragged her away from the hole. Jamie was weeping with fear and with relief that someone had rescued her. Judah Weston ripped off his coat and wrapped her in it. By then, several people had hurried over, among them Billy Ritchfield.

"What happened?"

"She went too close to the dock." Judah snapped. "Give me your coat."

Billy quickly unzipped his down coat and threw it over Jamie. "I'll get Ben."

"Put me down," Jamie recovered herself. "I am fine. You're embarrassing me."

Judah ignored her and carried her toward the cars. Ben and Thomas signalled Judah to bring her over to their cars.

"My car heats up fast," yelled Ben. "Put her in here. Thomas is going for the doctor. We've got to get her home immediately."

Jamie protested, but she was shivering uncontrollably. Judah tightened his grip on her and headed for Ben's car. She was about to say something sarcastic, but the look on Judah's face stopped her short. He looked frightened and concerned, as if he knew it could have been much worse. She could have slipped beneath the ice and—

At the thought of such a horror, Jamie passed out in Judah's arms.

Chapter Nine

When Kate King pulled into her driveway, she saw Judah's truck and four other vehicles parked in front of the house. She recognized the doctor's car. He rarely made social calls. Her heart started to pound.

"Jamie!"

She jumped out of her car and ran to the front door. Ben opened the door and tried to reassure her.

"She's all right, Kate," he said firmly.

Kate ignored him and started for the stairs. She didn't see Judah and Billy holding blankets in front of the fireplace.

"Bring up one of those blankets and be quick about it!" the doctor commanded from upstairs.

Kate rushed into Jamie's bedroom. The doctor was bending over her, taking her pulse.

"Grandma!" Jamie said. She tried to sit up but the doctor promptly forbade her to do so. He turned to look at Kate and frowned.

"I don't need you fluttering around in here. Go back downstairs," he growled.

"I will not," Kate retorted. She took Jamie by the hand and kissed her on the forehead. "What happened?"

"She fell through the ice," Judah replied as he walked in the room. He handed the doctor a blanket. The physician removed the blanket on Jamie and covered her with the newly warmed one.

"It was all my fault," Billy said woefully, following Judah into the room. "If only I hadn't left her alone. But I went to get the cocoa and the doughnuts and then I heard a commotion and—"

"'If only I hadn't left her alone'," Jamie mimicked Billy with a whine. "For Pete's sake, I'm not a child! So the ice broke, big deal! If you had been with me, the whole lake would have caved in and then we'd all be under the care of this charming doctor."

"That's not funny!" protested Billy. "I'm not that heavy, and besides, you shouldn't be—"

"What in the blazes is everyone doing in this room?" barked the doctor. "Everybody out or I'll throw you out." He nodded at Kate. "Go see what the devil's taking so long for Ben to make that hot water and whiskey."

The three visitors walked obediently out of Jamie's room and down the stairs. In the kitchen Ben was sputtering over the stove. The teakettle finally began to whistle.

"It's about time," the pharmacist grunted. He took the bottle of whiskey on the table and poured some into the cup. Then he added a dollop of sugar.

"Doc Stanton wants that right away," said Kate.

"I would have had it right away if you didn't keep your whiskey in some forgotten corner of your cupboards. I found it behind a fossilized jar of honey."

Kate reached for the cup, but Ben refused.

"I'm taking it up," he said. "I need to talk to Stanton about medication for her in case she gets sick."

Kate sat down wearily at the table. Judah joined her while Billy warmed another blanket. Cupping his hand over hers, Judah smiled at the shaken woman.

"She'll be fine," he said.

"I know," responded Kate. "It's just such a frightful thing. Who pulled her out?"

"I did," said Judah. His black eyes narrowed for a moment. "I shouldn't have let her go near the docks."

"You heard her, Judah," Kate reminded the young man. "She's got a mind of her own. I just hope this is the worst trouble she gets into."

Judah nodded and his jaw tightened. He thought of Chad Braxton and his smooth ways. How he wished Braxton had never showed his face in Caderville. If he ever caught that creep doing anything underhanded to Jamie he'd—his hands clenched.

"Judah!" Kate intervened. "Calm down." She studied his face. "I know what you're thinking. You're just going to have to trust the Lord to watch over her. He was watching over Jamie today. You were there to pull her out and bring her home safely. I pray for her every day. And today you were part of an answer to my prayer. Thank you."

She smiled. Judah blushed and ran a hand through his tousled black hair.

"Where's that other blanket!" came a familiar shout from upstairs.

Billy Ritchfield ran up the stairs and back down again. He joined Judah and Kate in the kitchen.

"That man has the disposition of a camel!" he whispered.

Kate laughed. "Yes, but he's saved more lives in this county than any other doctor I've known. He can read a situation like a book and solve it in a matter of minutes. It's something to see."

"Well, he could at least be civil," Billy complained. "I hate getting yelled at. It makes me feel like a kid."

"Buck up, soldier," Judah slapped Billy on the back. "The night is young."

Kate got up to look out the window over the sink. The sun had already gone down. She reached over and turned on the back light. Shadows from the house stretched to join the darkness in the outer edges of the yard. The dim shape of the darkened barn brooded in the background. It was going to be a long night.

Before going back upstairs, she whispered a prayer of thanks that Jamie was all right.

"She wasn't in the water long enough to warrant taking her to the hospital," Dr. Stanton explained, "however, she was in long enough to get chilled to the bone."

"You can say that again," said Jamie. "Can I have some more of that hot toddy stuff?"

The doctor nodded, and Ben left to make more of the hot drink for the patient.

"As I was saying," the doctor continued, "she was in long enough to get chilled to the bone. She'll be fine, but in all likelihood she will probably come down with a sore throat and fever, then a full blown case of the flu. What is your history with fevers, young lady?"

"Oh, we go way back," replied Jamie with a grin.

"She has a tendency to get high fevers," interjected Kate. "At least she did when she was a child."

"That doesn't help me now," the doctor said brusquely. "What about as an adult?"

"Still high," said Jamie. She frowned at the thought of it. "The last time I was sick, my fever was so high I—" She shivered. "It was awful."

"Then you can expect the same," said the doctor. "Just give her extra-strength acetaminophen every four hours and keep cool compresses on her head. That should help. I've given Ben a prescription for an antibiotic. Just follow the directions. She'll be fine."

He picked up his bag and headed down the stairs. Kate walked him to the door.

"Thanks for coming, Doctor," she said.

He grunted and put on his coat and hat. "You know I don't often make house calls. But Wheelock wouldn't take no for an answer. Make sure the girl doesn't do something foolish like galavanting out of bed too soon. I don't want to medicate her now in case she gets by without getting sick. That's not likely, though. She'll probably get ill, but she'll be okay. Call me if you have any doubts about the situation."

Giving Kate a mere hint of a smile, he was gone.

"Grandma!" Jamie called. "Get these people out of here!"

Kate smiled and shooed the men out of Jamie's room. She adjusted Jamie's pillows and checked her blankets.

"How do you feel?"

"I feel fine, Mommy. Now where is my teddy bear?" Jamie sighed. "Grandma, you don't need to fuss over me. That hot toddy really warmed me up. I'm just tired now, that's all."

"Okay, dear, you go to sleep. I'll send everyone home," said Kate. She turned off the light on Jamie's bedstand. "I'll leave the hall light on."

"Good," said Jamie. "I wouldn't want the bogeyman to get me!"

"Stop being silly! I'll get that old bell we used to use whenever Ellen or Frank were ill. You can ring that if you need me."

Down in the kitchen, Kate tried to persuade Judah, Billy, and Ben to go home. "She's going to sleep now," she said. "It's not necessary for you to stay any longer."

"If you're sure you don't need us," said Judah.

"We're not in any hurry," Billy volunteered.

Kate smiled. "We'll be fine."

The two young men reluctantly put on their coats.

"I'll be back tomorrow," said Judah.

"Yes, we'll be back tomorrow," agreed Billy, shutting the door behind them.

Ben stood his ground. "I'm going to run over to the store and fill this prescription. I'll pick up some extra-strength acetaminophen too." He put on his coat. "Be back in a few minutes. I'll be sleeping on the couch."

"Ben Wheelock!" Kate exclaimed. "I really don't think that's necessary. I appreciate your kindness, but I can't expect you to stay here tonight."

"I'm staying," he said matter-of-factly. "You may need me."

Kate threw her hands into the air. "Can't talk sense to you when you're like that," she sighed. "I'll fix the couch for you. Just let yourself in. I'm going to check on Jamie and go to bed."

Jamie was sound asleep. Kate placed her hand on the young woman's forehead. It felt normal.

"Sweet dreams, and the Lord bless you," she whispered. Then she got ready for bed herself.

Ben returned from his mission and called quietly up the stairs to Kate. "I'm here now," he said. "Good night."

"Good night," Kate whispered loudly from the top of the stairs.

Jamie woke up to see a tall man in a large orange parka standing next to her bed.

"Who are you?" she whispered, her heart pounding.

"The bogeyman," he said calmly.

"Oh," Jamie turned on to her side. "Good night."

Suddenly her eyes flew open. The bogeyman! What? She turned around and he was gone. Billy Ritchfield was sitting on a bench eating lemon meringue pie.

"Billy, what are you doing here? It's late, and I'm trying to sleep!"

Billy just ignored her and continued eating.

Violet Cranberry came out from behind Billy and offered Jamie a pillow. "Here, dear, you'll feel better." She put the pillow over Jamie's face.

"I can't breathe!" Jamie cried. "Get it off me!"

She struggled for a moment and finally climbed out of bed. The floor felt cold to her feet. "Wait a minute," Jamie panted. "This isn't my floor! This is ice!"

She slipped and fell. The ice cracked, and Jamie felt herself falling and falling into hot water. It was so hot.

"Help," she cried. "I'm drowning!"

Judah pulled her out and placed her back in bed. He started piling blankets on her. It was so hot.

"No more blankets," Jamie muttered. "Too hot."

"Doctor's orders," said Dr. Stanton. "Here, put this on." He handed her the orange parka.

"Want a doughnut?" asked Billy.

"Help!" cried Jamie, gasping for air. "It's too hot. I can't breathe. Somebody help me!" She reached over to ring the bell, but she dropped it. Jamie watched it fall into a large hole in the ice. "Help!"

Her cries for help jerked Kate awake. She ran into Jamie's room. Her granddaughter was writhing on the bed, moaning. Kate touched Jamie's forehead.

"She's burning up! Ben! Get up here!"

Ben bounded up the stairs, medicine in hand.

"Try to hold her still, and I'll get this stuff down her," he ordered.

Katherine put her hands on Jamie's shoulders and spoke soothingly to her. "It's okay, honey. I'm right here. It's okay." Jamie responded long enough for Ben to administer the medicine.

"Ben, you stay here while I get a washcloth," Kate instructed. She ran to the bathroom, grabbed a cloth, and stuck it under cool water. She hurried back to the room and placed it on Jamie's feverish head.

"Too hot," the young woman mumbled. "Too many blankets. Watch out for the ice," she warned.

"It's okay, Jamie. You're going to be fine." Kate turned to Ben. "There's a basin under the bathroom sink. Fill it with—"

Ben was out of the room before she could finish. He returned with lukewarm water and extra washcloths.

"We've got to be careful not to give her a chill," he said. "Keep up the washcloths until the medicine kicks in. Then she should be better."

Kate smiled and handed the pharmacist the washcloth. "Thanks for staying, Ben."

He wrung out a fresh cloth and gave it Kate.

"I told you so," he said.

Ben sat down in a chair with the basin on his lap. They continued the washcloth treatment. Jamie tossed and turned, moaning with fever. Finally, the young woman quieted down and fell into a deep sleep.

The next morning, Jamie awoke with a sore throat and the aches and pains of flu. She felt like she'd been through a war.

"Oh, my aching head," she muttered. She tried to sit up but found herself too weak and dizzy.

Kate bustled into the room.

"Good morning, dear," she said, checking Jamie's forehead for fever.

"What's so good about it?"

"You had quite a night," her grandmother said softly. "Scared me half to death!"

Jamie frowned. "Did I act strangely?"

"Well, you were hallucinating because of the fever. That's all. You kept talking about the ice and the blankets."

"Oh no. I was afraid of that. I remember something about the bogeyman and Billy. It's vague to me. I hate that!"

"You mean to tell me that's what happens when you get a fever? Why didn't you tell me?" Kate shook her head. "At least I would have been prepared!"

Jamie sighed and closed her eyes. "I didn't want to worry you. And I was hoping it wouldn't happen, anyway."

"It's over now. Can I bring you something to eat?"

"No, just something to drink. My throat is killing me."

Ben knocked on the open door. "May I come in?" he asked. "It's time for your medicine."

"Mr. Wheelock!" the patient exclaimed. "What are you doing here?"

"It's a long story," he replied, handing her three pills. "Antibiotic and something for your headache and sore throat pain."

"How did you know I—? I give up."

Kate helped Jamie with the medication. After taking a drink of cool water, Jamie put her head back on the pillow.

"How's the fever? Gone?" asked Ben.

"Yes, thank goodness," responded Kate.

"Judah and Billy are here," Ben said. "They wanted to see how you are doing."

There was no response.

"She's asleep, Ben," whispered Kate. "Let's go."

Down in the kitchen, Judah and Billy sat at the table talking quietly.

"This isn't a funeral home," laughed Kate as she entered the kitchen. "You don't have to whisper!"

"We didn't want to disturb Jamie, Mrs. King," said Billy.

"How is she?" asked Judah, his voice reflecting the concern he felt.

"She's sick, just like the doc said she'd be," Ben replied.

"Yes, but it's flu, not the plague, so everybody cheer up, for heaven's sake," exhorted Kate. "Now who wants pancakes?"

"No, Katherine, you are not cooking for us this morning," Ben spoke firmly. "You had a rough night. You need to rest yourself. We were just leaving, right men?"

Judah and Billy hastily agreed and headed for the door.

"If you need anything, just give me a buzz," said Ben as he pulled on his coat. "Tell Jamie not to worry about work this week. I can handle it until she gets better."

"Thank you, Ben." Kate smiled at her old friend. "Thanks again for helping us out."

Billy pulled open the door, and there stood the pastor, his hand raised, ready to knock.

"Good morning, Reverend Jacobsen," Billy greeted him.

"Good morning, Billy. I've come to see how the young lady is doing." He looked around at the men in the foyer. "Apparently so has the rest of Caderville."

"Come on in," said Kate. "They were all just leaving."

The three men left, and Kate escorted the pastor into the parlor.

"I'm sorry I've come so early this morning, but I was concerned. How is Jamie?"

"She's not feeling well, but she'll be fine. She's come down with the flu."

"I'm glad to hear it worked out all right. She gave us quite a scare. I was afraid she'd end up with pneumonia or something."

"No, thank the Lord. It was like you described in your sermon yesterday. The Lord certainly was watching over Jamie at the lake. I want to share it with Jamie."

The pastor gently took Kate's hand. "Be careful what you say, Kate," he said hesitantly. "Now don't take offense, but I don't think she's quite ready to hear it. If we overstep our bounds, it might push her farther away. We each have to find our own way."

"You are a wise man, Reverend Jacobsen," Kate replied. "I know I can be kind of pushy sometimes. Jamie already talked to me about my preaching."

"Good! I'm glad you two can talk! You tell her I was here and that we're praying for her." The pastor stood up. "You look like you could use some rest yourself, Mrs. King. I'll let myself out."

Kate thanked him and sighed with relief after he was gone. She appreciated everyone's concern, but right now all she wanted to do was sleep. The weary grandmother closed her eyes and fell asleep on the green sofa. The old farmhouse sheltered the two exhausted women, and the trouble of the night before dissolved in deep sleep.

Chapter Ten

"You can't use that! Since when is 'en' a word?" Jamie said accusingly.

"It's right here," replied her grandmother. "Mr. Webster will prove me right." She proceeded to read the definition. " 'An en is half the space of an em.' It's right here. Want to read it?"

"Never mind," said Jamie. "Now you're out, and you get four points for it. You win again."

"Better luck next time," Kate said.

"What next time? You always beat me at Scrabble. I only won once, and I think you let me win that time."

"Well, I didn't want you to get discouraged."

"Thanks." Jamie pushed back her covers. "I feel much better. It's been three days. I'm going to get dressed."

"All right, Jamie. I'll fix lunch."

Jamie felt a little weak-kneed as she climbed down the stairs. She settled herself in the living room. The phone rang, and Kate answered it.

"It's for you," she called to Jamie. Jamie could tell by the tone of her grandmother's voice that she wasn't too pleased with the caller. Jamie picked up the phone in the study.

"Hi Chad!" she with a smile in her voice. She heard the click of the kitchen phone as Kate hung up.

"How'd you know it was me?" Chad's voice was a welcome sound to Jamie's ears.

"Never mind how I knew. What's new?"

"What's new? There's been talk all over town about the young woman from California who fell through the ice and barely escaped with her life." Chad sighed. "I turn my back on you for one moment, and you try to kill yourself. Really Jamie, I didn't know you cared!"

Jamie laughed. "You are so vain! I thought you'd be in school today. What's up?"

"They canceled classes this afternoon. So here I am, at home with nothing to do."

"Why don't you come over?"

"Do you think your grandmother would let me in?" asked Chad.

"Of course she will!" said Jamie. "Don't worry about Grandma. Besides, I am bored out of my mind and suffering from a severe case of cabin fever. Maybe you could cheer me up."

"I shall do my best, fair maiden. I'll be over at two o'clock."

Jamie hung up and hugged herself. Chad Braxton was coming! Whenever she thought of him, her heart fairly skipped a beat.

"Those eyes of his! He is so gorgeous," she said to herself. "Jamie, get a grip on yourself. Looks aren't everything." She paused for a moment. "Looks!" she shrieked. "What about me? I'm a total wreck! I must look like something the cat dragged in."

"You don't look that bad," Kate said. She put a tray in front of her grand-daughter. "Cold chicken and mayonnaise, just the way you like it."

"Thanks," Jamie said. "Chad's coming over this afternoon. I hope you don't mind." She braced herself for an argument.

"That's fine, dear. I've got a lot to do this afternoon. I'll stay out of your way." Kate ignored the shocked look on her granddaughter's face. "Besides, it will be nice for you to have some company."

Kate left the room humming a tune. Jamie finished her lunch, trying to digest her grandmother's behavior. Her grandmother had acted a little different all week. Jamie had waited for a sermon about God watching over the sparrows, and how He had watched over Jamie that Sunday. But the sermon had never been delivered, and now Kate was not even protesting Chad Braxton's visit. For a moment, Jamie felt a little disappointed and perhaps unsure of herself. She shrugged off her feelings and climbed the stairs to get ready for Chad. At two o'clock, the blue BMW pulled into the driveway. Jamie let Chad in and showed him to the living room. He looked around the room and through the door.

"Where's your grandmother?" he whispered.

"She's upstairs working on something," Jamie whispered back. "And you don't have to whisper," she laughed aloud.

"What's she doing? Polishing her shotgun?"

"Stop it! She's not that bad," Jamie smiled.

Chad sat down on a rocking chair and looked Jamie over.

"You look a little pale, Jamie," he said with concern. "Maybe I shouldn't have come."

Jamie shook her head. "I'm glad you came. I've got a bad case of cabin fever, but I'm not quite strong enough to hit the road."

Chad leaned forward in the chair. "What can I do to entertain you?" he asked.

The sincerity in Chad's grey eyes touched Jamie's heart. He made her feel special. The young woman's heart stirred with feelings she struggled to ignore.

"Aha!" Chad exclaimed, his eyes catching sight of the Scrabble box. "I haven't played this in years! When I was at Penn State, I was the champ of my dormitory."

He picked up the game and set it up on the coffee table.

"Wonderful," Jamie muttered. "Now I can be soundly beaten by someone other than Grandma."

"Chin up, old girl. Let me dazzle you with my fabulous vocabulary!"

Jamie put up a good fight, but when Chad managed to use all his letters by spelling out "quicken" on a triple word space, she gave up.

"Let's see," figured Chad, engrossed in totalling up his score. "Well, the Q is on a double letter space, so that's twenty; hmm, all together that's thirty-two points. And it's on a triple word space, so that's three times thirty-two. Now what's that?"

"Ninety-six, to be exact," replied a disgusted Jamie.

"Oh, yes, I almost forgot! I get fifty points for playing all my letters! Isn't that wild?"

"Wild. Really wild. You just made one hundred and forty-six points with one play. Can we quit now?"

"How about a coffee break?" Kate walked in with a tray laden with pie and cookies.

"Wow! That smells great!" said Chad. "Good afternoon, Mrs. King."

"Hello, Chad," said Kate. "Would you two like coffee or cocoa?" Emptying the tray's contents on the other end of the coffee table, she glanced at the game. "Whoa! Who made 'quicken'? That's a whopper!"

Jamie flopped back on the couch. "Take a wild guess!"

"Well, it couldn't be you. Must have been Chad."

Chad laughed. "Sounds like you have quite a Scrabble reputation, Jamie."

"Yeah," replied Jamie, "a bad one."

A knock at the back door in the kitchen called Kate away from the post-game analysis.

"Hello, Judah," Jamie heard her grandmother say in the kitchen. "Come on in."

"I can't stay," Judah said. "I'm on my break. I just stopped by for a minute to see how Jamie is doing."

"Come and see for yourself!" said Kate.

"Oh, no, Mrs. K. I'm a mess, I mean I came straight from work, you know, and . . . " He looked down at his grease-stained overalls.

"Who cares? Come on in to the living room." She looked him over. "Just don't sit down or touch anything," she said with a laugh.

Judah reluctantly followed his hostess to the parlor. He knew what to expect. He had seen the BMW in the driveway. He braced himself to be polite to Chad Braxton.

"Hello, Jamie," Judah greeted the young woman. "Braxton."

"Hello, Judah," Jamie said. She had not seen the tall, dark man since he had pulled her from the lake. Somehow, Jamie didn't feel quite so aggravated to see him as she had thought she would be.

"Sorry to interrupt. I just wanted to see—"

"I'm just fine," the young woman replied. "I'll be back to work on Monday."

"You sure you'll be ready?" asked Judah. "You don't want to overdo it."

Jamie smiled and shook her head. "I'll be fine. Thanks for asking."

The gentleness in her voice made Judah's heart pound. Jamie surprised herself with the way she was talking.

"Ever play Scrabble, Weston?" Chad's voice snapped through the air.

Jamie was startled by Chad's tone. Judah merely ignored it.

"No, as a matter of fact I don't," said Judah.

"Oh, that's right. I guess the vocabulary of a mechanic wouldn't cut it, would it?" sneered Chad.

"You're rather an imperious fellow, aren't you, Braxton?" Judah replied smoothly.

"Touché!" said Kate under her breath.

"I've got to get back to work," Judah said. "I'm glad you're feeling better, Jamie."

"I'll walk you out," Kate volunteered hastily.

After Judah left, Jamie turned to Chad with a questioning look. "What was that all about?" she demanded.

"What?" asked Chad innocently.

" 'Do you play Scrabble, Judah?' Mechanic's vocabulary? Why were you baiting him?" She stared at him in amazement.

"Oh, that! I just like to rile the guy, that's all. He is such an uptight dude," Chad said. "Besides, maybe I should ask you the same question."

"What?"

"What was that all about? Your sweet alluring voice when you spoke to that idiot," challenged Chad. "Do you have a crush on him?"

Jamie turned bright red. "You're crazy, Chad Braxton!" She threw a pillow at him. Then she stopped short of throwing another one.

"Wait a second," she said accusingly. "Do I detect a hint of jealousy here?"

Chad bit his lip. "Ouch," he said. "You weren't supposed to notice." He sat down next to Jamie on the sofa. "I know he saved you from the evil clutches of Blueberry Swamp, but that doesn't mean you have to fall for the guy." He moved closer to her. "After all, I'm better looking, more suave, and a lot more fun, don't you think?"

He gazed intently into Jamie's eyes with a look of sincere desire. Jamie swallowed hard. He was so hard to resist. She took in his perfect hair, his perfect eyes, his perfect lips. Chad seized the moment and leaned over to kiss her. Jamie closed her eyes in anticipation.

Smash! Clatter! Clang! The kiss never came. Kate dropped the large metal serving tray just outside the parlor door. Chad nearly jumped out of his skin.

"Oops!" Katherine apologized. "Dropped my teeth!"

She picked up the tray and walked through the livingroom doorway, laughing. "That's what my father used to say if anyone dropped something that made a huge noise: 'Did you drop your teeth?' He was a jokester, my father."

"I thought it was a shotgun," Chad blurted out, with an emphasis on the word shotgun.

"Silly boy!" Kate busied herself with cups and plates.

Jamie suddenly felt very tired. *I don't believe this is happening,* she thought.

"I'll take that," Chad said. He picked up the tray to carry it to the kitchen. "I better be going now, anyway. You look tired, Jamie."

Jamie nodded and let out a long sigh. "You're right. All this excitement has drained my energy."

"Don't get up," smiled Chad. "Your grandmother will see me out, I'm sure."

Jamie laughed. "Thanks for coming Chad."

"My pleasure," he said aloud. "Almost," he whispered.

"Stop!" Jamie hushed him. "She's not deaf, you know."

He grinned, balanced the tray on one hand, and tipped an imaginary hat.

"Don't drop that tray!" Kate called from the kitchen.

"I'm coming," responded Chad. He winked at Jamie and left her alone in the parlor with her thoughts.

When she heard his car start up, Jamie lay down and closed her eyes. The last thing she heard before she fell asleep was her grandmother in the kitchen whistling "Onward, Christian Soldiers."

Chapter Eleven

"Jamie! Your dad's on the phone!" Kate called upstairs to her granddaughter.

Jamie went into her grandmother's room and picked up the extension. "I've got it, Grandma," she said into the receiver.

"Dad?"

"Jamie girl! How are you? Been ice skating lately?" Her father's deep laugh filled Jamie's ear.

"Very funny, Dad," Jamie said. "That was two months ago."

"So how's everything?"

"Fine. I work, I eat, I sleep. I play Scrabble."

"No excitement?"

"Well, not really," Jamie hesitated. *What was he driving at?*

"Your grandmother tells us there's a new man in your life!" Her father's voice sounded ever so slightly agitated.

Jamie let go an audible sigh. "You mean Chad?"

"That's the one. Chad Braxton, I believe?"

"What about him?"

"Kate doesn't seem to like him very much, Jamie girl. And that must mean he's like one of the good-for-nothing jerks you hung around with at college." His voice tightened with displeasure. "Who is he?"

"Dad," Jamie began, her blood beginning to boil, "his father owns the theater, he's a senior at SUNY Lamberton, it happens to be none of your business, and I would hang up on you but you're my father!"

There was silence on the other end of the line. Jamie's father cleared his throat. Jamie could hear her mother's frustrated "Dan!" in the background.

"I'm sorry, Jamie. I didn't intend to call and interfere. You know I care about you, and I worry about who you spend your time with. You know what your mother always says—"

" 'He who walks with the wise grows wise, but a companion of fools suffers harm.' Proverbs 13:20," Jamie quoted in a singsong voice. "She made me memorize it when I was a kid. Give me a break. Dad, I'm twenty-two, remember? When are you going to accept the fact that I am not your little girl anymore?"

"Okay, okay, let's not get started again on the 'I'm not a child anymore' argument. We've been over that enough as it is. But as for it being none of my business, you will always be my business, even when you're fifty-two." He paused a moment. "Let's make a deal. I'll let you know what I think, but I won't tell you what to do, how's that?"

"Deal," responded Jamie. "Now, how's mom?"

"She's uh, fine."

Jamie noticed a slight change in her father's voice. "What's the matter, Dad? Is she all right?"

"Yes, she's fine," he said quickly, handing his wife the phone.

"Hi honey, how's it going?" Ellen Carrigan's voice was strained.

"What's the matter, Mom? You sound funny. What's going on?"

Jamie's mother ignored the question. "We've got a surprise for you. We're flying out for Easter."

"Great!" Jamie exclaimed. As much as she was glad to be away from home, she did miss her parents. "That's only a few weeks away."

"I've got another surprise as well," said Ellen. "Your friend from college wants to come and spend a few weeks with you this summer."

"You mean Cassie? Fantastic!" Jamie fairly shrieked.

"We'll talk about it at Easter. I don't want Grandma to get worn out."

"Grandma won't mind! You know, the more the merrier. It'll be great!"

"We'll discuss it then. Take care of yourself. Now let me talk to Grandma."

Jamie called down to Kate, and then she hung up the phone. She went back to her own room and flopped onto her bed. In her excitement about seeing everyone, she had forgotten to pursue the subject of her mother. *Why did she sound so strange? And what was up with Dad?* Jamie felt a knot form in her stomach.

"I don't know," she thought aloud. "I've got a bad feeling that something's really wrong. What could it possibly be?"

"Jamie, can you come here?" Kate called up the stairs.

"Coming!" Jamie answered. She bounded down the stairs and into the kitchen. "What's up?"

Katherine stood over the stove, stirring up something in an old iron pot.

"Take this out to Merlin, would you?" she asked. She poured the contents of the pot into a large dog-food bowl.

"What kind of concoction is that?" Jamie asked, wrinkling her nose.

"It's a special mush for Merlin. I think he's feeling a bit poorly today. Your grandfather used to make this for the animals whenever they took sick. It works wonders."

"Wonder Mush. Why don't you market it?" Jamie laughed over her shoulder. She got her coat and pulled it on.

Kate handed her the bowl. "Here. Nurse for a day."

Jamie took the bowl and hesitated. "Grandma, did you notice anything strange today about Mom and Dad?"

A serious look flitted across Kate's face and was gone. "No, I don't think there was anything really—"

"Grandma!" demanded Jamie. "I can tell when you're avoiding an issue. What's going on?"

Kate patted Jamie's cheek. "Nothing your Mom and Dad can't handle," she said. But her eyebrows knit together betrayed the concern she felt in her heart.

Jamie braved the cold March wind and pulled open the barn door. Azalia and Merlin both turned their heads to see who was their latest visitor. The annoyed look on their faces said, "Shut the door and be quick about it."

"You old dears," Jamie murmured sweetly to the pair of animals. "Look Merlin, I've got just what the doctor ordered: Wonder Mush."

She stuck the bowl in front of the elderly horse. He nodded his thanks and began to eat, with a jealous Azalia looking on.

"Good morning, Jamie," a voice spoke from the back of the barn.

"Judah!" Jamie sucked in her breath. "Why do you insist on sneaking around and scaring me half to death all the time?"

"If you call parking a fire-engine-red truck in plain view of the house, sneaking around, I guess I'm guilty. Sorry I startled you. Again."

"It's okay," Jamie said. She peered over into the corner of the barn. "How's your wild horse doing?"

Judah came out from among the shadows and smiled at Jamie. "He's not wild, honest. Come here and feed him some sugar."

Jamie hesitated. "I'd rather keep my distance."

"Come on," Judah insisted. "Come here."

The young woman walked slowly toward the back of the barn.

"Hold out your hand," Judah said.

Jamie held out her hand, and Judah placed two lumps of sugar on her palm. Speaking softly to the stallion, Judah cupped his own hand beneath Jamie's and guided it close to the horse's mouth. Shadow eyed Jamie for a moment and then took the sugar.

"See, he's not wild. He just needs to get to know you. Let's try it again."

Out came more sugar, and Judah cradled Jamie's hand in his own. Jamie thought she felt his hand tremble for a moment. She studied his face. He didn't look at her but concentrated on the horse. *I wonder what you're thinking, right now,* the young woman thought. At his touch, Jamie herself felt something faintly stir in her heart. *No way,* she thought.

"Mother Teresa," she said aloud, trying to snap herself out of the gentle intimacy of the moment. "St. Francis of Assisi."

"What?" Judah stood back. "What in the world are you talking about?"

"I'm talking about you. You are too nice, too good. You're a perfect saint."

Judah shook his head and leaned against the stall.

"I'm not perfect, Jamie," he said seriously. "I've made my share of mistakes."

"You mean you have sinned?" Jamie questioned in mock horror. "What did you do? Sing the wrong note at choir rehearsal? Set the table wrong at the church potluck dinner?"

"No, Jamie. It doesn't matter. What matters is I'm forgiven."

Jamie smirked, glad to get back to reality with Judah. "Spare me," she responded.

"Anyway," smiled Judah, "see, Shadow isn't wild. You can probably feed him sugar by yourself the next time. Once he gets to know you, he's a friend for life."

Jamie looked admiringly at the horse. "He is beautiful," she said.

"Yeah," Judah said, looking at Jamie. "Beautiful."

The young woman blushed. "I've got to go," she said. She grabbed the emptied bowl from Merlin and turned to leave. "See you later."

"Bye, Princess."

Jamie hurried out of the barn. It was a relief to feel the cold wind against her face. *I have got to snap out of this,* she thought. *Seems like every time I'm with Judah I get confused. This is ridiculous. You'd think I had a crush on him or something.*

At such a thought Jamie stopped short and dropped Merlin's bowl.

"No way, heart of mine," she commanded aloud. "Remember the dream I had, chains and all. No way!"

Judah stood in the barn, with the feel of Jamie's hand still burning on his own.

Chapter Twelve

The air was clear and sweet with the aroma of spring. Jamie breathed in slowly and savored her favorite herald of the new season. The smell of mud and rain and new grass invigorated Jamie's senses. Winter was over!

It was visiting day. Grandmother and granddaughter were on their way to Sadie Atkins' house. Jamie always enjoyed these times with her grandmother. Whoever they visited always had stories to tell, stories that gave Jamie a glimpse into the past.

"I'll drive," Jamie volunteered. "I bet that road up to Sadie's is a mess with mud."

"I will gladly yield the wheel to you, my dear. If we end up in a ditch, it will be your fault."

"Never fear, Richard Petty is here!" Jamie announced.

"Richard who?" Kate asked.

"Never mind," Jamie groaned. "Let's go."

Sadie lived up on Jasmine Hill Road, five miles out of town. The road was paved only part way, and Sadie's was the last house on the route. Jamie carefully maneuvered the car over muddy bumps and ridges. At last they reached the top of the hill. Sadie's house perched on the hill like a lone bird. Despite its peeling paint, the old house had a sturdy look that declared it would be there another hundred years. The windows of the Atkins' home were framed precariously by dark green shutters which had obviously seen better days. A couple of vagrant shutters were leaned up against the foot of the house. Stretched lazily across the front of the building was a long inviting porch.

Katherine and Jamie climbed the porch steps. A pleasant-faced, middle-aged woman greeted the two visitors at the door.

"So glad you could come," the woman said warmly. She smiled at Jamie. "You must be Katherine's granddaughter. How are you feeling? We heard about your fall."

"I'm just fine," replied Jamie. *Good grief,* she thought. *Branded for life. They'll probably put it on my tombstone: Jamie Carrigan: The Girl Who Fell Through the Ice.*

"My name's Margret. I'm Sadie's granddaughter."

"How are you holding up, Margret?" Kate gave her a kiss. "Is Sadie behaving herself?"

"Oh, you know Grandma Sadie. She's got a mind of her own!"

"And a clear mind it is, too!" Sadie said indignantly. She stepped out from behind Margret. "Thank your stars I'm not a brainless wonder like old Ed

Calhoun. Sits around his house all day, doin' nothin' but watch game shows and talk to his dog. Why, at his age, you'd think he'd be up and about doin' somethin'!"

"Grandma," Margret said gently. "The man is eighty-five years old. He's not a spring chicken! And what are you doing out of your chair? You're supposed to call me when you want to get up!"

Sadie ignored her granddaughter and hit the floor with her cane. "At eighty-five I was helpin' out at the library every Tuesday. Why, I bet Ed Calhoun hasn't cracked open a book in twenty years." Sadie pursed her lips and shook her head. "He came here the other day, looking for all the world like a string of suckers."

"A string of suckers!" Jamie blurted out. All she could picture in her mind was a row of lollipops.

Margret guided Sadie back into the parlor. Kate and Jamie followed them.

"A string of suckers, young lady, refers to a line of fish." Sadie sat down slowly into her rocking chair. "Suckers," she explained, "are good-for-nothing fish with thick lips that stick out like a princess looking for a frog. You can eat 'em, but they're so darned bony it takes about ten to make a mouthful. People used to fish 'em out of the river here and hang a bunch all in a row on a fishing string. Pitiful lookin' thing, a string of suckers, their fleshy lips and skinny bodies just a hangin' there, eyes all staring at nothing. Anyway, I asked old Calhoun what was the matter, did his dog die, or what. Well, he set his mournful eyes on me and said his TV was broken. Said it would be days before it would be fixed." She snorted in disgust. "I guess Vanna White keeps his heart beatin'."

Jamie tried very hard not to laugh out loud, but she couldn't help it. Sadie smiled and peered through her glasses at Jamie, looking her up and down.

"Why don't you do something with your hair?" she asked abruptly. "Hangs there like a mane. You're not a horse are you? Anyhow, you don't look like a horse."

The surprised young woman gulped and shot a questioning look at Kate. Grandma Kate winked at Jamie in an effort to put her at ease.

"Sadie! You certainly do have a way of speaking whatever's on your mind, don't you?"

"Rude, that's what Margret calls it. She says I'm as rude as a blue jay in winter when the feeder's full." The old woman pulled her soft blue sweater closed and folded her arms across her chest. "And at my age, I don't care. I'll say what I think if I feel like it. Otherwise I'll keep quiet." She smiled at Jamie. "Never mean any harm, though."

The young woman smiled back. She was getting used to Sadie. She hoped Mrs. Atkins would tell some of her stories about Caderville at the turn of the century. Jamie was beginning to realize she had a deepening interest in history and storytelling. Perhaps her time with Grandma Kate was bearing fruit after all. At least if she went back to college in the fall, she knew what her major would be.

Margret walked into the parlor with her coat in hand. "I hope you don't mind, but I'm going to run to the store while you all are here. We need a few things, and I can't leave Grandma alone. Do you mind?"

"Of course not," Kate responded. "You take your time." She got up and walked Margret to the door. "Why don't you stop somewhere and have yourself a nice sandwich, or something?" Kate whispered. "I know you must need a little break from being cooped up here all week."

Margret sighed wearily and nodded. "I sure could use a little pampering myself! Between tending to Grandma during the day and the kids at night, I'm beat!"

"Run along, then," Kate gave her a friendly push toward the door. "We'll be here when you get back."

Kate returned to the parlor to find Sadie and Jamie poring over an old photo album.

"Now what family secrets are you going to tell us today, Sadie?" she asked.

"Pshaw!" Sadie chuckled. "We don't really have too many skeletons in our closets." She paused and then pointed to a faded picture of a young man leaning against a tree. "Unless you count Jackson Atkins. He was my husband's uncle. He was a gambler. They used to say he'd gamble away his own mother if he was desperate enough. And he usually was. Desperate, I mean.

"Why, my husband used to tell how Uncle Jackson bet their father's chicken coop in a game of twenty-one. And he lost. The next morning, two strangers came and started dismantlin' the coop. Right in front of Jackson's father. He didn't take too kindly to that and run 'em off with a loaded shotgun. He told 'em they had a choice: either all bets were off or their heads were! Well, they hightailed it out of there and never came back." Sadie sighed. "Not long after, Jackson left the farm and headed for Nevada."

Jamie pointed to an oval photograph mounted on faded brown cardboard. "Who's that?"

A warm smile brightened Sadie Atkins' face.

"That's my Charlie."

"Charles T. Atkins," Kate chimed in. "He was a fine man, Sadie."

Sadie nodded and lay a gnarled finger gently on the picture. "Charlie was a good man, Kate, one of the best. Like your John was." The elderly woman reached over and patted Kate on the hand.

"We met at the county fair in 1910. I was fifteen years old." Sadie looked up and her blue eyes seemed to gaze right back into the past.

"He was showin' a calf at the fair, and my daddy was in the market for a calf.

That's where I first saw him. He was brushin' his calf and looked right over at me. The bluest eyes I'd ever seen. He had the Atkins nose, though. You could hang your hat on it. But anyhow, it was love at first sight. We got married two years later."

Kate reached for an old tintype tucked in the back of the album and placed it in Sadie's hand. "Tell Jamie about her."

Sadie fingered the tintype carefully. Jamie leaned forward to get a better look. Despite the deterioration, it was clear that the young woman in the picture had been beautiful. Her hair was swept up in a bun, and her features were delicate.

"Emily Reed," said Sadie.

Emily. That name rang a bell.

"The young pastor and the logger's Emily!" Jamie exclaimed.

Sadie eyes twinkled with amusement at the sight of Jamie's enthusiasm.

"I see you've told her the story," she said to Kate.

"Oh, yes," replied her friend. "Many times. I guess she finds it hard to believe anything exciting or romantic could happen in Caderville."

Sadie shook her head. "There's lots of love stories to be told about Caderville, young lady," she said. "Loves found, loves lost, loves that just plain dwindled away. Like any other town, I suppose."

"What about Emily?" Jamie asked expectantly. "Did your family know her? And did your grandmother really get a letter from the pastor and her? Or is that just a rumor?"

"Whoa, slow down. Give me a chance, and I'll tell you what I know."

Jamie was all ears.

"My family has a long tradition of handing down stories, stories about the family and the country they live in. My mother and her mother before her could describe the lives and happenings of our people down to the smallest detail. Of course, I never knew Emily. I wasn't even born then! But I know what she was like and what happened to her. I never saw that young pastor, but in my mind's eyes I can see his flaming eyes and curly hair. They said he had a voice like an angel when he preached, and he'd get so fired up with the Word of God that he'd pace around the pulpit, his black curls falling over his forehead, his eyes flashin'.

"Anyway, you know the story. He fell in love with Emily and she with him, and they left Caderville."

"But what about the fire and the letter—"

"Emily's fiancé, Tom Sanders, was a cruel man. Emily knew Tom would try to stop the reverend and her, so they made plans to leave. On the night the pastor usually had his prayer time, he left a lamp on in the church to make it look like he was there. Now, Tom Sanders could burn down a barn in twenty minutes. He knew just what to do. They say he must have sneaked into the church and locked the study door from the outside, thinking the reverend was there. Then he set the church afire. It was burnt almost to the ground by the time anyone even knew it was on fire."

Katherine had disappeared and returned with a cup of tea for Sadie. The old woman accepted it gratefully. The room was quiet for a few minutes as the old woman warmed herself with the tea. Jamie looked around at the antique furnishings. There was a large china closet filled with all kinds of plates, cups, saucers, and pitchers. Some were blue willow, others were creamy white with pink roses painted in garlands along the rims.

Sadie continued her story: "Of course, everyone was mortified. They began planning a funeral until it was discovered that Emily and her few belongings were gone too. Well, they ran Tom Sanders out of town. Mr. Cader rebuilt the church. And that was that."

"What about the letter? Was there really a letter sent to someone from India?"

Sadie adjusted the glasses on her nose and continued. "My grandmother and Emily were—"

"Just let us know when you get tired, Sadie," Kate interjected. "We don't want to wear you out."

Sadie frowned at Kate. "I'd rather be tired from doing somethin' than tired from doin' nothin'."

"Anyway," she began again, "my grandmother and Emily were best friends. One day, several months after the fire, my grandmother received a letter from Emily and the reverend."

Jamie almost fell off her chair with excitement.

"Really?" Jamie exclaimed. "Your grandmother?"

The old woman scowled. "You think I'm making this up?" She sniffed and went on with the story.

"The return address was labeled Serampore, India. They asked that only their close friends be told what they were doing. Well, Grandma made the mistake of telling Luella Haverstraw. Luella was a talker. She could talk and talk. It didn't matter if she was a talkin' to an adult or a child. As long as it was breathin', she was talkin'. When Mama was a child, she used to hide under the kitchen table whenever Luella came to call on Grandma. Once she had your ear, she wouldn't let go!"

Sadie let go a laugh that crackled in the air. "Pretty soon it was all over town about the reverend and his new bride." Jamie smiled and soaked in the history. Her mind wandered to the young couple who had escaped to fulfill their love for each other. And for God, Jamie guessed. She tried to imagine the trip across the ocean to India. It must have been frightening, but they had had each other.

Sadie saw the look in Jamie's eyes and got up slowly from her rocking chair. She walked over to the china closet that stood in the corner of the room. She opened the glass door and carefully pulled a long manila envelope from beneath a rose-covered gravy boat.

"I haven't shown this letter to anyone in thirty-five years," said Sadie abruptly, "and now I'm a-showin' it to you." Jamie's eyes grew wide with the realization that she was about to see *the* letter. Sadie sat down and painstakingly pulled some papers from the envelope. She handed Jamie a carefully preserved envelope dated 1852.

The young woman fingered the envelope and stared at the words, "Serampore, India." *I'm touching history,* she thought. Then Sadie gave her the letter. The handwriting was graceful but faded. It was hard to make out the words. She squinted, trying to make out the name signed at the bottom.

"That's his name," Sadie explained. "He wrote the letter. Here." She handed another paper to Jamie. "This is a copy of the letter one of my daughters typed out for me years ago."

Jamie eagerly read the letter. She felt a little guilty, as if she were intruding on someone's privacy. The letter briefly described their hurried wedding, presided over by a pastor friend in New York City, and then recounted the tumultuous passage to India.

But one paragraph in particular leapt out at Jamie: "I cannot say what we did was right. I am ashamed and worried that perhaps you will think less of me. Yet I would cross the ocean again for her. Indeed it was out of fear for her life, not mine, that I took her away. As dear as our love is, however, we have both discovered how precious is another treasure we brought with us to this land—the Gospel of our Lord Jesus Christ. The people here flock pitifully around us to see His light, and I am put to tears at the sight of their earnest desire. O that I would handle His Gospel with the care and love that it demands, whether I be in the valleys of the Delaware or the darkened byways of Serampore."

Jamie finished the letter and glanced at the name of its writer. Isaac Weston.

"Weston?" Jamie questioned. "You mean like in—"

"Judah Weston. No, not necessarily any relation to the Westons of Hillside," Kate could read her granddaughter's mind.

"You never know," Sadie piped up. "No one ever asked those Westons about where they came from."

The young woman examined the original letter again. She lightly traced the flowing letters that formed the young man's name.

"Okay, Juliet, I think we've had enough romance for today," Kate said, getting up from her chair. "I think I hear Margret's car. We'd better get going so Sadie can take a nap."

Sadie restored the letters to the safety of the breakfront. A car horn honked in the front yard. Almost simultaneously, a loud crash ripped through the air with a bang.

"Good glory!" Sadie yelled.

Kate ran out to the front of the house. "The roof?" she cried over her shoulder.

Jamie quickly followed her grandmother. She stopped at the sound of Sadie laughing, laughing so hard she was doubled over in her rocking chair.

"It's not the roof!" she cackled. "It's one of those blamed shutters." The ninety-three-year-old woman wiped tears of laughter from her eyes. Kate returned. "It's a shutter," she started to explain, "one of 'em must've fallen off and hit the roof of the porch—" She stopped and looked at Sadie. "What are you laughing at?"

"You!" she crowed. "You ran out of here like Chicken Little on Judgment Day! I haven't seen you move so fast since that time old Bob Henderson tried to ask you out on a date at the church bazaar."

Sadie started laughing again, and this time Jamie joined her. "You should have seen your face, Grandma."

Margret entered with an armful of groceries.

"What's so funny?" she asked.

"You don't want to know," replied Kate. She smiled and gave Sadie a hug. "We've got to go now. You'd better lie down." She turned to Margret. "I think we've worn her out. She's been telling Jamie all about Emily and Isaac."

Margret smiled at Jamie. "Romantic story, isn't it?" she asked. "I used to make her tell me that story over and over."

After thanking their hostess for a lovely time and promising to come again, grandmother and granddaughter drove back down the hill and headed toward home.

"Bob Henderson?" Jamie inquired sweetly.

"Never mind," Kate muttered.

"Is he cute?"

"Jamie!"

Chapter Thirteen

The canary yellow rent-a-car drove determinedly through Caderville without stopping. A mile from town, it turned left onto a dirt road and soon approached the red mailbox. It hesitated at the mouth of the driveway. The occupants of the car were engaged in a heated discussion, words and emotions flying.

In an effort to buy time, the car passed the mailbox and continued for another mile. The couple reached a temporary truce and bottled up their feelings for the time being. The car turned around and reapproached the red mailbox. It turned up the driveway and came to a stop. Silent and reluctant, the man and woman sat for a moment, enclosed by the brightly colored automobile.

The front door of the house flew open. Jamie ran down the walk with a yell. "Mom! Dad!"

Ellen took a deep breath and pushed open her door. She threw her arms around her only child and held her tight. Dan Carrigan waited his turn and kissed his daughter on the cheek.

"Jamie girl, you look great!" he said with genuine affection. "I guess all this fresh air is doing you some good after all!"

"Oh, Dad," said Jamie. She studied her parents' faces to see if there was anything different. Since their last conversation, Jamie had never been able to shake the feeling that something was wrong. Right now they just looked tired. Probably tired from the trip.

"Come on inside," Jamie directed. "Grandma's got a big dinner ready for you city slickers."

They laughed and followed Jamie into the farmhouse. Kate gave them a warm welcome, and they sat down to a delicious meal. On the surface, everything appeared to be normal. The family caught up on each other's lives, but in the most general terms. Jamie could sense an undercurrent of tension between her parents; so could Katherine.

In an effort to break the tension, Jamie talked about college. "I think I know what I want to major in," she said excitedly.

Dan and Ellen perked up. "You mean you actually have some direction to go in?" Jamie's father teased.

"Dad!" Jamie exclaimed in exasperation. "I'm serious. I want to study history and literature."

"That sounds wonderful," said Ellen warmly.

"What are you going to do with it?" Dan asked, ever the practical voice of reason.

"I want to write," his daughter replied.

"Write what?"

"Dan!" Ellen scolded. "Write stories, of course, maybe a novel or two, right Jamie?"

"That's it," Jamie nodded enthusiastically. "Maybe I'll try some journalism too. At any rate, that is the direction I'm shooting for. I want to be a writer."

"Not much money in writing, is there? Unless you write macabre stuff or that lusty love junk that sells today," mused Dan.

"How about macabre lusty junk?" Jamie laughed.

"Very funny," Kate chimed in. "There's enough trash out there today as it is!"

"Actually, Jamie, you were always making up stories when you were little," Ellen reminded her.

"Yeah, like the time you said it was your Raggedy Ann who wet the bed," Dan grinned.

"Dad!"

"No, I don't mean like that! I mean you used to make up stories about princes and princesses and your dog Buffy, things like that."

Jamie sat back in her chair. "I'd forgotten all about that!" she exclaimed. "Maybe it's in my blood to tell stories, like Sadie Atkins and her family."

"Sadie who?" Dan asked.

"Never mind," said Jamie. "Enough about me. What have you two been up to besides work and church?"

Dan and Ellen fell over each other in an effort to sound normal.

"Oh, nothing much," Dan replied. "just the usual. Golfing with the guys. Keeping up with the yard. Dodging earthquakes. I just love California!" he smirked.

"What about you, Mom?"

"Well, Jamie, your Dad's been working a lot of overtime lately. So if I'm not working at the church, I'm just sitting at home," her voice cracked. "Excuse me," she said, getting up from the table. "I'm not feeling well. I've got to lie down."

"You go right ahead, dear. It's a long trip from California. You must be exhausted."

Ellen fairly ran up the stairs. Jamie could hear the door close with a bang. She looked over at her father.

"What's going on, Dad," Jamie demanded. "Something is wrong, and I want to know what it is. Is Mom sick or something?"

Dan Carrigan put his elbows on the table and covered his face with his hands. "No, she's not sick," he said with resignation. He rubbed his eyes and yawned. "I don't want to talk about it right now, okay Jamie? Besides," he reached across the table and patted Jamie's hand. "It's nothing for you to worry about. She'll be just fine."

Kate didn't say a word but began to clear the table. Jamie sat staring at her father. "I want to know what's going on," she insisted.

"And I said I don't want to talk about it!" Dan snapped. He got up abruptly and stomped through the kitchen and out the back door.

Kate's troubled look only succeeded in fomenting Jamie's anxiety. "Oh Grandma," she whispered. "You don't think it's serious, do you?"

Kate stopped clearing and sat down next to Jamie. "It's obvious they're having problems, but how serious it is I don't know. Only they know, and only they can work it out." She took Jamie by the hand. "You've got to try and stay out of it."

Jamie felt like she was going to throw up. "But Mom looks so upset, and Dad seems like he's going to explode. What if—"

"No 'what ifs' allowed, young lady. Jesus said not to worry about tomorrow, but to let tomorrow worry about itself."

Jamie sighed. "I'll try, Grandma. But it's not going to be easy."

Out in the yard, Dan Carrigan stopped midstride at the sight of Judah leading Shadow out of the barn. "He's a beautiful horse," Dan commented. He took a deep breath of the early evening air. He was glad to be out of the house, away from everybody.

"Thanks," said Judah. He turned the stallion loose in the corral behind the barn. "Judah Weston," he said, offering Dan a handshake.

"Dan Carrigan. So you're Judah. Kate's often spoken of you. Says you're a big help to her."

"I try to help out as much as I can." Judah disappeared into the barn and returned with a saddle. He whistled for Shadow who immediately obeyed, submitting to blanket and saddle.

"So you're Jamie's father," Judah said as he tightened the saddle.

"Yes, Jamie's my little girl." He laughed. "She'd have a fit if she knew I said that."

"You're not kidding," Judah said, half to himself. "Your wife must be beautiful."

"What?"

"Jamie is a beautiful girl. I figure her mom is probably pretty too."

"Uh, yeah, Ellen is—" he spoke haltingly, as if he hadn't thought about it in a long time. "Yes, she is pretty. Like mother, like daughter."

Judah mounted his horse with ease and looked down at Jamie's father. "Nice meeting you, Mr. Carrigan."

"It's Dan. And by the way, how's Jamie doing, anyway? Do you spend much time with her?"

Judah shook his head. "She and I don't see eye-to-eye on too many things. I try to steer clear of her. Besides, I've been told more than once to mind my own business."

"Sounds like Jamie," sighed Dan. "I don't want to sound like a detective, but what about a guy named Chad Braxton? Kate's mentioned him and—"

"That's another whole subject," Judah replied. Dan noticed a hint of fire in the young man's eyes. "I've got to go." Judah nudged Shadow and steered him toward the road. "Have a nice evening, sir."

"Thanks." He watched Judah disappear down the road in the muted light of dusk. Shoving his hands into his pockets, Dan turned reluctantly toward the house.

Chapter Fourteen

Jamie awoke the next morning and for a moment forgot why she felt so down. Then yesterday's scenario replayed itself in her mind and she remembered.

"Mom and Dad," she whispered.

During the night, Jamie thought she had heard the muffled sounds of her mother weeping.

"I'm so glad they came to visit," she said wryly.

At the breakfast table, Dan was missing.

"He went out for the paper," Ellen answered the question in Jamie's eyes.

"Want some pancakes?" Kate asked her granddaughter.

"No thanks," Jamie answered. "I'm not hungry."

"Even if I make it into the shape of a kangaroo? Remember how I used to do that when you were little?"

"No thanks, Grandma." Jamie retreated to the living room.

Ellen followed her daughter and signalled Kate to join them.

"I have something I want to say to you," Ellen said quietly.

Kate sat down. Jamie stayed in front of the fireplace, staring intently into the flames.

"Jamie, I know you realize there is something wrong between me and your Dad. I'm not going to get into the details with you, but I will say this much. Every marriage has its rough spots. We're not immune, and right now we happen to be having a difficult time." Ellen walked over to Jamie and put an arm around her. "I don't want you to worry. Everything will be all right."

Jamie looked at her mother with tears in her eyes. "You don't sound so convincing, Mom. How do you know it's going to be okay? How do you know?"

Ellen turned away, unable to speak. Kate hurried over to her daughter and drew her into her arms. Jamie looked at the two standing there, mother and daughter crying together. She couldn't take it. She bolted from the room.

Jamie ran out of the house and into the field. Her tears blurred her vision. She couldn't see the trees dressed in April buds of promise. Jamie felt as though the foundations of her life were crumbling beneath her feet. Nothing made sense. One minute she was in a ship heading somewhere, then suddenly she was lost on a storm-tossed dingy. There had to be more to life than this. This was crazy.

Just then a horn honked and a car pulled into the driveway. *Chad!* Jamie quickly wiped her tears and ran to his car.

"Hey baby, how about going for a ride?" proposed the young man.

"I'd love to!" Jamie pulled open the passenger door. "Get me out of here!"

Chad looked quizzically at Jamie, shrugged, and threw the car into gear.

"Your wish is my command!"

The BMW flew out the driveway, barely missing the yellow car that was just pulling in.

By the time they reached town, Jamie had pulled herself together.

"You're out and about early this morning," she said to Chad.

"Yeah, well, it's Easter break and there's nothing going on. Thought I'd see if you and I could stir up some action in good old Caderville." He glanced at his passenger. "Are you okay?"

"I'm fine," Jamie replied. "Family problems. That's all."

"Don't say another word about it," said Chad. "I make it a policy never to get involved in family problems."

His words seemed a little cold to Jamie, but she didn't really want to talk about it anyway. She opened her window and let the morning air bathe her face with coolness. *Maybe I'm overreacting,* she thought. *Maybe it is just a rough time and they'll work it out. Don't worry, Grandma Kate always said. "The only thing worrying changes is the look on your face. It gives you wrinkles."* Jamie had to agree. Her anxiety over her parents was draining her energy. She decided to put the problem out of her mind. At least she'd try.

Chad stopped at one of the two traffic lights in Caderville. A black mustang pulled up beside the blue BMW.

"Who's the babe?" asked the driver of the mustang.

"This is Jamie," Chad replied. "Say hello, Jamie."

"Hello Jamie," Jamie said.

"Hey, a real comedienne!"

"That's kind of a long word for you, Luger."

"Very funny, Braxton. How about a little race?"

Chad's eyes gleamed at the prospect. "And the stakes?" he asked.

"Case of beer?"

"You're on!"

They revved their engines. Jamie grabbed Chad's arm.

"Are you crazy?" she asked incredulously. "We're in the middle of town!"

"Who cares?" Chad laughed. "By the time the local yokel sheriff wakes up and gets his shoes on, we'll be halfway to Lamberton!"

"Oh, great, just great," Jamie said sarcastically. "Drag racing at 8 a.m in the middle of town. Brilliant. Do you suppose your father will spring for bail?"

"Lighten up! I told you we'd stir up some excitement. And I'm a man of my word!"

"Hey, let's cut the conference," demanded Luger. "Are we on or what?"

"We're on."

They gunned their engines. The light turned green. They took off, tires squealing.

"Yeehaw!" Chad whooped.

Both cars hit seventy in a matter of seconds. Jamie watched the speedometer tip toward eighty. The mustang straddled the yellow line while Chad maintained the lane. Jamie's heart was pounding. Caderville passed by in a blur. Luckily the road was clear, and in two minutes they were out of town. They raced up the ramp to route 17. The mustang pulled ahead. Chad chased him for several miles, then gave up with a laugh.

"That Luger! He's got quite an engine under that hood!" Chad slowed the car down to sixty-five. He looked over at Jamie. Her hands were covering her face.

"Are we dead yet?" she asked, her voice muffled by her hands.

"Jamie, lighten up! Wasn't that fun? Didn't your heart beat faster and your palms sweat and your mind swim with that fabulous dizziness that comes from flirting with the edge?"

"The edge of what? A cliff? Chad, you scared me half to death. And besides, I'm not into life-threatening sports."

Chad reached over and put his hand on Jamie's leg.

"I'm sorry, fair maiden," he apologized warmly. "I thought you could use a little excitement, that's all."

"Next time just take me to another horror movie."

Chad took the next exit and turned back toward Caderville. To his surprise and Jamie's mortification, there was a road block on the outskirts of town. The sheriff stood next to his car, arms folded, waiting patiently.

Chad cursed under his breath.

"Great. Just great," Jamie groaned. "I guess the local yokel sheriff got his shoes on after all," she jabbed at Chad.

"Don't rub it in," he muttered.

He pulled over, and the sheriff approached the car.

"Nice little show you put on," he said to Chad.

"Got any proof?" Chad growled.

The sheriff laughed. "Proof! Just about every store owner in Caderville saw you, that's all." He adjusted his glasses and leaned back on his heels, as if he had all the time in the world. "I was at Joe's getting my haircut, when lo and behold, I see a blue BMW and a black Mustang go flying through town. I'd know those two cars anywhere. I figured you'd be coming back. You and I aren't strangers, eh Braxton?"

The sheriff removed his glasses and started cleaning them with painstaking accuracy. "I'm extremely angry with you," he said evenly. "You could have killed someone, including yourself and your buddy there." He peered into the car to see who was with Braxton. "Hey, aren't you the girl who fell through the ice this winter over at Blueberry Lake? Katherine King's granddaughter?"

Jamie nodded. "Jamie Carrigan," she said weakly. *I can't believe this is happening,* she thought. *I'm in trouble with the police. It's California all over again. Grandma's going to kill me. Grandma, nothing! She sat bolt upright.*

Mom and Dad! They're going to throw a fit!

"Well, I'll tell you what I'm going to do," drawled the lawman. "I won't put any heat on you, young lady. I'm sure you're feeling enough heat as it is." He smiled at Jamie. "You're looking a little green. I know it's none of my business, but if I were you, I'd steer clear of this guy. You're liable to get into trouble."

Jamie sunk into her seat, hoping to disappear.

"As for you, Braxton. Here's the deal: I'm slapping you with a hundred dollar fine. Here's your ticket." He handed Chad a slip of paper. "And if I so much as see you spit in the street, I'll land you in jail so fast you won't know what hit you."

Chad took back his license without saying a word. The sheriff tipped his hat to Jamie and returned to his car.

Chad drove slowly through town and back to the King house, cursing all the way. Jamie was shaking her head and staring at Chad as if she had never seen him before.

"You're crazy," she said. "Nuts. Totally gone. The sheriff's right. We could have gotten killed, for Pete's sake. And you know it's going to be all over town, probably before I even get to the front door. I'm doomed. My family's going to kill me."

Chad pulled out a cigarette and lit it. "So you take some heat from your folks. Big deal! You know something, Jamie. You are always blowing things way out of proportion. So we got caught, big deal! Nobody got hurt."

He pulled the car over to the side of the road, not far from the King property. "I wouldn't do anything to hurt you," he said softly, his grey eyes pleading for mercy. "You are so special."

Jamie looked at Chad and swallowed hard. It was so hard to stay angry at him. He reached over and touched her hair. "Forgive me?" he asked.

"Okay," Jamie whispered.

He leaned over to kiss her.

Blast! A car horn blared through the air with a vengeance. A yellow car pulled up to the BMW.

"I don't believe this," Chad snarled. "Who the—"

"Dad!" Jamie exclaimed.

Jamie's father jumped out of the car. "Jamie where have you been? I've been looking all over for you! You shouldn't just take off like that. Your mother—"

"My mother is a basket case, probably because of you!" Jamie fired back at him.

Her words startled him. He stopped and looked at Chad. "Who are you?"

"Chad Braxton," the young man replied. "I'm a friend of Jamie's."

"I bet," Dan Carrigan snorted.

Jamie got out of the car and slammed the door shut. "Thanks for the ride,

Chad. I'll walk the rest of the way."

"Whatever you say, Jamie," Chad said. "See you later!" he called out as she walked away.

Dan glared at him. "Jamie!" he bellowed. "I'm talking to you! You get back here!"

Jamie ignored him and kept walking. Dan got back into his rental car and drove slowly back to the house. In the rearview mirror, he could see his daughter's face. His stomach turned as he saw the hurt and anger that was written there.

Chapter Fifteen

A rousing rendition of "Welcome Happy Morning" filled the sanctuary on Easter Sunday. The people who attended services only on Easter and Christmas helped pack out the church. The happy tune and the happy faces of the congregants grated on Jamie's nerves. Her father stood next to her, fidgeting with his tie. Ellen's hands were folded tightly as she quietly sang the hymn. Kate sang with gusto, joy shining on her face.

Jamie looked over at her grandmother. *She must know something I don't know,* Jamie thought. *How can she sing like that when everything is upside down?*

The pastor called the children down to the front of the church. It was time for the children's sermon. The little people walked, skipped, and ran toward the pastor in gleeful anticipation of speaking into the microphone.

"Who knows what today is?" Pastor Jacobsen asked.

Several children raised their hands and answered in unison. "Easter Sunday!"

"Easter Sunday!" Little Tommy Garnett's voice trailed behind the others', his face beaming.

"That's right," responded the pastor. "Now, who can tell me what Easter is all about?"

"It's about Jesus," five-year-old Clarissa Newcome piped up.

"Jesus," echoed Tommy.

Clarissa gave the little boy a dirty look and continued her exposition. "He got dead because of some bad men and they stuck Him in a hole and on Easter He crawled out of that hole, good as new."

"Good as new," echoed Pastor Jacobsen. "That's right Clarissa. That's what Easter is all about. We celebrate together because Jesus rose from the dead. Good as new," he said with a smile.

The service continued and Jamie's mind wandered out of the sanctuary and back to the day before. Her parents had tried to reassure her that things were not as bad as they seemed. Jamie had listened politely and decided there was nothing she could do about it any way. What happens, happens. It's not like they were getting a divorce. At least she hoped not. And at least no one had found out about the drag racing. Not yet, anyway. Jamie looked over at the back of Sheriff James T. Watson's head. Figured he attended First Baptist. He had greeted Jamie that morning with a serious sort of smile. Maybe he was keeping Jamie's involvement to himself. Maybe no one would ever know.

"Praise be to the God and Father of our Lord Jesus Christ! In his great mercy he has given us new birth into a living hope through the resurrection of Jesus

Christ from the dead, and into an inheritance that can never perish, spoil or fade—kept in heaven for you." Reverend Jacobsen read the Scripture jubilantly.

"I like those words 'living hope.' In Christ we have a hope that never dies! And what about the word "new"? He makes all things new! This not only applies to being born anew into the kingdom of God. It applies to our everyday lives as well. He can resurrect our broken dreams, our broken hearts. Why? Because He loves us all dearly. The power of the resurrection of Christ can affect every area of our lives, if we will let it."

Without her knowing it, the fervent words of the pastor fell like seeds into Jamie's heart and mind.

"What the world gives us can pass away," the pastor continued. "People change, circumstances change. But what God gives us through Christ can never perish, spoil, or fade."

Jamie glanced over at her mother and was in for a surprise. Ellen looked relaxed for the first time since she had arrived from California. There were silent tears running down her face, but Jamie could sense that they were not tears of sorrow. Something the pastor had said was touching Ellen, giving her something to hold on to. On the other hand, Dan Carrigan sat uncomfortably in the pew, acting as if he wasn't listening to what he knew he was hearing.

After the service, Kate King and the Carrigans stopped in the parking lot for a powwow. "I've invited Billy Ritchfield and Judah for Easter dinner today," she announced.

Ellen started to protest but Kate cut her off. "I won't sit around and mope like the rest of you. I love you dearly. I feel your pain. But I trust the Lord. He is faithful. The Lord answers prayer. 'And I'm a-prayin' like thunder' as Sadie would say. We could stand for some nice company and light conversation, don't you think?"

Ellen smiled at her indomitable mother. "I'm not going to argue with you, Mom."

Behind Kate's back, Dan mouthed "Oh, great!" and Jamie rolled her eyes. Katherine turned around.

"And you two will have to behave yourselves."

Judah and Billy showed up just as Jamie and Ellen were putting the finishing touches on the table. The good china and silver candlesticks made a lovely setting for the Sunday dinner. Kate added an arrangement of lilies to the center of the table.

"Aren't they pretty?" She stepped back to admire the flowers.

"That smell reminds me of a funeral home," said Jamie.

"Ditto," agreed Dan.

"Fiddle dee dee," huffed Kate. "I think they smell lovely!"

"I vote for the food smelling lovely," Billy commented from the doorway.

"You would," Jamie laughed. "Mom, Dad, this is my friend Billy Ritchfield. We used to play together whenever I stayed with Grandma."

They shook hands all around. "And this is Judah Weston, my right-hand man," Kate added warmly. "Don't know what I'd do without him."

Judah smiled and joined the group in the dining room. Kate motioned for everyone to take a seat. Jamie ended up between Billy and Judah.

"A rose between two thorns, eh Jamie girl?" Dan teased.

"You can say that again," said Billy admiringly.

"A rose between two thorns, eh Jamie?"

"Cut it out!" Jamie protested.

"So," Dan continued, "what do you two thorns do for a living?"

"I'm a lawyer," Billy replied. "I studied at Harvard and then came back here to open an office."

"Harvard? And you came back to Caderville?" Dan was incredulous.

"I don't care much for the big city," responded Billy. "Besides, there's a scarcity of good lawyers in this area."

"Here, here," Jamie applauded. "You are a noble and good man!"

Ellen hushed her daughter. "No, Billy, that really is a great thing you've done. I admire a man who thinks of other people besides himself."

Ellen's words made Dan squirm. He turned to Judah.

"And you?"

"Mechanic," replied Judah.

"And a good one!" said Kate.

Dan nodded his approval. "There will always be cars to fix, right?"

"He's a cowboy, too, right Judah?" said Jamie.

Judah's lips curved in a slow, patient smile, and he looked into the young woman's brown eyes. "Yes, I guess you could say that, Jamie."

Jamie looked away. She couldn't look into his blue eyes. Something in them made her feel like a child, like there was something she needed to learn.

"So Jamie," Billy changed the subject, "do you ever have any nightmares about falling through—"

"Billy!" Jamie cried. "If one more person mentions the falling-through-the-ice incident, I think I'll scream!"

Ellen ignored her daughter's aggravation. "That reminds me, Judah," she said. "We wanted to thank you for helping Jamie that day. I'm sure it was terribly frightening. Thank goodness you were nearby to pull her out."

"Let's not forget Billy," said Jamie sweetly. "His tremendously ugly and painfully orange down coat probably saved me from freezing to death, right Billy?"

Billy straightened up in his seat. "Hey, I never thought of that!" he said brightly. "I'm a hero, and I didn't even know it!"

There was a round of applause for the heroes. The table was cleared away, and the party withdrew to the living room.

"If you'll excuse us, Mom and I are going to do the dishes," Ellen said. "We have some more catching up to do before Dan and I leave tomorrow."

Jamie sat with the men for awhile, totally bored with their enthusiastic talk of touchdowns and quarterbacks. Eventually she slipped out of the room and out of the house. She went to the barn and sat down on the top of an old barrel. Through the open doors, Jamie watched the air turn golden as the sun journeyed toward the other side of the western hills. The white farmhouse glowed pale yellow in the retreating rays of light. She could see lights begin to glimmer in the windows of the house.

"Life can be strange," Jamie said to Merlin and Azalia. "You think certain things will stay the same forever, and then wham! Something rocks the boat." She patted Merlin's nose. "I just hope the boat doesn't sink."

In the far corner, Shadow snorted. Jamie approached the black horse slowly and then gingerly reached out her hand to pet him. To her relief, he stood still for her and even nuzzled her hand.

"Judah was right!" Jamie spoke quietly to the horse. "He said once you'd get to know me, we'd be friends for life!" She ventured a hug around the horse's neck. "I wish some of my friendships with people made sense! I'm not so sure about Chad anymore. He's so . . . so careless about things. I can't put my finger on it, but I don't feel right about some of things he says and does."

"I'll tell you why you don't feel right about Chad," Judah's voice carried from the door of the barn.

"You've got this sneaking business down to a science, don't you," said Jamie.

Judah ignored her comment and pursued the subject of Chad.

"You feel funny because Chad is a self-centered jerk. He doesn't care about you or respect you, Jamie."

"How do you know that?" Jamie asked angrily. She was angry because she knew instantly that he was right.

"The perfect example is the drag race. You could have gotten hurt badly, or even killed. But Chad didn't take that into consideration. He doesn't care about anyone but himself!" It was Judah's turn to be angry.

Jamie walked slowly over to Judah. "How did you know about the race?" she asked weakly.

"Ben told me. And he's fit to be tied. But he doesn't want Katherine to know. It would upset her too much."

"Great. I'm really looking forward to going to work tomorrow." Jamie suddenly felt very weak and very small. It was all too much for her. She hid her face in her hands and began to cry.

Her tears shocked Judah. He hesitated for a moment. Then he awkwardly put his arms around her. "Don't cry," he said. "I didn't mean to upset you."

"It's not you," she said through her tears. "It's everything, it's my parents—"

Judah brushed Jamie's hair out of her eyes and looked at her with concern in his eyes. "I don't know what's going on, but I'm sure your mom and dad can work it out."

Jamie hid her face in Judah's shirt. "I'm not so sure," she said brokenly. "One minute I decide not to worry about it, and the next minute I'm going nuts." She pulled away from him and wiped her face with her sleeve.

"Judah, I'm going to be flat out honest with you. You make me feel like a little kid. You make me feel like there's something I don't know, but that you know. Like you're waiting for me to find out what it is."

Judah looked at her a moment. He ran a hand through his black hair and nodded. "You'll see," he said. "I know you'll find out one day."

An indignant Jamie put her hands on her hips. "And how do you know that, O Great and Mighty Know-It-All?"

"Because I'm praying for you," he replied firmly.

Jamie groaned with exasperation. "Judah," she said matter-of-factly, "thanks for the shoulder to cry on. But let's forget this conversation ever happened, okay?"

Judah bowed to the young woman. "No problem," he said graciously.

"Thank you." Jamie stomped out of the barn.

Judah watched her walk to the house.

Once out of earshot, the tall young man with the cowboy boots had the last word.

"And on top of all that," he said aloud. "Billy's going to be my best man."

Chapter Sixteen

"Cassie!"

"Jamie, darling!"

The two young women hugged each other. Cassie stepped back to take a look at her friend.

"Well, you don't look like a hillbilly!" she laughed.

"Thanks a lot, Cassie," Jamie said. "Did you think I would turn into a bumpkin or something, living out here in the boonies?"

"Something like that," Cassie sniffed. "But you look great, kind of wholesome-looking, you know?" She ran her fingers through her short, curly black hair. "So who's going to help us with my luggage?"

Jamie looked at the large pile of travel bags and suitcases. "I thought you were staying for three weeks, not three months!"

"Hey, you're lucky! I only brought the essentials," Cassie pouted.

"And it's essential that you have a different outfit for each and every day, right, my friend?"

"Mais oui, darling!"

Jamie picked up two suitcases and started lugging them to the car. Cassie picked up a small satchel. She waited while Jamie put her load into the trunk.

"Don't strain yourself," said Jamie, taking the satchel from her girlfriend.

"I don't want to break a nail!" Cassie cried.

"Oh brother!" muttered Jamie. She grabbed the handle of an extra large piece of luggage and tried dragging it to the car.

"Need some help?" a man's voice inquired.

Jamie turned around. "Hello Chad."

"Hello Chad?" he echoed. "No big hug, no kiss after we faced the threat of death together?"

"What are you talking about?" Cassie asked, dying of curiosity.

"You don't want to know," Jamie muttered.

"She's so reserved, isn't she?" said Chad. "It's what I love about her!"

Cassie started to laugh and Chad joined her.

"Chad, Cassie. Cassie, Chad," Jamie introduced them. "Now if you two are through goofing around, I could use some help."

Chad saluted Jamie and went straight to work. He filled the trunk and most of the back seat with Cassie's things.

"How about we celebrate the arrival of your friend, Jamie?" suggested Chad.

"How sweet!" Cassie purred.

"How about we all take in a movie? My treat!"

Jamie snickered. "His father owns the theater," she informed Cassie.

"I like your style, Chad," Cassie giggled. "We accept."

"Saturday night? Nine o'clock?"

"We'll be there!"

Jamie shrugged. "Why not? We'll see you then, Chad."

Chad reached for Jamie's handed and gently planted a kiss. "Until then, fair maiden."

"You're nuts," Jamie grinned at Chad's handsome face.

"She loves me, can you tell?" Chad sighed dramatically. "See you, Cassie."

Jamie and Cassie slipped into the car, and Jamie drove to the drugstore.

"Ooh, that Chad is a stunner!" Cassie cooed.

Jamie ignored her.

"I want you to meet Ben, my boss, and see where I'll be working while you sit around and paint your nails."

There was parking right in front of the pharmacy. As they got out of the car, Cassie let out a low whistle. She grabbed Jamie by the arm.

"Be still my heart, I think I'm falling in love! Who is that gorgeous dream walking our way?"

Jamie turned to look down the street. She saw ten-year-old Clarence Sunderman, Jr., sweeping the walk in front of the grocery.

"Cassie, I hardly think CJ is your type," responded Jamie. She kept looking and saw Judah crossing the street. "I don't see anybody. Who are you talking—"

"Him! Him!" Cassie hissed. "He's coming our way! I've just got to meet him!"

With a jolt Jamie realized Cassie was talking about Judah. Judah? A gorgeous dream?

"Hello, Jamie," Judah greeted her as he approached the two women.

"You know him?" Cassie whispered excitedly in Jamie's ear.

"Uh, hi uh, Judah," Jamie stuttered. "This is my friend Cassie Templeton. Cassie, this is Judah Weston. He works for my grandmother."

Judah held out his hand. "Nice to meet you. Welcome to Caderville."

"Why, thank you," Cassie said sweetly.

Jamie stared in amazement at her friend who was drooling over Judah Weston. Then she looked at Judah as if seeing him for the first time. His strong build, his wavy jet-black hair, his pale blue eyes.

Judah began to feel a little uncomfortable, like a bug under a magnifying glass.

"You'll have to excuse me, ladies, I'm on my way to the hardware store. See you later."

"I hope so," Cassie beamed.

Jamie took Cassie by the arm and dragged her toward the drugstore. Ben met them in the front of the store.

"Well, well, another beautiful young woman from California." He tilted his head toward the front window. "I see you already met Judah." He extended his hand. "Ben Wheelock, pharmacist."

"Also spy, eavesdropper, and general snoop," Jamie added.

"Jamie!" Ben cried. "How could you say such a thing?" He grinned at Cassie. "Don't believe a word of it!"

"Pleased to meet you," smiled Cassie.

Jamie gave her the grand tour. On their way out, Chad came into the drugstore. Cassie and Jamie acknowledged their date again for Saturday night, waved good-bye, and left for Kate's.

Chad paid for his purchase and was out the door. Ben stood looking after him, twirling his pencil behind his ear. He reached down and fingered the receipt Chad had left behind on the counter. Something wasn't right. The pharmacist had a hunch, a terrible hunch. He hoped he was wrong.

Kate King greeted the girls at the door with a big smile. She showed Cassie to the guest room and served the girls lunch on the side porch. The June air was mild and sweet with the fragrance of the sweet peas thriving nearby.

"Your grandma's a sweetheart," Cassie said. "She really makes me feel at home."

Jamie smiled at her friend. "Yes, she's great. I've really enjoyed my time here."

"So tell me all about these positively beautiful men you've surrounded yourself with! That blond guy is a knockout. Sounds like he's lots of fun too."

Jamie picked up a cookie and took a bite.

"I'm hardly surrounded," she said dryly. "Chad is sweet, and he is certainly not boring. Now Judah, on the other hand . . ."

"Wait a second," said Cassie, studying Jamie's face. "Chad isn't the guy you wrote me about is he? In your letter you were so excited about him, he absolutely made you dizzy! What happened? You don't look too excited now." Cassie leaned over with concern on her face. "You know, I hate to sound like your analyst and spoil this nice day, but you look like Courtney Smith looks without her makeup. Kind of sad-looking. What's the matter?"

Jamie smiled. "How is Courtney?"

"Don't change the subject!"

Jamie looked away. "My parents are having problems in their marriage."

"Get outta here, Ms. Carrigan. Your parents? The John and Olivia Walton of Santa Clara? Our very own Cliff and Claire Huxtable?"

"Try Sonny and Cher," Jamie groaned.

"No way," Cassie was vehement. "What makes you think so, anyway?"

"When they were here, Mom looked and sounded awful. Seemed like she was always on the brink of tears. And Dad was real uptight."

"Oh," responded Cassie. "Well, you're probably just making a mountain out of a mole hill. They'll be fine." Cassie reached over and squeezed Jamie's hand. "Don't worry, Jamie. It's going to be all right."

"I hope so."

"Aren't they Christians? I mean like your grandmother is?"

"Yeah," said Jamie. "They go to church and the whole bit."

"Maybe they can work it out then, you know? I thought Christians weren't supposed to have problems like that."

Jamie frowned. "I guess there're just no guarantees."

"Guarantees?" Kate spoke through the screen door. "Guarantees for what?" She opened the door and joined the young women on the porch.

"Marriage guarantees," Cassie said. "We were talking about Christian people and marriage."

"Yeah, Grandma. If Dad and Mom are such great Christians, why are they having problems in their marriage?" Jamie asked accusingly.

Katherine shook her head. "You don't understand, girls. When you become a Christian, Christ doesn't come into your life and make you a sanctified automaton. It's a relationship. We are to walk with Christ, keep in step with Him. If at some point a person gets self-centered and starts focusing on him or herself all the time, you sort of lose your hearing. It's like with each step you're getting farther from the Lord and you can't hear what He's saying. That can turn your life and other relationships into a real mess. No, there are no guarantees for the behavior of the people we live with and love. The only guarantees we have are for God's behavior. He'll always be faithful, loving, and merciful to His children. I think those are the only guarantees we'll ever need."

Cassie smiled at Kate. "You sound just like a preacher. Not a bad one, either!"

"Why thank you, my dear!" Kate replied.

"I just don't get it," said Jamie. "It doesn't make sense to me." She got up from her white wicker chair and turned toward Cassie. "I guess we better start hauling your suitcases in."

"Some of them are really heavy," Cassie said, following Jamie down the steps. "We're going to need a man to carry them up those stairs. Any suggestions?" she asked hopefully.

"Judah can do it," Jamie answered without turning around. She took a smaller case from the car. "He'll be by to feed the animals later today."

Cassie screamed. "Really?" She grabbed Jamie by the hand and danced her around the front yard. "This is going to be a great three weeks!"

True to schedule, Judah arrived to tend the animals. Kate went out to the barn to invite him in for dessert.

"I better warn you, though," she said in mock seriousness. "There may be man-eating sharks in the area!"

Judah blushed and shook his head. "I'm afraid I'm not much bait, Mrs. K."

Kate smiled and headed out the barn door. "That's what you think," she said under her breath.

Meanwhile in the kitchen, it was all Jamie could do to keep Cassie in her seat. "What has gotten into you?" Jamie asked. "You're acting like a teenager! You'd think Judah was some movie star or something! You're acting crazy."

"What do you care how I'm acting? I thought you didn't particularly care for Judah."

"Well, I don't care," Jamie said, beginning to choke on her words. "It doesn't matter to me how you act. I don't care—" As soon as the words were out of her mouth, she realized she did care. A lot.

The kitchen door swung open. "Here we are!" sang Kate. "Judah has agreed to join us for apple pie."

Cassie gave the young man her best smile and motioned for him to sit next to her. He sat down as if he were trying to avoid a porcupine.

"Isn't this cozy!" Cassie exclaimed, pulling her chair closer to Judah.

Judah moved his chair a little to the left, trying to flee Cassie as subtly as he could. Jamie glared at Cassie. Kate turned to the sink, her back to her guests, so they could not see her silently dying from laughter.

It was the longest dessert of Judah's life.

Suddenly, Cassie had a brilliant idea. "Why don't you come with us to the movies Saturday night?"

Jamie tried to kick Cassie under the table but hit Judah by mistake.

"Ouch!" He rubbed his shin.

"What's so painful about the movies?" Cassie asked.

Kate, who by now was seated next to Jamie, nearly choked on her coffee. She finally had to excuse herself from the room.

Cassie looked after her with concern. "Is your grandmother all right?"

Muffled laughter erupted from the direction of the living room.

"She's fine," said Jamie flatly.

"Now, about the movies?" Cassie leaned toward Judah.

"I don't think Judah would want to go," Jamie said, trying to give Cassie a shut-up-already look.

"Why not?"

"Because Chad and he don't exactly get along. To put it mildly."

Cassie laughed. "Why, Judah, you wouldn't be Chad's date! You would be mine!"

Judah pushed his chair away from the table and stood up. "No, I really couldn't," he said apologetically. "I already promised Billy I'd go to Lamberton."

Cassie's eyes narrowed. "Billy? Do we know her?" she turned to Jamie.

The sound of laughter pealed again from the other room. Judah excused himself and hurried out the door.

Chapter Seventeen

It didn't take long for Cassie Templeton to realize that Judah was not interested; not interested in her, anyway. She gave up the chase and settled down to enjoy her time with her best friend. Jamie introduced her to Billy Ritchfield, and together they formed a threesome. Billy stopped by regularly, games in hand. They played Scrabble, Trivial Pursuit, and Parcheesi for hours into the night. Sometimes Kate joined them, but mostly she sat in her chair and watched. Judah occasionally dropped by, but in the summer he was busy with Shadow, riding him in shows and exhibitions. Jamie missed not seeing him as often, but she figured fair was fair. She hadn't really encouraged him to come around. On the other hand, she could tell he seemed to be avoiding her. Maybe it was just as well. It was hard for Jamie to sort her feelings out.

Chad Braxton was busy working full time at his job in the stockbrokers' office in Lamberton. Jamie was relieved. She really didn't want to see him anymore. Ever since the drag race, she had realized what a selfish person he could be. He was hanging out with some new friends in Lamberton. Jamie had met them once at the theater, and they had given her the creeps.

"Want to go for a walk?" Jamie asked Cassie one afternoon. "Sitting on the porch is getting us nowhere."

"A walk? How quaint," said Cassie. She stood up with a stretch. "You know I'm missing three weeks of aerobics for you, darling."

Jamie clutched her heart. "I am truly and deeply touched."

"You're touched all right," said Cassie, thumping Jamie's head.

"Hey, look who's talking," Jamie nudged her. "You're the one seeing a shrink."

"Don't knock Bernie! He's a sweetheart. I get to talk about anything I want. He's a good listener."

The girls headed for the meadow. The summer sun splashed the afternoon with brightness. Blue as a jewel on a king's hand, the sky stretched overhead in a stunning band of color. Dressed for summer, the hills wore variegated greens blending in muted tones. Scattered wild flowers greeted the day with shouts of color, yellows, blues, pinks.

Cassie took a deep breath. "I must admit, the air is definitely cleaner here."

"Does it work?"

"Breathing? Oh, yes you should try it."

"No, therapy, I mean. Does it help? Do you ever discuss things like, well, the meaning of life?"

"The meaning of life! Jamie Carrigan. I think all this fresh air has gone to your head!" Cassie laughed. "Yeah, I think about life. I think about all the things I want. You know. So many malls, so little time."

"Forget it," said Jamie. "You are in no condition to talk about serious things. You'd better watch your step."

"Jamie, don't you worry about me," retorted Cassie indignantly. "Life and I are doing just fine."

"No, I mean really watch your step—"

Squish. "Too late," Jamie sighed.

"What in the world?" Cassie cried.

"Cow patty. You are now an official member of our family here on the farm. Congratulations!"

Cassie could only shriek in horror. She ran to the house. Jamie ran after her laughing and yelling, "It's not fatal!"

Cassie was sitting on the porch steps, trying to get her shoe off without touching it, when a white car pulled into the driveway. The driver honked at the two young women.

"Hi Billy," they said in unison.

"Want to go over to Sadie's and help Judah and I fix her shutters?"

"Sounds positively exciting," said Cassie limply.

"Yes, we'd love to," responded Jamie. "Just give Cassie time to change her shoes."

"You've got to watch your step around here," said Billy cheerfully, eyeing the offending shoe.

"Thank you, Spock. Your insight and timing are impeccable."

Kate came out the front door with a dish of cookies in her hand. "Did I hear you say you were all going to Sadie's? Can you take these cookies with you? They're her favorite."

"Sure, no problem, Mrs. King."

"I'll carry them, Grandma," said Jamie. "Between Cassie and Billy, those cookies might disappear before we get there."

They piled into Billy's car and drove to Sadie's. When they arrived, Judah was already on the roof pounding nails. He waved with his hammer and then resumed his work.

"Friendly fellow, isn't he?" remarked Cassie.

"When there's a job to be done, he's all business," sighed Billy. "I guess I'd better get up there."

He climbed slowly up the ladder, urging Cassie and Jamie to hold the ladder still. He reached the top and immediately sat down on the roof of the porch.

"What do I do now?" they heard him ask in a shaky voice.

Judah laughed. "Calm down, Ritchfield. You won't fall. Hand me that box of nails and that other shutter."

Sadie came out on to the porch accompanied by Margret. She sat down on the green rocker.

"Hello girls."

"Hi, Mrs. Atkins," said Jamie. "Hi, Margret." Jamie retrieved the cookies from the top of the car and handed them to Sadie.

"Thank you." Sadie's face lit up. "Sugar cookies. My favorite." She looked over at Cassie. "Enjoyin' your stay?"

"Yes," replied Cassie. "I'm really enjoying this country living. Makes for a nice vacation."

"Well, I'm glad. It's a sight better than livin' in the city. Too noisy there. And dangerous, I might add."

"We came to help Judah and Billy with the roof," said Jamie. "I guess we better check and see what they need."

Jamie stepped back and cupped her hands over her eyes.

"What do you want us to do?" she called up to the men.

"Nothing," said Judah. "It will only take two of us. We can handle it."

"William Ritchfield. I thought you said—"

"Oh, never mind," said Billy. "You can help us by just sitting there and looking pretty."

"You're lucky you're out of reach," Jamie retorted.

"I know something you can do," suggested Sadie. "You can feed Peggy Sue."

"Peggy Sue?" Cassie asked. "Is she a little lamb? A baby calf?"

"A sow," replied Sadie. "A sow as big as a black bear. And twice as mean."

"Sounds like loads of fun," shuddered Cassie. "I think I'll pass."

"We'd love to," said Jamie, pulling Cassie to her feet. "Come on, Cassie. "It's a piece of cake. When you go back to California, you can wow your friends and tell them you actually did some chores on a farm. They'll probably all pass out from shock."

Margret showed them where the feed was and pointed them in the direction of the pig pen. Jamie carried the bucket of food. Cassie reluctantly followed her. When they arrived at the pen, Cassie gasped.

"That thing is huge!" she cried. "I'm not getting anywhere near it!" Peggy Sue snorted up at the girls.

"Come on, it can't get out. Just dump the feed over the side into that trough there," instructed Jamie.

"Why I am listening to you?" complained Cassie. She picked up the bucket and gingerly poured its contents into the trough. Suddenly the sow started squealing and snorting wildly. Cassie dropped the bucket and Jamie screamed. The sow rammed up against the wooden slats of the fence and broke through. Cassie and Jamie took off like lightning, running for the nearest thing they could climb.

Billy was halfway down the ladder when he heard the two women scream. "What in the world?"

"Peggy's loose, I figure," said Sadie calmly. Judah scrambled down after Billy. They rounded the corner of the barn in time to see Cassie and Jamie frantically clambering over the side of Judah's truck. Peggy Sue was desperately trying to reach them, snorting and jerking and jumping as best she could.

"Do something!" Cassie screamed.

Jamie was doubled over, laughing hysterically.

"Go get the hammer and nails," Judah told Billy.

"Gladly," he said, eyeing the sow.

Judah grabbed a stick and a handful of feed and herded the animal back to its pen. Billy brought him the hammer and nails, and Judah quickly repaired the fence.

Billy helped Cassie and Jamie out of the truck.

"Piece of cake. Wow your friends." Cassie seethed. "Jamie Carrigan, I'll never forgive you. We almost got killed."

Jamie was still choking from laughter.

Billy tried to maintain a straight face. "It's not funny, Jamie. Cassie was really frightened." He cleared his throat. "Imagine your epitaph." He recited: "Our friends have departed/ We all know how/ They were hit and run over/ By Peggy Sue Sow."

Jamie fell to the ground, holding her sides. "Stop!" she cried, "It's too much!" Tears of laughter streamed down her cheeks.

"I am not amused," said Cassie, fighting a smile. She climbed up on the porch and sat down.

Judah returned, hammer in hand. "Are you two all right?" he asked.

Jamie nodded, gasping for breath. Cassie rolled her eyes. "I'm fine. Miss Carrigan seems to be having a breakdown."

"Honeysuckle," said Sadie.

"What?" All eyes were on Sadie.

"Someone must be wearing honeysuckle. Drives Peggy Sue wild. She just loves it."

Cassie looked a little pale. "I'm wearing a perfume that is a blend of honeysuckle and musk."

"An expensive perfume, I bet," reported Jamie.

"Very," said Billy. "It almost cost Cassie her life."

At that, Jamie and Billy broke up laughing.

"My father used to have a sow just like Peggy Sue," reminisced Sadie. "Her name was Belinda. One day, my cousin Orville and his wife Kitty came up from the city for a visit. Kitty was real prim and proper and citified. Well, unbeknownst to us, she was wearin' honeysuckle perfume. Belinda got one whiff of that and broke out of her pen. She chased Kitty clear to the other side of the field. Knocked down nearly an acre of corn before we could stop her." Sadie slapped her knee and let out a laugh. "An acre of corn!"

Cassie shot Jamie a dirty look.

"And then there was the time Belinda went after the judge's wife. Marilyn Parker, that was her name. She came one day to bring over some molasses for my mother. Well, sir, Belinda got loose and chased that woman up a tree. Never saw a woman her age climb a tree before, but Marilyn Parker did it. And fast. She would've made a monkey proud."

Sadie stopped for a moment, remembering. "Mother had to call the fire department. Mrs. Parker wouldn't let my father get her down on account she thought he'd drop her. My father never liked the judge. You know, come to think of it, Marilyn wasn't even wearin' perfume. I expect Belinda chased her out of sheer meanness."

"I'm getting a headache," said Cassie.

"I'll drive you girls home," Billy volunteered.

"We're done with the shutters, Mrs. Atkins," said Judah. "They shouldn't be falling down any more."

"Thanks so much, boys," said Sadie. "I don't know how to thank you. My grandsons couldn't hammer a nail straight if their lives depended on it."

Judah smiled and put his tools back in the truck.

"Come again!" Sadie called after the girls. "And thank Kate for the cookies!"

That evening after they ate, Jamie and Cassie settled in the guest room to talk. Jamie hugged a pillow and watched as Cassie carefully painted her nails. Her lips pursed with concentration, Cassie stroked the color on with admirable precision.

"You ought to go into business," said Jamie. "Nails By Cassie".

"Very funny, darling, but don't laugh. There's money to be made in the beauty business."

"What is that awful color, anyway?"

"Sparkling fuchsia."

"Good grief," Jamie responded.

"It happens to be a very hot color right now," retorted Cassie. You really should try it."

"No thanks," Jamie replied. "You know I hate fussing with my nails."

"Obviously," said Cassie, wrinkling her nose at the sight of Jamie's short nails. Jamie leaned back and took a deep breath. "Cassie?"

Cassie looked up from her nails and eyed her friend. "Now what? You've got that 'I need to ask you a very important question' look on your face."

Jamie nodded. "What was it like when your parents went through their divorce?"

Cassie's eyebrows shot up and she leaned back on the post of the bed. "Wow! Talk about left field."

"Come on, tell me how it was. How did you feel? What happened?"

Cassie sighed and resumed her painting. "Well, I was twelve at the time. Mom and Dad had been fighting on and off for a long time. Seemed like every fight got worse until one day it stopped."

"It stopped?"

"Yeah, they stopped talking altogether. The silence in the house was unbearable. Shortly after that, Dad left. With his baby-faced secretary on his arm, if you know what I mean." Cassie snickered. "You'd think he'd have had more imagination than that! Seems like it's always the secretary. Not very original."

Jamie felt sick to her stomach. "What about your mom?"

Cassie frowned and replaced the brush in the bottle.

"Mom was devastated. She cried a lot. For a long time." Cassie looked away for a moment. "I think that was the hardest part," she said, her voice trembling. "To see Mom suffer so much. I used to hear her at night in her room, trying to cry in her pillow so we wouldn't hear her. It was awful." Cassie cleared her throat. "But she got over it. She pulled herself together and got on with her life. She's a very together lady. She always looks put together, from her hair to her nails. Very stylish. She's got her friends and her clubs and her boyfriends."

Jamie smiled. "What about you?"

"What about me?"

"Did you get over it?"

"Of course," Cassie said simply. "I made up my mind to hate my father. That helped take away the hurt and betrayal I felt through all that garbage. Bernie says I need to get rid of the hate, but so far it works just fine."

Jamie swallowed hard. "I don't know, Cass. That doesn't sound like the right way to deal with something like that."

"And what do you know about it?" snapped Cassie. "You don't what it's like to wake up in the middle of the night and feel like the whole universe is falling apart. You don't know what it feels like to be so lonely you don't think you can get out of bed in the morning." Tears were streaming down her face. "I used to feel like it was my fault, like if maybe I was a nicer kid or better student, my parents would have stayed together. I felt like the ugliest, dumbest kid in the world. It was awful.

"Oh, now look what you made me do! I've smeared the polish on my thumbnail." Cassie wiped her eyes and grabbed the polish remover. She blinked away her tears and concentrated on her nails.

Jamie reached over and put her arms around her friend. "I'm sorry," Jamie whispered. "It's just that I'm afraid my parents—" She couldn't say another word.

Cassie closed her bottle of color and held Jamie at arm's length. "I told you before, don't worry about it. Besides, you're an adult now. It might not be so hard to deal with when you can understand what's going on." She got up from the bed and blew on her nails. "All this gloomy talk has got me starved. Let's go beg your grandmother for a late night snack."

Jamie followed her friend down the stairs. Kate greeted the two young women in the kitchen. "What long faces!" she exclaimed. "Who died?"

"True love," said Cassie ruefully. "We were discussing an obsolete concept."

"Oh my!" said Kate, rising to the occasion. "That's simply not true!"

"Oh no," muttered Jamie. "Here she goes."

"True love is God's love. And that never dies. Never! He says in His Word He'll never leave us or forsake us. And it's true."

"Well, Mrs. King, that sounds real nice, but I can't get into that," said Cassie. "I guess I just don't see how that fits into real life."

Kate smiled. "Well, I shall pray you come to see it. He loves you Cassie. Just the way you are."

"Grandma!" Jamie sighed.

"No Jamie, I like to hear your grandmother talk about her faith. It's nice."

Jamie rolled her eyes. "You shouldn't have said that."

"Let's make some sandwiches, and I'll tell you all about it," said Kate enthusiastically.

"Deal!" said Cassie.

"Oh boy," lamented Jamie.

Kate patted her granddaughter on the cheek. "Get out the mayonnaise, dear. This is going to be fun!"

The faithful clock on the mantel in the darkened living room kept pace with the approach of midnight. Light from the kitchen vainly tried to reach around the corner of the hall to spread its warm glow, its edges swallowed by the shadows of nighttime. In the kitchen, the unseen light of another kind shone brightly around the three women at the table, the air dancing with words of love and hope and promises kept.

All too quickly, Cassie's vacation ended. "I can't believe three weeks is over already," she sighed. She straightened her large sun hat and put on her sunglasses. Her luggage was being loaded on the train.

Jamie gave her a big hug. "I'll miss you, Cass. I'm so glad you came."

"I really enjoyed myself," said Cassie. "This simple country living almost has me hooked!"

"Good!" exclaimed Billy. "Why don't you move here?"

Cassie looked over the top of her sunglasses. "I said almost, Billy dear."

Kate gave Cassie a kiss. "Any time you want to stay with me, you just give me a call."

"You have a safe trip, now Miss Templeton," Judah shook her hand.

Cassie motioned for Judah to come closer. "You keep an eye on that girl," she said quietly, pointing to Jamie. "She is one of a kind."

Judah nodded. "I will," he replied. "That's a promise."

Jamie blushed and gave her friend another hug. "Thanks for the listening ear, Cassie. You are the best."

"I'm only going to California," Cassie protested. "You all make it sound like I'm falling off the edge of the earth!"

"Well," mused Billy, "from what I've heard about those earthquakes, you know, and California . . . " He made a motion with his hand. "Splash! Right in the Pacific Ocean."

Cassie batted him on the head, waved good-bye, and boarded the train.

Chapter Eighteen

"Hello, Jamie," Chad called to her as she walked down Main Street.

"Hi Chad. What's with the jeep?" Jamie asked. She stepped over to the jeep and looked inside. "Looks new. Tired of the BMW?"

Chad patted the steering wheel. "It's my Dad's latest toy. Thought I'd give it a spin. Want to come?"

"Sorry. Can't do it. Ben's going out for the afternoon so I'll be covering the store myself."

"Oh," said Chad thoughtfully. "So you'll be closing up the place?"

"No, my grandmother's going to do it! Of course I'll be closing up the place!" She gave him a quizzical look. "Why do you ask?"

"Uh, well," Chad cleared his throat. "I was wondering if you wanted to have dinner over at the diner. I could pick you up after work."

"I don't know Chad, I'm kind of tired today, and I know by tonight I'll be bushed. Maybe another time."

"Why Jamie Carrigan! If I didn't know better, I'd say you were trying to avoid me!" He pursed his lips. "I'm hurt."

"Save your puppy dog face for the other girls, Chad. I'm immune," she laughed.

"Please, Jamie, pretty please with a hot-fudge-sundae-I-know-it's-your-favorite on top?" He gazed into her eyes.

There it was again. There was something about Chad's face that was different. She just couldn't put her finger on it. What was it? Maybe his eyes? Did the familiar gray eyes seem a little cloudy or something?

"Come on Jamie," Chad pleaded. "We'll just go to the diner. No big deal!"

"Okay," Jamie gave in. "I'm through here at five."

"Great!" Chad grinned. "See you then!"

Jamie watched him drive away in the new jeep. His grin stayed fixed in her mind. It had seemed kind of strange. In fact, it hadn't looked like Chad at all.

"I must be tired," she thought.

Jamie returned to the pharmacy. Ben gave her the key and instructions for closing up shop. "Now the meeting I'm going to is in Lamberton. It should be over by four. Here's the phone number in case something comes up. If the meeting ends on time, I'm going fishing. So you won't see me until tomorrow. Any questions?"

Jamie couldn't think of any. "Don't worry about a thing."

"I won't," Ben smiled. "Thanks to you!" He walked toward the door. "Just bring the key with you tomorrow," he said over his shoulder.

"Okay. Hope you catch a big one!" she called after him.

Jamie busied herself around the store, dusting shelves and waiting on customers. No prescriptions could be filled, but there were plenty of other things to do. It seemed like every customer wanted something they couldn't find themselves, and everyone wanted to know where Ben was.

"Yoo hoo," a voice sang across the aisles to Jamie. "Young lady!"

Jamie looked up from the cash register to see a plump woman dressed in purple. She was signalling to Jamie to join her in the second aisle.

"Can I help you?" asked Jamie.

"Shhh!" the woman hushed her. "Not so loud!"

Jamie looked at the woman in surprise. "What seems to be the problem?" she asked quietly.

"Well," spoke the woman in a loud whisper. "I've run out of dye for my hair."

Jamie looked at the woman. Her hair was jet black except for the tattle tale gray roots.

"How can I help you?"

"I can't seem to find the brand I always buy." She looked furtively up and down the aisle. "I'm glad Ben's not here. I never buy it when he's around. He's such a snoop and a talker. No one knows, of course, that I dye my hair. Naturally, my hair is not all that gray. I really just need to touch it up." She primped her hair and handed Jamie an empty box of the dye she used. "Here it is," she whispered. "See if you can find it."

Jamie began her search. *I feel like James Bond,* she thought. *Any minute someone with a briefcase machine gun is going to turn down this aisle and let us have it.*

"Hurry!" hissed the woman. "I can see Alma Stack walking down the street! She's probably coming here!"

Jamie found a box behind a package of blond dye and handed it over to her customer. The woman nodded toward the cash register. "Let's go."

Jamie rang up her purchase and put the secret in a bag. She handed it to the woman, who sighed with relief.

"You must be Kate's granddaughter," the woman smiled.

"That's right. I'm Jamie Carrigan."

"You're the one who fell through the ice this past winter, aren't you?"

"Yes, ma'am, that's me," Jamie sighed.

The woman shook her head. "I used to skate. That is until Benjamin Wheelock nearly killed me."

Jamie coughed, trying to not laugh. "You must be Violet Cranberry."

"Yes, dear, that's me," she smiled and primped her hair again. She leaned close to Jamie and whispered in her ear. "Benjamin had quite a crush on me, don't you know? But of course, after the accident, it was all over between us."

Violet turned to leave. "Now don't you tell anyone now, okay dear? I mean about my hair, of course."

Jamie nodded. "Not a word!"

"Bye now!"

She watched the lady in purple walk grandly out the door. "Yoo hoo! Alma!"

Jamie smiled and leaned against the counter. She was really feeling at home in Caderville.

There was no letup in customers for the rest of the afternoon. At five o'clock, it was with great relief Jamie finally put the closed sign in the window. She locked the door so no one could slip in for one last purchase. She was about to lock up the cash register when there was a knock on the window. It was Chad.

Rats! She had forgotten about their dinner date. *What I'd really like to do is go home and soak in a hot tub,* she thought.

She opened the door for Chad and let him in.

"I just have a couple of things to do, and I'll be right with you," she said.

"Take your time," he smiled.

Jamie locked the cash register and then walked to the back of the store. Ben always double-checked the back room where the drugs were kept. A couple of cabinets he kept under lock and key. Jamie quickly scanned the room. Everything looked in order. She turned to leave and nearly bumped into Chad.

"What are you doing, Chad?" she asked. "I didn't even hear you follow me. You scared me half to death!"

"I'm sorry, Jamie," he said. His voice sounded thin. "I didn't mean to frighten you."

She looked at his face. His pupils were dilated and his breathing was loud, almost labored. Jamie felt prickles of fear rise on the back of her neck.

"We can go now, Chad," she said weakly. "I'm finished."

He fervently shook his head. "No, we can't go now. You're not finished. We have to pick up a few things for our journey."

Jamie laughed nervously. "We're just going to the diner, Chad."

"No," he said sharply. Then his voice softened. "We're going to our castle, you and I. And we'll need some very special supplies."

He pushed his way into the back room. "We'll need some footballs and yellow jackets."

"What?" Jamie's voice trembled.

"Uppers and downers, come on, pills. You know where they are. Get them."

"You mean—" Jamie's brain was starting to freeze with fear.

Chad snorted in disgust. "Amphetamines and barbiturates, if you must have the technical terms. Now find them. We're going to need them."

"But I don't have the keys—"

"Hurry up!" the man fairly shrieked.

Suddenly, the sound of footsteps clacked hurriedly down the main aisle of the store.

"What's going on around here?" Ben Wheelock demanded. "What are you doing back here, Braxton?"

"Ben!" Jamie cried.

As Chad turned slowly around, he pulled a small pistol from inside his shirt.

"Calm down, Wheelock. We're merely shopping for supplies."

Ben looked down at the pistol. "Have you gone mad?"

"Shut up!" A smile spread over Chad's face. "How good of you to stop by and lend us a hand." He grabbed Jamie and moved away from Ben. He directed Ben with his pistol. "Give us all the pills you've got. You know what I mean."

"I'll give you whatever you want, just let Jamie go."

"No!" Chad hissed. "She's coming with me."

Ben hesitated. He looked at Jamie. She was shaking with fear. "Let her go!"

"Don't make me angry, Wheelock!"

"Ben, please, just do as he says," whispered Jamie.

The druggist took two keys from his pocket and reluctantly unlocked two of the cabinets. He removed two bottles of pills and handed them over to Chad. Chad grabbed them and in one quick motion hit Ben on the head with the butt of the pistol. Ben fell to the floor. He wasn't moving.

"No!" Jamie screamed.

Chad jerked her back and threatened her with the gun.

"Be quiet, or I'll do something worse." He handed her the jar of yellow pills. "Open it up and take one."

"No way," Jamie shot back. At the sight of Ben lying on the floor, she was beginning to burn with anger.

"Just say no. Pity that's not going to work this time." He pointed the gun toward Ben's head. "If you don't do as I say, I'll just have to kill Mr. Wheelock. Now that would make it your fault, wouldn't it?"

Jamie opened the bottle with shaking hands.

"Now just take two," Chad said softly. His voice was suddenly sweet. "It's just to relax you."

Jamie looked at the pills in her hand.

"Take it," he said sternly.

Jamie swallowed the pills. She looked down at Ben. Tears streamed down her face.

Chad took her by the hand and hid the pistol behind her back. "We're going to leave now. Walk very carefully out of the store. Lock the door. Then we'll get into the jeep."

Jamie obeyed. There were people in the street, but the cold nozzle of the gun reminded her to act normally. She climbed into the jeep with Chad close behind.

"Hold your hands out."

Jamie obeyed.

"That's a girl." He quickly tied a rope around her hands.

Chad started up the jeep. He laughed out loud. "Broad daylight," he chortled. "Everyone sees us and no one knows!" He shivered with excitement. "I love the edge," he whispered gleefully. He threw the jeep into gear and drove through town, obeying the speed limit.

Jamie tried to see where Chad was taking her. He drove out the southern end of town and followed River Road for several miles. Jamie was starting to feel drowsy. She felt her head drop to the back of the seat. *No, no, stay awake, awake.* It was too hard to keep her head up.

Chad slowed down and turned onto a dirt road that was obscured by trees and overgrowth. Jamie didn't recognize the road. It was difficult to keep her eyes focused. The road climbed the side of a mountain, turning into a narrow path barely wide enough for a vehicle to drive on. The jeep jerked along the rough terrain, helping to keep Jamie awake. After what seemed like hours, Chad pulled up to a cabin hidden among a cluster of evergreens. There was a motorcycle parked in front.

"Here we are, fair maiden! Our very own home away from home. Our castle." Chad opened the passenger door and helped Jamie out of the jeep. Her legs were like rubber, and she fell against him.

"Whoa, darling! Not in public!" He propped her up and led her to the front door of the cabin. After lifting up the large slat that barred the door, Chad whisked Jamie up into his arms, carrying her over the threshold.

"Here we are!" he cried. He put Jamie down. With a dramatic sweep of his arms, Chad showed off the interior of the cabin. "Like it?" he asked anxiously.

Jamie couldn't answer. She struggled with the rope around her wrists.

"Now, now, leave those on, my dear. We wouldn't want any accidents to happen." He ran over to a dilapidated coffee table. "Look!" he said excitedly. "Look what I bought for you!"

He held up a Scrabble game. Jamie shook her head. *This isn't happening,* she thought. *I must have a fever. I'm hallucinating.*

"You look like you need a nap," Chad said matter-of-factly. "I guess you not only can't hold your liquor, you can't hold your barbs. Poor baby."

He led her over to an old cot and ordered her to lay down. As she put up her feet, he pulled out some rope from underneath the cot. "Now be a good girl and let me tie your feet together." He knelt down to secure the rope around her ankles.

Jamie mustered what strength she had and kicked Chad in the face. He flew into a rage.

"Don't do that! You hurt me!" His face turned bright red. The veins on his neck popped out and throbbed. He raised his hand to hit Jamie across the face. She closed her eyes and stiffened in anticipation of his fist.

No fist came. Jamie opened her eyes. Chad was shaking his head, smiling crookedly at her. "No, no, my dear. I mustn't hurt you. You must be in top shape for our journey."

"Chad, what are you talking about?" Jamie's speech was slurred. "You're crazy. You're on something, aren't you?"

Chad laughed and commenced tying Jamie's feet together.

"Yes, my dear, I have found the way to paradise. And I want you to come with me." He finished his job, pulling the roped tightly. "Some people call it Snow," he said. He paused, folding his arms across his chest. "Let's see, now," he searched his memory. "Some call it Lady, the Big C, Flake." He leaned over Jamie. "I prefer to call it the Ultimate Edge."

Jamie was losing the battle to stay awake. Chad covered her with a blanket. "Sweet dreams," he whispered. "While you nap, I'll fix dinner." He stood over the sleeping young woman for a few moments, perched like a vulture. He wiped his running nose with a white handkerchief elegantly emblazoned with the letters CB.

Chapter Nineteen

Ben groaned. He sat up slowly, rubbing his head.

"Jamie," he uttered her name. Looking at his watch, he figured he'd been lying there long enough for Chad to disappear without a trace. Grabbing the back of a chair, Ben pulled himself to his feet. He plucked up the receiver of his phone and dialed the police.

Ben quickly related the incident to Sheriff Watson.

"You'd better go to Kate's and break the news to her," the sheriff said. "I'll send John over to check out your place, Ben. I'm on my way to Braxton's."

"So am I," Ben seethed, banging the receiver down.

When Kate opened the front door, she knew something was terribly wrong. "Ben? Is it Jamie?"

"Come and sit down, Kate."

"Ben? What is it? Just tell me!"

"Kate," Ben began to choke on his words. "Jamie is missing."

"What?" Kate gasped. "What are you talking about? I don't understand!"

"Mrs. K!" Judah's voice sounded from the kitchen. He walked into the living room. "I knocked but you didn't hear me. I was wondering if—Oh, hello Ben." Judah looked at Kate. "What's wrong?"

Kate could only respond by breaking down, a torrent of tears covering her face.

Ben stood up. "It's Jamie, Judah. She's missing. Chad Braxton's got her. He came to the store. He knocked me out." Ben rubbed the back of his head. "I couldn't help her. I let him get away," he said angrily.

Judah's face paled for a moment, his mouth formed a grim straight line. "Braxton," Judah spat the name. He headed for the door. Ben followed him. Judah turned and stopped him. "You stay here, Ben. Kate's going to need you. Call Reverend Jacobsen and Billy and anyone else you can think of."

Ben nodded. "Watson's over there now. Have him call me with the plan of attack."

Kate looked up at Ben. "I've never been this frightened, not since the day we took John to the hospital. God gave me peace then. He'll give me peace now. I just wish I could have done something. I tried to tell her, but—" Tears began to flow again.

Ben put his arms around her. "Now, Kate, you've got to be strong. You know your faith has gotten you through a lot of things. You'll get through this."

Jamie's grandmother shook her head. "No, Ben. It's not my faith that sees me through. It's the Lord."

Just saying those words aloud gave Katherine a surge of strength. Her face brightened. "I don't have to rely on my own strength, Ben. I can rely on His!"

Ignoring the confused look on Ben's face, Katherine continued. "I have always told Jamie that God will never leave us or forsake us. And she's heard Reverend Jacobsen's sermons. We'll just pray that Jamie remembers these things. Yes! That is our plan of attack, Mr. Wheelock. Start praying for God's Word to come to Jamie wherever she is. It's what she needs right now. I know God will hear our prayers."

Ben nodded. "Okay Kate. Whatever you say."

Kate took a deep breath and got up from the sofa.

"I've got to call Ellen and Dan first," she said.

She walked into the study and picked up the phone. "Be calm, Kate," she said to herself. She dialed California. "Hello, Dan Carrigan," Jamie's father answered the phone.

"Dan, this is Kate. Where's Ellen? Tell her to get on the other phone."

"What's the matter, Kate?" Dan asked. "You sound upset."

"Get Ellen."

The other line clicked. "Hello, Mom, what's the matter? It's Jamie, isn't it? What happened!"

"She's missing. Chad Braxton has kidnapped her."

The silence at the other end of the line cut Kate's heart.

"The police are looking for her, and we're praying and—"

"We'll catch the next flight out of here," said Dan hoarsely.

Dan hung up the phone and rushed to the room where Ellen stood. She was clinging to the phone, hands shaking, tears streaming down her face. Dan took the phone from her and gathered his wife in his arms.

"It's okay, Ellen. It's going to be okay. You go pack some stuff while I call the airport."

Ellen composed herself and headed for the bedroom.

"If anything happens to her, I'll—" Dan stood alone in the room. Everything seemed to crash in around him. Thoughts of Jamie swarmed his mind. He could see her take her first step. Her first day of school. The look on her face on Christmas morning. Walking down the country road at Grandma's, hurt and angry. "Oh, my God. If anything happens to her . . ." He stopped himself and shoved his thoughts aside. "We're coming, Jamie," he said picking up the phone. "We're coming."

Kate returned to the sofa. Ben began to make the other phone calls. Billy was the first to arrive, followed by Kate's friend Louise Hanson and Pastor Jacobsen.

"Everyone in Caderville's praying," spoke the pastor.

"The whole valley," added Billy. "They're going to find her. Don't worry Mrs. King."

Kate smiled. "How can I worry when the saints are storming the throne?"

"On the way over here, I got to thinking about some verses in Psalm 46," said Louise quietly. "Would it be okay if I read them to you?"

Kate nodded. "Please do."

"God is our refuge and strength, an ever present help in trouble. Therefore we will not fear, though the earth give way and the mountains fall into the heart of the sea, though its waters roar and foam and the mountains quake with their surging."

Pastor Jacobsen took Kate by the hand.

"He's sending help, Katherine. I just know it."

Judah sped over to the Braxton residence. The sheriff's car was parked in front. Judah burst through the front door. Sheriff Watson stood in the large front hall with a piece of paper in his hand. The Braxtons stood with him, looking terrified.

"What have you got?" Judah demanded. "What's going on?"

"Hold on a minute, Judah. We're handling it."

Joseph Braxton spoke up, perspiration running down his face. "He left me a note," he explained, pointing to the paper in the sheriff's hand. "Said he was borrowing the jeep to take Jamie shopping in Lamberton."

"Jeep?" Judah asked.

"Yes," said Joseph. "It's new. It's green with black interior . . . " His voice trailed. "I am so sorry about all this. I should have seen it coming."

"What do you mean?" the sheriff asked sharply.

"Well, my son, Chad," Joseph Braxton's voice broke. "He's been acting strangely the last few days. Kind of spacey, volatile. Even paranoid."

"Drugs?" the sheriff snapped.

"I'm not sure, but yes, I think so."

Judah headed out the door. The sheriff followed him.

"Hold on, Judah. I've called the troopers and the boys in Lamberton already. I've got an APB out on both Chad and Jamie. He's probably hiding out somewhere in Lamberton. There's nothing much we can do but wait."

"Yeah, well you can wait all you want." Judah jumped into his truck. "I'm looking for Jamie."

"Judah, you just hold on a minute. We will handle this. I've got my men out questioning people. We'll see if we can dig anything up. In the meantime, you stay out of this. Go back to Mrs. King's place. I don't want you running around half-cocked. I'll call you as soon as we hear anything."

Judah punched the steering wheel. "I'm warning you, Judah. Stay out of the way. We'll handle it."

Jamie awoke to see Chad sitting at a table with a plate of sandwiches.

"It's about time, Jamie! I want to feed you dinner. I've so many things to do," he chattered. "So much to do, so little time!"

Jamie's head was finally clear, and she struggled to sit up.

"Let me help you," Chad said sweetly.

"Get away from me!" Jamie screamed. She pulled her legs over the side of the cot and sat up herself. "Get away from me!"

"No no! That will never do!" Chad clucked. He picked up a cloth and gagged the young woman. "I can't think straight when you're screaming!" He shook his head. "Just for that, no lunch for you!" he pouted.

Jamie tried to stand up. She fell to the ground with a thud. Chad grabbed her and dragged her across the room. He propped her up against the wall.

"Stay, Sheba!" He snickered. "Get it? Sit, Sheba, heel."

Chad busied himself on the other side of the room. Jamie felt panic rising within her. This guy was crazy. He was obviously on something. What was he talking about before? A ticket to paradise? What did he call it? Snow? The Big C? She'd heard those words somewhere.

It hit Jamie like a blow to her stomach. Her blood ran cold. Cocaine. The man was hooked, and he was going to take Jamie with him.

Her eyes darted around the room. There were all kinds of supplies, magazines, books, food. Chad had fully stocked the place, as if he were planning on staying for a long time.

Chad walked over to Jamie and knelt down beside her. His hands were shaking.

"A friend of mine is going to drop off our ticket to Paradise, at an undisclosed location, of course. I must go now and pick it up." He rubbed his hands together. "And of course I'll take the motorcycle. The fools in town will be looking for a green jeep." Chad convulsed with cruel laughter. "Besides, the idiots think we're in Lamberton, shopping at the mall."

Suddenly serious, Chad leaned close to Jamie.

"You know that old question everybody discusses in high school, the one about if a tree falls in the forest, and there's no one to hear it, does it make a sound?"

Jamie looked at him in confusion and fear.

"Well," he continued, "I've been thinking. Let's do a little experiment. You like experiments don't you?" He removed the gag from around her mouth. "While I'm running my little errand, you can scream all you want. There's no one around here for miles. The question is, will your screams make a sound?" He laughed hysterically and hugged himself with fiendish glee. "I am so, so funny!"

The young woman stared at him in disbelief.

"Speechless, my dear? Good. We don't have time to talk. I've got to go." He paused and smiled at his captive. "I'll be back in a little while, fair maiden.

"While I'm gone, think of me!"

Jamie heard him bar the door on the outside. The sound of the motorcycle's engine signalled his leaving.

Jamie sat for a moment, completely terrified. Her mind was frozen with shock. She thought if she moved or made the slightest sound, Chad would burst through the door.

Tears began to course down her cheeks.

"What am I going to do?" She struggled to get up, but promptly fell back against the wall. She started to weep uncontrollably. Suddenly, a memory pushed its way to the front of her mind. She could see herself in her backyard as a child. Her father was teaching her to ride a bike. Having fallen hard on the first try, six-year-old Jamie lay crying on the lawn. Her father scooped her up and made her try again. "Don't give up, Jamie girl," Dad had said. "Keep trying."

Jamie forced back the tears. She took several deep breaths in an effort to calm herself.

"I've got to get out of here before he gets back," she whispered.

The young woman began to work frantically to undo the rope around her wrists. In his zoned state, Chad hadn't tied them too well. Her heart pounding in her ears, she finally pulled the knots loose.

"Come on, come on!" she pleaded, grabbing at the rope around her ankles. It was tied much tighter than the other rope. Her hands began to burn and bleed with effort. Jamie stopped and pulled herself upright. Hopping over to the kitchen area, she searched for and found an old knife. She sawed at the rope with the dull blade. Persistence prevailed, and she jumped to her feet.

Jamie scanned the cabin for a way out. She knew Braxton had barred the door. There was no way she could force it open. Her only alternatives were the small square windows. They pulled open easily enough, but they were boarded shut from the outside. Grabbing an iron poker from the fireplace, Jamie began pounding on the boards. They gave way, and she hoisted herself through the opening.

The cabin was completely surrounded by thick woods. There was scarcely space to park a car. Jamie headed for the narrow road that led up to the cabin. She stopped.

I can't go that way, she thought. *Chad may be back any minute.* She turned herself around and surveyed the area. Panic surged through her. Behind the cabin, the mountain continued its steep climb.

"There's no other way but to go down," she told herself. "I'll just have to go through the woods and steer clear of the road."

She bolted into a run. A myriad of branches plucked at her clothes. She shielded her face as best she could, but soon she was covered with scratches.

She didn't care. Her only thought was to get as far away from the cabin as possible.

Her hair caught on the sweeping bough of a prickly bush. She stopped and pulled at it, cursing the length of her hair. Finally tearing herself loose, she continued her flight. Trees, branches, and leaves passed by her in a blur. A gnarled root clutched Jamie's foot, and she went tumbling to the ground.

I hate that, she thought, jumping up and dusting herself off. *It's just like in the movies. Terrified girl running from monster trips and falls, hurting her ankle. You yell at her to get up, you idiot.*

Jamie started to laugh and cry at the same time.

"I'm losing it," she said aloud. "Get a grip on yourself, Jamie. This is not a movie."

Shafts of sunlight flickered through the trees, creating patches of glowing green.

"Sun will be going down soon," Jamie said to herself. "I better get moving."

The young woman began to run again. The downward slope of the mountain seemed to go on forever. She ran until her side flared with painful cramps. Dropping to the ground, the young woman closed her eyes.

"Got to rest," she panted. "Got to rest." This time she let the tears come freely. Feelings of isolation and loneliness nearly suffocated her. Thoughts of her family stabbed her heart. She was miles and miles from love and help.

Finally her crying subsided. The sounds of the forest filled her ears. Tree frogs chirped and hummed incessantly. An occasional squirrel chattered noisily over some perennial feud. Birds called and sang, snatches of melody threading through the trees with a serendipitous harmony. *Birds. Birds. What about them?* Jamie lifted her head. Somebody had said something once about some kind of bird.

Sparrows, she remembered. *Reverend Jacobsen said God watches over the sparrows. And us. He watches us. He knows the hairs on our heads. He knows and sees everything.*

Jamie sat up. Like a whisper quietly reverberating from ages past, the thought came: *You are not alone.* She closed her eyes and listened more intently to the birds. Maybe this stuff about God was not so crazy after all. She was beginning to feel peaceful for the first time in a long time. *He sees me.*

The baying of a hound ripped through the air. Startled, Jamie jumped to her feet. She was about to run when the dog crashed through the undergrowth. It barked and howled, insanely elated with its discovery. Jamie was so shocked by the dog that she failed to see the figure emerging from behind the trees.

"I had a feeling you might play hard to get," Chad Braxton mused from the other end of a rifle. "Tsk, tsk, don't you like me, fair maiden? Or are you being coy to arouse my passion?"

"Chad, you son of a—"

"Now, now! No name-calling. That would bespoil your beauty." He called the dog away. "How do you like my little helper? Snoozer is my Dad's best hunting dog. Dad's things certainly come in handy," he said, patting the handle of the rifle. He stopped and looked furtively around, as if he thought someone might be nearby.

"Come on," he commanded, grabbing Jamie by the arm. "We've got to get back to the castle."

Chapter Twenty

The farmhouse kitchen was full of people. Pastor Jacobsen and Louise sat beside Kate, praying silently with her. Billy was pacing the floor. Ben and Judah sat near the phone, waiting.

The jangle of the phone made everyone jump. Ben snatched the phone. "Watson?"

Ben listened to what the sheriff had to say and hung up. He shook his head and flopped down in a chair. "Nothing. Not a thing. Nobody's seen anything. Nobody here. Nobody in Lamberton. Nothing."

Judah stood up and looked out the back window. The sun would soon be setting. He looked out at the hills that graced the edges of the valley. A thought struck him.

"Maybe they're not in Lamberton."

All eyes were on Judah.

"Where would you hide out around here?" Judah asked.

Ben jumped up. "Somewhere in the hills, of course."

"But where could we possibly begin to search?" Billy asked. "We're surrounded by hills. They could be anywhere."

"Wait a second!" Ben pounded on the table. "Why didn't I think of that before! I've seen that jeep! I've seen it! I was fishing. You know the eddy just below town, about five miles down River Road? I've been fishing over there for a couple weeks."

"Cut to the chase, Ben," prodded Judah.

"A couple times while I was there, I saw a green jeep drive by and turn up one of the old mountain roads."

"Which road?" asked Judah, his voice tense, his mind about to explode.

"The road that goes up to the old Fisher place, that hunting cabin."

Billy hurried to the phone. "I'm calling Watson."

"Wait a minute," cautioned Judah. "If they go driving up there in their cars, they'll scare Chad half to death. He might—" Judah caught Kate's eye and hesitated. "He might do something crazy. I know a better and quieter way. Shadow and I have been on that road a hundred times. Call Watson and tell him I'm going on ahead. Tell him to come, but no sirens."

Judah was out the door. In a matter of minutes, he was flying down the road, Shadow's legs a pounding blur of black.

Chad prepared the cocaine while Jamie watched. Time seemed to stand still, roaring in her ears.

"This stuff will take us to the moon!" Chad cried ecstatically.

Life is so fragile, Jamie thought. There's got to be more. It can't just end like this. I'm going to die. The thoughts turned over and over in her mind. Pictures of her mom and dad flashed across her mind. *Maybe they're going to get a divorce. I guess that doesn't matter now. Nothing is ever certain.* Then she thought of her grandmother. There was something certain about her. What was it? Jamie's mind was cloudy with fear and shock. What was it about Grandma that never changed. Oh yeah. Her faith. She never lost faith in God. Said so many times that God had never let her down. Even when Grandpa died.

"Jamie," Katie had spoken to her after John's death. "Sometimes I get mad at God for taking your grandpa first. But then I remember He's God, I'm not. He's here with me, I'm not alone. He'll never leave me or forsake me."

Not alone. Jamie remembered her feelings in the woods. *Oh, God,* she prayed in her heart. *Please help me.* Words from Pastor Jacobsen began to permeate her mind like a forgotten song. "Don't be afraid of those who can kill the body," the pastor had said. "Fear God. What Christ gives is eternal, unchanging. Certain. That which is hidden will be revealed. In the hidden places of the heart we can experience God's love."

An image of the stainedglassed window in the church flashed in her mind. She could see the storm-tossed boat and the resolute Christ. The turmoil of the moment, the uncertainty of life swirled around Jamie like relentless waves. In the midst of clamoring insanity, the hidden need of her heart was laid bare. She saw a rock immovable, a passage out of the darkness and into the light. She saw Christ.

In the dimming light of the cabin, while a madman concocted a nightmare, Jamie Carrigan realized the truth of God's love. For the first time in her life, she called out to Christ, and God became her Father. In the power of that moment, the truth of His nearness struck her in the depths of her being.

"Eureka!" yelped Chad. "We're all set!" Holding a syringe, he walked over to Jamie. "I'm going to snort my snow but I know I can't make you snort it. So I'm going have to inject you. That way we can go over the edge together. Isn't that sweet?" Chad's entire body was shaking. His face was flushed. "Are you ready?"

Jamie looked into his eyes. "Why, Chad? Why are you doing this?"

A smile slowly spread across the young man's troubled face. "Because I love you, fair maiden. And you love me. And this way, we can be together always. I told you before, I always get what I want. And I want you. Now, hold still."

"He's here, you know," said Jamie. "He sees us."

Chad twirled around frantically looking for an intruder. "Who? Where is he?"

"You can't see Him. It's the Lord. He's here."

Chad shook his head and clucked his tongue. "I never would have guessed it, Jamie dear. You, of all people, grabbing on to faith in a crisis. That's such a cowardly and escapist thing to do, don't you think?"

Jamie looked into Chad's eyes. "What do you call what you're doing? Aren't you trying to escape? What are you escaping from, Chad?" she asked, trying to buy time.

"I'm not escaping," he snapped. "I just like living on the edge, that's all. Besides, nobody cares what I do. Everyone is so narrow-minded. They don't understand me. Nobody cares what I do."

"Your parents care about you, Chad."

"That doesn't count," he retorted, sweat dripping down his face. "They're my parents. They have to care."

"I care what happens to you," said Jamie softly.

"I know you do!" Chad hugged himself. "That's why I brought you here. So we could be together. I told you that already. Are you going deaf or something?"

"Chad, why don't we go down to the diner and get something to eat? We can talk things over. Maybe we could go over to your house and see your mom and dad."

"Go to the diner?" said Chad, his brow furrowed with thought. "Maybe we could, maybe. We could go to the movies, too." He stopped and slapped the side of his face. "Aha! You're just trying to confuse me. You're just stalling for time! I caught you in the act! Na, na, na, na, na," he sang in a sing-song voice. Chad wiped the sweat off his face with his sleeve. "No way, fair maiden. You can't fool me! I'm the master of trickery." He frowned. "Now hold still, I said. It's time for paradise!"

Jamie looked down at her hands and feet. Chad had tied her up again. As Chad bent toward her, she threw herself on the floor, screaming. She thrashed around as hard as she could.

"Stop it!" screeched Chad. "Stop it!" He ran over to the table and put down the syringe. He grabbed a cloth to gag Jamie. She tried to pull away from him. He slapped her hard across the face. It stunned her. "Jamie!" he hissed, putting his face next to hers. "Remember this?" He waved the pistol in front of her. "You mustn't be a naughty girl." His breath felt hot against her face. "You must be a good girl!" He tied the gag painfully tight.

Jamie was dazed. Chad leapt up to retrieve the syringe, when suddenly the front door smashed open. Without stopping, Judah threw his body against Chad. Chad went flying into the wall with a crash. He jumped to his feet and tried for the pistol on the table. Judah blocked Chad's arms with a powerful swipe, pushed Chad away, and grabbed the pistol himself. Chad lunged for Judah, but Judah dodged him. Braxton fell against the table and knocked it over. Powdered cocaine fell in a shower of white all over the floor. The syringe clattered down and rolled along the floor. Judah smashed it with his boot.

"No!" screamed Chad as he watched his dream scatter and fall between the rough-hewn boards of the wooden floor. He scrambled around, clutching at the elusive powder with trembling hands. "No, no." His voice trailed to a despairing whisper. He looked wearily at Jamie. "Now we can't go," he whined quietly. He sat on the floor and put his head in his hands. Judah watched as the man finally collapsed in a quivering heap.

"Jamie!" Judah cried. He rushed over and began to untie the gag. Jamie looked up at him, her eyes wide with shock and relief. She couldn't speak. Judah didn't wait to untie her but swept her into his arms. As he held Jamie close, he hid his face in her long brown hair. Jamie suddenly felt her hair getting wet with his tears. The man was weeping.

"Oh, dear God. Jamie. I almost lost you." he cried. He held her tighter as if he'd never let her go. Jamie felt the strength of the man's love coursing through his arms, flowing through his silent tears. She began to tremble with the realization that the nightmare was over.

"Very, very touching," Chad's voice slithered across the room. Jamie's heart leaped to her throat.

Judah instinctively grabbed the pistol and whipped around to face Braxton.

"Stalemate," said Chad gleefully. He was standing near the door with his father's rifle in hand. "You can't shoot me, because I'll shoot you. Sounds like a nursery rhyme, doesn't it?"

"What do you want?" Judah barked.

"How did you get up here so sneakily?" asked Chad.

"Why?"

"Just answer me or I'll aim at the little pheasant you have there under your arm." He grinned at Jamie.

"Horse." Judah answered. "I came by horse."

Chad's eyes widened. "Fabulous! I'll just borrow your horse, if you don't mind. Where is it?"

"Out front," Judah replied.

Chad backed up to the door facing Judah and Jamie. He slowly opened it. "Now don't do anything rash!"

"Oh, we won't," muttered Judah under his breath, a gleam in his eyes.

Braxton slammed the door shut and found the horse next to the jeep. He ran toward Shadow, reaching for the rein. Judah ran to the door in time to see Shadow promptly rear up and knock Chad to the ground. His rifle flew out of his hand into the grass. The agitated horse paced nearby, snorting angrily at the stranger.

Judah sprinted over and picked up the rifle. Chad didn't move. Shadow had knocked the wind out of him.

The sounds of car engines signalled the arrival of the police. Sheriff Watson and his men poured on their searchlights. They jumped out of their cars, guns pulled and trained on Chad Braxton.

"I don't think you need the guns," Judah said quietly.

Watson looked at the man slumped over on the ground. He signalled his deputies, who hurried over and handcuffed Braxton. They pulled the man to his feet and led him to one of the squad cars.

The sheriff entered the cabin, scanning the scene.

"Are you all right, Miss Carrigan?" he asked.

Jamie nodded. "Do you think you could get these ropes off me sometime today?"

"Oh, yeah, I forgot," said Judah. He quickly untied them. Jamie got up, rubbing her wrists. Looking around the mess, her eyes fell on the broken syringe. She shuddered and turned away. "I want to go home."

"You can ride in one of the squad cars, Miss Carrigan. John here will take you. I want to have a word with the Lone Ranger here."

Jamie smiled at Judah. "Go easy on him, Mr. Watson. He saved my life."

"See you at the house," said Judah.

The young policeman guided Jamie out the door. Watson pointed a long finger at Judah. "What in blazes got into you? You could have gotten yourself, and possibly Miss Carrigan, killed! I ought to haul you in for interfering with police work."

Judah simply nodded. "Yes. I guess you're right."

"We were handling it. You have no business interfering with a police investigation."

"Yes, you're right."

"Riding a horse to the rescue. This isn't a cowboy movie!"

"Right again."

"Well, just don't do it again."

"I promise."

Chapter Twenty-One

As the squad car pulled into the King driveway, Kate and Ben burst out the front door of the house. They helped Jamie out of the car and practically carried her into the house. Katherine and Louise surrounded her, crying for joy. Billy and Ben started whooping and hollering. Pastor Jacobsen stood in the corner, grinning from ear to ear and praising the Lord. At the sight of such dear family and friends, Jamie let herself go. All the tension and terror of the day drained out of her in racking sobs.

The tears subsided. A deep sense of peace stirred in Jamie's heart. She knew it was from more than being safe.

"Oh, Grandma. So much has happened."

Kate saw the sparkle in her granddaughter's eyes. "I think I already know what you're going to say."

Jamie nodded. "You were right. Judah was right. Billy tried to tell me. It's real! God's love is real! Oh Grandma! It's like I've finally found my home. A home I'll never have to leave!" She looked over at the pastor. "And you, Reverend Jacobsen—your sermons. Your words reached me in the middle of the woods when I thought I was going to die." She leaned back on the green sofa. "I'm so grateful for all of you."

"And Toto, too?" Billy quipped. At that, everyone laughed. Jamie threw a pillow in his direction.

"I think we'd better take care of your face now, young lady," Ben said briskly. "We'd better clean up those scratches and put some ice on the swelling."

"Yes, Dr. Wheelock, whatever you say," Jamie smiled.

"Jamie, I'm so glad you're okay," Ben said somberly. "I can't help but feel this is somehow my fault."

"Mr. Wheelock!" Jamie objected.

"Ben! Don't be ridiculous!" Kate exclaimed. "How could this possibly have anything to do with you!"

"Chad Braxton came into the shop for antihistamines starting in January. That's okay, it's winter time, cold and flu season. But then he kept coming. And it was always the same. I finally got a hunch that he was dabbling in drugs. Certain drugs cause nasal discomfort and congestion." Ben shook his head. "I should have said something to you, Jamie. I should have warned you."

Jamie reached out for Ben's hand. "Stop thinking that way. You know I probably wouldn't have listened to you, anyway."

"If it weren't for Ben, we may not have found Jamie in time," a voice said firmly from the living room door.

"Judah!" Everyone clapped and cheered and slapped him on the back. Judah grabbed Ben's hand and lifted it in a victory sign. The room was buzzing with joy.

Kate took the opportunity for some last-minute scheming. "Why don't we all go in the kitchen and whip up a meal for Judah and Jamie? They must be tired and hungry!"

Everyone took the hint, although Billy had to be dragged out by Pastor Jacobsen. Suddenly, the room was quiet. Judah and Jamie were alone. Jamie stood up and rushed into Judah's arms.

"Judah," she whispered. At last, she rested in his arms, knowing that it was where she belonged. She looked up into his rugged, honest face. "Thank you for praying for me. I found His love, Judah. It was just like you said. I really did find it. Or maybe He found me!" She laughed and hugged Judah tightly.

Judah's blue eyes were warm with love. "I told you so," he teased.

"And I discovered something else this summer."

"Oh?" His heart pounded, and Jamie felt him tremble. "What's that?" he asked huskily.

"I love you, Cowboy."

Judah breathed a deep sigh of relief.

"I love you too, Princess," he whispered. "But I think you know that."

Judah hesitated. Then he shyly leaned down and kissed Jamie gently on the lips. No tray clattered to the floor, no horn blared angrily, but the five people standing in the hallway did applaud. Even Billy Ritchfield.

"And on top of all that," Jamie whispered into Judah's ear, "Billy's going to be your best man."

Judah looked at her in surprise. Then he threw his hat in the air with a whoop.

"All right, all right, enough of that," Ben interrupted. "Jamie's face needs fixing. Now come on in the kitchen and sit down."

Jamie obeyed, and everyone stood around the table staring at her. They watched as Ben carefully cleaned her scratches and applied antiseptic. Kate prepared an ice pack for the swollen side of Jamie's face.

"He hit you, Jamie?" asked Billy. His voice was shaking with anger at the sight of her bruised cheek and eye. "If I ever get my hands on him, he'll regret the day he was born!"

"Billy!" admonished Kate. "Calm down. You're going to upset her."

"That's okay," responded Jamie. "But you know what? I feel sorry for Chad Braxton. If you could have seen him at the cabin, you'd feel sorry for him too. He was confused and messed up. He's lonely, and his brain is fried from drugs. It's a shame."

Judah nodded. "She's right, you know. I never thought I'd be saying this, but I feel sorry for him too. It makes me more thankful for what I have now."

"We'll put him on the prayer list," suggested Reverend Jacobsen.

"Well," spat Ben Wheelock. "You lovely, holy Christians can spout all the forgiveness you want! I'm mad, and I'm mad as h-e-double-toothpicks, and I don't care who knows it!"

"H-e-double-toothpicks?" laughed Jamie.

Kate put her hand on Ben's shoulder. "I'm mad too," she said. "But when I'm done being mad, I'll forgive the boy. But I'll tell who we're going to have to tie down when he gets here."

"Who?" asked Jamie, holding the pack over her eye.

"Your father. I called your parents when we first found out you were missing. They caught the first flight out here. Probably won't arrive until after midnight, though."

Jamie suddenly felt a little dizzy. "I think I better lie down," she said.

"Good idea," said Ben. "And I think everybody should clear out and let you rest."

"You're the boss," said Jamie. "By the way. Violet Cranberry came by the store today. Told me some interesting stories about you."

"Fiddlesticks," was all Ben would say.

"You should try to eat something," said Louise as she got ready to leave. She gave Jamie a kiss. "I'm so glad you're safe, dear."

Pastor Jacobsen nodded. "Ditto!" he said. "What a story we'll have to tell on Sunday morning!

Jamie smiled. "Tell it all." She got up walked to the foyer.

"I don't want to go upstairs yet," she said. "I want to sit in the living room. Do you think we could have a fire in the fireplace?"

"I'll make it," Billy volunteered.

"I'll be going now," said Ben. "You take care of yourself, young lady."

Kate walked him to the door. "Thanks Ben," she said. "You saved Jamie's life when you remembered the jeep. I will never tease you about your fishing again!" She slapped him on the back of his head.

"Ouch!" Ben exclaimed. "I'm still sore, you know."

"I forgot! You'd better put more ice on that bump, Dr. Wheelock."

"All right, all right," said Ben, rubbing the back of his head. "And Kate, I guess there really is power in prayer, eh? Maybe there's hope for my poor old soul after all."

Kate laughed and shooed him out the door.

Billy had a fire blazing in the fireplace. Jamie sat on the couch, soaking in the warmth. Judah sat next to her with his arm around her.

"Best man," Billy muttered. "I'm always somebody's best man."

"You mean, like " 'always the bridesmaid, never the bride'?" Jamie teased.

"Very funny," scowled Billy. He leaned back in the rocking chair and looked at Jamie. "Some day, I'll sweep the heroine off her feet, and it'll be time for paradise!"

Jamie looked at Billy. At the sound of his words, she suddenly saw Chad's face. *It's time for paradise.* Her hand flew to her throat and she began to tremble violently.

"Jamie! Are you all right?" asked Judah.

She shook her head. Her eyes filled with fear.

"He said he was going to take me to paradise. He was going to give me cocaine. He was going to kill me!" She bent over sobbing.

"Jamie, I'm sorry! I didn't mean to—" Billy pleaded.

"It's okay, Billy," said Judah. "She's still suffering from shock."

Kate hurried in from the kitchen. She sat down with her granddaughter and tried to soothe her. Jamie quieted down.

"We'd better go," said Judah to Billy.

"Yes, I better go before I say something stupid again."

"Come here, Billy Ritchfield," said Jamie. She signalled to him to come close. She kissed him on the cheek. "You're a great friend," she said. "The greatest."

Billy blushed and followed Judah out the door.

"Great friend," they heard him complain as he walked out the front door. "I'm always the great friend."

Just after midnight, Jamie's parents arrived and rushed in to assure themselves that she was alright. Dan Carrigan cursed every time he looked at his daughter's bruised face. Ellen sat holding Jamie's hand, tears running down her cheeks.

"You're safe, and that's all that matters," said Ellen.

"I'm okay, Dad. Stop staring at me."

"I'm sorry. I can't help it. When I think of that creep and what he tried to do—"

"Dan," Ellen implored him. "Jamie's had enough excitement for one day."

"Look," Jamie intervenes. "It's almost one o' clock. I'm going to bed. Can I sleep in your room tonight, Grandma? Just for tonight."

"Sure, dear. It's perfectly understandable. I'll go get your pillows."

Kate headed for the stairs, and Jamie got up to follow her. Dan gently took her arm.

"Just a minute, Jamie girl. There's something I want to say to you."

Jamie stopped and looked at her father. *Oh great,* she thought. *Of all the nights he picks to tell me he's leaving mom, it has to be this night.*

"Sit down Jamie."

She sat next to her mother. Ellen squeezed her daughter's hand.

"I know you've been worried about your mom and me. Things haven't been very good between us. In fact, they've been awful." He shoved his hands in his pockets. "I want you to know it was my fault. Your mom has been great. I just got real selfish and only thought about myself." He turned to look into his daughter's eyes.

"I almost lost her, Jamie," his voice broke. "I almost lost your mom. But I woke up, that's what I'm trying to tell you. I woke up, and I'm trying to make it up to her. And now this happens. I almost lost you." Tears coursed silently down the man's cheeks. "You sort of get things in perspective when your life falls apart. You figure out real quick what's important and what's not."

"I know," said Jamie.

He cleared his throat. "I'm trying to say I'm sorry." He looked at Ellen.

"Dan," she whispered. "I love you."

Jamie looked from one parent to the other. Her heart was bursting with relief and joy. But even as she looked at the two of them, she realized that the change in her own heart did not hinge on whether or not her parents reconciled, or whether or not she had been saved from Chad Braxton. Her heart would forever find its home in Christ, regardless of what life would bring.

Jamie got up and kissed her father on the cheek.

"Thanks, Dad," she said. "I'm glad things are working out. I was real worried. The Lord is so good to us."

Ellen's eyebrows shot up. "The Lord is good? That came out of our Jamie's mouth?"

Jamie smiled. "I'll tell you all about it tomorrow. I'm going to bed!"

Epilogue

"Good morning, Violet. Can I help you with something?" Jamie gave the woman a knowing wink.

Violet giggled and nodded her head. "Yes, dear. You're not too busy, are you?" She lowered her voice. "Where's Ben?" she hissed.

"He's in the back," Jamie whispered back. "He probably doesn't even know you're here!"

"Good morning, Violet!" Ben called from the back of the store.

"Oh, drat that man!" Violet scowled.

"Come on," said Jamie. "He won't even see us!"

Jamie and her accomplice handled their mission with speed. In a matter of minutes, Violet was on her way with her package.

"See you later Violet!" yelled the pharmacist from behind his partition.

"Humph!" Miss Cranberry gave one last primp to her hair and stomped out the door.

"I'm impressed!" said Judah from his stool at the counter. "You're really good with people."

"She's a prize, all right," chimed in Ben. "I don't think I'm going to let you have her, Judah. After all, I saw her first."

"Want to arm wrestle for her?" inquired Judah. He put his elbow up on the counter. Ben eyed Judah's muscular arm.

"On second thought, I'll settle for being godfather to your first kid. Deal?"

"Deal," said Judah with a grin.

"Hey wait a minute, don't I have any say in this?" Jamie piped up.

"No," the two men spoke in unison.

Jamie shrugged. "I can't fight both of you. Hey, it's five o'clock. I feel like walking home today. Who wants to be my escort?"

"Not me," replied Ben. "Exercise is bad for my health."

"I guess it's up to me," said Judah. He held out his arm, and Jamie curled hers through it.

"See you later, Ben."

Judah and Jamie walked through town. The air was warm and sweet with the smell of newly-mown hay. Jamie took a deep breath.

"That's my favorite smell," she said.

Judah looked over Jamie. The sunlight brought out the golden highlights in her brown hair. Her eyes were peaceful and happy. He stopped her at the turn off to Ryder road. "You look beautiful," he said.

Jamie blushed and looked down the road that led to her grandmother's. The trees on either side of the road merged in a canopy of green. Shafts of light streaming through the trees scattered the road with gold.

"So will you?" Judah asked.

"Will I what?"

"Marry me."

"I don't know," teased Jamie. "I hear there's a wise old woman who lives down that path of gold down there. Maybe I should go ask her what she thinks."

"Let's go," smiled Judah. He clasped her hand tightly in his own.

Together they walked down the road toward Kate's home. Jamie couldn't help feeling that her time spent with her grandmother had been a road her heart had needed to travel. Like the contrasting light and shadows that pulsed beneath the canopy of leaves, Jamie's journey traced moments of brightness and profound darkness. At journey's end, she found her heart was where it always should have been. Hidden in the arms of her Creator.

As they approached the red mailbox, Jamie could see her grandmother inspecting her flowers in the front yard. She squeezed Judah's hand and kissed him gently on the cheek.

"I'm home," called Jamie to her grandmother. "I know," Katherine King called back to her granddaughter with a warm smile. "I know."

"I'll take that as a yes," shouted Judah.

The Delaware Valley resounded with the shout of the cowboy and the laughter of the princess. The wise, silver-haired woman looked on and smiled.

About the Authors

Sara Mitchell is the author of seven inspirational romances and a new historical suspense series (Bethany). Sara feels called to share her faith through writing the kinds of books which offer sunshine instead of clouds, a smile instead of a scowl...and create a desire to seek God instead of shun Him. In addition to her writing of novels, Sara has also authored several musical dramas. She and her husband and children reside in Burke, Virginia.

Irene B. Brand is an award-winning inspirational romance novelist who has written ten novels as well as articles for numerous historical and religious periodicals. A retired teacher, Mrs. Brand resides in West Virginia when she isn't pursuing her other active pastime, international travel.

Susannah Hayden is a popular author of both fiction and nonfiction for adults and children. She recently completed a biography of missionary Jim Elliot for the popular, new series, "Heroes of the Faith," and has authored several titles in the "Young Reader's Christian Library" series for readers ages eight to twelve. Besides being a wife, mom, and author, Susannah is the manager of Publishing Services for the international division of Cook Communications (part of David C. Cook Publishers). Susannah lives with her husband and two children in Elgin, Illinois.

Kjersti Hoff Baez has established herself as a prominent inspirational romance writer with *Passage of the Heart*. In addition to writing love stories, Kjersti also writes children's books and has three titles, *Corrie ten Boom, Ruth,* and *Miriam* in the best-selling "Young Reader's Christian Library" series. She lives in Ossining, NY, with her husband and three children.